Jakob Ejersbo

LIBERTY

BOOK THREE OF
The Africa Trilogy

Translated from the Danish by
Mette Petersen

MACLEHOSE PRESS
QUERCUS · LONDON

First published in Denmark as *Liberty*
by Gyldendal, Copenhagen, 2009
First published in Great Britain in 2014 by

MacLehose Press
an imprint of Quercus
55 Baker Street
7th Floor, South Block
London W1U 8EW

STATENS
KUNSTRÅD
DANISH ARTS COUNCIL

Supported by the Danish Arts Council's Committee for Literature

A CIP catalogue record for this book is available from the British Library

ISBN (MMP) 978 0 85705 128 8
ISBN (EBOOK) 978 0 85738 659 5

10 9 8 7 6 5 4 3 2 1

Designed in Collis and Quadraat Sans by Libanus Press
Typeset by IDSUK (DataConnection) Ltd
Printed and bound in India by Replika Press Pvt. Ltd.

A big thank you is due to my first reader Christian Kirk
Muff for stoking the fire and kicking my arse to bits.
Thanks are also due to Ole Christian Madsen
for tune-ups. And to Morten Alsinger
for a thousand coffee breaks.

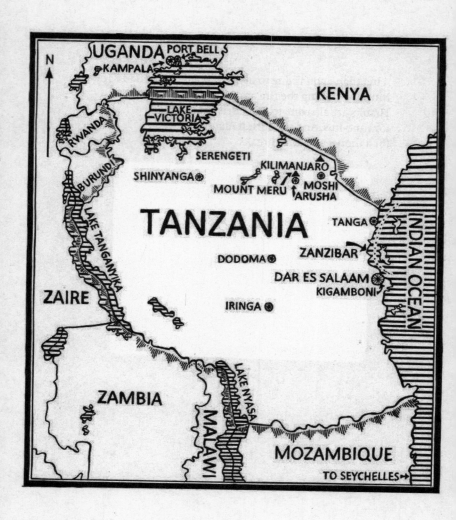

For
Gary Dread
&
the strangers

1980

Christian

As I step out of the aeroplane tropical heat sweeps around me – in the distance I can see Kilimanjaro's snow-capped crown in the twilight. A group of black men are lounging about outside the single-storey airport terminal, smoking cigarettes next to a couple of scarred luggage vans.

"Welcome to Africa," Dad says, putting a hand on my shoulder as I step onto the tarmac. The aircraft engines have stopped. The only sound is that of cicadas. The airport has a single landing strip, and there is no plane there but ours.

I look at the black men. A fat black woman is telling them off in Swahili. They grin and slowly lug the clattering luggage vans towards the plane's belly. Their faces are blank now.

When I got up this morning it was the day after Boxing Day, and I was a Danish boy who lived with my mother on the outskirts of Køge. Now I'm going to be living in Tanzania and attending an international school. Our family will be together again soon. Dad's days of being a Mærsk man stationed in the Far East are over. My baby sister was born in October and Mum will be bringing her down in a few months. Everything has been turned upside down.

"It'll be a while before the luggage arrives," Dad says. We pass some shoulder-high plants with leathery leaves and enter the concrete building, which is blacked out.

"Why is there no light?" I ask.

"I expect there's a power cut," Dad says. "They probably just need to start the back-up generator." I stay close to him while the other white people, a few blacks and quite a few Indians enter the dark arrivals hall. We changed planes in Amsterdam and there were stopovers in Rome and Oman. Somewhere in the building an engine sputters into action, and a few seconds later some of the light bulbs in the ceiling start glowing faintly.

"Niels, Niels," a woman calls. Dad turns.

"Hi," he calls back and waves. "That's Katriina," he tells me, walking towards the glass partition. He'd told me that a Swedish family had taken him to the airport, and that they would be there to pick us up in his car. I look at the police officers, standing idly by with their machine guns strapped across their chests. I follow Dad.

"So this is Christian," the woman says and nods, smiling. "Hello, I'm Katriina." She is wearing a flimsy summer dress and sandals.

"Hello," I say and try to smile. Dad tells her something about our trip here, and it seems odd that he should be standing chatting to a woman I don't know and that Mum should be in Denmark.

"Was it good to see your new daughter?" Katriina asks.

"Yes, it was lovely," Dad says. "And my wife is looking forward to coming down." A sound makes me turn. The baggage carousel isn't moving and suitcases are flying through the hole in the wall. A skinny black man in a grubby pale blue uniform crawls through the hole and scrambles over the suitcases, which he starts hurling onto the floor.

We get our bags together and walk over to passport control. The officer stares for a long time at the photograph and then at me. I try to smile at him. Suddenly he grabs a stamp and hammers it onto an inkpad and then into my passport – three different stamps before he takes a pen and adds a few scribbled words. He hands me back my passport.

"Welcome to Tanzania," he says in strange English, smiling broadly. At customs control we come across a fat man who is sweating profusely. He signals for me to open my bag. He kneads my luggage with his meaty hands, grabbing my football and saying a lot of things I don't understand. He smiles, slamming the ball into the ground and catching it again.

"He thinks it's a good ball," Dad says.

"It is," I say, smiling at the man. I'm nervous. I don't know what his smile means. Is there a problem? He puts the ball back, makes a quick mark on my bag with chalk and pushes it towards me, nodding:

"Football, very good," he says. Dad has gone on ahead. The Swedish woman is hugging him. Luckily she only shakes my hand. She has large breasts.

"How old are you?" she asks in Swedish.

"Thirteen," I say.

"I have a daughter who is eight. And my fifteen-year-old nephew is staying with us. Solja and Mika," she says, grabbing one of my bags.

"We're going back to our place now for a bite to eat – we're having a small welcome party for you. We've moved to a new house."

"One without rats?" Dad asks.

"Yes," Katriina says. "And we have a nanny called Marcus."

"A man?" Dad asks.

"A boy," Katriina says. "He's an orphan and used to live with some Germans but they went home. Solja and Mika found him. He was living with a local parson in Moshi who had put him to work in his fields."

We go out to the car – a white Peugeot 504 with the steering wheel on the wrong side. The darkness is solid and as soft as velvet. We pass a guard at a barrier – leave the airport and drive through the night. The road is straight, the landscape flat. No street lamps, no buildings. The headlights sweep over greyish-green shrubs at the side of the road.

Three months ago Dad started working as Head of Accounts at a sugar plantation called T.P.C. – Tanzania Planting Corporation. It used to be owned by Mærsk but has now been nationalized by the Tanzanian state, and Mærsk have been contracted for the next few years to teach the locals how to run it. It's just outside Moshi, which is where my school is. Dad turns around in the front seat.

"Are you alright, Christian?" he asks.

"When will we be going out to the house then?" I ask.

"We'll go later," Dad says. "It's only seven." He has told me it gets dark early and that it happens very quickly because we're so close to the Equator. I feel lightheaded. What I wouldn't do for a cigarette.

"Alright," I say and look out of the window and up to the sky, studded with bright stars stretching all the way to the horizon.

We reach a T-junction. Wooden shacks and little brick houses cast faint light into the darkness. There are shops on the bare ground. Dark shapes move around between them. We turn right, towards Moshi.

"This is one of the best roads in the country," Dad tells me. "Almost no potholes." The darkness envelops us completely. There is almost no traffic, and Katriina is going fast. There's a bend in the road, then it dips into a ravine – our headlights illuminate the steep rock walls on both sides.

"What?" Katriina shouts and steps on the brakes, turning the wheel to avoid slamming into a large leafy branch lying across our side of the road. The brakes lock, and the car skids into the branch, pushing it ahead of us until we come to a complete standstill.

"There's someone there," Dad says. I can just make out a dark shape a bit further ahead, but with the leaves of the branch in the way, our headlights don't provide much light.

"Is it highway robbers?" Katriina asks.

"I don't think so," Dad says, opening his door. "The branch is a Tanzanian warning triangle." I get out with Dad and help him pull the branch away from the front of the car while Katriina reverses. Now I can see that the shape is in fact a lorry that has slammed into one of the rock walls and is blocking the road – a large fresh branch is poking from under the rear bumper. We lug the branch back to its position on the road. There is no-one to be seen.

"What do you think happened?" I ask.

"Dodgy brakes," Dad says. "The driver probably drove into the rock wall to stop." We get back into the car.

"*Fa'n!*" Katriina says – damn, hitting the wheel before getting the car in gear and driving on more slowly. We can just about edge past the lorry. As the road straightens out again at the bottom of the ravine, Dad turns to me:

"When you drive through here during the day, you'll see a load of wrecked cars," he says.

After twenty minutes we reach the outskirts of the city and drive down some smaller roads.

"Why does it smell of cow dung?" I ask.

"The Maasai drive their cattle through here when they're going to the abattoir at the other end of the city," Dad says.

"Almost there," Katriina says as we turn into a bumpy dirt road that runs between two rows of white villas behind tall fences and gates.

Marcus

MARABU

"Hey, are you there?" *bwana* Jonas shouts from the veranda.

"Yes, *bwana*," I call back from the kitchen where I am sitting, waiting for Katriina to return from the airport.

"Bring out some beer," *bwana* Jonas shouts.

"Right away," I answer and dash to the fridge. Solja comes out into the kitchen.

"I am hungry," she says – already she is good with the English language, even though this Swedish family has only been here four months.

"I will fry some meat for you in a minute," I tell her and run out with the beer to the veranda, where *bwana* Jonas is sitting with his colleague Asko and his wife from Finland. I put the beer down on the table. Asko is very big and fat. His wife, Tita, titters like a bird:

"Thank you so much."

"Do you want me to make some food for Solja?" I ask.

"If she's hungry," *bwana* Jonas mutters with his Swedish tobacco-dirt in his mouth, shrugging without even looking at me. I hurry back to the kitchen and take the chicken outside and put it on the barbecue. Looking after this eight-year-old girl is my ticket to the good life. I have been with this family for only two weeks, and it's hard to understand what my role is. Am I a nanny, or am I being adopted? Life is hard when you have abandoned your own parents. I turn the chicken on the barbecue.

"Do you like chicken?" Solja asks.

"Yes, very much." I love meat. When I was born – in 1965 – my family lived like marabous, scavenging for meat in Serengeti National Park. My father worked there because even though we are of the Chagga tribe from the slopes of Kilimanjaro we have no land. As a child I was almost a wild animal – running about in the dust while the tourists came in little planes to be driven around in Serengeti for one day only. They brought lunchboxes from the hotel in Nairobi – big white cardboard boxes. They want to sit down and eat, and us blacks, we keep an eye on them. We live on corn porridge and spinach – and these boxes contain white meat from the chicken, dark meat from the cow, they have lovely strong breads, a golden apple – loads of flavour. But meat is the most important thing – we are starving for meat in a place where meat is walking around on all fours. We're not allowed to kill the meat, because the tourists want to see living animals. We keep an eye out for when these *wazungu* are done eating, and as soon as they leave the table we make a run for the boxes. The tourists laugh at us, call out to us. Sometimes they throw the chicken on the ground, so it becomes dusty and we must fight for it. We can wash the chicken, but we can also eat it with dust on. At other times the tourists throw the good food into a bin for rubbish, where the winged marabous come to feast. We throw stones at the birds. We fight for the food. The white people take photos of us as if we were strange monkeys. We're not strange. We're just hungry.

The smell of grilled chicken rises to my nose. I dash over to the Swedish sauna hut next to the house and make sure there is a good fire in the oven so the white people can sweat a little more in the warm country. Then I set out a plate for Solja with chicken and bread and butter – and salad, which she never eats.

"And a Coke," she says. I take a Coke from the fridge and open it for her. She takes her food to the veranda to listen to the adults talking. But what should I do now? Should I get started on the rest of the food, so it's ready when Katriina gets back from the airport with *bwana* Knudsen and his son?

DANISH BOY

"Thanks for dinner," Solja says. Like the good girl she is, she brings her plate back to the kitchen. I take the chicken scraps and gnaw off the last bit of meat – lovely and fatty. Until two weeks ago I was living with the Lutheran parson in Moshi, who made me work in his fields. I have told these Swedes that I don't have parents – they are dead from disease and a traffic accident. It's safer to lie – maybe the whites can't understand that my parents were so bad it would be better if they really were dead.

A car honks its horn at the gate; the guard dashes out. Katriina is bringing *bwana* Knudsen and his son, who is my size and very quiet; not wild in the eyes like Mika, who has run into town saying he was going to the cinema. This Danish boy looks like Gerhard, my German child-hood friend from Serengeti.

I call on the house girl from the servants' quarters, our shared ghetto. She is to help me in the kitchen, so the white people can eat. I put more meat on the barbecue and carry drinks to the veranda.

"Coke?" I ask *bwana* Knudsen's son, handing him the bottle.

Christian

Katriina's husband is called Jonas. He is sitting on the veranda with a fat Finnish man – Asko – and Asko's tiny wife, who is called Tita. They're speaking a strange language I don't understand at all.

"Do you understand what we're saying?" Katriina asks slowly in Swedish. I shake my head.

"Swedish with a Finnish accent," Dad says, laughing. A young black guy appears on the veranda and hands me a Coke before leaving again.

"Is that the new nanny?" Dad asks.

"I'm damned if I know what he is," Jonas says.

"Don't say that," Katriina says. "Marcus is very helpful, and we only give him food and lodgings."

"And his school fees," Jonas mutters.

"It's nothing," Katriina says.

"Marcus is my friend," says a little girl who has just appeared on the veranda – she must be Solja.

Not long after, Marcus and a black girl bring the food. The black girl is young and silent, wrapped in a brightly coloured piece of thin fabric. We eat on the veranda with our plates in our laps. The adults drink beer, smoke cigarettes. The cicadas sing, the bats scurry through the air.

"The sauna is ready," Katriina says. They're all talking and smiling as they get up – Dad too. People go into the sitting room.

"The sauna?" I ask Dad.

"The Swedes and the Finns are very keen on their saunas. Come along," he says.

"I'm not going in there," I say and stay in my seat. He looks at me for a moment. I can't read his look when it's so dark on the veranda.

"Alright," he says and follows the others. Solja has gone – maybe she's been put to bed. I look into the sitting room. They're all undressing. I see Asko's cock under his big paunch and look away. So weird. I look again. Dad has wrapped a towel around his waist and is going into the sauna, which has been added to the back of the house. I wonder what Dad has been up to for the five years he was stationed in the Far East without Mum? Going to bed early?

Asko has left his cigarettes on the table. I started smoking last year with the other outsiders in my class. I can tell myself that I want to wake up at three a.m. Then I sneak out and go the corner shop, put coins in the machine and draw a ten-pack of Princes. When the drawer is open, my hands are just small enough that I can push my fingers in and grab onto the next pack and pull it out; I can empty an entire column for the price of just one pack. Or I could. Down here I have no idea how to get cigarettes. Asko's cigarettes are called Sportsman. It's quiet here –

everyone's in the sauna. Do I take one? But I'm afraid to. I wish Mum was here.

My parents almost got divorced a year ago. Late one night my mum came into my room – I was already in bed. There had been a lot of rows on the phone with Dad in Singapore when she thought I was asleep. Mum sat down on the edge of the bed.

"Christian, I need to talk to you about something serious," she says.

"Are you guys splitting up?" I asked.

"No, of course not," Mum said. She looked at me then turned away, holding a hand up to her mouth and swallowing. "No," she said again. I knew they were getting a divorce.

"Then where will I live?" I asked.

"We're not getting a divorce – I'm pregnant," Mum said, smiling in a strange way. Once, when he was drunk, my dad had told me there was something wrong with Mum's plumbing. She couldn't have any more children.

"Pregnant?" I asked.

"Yes – you're going to have a little brother or sister," Mum said.

"Is Dad coming home then? To stay?" I asked.

"You bet he is," Mum said.

"O.K.," I said.

"Aren't you pleased?" Mum asked.

"Yes," I said. The plan was for Dad to come back to Køge and work for Mærsk on Esplanaden in Copenhagen. I would believe that when I saw it.

Mum arranged a party for the day he was to arrive. The day before, I heard her screaming into the phone:

"We *are* divorced. We have been for ages. If you don't want to be with us, I'll sell the house and send you your half. I can't do this anymore." There's a break – Dad is saying something from Singapore – and I hurriedly open my door just enough to listen in. Mum is speaking quite calmly again:

"Either you get here, or I'm through with you." She puts down the phone and comes to my room to say goodnight. I don't ask her until she is almost out of the door again:

"Isn't Dad coming to the party tomorrow night?"

She stops without turning.

"I don't know," she says and leaves. Not long after I hear the car starting. When I turned twelve, she started working nights – it's fine to leave me home alone. I get up and go outside, smoke a cigarette. I go inside and flick through all the pages in the notebook by the phone. Tap in the numbers.

"Knudsen speaking." The connection to Singapore crackles.

"Dad?" I say.

"Christian! Do you know what time it is here?"

"Are you coming home?" I ask.

"Where is your mum?" he asks.

"At work," I say. He sighs.

"Something's come up. I can't leave for another few days. I'm sorry, Christian," he says.

"No," I say.

"Christian," he says, "your mum is . . ." He doesn't go on.

"You said you'd be here," I say.

"There's nothing I can do about it," he says.

"But . . ." I say.

"I'll be there as soon as I can," he says.

"Goodbye," I say and hang up. My hand is shaking.

The next day Mum had her party. She was dancing tight with a tall doctor – I hated her for it. Dad came through the door. I looked at him, he looked at her. He had made it. He raised his hand and smiled. She looked at him and went on dancing. She was pregnant, but it didn't show yet. Why was she still dancing with that doctor when Dad was here? The doctor looked at my dad and stopped – let go of her. She smiled at the doctor and looked vacantly at Dad without moving. He was standing just inside the sitting-room door, still had his coat on and everything. I hurried over to him.

"Dad," I said.

"Christian," he said and held me up high in the air even though I'm too big to be lifted. Mum came over to us.

Now I'm going to be living with him for a few months until Mum comes down. It's a bit odd. I don't really know the man. And when Mum comes down with my little sister, we'll all be together, like a proper family.

I hear a squeal from the other side of the house. Get up and take a couple of steps into the sitting room, look through the windowpane in the back door. Katriina is skipping about on the lawn. Her full breasts bob up and down – her nipples are very dark. Dad appears from the sauna with a garden hose in his hand. Its jet of water sprays onto Katriina, who stops, breathes heavily, shakes a bit. She's standing still, letting the water wash over her – I can see the large dark bush between her legs. The jet of water hits her upper body, and she twirls into it. I look at Dad, who is smiling and holding the garden hose over his own head so the water flows over his naked body.

I quickly go back to the veranda before they see me. Sit down for a bit.

"Come out here, Christian," Dad calls from the other side of the house.

"Why?" I shout.

"Don't worry, no-one's naked now," he shouts. I go out. They're sitting on benches around a table in a small fenced-off area just outside the sauna. The men with towels around their waists, the women wrapped in brightly coloured cloths like the one the black house girl was wearing. Katriina is sitting next to Dad. She takes his hand in hers.

"I can't wait till your wife brings your little daughter down," she says.

"Why is that?" Dad asks.

"Because I'm pregnant as well," Katriina says. Tita sighs and looks sad. She looks down. I look over at her husband, Asko. He looks ticked off. Maybe she would like to be pregnant as well.

"Congratulations," Dad says. "When are you flying back to Sweden then?"

"I'll be having the baby at K.C.M.C.," Katriina says. "There are so many white doctors there."

Asko and Jonas are talking in Swedish. Tita doesn't say anything. I look at Jonas. He is tucking chewing tobacco behind his upper lip, moving it around with his tongue and fixing his eyes on something in the darkness. I turn my head and follow his gaze. It's the house girl. She's standing at the corner of the house, bent over, scrubbing the barbecue grill – her arse is sticking out, bobbing up and down as she works.

"What are you looking at?" Dad asks, laughing. "Do you like the look of her?"

"I don't know," I say. I don't tell him that I'm looking at what Jonas is looking at, just get up and step out into the garden.

"Where are you going?" Dad asks.

"I'm just going to have a look around," I say.

"Don't get lost," Dad says.

Marcus

MY MZUNGU

All the *wazungu* have gone naked into the sauna – a big production in pink flesh. Katriina comes into the house:

"Marcus, will you be sure to brush Solja's teeth?"

"I will do it," I say, and Katriina goes back to the sauna party.

"But I want Mummy to do it," Solja says – she is eight, old enough to do it herself. Afterwards she goes to her room. But right away she calls:

"I can't find my nightie." I go to her. Her nightie is in her wardrobe, right in front of her, but the girl wants the attention, so the negro must do his bit. Solja starts putting on her nightie.

"Goodnight," I say, leaving.

"I can't sleep, Marcus," she says. "They're being noisy." It's true, they've left the sauna and are sitting on the small wooden veranda, talking, drinking, shouting. "Can I sleep at your place?"

"No, that won't do," I say. How will this *bwana* Jonas react if Solja sleeps in my ghetto? – I think he wants white and black to be kept well apart. I go to her bed and hold up the duvet up for her. She gets in and I smooth down her hair.

"Tell me a bedtime story," Solja says.

"O.K." I lie down next to her on the bed, and she puts her head on my shoulder. What should I tell her? About the marabou in Serengeti? About slaving for the Reverend? About the teacher's rod at school? No. I must think of another story.

"Go on," Solja says next to me in bed. So I tell her about Bob Marley; how his father was a white man who soon went away and his mother was black, and Bob grew up in poverty and came to Kingston in Jamaica and sang about freedom. I sing quietly:

"*Won't you help to sing, these songs of freedom, 'cause all I ever had, redemption songs.*"

"That's a good song," Solja mutters. I tell her about the descendants of the African slaves on Jamaica who created the Rastafarian religion. They call God "Jah", which is short for Jehovah from the Bible. The religion took its name from the Emperor of Ethiopia, Haile Selassie I, who was christened Ras Tafari. They see the emperor as God's incarnation on earth, because Haile Selassie was head of the only African state that was completely independent of white people. Rastafarians don't accept that Haile Selassie is dead.

Solja breathes quietly; but it's too soon for me to move – she might wake up. This girl child is very important – I have to look after her.

My first *mzungu* was Gerherd from Germany – his parents came to study wild animals. We lived in Seronera, and all the children used to play together, black and white. Gerherd is like me, except for the colour of his skin. His skin is always covered by sneakers, blue jeans, jeans jacket. My skin is on show. I only have old school shorts and a worn-out T-shirt with the word BAYER printed on it, a hand-me-down from Gerhard. We kids are bored because Seronera is just a small cluster of buildings surrounded by Serengeti National Park.

"What should we do?" Gerhard asks.

"We could play football," I say.

"But we're not enough to make up two teams," he says.

"We'll just go over to the village – there are plenty of children there," an English boy suggests. It's the village where the guards live with their families. You have to cross the grasslands to get there.

"We're not allowed; it's dangerous," Gerhard says.

"I am not afraid of those animals," the English boy says. "It's the animals that are worried when they see so many two-legged beasts."

"What do you think, Marcus?" Gerhard says.

"I'm used to the animals," I say. We're seven children who set off; *waafrika*, German *mzungu*, English *mzungu* – we don't ask the adults, we go quickly. Then the earth shakes – it's the heavy thunder of hoofs. Gerhard is next to me.

"Rhino," he shouts. The beast is coming at us at full speed. We're running to all sides; Gerhard one way, me another. With a rhino you have to stand still – we know that. The animal doesn't see at all well – it can only see movement. If we're standing still, we could be trees. If it comes at me, I must jump out of the way at the very last moment, right before the burning spear rams into me. If I jump too soon, it has time to change direction. But can you stand still when the earth is trembling and you're staring Death in face? We scatter, the rhino swings its lowered head; there's Gerhard – on top of the horn now. The beast throws him into the air – he is simply flying, landing like a sack of rice on the ground. The rhino jogs off. We run over to Gerhard – a big hole in his stomach, bloody with white things hanging out – maybe from the chicken he had in the box today when he pretended to be hungry.

"Start carrying him back, then I'll run for help," the English boy shouts and scrambles off through the grass. Along with the other *waafrika* I start to carry Gerhard back – he is even whiter now.

"Marcus," he says. "Don't let me die here."

"Don't worry – it's only a small hole," I say. But the hole is a big one.

The adults bring a Land Rover, but the car only makes things worse on the bumpy road. Gerhard has passed out by now. Luckily there is a tourist plane – a small one. They carry him into it, take off. But he dies in the air above Arusha. Who will get Gerhard's special shoes with bumps under them for playing football? I will. Gerhard's father and mother want to be visited; they have two little girls, but I can play the part of the boy, even though he is dead in the ground.

Soon I am wearing Gerhard's clothes, and it makes my father angry. He thinks I am letting my own family down in order to be with the white people. My father beats me so hard I run to the safety of Gerhard's mother and am adopted into a white life with my dead friend's family.

Gerhard's parents are strange. All fruits must be scrubbed with washing-up liquid, and all vegetables must be rinsed in chlorinated water which stinks badly; otherwise they are dangerous for the white stomach. The woman sits all day, drinking coffee and reading books. She has *waafrika* for every job: washing, cleaning, cooking. But she pays them far too much and doesn't see that they steal sugar and flour. At night the white woman sits on her sofa, drinking alcohol and smoking cigarettes like the man, and sometimes she speaks to him in a nasty way, but he never hits her while I'm there – at worst he sneers at her like a grumpy monkey. Sometimes the man kisses her, right in front of me – whatever will they do next?

Then the Germans leave for another national park to study the hyena. They like to count the animals. I go with them, like a piece of luggage in their trunk. They take good care of me. Being fed well, having fun, riding bicycles – it overpowers my brain; I am being carried forward in life. If I just play with their children, they are happy. They even teach me to drive a car, so I sit behind the wheel in the national park while the German man uses the binoculars. But after a year their research is done, and they must go home to the white country. I am shocked. What will happen now? I thought they would take me with them to Europe. But the man sends me by car to Seronera like a tourist. They have given me money; I am wearing sneakers and jeans and a jeans jacket; my packed lunch has the white meat.

My parents left Seronera – the work was over; they went back to Moshi. They couldn't take me – how would they find me? I am fourteen. I take a bus to Moshi – several hundred kilometres, all alone in the world. I find the house my parents have rented in Soweto. The walls are sticks and mud, the floor is dirt, and the roof is a large tin can for cooking oil which has been cut open and tapped out flat – eaten by rust. My younger siblings are running around outside, dirty and half naked – grown like weeds in the year that has passed. Inside it is dark and it smells dirty. My mother looks almost like a stranger.

"The Germans went to Europe," I explain.

"You can't stay here," she says. "You have to leave before your father returns – he'll kill you."

"Why? He is my father," I say.

"You never do as you're told, Marcus. You're the oldest, so it's important to the entire family that you be good. Otherwise the other children will be bad as well."

"I can behave."

"No," she says. "You're like the *wazungu* children; no respect for your parents. You can't live here."

"But where will I go?" I ask.

"Go to my sister in Majengo," my mother says. "You can live with her – there's no man in the house."

From that day I am alone in life and seek my fortune – preferably with white people.

"Wh-wh-wh-wh-what is your n-n-n-name?" Mika asks outside – he is back from the cinema and is talking to *bwana* Knudsen's boy.

"Christian," the boy says. I get up carefully from Solja's bed and go out to them.

Christian

"A-a-a-a-are you a man or a mouse?" a young guy who must be Katriina's nephew Mika asks, holding out a roll-up. He has appeared from the darkness in the garden and smells of beer, even though he is only a few years older than me. I don't want to be a baby. I take a quick look into the sitting room to see if there are any adults. No. I take the cigarette – Mika holds a match towards me and smiles. The tobacco tastes strange.

The black kid, Marcus, appears from the sitting room.

"*Tsk*, Mika," he says, taking the hand-rolled cigarette from my hand. He smells it and hands it to Mika, shaking his head.

"It's *bhangi*," he tells me. "It'll make you crazy." He digs out a pack of filter cigarettes from his pocket. Sportsmans. Holds the pack towards me. I take one. I've just had my first drag of weed; how cool is that?

"Thanks," I say.

"Let's go down to my ghetto, so your father doesn't see you," Marcus says. It's difficult to understand what he's saying, because his English is heavily accented. I was taught English in school for two and a half years. And I've practised with Mum by repeating things from a cassette we borrowed from the library, and she's played me records with Bob Dylan and the Rolling Stones and the Beatles and tried to teach me the words. Mika has disappeared into the house.

"Alright," I tell Marcus and follow him down towards a smaller brick building at the back of the garden. "Is this where you live?" I ask. I'm feeling a bit faint, and my feet don't seem to touch the ground.

"Yes," he says. "It's the servants' quarters, for me and the house girl. The black ghetto." He smiles at me in the dark, opens his door and goes inside. The room is pitch black. He lights a bat light – apparently they haven't got electricity.

"Do you like music?" he asks.

"Yes," I say. "Bob."

"Do you know Bob Marley?" he asks, surprised. I don't really.

"Bob Dylan," I say.

"I don't know him. You should listen to Bob Marley," Marcus says and puts on a small tape recorder that runs on batteries. The music has a slow pumping sound that enters my body. I light my cigarette and have to lean against the table.

"Wow," I say.

"Are you feeling the *bhangi*?" Marcus asks.

25

"I can't feel the ground," I say. Marcus grins. I hear a sound and turn nervously, trying to hide the cigarette.

"It's Mika," Marcus says. The Finnish kid enters the room with a can of Carlsberg in his hand.

"Ch-ch-ch-cheers," he says.

"You're not allowed to take those beers," Marcus says. Mika hands me the can, watching me coolly. What can I do? I take a gulp. Smoke my cigarette. Mika takes the beer from me and leaves. I get up unsteadily. Put out the cigarette in an ashtray.

"I'm going out," I say.

"Are you not well?" Marcus asks

"I'm going out," I say again and stumble through the door, onto the ground, across it. My legs feel rubbery, and my head is reeling. I lean against the fence around the property and weave my fingers into the wire. Take deep breaths, letting them roll through my guts, and sit down on the grass. Marcus comes out.

"Are you alright?" he asks.

"Yes," I say.

"Wait here," he says.

"Don't fetch anyone, alright?" I say.

"I'm fetching you a Coke," he says. I feel alright, I'm just very tired. What should I do? He brings the Coke. I nod and drink. I don't want to have to explain anything to anyone. I raise my hand in a wave for Marcus and aim for Dad's car, which is shining white in the darkness. The adults are still at the sauna at the back of the house. Luckily the car is open. I climb in on the back seat and shut the door.

Dad coming back from Singapore didn't change much. He was still working for Mærsk, only now it was at their head office on Esplanaden in Copenhagen. He got up before I woke up and came home just as I was going to bed. I could hear Mum at night:

"But he needs you here. I can't be his dad. I have no idea what he's getting up to."

"Does he do things he's not allowed to?" Dad asks.

"I don't know. I think so. I am sure he has started smoking, and sometimes his clothes smell of petrol. And I don't know if he is alright, because he never tells me how he's doing at school. I'm afraid he's a bit of an outsider," Mum says.

"He'll be alright," Dad says. I don't know. We *are* outsiders. We don't wear polo shirts; we wear wooden-soled boots with steel fastenings. We fiddle about with an old Puch Maxi. And even though John Travolta has a cool walk in "Saturday Night Fever", we don't like the castrato singing of the Bee Gees – we prefer Pink Floyd.

"What's the use of you being here, if you're always at work?" Mum shouts in the kitchen. I get out of bed and go in. They go silent – act like nothing's happening.

"Aren't you asleep?" Mum asks.

"You were being loud," I say and go to the loo.

"I'm sorry," Dad says.

"You do speak very loudly, Niels," Mum says.

"I'm not happy at Esplanaden either," Dad says. "You have to be very aggressive all the time to fit in."

"Then get yourself something in a smaller company," Mum says. "We're having a baby, Niels. Finally. They don't understand that at Mærsk. To them wives are just people who do what they're told, look nice and iron their husband's shirts to perfection."

"I'll see what I can do," Dad says. I go back to my room.

"Goodnight," Mum says.

It went on like that. One night Mum was working the night shift and Dad was away on business in Los Angeles. I was standing at a Texaco petrol station at one in the morning with a friend. He was holding the nozzle of the hose to an empty Coke bottle, and I was jumping up and down on the petrol hose – the small vacuum created by my bodyweight pulled petrol from the hose so we could fill the bottle. At the crossing we poured petrol onto the road and waited a moment. Headlights approached, we lit the petrol; brakes jamming, tyres screeching, a sideways collision with a lamppost. We made a run for it. The next day the T.V. news reports a serious prank in Køge that might have gone very wrong. Mum gives me a weird look.

"Your shoes smell of petrol," she says.

"Moped fuel," I tell her.

"You're not allowed to ride a moped," she says.

"I was on the back of it," I say.

"You're not allowed to do that either," she says and confiscates my allowance.

27

Dad returns. They row at night. Mum cries.

"Sit down," Dad says when he comes home from work one night. We sit down. He is standing, leaning forward with both palms on the dining table.

"Africa," he says.

"What?" Mum says.

"Mærsk runs a sugar plantation in Tanzania," he says. "And the Head of Accounts has come down with a bad case of malaria. They need a replacement right away. Two years." He looks at Mum. Mum looks at me. I shrug.

"Is there a school?" Mum asks.

"Yes," Dad says. "A big international school. Lots of Scandinavians. Excellent place."

"Where would we live?" Mum asks.

"You know, the sugar plantation has a number of houses – like detached houses with gardens," Dad says.

"I want to have the baby in Denmark," Mum says. "Christian can go as soon as you've got yourself sorted down there."

"What do you say, Christian?" What could I say? I didn't know.

"Alright," I said.

I'm lying on my back in a Peugeot. Above me is the starry African sky. The Coke feels good in my stomach. I close my eyes.

Marcus

KNEADING

"Hello?" *bwana* Knudsen says, knocking on my ghetto door. "Have you seen my boy – Christian?" he asks, standing at the door.

"He's on the backseat of your car, he's tired," I say.

"Well, that's practical at least," *bwana* Knudsen says and adds: "Goodnight, then."

"Goodnight," I say. *Bwana* Knudsen leaves. I can hear the Swedish ABBA music coming from the house. I go into the garden so I can spy through the windows. I have seen it once before. *Bwana* Jonas is never nice, but when he's had something to drink, he pushes the furniture aside and takes Katriina in his arms, and then they fly about the floor in a very European style, and Katriina's eyes swim with honey as she dances with this strange man.

Soon the music stops. The party is over. I must get to bed, because the slave is the last one to go to bed and the first one up when the masters are hungover. Yes, my situation is unsure – I must hop to it so I can be key to a flowering of the joy that will carry me with it to a better life.

I wake up with the thought of God's white foot kicking my black arse. Leap into the kitchen to make toast for Solja, boil an egg, make orange juice for my white daughter.

"Mum and Dad are hungover," she says. Yes, it's wonderful. They need a helper, and Solja likes me. She eats her breakfast, and *bwana* Jonas gets up, with a hangover that feels like a saw in his head. Should I stay or should I go?

"Go down to your own house," he says without looking at me, so I get out as quick as I can, until Katriina comes to my ghetto:

"We're taking Solja to see one of her friends, and then I'll come back for you. We're going shopping with Tita," she says.

"Yes," I say. The car leaves. The house girl has gone up to clean after the night's festivities. Finally Marcus the Marabou has a moment to attend to his own nutrition. I hurry to the kitchen in the main house and through the door I hear a squeal from the house girl. What's going on in that kitchen? I look through the grille in the door. *Bwana* Jonas is standing at her side – kneading her bottom like dough with his hands. Very scared, I turn to leave without a sound, but I'm nervous so I stumble over the basket of clothes pegs on the back stairs. *Eeehhh*, it makes a terrible noise.

"Marcus!" *bwana* Jonas shouts from the kitchen. I stop, turn around, a completely innocent look on my face.

"Yes?" I say. *Bwana* Jonas opens the door and holds up his finger.

"Don't you breathe a word of this," he says.

"No, I won't say a word," I say and nod energetically.

"If you do, you're out of here," *bwana* Jonas says.

"I never say anything to anyone about anything." I keep nodding with great energy. What do I have to offer? I'm not exciting like the house girl. On my way to my ghetto I see Jonas' big Yamaha 350cc in the garage. *Eeehhh*, but it's me who's being stupid. Before I go into the house, it's important I make absolutely sure who might be inside.

I sit down outside my ghetto, so I won't disturb the kneading of the black dough. When the house girl returns, she's got a very proud and dismissive face on. She wants to go straight to her room without talking to me.

"He is already a married man. Why do you let him knead your bottom?" I ask.

"*Tsk*," she says. "The man likes me – soon he will make me a present."

Christian

I open my eyes and see a white mosquito net. Am in a bed. It's daylight. A bright room with terrazzo flooring. A desk and a chair. In front of the wardrobe is my Diadora bag and suitcase. It's clean, freshly painted. Dad must have carried me in last night. I must be in the house in the sugar plantation. I get up. The floor is cool under my feet. I peer into the garden – the lawn is well tended, very green, surrounded by flower-beds. My head feels odd. I put on my jeans. Dad must have pulled them off me. Open the door quietly, hear sounds in the kitchen, go down the hall into a sitting room. There's a note on the coffee table. "Hi, Christian. I'm at the office. Will be back at two. The cook will make you breakfast. Love, Dad." The cook? I hear footsteps. Turn around. A black man with an apron and bare feet. He smiles and says something. I raise my hand in a sort of greeting. He invites me to come closer with a gesture – he wants me to follow him. Into the kitchen. He pulls out a chair at the dining table – I sit down. He opens the fridge and holds up an egg, looks questioning at me while speaking in something that could be Swahili. I nod. He holds up one finger, then two, then one again – looks as if he is posing a question. I hold up two fingers. Two eggs. He holds up a saucepan and a frying pan. I choose the frying pan. He smiles and nods. He serves toast, juice, coffee in a cup. Mum says I'm too young to have coffee. I drink it while the cook watches me. It's strong. I sip the juice. The eggs are nice. I nod and smile at him. He smiles back.

Marcus

LITTLE BLACK HELPER

Katriina returns in their red Peugeot estate, and we go to the Y.M.C.A., where Asko and Tita are staying while they wait for a house. We drive to the market on the edge of Swahilitown. If there are things in the car, I stay with it so it won't be emptied, because the tailors sewing under the sunscreen across from the main entrance never see anything, even if you return to find the car has been stripped of its wheels.

First the white ladies want to look at the brilliantly coloured fabrics at the tailors', so I run over to the Rasta guy Phantom, who has a small kiosk at the entrance to the market, selling cigarettes, moisturizer, soap, pens, toilet paper, batteries, hair slides, chewing gum, razor blades, bits and bobs. The other day a little bit of money went missing in the Swedes' house – it might have been Mika or the house girl who took it. I buy a cassette of Bob Marley music and five pieces of Big G gum for Solja and cigarettes I can give to Mika.

I say goodbye to Phantom and go to the tailors' to find my white ladies. But who is that? My mother, sitting on the ground with the two youngest children, who have runny noses and clothes in tatters. Mother is selling things right on the street outside the market, where you don't have to pay to have a stall, and where the police can kick you off the kerb and confiscate everything you have. A piece of burlap on the ground with a few tomatoes and onions and bananas from the field my parents have in North Pare Mountains, because even though we are of the Chagga tribe from the slopes of Mount Kilimanjaro, our family has lost all its land.

"Marcus, you have to help me," she says. "Your father has lost his good job as a driver. There is no money for food now."

"Only because your husband is wasting all his money on drink," I say.

"It's his worries with so many children to feed," she says. "You're doing well in life now – you have to help us, like we helped you."

"Is it a help if I hit you with a rod until you bleed all over like you beat me?" I say.

BEATING

During my childhood in Serengeti my father managed the youth hostel in Seronera. *Wazungu* and *waafrika* alike stayed there. My father was their guide as well; he knew where the elephant was, the lion, the hyena. Afterwards he showed the films made by people like Michael Grzimek and the other *wazungu* who created the park – European researchers of wildlife. I went to the school for the children of the staff – black and white mixed together. And the white wives taught us in English.

"Now we decide everything for ourselves," Father told me, "because our president, Teacher Nyerere, took our country back from the English

31

before you were born and gave us *uhuru*." Freedom. But it's not true. The boss of Seronera was *mwafrika*, but who decides the quality of life?

In school I mixed with the white children, and I was drawn to the foreign way of life. Their parents said: "It's good that you play together." I thought that I was happy, and I didn't know anything about what would come later. I learned new things. Riding a bicycle. Eating special food from tins. Drinking cocoa, eating biscuits. The white children had money for fizzy drinks from the shop, owned by a cranky *mhindi* – if I came to the shop on my own, he would have his rod speak directly to my skin.

My father changed jobs and went on expeditions to catch poachers. We children were alone with Mother. I was the firstborn but was busy at school and with my German friends, and I thought it was wrong that Mother was always sending me to the shop and to fetch wood and water and that she wanted me to mind the little ones who were screaming and shitting – I'm not a girl.

When Father came home, he brought lovely joints of meat confiscated from the poachers, but I never got a single scrap. Mother told him plainly how I had refused to do my chores, and he invited me into the bedroom to talk to the rod.

Mother was at home with the children. In the evening my father's pipe filled the whole house with its stink, and his gaze became weird.

"What is that you're smoking?" I asked.

"Dried elephant turds," he said and laughed loudly, swinging for me, PAH – a blow over the back of my head.

At the white people's it was different. No stinking elephant turds, but posh white cigarettes. No blows, but fizzy drinks and biscuits.

"Go and tidy your room," the white lady told her son, Gerhard.

"*NO* – I won't do it," Gerhard screamed. And then the house girl did it, while me and Gerhard had fizzy drinks.

Now I start to ignore my parents totally, because I think they do the wrong things; they don't have any fizzy drinks.

"Marcus – you must sweep in front of the house and mind your little sister while I go to the shop," Mother says.

"*NO*," I say.

"You're as hopeless as a *mzungu* brat," Mother says. But I won't give in. Until Father comes home and has had his dinner so his strength is up again. Then he invites me into the bedroom where we all sleep – the other children stay in the sitting room. A beating to make the skin come off the flesh like on a slaughtered animal. I run away. Sleep in a storage room on the grounds. I am hungry and shaking with fever when I go back to my parents.

"Where have you been?" Mother asks.

"At my friends'," I answer.

"Out!" Father kicks me. "You go and stay with your *wazungu* friends." I go to the German family. The T-shirt is stuck to my bloodied back. They wash me. The woman puts the white ointment on my back and gives me pills against the fever for many days. I explain to them what happened to me. They say:

"Ah, but that's very wrong. You stay with us." Then I just sleep somewhere in their house like a sort of pet.

Primary school ended after Year Seven – I was thirteen. There was no secondary school in Seronera, and my family didn't have any money and didn't care about me. My white friends went to an international boarding school in Nairobi. My future was different. I went with Gerhard's parents to a new national park to amuse their little children. But this German family disappeared and left me on a stony road in life. Until now – now I am struggling to become a member of the Larsson family from Sweden.

PROTEIN

After our shopping trip we drive to Kibo Coffee House by the Clock Tower roundabout – the place you go to meet people in this town. It's wonderful to be with white people. I drink lovely coffee, eat lovely snacks; doughnuts – this is the life. Catch a wave, ride it. There's good ice cream, there's coffee, and coffee ice cream, and iced coffee with milk and cane sugar from T.P.C. and a spoonful of ice cream on top. And the car is right outside, so I can keep an eye on it, and the shopping baskets are full of protein, which I have been told is the best sort of nutrition.

Back when Gerhard's parents had gone away, I found my parents' shack in Moshi's slum, Soweto, but my mother sent me to Auntie so Father wouldn't destroy me with his rod. Auntie had no money, but she is Christian and knows people. She sent me to K.C.M.C. – Kilimanjaro Christian Medical Centre – to apply for a job. I walked all the way on my thin legs. A great white building, the best hospital in Tanzania, constructed by the Israelis with money from God.

33

I get a job at N.U.R.U., the Nutrition Rehabilitation Unit. *Nuru* means light in Swahili. The bosses are from England and train mothers to feed their children proper food. For weeks they live in barracks and are told that shit from animals and humans mustn't fall close to the porridge pot. We have nurses showing how to be ready to give birth to a baby and about diseases like worms and bilharziasis. And the fathers must come to be taught how to build safe fires for cooking so it isn't the children that end up being cooked.

I work for George in the vegetable garden growing food for the children. The nurse shows the mothers how to combine things so the belly doesn't stick out while the hair goes red and arms and legs go thin like matchsticks. I tell her about the time I was hungry for meat.

"You were lacking proteins – they don't have to come from meat," she says. "You need eggs or beans or meat to build your muscle. And you need greens, rabbit food, which make the brain work well, milk for your bones and corn porridge for energy to make you run like a gazelle."

Every day I walk. That too is an education in the way life is meted out. In Majengo we have dirt roads and poor housing with no water or electricity, and lots of bars where men drink *mbege* and women can be bought. But beyond the roundabout by the Y.M.C.A., there's Shanty Town, with big houses, good tarmac, posh cars. Auntie says that Shanty Town was a real shanty town when her father was young, but then the Germans brought the railway and Moshi grew. The important people had the shanty town removed so they could live there themselves.

These days the area has many white people who are only here to help the negro, but wealthy black people live there as well, with their good clothes and stomachs that are never hungry.

I like playing with the children in N.U.R.U. And I help George – the local man who manages the hospital's farm. He teaches me. I look after the rabbits, the chickens, the vegetables. I give the money to Auntie, who almost doesn't have room for me in her house, because it only has one room, and she already has two daughters and no husband. So I start to look for a new place to live where I can make myself useful all the time in return for a lift in life.

Now I am sitting with two white ladies at Kibo Coffee House. Tita keeps looking at me. Her husband Asko is fat and pink like a pig with sunburn. Maybe Tita is doing a study of the black skin?

Christian

I go out into the garden. The sun is beating down on my head. There's a faint smell of burnt sugar. At the end of the drive I stop. There's a gravel road with detached houses behind well-tended hedges as tall as a man. I don't know where I am. In the distance I see a tall, silvery chimney with the letters T.P.C. vertically down its front. That must be the sugar factory. I go back inside. My suitcase is empty. I open my wardrobe – all my clothes have been freshly ironed and are neatly stacked on the shelves; the cook has seen to that. So what am I going to do? A door opens.

"Welcome to T.P.C.," Dad says.

"Hi," I say, smiling.

"Have you had breakfast?"

"Yes," I say.

"Then come along." We go down the street with detached houses on either side towards the chimney. "This is where the white-collar staff live," Dad says. "You know, I took over the Head of Account's house, and since he didn't bring his family, we're the ones without a swimming pool. But two houses down that way," Dad say, pointing, "there's the Rasmussens and their daughter, Nanna, who is about your age. They're still on holiday, but you can go there and have a swim if you like." We leave the detached houses behind.

"These are the workers' cottages," Dad says and points at rows of little yellow houses with tin roofs. "There's a family at either end of each of those small buildings." The little houses have numbers, like cells. The bricks are sooty above the doors from the wood smoke that seeps out. Dirty children run around among the free-range goats and chickens. "It's a good place to live if you're an unskilled worker," Dad says.

We reach the factory area, and Dad greets the guard at the gate, saying in English: "This is my son."

"Ohhh," the guard says, smiling. "Welcome to T.P.C."

"Thanks," I say. The smell of burnt sugar is quite strong here. The factory seems very run-down. Inside we meet the factory manager, Mr Makundi, who has been here since T.P.C. was started in 1954. "You must call him *mzee* Makundi, because he is an old man," Dad explains.

"Yes, the old Mr Møller was clever," Makundi says. "He came here to hunt, and then he had the idea of irrigating the dry soil with water from the rivers and growing sugar canes. T.P.C. was just a small garden where

Mr Møller would holiday." Makundi also tells us that he has a son of my age called Rogarth. He is at the school in Moshi as well.

"I am going to have to work a little more. Can you find your own way back?" Dad asks. "Yes," I say. "I can." He hands me some money. "What do I need that for?" I ask.

"There are some kiosks near the workers' houses where you can get fizzy drinks. You can get them at the workers' canteen right across from the factory as well. I'll be back in two hours."

"Alright," I say and leave, passing the workers' canteen without going inside. Back to the house. What should I do? I need a cigarette. I find an open pack and some matches in the sitting room. The cook is in the kitchen. I go out and round to the back of the house, but you could see me from next door. There's a hole in the hedge – I go over to it and push through. The golf course. Dad has mentioned it. Mum would like to play. No-one in sight. The grass is ankle-high – I wonder if there could be snakes here. I squat down and smoke.

Later I go exploring. A few black men are walking around on foot. Most of them don't pay me any particular attention. The ones that do nod and smile. I smile back. Their teeth are white as freshly fallen snow. I go to the workers' canteen and walk over to the counter.

"Hi," I say in English to the large black lady standing behind it. She smiles. "Could I have a Fanta, please?" I ask, handing her my money. She takes some of it and nods, handing me the bottle and the change. I can see a small dirt field where there are some boys playing with a ball of sorts. I finish my drink and go over to them. The ball is made of strips of plastic and fabric that have been tied together into a ball with string and elastic bands. The boys are my age and slightly younger. They have bare feet. When they see me, one of them kicks the ball over to me. I flip it up with my foot and juggle it; foot, thigh, foot, head, thigh, foot, before kicking it back to them. They laugh, speak in Swahili, point at me. I grin. One of them divides us into two teams by pushing us together in groups. My team doesn't wear T-shirts – we use them for goalposts. We play – they seem not to notice that they're not wearing shoes; I can see that the soles of their feet are thick with callused skin. A boy my size points at himself:

"Emmanuel," he says and then points at me.

"Christian," I say.

"*Huyo jina lake ni Christian*," he tells the others, who all tell me their names.

"I speak English, almost," Emmanuel says.

"Me too," I say, and we laugh and go on playing. A guy in a shirt and gabardine trousers and freshly polished shoes approaches the playing field.

"Hello," he says. "My name is Rogarth. My father is the manager here."

"Hi," I say and hold out my hand, saying my name. The other boys keep their distance and don't speak to him.

"Maybe you'll be in my class at the international school," Rogarth says.

"Alright," I say, nodding.

"You'd better be careful with those guys," he says with a gesture towards the footballers.

"Why?"

"They're thieves," he says. I don't say anything. "I could teach you to play golf," he says.

"I'd like that," I say.

"Christian." That's my dad's voice – he is standing by the road.

"Yes," I say and go to him.

"So, you've met the lads," Dad says.

"Be back tomorrow," Emmanuel shouts.

"Yes," I shout. We go to the house to have lunch.

"Dad, that Rogarth told me to be careful with the guys I was playing football with – that they were thieves." Dad laughs:

"Perhaps they are," he says. "But Rogarth's dad is an even bigger thief, or Rogarth wouldn't be able to go to the international school."

For lunch the cook's made a sort of curry, served with rice – it's nice.

"I thought we might go into town and have a look at your school," Dad says. "And tonight we've been asked for dinner with some English people here at T.P.C."

"Alright," I say. We drive past the factory. Dad points out different things. The administration building where he has his office. The workers' sickbay and canteen. The garages. The workers' canteen is known as the messroom – something to do with when Mærsk founded the plantation. We're driving on a tarmac road with fields of sugar on either side. The trees edging the road are full of purple flowers. On the roadside there are concrete canals for irrigation, and we keep passing railway tracks. At one point the road and the rails run parallel – a long cortege of open trucks loaded with sugar cane rumbles by.

"The trains are coming into the factory around the clock," Dad says. Here and there water from sprinklers in the fields sprays onto the road. We pass a clearing where men, sweaty and slim, walk around and slice through the sugar canes close to the ground with a long knife with a broad blade. "The knife is called a *panga*," Dad says.

"Don't they have any harvesters?" I ask.

"They broke down a long time ago, and the country has no foreign currency with which to buy spare parts. A *panga* and manual labour is cheaper." The men's clothes are filthy and tattered.

"Do they come here every morning for work then?" I ask.

"No, they live on the plantation in villages – 4,000 men and their families, schools, shops, everything." We approach a roadblock and are waved through. The sugar fields are replaced by dry bushland. "That was the entrance to T.P.C.," Dad says. Soon we see little brick buildings along the side of the road. We reach a roundabout. "T.P.C. roundabout," Dad says. There are more and more buildings. Black people everywhere. Most of the men wear white shirts and gabardine trousers, the women flowery dresses – some of them carry babies on their backs. Quite a few Indians. "There are about 80,000 people in Moshi," Dad says. We pass a large market, roundabouts with flowerbeds, leave the city centre through an old part of town and reach the school via a wide dirt road. It's called I.S.M. – International School of Moshi. The school's grounds are nice and green. There are classrooms, a sports hall, a dining hall for the boarders and buildings where they live. A playground for the youngest, a swimming pool, playing fields. The Christmas break won't be over for another few days – there's no-one here. It makes my tummy ache.

"It'll all be in English," I say.

"But no uniforms and no physical punishment. At first you'll be in their special class, so you pick up the language quickly. You'll be fine," Dad says and puts his arm around my shoulder.

That night we have dinner at John and Miriam's, the English couple.

"They were both born in Kenya. He is the plantation's works manager," Dad says. The grown-ups have gin and tonics; I have a Coke. Dinner is served. Potatoes boiled to oblivion, cauliflower boiled to kingdom come and a lamb that is excessively dead. Dad speaks to me in Danish:

"This animal has been desecrated in the fine tradition of English cooking," Dad says.

"Do you like it?" Miriam asks.

"Very much," Dad says. After dinner John sits twirling the brandy in his glass. He gets out cigars, offers my dad one. Dad takes it and gets out his lighter.

"Wait," John says, holding up his hand.

"Oh, stop it," Miriam says with a silly titter – I think she's tipsy. John takes a bell from the coffee table and rings it. The cook comes into the sitting room, takes a few quick steps towards John before falling to his knees so that he slides the last three metres across the polished floor, raising a lighter in his hand, and as he come to a halt beside John's armrest, he lights it – giving John a flame for his cigar. Dad puts his cigar in the front pocket of his shirt.

"I'll have mine later," he says. "We have to go home to call Christian's mum." We get up to leave. Dad puts his arm around my shoulder as we walk home. We can't get through to Mum. Dad sits down and takes out his cigar. "Brits! They're bloody mad," he says.

"Wait," I say, snatching his lighter. I make a quick run for it, slide across the floor and light the cigar. We laugh.

Marcus

GOD'S WRATH

Colonialism. The white man has electricity in his house and can sit in relaxation when he empties his bowels; use soft white paper to wipe away the filth. The black man must squat in the darkness of the ghetto-bog while cockroaches run over his feet, and he must wash his arse with his hand and water and get filth under his nails. And my tape recorder keeps getting tired – batteries are expensive to buy. I take a wire from the kitchen in the house, pull it to my room from the roof of the main house via a tree and in under my own roof. The light in my room creates its own problems.

"Why don't I have any electricity?" the house girl asks. She didn't want to speak to me before, but now she sees me as her electrician.

"I want a ceiling," she says. "I can't live in a way that lets you look over the partition wall while I'm getting changed."

"I'm not watching you," I say.

She pulls a face at me.

"Then tell them you want a ceiling," I say.

"You're the one who knows the *wazungu*," she says. But I don't know them. I just hope they are better than *waafrika*. After my stay with Auntie in Majengo I went straight back to the black hell. When I was at the N.U.R.U. farm at the hospital, I was observed for many months by a Lutheran parson. He came to speak to the sick Lutherans at the hospital and saw me working. He talked to the manager of the farm, George. George says I'm good. So the Reverend decides to take me. He lives close to Uhuru Hotel in Shanty Town. He goes from school to school and preaches, visits the sick and prays for them.

The Reverend takes me to his private farm in Kahe, close to the T.P.C. sugar plantation. It's hard; he wants labour, a slave. He gives me a triangular milk carton and bread. I must stand there and oversee the people who are growing corn and beans to make sure they do it right.

"You have to water that. Remove the weeds," I tell a man old enough to be my father – only the fear of God's wrath stops him from beating me to the ground. Fifteen years old. You can imagine how popular I would be if I should tell of their laziness. My food is bread and milk that has gone off. I sleep in a shed. In Tanzania you cannot question the acts of great men, but I have experienced the white ways.

I speak to the Reverend directly:

"I must go back to school." And my work is good, so the Reverend signs me up for Kibo Secondary School in Moshi and pays for the first year. The Reverend shows me the servants' quarters behind his house: a small building with two rooms – the house girl is already living in one of them. At the end of the building is an entrance to a shower and the hole in the ground – it even has a flush. I'd have my own room, which is better than our whole house in Seronera. A step up in life, because I have left Auntie's crowded house behind.

"Alright," the Reverend says. "You can live here while you go to school and learn things. But during your holidays you must help out at the farm."

"Very well, I will do it."

But school is a surprise for me. In Seronera we were allowed speak to the teacher like human beings. At Kibo Secondary School I am like a cow – if I step out of line, the teacher will adjust my direction with his stick, *eeehhh*.

My good fortune led to tension at school, because the Reverend is an important man. "I'm an expert on fields, so he has taken me in and is paying my school fees so I can teach his employees to grow things," I boasted. But boasting didn't feel quite so good when the others went home to their mothers who had made them tea with milk and sugar and a snack, and they had time to play and a family around them. I went home to my work. I wanted to get away. From my time with the Germans in the national park, I had been used to a white life without dust and poverty. The Reverend was black, but he prayed to the white god, and his neighbours were white missionaries – some of them from the German country.

Christian

Rogarth comes to fetch me the next morning with a golf bag over his shoulder. I have one too; it was left in the house when Dad moved in. We go out – goats and cattle are grazing on a fairway, watched by a young shepherd.

"It's not a very good golf course," Rogarth says.

"Full of cowshit," I say.

"Yes," Rogarth says. "There are special African rules. You're not allowed to hit the animals, and you have to find your ball quickly, or it might be trod into a cowpat." Boys in rags come running over to us. "Caddies," Rogarth says.

"Can't we carry our bags ourselves?" I ask.

"No, we can't," Rogarth says. I recognize Emmanuel and hire him. The caddies haul our bags, catch the balls and are always ready with the club you need. I end up in the middle of a herd of drowsy-looking zebu cattle grazing around my ball. I have to roll it out carefully.

"Difficult conditions," I say.

"You're allowed to take a free drop if your ball is eaten by a snake thinking it's a bird's egg," Rogarth says.

"Do you play?" I ask Emmanuel.

"Yes," he says, grinning. "But I only have one club."

Rogarth doesn't speak to his caddie. When he's ready to swing, he just reaches his arm back with his hand held out, and the caddie places the right golf club into it with the handle in his palm. Suddenly Emmanuel runs off, waving his arms about – screaming and shouting.

"Monkeys," Rogarth says, and then I see them. "They steal the balls." Rogarth helps me with my grip. He plays well. I play very badly.

After lunch I am bored. Dad is busy at work, so he doesn't have time for anything. I tuck cigarettes and matches into my pocket, grab my old leather football and go over to play with the lads. I start picking up some Swahili.

The next morning I go over to see Rogarth, but his mother says he isn't home. I go to the golf course, and Emmanuel comes running. I give him the golf bag. We go to the first hole.

"Would you like to play?" I ask.

"Yes, very much," he says. So we take turns. He hands me the club first – I hand it back to him so he can take a swing. It feels strange that he must carry the bag all the time – walk around with its weight on his bare feet. It makes the game rather unfair. As he swings, I throw the bag up on my shoulder.

"No, let me take that," Emmanuel says.

"I can carry – no problem," I say.

"It's better that I take it," he says with a worried look. Alright. Some way behind us two white ladies appear – one of them is Miriam the Brit, with the cigar and the sliding cook. Emmanuel doesn't want to take his swing when it's his turn. "It's not good if she sees me playing," he says.

"Why not?" I ask.

"It's not good. She doesn't like it."

"Who bloody cares?" I say. He shakes his head.

"She's got a hunting rifle in her bag," he says in a low voice because the ladies are approaching. "Have a look between her clubs." I look: a bluish metal pipe.

"Do you think she'll shoot you if you play?"

"No, no," Emmanuel says and laughs. "It's only if she sees an angry lion."

I play golf all morning, and after lunch I play football. That night my face is red, and I have large blisters on my shoulders and back – you can pull off my skin in large flakes.

We call Mum at home.

"Please don't tell her you've got sunburn," Dad says. "She'll be so cross with me if you do."

"I promise I won't." Afterwards we go towards the messroom to eat.

"We must say hello to the Rasmussens," Dad says. "They're back from Denmark." Nanna reminds me of the girls who wouldn't talk to me at school in Køge – beautiful and snooty.

"Hi," I say.

"Hi," she says. Her mum speaks:

"Come over anytime and use our swimming pool – whenever you feel like it."

"Thanks," I say. Nanna looks mopey. Her mum continues talking:

"Nanna, you could tell Christian a bit about the school." Nanna looks at her crossly:

"What do you want me to tell him?" she asks. "It's just a school."

"Rogarth told me about it," I say.

John and Miriam enter the messroom terrace. Sit down at the table next to ours. Miriam addresses my dad:

"It's not good that your son allows the caddies to play on the course," she says. "It doesn't look right."

"Why not?" Dad asks.

"Because they must know their place. If we don't show them their place, they get confused. Then they think that our place is their place. That we're the same. And we're really not," Miriam says.

"I see," Dad says, looking at me. "Do you understand what she says?" he asks me in Danish.

"Well, yes and no," I say. Dad laughs.

"What's so funny?" Miriam asks in English.

"Christian decides who he wants to play golf with," Dad says.

"You'll find soon enough that I'm right," Miriam tells him and looks away.

The next morning Rogarth returns.

"You mustn't let the caddie play," he says as we climb through the hole in the hedge.

"Why not?" I ask, stopping.

"He'll get the wrong idea," Rogarth says. "Now the caddie will think he's like you. Then he won't know his place."

"He is like me," I say.

"No," Rogarth says. "The caddie is paid to work for you – that's all; he's not your friend. He's just a negro from the bush." Rogarth is a negro as well. Should I remind him of it?

"And so what if he's from the bush?" I ask.

"He is without knowledge. He will steal the moment you turn your back."

"I don't agree," I say.

"You'll see," Rogarth says. I change the subject. I need a cigarette. Maybe Rogarth will tell on me if he sees me smoking. I take the chance and get out my cigarettes, holding out the pack to him. He takes a quick look around and takes one. We light up, smoke in silence and go out onto the course. The caddies come running over to us. Emmanuel carries my bag. Rogarth and I play more or less in silence. Kilimanjaro is clearly visible. At the sixteenth hole you swing straight at the mountain – it looks different every day depending on the light and the clouds.

That afternoon I go over to the Rasmussens' house. My heart is pounding. Girls are incomprehensible. The mother opens the door to me.

"Oh, you came. Nanna is out by the pool," she says. I go through the house. Nanna is sunbathing in a bikini and sunglasses. She is starting to grow breasts, and I concentrate on not looking at them.

"Hi," I say.

"Hi," she says, not moving a muscle.

"I thought I might take a dip," I say.

"Right, O.K.," she says – nothing more. I let my towel drop on a chair and get in. Do laps. Her mum brings us fizzy drinks. I have one. I need a cigarette. Her mum is nowhere to be seen.

"Do you smoke?" I ask.

"No, yuck," Nanna says.

"Well, thanks for the loan of your . . . water," I say with a gesture towards the pool. I go home and out through the hedge. African women walk past the golf course with things on their head; large bundles of firewood, several metres long; tubs full of water. Nice and easy down the paths that cross the fairway.

Marcus

WRONG PERSON

Solja and Mika say to me: "Are you alright? Have you eaten? You can ride my bicycle." But *bwana* Jonas sits on the veranda and says: "Don't give your bike to that brat – he'll just break it." Jonas has bought an 80cc Yamaha for Mika. I'm not allowed to ride it, because it's been bought with Jonas' money. Mika will let me ride it, but not if Jonas is there. If Jonas comes, I have to get off.

But Mika didn't come to Africa to sit on an 80cc when there's a 350cc around – Yamaha, as red as blood. No-one else is at home, and Mika wants to ride it. You have to eat first to have the strength to kick it started. And if does start, it doesn't just go – it flies like a feather. It rears up, and then Mika is on his back in the drive and the Yamaha is scratched.

"What were you thinking?" Jonas screams; the dirt in his mouth sprays onto my skin – I become an ashtray. "It's your ruddy job to stop him."

First I'm a niggerboy, not allowed to borrow a bicycle, and then I am a king who must tell the white boy what he can and cannot do. I will never understand Jonas.

"If I hadn't been here, you would all be dead," he roars into the night, drunk on the veranda. Apart from that, no-one tells me anything. What jobs must I do? I have to guess. That is the most dangerous thing that can happen to you: having a person control your life without directing it.

There's a knock on my ghetto-door. I open. The house girl is outside with my clothes in her arms. I put them in the laundry basket in the house. She takes them out and lets them drop to the floor.

"I'm not your house girl – you can wash your own clothes," she says.

"You must wash my clothes," I say. "The white people say so."

"I don't believe that," she says.

"Then ask them."

"I'm not going to do that," she says.

"Do you want me to go and fetch them so they can come down here and tell you that, yes, it's true – you must wash my clothes?" She pulls a face at me but picks up my clothes. Washes them.

VODKA AIR

In the evening Katriina and Jonas are going for a dinner party, and they take Solja with them.

"My stomach hurts," Mika says, because he doesn't want to go. As soon as they have left, he lights the sauna. "You must come," he tells me.

"I'm not cold," I say. But I go down into the shed with him to try out their foreign customs. There are two wooden benches – one on the floor

45

and one right under the ceiling. In the corner is an oven, and there are hot stones on top of it. Hot as hell! Sweat is pouring from me. Mika throws water onto the stones – the steam tears at my lungs.

"Wait," he says and leaves. Not long after he returns with a glass of water. "When I pour it on the stones, you must breathe deeply." I do it. A fire in my lungs and right away I am high. He has poured vodka onto the stones. "It goes straight into your system through the blood vessels in the lungs," Mika says. He knows all about these things. Afterwards we must stand under the cold shower – your body becomes very alert and very tired at the same time. And when we have sat down on the bench outside the sauna under the open sky, Mika runs into the house and brings back Carlsberg beer in the special cans.

"Here," Mika says.

"We're not allowed to drink Jonas' beer," I say. "It's very expensive."

"He'll never know," Mika says and opens one. He asks me if I have ever been with a girl.

"No," I say.

"I have," Mika says. "It hurt her badly, and she bled all over the bed. Her parents were SO mad at me." He shakes his head. "But damn, it was good!" he says and makes the pumping movement. Me, I am thinking that the school holidays will be over soon and then I'll see Rosie again. She is the most beautiful girl in my class, and now I am dreaming of kneading her bottom.

DRINK

Mika has been sent pocket money from Sweden. He gets it in dollars. I have introduced Mika to Phantom at the market, who does a black-market money exchange and makes Mika a Tanzanian millionaire. Mika is fifteen years old like me, but he is very tall and big.

On New Year's Eve he tells Katriina we'll spend the day at the cinema. The idea that Mika could have a normal life is an idle one, because he drags me to the bar at Moshi Hotel. It's very private on the first floor, so we can hide out there until the big New Year's celebration. We drink until two a.m. The taxi has no petrol, so we walk all the way home under the street lamps. The regional commissioner has had all the lamps on Kilimanjaro Road fixed. It's the only road outside the city centre that has any, because that's the route the regional commissioner takes for his evening jog and he wants people to see him. He is the greatest thief – much respect to him – he has built a squash court for himself in his home village. If a white man says the regional commissioner is an idiot then that white man is on a plane to Europe within twenty-four hours. If the man is black, he is in the Karanga Prison on false charges, because the judge is the regional commissioner's partner in crime when it comes to drinking beer and being corrupt.

Mika and me, we struggle from lamppost to lamppost, hugging each of them until we feel a bit better and can stagger on to the next bright light. Then we have to rest and be sick. I am just waiting for the commissioner to come jogging past us.

"Ma-Ma-Ma-Marcus, are you al-al-al-al-alright?" Mika stutters.

You could ask: Why did I go? He's a European, and I'm African – how could I say no? After all, he must know when things are right and when they are not, and how they should be done.

We're very noisy; we almost can't see. They drag us to the bathroom, they fill the bathtub with cold water and dump us into it. We're like dead people. We are sick down our own fronts without even knowing it. They let Mika have pocket money and let us run around at night, and now they're mad at us.

WHITE MADNESS

I go to school and am paid neither by the Larssons, the Swedish aid organization, S.I.D.A., nor by the state. But I am allowed to look after Solja and be involved in *bwana* Jonas' aid project, which is called F.I.T.I. – the Forest Industries Training Institute. I can never borrow the Larssons' private bikes, but the project motorbikes – 125cc Yamahas – those I can ride – to get cigarettes in town for Katriina, to pick Solja up at school, to fetch meat from Karim's.

Jonas teaches the negro to fell the trees in the forest. They work southeast of the city on the other side of the railway on the fringes of the Elephant Forest. Once the rainforest here was full of elephants – now it's full of bandits. The police are afraid to even set foot in there unless they are at least ten men. The bandits live in huts and produce *gongo*. On the road to the forest is that mad place the Hindus go, where they put their dead on a platform with a bonfire underneath, and then gather in a group and stare as they torch a friend or a father – they call it *Garden of Heaven*.

F.I.T.I. has an entire group of Swedes and Finns who teach: felling trees, cutting timber and boards from the logs, making plywood.

When Jonas and Asko speak English, all you hear is a building collapsing. Soon my job includes keeping an eye on the local builders who are building the storage rooms for F.I.T.I.'s sawmill. I hurry to work straight from school. If I'm just five minutes late, Jonas roars: "We're not working according to African time here." White time – every second counts. If you meet your auntie on the road in the sun and she's lugging groceries like a mule, you must simply honk your horn and drive on. You mustn't stop and say hello. You mustn't help. *Tsk*, madness.

I have to skive off from school to do the Swedes' jobs for them, and afterwards the teacher beats me, but I make no sound. I know how it works from my father: if I am noisy, the excitement grows, and the blows rain down on me. When I am silent, the beating becomes dull. But the project motorbike lifts me into a new category at school. Before I was dirt poor, almost a beggar. I couldn't even speak to Rosie, the princess of the class. Now she wants a ride on the back. Rosie so close to my back – her soft *titi* make my heart race. *Eeehhhh*. I stop at a kiosk and buy her a fizzy drink. We sit on a bench.

"How is it, living with *wazungu*?" Rosie asks.

"It's very excellent," I say. "A good house with high-fidelity music system, special food from Europe, imported beer – a relaxed lifestyle."

"It sounds lovely," Rosie says and scooches closer to me. *Eeehhh* – the dream of Europe makes her cuddly. "Do they have the lovely music with ABBA?" she asks.

"Yes, of course. They are Swedes – ABBA is from their own country," I say.

"Really?" Rosie says. "I am crazy about that music – do you think I can come over and listen to it?"

"I will make you a cassette of it," I say.

"Really?" Rosie says. "That will make me very happy." I am already very happy just thinking about how happy she will be when she gets the cassette. But I have to cut this bliss short, take Rosie home and dash off to F.I.T.I. to manage the builders.

MASH

Finally it is too dark for us to work, and I can go home, tired, tired. I switch off the motorbike before I reach the gate so my arrival is secret;

I put it in neutral and roll down the drive. Jonas' Yamaha is outside the house. The car isn't there. The house girl mustn't hear me either, because then she will argue about why I have electricity while she lives in the darkness like a negro. I park the motorbike in the garage and sneak into my ghetto, as quiet as a mouse. Lock my door and draw the curtains and lie down on my bed. The cicadas and insects are as noisy as hell – I hope the house girl doesn't wake up and make her speech about ceilings and electricity. I can't hear anything from her side, and soon I am asleep. There's a flickering light when I wake up; the house girl's paraffin lamp throws its light up onto the roof, and I'm thinking that if Jonas' won't pay for that ceiling then I'll have to find the money for it myself. I can't live the house girl's life as well as my own. The two have to be separate.

The dogs in the neighbourhood are barking like mad – it's already pitch black outside, but I can hear another sound as well. What is she doing? Is that Jonas? The voice is thick, something about *sawadi* – a present. Very quietly I climb – from my bed to the floor and up onto the desk. I stand up – when I'm on my tiptoes, I can look over the wall into her room. *Eeehhh*, it is Jonas who is sitting on her bed, but what? Are my eyes deceiving me? His pump is sticking out of his trousers, and she is working her hand like a whisp making mash.

"*Nzuri sana*," he says – very nice. He has lifted her T-shirt, and he is groping her *titi* – they're jutting out. Now he is trying to push her head down to his pump.

"Ah-ahhhh," she says, shaking her head, and letting go of the pump, she goes to the door and puts her hand on the doorknob. Where is she going? He knows next to no Swahili, so he holds up his hands as if surrendering, then pats the bed where she was before. She comes back, grabs his pump and goes on making mash. Now he wants to kiss her *titi*. "Ah-ahhhh." He tries to run his hand up her leg under her *kanga*, but her legs are as closed as if it was Sunday and she was at church. She pulls hard, fast and mechanically at the pump until it sprouts the white seed. It's very ugly to look at, but my pump, it also rises – like a little soldier it stands to attention before her *titi*. His pump is limp now. She pulls out a handkerchief and wipes his seed off the pump, off her hand. He gets up at once – his face is cross as he zips his trousers with his back turned to her. I am afraid he will look up, afraid to move and make a sound.

"*Asante*," he says – thank you – and leaves. She throws the handkerchief on the floor. His footsteps fade away as he reaches the house. She

49

makes the testy sound "tsk", and now her shoulders are shaking. She doesn't hide her face in her hands, because the black hand has whipped up a mash and is dirty with the white seed. She hides her face behind her arm, and she sobs. And now I think that I must be silent until she goes out, because otherwise she will know that I have been here all along, and then she will have me kicked out in five seconds flat.

"Ah," she sneers, grabbing her towel and her soap, turning off her paraffin lamp and, locking the door behind her, going around to the gable end of the servants' house, opposite the garage, where we have our shower and hole in the ground. I jump down from the desk. She doesn't know I was there. I can hear Jonas starting his motorbike, driving off. This man is a hunter of house girls. He is going to Moshi Club, where the rich people drink. At Moshi Club the white man can play golf, tennis and squash, but more than anything he can give his eyes a rest from poverty and stupidity; the waafrika and wahindi who go to the club are all rich and corrupt.

I open my door quietly and sneak around to the garage. I pull the motorbike all the way out and some way down the street. I start it and drive back, making a great noise, parking in front of the niche where are doors are, slamming open my door, turning on my electrical light and my tape recorder with Burning Spear singing "Do you remember the days of slavery?"

SPYING ON THE GIRAFFE

I sit down outside the door and smoke a cigarette. This house girl used to work for wahindi. Indians are strict with house girls. Work from morning to midnight, the children badgering her every minute, and whenever the man is alone with her he will grab her bottom, try to stick his pump in. But worst of all is working for waafrika – they treat the house girl like a scabby dog. Now she is with wazungu – everything is easy, if only she will whip up a bit of mash. And everyone says that wazungu are soft. You can borrow money from them if you say that your mother is very ill, and if you can't repay them, it doesn't matter.

The house girl returns from the shower with her towel wrapped around her.

"I'll get you your electricity tomorrow – I'll make it for you," I say. She mutters something inaudible and goes inside. Not long after she asks from inside:

"Do you think our *mzungu* is very rich?"

"Yes," I say. All *wazungu* are. The next day I go to Katriina and explain it to her: "The house girl wants a ceiling where we sleep."

"Why – is she afraid of snakes?"

"No, she's afraid that I will spy on her when she undresses."

"And do you, Marcus?" Katriina asks with a smile.

"Me?" I point at myself. "No, she is half Maasai – I might as well look at a giraffe." But I have seen her. That is why she is always cross – the Maasai say she is short with an arse as wide as hippo's, and flat-nosed like a bantu, and we Chagga see her as a giraffe in the national park.

"I will ask Jonas," Katriina say. Already the next day she comes to me and says:

"Marcus, we'll pay for your ceiling – just you organize it."

"Thanks," I say. "That won't be a problem."

1981

Christian

"You don't have to," I say the night before my first day at school.

"But I'd like to take you," Dad says.

"You don't have to. I know where the office is – I'll just go there and register. And Rogarth will be there. And Nanna."

"Righto," Dad says and adds, "It'll be fine." He gives me an awkward pat on the back.

"Yes, of course it will," I say, even though my stomach hurts. What good would it do if he did take me to school? The classroom is the real battlefield, and the halls. He won't be there for that.

It's chilly in the mornings. I am quick to dispatch breakfast. T-shirt, jeans, sneakers – off to the edge of the T.P.C. residential area. Nanna, Rogarth and a few younger kids show up. The T.P.C. car arrives, we get in and are taken to school. I don't say anything.

I report at the office. The bell goes as a black lady shows me to my class. There's black, brown and white children everywhere – from first-year infants to their version of *gymnasiet*. I make sure to keep a poker face and look around the classroom when they introduce me. Rogarth and Nanna aren't here – they must be in a different set. During break the teacher takes me along so I can be given books. During the next break I go into the hall, which is merely a stretch of concrete decking under the eaves. There's grass and flowerbeds between the school build-ings, and children and young people of all colours and sizes.

Rogarth comes over.

"You alright?" he asks.

"I'm fine," I say. Nanna gives me a look and nods while passing with a friend; she probably won't speak to me before she knows whether I pass muster with the other kids. Mika sees me and pulls a nasty smile:

"The little Dane," he says and makes as if he's being sick – he must have seen me that night. Tosser. A white long-haired chap from my class comes over.

"I'm Jarno," he says. "Finnish. Do you play football?"

"Goalie," I say.

"Any good?" he asks.

"Give me a try," I say.

"We have an All Stars team which plays the local schools," Jarno says and tells me when there's practice.

There's a moment's silence while the world hums about our ears.

"Do you smoke?" Jarno asks.

"As much as I can," I say.

"I'll show you all the good spots after practice," he says.

Next lesson is English, and I am sent to a special class with some Germans and a Norwegian who are also new. The teacher is a rather wizened lady, but very sweet. Later we have P.E. with the class above us. First it's running. I go towards the games field next to Jarno. In front of me is a black girl with bare feet. She already has breasts and a good-sized arse. Her eyes are beautiful.

"She can't run like that, can she?" I say.

"Shakila. Just you wait and see. She's the fastest in the school," Jarno says. And he's right. The track is covered in weeds, and their seeds are little prickly burrs. But Shakila runs faster on her bare feet than anyone else. After running practice we play football. The teacher is English. He comes over to me.

"What position do you play?" he asks.

"Goalie," I say.

"There's football practice Tuesday and Thursday afternoons. Welcome to the team," he says.

After school we are picked up by the T.P.C. car. On our way through the fields of sugar cane, the young children wave at the conductors on the passing trains. They wave back, and it seems there's a sort of game involving counting how many fingers they have. Rogarth explains it to me:

"The point blades are worn down, so they get off the train and run in front of it so they can tap down the point, and then they put sugar canes down to hold them in place. If they're not fast enough, they sometimes lose a finger."

*

In the afternoon Rogarth shows me the way to the river. We sit there, smoking cigarettes, while women in shabby dresses wade into the water to fish with large nets held between them. On the bank children watch out for crocodiles. I am relieved about school. It went well.

Afterwards I go home. Dad is there.

"It was alright," I say.

"Good," he says. "Shall we look at your homework?"

"Alright," I say and get my books. Dad never used to do prep with me. We sit at the dining table. It feels odd. I do it as best I can. It grows dark. We eat in the messroom and then go for a drive in the fields.

"Watch out for lights pointing at the sky," Dad says.

"There," I say, pointing. We find a dirt road between the sugar fields and make our way to the place where the plantation trains are loaded with sugar canes, which are taken to the factory around the clock. They only stop when it's time to clean the machinery. We stand there watching while the stars shine brightly above our heads and the bats flit through the sky.

Marcus

ORGANIZER

This home is insane. The house girl lives like a queen – she is always being given the day off by Jonas while I work late into the night minding Solja, and the rest of them are at Moshi Club. Everyone is hungry. I am hungry. Mika and Solja are hungry as well. Did anyone plan for dinner? Who must make it? So I prepare it because I have seen it done at the Germans'. And Jonas returns on the big Yamaha 350cc. We eat at the table. He says: "I'm out of here. I don't like this food." But no explanation as to why. And what does he want instead?

Still, I have to make myself useful every day. The white people must understand that without Marcus they will be lost in the black land.

The garden is dull on the eye, so with the help of the gardener I make arrangements; I explain how to plant flowers and shrubs in the beds. And sometimes I want to take part in the practical work, because a Chagga likes to root around in the soil. I have sunflowers by my ghetto, and once they come up, I sow a few *bhangi* seeds between them, hidden away. *Bhangi* plants help keep mosquitos away. I speak to the guard, who promises to water them late at night when there's no water shortage. Him knowing isn't a problem, because the guard smokes every night. They grow very well. Soon I will be able to harvest them.

Every night here, some new oddity. Katriina is going to have the baby at K.C.M.C. She's not afraid of the local hospital, because there are white doctors there as well. Doctor Freeman from Australia is going to be getting the baby out. He comes to the house. Into the sitting room. Right there, while Jonas is in the chair, the doctor makes Katriina lie down on the sofa, lifts up her top, touches her stomach everywhere, listens with special headphones that have a sort of trunk which reaches her navel.

DREADLOCK

Mika has met Alwyn at I.S.M. – he is the son of a great Chagga farmer who owns an enormous farm on West Kilimanjaro. He has cattle which produce milk for a hopeless cheese factory, and he grows wheat for the breweries. His son grows dreadlocks on his head and smokes a lot of *bhangi* and thinks he's a Rastafarian.

To me Alwyn's lion's mane is heresy – Bob Marley is a freedom fighter; Alwyn is just his father's spoiled son.

Out on his father's land Alwyn throws seed on the ground far from the house, and the plants come up during the rains. Alwyn sells *bhangi* to the *wazungu* kids at school, and Mika is his best customer. Now Mika can smoke as well as drink – Africa has become a disaster for Mika. He almost only comes home to sleep. In the afternoons Mika stays at school. "I have games," he tells Katriina. At night he dashes off to the city centre. "I'm going to the cinema," he says, or "Alwyn and I are doing prep together at Alwyn's." Because Alwyn lives with an aunt in the city centre. It saves money that he doesn't have to board. They don't do prep. Mika comes home late, shifty-eyed from too much *bhangi*, but the grown-ups suspect nothing.

One night I am sitting there leafing through a European magazine full of people in posh clothes in posh houses with posh furniture. Solja is sleeping like an angel, and the parents are at the club. There's a car honking at the gate – Asko in the project Land Cruiser. I go outside. The guard has opened the gate. Asko parks right in front of the veranda, and out staggers Mika – drunk, stoned. In the back of the car is Mika's 80cc motorbike.

"Where are Jonas and Katriina?" Asko asks.

"They're at the club. What's happened?" I ask. Mika grins goofily.

"He was sitting in a bar in Majengo, drunk out of his head," Asko says.

"And what if I was?" Mika says – so drunk he doesn't stammer.

"He shouldn't be in Majengo," Asko says. "Get him to bed. I'm going out to speak with Jonas."

"They bleeding well don't decide what I can do, Marcus," Mika snickers and staggers into the house. Asko has already started the car. The question remains unanswered. Why was Asko in Majengo, when he has his fine wife, Tita?

THE BIBLE

In our house the Bible is called *Ostermann Tax & Duty Free*; a big book full of everything: clothes, furniture, sweets, tinned food, Hi-Fi decks . . . everything. It's a Danish company that sells things to embassies all over the world. When *wazungu* find work in Tanzania, they are allowed to bring a container into the country full of all their things: fridge, freezer, car, stereo . . . everything, because you can't buy anything here. They're allowed to do it once – free of charge. Jonas goes to Dar es Salaam for four days and brings home the container. It's not their own things, but things they have ordered through the Bible: strange tins of food, packets of chocolate, many Carlsberg beers, a very powerful vacuum cleaner. It is a feast to the eyes, and the sound of the stereo is crisp and clear.

There is a big tube with paper inside it – a great big picture of a forest. Grass at the bottom and a lake, tall green trees, sunshine, but the gentle sort – not like the African sun. We're going paste the picture onto the wall at the end of the room, so that the forest is inside the house – a strange white custom. I help Katriina do it, because her stomach is very round now. She smiles a lot.

"This is how the forest looks at home in Sweden."

Asko and Tita have also had a container sent with a car and everything. They arrive in their car to see the forest on the wall; *eeehhh* – a very fine Mercedes Benz, like a dictator's. But we still have to pick Tita up at the market while Asko rides his motorbike. If he's going somewhere with Tita, he borrows the project's Land Cruiser even though it's illegal for the staff to use it in their own time. Where is the Mercedes? It's in the garage at the F.I.T.I. forestry school on wooden blocks, with the wheels taken off and a large blanket over it to keep it warm.

"Why must Asko's car always sleep in the garage?" I ask Katriina. She sighs and smiles:

"Because Asko is allowed to take it back to Finland without paying taxes and duties if he has had it at least a year while living abroad," she says. So Asko's help for the negro is also a big help for Asko himself – he will be *bwana mkubwa* in Finland, driving a big Mercedes – completely new and never exposed to the Tanzanian dust.

At night I am standing in the kitchen with Solja, making popcorn as a snack. The ABBA music starts playing in the sitting room.

"Now Mum and Dad are going to dance," Solja says in English and smiles at me. I can hear them speaking the Swedish language in the sitting room. Solja's face looks wrong as she listens to them.

"What are they saying?" I ask, because Katriina has started sobbing in the sitting room.

"Dad is being mean," Solja says. "He says Mum's too fat to dance. But Mum says it's his baby that's making her fat."

ABBA POWER

Sunday. Solja is sitting in front of me on the motorbike's fuel tank, holding on to the handlebars while I take her to a friend.

"*Haraka, haraka,*" she shouts – fast, fast. The girl likes speed. Now I have the motorbike all day until it's time to pick her up. I am wearing my good shirt and sunglasses I have borrowed from Mika – I am looking very sharp. I whizz off to Nechi's family home across the street from the Police Academy. I hope Rosie will be there. The first thing I see is Edson the Acrobat walking on his hands on the drive. Why is he doing that? On the front steps Rosie is sitting between Claire's knees, and Claire is plaiting Rosie's hair into pretty narrow cornrows across her perfect head.

"Do something else," Rosie tells Edson, who immediately starts doing cartwheels into somersaults, and one-armed press-ups. Yes, he is very acrobatic and wants to impress Rosie with his strength – *tsk*. The girls giggle, and Claire whispers something in Rosie's ear that makes her laugh and clap her hands. I sit down on the steps next to Nechi and offer him a cigarette.

"Your hair is going to look nice," I tell Rosie. She looks at me. I put my hand into my pocket. "Oh yes, I have that tape for you," I say very casually and hand her the ABBA cassette.

"Ohhh," Rosie says and flies from her seat and kisses my cheek. "Thank you, Marcus."

"You're welcome," I say. Edson has stopped doing his cartwheels and is looking at Rosie – suddenly he's looking tired.

"Will you take me home, Marcus?" Rosie asks.

"Yes, of course," I say and start the engine. *Eeehhh*, it's amazing when she puts her arms around me.

NO LAND OF MY OWN

"Marcus?" the gardener calls. "Your mother is here to see you." What? I leave my ghetto, and my mother is standing in her Sunday best with my youngest sister on her back.

"What are you doing here?" I say.

"I just wanted to see if my oldest son was well," Mother says.

"I am well. Now you can go again," I say. I won't offer her so much as a chair to sit on. She looks at the ground. Here it comes:

"You have to help me – just a little – I need money to feed the children."

"They're not my children. You must speak to your husband – getting the money is his job," I say.

"But he has lost his good job, and there's no work to be found," Mother says.

"No-one wants a driver who is drunk," I say.

"But the white people – you help them. They have lots of money," Mother says.

"It's their money – not mine."

"But you can take a little. They must understand that you have to help your family."

"They pay for my food and my school and give me a house to live in. I mustn't beg for money for my father's drinking," I say.

"What have they done for you? They cheat you. They'll leave just like the Germans. We're your parents," Mother says.

"Yes, I know. Every night I must sleep on my front, otherwise I will feel the mess of skin my father made on my back."

"What should I do?" my mother asks and starts crying like at a funeral.

"You have your *shamba*," I say, because they have a good field in North Pare Mountains where land is cheap – food for the family and a little bit to sell.

"He has sold the land to get money for drink," she says.

I ask about her family in the village on the mountain.

"They don't have room for us," she says.

It's true. The mountain is swarming with Chaggas, because now the white people have been here for a hundred years, the babies hardly die – almost all children live to grow up and produce little Chaggas of their own. White medicine keeps death at bay, and the white missionaries have always lived in packs in the highlands. The lowlands are hot, but the mountain is cool like the white country.

But when a Chagga has ten children and they all survive, then his land must be split into ten. In the end each family owns a stamp-sized bit of land, not big enough to feed half a cow, and the clever ones buy land from the less clever ones, and suddenly there's a man like my father: a Chagga with no land on the mountain, *pfffiii*. He is nothing, has to leave the mountain, go out into the world. Now he can no longer be helped by his family, because the family has been scattered, and who wants to help a drunken Chagga who doesn't even have land of his own to put his feet on, but is slinking around in the burning dust of the lowlands like a snake?

I give Mother whatever money I have and send her away.

Christian

Football practice. Jarno points everyone out:

"That mulatto there is Panos – our half-Greek centre-back. Stefano is Italian – midfielder. Baltazar – that blue-black guy over there – is on the wing; son of Angola's ambassador. And then there's the Arab, Sharif – our libero."

"And you?" I ask.

"Central midfield," Jarno says. After practice I go with him and Panos to the river and smoke cigarettes, talk about girls and music.

Dad picks me up late afternoon.

"Congratulations," he says.

"On what?" I ask.

"Your sister was christened," Dad says.

"Right," I say, smiling. "So what's her name?"

"We decided on Annemette," Dad says.

"How are they? Alright?" I ask.

"Yes, fine," Dad says. "Your mum is looking forward to coming down."

We drive from the school to the Larssons'. Dad needs to talk to Jonas about a trip to Arusha National Park. "We have to go on safari now, before your mum arrives. You can't drive on those wretched roads with a baby," Dad says. Soon Jonas will have a Swedish friend coming down for a visit – Andreas. And Andreas will want to see wild animals as well. John and Miriam from T.P.C. will tag along, but Katriina is heavily pregnant and is going to stay at home. We arrive at the Larssons', but Jonas isn't there.

"He called and said he would be late. He won't be here for another few hours," Katriina says.

"Well, in that case we'd better go home," Dad says.

"Why don't you stay for supper?" Katriina says.

"Can I go to the cinema then?" I ask.

"Of course," Dad says. Mika would like to go to the cinema as well. Solja badgers her mother to let her come with us, even though she is only nine years old.

"Alright," Katriina says and calls Marcus – I don't think she trusts Mika. Dad takes us to ABC Theatre on Rengua Road; he gives me money before driving off again. We go into the foyer. Mika lights a cigarette and looks at us.

"I can't be arsed to see that film," he says and walks out.

"*Tsk*," Marcus says. "Now he'll be going to the bar." We get tickets for expensive seats on the balcony where the chairs are upholstered. The film is brilliant: "Vanishing Point".

"That was stupid," Solja says when we come out again. "All he did was go around in that car."

It was the coolest thing: the guy in the car playing hide-and-seek with the police. Marcus liked the blind black radio D.J. It's late, and we'd promised to bring Solja straight home. We pass the Arusha roundabout and walk down the small residential streets in Shanty Town, take the back way so we can sneak through the hole in the fence behind the house. A bit further down the street there's a red Toyota Land Cruiser. "That's our car," Solja says.

"No, it's not yours," Marcus says. "It's another car." There are no street lamps here, but it does look like their car, and it looks as if it's rocking slightly even though the engine is switched off.

"But it is ours," Solja says.

"No, your car is different," Marcus says firmly. I don't know, but it could be their car. We're just a hundred metres from it. Marcus puts his arm around Solja's shoulder: "Let's get home and have a snack." He tries to guide her to the other side of the street from where we cross the undeveloped plot behind their house where people have planted corn.

"It is ours," Solja says, shaking his arm from her shoulder, half running towards the car.

"*Tsk*," Marcus says in a low voice.

"But isn't it theirs?" I ask.

"Ssshhhh," Marcus whispers. Solja has almost reached the car. Her feet crush some dry twigs on the roadside – making a sound; the car stops rocking, she stops running; sneaks the last few feet on the tarmac. "It's Jonas," Marcus says. "Solja mustn't see him."

"In the car?" I ask.

"Yes," Marcus says. I'm about to ask what he's doing there, but I think I know. Solja is squatting by the rear bumper. What should we do? If we call to her or go over and pull her away, Jonas will hear us and know that we know. And she will know it as well. Silence. Then the car starts rocking again. Marcus stands stock-still. Solja has positioned herself on the roadside next to the car. There's a taxi coming from the opposite direction. Marcus turning into the cornfield leading up to the back garden is something I hear more than I see. Someone is moaning inside the car – a woman. The taxi approaches; Solja gets up and presses her face against the side window. For a brief moment the taxi headlights illuminate the cabin of the Land Cruiser. On the backseat, but facing the wrong way: a black woman with her shirt open. The black breasts bob up and down – she is leaning back towards the seat in front, moving up and down. She is sitting on top of Jonas. Solja squats down abruptly, leaning in towards into the back tyre. Fuck, this is not good. I reach out to take her hand, to get her out of there. Just as I grab hold of her, she pulls away. My turn to squat – I look at her dark silhouette. The moaning from inside the car grows louder and louder.

"*Jävla hora*," I hear Jonas saying inside the car – you fucking whore. Solja gets up abruptly, walks past me. Finally we get out of there – I follow her; she is walking stiffly, slowly. By the time we reach the edge of the cornfield I have passed her and stop to make sure she is coming. She is bent over.

"Come on," I whisper. She gets up, turning her back to me, raising her hand. Bollocks. A stone. There's just enough time for me to say, "No," before she has swung her arm, thrown the stone. The sound of glass shattering. She turns around, runs past me through the corn stalks. We hear car doors opening.

"Who's there?" Jonas shouts in English. The cornfield has already gobbled us up.

The neighbour's dog discovers us as we squeeze through the fence, and Katriina sees us from the veranda.

"Hey," she calls. "Was it a good film?" Solja doesn't say anything. We're standing in the corner of the garden. I don't know what Solja will do next. What could she possibly do? Maybe she'll tell her mum everything.

"Yes, it was fine," I say.

"We have to go soon," Dad says. We have to get back to T.P.C., because I have school tomorrow, and it's already nine-thirty.

"Is Jonas not back yet?" Marcus asks – I don't know why he would ask.

"No, maybe his car is acting up," Katriina says. Marcus walks towards his servants' quarters.

"What are you doing?" Katriina asks, because we're standing by the fence without moving, still not coming towards the house.

"We'll be right there," I say, putting my arm around Solja's shoulder, walking towards the veranda.

"What's the matter, darling?" Katriina says as soon as she sees Solja.

"Nothing. I'm going to bed," Solja mutters and goes inside the house. Katriina looks at me. What should I do? I shrug. She gets up and follows Solja into the house.

"What was that about?" Dad asks.

"I don't know," I say and sit down on the edge of a chair. "Can we go now?" I ask.

"Was it a violent film?" Dad asks.

"No, it was perfectly nice," I say. Now I can hear Solja crying inside the house and the sound of Katriina's voice – she is worried.

"But what happened?" Dad asks.

"*Nothing* happened. How the hell should I know what's got into her?" I say.

"No need for that language," Dad says.

"I'm going down to Marcus."

"You're not going anywhere," Dad says. Katriina comes out on the veranda.

"Christian," Dad says, "what happened?" I look at the floor.

"I don't know what's going on with her," I say and look up. My cheeks are burning, but I don't think they can see that in the dark.

"What does she say?" Dad asks Katriina.

"But that's just it – she won't say. She's just crying." Katriina's standing there, wringing her hands. "Marcus!" she calls. Just then we see headlights across the dirt road. It's Jonas' Land Cruiser. The guard runs to open the gate for him. I can see that Marcus is coming slowly across the lawn from the servants' quarters. Jonas parks the car in front of the veranda – one of the side windows in the back is shattered. The others don't notice it in the dark.

"Hello," he says in a dull voice. He looks at us, letting his eyes rest on me for a moment, trying to read the situation. Marcus is coming towards us. Katriina breaks the silence:

"Solja is inconsolable. She's in her bed crying, and she won't speak to me."

"Did something happen?" Jonas asks.

"She went to the cinema with Christian and Marcus, and then when they came home – only a little while ago – she went to bed right away and . . . just cried." Jonas looks at Marcus.

"What happened?" he asks. Marcus doesn't say anything for a moment.

"Maybe they've been cruel to her at school," he says. "Nothing happened at the cinema."

"Did you go straight home afterwards?" Jonas asks.

"Yes, but . . ." Marcus says.

"What?" Jonas says.

"When we came through the fence back there," Marcus says and points towards the corner of the garden. Jonas interrupts him:

"I've told you not to use that hole in the fence. It must be closed up." Marcus doesn't say anything. "Then what?" Jonas says.

"Well – she wanted to take some corncobs from the field, and I told her not to steal them, because they belong to poor people who need to have to something to eat every day, but she said she didn't care and ran into the field, and I lost sight of her. And then we waited for a little while, and I called her and was going to go into the field to look for her, but then she came back and we went through the fence." Marcus says too much and much too quickly. It seems suspicious, because he doesn't normally speak like that.

"And then what?" Jonas says.

"But perhaps that's what upset her, because I spoke to her gruffly about not stealing," Marcus says. Jonas looks at me.

"Is it true?"

"Yes," I say.

"Why didn't you just say that at once?" Dad asks. What a fool he is.

"I didn't think it could have anything to do with that," I say.

"You'd better go and look in on her," Katriina says. Jonas goes into the house. We're all quiet.

"Was there anything else?"

"No, just go," Katriina says angrily.

"Bye," Marcus says.

"Bye," I say. Jonas comes out again.

"She's already asleep." I don't believe for a minute that she's sleeping – she's just pretending. Dad looks at his watch.

"We'd better be going," he says.

"Alright then, bye," Katriina says in a monotone and goes into the house.

"Right, well," Jonas says. "I'm sure we'll meet at the club." I go over to the car, get in on the passenger side. Dad gets in behind the wheel. Starts, drives, doesn't say a word until we reach T.P.C. The guard at the gate recognizes the car and raises the bar. As soon as we're on the other side Dad stops the car and turns off the engine. A guard comes right over.

"*Shikamoo mzee,*" he says.

"*Marahaba,*" my dad says. "*Hamna shida.*" No problems – to get him to leave. The guard walks away. "What happened?" Dad asks.

"What?" I say.

"Don't be stupid," he says.

"But . . ." I start; I feel as if I'm going to be sick. "Nothing happened." My throat is constricted.

"Get out of the car," he says. I do, shutting the door behind me, standing there looking in through the open window – my dad in the faint light from the dashboard. "It's a 25-kilometre walk home," he says. "You can either walk, or you can tell me what happened." I turn away from him, starting to walk – my shadow moving in jolts ahead of me, long and slender in the light from the headlights. Tears are coming into my eyes, and I bite back a sob, because I don't want the guards to hear.

Dad starts the engine and drives up next to me. "Are you sure you wouldn't rather talk?" he asks. I shake my head. He keeps driving next to me. Fucking idiot, what's he thinking? I stop, he brakes a little ahead of me. Marcus gave me some cigarettes – I get one out and my box of matches, stuffed with cotton wool to stop them rattling in my pocket. Get one out of the box, light it, light the cigarette, take a nice deep drag, wipe my eyes with the back of my hand, start walking again, pass the car. Exhale a cloud of smoke. Dad opens the car door.

"I've damn well had it with you," he shouts. I stop with my back to him. I can hear him getting out. I walk back towards the car; the head-lights blind me, so I can only see his silhouette. He's standing by the door – I go to the passenger side. He turns. We're looking at each other over the roof of the car. I look away. Take the cigarette from my mouth, saying:

"Jonas was fucking one of his whores in the Land Cruiser down on the backstreet when we came back from the cinema."

"No," Dad says.

"Yes." I open the passenger door, get in and shut the door.

"Did Solja see it?" Dad asks as he gets in.

"What do you think?"

"Did Jonas see you?" Dad asks.

"No, but he heard something," I say, sucking on my cigarette, which is stodgy at one end and tapers off at the tip like a bull's cock. I snivel. "She threw a stone which broke one of the car windows."

"You shouldn't smoke," Dad says.

"Really."

"It's not good for you," he says.

"You're surrounded by idiots," I say and keep smoking until I can shoot the butt out into the sugar fields. Dad doesn't say anything else. We drive home in silence.

Marcus

SMART CHILD

Solja doesn't speak for four days. Katriina takes the child to the *wazungu* doctors at K.C.M.C., but they can't discover anything wrong with her. I sit with Solja next to me on the veranda and read to her from an English children's book. Then Solja looks up at her mother.

"*Ninataka umbwa*," the girl says in Swahili – she's completely mastered the language already. Katriina jumps up and says something in Swedish, clasping her hands. Solja just looks at her mother, who looks at me:

"What is she saying, Marcus?" Katriina asks nervously.

"She says she wants a dog," I say.

"Why?" Katriina asks.

"*Kwa sababu ya wezi*," Solja says.

"She says it's because of the thieves," I say.

"Do we have to have a dog?" Katriina asks, very confused.

"Having a dog is good," I say. "You see, we blacks are afraid of dogs."

"But we have a guard," Katriina says, and goes over to stroke Solja's cheek, muttering to her in Swedish. I explain:

"The dog isn't to stop the thief. It's an alarm clock for the guard to wake him up when the thief is coming."

"Do you think the guard sleeps on the job?" Katriina asks.

"What do you think he does?" I ask.

"Say something else," Katriina says to Solja.

"*Ninataka umbwa*," the child says.

"Can you get us a dog?" Katriina asks.

"Yes," I say. Solja speaks in Swedish, words I can understand:

"Thank you, Mother," she says. Clever girl.

DECAPITATED HEADS

The parents think that everything is wild and dangerous in Africa; the children are not allowed to move around freely. "Idi Amin was a barbarian," the grown-ups tell each other. Tanzania booted Big Daddy out of Uganda in 1979 because he attacked our country. And now come the stories about Amin's insanity; he killed and tortured 300,000 people; he kept decapitated heads in his freezer so he could take them out and talk to them. He ate his wife. He buried his enemies alive or fed them to the crocodiles. People who were still alive were tied down and a metal bucket was put upside down on the bellies with a rat inside it, and then a fire was lit to make the rat escape the fire by eating its way through the living belly. Amin was black, and now *wazungu* think that all blacks carry the same barbarity in their blood.

When I lived with the Reverend I became a small guard for the German children, because I knew my way in the black wilderness. The missionary children attend I.S.M. – International School of Moshi; that is where all the *wazungu* children and children of diplomats and the *wahindi* children and children of the most corrupt politicians go – the ones whose parents can afford to pay very great school fees.

When I came home from school, I would play with the German children. I was only slightly older than them – three years. It was odd to eat at the same table as a new German family. They didn't even know whether I could hold a spoon. How would I behave? It frightens them, because it is in their blood to be racist. One child would ask another child, "The black monkey – has it eaten?" The child points to me – forgetting that I know many words. Even the mother would say, "Has the black one had a shower? I think I can smell negro sweat." But I start with the children – they have dinner at my place, but only when the Reverend isn't around. Because if the Reverend comes and finds me playing with the Germans – that's when it's dangerous.

The Reverend will come home late at night and find that the light is on in my room, and he will come down and remove the light bulb, because I am stealing his electricity for my homework, when my destiny is to work in his stupid fields. But first he will leave the light on so that he can see where to slap my face. God uses the bishop as his slave, and the bishop uses the Reverend. The Reverend needs a slave to beat so that he too can feel like a big man.

CORRUPTION

I gambled on being adopted by the German missionaries, but they ended up caught between the devil and the deep blue sea, or at least between the will of God and man's earthly desires. The Germans worked in the same office as the Reverend. The German woman is the bishop's secretary, and the man works as an engineer and architect. The man tells the Reverend:

"Why do you fiddle the money from the European sponsors?"

"What?" the Reverend says. "I don't fiddle anything. The money goes towards paying for God's kingdom on earth."

"No," the German says. "The books say that a school has been built, but the school isn't there. The money must have gone into someone's pocket."

"*Tsk*," the Reverend says. "Don't bring your false allegations to me." And the Reverend leaves the office with his pockets well lined, treating the German like an imbecile, ignoring him.

To make matters worse, the German starts kicking up dust with the bishop. The German doesn't understand that when the Reverend takes the money, the bishop's wallet also grows fatter. And the white man is only a visitor to the black country. We have an apartheid of our own.

"We can't prove anything," the bishop tells the German. "But we think that you have taken the money for yourself." The German is given an hour to clear his desk and leave the office. At the same time, the bishop is building a new house in Old Moshi.

But by the time that happens I have already seen the Larsson family, who had moved into a wooden house across from the Reverend. The new children see me as one of the Germans. I turn up at their school in the afternoon to ride horses, even though the Germans are already packing up. The Swedish family is a door to a better life, but the door is locked, and I am looking for the key. I am the little black helper who must be candid and kind.

If I go to I.S.M. alone, they won't even let me through the gates. Who must I challenge? The Headmaster?

"Have you paid your school fees?"

"No." And yet I am sitting on his horse.

DIRT IN THE MOUTH

Mika explained how I am suffering with the Reverend. So Katriina spoke to her husband. I remember. Jonas was sitting with dirt in his mouth. Satanic Swedish *juju*. He popped his index finger in and pushed the dirt around between his lips and his teeth; when he opened his mouth his teeth were black. I didn't understand a word, just that the man was hostile. Mika stutters at Katriina:

"I-i-i-if you can't help him, then that's cr-cr-cr-cr-cruel." And then Katriina speaks to me.

"What's your name?" she asks.

"Marcus Kamoti."

"How old are you?"

"Fifteen years old," I say.

"But you're so . . . small," she says.

"When I was little, we didn't have a lot of food in my family."

"Where are your parents?"

"Dead," I say and weep a single crocodile tear.

"What do you want?"

"I want to go to school, but the Reverend refuses to pay my school fees because he wants me to be a slave in his fields," I lie. The fees have been paid, but life with the Reverend is not good.

"I'll see what I can do," Katriina says. *Bwana* Jonas remains a problem. First he wants to know where I am from, which village, so he knows where to find me if I steal. He never asks me directly – he asks Katriina to find out while he himself whizzes off on his big Yamaha motorbike. And I grease Katriina's mind with my helpfulness.

The Larssons had only just arrived in Tanzania, and times were hard. You can't get anything; sometimes you can't even get toilet paper. But I can find these things for them; I know the prices and understand the Tanzanian ways.

The timber house was full of rats, and the Larssons had complained to the government office – they wanted to move to a brick house. I stole rat poison from the Reverend and got under the floorboards, spreading the poison – solving the white people's problem.

Solja was my key to the opening of Katriina's heart. Solja liked me. She went straight into the kitchen and ate everything she wanted.

"*Toka!*" said the Larssons' cook – get lost. He was old and didn't want children on his turf. Solja was naughty. Soon she put her hand into the cake batter he was making and started eating.

"Enough!" the cook said and pushed her away. She leapt forward and pushed the entire earthenware bowl onto the floor so that it broke, and then she stood there staring at the cook. WHAP! – he slapped her, and she screamed for Katriina who in turn was very furious and fired the cook on the spot. This was my chance. Who would now cook dinner? I had picked something up from the cook in the German home, and right away I turned myself into the useful negro boy: I helped with dinner. And while Katriina was looking for a new cook, I was always around, whenever *bwana* Jonas was out. Their shoes were dusty; I polished them. And washed the motorbike, sorted out food and coffee for the guard at night. No-one had to explain me anything – helpful and attentive; in no time at all they found they couldn't do without me even if they wanted to, if they wanted their lives to run smoothly. The Reverend beat me every time I neglected my duties, but my investment in the Larsson house was my hope for a better future.

After a while the Swedish door was opened completely.

"You can stay in the servants' quarters in the new house," Katriina said. "And I'll pay your school fees." I moved in with them straightaway, and the Reverend was disappointed. His slave had gone missing – the beans withered in his garden. First chance I got, I popped a bit of *bwana* Jonas' dirt in my mouth; it was like chewing on an old ashtray; my stomach was dizzy until all the food came out the wrong way, through my mouth.

I began the artificial lifestyle of the servant. When *bwana* Jonas is around I try to be as invisible as possible. And I never speak to other people about the Larsson family; whenever anyone asks I always tell them everything is fine. My hypocritical mask is complete. Yes, soon it's like I have the slave-owners hypnotized. When the black people don't speak and gossip and grumble about the white peculiarities, it's because we are as stupid as cattle. But in fact, we know everything. Do you want to know whether the egg is fresh, Katriina? – I know; the house girl knows. Do you want to know whether *bwana* Jonas has done his job or been as lazy as a dog? – we know.

If *bwana* Jonas sees me, I am a lamb: "*Shikamoo,*" I say; Swahili for *I hold your feet* – the respectful way to greet one's elders. "Would you like me to wash your motorbike, *bwana* Jonas?" "Would you like some coffee, *bwana* Jonas?" Every time he sees me, I beg for a new little job that can add pleasure to his existence. At first Katriina would laugh at me:

"Don't call him *bwana*. We're all equals. His name is Jonas."

"As you please," I say, because I thought the woman was good, but mad at the same time. Should I tell *bwana* Jonas to polish my shoes, so we could see a real flowering of equality?

ROTTEN MOUTH

Katriina has given me some pocket money, which I take to my auntie in Majengo as a present and a thank you for all her help when I first came to Moshi. I have to stay and eat corn porridge and fish with her and her daughters, because it would be rude not to. The corn porridge sticks to my teeth and feels like concrete when it lands in my stomach, while the fish gives a taste of rotten acid; I have now got totally used to the white food, nice and light.

On my way back I pass the bars with drunken men and girls for sale. There's one man whom I recognize … *eeehhhh*, it's my own father, dirty, worn out, tottering even. And he has seen me, so I change my direction and go to greet him. The smell from his mouth is of rotten *mbege*.

"Where is my present?" he asks me straight out, holding out his hand.

"I don't have one," I say.

"You live with *wazungu*, and you can't even give your own father a small present after he has carried you through life on his shoulders?" he shouts and stumbles. The customers at the bar stop talking – they want to see if there is to be a show as well.

"They pay for my school and my food – they don't give me money," I say.

"You're lying," my father shouts and spits at me. "You're not my son." He reaches out an arm to push me away, but the link between his eye and his arm is disturbed by *mbege* – his arm slaps nothing but air, because I have stepped aside. My father lands on his face in the dust. People laugh because it is always jollifying to watch other people fall. Father mutters and reaches up an arm to be lifted from the ground. I turn and walk away while I light a cigarette and smoke it. I set my sights on the white family, my benefactors.

THIGHS LIKE CREAM

Tita and fat Asko finally have their own house and have moved out of the Y.M.C.A., but they still need a sauna.

"I haven't got the time to build it," Asko says. He is the saw doctor at F.I.T.I.; he teaches black people to sand timber down, so that they can cut it out into planks and things.

Tita twitters like a bird; she wants the sauna soon, otherwise it's just impossible to live in the hot country. At the sawmill school Asko has his students practise their craft by cutting boards for the sauna. The boards are then taken to Asko and Tita's house, and I am sent there to supervise the local builders, even though it means I have to skive off from school. And today is my birthday – sixteen years old. No-one knows, so the celebration takes place only in my mind. Tita explains in strange English how she wants the walls and the ceiling, and I pass the information on in Swahili.

"Marcus," she calls from the veranda on the front of the house. I go over. She's lying on her front on a sunbed, almost naked in the sun. Skimpy yellow knickers, thighs like cream, lovely and round, her legs like a V, and I can see little blonde hairs sticking out of her flower. Her back is entirely bare. I don't stand too close. That arse of hers isn't as flat and dreary as that of other white women – Tita's arse: it's ready to dance.

"What is it?" I say. She raises her upper body and looks at me. Out of the corner of my eye I see her breast, small and smooth.

"Come here, do," she says and sounds impatient. She points at an orange plastic bottle. "Take some of that and put it on my back." I put some on my hand, smearing it onto her shoulder blades and down her back, but only along the middle, so that my black hand is nowhere near her titi and bottom. "Go on. Do it properly," she says. "The sides as well." The white skin says what the black hand must do on top of it. The sauna hasn't been built yet, but inside me it is lit all the same – a great big fire. Is that my birthday present? "That wasn't so bad, was it?" Tita says.

"No," I say.

"You're a good boy," she says.

"Yes," I say.

Christian

Arusha National Park. Dad has borrowed a Land Rover, and we go around in it, looking at the wildlife. Jonas is in their Land Cruiser with Andreas. John and Miriam from T.P.C. have come along as well with Miriam's little sister, Vera, who has come to visit from Kenya.

We are back at the lodge before sundown. Shower in water that has been heated all day by the sun in the water tank.

Everyone gathers on the veranda outside the restaurant for a "sundowner". I go there with Dad. Jonas and Andreas are sitting with John, Miriam and Vera. Mika and Solja have both stayed at home in Moshi.

"So, what soup are we having today?" Dad asks.

"They're calling it potato soup," John grins.

"I do miss the time when it was chicken soup," Andreas says. We have the same soup for starters every night. The name has changed every day, but the soup is the same. Bouillon. At first they called it chicken soup – it had some meaty scraps in it. Then they ran out of chicken and dumped in a handful of carrots – carrot soup. Today – potato soup. The main course is the same every night. Tough beef with ketchup and chips and coleslaw.

Andreas is a journalist from Sweden. He is here to write articles about how Jonas is training sawmill workers with Swedish aid money. Andreas leans towards Vera and speaks to her in a low voice. She titters, and it makes her breasts bob up and down behind the fabric of her dress. I gape at them. When we've finished eating, the grown-ups sit and drink. I go to my room to read Ian Fleming. From the way they're laughing, I can tell they're getting more and more drunk. Andreas is talking out of his arse – Vera laughs. I fall asleep before the old man gets back.

I sleep until late. Today we're driving back to Moshi and T.P.C. I go over to the restaurant.

"You bastard!" I hear Vera's voice as I step onto the veranda, and she rushes past me with tears in her eyes. I look after her, go inside, look at Jonas and Andreas and Dad who are all sitting there. Jonas is staring at nothing in particular.

"There's no reason not to be polite to her, is there?" Dad says to Andreas.

"We slept together, that's all," Andreas says. When we're about to leave, Vera comes over to our car.

"Can I ride with you?" she asks.

"Yes, of course," Dad says. The Land Rover has no back seat – it has three seats in front instead – I have to sit with the gear lever between my knees. The dirt roads are beat up, the car tips and tilts; sitting like that is not very practical when the gears have to be changed constantly and there are no proper seatbelts – I keep bumping into them, first Dad and then Vera.

"Sit up here," Vera says and pulls me onto her lap so Dad can drive more easily. She snivels: "Why was he so mean to me?"

"I don't know," Dad says. "It was stupid of him."

"Yes, I don't understand it . . ." Vera starts but then stops, snivels, composes herself. "Christian shouldn't have to listen to these things – he wouldn't understand."

"Oh? I think he understands rather more than I like to think," Dad says. I don't say anything.

"Perhaps," Vera says and pulls me closer. Her sturdy soft thighs right under my bare legs – just the thin fabric of her dress between them. Vera bends in across me – tries to look at my face. I am thirteen years old. What does she think I'm feeling?

"It's not that I want to marry him," she says. "Just that we were having so much fun and then suddenly . . ." She shakes her head, drying her eyes with a quick, almost furious movement of her hand. "Suddenly he treats me like some sort of whore. Why would he do that, do you think?" she asks.

"You know – Scandinavian men; afraid of showing any emotion," Dad says. Vera smoothes down my hair. The heat from her thighs is penetrating me. I am afraid she'll notice my erection.

"It's not just Scandinavian men," Vera says.

"What?" Dad says.

"Men. Who have a hard time showing emotions."

"No. I suppose not," Dad says.

"Why is that?" she asks.

"I don't know," Dad says.

"I want to be treated like a human being," Vera says. My dad nods. I can feel the heat between our thighs. "I am a human being," she says. Yes, you are. So am I.

Marcus

BRAIN

I am very confused by my life with these *wazungu*, but the most important things work – Katriina is paying my school fees, so I can learn.

But school is difficult as well: khaki shorts and a white shirt, be polite, sit still. If you're noisy during lessons, you'll have to meet the rod. Listen very carefully, because Teacher almost doesn't care whether you understand anything – the salary is so bad.

Kibo Secondary School has gone to rack and ruin, and yet it still costs money; in Tanzania only primary school is free. The blackboard in our class is so worn no-one can see the lines the teacher draws. How will we ever learn?

At school you can buy yourself a good brain. If your parents give the teacher a present, your grades will skyrocket, even if your head is made of stone. But without money, your grade counts for little, even if your head is screwed on tight. You are but a cow, and your teacher is a stick. Edson is the only poor pupil who isn't beaten. He is on a government scholarship because he is a master at acrobatics – very strong – and the teacher understands that Edson is so very stupid he might actually hit him back. Big Man Ibrahim is almost never beaten, because he only smiles when the rod hits him. I am beaten every time I boast of my wealth by driving my motorbike past the teacher as he walks in the dust. Nechi's grades are good, because the family is powerful, so even though he is naughty, he is never slapped. Rose gets good grades as well, because she is very beautiful. I am at the very bottom of the class with Edson and Big Man Ibrahim, despite working very hard.

SURVIVAL

Have I moved forwards in life by attaching myself to the white confusion? For me it's all about survival. Bob Marley puts it very accurately. First time I heard him, I was living with the Reverend. Every day I would run over to my German friends in the missionaries' village to play. They gave me a tape recorder, and whenever the Reverend wasn't around, I got it out and started listening to my tapes and doing my homework. I had the music of the Germans – ABBA, who are also white, and Boney M., who are black people that sound white.

The German missionary heard me speaking German to his children, so he arranged with the Reverend to use me as an interpreter:

"You're to go on tours with some German tourists, Marcus," he told me. An odd sort of lorry with very large wheels had arrived, full of Germans, who travelled with tents like poachers all over Africa. They were going to Marangu one day to walk to the first cabin on Kilimanjaro – not to the top because some of them had brought pregnant wives. I was to help them with the language.

"Would you like some chocolate?" one lady in the lorry asked in German.

"*Ja, danke schön*," I say in German, and everyone laughs and they give me this amazing thing called a Mars bar, which I eat very quickly: if they had second thoughts, they could take it back. We're driving on the main road towards Himo.

"Do you like reggae music?" the German guide asks.

"Yes, I like it very much," I say because I have heard it in Phantom's kiosk at the market. But I haven't got the money for cassettes or recordings.

"This is the new record by Bob Marley and the Wailers," he says and puts a cassette on the car stereo. *Eeehhh*, a nice sound – not the stiff white music, but rhythmic, alive. "*So much trouble in the world now*," Bob sings with a warm voice – not like ice cubes like that Boney M. The German shows me the cassette. "Survival" it's called, the cover is covered in flags – even the Tanzanian flag is there. All the African flags are there.

The German explains that under the word "Survival" there's a picture of the slaves – how they lay very close together in the ships that took them to America.

"But they went to America," I say, because that's better than here where the black boy is a slave to the Reverend. Bob sings: "*Babylon system is the vampire. Sucking the blood of the sufferers.*"

When we return to Moshi, the German gives me the Bob Marley cassette. I am very happy and listen to it until late in the night.

But the Reverend finds my tape recorder and takes it. I am given some sleeping bags by the Germans, and the Reverend takes them too. He has a family of his own – a boy, two girls, his wife. And he takes my things to give to them.

At one point I told the Reverend that I want to travel with the German missionaries to Pangani on holiday.

"No," he said. "You must go to the farm in Kahe to work." When I returned from Pangani, the Reverend kicked me out with God's own foot – I'd had enough of living under his regime.

Now I am under a new, white regime, with a Swedish man who is fooling around with the house girl and perhaps chasing *malaya*. Perhaps I have chosen the wrong path?

SLAVE MUSIC

I need to be instructed in the white ways. Who can I ask? From my time with the Reverend I know an American missionary family who live close to Uhuru Hotel. They have no children, just a little black dog from America, a shaggy one. It's not coping well with the heat, so the man shaves it once a week – the dog looks like a plucked chicken in the oven.

I have important questions, so I go to visit the Americans. But in the sitting room my eyes are caught by Hi-Fi electronics that spellbind me.

"Do you know black American music?" the man asks.

"I know Boney M. and Bob Marley."

"Bob Marley is from Jamaica and Boney M. suck," he says. "It's is nothing like that." And he gets out cassettes – a full box of them – and he puts them on. The sound, *eeehhhh* – it's wild. It's honey and warm sweat and taut muscles. It is the sound of Africa combined with a very soft comfy chair and a sword of steel. It is Bill Withers, who can make the lady cry; Marvin Gaye for the lady's heart; Isaac Hayes, who goes straight to her papaya; Stevie Wonder, who gives great spirituality; Jimi Hendrix, the mad witch doctor at a blood ceremony; Otis Redding, who makes everyone dance close. But they also have ladies singing: Dionne Warwick, who makes the man nice and sweet, while Donna Summer makes your pants lively. And Nina Simone – you wouldn't want to run into her at night: she would bite you to death and eat your flesh raw.

"Do you like it, even . . . though you're white?" I ask. He roars with laughter.

"Yes," he says.

"The black people in America – do they speak any African language?" I ask. He looks surprised at me.

"No, no, no. They speak English like I do. They don't come from Tanzania. They were taken as slaves more than two hundred years ago from West Africa, far from here."

"Weren't there any slaves from Tanzania?" I ask.

"Yes, but most of them were taken by the Arabs and sailed to Zanzibar to work on the clove plantations. And some of them were taken to the Arabian Peninsula to be slaves to the Muslims. Swahili is very similar to the Arab language. There weren't many people from Tanzania sent to America." This white chap knows everything. It doesn't matter what I ask him, he always has an answer. Now his wife comes in:

"How is Katriina's tummy?" she asks.

"Very well," I say, smiling a lot, because I can't ask hard questions in this house. I am floating in between; not white, not black, not child, not adult – without a home, but not on the street. If I try to be understood, it will come at a price. How can I get all these people to sit down and listen to me? Impossible. I allow myself to be used in order to use. Should I go to Katriina? "Hello, your husband is mad – he's pumping all the black holes." Throwing stones in the glass house. If I tell the Americans, it may travel straight to Jonas' ear. Like flushing myself down the toilet never to be seen again. Can I ask this American man for a job? The only job here is shaving the dog, and the man does that himself.

The dog I am getting for Solja is German, a German shepherd – a bitch, an ugly beast.

"I am calling it Lille Gubben," Solja says – it means Little Old Man and it's the name of a horse in a Swedish children's book. The only condition is that the dog is not allowed inside the house – it can live on the veranda in a big basket with a blanket.

Christian

Dad points to the sofa. Mum is arriving with Annemette tomorrow.

"Sit down," he says. Now what? Has he found out that I am smoking? But surely he knew that. I sit down.

"What?" I say.

"Christian," he says, "if you're going to smoke, drink or . . . mess around with girls, you can do it right where you're sitting." I look down at the sofa cushions, then up at Dad.

"What do you mean?"

"They've talked me into joining the school board as their accountant, so I'll have to sit and vote about whether to suspend misbehaving pupils for a week or two or boot them out permanently. I want you to know that if your name were ever to come up, I would vote for the maximum penalty for you, just so that there'll be no misunderstandings."

"Right," I say.

"Yes. And your mum told me that you got in pretty deep during those last few months in Denmark."

"You'll vote for the maximum penalty?" I say.

"I don't want anyone to question my impartiality," he says. Is he off his rocker? Thank God Mum is coming down now.

"Alright then. Now I know," I say, getting up.

"Wait," Dad says.

"What else?" I ask.

"Christian – all that stuff about Jonas Larsson fooling around – don't tell your mum."

"Why not?" I ask.

"She's just had a baby, and now she's coming down to a whole new life – that can make a woman a bit touchy," he says.

"Alright. Goodnight," I say. Why is he being so odd?

We're standing on the viewing platform, watching the plane land. Mum is carrying Annemette off the plane. She's pretty and noisy.

"That's how it is with babies – they spend most of the time screaming, shitting and sleeping," Dad tells me.

Miriam helps Mum hire a young woman who recently had a baby herself. The woman must be addressed as *mama* Brian – named after her firstborn – a little boy called Brian, who is hanging wrapped in a piece of cloth on her back. *Mama* Brian is to help Mum with Annemette as well as cleaning the house and doing the washing. Mum wants to do the cooking herself.

The screaming is hurting my ears. I go out into the garden. A worker is busy mowing our lawn. Normally he would be felling sugar canes with his *panga*, but he's on sick leave from the fields because he cut his leg. When workers who are ill are well enough to leave the T.P.C. sickbay, they are given the job of mowing the lawns on the golf course or in the staff gardens.

Mum starts working a couple of hours a day at the T.P.C. hospital. The field workers are treated for minor cuts and the occasional snake bite. And then there are all the usual things: malaria, worms, diarrhoea, bilharziasis, malnutrition and typhus.

"Your mum is nothing if not dedicated," Dad tells me, smiling.

"I can't just go about being a grand lady," Mum says. She is starting a programme where she and a local nurse go to the workers' villages to examine their children. She advises new mothers on natal care, nutrition and hygiene. She finds old car and motorcycle tyres which she brings as gifts so that they can make car-tyre sandals. There's a big problem with children and adults alike getting worms and thorns into their bodies through their feet.

I slip out to smoke and play some golf. A young Maasai is standing on one leg leaning against his long cowherd's staff, looking at me while I strike out. The ball lands in the long grass, and I can't find it. When I have looked for a while, he goes straight over, picks it up and comes over, putting it in my hand. I thank him. He doesn't move a muscle. I wonder what he's thinking.

Marcus

COLD CASH

Katriina receives a visit from Miriam, a British lady from T.P.C. I am given the job of looking after Solja and preparing tea and sandwiches in the kitchen. Tita is here as well, and I think about her creamy thighs.

"Do you have children?" Tita asks the British lady.

"Yes, two girls of eight and ten. They're at boarding school in Kenya," Miriam says.

"Why in Kenya?" Tita asks.

"John and I were both born in Kenya – our parents are farmers," Miriam says. "What about you – do you have children?"

"No," Tita says with a deep sigh.

"Aren't you having children?" Miriam asks.

"My husband, he doesn't . . .'"

"Asko shoots blanks," Katriina says.

"No, really?" Miriam says.

"Yes, I'm afraid so," Tita says, sighing.

THE PORTUGUESE INDIAN

Jonas returns from Moshi Club with a bald man from Goa, *bwana* D'Souza; the tips of his moustaches reach past his mouth and stretch out to the sides where they join great big mutton chops – but on his head there's only a scant circle of hair. His white shirt is stretched out by his beer gut but is left open at the neck, so you can see curly hair on his chest. His belt sits under his paunch. His collar outside his jacket. Pinstriped, flared gabardine trousers. Highly polished tan leather shoes. "I am a Portuguese and a Catholic," he says if you ask him. He is a colonialized Indian from Goa who has come to East Africa to cheat the negro.

D'Souza and Jonas negotiate. D'Souza is going to buy some things and will find a local *bwana mkubwa* who will buy the rest but won't take them home. Payment over twenty-four months; the fridge and washing machine only to be handed over when the *wazungu* family go back to Sweden.

D'Souza sees me in the house. I go to the kitchen to make Solja a sandwich. I can hear him speaking:

"Your house boy – don't trust him too much. They all steal," D'Souza says.

"Don't worry. I don't leave anything lying around," Jonas says. Don't leave a handful of coins out – the house boy might steal it; but do let him watch over your child every night – that after all has no value.

The Australian Dr Freeman comes to the house to examine Katriina. She is like a fish on land, snapping for air – the new *mtoto* inside her makes her stomach a balloon. And the doctor is standing right in the sitting room, feeling Katriina with his hands while Jonas watches.

In my own ghetto, workers have built a roof over the house girl's room. Sometimes I hear her go in and then later I hear the door opening again. Now she's going out, I think – I wonder where she's going? But no. She's not going out. It's Jonas coming in.

ROSIE'S PARTY

"Will you invite us to a party at your house soon?" Rosie asks at break. Does she think it's hard for me?

"Yes," I say. "We can do it on Saturday."

"Really?" Rosie says.

"I'll fix some food and some imported beer. Then we can have a small disco," I say. Later I leave school with Big Man Ibrahim.

"That girl is going to get you into big trouble with your *wazungu*," he says, laughing.

"They're going to Hotel Tanzanite in Arusha from Saturday to Sunday," I say. And I make the arrangements. I sneak Carlsberg out of the larder, and a packet of triangular chocolate, Toblerone. And I have a package of Asko's cigarettes which he forgot one day when he was drunk and is almost full.

Saturday the Larssons drive off to Hotel Tanzanite, and I buy chicken and vegetables at the market for a good dinner.

"Come and help me make dinner," I tell the house girl.

"You can't use the house for your friends. When you are unkind to me again, I will tell *mama* Katriina," she says.

"I am always nice to you – already I have made sure you have a roof built so that you can keep your activities private," I say.

"*Tsk*," she says. "You're against me, just because *bwana* Jonas likes me better than he likes you. I will tell *mama*."

"I could tell *mama* Katriina stories as well," I say. The house girl looks very confused. But luckily Big Man Ibrahim comes just then, and his tongue is very smooth:

"*Eeehhh*," he says, looking her up and down. "Your dress is very nice. I hope you will dance with me tonight."

Nechi arrives with Vicky – she is two years below us at school, and her father is a teacher at the Police Academy with Nechi's brother. Nechi helps us operate the barbecue while the girls lay the table and Edson makes himself useful as entertainment.

"What's that in the shed?" Rosie's friend Claire asks, pointing at the sauna. I explain about the Swedish activity.

84

"Naked? Men and women together?" Claire asks. She is very shocked. I nod. Big Man Ibrahim laughs and slaps his thighs.

"They'll be as dry as twigs," he says.

"Afterwards they fill themselves with beer," I say.

"But why would they want to sweat?" Claire asks.

"They say it purifies the body," I say.

"But sweat is dirty," Claire says.

"Perhaps it's something unique to the white skin," Rosie says.

We eat the good food, and I have a Carlsberg for each guest, and afterwards I pass around the special triangular Toblerone chocolate and offer them cigarettes from the pack of American wonderful Marlboro while the music plays in high-fidelity quality in our ears.

Later Ibrahim ends up under the house girl's private roof – perhaps she shows him her methods for making mash. Edson is on the veranda with Claire, but she is too Christian to go with him in the darkness. Nechi walks little Vicky home to her house by the Police Academy. For myself, I have Rosie in my arms, all soft and warm, as we dance in the sitting room to ABBA's music.

The next day I am one big cleaning machine removing all traces. The house girl doesn't help – she has run to church to confess her wickedness. The cushion covers have to come off to be soaked, because there was naughtiness with hands and tongues and titi, so much that Rosie spilt my tomato juice and vodka – a large red stain.

When the Swedes come through the door, all the covers are hanging on the clothes line, and I immediately dish up an explanation:

"I am doing a big clean while you're away." Jonas sniffs like a sceptical hyena – can he smell the negro's *joie de vivre*?

The next day Katriina calls me to the house:

"You have had a party in our house while we were away," she says.

"What? How do you know?" I ask.

"The neighbours are talking," Katriina says. Tsk, the other *wazungu* on the street know that the Larsson family was in Arusha, and yet there was great disco-noise from the house.

"I am sorry," I say.

"You had girls here," Katriina says.

"They were only some friends from school," I say. Katriina sighs:

"Marcus. Don't you know that one must always be very careful with girls?" she asks.

"I'm always kind to girls," I say.

"Careful," Katriina says. "Do you know how to be careful so that the girl doesn't get in trouble?" I look down – Katriina thinks we do that sort of wickedness. Maybe she herself got in trouble with *bwana* Jonas when she was young.

"I know. But we don't do that sort of thing at all," I say.

"Suddenly you will be doing it – then it's best to be prepared."

"Certainly," I say. Like she's a sort of father to me and I am the wicked son.

GREAT THIEF

"There is an enormous forest. The trees are ready for felling. There are great opportunities, and no-one has touched it," Jonas says, very excited. He has been to West Kilimanjaro with Asko and seen the forest which was planted by the Norwegian people in the 1960s. Since then the trees have grown big and fat. The mountain also has precious African trees – ancient. You can pick money straight off those trees. And Jonas is fed up with teaching at F.I.T.I. "The students don't understand what I say," he says. Because Jonas speaks English with a heavy Swedish accent and Swahili like a deaf man. But the students – they do understand him. The problem is Jonas – he doesn't understand English with an African accent, because he can't listen when his head is full of hangovers from Moshi Club, and on top of that comes the paranoia from smoking *bhangi*. And the teaching starts early in the morning – Jonas can't get out of bed in time.

"It could be done," *bwana* D'Souza says. He has a small sawmill on the other side of the mountain at Rongai. Jonas meets him at Moshi Club and asks him about labour, the timber market, transport, government contracts – because it is the government who owns all land in Tanzania. Whose palm must be greased?

D'Souza knows everything; he even has children at International School of Moshi – that's how corrupt and how great a thief he is. I.S.M. is very expensive. The parents of the local children at the school are wealthy *wahindi* businessmen, Maasai with more cattle that you could count, or corrupt politicians and government officials. Their only thought is that their child must have the white education so that it can escape the mess that is Africa. And if you fail to escape, then you will still have learnt enough to cheat the poor negro.

So now Jonas is hatching a great plan to set up portable sawmills on West Kilimanjaro to supply the Tanzanian market and perhaps even for export. And who is to be the boss of it all? Yes. That's right. Jonas.

BABYSITTING

Katriina is due to give birth soon, but she is still running around at night as her husband's personal guard. I must look after Solja if her parents are going to Moshi Club or somewhere else. That's what I'm there for. I come home at five after a long day at school and more work at F.I.T.I. Then the family goes to the club to hang out, play squash, tennis, golf – drink. They return again at seven, all of them. Later the parents go out again to visit their own friends, either at their homes or at the club. Sometimes Solja is simply left with me.

"Tell the house girl to make Solja some dinner," Katriina says.

"But the house girl has been given the night off," I say.

"Who has given her the night off?" Katriina asks.

"Jonas did. He told her to take the rest of the day off."

"Why did he do that?" Katriina asks.

"I don't know anything about that."

"Oh well, then you'll just have to make her something, Marcus." And Katriina drives off. I make the food for Solja; I brush the teeth in her mouth. If she is too dirty, I put her in the bathtub. And then I sit with her the whole long night. Perhaps her parents aren't back until two or three a.m. I have to make sure Solja is happy and safe in her bed; I have to half-sleep on the sofa while with one ear I listen out for the car. I am bored and don't get proper sleep. The next day I am tired at school. Working for *wazungu* is hard.

What should I do with my time? I read all the books on the shelf, I read American *Newsweek* and the lies in the Tanzanian *Daily News*.

"What's that you're reading?" the house girl says.

"A story about life in the world – the things that happen in other places," I say.

"Why?" she asks. Why would I want knowledge she doesn't have? What sort of knowledge is that? Why do I think I'm better than her? But mostly she doesn't say very much to me, because Jonas is always giving her time off in return for her making mash for him.

At night I get so bored I go into the larder and steal some beer, some cans of Carlsberg – rearranging the cans so no-one notices. And there is a lot of imported food: crispbread, biscuits, macaroni, spaghetti, all the tinned food you can't get in town: tuna, mackerel, liver pâté, ham, cod roe – imported via Ostermann. I am very good at eating it.

At school Rosie comes up to me, grabbing my arm at break.

"Are the Swedes going to send you to their country in Europe soon?" she asks.

"No, I only babysit their children," I say.

"Stop it," Rosie says, tapping my chest. "All the time I see you on that project motorbike."

"Yes," I say. "I may get a job on the project when school finishes. Then I'll probably be going to Europe for some training." And Rosie guides me round the corner of the school building and puts her tongue into my mouth, very lively. Have I lied? No. The girl is dreaming about Europe, just like me. We both hope our dream will become reality.

"I'll come visit you soon," Rosie whispers before going back to class.

Christian

"What sort of cart is that?" Emmanuel says in the middle of a game of football one Saturday afternoon. I follow his gaze and see Dad walking the pram, which has a flowery mini-parasol with laces and frills so Annemette's pale legs don't come into contact with so much as a sunbeam.

"Tsk," I say, as Emmanuel runs over to see what's inside the box with wheels. He sees the child and laughs out loud.

"What are you doing with the baby?" he asks Dad.

"I am taking it for a walk," Dad says. Emmanuel looks worried:

"But then what's happened to your wife? Is she very ill?" he asks.

"No. She's playing golf," Dad says.

Emmanuel looks at him. He seems quite confused.

My dad rolls on. Emmanuel looks after him.

"Your father is going to have to beat that woman harder," he says. Then he laughs and takes a couple of steps as if pushing a pram. "Box on wheels," he says, slapping his thighs. It's absurd. And incredibly embarrassing.

We go back to playing football, but there is a weird atmosphere. Later I go with Emmanuel to the river to smoke cigarettes and look at the women and the older girls fishing in the river with their long nets. When they come back to the bank, their thin dresses stick to their bodies – I can see everything.

When I come home, Dad has just come out of the shower.

"Get yourself a shower and get ready – we're going to the messroom for supper," he says. I go to their bathroom to take a dry towel from the cupboard. Leap back. Some little critter? – something wet under my foot. Scorpion?

"*Eeeeeewww!*" I shout. A condom. Limp. On the floor. Full. Mum comes in.

"It's not that bad," she laughs.

"But you can't just leave it there. Do you want *mama* Brian to step on it?"

"No, no," Mum says. I go to my own bathroom. They're lying there ... fucking in the afternoon. Christ, that's gross.

My dad and Nanna's dad have gone to a meeting at the embassy in Dar es Salaam. I go with Mum to have dinner with Nanna's mum.

"Kirsten," Nanna's mum says during dinner. "Wouldn't you like to take over the Danish first language course at school?" I.S.M. used to have twice-weekly language lessons for native speakers, but at the moment they can't find anyone to teach it. I hold my breath.

"No," Mum says. "Not while Annemette is so little."

"Thank heavens," I say.

"Why would you say that?" Mum asks.

"I don't want you for my teacher," I say. "That would be really odd."

"Yes, it certainly would make skiving off or forgetting homework very difficult," Nanna's mum says. I don't say anything to that. I glare at Nanna, who seems to find it funny. After we've finished eating, I go with Nanna to her room to listen to some music. She puts on an ABBA cassette. I sit some distance from Nanna on her bed – I'd like to move closer.

"But why do you want to go home in a year?" my mum asks on the veranda – the sound carries through the open window.

"You know. Nanna will have finished Year Eight by then – it's the very latest we can return if she is to get a feel for Denmark before finishing Danish primary school," Nanna's mum says. "I mean, that way she'll have time to find out what she wants to do with her life. She'll get a better idea of what her options are."

"But won't she just go straight on to *gymnasiet*?" Mum asks.

"Yes, but there's no vocational counselling here," Nanna's mum says. "They're just big children. While they're down here, they have no way of even *seeing* what their choices will be when they grow up." Nanna shrugs and sighs.

"They're so busy fretting about what I'll be when I grow up," she says.

"Fuck 'em," I say. We sit a bit more closely – her leg against mine. We talk a bit about what we might be. Her clean scent rises to my nostrils – I am so close to her.

"Do you want more children?" Nanna's mum asks outside.

"No," Mum says. "It's fine with the two we've got, so now we have to be careful."

"Then I hope you've brought plenty of supplies, because you can't get anything here," Nanna's mum says.

"I think I've got plenty," Mum says, laughing.

"Oh? What does that mean?" Nanna's mum asks. Nanna has moved away from me on the bed. No more skin against skin. Now she gets up and walks around a bit.

"Well, I went into the pharmacy," Mum is saying outside, "and then I went up to the youngest male pharmacist – on purpose, you know – and said to him, very loudly: 'I want four hundred condoms.'" My mum laughs. "You should have seen his face – fiery red." They're laughing outside. Nanna is standing by the door with her back turned to me.

"I want another Coke," she says and leaves, walking down the corridor. Bollocks.

Marcus

SPIRITUAL

Babylonian disaster. Bob Marley is dead: 6 February, 1945 – 11 May, 1981. Exodus from this dust and blood. It was cancer, the *Daily News* says – only thirty-six years old. We have been spiritually amputated.

The European people try to be spiritual as well. The Swedes think that the powder is out of reach in Africa, but Mika talks such a damned lot, everyone does what he wants in the end. There is brown sugar here – you can get it in all the big cities. It comes from India, Pakistan, and Mika goes to a few of the older pupils at I.S.M. – *wahindi* – they can get it for him, because their fathers are businessmen with an import–export business. Mika has a radar for trouble. I know that, because he always wants to fight. "It's only a bit of fun," he says, but I don't understand at all. When no-one's looking, he sniffs powder up his nose and goes crazy. His eyes are open all day long, but all he sees is dreams.

But Mika isn't the only one who wants to take spiritual shortcuts.

I want to harvest my *bhangi*, but what do I see? The plants have gone – all of them – gone.

"You've stolen my *bhangi*," I tell the guard. "If you don't give it back, I'll have you fired."

"I haven't taken it," he says.

"Then who has? Ghosts?"

"I haven't taken it."

"You smoke every night – you've filched it."

"I haven't touched it – only watered it every night like you said."

The next day Katriina comes down to my ghetto.

"Marcus, could you give the house a good clean while we're at the club?"

"Yes," I say. That means that they're having people round, and the house is one big mess. I clean, clean, clean – *ehhh*; when I pull my broom out from under the bed, it brings some heavy shit out; big branches with leaves – all my *bhangi* plants are under the bed, and I have to push them back. How can I ask *bwana* about the journey it made from my garden to under the white man's bed? It's impossible.

PEEING IN THE GARDEN

Rosie visits me in my ghetto while these *wazungu* go to their sweat lodge. I serve Rosie fizzy drinks and European chocolate and the erotic sound of Bob Marley, who sings in Rosie's ear: "*Turn your lights down low. Never ever try to resist, oh no*". Soon our tongues are wrapped together, and my hands are on her wonderful breasts. I hear the sound of a door, voices.

"What's that?" Rosie asks.

"Wait," I say and go to the curtain, lifting a small corner so that I can look towards the kitchen door of the house. Rosie comes over and stands behind me. Jonas comes round from the corner of my ghetto and walks towards the main house. I realize that Solja is standing on the back stairs in her nightie with the dog, Lille Gubben.

"Where have you been?" she asks. Jonas stops in the middle of the lawn, looks up.

"I was just going out," he says. "You should be in bed."

"You're being so noisy. Where were you?" Solja asks.

"The loo was busy, so I had a pee in the garden," Jonas says.

"Can they not leave soon? I want to go to sleep," Solja asks.

"It probably won't be long, darling. But Marcus is at home. You could go sleep at his."

"I don't live there," Solja says and turns around to go back into the house with Lille Gubben.

"You can't take the dog into the house," Jonas says. But Solja doesn't answer. She loves that dog, and it adores her. How else is she going to get any love in this house? Jonas gives up trying to instil discipline in his child and walks towards the sweat lodge.

"Isn't he being a bit odd?" Rosie asks.

"Yes," I say and kiss her again.

PARANOIA

The morning after their party I am up before everyone else. At first I go to the house to see if Jonas has forgotten to put on the padlock on the larder door. It's open. I quickly take seven cans of Carlsberg beer down to my ghetto, hiding them behind my desk, taking my collection of empty cans and scattering them over the lawn with all the cans from the night before. Then I go up to the house to tidy it. When Jonas gets up, he doesn't want to see me.

"Out!" he says. "You must pick up all the cans and put them in one pile." I go outside and pick them up. He pokes his head out of the door. "*Don't* put them in the rubbish hole." I know why. He wants to examine them first like a scientist researching rubbish.

Later the family goes to the club. Jonas says he's not ready – he must have a shower first. Katriina goes in the car with Solja, Jonas follows them later on the motorbike. After an hour at the club he returns and goes to the bedroom. Now he's alone. He smokes and smokes and smokes – and then he comes out onto the lawn with a cigarette in his hand, taking small drags, squinting. I can't even say hello to him when I pass – he registers it only as an interruption.

Christian

Things are going well at school. My English has got quite good; I am the school team's goalie; I have friends. I go to the cornfield behind the dining hall or down to Karanga River and smoke cigarettes with Jarno. Sometimes Panos from the football team comes with us – nice guy. He's a mulatto; half Greek, a quarter English and a quarter black Tanzanian. At break I stare at Shakila – still the fastest girl in school. And I have football practice in the afternoon a few times a week. When I don't, I play football with Emmanuel and the other boys at T.P.C., even though Rogarth says they're thieves. I don't play golf anymore, because when I do, Mum wants to come, and being there with her and Rogarth is just too plain weird.

"Where's Mum?" I ask when I come home from school.

"At the workers' sickbay," Dad says.

"She's always at the sickbay," I say.

"I think she misses her work," Dad says.

"But she doesn't have to work," I say.

"Your mum is a modern woman," Dad says. "There's no great home-maker lost in her."

A little later Mum returns. Dad tells her he's invited Miriam and John over for drinks.

"Do you know how John treats the field workers?" Mum asks.

"What do you mean?" Dad asks.

"Their working conditions are completely insane. They don't even have proper shoes. They keep coming in with sores on their feet and legs," Mum says and takes little Annemette from *mama* Brian. We sit down to eat.

"But he's not the one who decides all that," Dad says.

"He could try to improve their conditions," Mum says.

"There are 4,000 field workers. They feed their families. The planta-tion gives them homes and schools and medical help. That's not bad for Africa," Dad says.

"I'm talking about John here. John's a bastard," Mum says.

"I'm going over to Nanna's to do prep," I say and hurry out of there.

I finally get to put my hand up Nanna's top and feel her little breasts. They're soft – feel wonderful. But I'm not allowed to lift up her top and look at them. She smells great. She pushes me off.

*

When I return, Miriam and John are in the sitting room. Mum is lecturing them on the rights of the field worker. John is speaking to her as if she were a naïve child:

"I treat them like the workers they are," he says.

"They're not animals," Mum says.

"Negroes," John says. "In Africa." Mum gets up and walks down the corridor.

"She's going to look in on the baby," Dad says. Miriam and John finish their drinks, say their goodbyes. Mum returns to the sitting room.

"I know it's grim," Dad says. "But by Tanzanian standards I really think it's not a bad job for an unskilled worker."

"Right," Mum says. "I know. It's just . . . I'm going to see if I can get some work at K.C.M.C. – do some good," she says. "Or teach Danish at the school in the afternoon."

"That's a good idea," Dad says.

"I can't just faff about out here at T.P.C. all day long – that much is certain," Mum says.

"In that case you'll have to learn to drive the Tanzanian way," Dad says.

"Yes," Mum says, sighing. She's still worried by the fact that Tanzanians drive on the left side of the road.

Annemette's tummy is acting up. *Mama* Brian looks after her in the mornings when Mum is at the T.P.C. sickbay. Both Dad and Mum are busy. They let me to do pretty much what I want. But sometimes Mum starts trying to tell me off:

"Really, Christian, the least you can do is clear away your own plate from the table," she says. Or when I return from playing football with the lads: "I can smell smoke on your clothes."

"Well, that's because some of the older boys smoke," I say.

"Are you sure you're not the one smoking?" she says.

"Yes," I say.

"Don't smoke," she says. "It's not good for you."

"You smoke," I say.

"Don't do as we do," Dad says, smiling at me. "Do as we say."

"Christ on a bike," I say.

*

Other than that very little happens at T.P.C.

"Do sit down and listen," Mum says. She and Dad are reading Karen Blixen's *Out of Africa* to each other in the evenings, while drinking gin and tonics and smoking cigarettes – there's no T.V. in Tanzania.

"I really can't be bothered to listen to that," I say.

"It wouldn't hurt you to sit with us a little," Mum says.

"I'm going to Nanna's," I say. It's like being in church on Christmas Eve when they read from that book.

At Nanna's we kiss, sitting on the edge of her bed. She parts her lips, but my tongue bumps against her teeth. And I've snuck my hand under her top, touching her tummy, moving it towards her breast, holding my breath.

"Don't. It tickles," Nanna says, pushing my hand away, getting up. Tickles? I hardly did anything.

Last day before the summer holidays. During lunch break a girl screams in the toilets. A teacher runs out – I follow with Jarno.

Mika is lying on the floor, frothing at the mouth.

"It must be a snake," the teacher shouts. One of the pupils has fetched the school nurse, *mama* Hussein. She sits down and does C.P.R. on Mika. He starts breathing again, but he seems very sluggish. Other teachers have come out as well, and they carry him to a car, take him to K.C.M.C. Rumours are rife, until the teachers tell us he is going to survive.

The next day Dad is at a board meeting at school. He seems shaken when he comes home.

"Damn me if it wasn't heroin," he says.

"What?" Mum says.

"Mika had taken heroin," he says.

"But . . ." Mum says.

"Apparently you can get it here in Arusha. Have you heard that as well, Christian?" Dad asks.

"No," I say.

"But . . . then what?" Mum asks.

"Not much to say. We had to kick him out. There was nothing else to be done."

*

We're at Moshi Club, sitting with the Larssons and Asko.

"How are you?" Asko asks.

"I'm on holiday," I say. "I'm bored." And I am. Dad works all hours, and Mum is busy with Annemette and the T.P.C. sickbay. I am bored shitless.

"You could always come out with us," Asko says. He and Jonas are going up to West Kilimanjaro to see the forest. And they're going to see Léon Wauters, a Dutchman who lives at Simba Farm. The farm is right below the large forest Jonas would like to put sawmills in.

"Yes, sure," I say.

I sleep on the sofa at Tita and Asko's. She's prancing around in a flimsy, short kimono made of yellow silk, and I can see her smooth golden legs. Falling asleep isn't easy.

We leave early the next morning. All the way up to the forest, where Jonas and Asko walk about looking at the trees, talking about sawmills. Afterwards we drive down to Simba Farm, which has some of the most fertile soil in the country. Léon Wauters grows flowers for a Dutch company who sell seeds. Aside from the flowers he grows wheat and hops for the breweries. The state needs bottled beer – it's only drunk by the upper classes: corrupt politicians and businessmen.

At Simba Farm the main house is full of antlers and pelts. We're served a warm lunch – ostrich steaks in a peanut-butter sauce with new potatoes and a salad from the farm's vegetable garden.

"I shot the ostrich myself," Léon says.

"Aren't they on the endangered species list?" Asko asks.

"Yes, but I have a deal with the park ranger – it's O.K. if they're taking my flowers."

For pudding we have banoffee pie. Later we go out on the neon green lawn, where you can see all the way down to the lowlands.

"Are you married?" Asko asks.

"Divorced," Léon says. "My ex-wife lives in Holland with our son."

"It must be lonely all the way up here," Asko says. "Do you sometimes come to Moshi?"

"No – it's too long a drive at night. Sometimes I go to Arusha for a few days to play golf," Léon says.

"Golf?" Asko says, raising his brows.

"Yes, golf," Léon says, grinning. He looks at me: "Do you play?"

"A little," I say. "At T.P.C."

"Want to shoot a few balls?" he asks, pointing: "I have a hole in the lawn over there, so I can practise my putt, and the rest of the time I shoot balls out over the fields."

"What about the balls?" I ask.

"The workers' children collect them. I pay them to."

"Doesn't it ruin the harvest – the flower heads?" I ask.

"During the growing season I only practise putting. Do your parents play at T.P.C.?" he asks.

"My mum mostly – she came down recently with my little sister," I say.

"Yes, I met her at the Larssons'. Do you think I could come out one day and play golf?"

"I'm sure you could," I say.

On the way back I sit on the back seat and stare out of the window. But I also listen to Asko and Jonas talking in Swedish:

"How are you and Tita doing?" Jonas asks.

"All she talks about is getting pregnant – I mean, like all the time," Asko says.

"Children – they're a damned nuisance," Jonas says.

"But that boy – Marcus – he babysits Solja in the evenings, doesn't he?" Asko asks.

"Yes, but he's a damned nuisance as well. He's just a stupid boy, but he pretends to be a part of the family, and I have to do all sorts of things for him. I don't think he'll be happy until I've got him a Swedish passport and a job with Volvo, damn it."

The following weekend Léon arrives on the Saturday. Dad is busy, so Léon does a full round with Mum. When Dad returns, they talk and have drinks on the veranda all three of them. There's a kudu roasting in the oven – Léon brought it. I disappear to have a smoke.

Marcus

THE INNERMOST PROCESSES

I wave goodbye to the plane. Mika is on board, on his way to Finland. The Larssons were the wrong family to solve his problems.

*

The child arrives at K.C.M.C. on 8 July, 1981. It's a little girl.

"Rebekka," Katriina says. "Her name is Rebekka." Jonas mutters something, visibly disappointed, because the man wanted a son – now he's alone in the family with three ladies.

Many people come by the house to see the baby, and I am constantly running around with Coke and coffee and beer and sandwiches for the guests. Tita and Asko come as well:

"Can you ask him?" Tita says when I pass the veranda.

"Yes. Marcus," Katriina says. "Tita needs some help around the house – a couple of little things that need fixing. Could you nip down one day and do it?"

"Yes. I'll do it," I say, nodding at Tita, who smiles. Asko is there, a beer in his hand, next to Jonas – they are looking down into the European cart that holds the new baby.

"I want a baby as well," Asko says – his voice sounds very drunk already.

"You'll have to work on it," Jonas says, grinning.

"I don't think anyone could make anything grow inside Tita," Asko says.

"Who says I'm the problem?" Tita says. I hurry away from their way of saying everything out in the open.

GARVEY DREAD

A local guy comes to my ghetto; Gaspar is his name – a street urchin, one of Mika's old friends via Alwyn the *bhangi*-pusher.

"You must send these to Mika in Europe," Gaspar says, handing me a box of Africafé tins from the factory on Karanga River.

"Why must I do that?" I ask. "You could send it yourself."

"It's not from me," Gaspar says.

"It's not from me either," I say.

"No, it's from Alwyn," Gaspar says. "He told me it was all arranged, that you were going to send the tins to Mika." Even though Alwyn attends I.S.M. and is the son of a *bwana mkubwa*, he's hanging out with the market filth and wants to use me as a coolie. Who's going to pay for the stamps?

"I don't know anything about that," I say. "What does Mika want with Africafé? – you can easily buy coffee in Europe."

"I don't know – I think perhaps he likes this coffee," Gaspar says. I take the tins and send Gaspar away. They're large Africafé tins, 450 grams in each. I tip open the lids with a screwdriver: yes, inside the lid the tins are factory-sealed with a special, thick layer of foil – no problems.

I write to Mika: "These things are very expensive to send, so I either want the money or some gifts, otherwise I won't send them." The tins sit on my shelves for a few weeks until I receive a package from Mika: a radio, underpants, sneakers. The good stuff I keep, the shitty crap from Korea I sell. And I go down and send the coffee, but Mika and Alwyn give me that paranoid feeling, so I put a fake postcode and the name Garvey Dread.

Gaspar brings Africafé several times – I send it. One day Jonas says:

"Have you been sending *bhangi* to Mika?"

"*Bhangi*?" I say. "No."

"Mika's mother writes to me that he's always crazy on *bhangi* – she thinks it must be coming from here."

"I don't know anything about that. I sent him some tins of Africafé – he asked for it."

"Africafé?" Jonas says. "Why would he want that? You can get coffee in Finland too."

"Maybe he likes the Tanzanian coffee," I say without explaining that the tins don't come from the shop but have been given to me by a street urchin. I go down to my ghetto – there are still four tins. I open one and break the seal under the lid. *Bhangi*, good stuff without sticks or anything, packed tight so when you shake the tin it sounds absolutely right, and the weight is good. Sealed in secret at the authorized coffee factory. That night I smoke such a lot of Africafé while listening to Bob Marley – together we are high, in heaven.

Now I ask around in town and learn that Gaspar has friends in the packing department at Africafé. But I am Garvey Dread – I can send the tins no problem, as long as Mika keeps sending me what I ask for.

Christian

The summer holidays are almost over. I go around, kicking the dust at T.P.C. Bored out of my head. Go to the garage where T.P.C.'s field machines are parked. There's a motorbike in the corner.

"Do you want to take it for a spin?" a voice asks me. I turn around. It's John.

"It might not be a very good idea," I say.

"It's a perfect idea," John says.

"My mum will have a cow."

"But you do know how to drive one of these things?"

"Of course I do."

"Your mum's not here," John says. "Have a go." He looks at me – wants to see if I'm afraid of my mum. I get up and kick-start it. Fuck it. Whizz down the street. Dad sees me from the window of his office. When he comes home, he looks around quickly to make sure we're alone. Raises his index finger and stares at me:

"Do you know what would happen if your mum saw you on that motorbike?" he asks.

"No," I say.

"She would make life damned uncomfortable for both of us."

Year Eight, first day after the holidays. I'm lounging about with Jarno, studying the new pupils, who are starting Year Seven. They all come from the Greek school in Arusha, where you can board from Year One. A fierce-looking white girl comes wriggling down the corridor. Another of the new girls says:

"So, Samantha, we'll see if you can manage when you're not the oldest."

"Truddi baby," the fierce Samantha says, walking towards the blonde girl who must be Norwegian. Samantha stops in front of Truddi, who stays where she is but looks nervous. Samantha smiles: "I'm the oldest here as well," she says. "I'm the only one here with any experience."

"What do you mean?" Truddi asks shrilly.

"Oh you old maid, you," Samantha says.

"You're so gross," Truddi says. Samantha smiles. She turns and walks on, but then stops and looks at me.

"What are you looking at?" she asks.

"You," I say without thinking. Samantha smiles:

"I don't blame you." She wriggles away, waving at me over her shoulder with her fingers. I'm in love.

"Do you like it here?" Mum asks one morning at breakfast.

"Yes," I say, munching my toast.

"And school?" she asks. I shrug.

"It's alright," I say.

"Are they nice? Are there any nice girls?" she asks. I stop chewing, take a sip of my coffee.

"A few – a fierce one and a very tanned one."

"I just want to be sure that you're alright."

"Really, everything's fine," I say.

"So you're in no hurry to get back to Denmark?" she asks.

"Denmark?" I ask.

"I'm just asking, just so I know," Mum says. Dad has more than a year left of his contract and he's talking about extending it. Why would she mention Denmark?

"Weren't you going to start working at K.C.M.C.?" I ask.

"I'll wait until Annemette is a little older," Mum says.

"But you don't want to go home, do you?" I ask – Mum hasn't even been here for six months.

"No, no," Mum says. "I just want to know if you're happy about things. "

"I could use a motorbike," I say.

"A motorbike?" Mum says.

"T.P.C. is really far from the city. That way I'd be able to get home from football practice and that on my own."

"You're not old enough to ride a motorbike," Mum says.

"John has one I could borrow," I say.

"You're not old enough," Mum says.

"I've ridden a moped in Denmark," I say.

"I can imagine," Mum says.

"When you were working nights," I say.

"Well, I'm not now," Mum says.

Marcus

INSURANCE FRAUD

Friday. First it's school, and then it's F.I.T.I., where I must translate Jonas' messages to the negroes in the office. Finally I'm home.

"You must get the sauna ready, Marcus," Katriina says.

"O.K.," I say. "But I'm going to have to leave at seven-thirty – I'm meeting someone." Edson's acrobatics troupe is performing at I.S.M. at eight, and I'm coming along to introduce the show in English so the audience can understand.

"We'll be here," Katriina says and drives off to the club with the children. Jonas is coming home tonight from a business safari. Later Katriina will return with guests from the club. On the lawn there's a pile of firewood which has been taken to the house from the school by some of the sawmill workers. I carry the firewood to the oven and start firing it up. It's a local, primitive type of oven, so I have to be around it, or the sauna may catch fire. You have to shut the oven very well and very carefully when you have loaded it with wood. When the oven is burning well, making bread rolls is the next thing: bread with butter, pork, tomato, green pepper and then cheese at the very top. When they are ready, I put them in the fridge, so they can be put straight in the oven, where the cheese will melt like a sort of glue, making it almost like a pizza. And I must put a lot of beer in the fridge; I may even have to taste one.

When I have got everything ready, it's almost seven-thirty, and Katriina isn't back yet. The troupe is coming to pick me up on their way to I.S.M. Today we're working on white time; every second counts. I take the guard to the oven and show him: "Put the firewood here and shut the grate."

Off we go to I.S.M., and the troupe gets ready. The audience is arriving.

"There's a house on fire, by Police Academy," a lady is shouting from the car park. I know it's our house. Right away I find Christian's mother, *mama* Knudsen, who can give me a lift. When we arrive, there's a big fire in the sauna shed but also on the roof at the back of the house, which the sauna is built up against. Flames reaching towards the sky. Miraculously the fire engine is already on its way, but no Katriina. *Mama* Knudsen goes straight to the club to fetch her. The guard is gone – he has run away. The firemen work to put out the fire. At the same time we try to carry out a lot of stuff: the furniture, the fridge, the freezer, the stereo – yes, we manage to get almost everything out, and the damage isn't so great. The sauna of course is wrecked. And the sitting room is a bit battered, the ceiling and roof burned on one side, and the entire room smells of smoke.

It is the way it always is: "How the hell could you leave the house with the sauna lit? Are you off your fucking trolley?" Jonas shouts when he returns not long after.

"It was me – I was home late," Katriina says. "Marcus had told me he had to leave. It's not his fault that the guard was so useless."

The next morning, while the slaves are tidying up, Jonas gets on the phone to *bwana* D'Souza for some tips on playing the insurance company African style.

I come along to the police station as interpreter. Jonas has made a list of things that have been ruined and reports the fire to the desk officer: he needs an official report from the police that can be sent to the insurance company in Sweden. Jonas asks: "How long will it be before you come and look at the damage?" They don't know. In order to get that answer you have to go and talk to the chief. Now Jonas enters the chief's office with me trailing behind him. The door is closed.

"Why didn't you call?" the chief asks.

"We did, but the phone didn't work – the line was fried, and the neighbours didn't have a connection either," I explain.

"Then why didn't you come and get us?" the chief asks.

"We were busy putting out the fire in the house and saving our things," I say.

"Yes, well, it will be a long time before the report is finished," the Police Commissioner explains: "First we'll have to examine the scene of the fire to see if all your things really have been damaged. There is a lot of paperwork to be done, and as you know we don't have many resources because our budgets are so small, so my estimate is that it will take three months – at least."

"I understand that," Jonas says. "But my problem is that my fridge has been ruined, and I can't afford to buy another before we get the insurance money. And all our clothes have been ruined."

"We don't mean to be unhelpful," the Police Commissioner says, "but we really haven't got the budget or the manpower to look into it right now. I can't just take people who are working on serious crimes and have them examine a fire that has been put out. And we can't afford to pay the overtime."

I set to work:

"What if this man were to help pay for the overtime? Could that be arranged?" I ask.

"Yes, perhaps that could be arranged," the Police Commissioner says.

"What would that cost?" I ask.

The Police Commissioner names a big figure.

"I can't afford that right now," Jonas says. "Because I am going to have to buy new mattresses and bed linen for the entire family. And some of my money burned in the fire. But I could give you half the sum."

"Alright. Give me the list of your ruined things. I will send a man with the paperwork." The Police Commissioner gets the list and the money. Nothing is examined, but the police report is soon finished, delivered by hand to Jonas' door. Jonas sends it to S.I.D.A. and everything is replaced, despite the fact that it all still works. Is S.I.D.A. going to send a man by plane all the way from Sweden to see if the stereo was melted by the flames? No. They send a lot of money. We start a new sauna further away from the house, in a corner of the garden. We run a hose over from the shower and the party starts again. That's the way we live.

THE OFFICE GIRL'S FLOWER

Katriina wants to stay at home with baby Rebekka, so I have to drive to the market in the car to shop for food. How can I do well at school when I have to look after an entire family at the same time? On the way I have to pick up Tita, who still hasn't got a driver's licence. At the Clock Tower roundabout we see Asko on his motorbike – and on the back, a black beauty. Tita goes very quiet. I drop her off with her groceries at her house. She doesn't want to come to the Larssons'.

Later Jonas returns with Asko. They start drinking beer. I have long since learnt to understand quite a few words of the Swedish language after having had lessons from Solja.

"Shall we have dinner together tonight?" Katriina asks. Asko just mutters in reply. "Will you go and fetch Tita?" she asks.

"Can't you just give her a ring?" Asko asks.

"Our phone's not working, and she can't drive your car," Katriina says.

"I've had too much beer," Asko says.

"That doesn't usually stop you," Katriina says.

"I can't drive now," he says.

"Marcus," Katriina calls. "Go down and pick Tita up. Tell her Asko's here and I'm cooking tonight." Katriina goes to the kitchen. I go over to the motorbike, which is parked outside the veranda.

I take off. Tita doesn't say very much, but she puts her arms around me and presses in close against my back on the motorbike. It feels lovely, but what does it mean? We go straight to the Larssons'.

Normally Tita speaks to Asko in Finnish, but now she wants everyone to understand.

"Who was that you were driving around with in town?" she asks in Swedish.

"Errrrrr . . ." Asko says. "That was . . ." He stops. "That was the office girl," he says in the end.

"Why are you driving around with the office girl?"

"She had to . . ." He hasn't rehearsed his untruth. "She had to . . . I had to take her with me so she could translate – at Tanesco; the electricity bill was off."

"They speak English at Tanesco," Tita says. She's right.

"Yes, a little. But she knows how to do these things," Asko says in his defence.

"I think I know how those things are done as well," Tita says.

That makes him angry:

"It's my job," he says. "You're being paranoid." Now she's crying. Because she's right. It wasn't the office girl. I've seen that beauty before – she hangs around in the bar at Moshi Hotel, selling her papaya for money. But the white man is allowed to pump for free, because as soon as the black girl talks to him she knows the rain will fall on her – making the field flower.

Later Asko asks me how to get a driving licence for Tita – she already knows how to control the car but won't understand the signs in the test.

"You tell the police she doesn't know English – that you have to translate for her at the test. Then the policeman asks his questions – you translate. Tita says something in Finnish. You tell the policeman the right answer. That's how it's done."

In town I gather information from Phantom by the market. Who is Asko's black beauty?

"It's Chantelle," he says. "Do you know her? Big bottom, big titi, very sensual. The Finnish man pumps her many times. She gets money for dresses, for taxis, for a grand life. Now she can eat meat in a restaurant and drink bottled beer in the bar."

And while that goes on the mash production goes ahead as well. The ceiling blocks the light from the house girl's room, but the boards are thin and don't cut out the sound of the mash-making. And it's normal when the woman is very fat or has just had a baby like Katriina has that the man is crazy for other women. But Jonas isn't normal. He is in the servants' quarters ten metres from his wife, sucking the house girl's titi, pert and firm. While his new baby daughter is sucking Katriina's titi, making them long and flat like a Maasai's. The happiest person is the big daughter, Solja, because now Katriina is often at home and is a real mother with time for her daughters.

LUMINOUS SKIN

The Larssons are going to a party at the Knudsens' at T.P.C. – it starts early and they're bringing their children.

"Marcus, you know how to drive a car, don't you?" she asks.

"Yes, very well," I say, even though I don't have a licence. But when Gerhard was killed by rhino and I was living with the Germans in the National Park, the German taught me how to drive the Land Rover so that he could concentrate on counting the animals.

"We'd like you to come with us to T.P.C. tonight, if you can?" Katriina says.

"Yes. I can do that." I'd like to see the nice houses where the Danes live.

"It's just that . . . Jonas might have a few, and I'd rather not drive, because I have to look after my little baby," she says.

"No problem at all," I say. *Wazungu* are strange that way. They decide what you can and can't do, and all they have to do is say the word and you do it, and yet they ask you as if you could say no.

Jonas drives there. I stay in the car, smoking a cigarette with their guard. The party drags on, but I'm only there as their driver. Then the Danish boy comes out – Christian.

"Marcus, I want you to see my stereo," he says.

"Do you think it's a good idea for me to go inside?"

"Yes, of course. Come on." He leads the way. I follow. Tita is there as well. She smiles when she sees me. We go down the corridor in the nice house. In his room are a white girl and a black boy. The girl is Danish and her name is Nanna. The boy is the son of a local T.P.C. boss. His name is Rogarth, and he is a black as pitch, but his behaviour is bad; when he feels the presence of his black brother Marcus in the white paradise, he doesn't want to say hello or in any way acknowledge that I exist.

Christian has a ghettoblaster of his own with a record player attached to it.

"Yes, I'm sorry, I don't have much reggae, but I'll get some the next time I'm back in Denmark," he says and plays some very strange music called Pink Floyd.

"I can make some cassettes for you – Bob Marley, Stevie Wonder, Eddy Grant," I say.

"Would you?"

"Yes, of course," I say. Christian wants to introduce me to his father. I come with him. Shake hands with *bwana* Knudsen – he's standing about smoking a cigar like the great socialist hero Fidel Castro; I have read about him at school – a good friend to both Angola and African socialism. Jonas goes to the ashtray and takes his lump of dirt out of his mouth. He dips it in the thick ash from the cigar and pops it back under his upper lip, looking smug. That man could eat death. *Bwana* Knudsen grins at him:

"Needed spiking, did it?" Jonas nods and leaves. *Bwana* Knudsen turns back to me:

"So you're the one who knows so much about music," he says.

"Yes," I say looking around the sitting room. These Danes don't have a stereo even though they have a great many L.P.s on their shelves, and the place is so nice. "Don't you listen to music?" I ask. *Bwana* Knudsen points to a sculpture in the sitting room:

"The music is there," he says. I can't see it. Christian laughs. On the shelf is a slab of wood with metal and coloured glass – very sleek, straight. A European Makonde. I go over and look at it. There are red lights inside the sculpture. Christian takes a small box in his hand and presses it; great music springs to life in the room. It's a stereo system called B. & O. – tight sound, remote control, it's a musical Makonde – you look at it for half an hour, and you still don't know where to push the button to start it because the button isn't there.

I can see it on Jonas' face, it annoys him that the driver mingles with the real people, so I want to leave.

"Just grab yourself something to eat," *bwana* Knudsen says, gesticulating.

"I'll bring some empty cassettes next time we come visit," Christian says.

"I'm going to go outside now," I say.

"You can stay if you want," Christian says.

"No, I have to watch the car," I say.

"But our guard is watching the car."

"Yes, I know, but I promised Jonas I'd do it."

"Oh. That's silly, isn't it?" Christian says.

"I'll see you in Moshi – remember the tapes," I say and quickly sneak out, taking food from the kitchen with the guard like two little monkeys. The white people and the local *mabwana makubwa* from T.P.C. chatter and dance and drink in the sitting room and on the veranda while the lushest sounds come from the Makonde-stereo. I am not a part of it, so it's not very nice to watch. I go to the other side of the house and sit down on the Land Rover's fender, light a Sportsman – thinking how can I get to live with parties like that, fine dining, bottled beer, Makonde-stereo, women who smell like flowers? Today I can watch but I'm not allowed to touch.

"Hello, Marcus. So this is where you're hiding?" *Eeehhh*, it's Tita coming towards me in the dark wearing a very flimsy dress – the tailor has so little fabric that her *titi* are almost jumping out of it. I get up. She comes over and stands in front of me. Her skin is like a lamp in the night.

"Won't you come inside and dance with me, Marcus?"

"I'm just here as the driver," I say. Tita moves her hips from side to side in front of me, raising her arms above her head. Her skin is luminous as she dances.

"Oh, come on." The scent from her mouth – gin and tonic with lime.

"Jonas doesn't like it if I come inside."

"Jonas is an old idiot, that's all," she says. "But we can dance out here instead." She dances closer to me. I quickly look around, don't move. She tilts her head to one side, smiling. "Don't be nervous, Marcus," she says.

"If Asko sees me standing close to his wife, I will be beaten," I say.

"Why don't you visit me anymore?" Tita asks.

"The sauna was finished a long time ago."

"That's no reason why you can't stop by and say hello," Tita says, winking at me. I swallow my spit. I'm afraid she will put her arms around me and discover that my pump is as hard as a rock. "Katriina has promised me that you'll come and help with a few things."

"Would you like a cigarette?" I ask, reaching down into my shirt pocket to take out the pack, so she'll be busy smoking and won't step closer. I look towards the house. I almost jump – Christian is standing at the corner of the house watching us. "I could be in trouble now." Tita looks around to see, but he's gone.

"What?" she says. I shake out a cigarette.

"The boy in the house – Christian – he was watching us." Tita laughs.

"And what did he see?" she asks, taking the cigarette. "That you offered me a cigarette." She puts it in her mouth. I light it for her. She turns around and walks away – looks over her shoulder.

"I'll be seeing you," she says.

FAULTY PLUG

The phone rings. Katriina speaks in Swedish. "Marcus," she calls afterwards, "could you pop down to Tita's?"

"Yes," I say. Perhaps I'm to explain to the guard that he mustn't get drunk at work and snore so loud it frightens the dogs.

"I think she has a technical problem with some electrical equipment," Katriina says. "You'd better bring some tools."

"Can't Asko fix it?" I ask.

"Asko is on safari," Katriina says. *Eeehhh*, is the sixteen-year-old negro boy going to be in the house while the husband is away?

Tita asks me to come in. Would I not like to sit down? I am polite to the white lady; I sit. Would I not like something to drink? Yes, I can drink. She serves gin and tonics. Tita has a plug – it's not working.

"Could you take a look at it? Perhaps you can fix it," she says.

"I can do that," I say. She gets up and walks down the corridor. I follow. Into the bedroom.

"The plug is behind there," Tita says, pointing at the bedside table next to the double bed. I pull out the bedside table so that I can get a better look. I get down on my knees to study the plug more closely, and Tita sits on the edge of the bed. Her skirt is up over her knees; if the negro turns his head, he can see the white flower. The curtains are drawn. The room is quiet dark.

"Is it not working at all?" I ask, turning my head because I can't help myself. Tita glides forwards on the edge of the bed, so her skirt is pushed up further, showing her thighs.

"Perhaps it can be made to work," Tita says, spreading her legs,

I want to look away, but my brain has no control over my eyes. I am looking straight at the flower. Tita is not wearing knickers. She leans forwards and takes the negro's hand. She puts it on her thigh – the black hand is almost no longer mine – she pulls it upwards towards the garden. *Eeehhhh*, what's happening? I'm thinking that when the black pump sows seeds in the white garden, the crop is a cocoa-fruit – everyone can see it. And already my fingers are noticing a wet sensation between Tita's legs, very warm. And Tita pulls her skirt up over her arse and spreads her legs completely. I am looking directly at the wet petals of the flower – pink in the midst of the blonde curls, the white skin.

"You have to kiss it," she says. And I do everything the white lady says – she must know – she must know how this is done right. "Use your tongue," she says. Yes. Everywhere I go with my tongue, like a swift propeller on the flower, which has a warm taste of the wildest honey. Tita points to the bud right above the pink petals. "Right there," she says. So I put my propeller on the bud, and Tita writhes with spasms – she catches my head between her hands, pressing my head hard against the spot. Tita moans and takes my face between her hands, lifting it from the licking. "We're going to make love now," she says.

"That's very dangerous," I say.

"It's not dangerous," Tita says, reaching towards the bedside table, opening the drawer and taking out a sock. "Get up," she says. I do it, my trousers like a tent because of my excitement. And Tita puts her hand there, holding the stiff pump through the trousers.

"No," I say. "It's too dangerous." But *mzungu* is deaf when Africa speaks. Because Tita opens the tent so that the black pump pokes out.

"It's stunning," she says. Yes, it is stunning, but what is Tita going to do with it? *Eeehhh*, the white woman takes the pump right into her mouth while her hand feels my sugarbag. She releases the pump and smiles at me as she opens the pack with the sock in it and pulls the sock onto the pump. I am shaking with excitement. "Lie down," she says, pulling off her top, making her pretty *titi* bob. "Kiss my breasts," she says. And everything she tells me – I do it. "Come inside me," she says. And even though the black man doesn't like being trapped inside rubber, he can make an exception today because the white woman is an adventure. No more handiwork and eternal damnation. The first time the pump parties indoors, it is in the white woman; white like the snow on Kibo's peaks.

THE KISS OF THE LEOPARD

The plans for the portable sawmills on West Kilimanjaro are going ahead and are given a stamp of approval by S.I.D.A. Asko flies to Sweden to buy the large forest machinery that will have to be sailed to Tanzania:

tractor, bulldozer, lorry with a crane that can pick up logs from the forest floor. When the sawmills are launched, there will be more *wazungu* who are experts in everything to do with trees. Already the project has started doing up the plywood factory in Boma la Mbuzi, which folded after it was nationalized in 1979. When it's up and running again, it will also house the sales office and the storage facilities for the timber from new sawmills. The forestry project is going to be called TanScan, named for the collaboration between Tanzanian and Scandinavia, because the *wazungu* workers will come from Sweden, Norway and Finland.

Asko's departure creates a new situation. Every day Tita needs something new – one day it's baking powder, the next day it's a tin of tuna. And always a black bag of sugar.

"It's dangerous if Asko comes home," I say.

"Don't worry – he won't be back for another few days," Tita says and does acrobatics in bed.

"He could even kill me," I say.

"Shush," she says, putting her tongue in my mouth so I can't say anything at all.

Yes, I know that situation. *Mzungu* only listen to their own needs. When I was a boy, still with my parents in Serengeti, my father's work was driving tourists around in the minibus.

Under his sunhat, which has a band of fake leopard skin, the tourist's head is red like a monkey's arse. And he wears the same sort of jacket and shorts as the white hunters, but he only shoots with his camera. The car is striped like a zebra and part of the roof can be raised so the tourist can stand up and look out at the animals. Father speaks to them as we drive:

"Don't stand with your whole body out of the hole – only your head. You're not allowed to stand on the seats – it is dangerous."

The tourists step down. Not long after they're standing on the seats again – with their entire upper body out of the car. Father stops the car. "You're only allowed to have your head up – otherwise it's dangerous when there are animals." They get down again. Father drives on. They get back up. He stops the car with not a single animal in sight.

"It's a rule," he says. "I'm not allowed to drive if you do it."

"O.K.," they say and get down again. My father doesn't drive on. He says:

"If you do it again, I'm taking you back to the lodge." Two *wazungu* men put their heads together. They hand my father something.

"Let's just get on, shall we? And no more talk about where we're standing." My father doesn't look back at the *mzungu* or at his hand, he just stuffs the thing into his pocket, starts the car and drives. The tourists climb up. Father finds a leopard resting in a tree. And a Japanese woman starts climbing out onto the roof. Father doesn't say anything – he too feels the hunger for meat. The *wazungu* have silenced him with their money. The Japanese woman has a large camera, it say *duku-duku-duku-duku*, almost like a pick-up truck. She is brave, standing on top of the roof taking pictures. I am below in the car looking out. The leopard stands up on its branch, leaps, its claws out. I can see up though the hatch in the roof; its paws land right on the Japanese *titi*. She falls over, rolls off the roof, and the leopard gives her the red kiss on the neck – no more Japanese.

Not long after my father was fired from his job as a driver. The tourists had complained about the greedy driver who was always telling them off and who had the Japanese woman killed. Instead he became a park ranger and was sent on raids to capture poachers.

Now I'm the leopard, with my claws on Tita's *titi*. But I don't give her the red kiss on her neck, I just obey her orders like a black machine in the white papaya.

QUAGMIRE

In the Larsson house the peculiarities reach new heights. Since the baby's birth Dr Freeman has come round one, two, three times. "How are you all doing?" he asks, studying baby Rebekka as an excuse to have Katriina's company. They talk and they talk a lot.

"We really don't need all these visits," Katriina says. "I'll call you if there's anything." Dr Freeman is like a wet dog – kicked away. This white doctor has access to all the black nurses at K.C.M.C., but he doesn't want to go native – he would rather try to steal another white man's wife for his lovemaking, because he wants to have the human companionship with the woman – not like Jonas and his mash-making.

Katriina can't go out at night when Jonas leaves, because Rebekka wakes up at night screaming, wanting to suck *titi*.

At night I sneak into the kitchen like the marabou.

"Is that you, Marcus?" Katriina calls from the sitting room.

"Yes," I say. "I was just going to get a slice of bread."

"Take the plate of meat and potatoes from the fridge and bring it here," she calls. I open the fridge, and there is a plate of food, arranged like it was at a restaurant. I know right then it is meant for Jonas, but it's too late – Jonas isn't here. In the sitting room I see the bottle of gin at once; Katriina is making short work of it; her eyes are as shiny as glass. "Sit down and eat," Katriina says, pointing at the dining table.

"Yes," I say.

"Do you know that I'm from Finland?" she says. "My entire family are refugees from Finland. We're Finnish Swedes. That means that Swedes think we're not as good people as they are. But Jonas, he's a real Swede. His father owns enormous forests in Sweden – a real *bwana mkubwa*. And Jonas is the prodigal son. You see?"

"What about your father?" I ask.

"My father worked in the forest," Katriina says. *Eeehhh*; Katriina has caught the big fish – the boss' son. But now the fish has become unpalatable.

"Yes," I say and eat while I nod, even though the important question hasn't been answered, because what is Katriina's role in this family? Katriina doesn't do anything – she drinks gin and has a house girl, Marcus the Babysitter, a gardener, the guard, everything. In Tanzanian families the woman is the one who looks after the children and the home and the fields – even if the man goes missing. Black women can fend for themselves, and it'll be tough on the men if the women discover this. But Katriina – I don't think she can fend for herself.

"Jonas' father's older sister will be down soon to see the little baby," Katriina says. I don't want to ask whether Jonas' father will be down – it's not for me to ask directly. "But Jonas' father doesn't want to see his grandchildren," Katriina says and leans forward for her glass, taking a big gulp. "You see?" she says. Yes, I understand these things. Jonas wants to be the king of the forest on West Kilimanjaro to prove himself to his father.

"Thanks for supper," I say and hurry back to my ghetto. How can I keep the problems of an entire Swedish family in my head when I have so many of my own to contend with? I try to hide, but these *wazungu* always drag me into their mess.

1982

Marcus

PUMPING FACTORY

Asko returns to Tanzania, and that puts a spanner in my work as a free *malaya* for Tita. Finally I can relax a little. Another Swede has come down with Asko to join the project – Gösta, with his wife Stina. The first job is to arrange a welcome party at the Larssons'.

I get on the motorbike and go to buy chickens to put on the barbecue. Then I drive back to the house to find the house girl standing outside the gate, crying.

"Marcus, Marcus," she calls. I stop the motorbike. She is standing with a number of different bags and says nervously: "*Mama* says I am fired, but . . ."

"Why has she fired you?" I ask. The house girl is very embarrassed and looks at the ground without answering. We both know the answer – Katriina has opened her eyes. "Have you been paid?" I ask.

"Yes, but the *mama* can't fire me. It's the man of the house who decides things," the house girl says, looking up.

"When you fiddle with the husband, the *mama* can even have you killed. You'd better leave quickly," I say.

"But he promised me he would—" I interrupt because I don't want to hear about his false promises:

"A man will always lie to you, when you're a whisk for his pump," I say and drive away from her – into the property. Katriina immediately comes out onto the veranda – her eyes are red. She wants to give me another job and I already know what it is: to fix all their problems.

"I've fired the house girl," Katriina says.

"*Eeehhh,*" I say like a total *mswahili*. What can I say?

"She couldn't cook," Katriina explains without looking at me. "We need to find ourselves an older woman, Marcus. One who has skills."

Then she turns and goes back inside without saying anything about the party; is it off, or am I cooking?

Christian

Saturday. The folks are going to a party at the Larssons'. It starts early and there's to be a dinner.

"I can't be arsed to go," I say.

"Of course you're going," Mum says. "You can talk to Solja." Mum goes to the bathroom.

"Solja's just a child," I say.

"So are you," Dad says.

"I'll be fifteen soon," I say.

"My point exactly," he says. No say in my own life.

Mama Brian has Annemette ready. When Mum is ready, we all go out to the car. I sit on the backseat with *mama* Brian. Annemette is on her lap in the carrycot. Dad sits on the passenger seat and hands the keys out of the window.

"Not now, surely," Mum says.

"You have to learn sometime," Dad says. Mum takes the keys, sits behind the wheel and starts. She goes the wrong way round the roundabout by the entrance to the T.P.C. residential area. "That wasn't right," Dad says.

"Oh drat," Mum says. "It feels completely topsy-turvy." Dad laughs. We go past the factory and down the T.P.C. road. There's a lot of heavy traffic at the moment. Almost all of the Tanzanian Railways' locomotives have broken down, so now the refined sugar is taken from the factory in lorries. The drivers are often off their heads with drink; you can buy *gongo* within the T.P.C. compound. Day and night the lorries drive down the T.P.C. road, many of them without headlights, because they have either been stolen or smashed by thrown-up pebbles, and it's impossible to get new ones. Some of the lorries crab sideways – they have been twisted out of shape in traffic accidents and haven't been straightened out properly. Dad explains:

"Hardly any of them have working indicators, so you have to be prepared for sudden brakes and turns. They have a system where you flash your right indicator if it's not advisable for the person behind you to overtake. And with your left if it's all clear," Dad says. We come up behind a lorry snailing along, but it's a straight road, it's got lights on and the driver is flashing his left indicator. "Come on," Dad says.

"Yes, yes," Mum says and starts overtaking the lorry, holding tight to the wheel until she swings back in front of it.

"It's not easy when you have to do it on the wrong side of the road," she says.

"Of course when they do indicate it might also mean that they want to turn. On the whole you've got to be pretty alert," Dad says.

"Yes, that's the impression I'm getting," Mum says.

We're not the first at the party – a number of people are already on the veranda, drinks in hand.

"I'm going down to Marcus'," I say and head straight towards the servants' quarters. Perhaps he has beer. But Marcus isn't there – the door is locked. I go towards the kitchen door. I can hear Jonas talking in there:

"Then how the hell do you imagine we're going to cook? It's not like *you* ever do anything."

"I won't have your whore in our house with the children," Katriina says.

"You're mad," Jonas says. "That's the house girl you're talking about!" I can hear Dad's voice:

"Calm down, both of you." Marcus opens the door and sneaks out on the back stairs.

"No, I bleeding well won't," Katriina screams. "The only thing he ever thinks about is shagging all the black girls." Marcus sees me in the twilight.

"She's fired the house girl," he says under his breath.

"We can easily sort out some food," Dad says inside the kitchen. I hear my mum's voice:

"What's going on?"

"Whoremonger," Katriina sobs.

"*Fa'n!*" Jonas shouts – damn. There's no music – everyone on the veranda must have heard them shouting. Then the power cuts out. Candles are lit, a bat light. Jonas leaves the veranda door and goes over to his motorbike, getting on it – "I don't need this shit." He takes off – probably to go to the club. The guests are standing silently on the veranda. Katriina is crying in the kitchen. Mum is comforting her. I haven't seen Solja – she must be with some friends of hers. My dad comes out on the veranda.

"It doesn't seem like there's going to be a party," he tells the other guests.

"We'll go to the club," one of them says. Another asks: "Is there no food? But we've just arrived? Is she not well?"

"There's no food," Dad says. "There's no power. And there are a few problems. I think it's best if we just leave." People drink up, stroll back to their cars. Muttering among themselves. Take off. I'm still standing outside with Marcus – we don't say anything.

"I want to go to the club," Katriina says doggedly from the veranda.

"Do you think that's a good idea?" Dad asks.

"He doesn't get to decide what I do and what I don't," Katriina says. Mum puts an arm around her shoulder.

"Let's go then," Dad says. They go towards the car. What should I do? No-one says anything or even seems to remember that I'm here. Katriina calls to Marcus:

"Keep an eye on Rebekka."

"I will do it," he calls back. How can Katriina leave a sleeping infant? But then Mum is leaving Annemette with *mama* Brian. Where is Solja?

"See you," I tell Marcus – go over to the car, get in the back seat next to Katriina, who calls out to him:

"Remember that Solja will be back at nine."

"Yes," he calls. Alright – then she is with friends.

We drive out to the club. Everyone from the aborted party is there. Sitting at the bar calling for grilled meat and chips from the kitchen. Jonas is there too, looking grim, talking to Asko, drinking beer. No Tita, though. Jonas only gives us a quick look as we come through the door – he ignores Katriina. I'm not old enough to be in the bar, so I go into the poolroom at the back. I open the latch to the bar just a little, peer in. Jonas is sitting at the bar with Asko – they're silent. Jonas signals the bartender, who pours beer into their glasses. Jonas makes another sign; the bartender grabs a bottle of Konyagi behind him and a jigger, pouring two slugs of Konyagi into each beer glass. Katriina is standing some distance away with my mum. Next to them are Gösta and Stina – they've just come down from Sweden and tonight was meant to be a welcome party for them. Katriina grabs Stina's arm:

"You must hire an old hag as your house girl," she says. Stina looks puzzled. "Or an ugly girl. So your husband isn't tempted. The young black girls . . . they . . ." Standing in the middle of the bar, Katriina starts crying again. Mum goes over and hugs her, smoothing down her hair. The Indian men stare at them testily; it's bad enough that white women come to the bar – do they really have to make a show of themselves? Jonas gets up from his barstool – goes outside. I go to the opposite side of the poolroom, watch him drive off on his motorbike. I go back to the hatch. Katriina is still crying. Asko gets up, leaves. He goes towards his car. I'm thinking about whether to run out and ask for a lift down to Marcus, but I don't want to ride with Asko. I leave the poolroom and go over to Mum.

"Can we eat soon?" I ask.

"Not right now, Christian," she says, turning back to Katriina. Dad is sitting at a table with Miriam and John from T.P.C. I go outside. I have no cigarettes. A Norwegian family call to their daughter to come back to them. She is my age and in my year, but we're in different sets.

"We're leaving," the Norwegian woman says in a firm voice. The man doesn't say anything. I wonder if I should ask them for a lift, but the Norwegian woman would certainly ask my mum if it was alright, and Mum would say no. I just want to get away from this mess and get back to Marcus. I start walking towards the golf players' driving range, which is right in front of the club. Soon I'm enveloped in darkness. I make my way between some trees and cross the field beyond until I reach the shrubbery on the side of Kilimanjaro Road. I walk along, keeping out of sight among the bushes, where the light from the street lamps doesn't reach me – it smells of the cowpats the cattle drop when the Maasai take them to the abattoir at the other end of town.

I make it down to Rombo Avenue – go to the gate.

"Guard?" I call. He comes over. I ask if Jonas is there. No. Marcus?

"Yes. He is with the children," the guard says and lets me in. The house is dark – still no power. I go to the main entrance by the veranda. Solja is reading by the light of two candles on the dining table. *Mama* Brian is in the sitting room with Annemette in the carrycot.

"Marcus is out back," Solja says. I walk through the dark house. It smells of fried chicken. I find him on the lawn outside the kitchen, lit up by the glowing charcoal in an oil barrel that has been cut in half; the grill above it is covered with chicken drumsticks and corncobs – it sizzles and smokes when the barbecue sauce drips onto the coals.

"Hi, Marcus," I say.

"Hi," he says and looks over my shoulder. "Are you all back?"

"Just me. I walked here," I say. "What are you doing?"

"I have to cook the meat. The fridge is dead – it'll rot otherwise. Where are the adult *wazungu*?"

"At the club. Except for Jonas and Asko – they left because Katriina said something about young house girls." Marcus shakes his head.

"What did she say?" he asks.

"She told Gösta's wife to hire an old and ugly house girl who Gösta wouldn't want to bonk."

"She's right," Marcus says.

"What are you talking about?" Solja has come out into the kitchen and is standing in the dark behind the door's mosquito netting.

"Nothing," Marcus says. "Are you hungry?"

"About my crazy parents, in other words," Solja says and comes onto the lawn.

"Yes," I say. And to Marcus: "I certainly am hungry."

"Get some plates then," Marcus says.

Sunday. The folks are in the sitting room. I'm out on the veranda looking at nothing in particular. Annemette is crawling about on the lawn, and *mama* Brian is squatting a few metres away. Benjamin the Gardener has the day off – I think he is probably in the servants' quarters. Mum is upset.

"Do you really think Jonas has been up to something with the house girl? Can't it be that she is simply . . . ?" Mum stops.

"I think it's true," Dad says.

"But . . . Why would you think that?" Mum asks. Dad sighs.

"Before you came down, Christian saw something," he says. It makes me shiver.

"Christian?" Mum says.

"Yes," Dad says and tells her about the rocking Land Cruiser on the back road. "Solja looked into the car. Solja saw her father with a . . . With a whore. Christian saw it."

"Why didn't you tell me?" Mum asks in a shrill voice.

"I didn't want you to worry," Dad says.

"Worry? What are you thinking? He's just a boy – he shouldn't be seeing that sort of thing."

"What's done is done," Dad says.

"But what did you do about it?" Mum asks.

"Nothing. What would you have me do?" Dad asks.

"Do you do that sort of thing as well?" Mum asks.

"Come off it," Dad says.

"O.K.," Mum says. "Ewww," she sneers. "It's so obvious. Jonas is the kind of man who's led a merry dance by his cock."

"Yes," Dad says, "There are people who lose all moral sense when you take them away from social constraints."

"What do you mean?" Mum asks.

"In Sweden his colleagues and family would keep an eye on him and protest if he were to let rip. Here he can get away with anything."

"But he can't just . . ." Mum stops again. *Mama* Brian has got up – she is taking clothes down from the clothesline.

"No," Dad says. "Someone ought to slap him about a little." Right. But Dad was stationed in the Far East several times. Away from social constraints. Sometimes he didn't see my mum for months on end. And Mum was at the hospital in Køge. Did she play nurse to the doctors? And Jonas isn't the only one who gets up to these games, is he?

"Katriina would like us to come and talk to them," Mum says.

"Yes," Dad says. "But what the hell are we supposed to talk to them about? He denies vehemently that anything's happened."

"I don't know," Mum says.

"*Nyoka, nyoka, nyoka!*" *mama* Brian screams. Snake! I look up. Annemette is over by the bougainvillea hedge. The woman is standing two metres from her, jumping and screaming, her eyes wild – the clothes she's just taking from the line lie strewn about her on the lawn. I'm out of my chair, see Benjamin rushing out from the servants' quarters with a *panga* in his hand. Mum is coming out onto the veranda.

"What's happening?" Dad shouts. Annemette starts bawling as Benjamin comes charging, and I'm hot on his heels, and *mama* Brian is screaming. Benjamin runs right over to the hedge, and I pick Annemette up – holding her and turning her in front of me. She's screaming hysterically as I check her to see if something's happened. Out of the corner of my eye I see something green slithering towards the hedge, and Benjamin is chopping violently at it with his *panga*.

"*Kufa!*" he shouts – die! Mum pulls Annemette out of my hands, squatting down, turning the screaming child this way and that – examining her limbs.

"Aaaaiiiiiiii!" Benjamin shouts, taking a few steps back on the lawn, letting go of his *panga*, sitting down in the grass, holding one of his legs and staring at it as beads of sweat break out on his forehead.

123

"Has she been bitten?" Dad asks.

"I can't see anything," Mum says.

"It bit me," Benjamin says, pointing at two small beads of blood growing on his calf.

"It was a dangerous snake," *mama* Brian says – she's looking limp and her arms hang at her sides.

"I don't think it bit the child," Benjamin says.

"Take her," Mum says and hands Annemette to Dad, and then she leaps over to Benjamin, putting her mouth to his calf, sucking, then spitting, then sucking again.

"Are you sure she wasn't bitten?" Dad asks and his voice breaks.

"She would have passed out already if it were poisonous," Mum says. "When she's so small." It might have been a grass snake, but it's impossible to know. Mum looks at me. "Fetch a knife, Christian." I run into the house, the kitchen, grab a kitchen knife and run back out. Mum is sitting in her vest, knotting her shirt at the top of Benjamin's thigh to slow down his circulation. I hold out the knife. Mum takes it, presses it against Benjamin's leg making a small cross, so the blood spills out. Mum drops the knife and presses the skin around the wound, sucking and spitting. She does it several times; her mouth is red.

"We have to go to A.&E.," she says. "Niels, you have to carry him. He mustn't put any weight on that leg." *Mama* Brian comes over to take Annemette from Dad. Mum points at her.

"*Toka!*" Mum says – get lost. She's picked up that much Swahili. I take Annemette, who is still whimpering. *Mama* Brian starts crying and speaking. Dad carries Benjamin to the car while Mum half runs next to them. "What sort of snake was it?" she asks. Benjamin's calf looks swollen.

"I couldn't see," he says. "It was green." A grass snake or a green mamba then. *Mama* Brian is still in the garden, looking heartbroken. I go inside. It's important to kill the snake that bites you, so you can be sure which species it is. Then you can be given the right serum. When you don't know, you have to be given a multi-serum, which can kill you in itself.

"You stay in the house," Mum calls to me before they drive off. I go back in and give Annemette a chocolate biscuit and some juice to take her mind off it and calm her down. *Mama* Brian knocks on the open veranda door.

"What?" I say.

"It wasn't my fault," she says.

"You didn't pick up the child when you saw the snake. You just stood there, screaming, scaring the snake," I say. "You have to leave."

"It wasn't my fault," she says.

"Get lost," I say.

"I must be paid," she says.

"Get lost," I say and go over to close the door.

Dad comes home a little later.

"Is she O.K.?" he asks, looking at Annemette, touching her arms, her head, her legs, her feet. She smiles.

"Yes," I say. "What about Benjamin?"

"He's as sick as a dog. They've given him the multi-serum," Dad says. "There's no guarantee he'll pull through. Where's *mama* Brian?"

"She left," I say.

"I don't bloody believe it. That she didn't just go over and pick up the kid," Dad says.

"Africans are very frightened of snakes," I say.

"It was her who made the snake panic, damn it. People say snakes don't normally attack children – only if they feel threatened."

"It probably felt threatened when Benjamin arrived on the scene," I say.

"Yes, but he didn't know that Annemette was alright. I think he knew you have to kill the snake, so you can show it to the doctor and get the right serum."

"I think so too," I say.

"Did you see him hacking away with his *panga* under the hedge. He really went for it," Dad says. "Your Mum too."

"Yes, that was something," I say. "She looked like a vampire." Dad smiles.

A Land Rover stops in the drive. Two policemen come to the door in the company of two men from T.P.C.'s guard service – they've come to pick up *mama* Brian.

"Did you call the police?" Mum asks, looking at Dad.

"No," he says.

"Why are you looking for *mama* Brian?" Dad asks.

"We've been told we have to come get her," one of the police officers says.

"Why are you coming to get her?" Mum asks.

"It's our orders," the officer says.

"But why?"

"It's an order," he says, and they leave.

"Now if that isn't strange, I don't know what is," Dad says.

"I'm going over to the sickbay – they might know what's going on," Mum says. I go with her. Benjamin is in a coma. We find the Indian doctor.

"Before he fell into a coma, Benjamin said I should call the police," the doctor says.

"Why?" Mum asks.

"Because your nanny wasn't doing her job," he says.

"But we don't want to report her," Mum says. "We've fired her."

"People have to do their jobs," the doctor says. "I'm sure they'll find her."

"But what are they going to do to her?" Mum asks. The doctor shakes his head, looking serious.

"She must wait in the cell while they wait for you to press charges for negligence with the baby."

"It was an accident," Mum says. The doctor shrugs.

"In that case you'd better speak to the police, so she can go home before she has a serious accident at the police station." Mum sighs and asks me:

"Do you know where *mama* Brian lives?"

"Yes, roughly." We go home and drive our Peugeot to a village which is a part of T.P.C but lies a few kilometres from the factory. The police have already picked her up. We go home. Dad goes to the police station to sort things out. He looks pale when he returns.

"They've worked her over. Her lips were broken, and you could see bruises under her skin," Dad says. Mum doesn't say anything. She's got Annemette on her lap. She's been sitting like that since she came back. Annemette wants to go down on the floor to play with her toy bricks, but Mum won't let go of her.

Marcus

MEATBALLS

For days on end I run around asking everyone for a house girl or cook who has worked for *wazungu*. Finally I come across Josephina, withered and old. She is a good cook, good with children. Katriina explains *köt-bullar* to Josephina.

"You take the mince, some boiled potatoes, an egg, finely chopped onion . . ." Josephina cuts her short:

"*Eeehhhh*, meatballs," she says, because Josephina used to work for Danes, who eat almost the same sort of Scandinavian food. Asko enters:

"It worked out fine, Marcus," he says, smiling, slapping my back, putting a pack of Marlboro in my hand. What worked out fine? Asko is on his motorbike and now I see what it is that worked out. Through the gate comes the nice Mercedes, Tita behind the wheel with a big smile on her face. Jonas and Katriina come out on the veranda with question marks on their faces.

"Congratulations," I say.

"Tita has passed her driver's test – both the theory test and the practical part," Asko explains. "The police officer pointed at the signs and I talked to Tita in Finnish for a bit, and then I explained in English to the man what the sign meant, as if I was translating."

"What about your Merc?" Jonas asks. "I thought you were saving it for Finland."

"Oh well, it does it no harm for it to have an airing every now and again," Asko shrugs.

"I can't just be stuck inside a house in Africa for years on end – I have to be able to get out and about," Tita says, jangling the keys.

They sit down at the table and have lunch; stinking Scandinavian fish on top of hard black bread, which they wash down with a clear European *gongo* which is called *schnapps*. I am in the kitchen, tidying up. At the table Asko is talking about Tita's theory test success. Asko is cut short by Jonas:

"You don't even have to take the test," he says. "You should have just asked me, then I could have bought her the licence."

"How?" Asko asks.

"You pay," Jonas says. "Money in an envelope to the man behind the desk. Of course you have to be in the office so no-one else sees that he's getting it, but . . . it's simple."

Jonas picked up these methods from D'Souza when the sauna burnt down and he needed to swindle the insurance company. But his methods are corrupt, and they corrupt the person using them as well. Doesn't Jonas see the consequences? If you yourself become a negro, you can't teach the negro how to become white.

THE BLESSED STENCH

The baby Rebekka is to be christened at the Protestant church, and she attracts a visit from Sweden. Jonas' father's older sister, Aunt Elna. The shock is great for me – when she steps into the house, the household is run to perfection. Solja wears clean clothes, the parents are home in the evenings – no noise or trouble. They even work in the kitchen and serve warm food to their aunt.

"Aunt Elna has lots of money," Solja whispers to me, pulling me to the fridge to taste a special Swedish speciality which comes in a tube: *Kalles Kaviar* – the aunt brought it with her. "It's very good," Solja says, squeezing a little bit out onto my finger and onto her own. I sniff the weirdness on my finger – it smells tart. I don't want to disappoint Solja, so I put my entire finger in my mouth – like sucking a girl who has peed all week and not washed once. These Swedes – barbarians.

The Swedish *mama*, Aunt Elna, wants me to come to church with them.

"But I'm a Catholic," I say.

"It doesn't matter – it's all the same God," she says. So now I'm sitting in the Protestant church with Aunt Elna and Josephina.

Aunt Elna wants to give Josephina money because Josephina is a god-fearing single mother who struggles to send money to the village, where Josephina's two big girls live with her sister. They should stay in school if possible.

Josephina invites Aunt Elna to come to the village and the hut, so Elna can meet her daughters and see what the village is like. Josephina's mind doesn't work according to the negro's plan of opening the *mzungu*'s wallet. Josephina's invitation is good old-fashioned, sincere hospitality. I go with them in the Land Cruiser, and Solja comes along as well. Aunt Elna is afraid of nothing. She goes straight into the old-fashioned Chagga hut with cattle at one end and people at the other. The stench from the cattle is a blessing that creates joy every minute of the day, because cattle means wealth and they are part of the family. I come from a Chagga tribe – in Josephina's house everything is in the old style, and I feel it warming my heart, but at the same time I am also pleased to be away from this way of life – soil and livestock.

Aunt Elna confuses me. She goes right to the side of the cow, squats down, pulling on a teat so that milk sprays into her mouth. She pats the cow, saying:

"These are some very good-looking cows you've got, Josephina." And all of us negroes laugh, because the old Swedish *mama* understands everything about cows.

"When I was a child, I helped milk the cows in the morning," she says.

Aunt Elna sees me with the children. She hears me speak the Swedish language with them. The old *mama* is wise. Even though the house is like a paradise now, she can see through the hypocrisy, because Solja goes straight to me or Josephina when she wants to eat, or a have bath, or help with her homework – her parents are like strangers come for a visit.

"What do you want to do in your life, Marcus?" she asks me one day.

"At the moment I go to school," I say.

"But what would you like to be? Or to do? When this family has gone home one day?"

"I would like to continue to go to school, as long as Katriina will pay for it. And then I hope Jonas can send me to Sweden with the project, so I can be trained in how to tame the forest."

"Don't rely on other people's help, Marcus. You can't ever be sure of it. You have to do it yourself," Aunt Elna says.

"But I have no-one to help me. My parents are dead. I have no house to live in, I have no professional training with papers, so I can't look for work with companies and get a job. I have to go to school, so that I know what I'm doing."

"Alright then, I'll see what I can do," she says.

As soon as Aunt Elna leaves, the old madness returns. Solja says she is hungry and Jonas shouts from the sitting room:

"Marcus! Make Solja some dinner. Must I tell you every time?"

"*Tsk*," Josephina says in the kitchen. "How are those children ever going to become human beings with a father like that?"

"We will make them human, Josephina," I say.

"We can't make them white humans – we don't know how," she says.

"We'll make them *waafrika*," I say.

"*Tsk*. It'll be a confusion," Josephina says, shaking her head.

MOTHER, THE DRUG FARMER

My little brother comes to the door. He has grown a great deal.

"You must help our family," he says.

"I don't have any money," I say.

"Our father is in prison for his drunken brawls, and our mother is living a dangerous life." He tells me Mother has started growing *mirungi*, which the Somali and the Arabs chew to get stoned; they call it *khat*. She sells it outside the market. It's illegal, like *bhangi*, but the police don't crack down on it quite as hard. If you go to Same on the bus, you will see people getting off in the middle of nowhere, and you don't understand why. What do they want to go there for? But they bring sacks and a knife – they grow it in the bush. And perhaps they hire people to help them carry it to the roadside, get on a bus to Moshi or Arusha or Dar – anywhere – to sell it while it's fresh and still works. Mostly it's Arabs chewing it on Sundays when everything is shut for the day. The men have a large lump of stalks in their cheek, working it with their mouth like a cow. Only sensible and calm people use it, because it requires the effort of the cow. And it looks like leaf greens – like salad, but *ehhh*, bitter – I know from my sample tastings. "If they arrest our mother, your little sisters will live like rats in the orphanage," my little brother says.

"How can I help them when I have no money?" I say.

"*Tsk*," he says. "You're the eldest, but you're a bad son who lets down his own mother to look after the *wazungu*'s children. Do you think they can make you white?" I give him whatever money I have and send him away.

THE EVIL EYE

Before Aunt Elna left, she said she would send me a package with some trousers and T-shirts to wear when I go to church. And some money. Every day I wait, looking forward to it. One day Solja calls me from the veranda – she's holding a brown paper bag in her hand.

"It's from Aunt Elna – for you," Solja says.

"Thank you," I say, taking the bag – it's all crumpled up, like rubbish. I open it and take out the clothes. Worn jeans and used underwear. I recognize the clothes. Solja wonders about it:

"But those are my dad's clothes," she says. Katriina talks inside the sitting room in Swedish, which I am on the way to understanding to the point of perfection:

"You must give him the nice parcel as well," she says. Solja fetches a package with smooth coloured paper. It contains two new T-shirts – not junk, the proper sort. But where are the trousers and the money?

*

Later D'Souza comes over with his son, who is given a package of clothes by Jonas; good underwear, sturdy new trousers. I think Aunt Elna sent those trousers for me, but Jonas looked at me and decided I am only fit for his worn-out clothes. The new clothes work better as a bribe – D'Souza can get him advantages in Africa.

"Marcus, Aunt Elna is on the phone," Katrina calls from the house. "She wants to say hello to you." I hurry up there.

"It was the best T-shirts you gave me. Very good. Thank you so much," I say into the phone. Soon she asks:

"What about the trousers – do they fit?"

"I don't know," I say – very conscious of Jonas, who is on the sofa listening.

"Didn't you get them?" Aunt Elna asks.

"Yes, things are very good at school," I say into the phone. She goes silent at the other end – only the whooshing sound on the line. She can guess that I'm not alone in the room. Now she becomes very diplomatic, so it won't cause any problems:

"Hmmm. That's odd. Perhaps . . ." She's thinking all the way up in Sweden. "You probably won't get them until later." Jonas is sitting on the sofa looking at me – in his eyes is the question of whether I should be beaten down like a sick dog.

"Yes, I'm sure you're right," I tell Aunt Elna, while Jonas gives me his evil eye, which tells me I'm not even a small axe: Hmmm, I give you everything – board and lodging – and yet you want more, eh?

I am hungry and go to the kitchen. Jonas cooks – first time I have seen him cooking.

"Do you want some help with that?" I ask, because I want to learn how to put the plants and the meat together in a new sort of tasty meal in the Swedish style. He doesn't look at me:

"This is for the family only," he says. "It's not something anyone can come and be a part of."

I go down and wait. When he has eaten, he sits out on the veranda to let the food settle in his stomach. Then I tiptoe in like a thief in the night and take the leftovers for my personal nutrition. Marabou.

Christian
Mum has hired a big, adult lady – *mama* Nasira, who has four children of her own, all of them at school. Annemette is no longer allowed to

totter around in the garden. Mum never lets her out of her sight. I think I should probably say something.

"I look forward to when she's a bit older," I say.

"Who?" Mum says, looking up.

"Annemette," I say.

"Right, yes," Mum says, looking at Annemette. "What then, when she's a bit older?"

"Then I'll teach her to swear and play football," I say.

Last day of school. Electricity in the air. The boarders are looking forward to going home. Panos comes over to me at lunch break.

"Want to come down to the river with me?" he asks in a low voice.

"Yeah, sure," I say. We cross the playing fields and walk between the trees so that no-one sees us leaving school grounds. We hurry down the slope.

"Boys," a voice calls to us.

"Samantha?" Panos says.

"Over here," she calls, getting up from behind a bush with a cigarette in her hand. We go over to her and squat down.

"Are your parents coming to pick you up?" Panos asks her.

"My dad's away on business, but Mum's coming," Samantha says. "How about you?"

"Taking the bus to Iringa," Panos says.

"Boredom at T.P.C.," I say. "What are you doing this half-term?" I ask her.

"I plan to drink G.&T.s and smoke cigarettes and dive," she says.

"That sounds pretty bloody good," I say. Samantha looks at me, squinting as she smiles.

"You could come to Tanga and dive with me," she says. "Go off the deep end."

"Cool it, you two," Panos says. Samantha grins and slaps him. I wish it were me she was slapping.

Summer holiday. I go over to Nanna's for a swim, but I don't try anything funny even though her dad's at work and her mum's in town.

"Thanks for letting me use your pool," I say afterwards. Nanna gets up from the sunbed, comes over to me and kisses me abruptly on the mouth, pushing her tongue between my teeth before turning and walking into the house, into her room. I follow her. We're kissing on the bed. I get my hand up under her top.

"No," she says when I try to pull it off her, but she keeps on snogging me. I take her hand and put it on my crotch outside my trousers. I want her to feel how hard it is.

"Ewww," she says, getting up and walking away.

"I'm sorry," I say, blushing.

"I think you should leave now," she says. She's not easy to work out, that one.

The next day Nanna flies to Denmark with her parents on holiday.

I'm sitting with Rogarth down by the river at T.P.C., smoking – he's leaving soon to visit some relatives.

"That John is a bad man," Rogarth says.

"Why's that?" I ask.

"He behaves like a colonialist – he speaks to all black Tanzanians as if they're dogs," Rogarth says.

"Yes, Mum says he treats the field workers very badly," I say.

"Not just the workers. The management as well. He must understand that Tanzania has nationalized T.P.C., that it's our country. He works for us – not the other way around," Rogarth says.

"What are you laughing at?" I ask.

"John's wife, Miriam, she's always drunk – did you know that?"

"Yes, it's hard to miss," I say.

"And John's always running around with whores in Moshi with another white man," Rogarth says.

"He is?" I ask. Perhaps the other man is Jonas.

"Yes," Rogarth says and laughs, shaking his head.

"Why is that funny?" I ask.

"He's chasing Tanzanian women like a randy dog, and he treats Tanzanian men as if they were bitches. He's not right in the head," Rogarth says.

We have gone to Dar es Salaam, the whole family. It's hot and humid. At first we stay a couple of days at Hotel Africana a little to the north of the city – a run-down place with a white sandy beach.

Then we move closer to the city. Through some people at the embassy we have rented a house in Valhalla – a fenced-in residential area where only Scandinavians live. Again, it's to the north of the city, on the Msasani peninsula, which is the well-to-do area of Dar es Salaam. The neighbours are Norwegian, and they invite us along to the yacht club, which is full of white people.

"We might as well be living in colonial times," Dad says.

"Black people aren't interested in sailing," the Norwegian says. I go down for a swim, drink a Coke, eat chips. I spot some people I've seen at school, but no-one I know. At night I call a number Jarno has given me – his father's project has a house in Dar where the family sometimes stays during school breaks when they want to get out of Morogoro. But they're not there.

We walk around the city centre, eat at restaurants, go down and look at the harbour where there are old merchant vessels with triangular sails.

"It's called a *dhow*," Dad says. "They're responsible for carrying freight between East Africa, Zanzibar and the Arab Peninsula – they're still in use."

Annemette is in her pushchair, chattering away – she'll be two in a few months and attracts a lot of attention.

Back to T.P.C. Dad can't stay away long. I go about and am bored silly. Rogarth is away on holiday. I play golf, football with the lads, smoke cigarettes by the river. I am stranded in the middle of a giant field of sugar canes. Dad is working and Mum is busy with Annemette, who goes about and touches everything and must be looked out for because of that incident with the snake. Mum doesn't trust the new nanny, *mama* Nasira, even though she seems very competent. Luckily there's only a week left until school starts again.

Marcus

SECRET PUSHER

The *bhangi* under his bed has been smoked, and Jonas needs his weed. He doesn't have any more tobacco dirt from Sweden to stuff into his mouth either, so now he is as grouchy and dangerous as an old rhino. I have to help him, just to protect myself from his madness. I go to Phantom's kiosk behind the market:

"Jonas needs *bhangi*," I say.

"I can bring some over tonight," he says.

"No, he can't know that it's you and me. Just use one of your little boys. When Jonas arrives at Kibo Coffee House the boy must go up to him and make him an offer. With a steep price," I say. Phantom grins.

"Alright," he says. I scratch his back, he scratches mine.

The next time I meet Phantom, he says:

"It's working. Jonas is my best customer."

One day I am at Kibo Coffee House, but out back where the toilets are. As I walk back along the corridor to the room with the high ceilings, I see Jonas; I stop, drawing back round the corner. Phantom's boy is standing next to him. Jonas looks around nervously – the strong Arusha-*bhangi* is making him as paranoid as pregnant gazelle. I see the boy sign to the guy outside. Jonas gets up, leaves the boy, goes out to start his motorbike, while another guy comes over to him, shaking his hand, and Jonas puts that same hand back into his shirt, stashes the small tightly folded brown paper bag and dashes home, home to smoke, his release, which has become his prison and my place of safety. Jonas sees me every day in his house, a black man who looks after his children, eats, moves around freely – it rouses his discontent. If his head ever gets really clear, if only for a single day – I will be kicked out on my arse.

Christian

"Aren't you going into town?" I ask Mum.

"No, not for another few days," she says.

"But I'm bored."

"Then you'll have to go yourself."

"But how am I going to get there?" I ask.

"I don't know," she says.

"I could borrow John's motorbike."

"Over my dead body."

"For fuck's sake," I say.

"Mind your language," she says. I go to the workers' canteen and drink a Coke.

Dad is elated when I come home:

"Our container will arrive in Tanga in two or three days," he says. "I'm driving down there tomorrow around noon. Do you want to come?"

"Yes, definitely." Finally something's happening. The container is from Ostermann. Usually the customs officers are bribed by a shipping agent in Dar es Salaam, but Dad has bargained on being able to get our stuff into the country through the harbour in Tanga himself – he knows the system from his time with Mærsk in Singapore. The container is full of tinned food, flour without weevils, Carlsberg beer, Princes cigarettes, sweets, blue jeans, sneakers and baby food.

Dad tells me he's going to borrow a Land Rover from a Norwegian man called Thorleif – he lives in Moshi – he's in on the order too.

"I'm going to a meeting in Arusha, and then I can swap cars with Thorleif at noon by the K.N.C.U. building – then I'll pick you up at Kibo Coffee House. Can you get to Moshi on your own?"

"Yes, of course," I say.

"But how are you going to get there?" Mum asks.

"I'll just get a lift with one of the lorries taking sugar into the city," I say.

"Don't go with someone who's drunk," Mum says.

"Don't worry, I'll be careful," I say.

The next morning I stand outside the factory waiting. Wave at the lorry driver when he comes out of the gate, shouting at him in Swahili:

"Can I get a ride into Moshi?"

"Jump on," he shouts without slowing down, so I run and jump up on the passenger side, open the door and climb in. He must be a Kichagga – his teeth are brown because there is too much fluorine in the water up on the mountain. He is sober. We can't talk because of the noise from the overworked diesel engine, but he offers me a cigarette. Lorry drivers have money, because there's always a bit of pilfering during transport, and the profit goes straight into their own pockets.

In Moshi I go up to see Marcus, but he's at work at Jonas' forestry school, F.I.T.I. I go down to the market and buy cigarettes from a Rasta guy in a small kiosk outside the market. Go up to Zahra's restaurant and eat samosas and then over to Kibo Coffee House to drink coffee while I wait for Dad. He doesn't show. It's past one. I go over to the K.N.C.U. building, where Thorleif works for the Nordic Project advising the farmers' co-operative movement. Our Peugeot is parked outside.

"Let's get going," Dad says, and we go down to the Land Rover together. We drive along North Pare Mountains down to Same. Every time a car comes towards us, we are enveloped in a cloud of dust which seeps into the cabin. Dad was told that the ship unloads early in the morning. We pass through Mombo. Even though Dad is going fast, it starts to get dark, and the road gets harder and harder to navigate. It's completely dark as we drive through Korogwe. Dad tries to keep up some semblance of speed, but time and again he has to step on the brakes or throw the car round a big pothole, and we still bump down into some of them, pushing the shock absorbers to the max.

"We're going to have to stop somewhere for the night," Dad says as we drive into Segera. We find a guesthouse which doesn't seem too scruffy and go to a restaurant and have grilled meat and grilled plantain.

Dad wakes me up before it's light, and we drive off in the grey dawn. The sun rises as we arrive at the harbour. We locate the harbour authority office. The freight ship is moored at the quay.

"Inside that cargo is all my lovely beer," Dad says. A large part of the container has been packed with Carlsberg. The brewery in Arusha has run out of bottle caps and Tanzania has no foreign currency with which to import a new shipment – the country is in crisis.

In principle you must pay sixty-five per cent import tax on the contents of the container. I wait outside while Dad talks to the head customs officer and passes him an envelope. Normally this kind of import is handled by Bimji, an Indian who works as a shipping agent in Dar es Salaam. But this is urgent – there's no beer in the country, and Bimji is having problems with the authorities – it seems he hasn't greased the wheels quite as well as he should have.

"It's taken care of," Dad says when he comes out. Things have become livelier on deck. We board it and go over to speak to the captain – another envelope changes hands. The hatches to the hold are opened and Dad is taken down to find the crate with our stuff, so he'll recognize it when it's hauled up. Floating in the shadow of the ship are seven small boats, tree trunks that have been hollowed out – outriggers traditionally used by the fishermen – they don't serve any purpose, they are just there. The Filipino man who operates the ship's crane adjusts his seat in the small cabin. Dad is standing next to him on the deck. The crane operator raises a crate from the hold and is about to swing it out over the railing and lower it onto the pier. He aims too low, so the crate crashes into the railing and shatters. The people in the little boats have had hawsers thrown down from the ship, and they climb up the sides like monkeys, flitting around on the deck picking up things from the shattered crate, hoisting them down to their partners below. Sail off with the loot. I have gone to stand next to Dad at the edge of the hold. Two Filipino sailors are putting chains around another crate, attaching them to the hooks at the end of the crane.

"That one's ours," Dad says and goes to the crane operator's cabin, where he leans in and talks to the man – an envelope changes hands. Our crate is guided beautifully over the railing, lowered onto the pier. It's too large to fit in the trunk of the Land Rover, so we have to take it apart with a hammer and a jemmy and open the pallet of beer cans so we can stack the boxes in the car. There's cigarettes, whisky, tinned food, clothes and sweets in there as well. We drive to a warehouse and buy some burlap to drape over the cargo so no-one can see what we've got in the back.

"I'm hungry," Dad says.

"What do you say we drive out to Baobab Hotel and have lunch there?" I ask.

"Is it good?" Dad asks.

"I know the owner's daughter from school," I say. "Samantha – they're English."

"What's she like?" Dad asks.

"She's alright," I say, blushing.

"Let's go," Dad says. We ask for directions and drive down a sandy road to the hotel, which is beautifully situated on the coast. I hope Samantha's there. I put a carton of Marlboro in my bag while we packed the car. Maybe I can sneak off and smoke a cigarette with her or just hand her a pack. She's fierce.

"I don't know where she is," the guy at reception says. I ask one of the waiters.

"I think she's around," he says.

"Where?"

"I don't know," he says. "Perhaps inside the house." I go over and ask, but the house girl doesn't know where she is.

"It doesn't look like she's here," I say and drop into one of the chairs on the restaurant's terrace.

"I've ordered Lobster Thermidor for us," Dad says. The hotel has neither beer nor fizzy drinks. The problem with the bottle caps effects the whole country. We have to drink water. There's a jug on the table –

no glasses. First a waiter brings a saltshaker and some napkins. There are already knives on the table.

"Might we also have some glasses and perhaps some forks?" Dad asks.

"I'll check," the waiter mutters. Times passes. Nothing happens. After a while a lady arrives with food on some plates.

"Thanks," Dad says, adding: "I asked for some forks and glasses a little while ago."

"Forks are a problem," she says.

"I'm happy to wash them myself," Dad says.

"Wait," she says and walks slowly back to the restaurant, the kitchen, her arse billowing. A little while later another lady brings us two forks.

"What about our glasses?" Dad asks. No reaction. She turns around and leaves.

"Well, at least we won't have to eat with our fingers," I say.

"Didn't you say it was an Englishman who owned this place?" Dad asks and prods at the odd-looking mass on his plate. Lobster cut into bits and boiled to oblivion. The chunks of meat put into the split lobster tail with a bland cheesy sauce poured over them. The sensation in the mouth: soft rubber mixed with porous plastic – the taste pretty much the same. And the sides? Haricots verts that have been boiled to within an inch of their lives and hash browns that – oddly enough – taste good. We should have ordered chicken and chips – that way you're on the safe side. The first waiter comes out of the restaurant again – empty-handed.

"I'll find those glasses," I say, getting up.

"Wait," Dad says, holding up a hand. "I want to see what will happen." The man sits down two tables away, lighting a cigarette. "Excuse me," Dad says. "We still haven't got our glasses."

"Wait," the man says and stays in his seat.

"I don't want to wait. Can't we have some of those teacups?" Dad asks. From where we're sitting we can see a bar counter inside the restaurant, stacked with teacups and coffee mugs.

"The glasses will be out soon," the man says without stirring. He looks away, smoking his cigarette. Samantha appears at the door.

"You'll give them some cups right now, you lazy bastard – or I'll make sure you never work again," she shouts in Swahili. "And put out that cigarette. *Kuma mamayo!*" she says – your mother's cunt, the worst insult imaginable. I remember saying it to our gardener, Benjamin, right after I had learnt it, and Benjamin told my dad not to thrash me too badly, because I didn't really know what it meant.

The waiter gets up slowly, taking another drag of his cigarette. Letting it fall to the ground even though there's an ashtray on the table, slouching towards the bar. "You're hopeless," Samantha sneers at him. Looks out towards us without meeting my eyes.

"The staff don't seem to be fully awake," Dad says to her. Why the hell did he say that? It's bloody well not her fault. She doesn't say hello – simply shrugs and goes into the restaurant. The man brings us our teacups.

"Was that the girl from school?" Dad asks.

"Don't take it out on her," I say. "It's not her sodding restaurant." I get up and go towards the restaurant.

"No, no," Dad says. Inside the restaurant I can hear Samantha in the kitchen. I go towards the door.

"You bleeding well can't treat the customers like that," she's shouting. I open the door slightly. The slow lady from before answers Samantha.

"That's none of your business – it's not your restaurant," the lady says.

"Well, it bleeding well isn't yours either," Samantha says, turning on her heel. She sees me – her eyes are wet. I hold the door open and she walks past me, storming out of the restaurant. She wipes her eyes with the back of her hand, and once she's outside she heads towards the coast. I follow her. She walks through the garden and out to the edge of the cliff, sitting down. I sit down next to her.

"I'm sorry about that," I say. She turns her face away. "My dad . . ." I add. She waves dismissively, doesn't say anything. I fish a pack of cigarettes out of my breast pocket where it's hidden by a T-shirt which I've put on over it, light two and hand her one. She takes it. "Sorry," I say again. Her skin's radiant.

"Don't apologize," Samantha says, looking at me. "It's not your fault." She spits out over the edge of the cliff, smokes, looks with bewilderment at the cigarette. "Marlboro," she says, smiling. Takes another drag.

"Where are your parents?" I ask.

"Dad's away on business, and Mum's in town, shopping."

"The holidays are almost over," I say.

"Yes, thank Christ," she says. "Some holiday." She gives me a crooked smile. Asks what I'm doing in Tanga. I tell her about the harbour. "Carlsberg," she says. "What I wouldn't give to get my hands on a crate – you can't begin to imagine."

"We're going back to Moshi any minute," I say. To be honest I had thought about perhaps staying there and getting a bus back with her, because that day with Panos, Samantha said that they always had loads of empty rooms, but I can't ask her – the mood is wrong.

"Can I come along to T.P.C. and stay with you until school starts?" Samantha asks.

"That'd be wicked," I say. Samantha at T.P.C. The pool – her in a bikini. John's motorbike – nicking a few Carlsbergs and going down to the river near Kahe to hang out with the crocodiles or out to Nyumba ya Mungu or into Moshi to visit Marcus. I stand and pull her up. We go over to Dad. The pudding on the table is looking rather weird – he hasn't so much as touched it.

"If your parents don't mind," Dad says.

"They're not here," Samantha says.

"Then who's looking after you?" Dad asks.

"I just hang around the house – it's pretty boring," Samantha says.

"But is there no-one here?"

"Yes, my mum is in town shopping – I'm sure she'll be back soon," Samantha says.

"We're going to have to leave soon," Dad says.

"Surely we can wait a bit," I say.

"We can't drive in the dark," Dad says, looking at his watch. "Half an hour."

"Alright," Samantha says. I go with her to the house, but her mum isn't back. Samantha is packing a backpack angrily. What can I say? I know the old man won't take her unless he has a written permit signed in triplicate. We go back.

"She's still in town, but it's alright – I've written her a note."

"I can't take you without having talked to her," Dad says.

"Oh come on! She'll be pleased to be rid of me. She hates me," Samantha says.

"I really can't," Dad says.

"Come on, Dad. For fuck's sake," I say.

"It's no good."

"Tosser," I say, walking away,

"Don't you . . ." Dad starts. Samantha comes after me. She puts her arm around my shoulder. All the things we could have done together – all the things we would do if we had just a little influence. But we're allowed to do fuck-all.

"Grown-ups," she says. "Useless fuckers, the lot of them."

We drive off. Not a word until Dad says: "Oh, bugger." I look up – a road-block. There's a bar across the road and three armed police officers, two men and a woman; on either side of the bar the verge has been blocked with oil drums filled with rocks. We should have had a U.N. car with flags on it – they let you straight through then: diplomatic immunity. We stop. One of the officers strolls over to us; his Kalashnikov is hanging across his stomach.

African socialism: the government is responsible for the purchase and distribution of the vast majority of goods, which means that you can't get cooking oil at one end of the country, while at the other end people have cooking oil aplenty but nothing to cook in it. The police carry out controls to make sure that no private initiative changes that situation.

Dad greets the officer very politely. The policeman looks at the burlap covering our goods.

"What's that?" the man asks. Dad hands him the customs papers – signed and stamped, bought and paid for. The police officer doesn't dignify them with so much as a glance – he may be illiterate.

"My goods are legal," Dad says.

"Please get out of the car and open the back," the man says. Dad opens the car door.

"Are you the commanding officer?" he asks.

"The commanding officer is over there," the man says with an indecipherable toss of his head.

"We're very short on time – I'd like to speak to him," Dad says. I get out of the car and walk round to the front.

"Open the back," the policeman says.

"Would you call your commanding officer?" Dad asks. The policeman calls towards a small shack under some trees.

"I'm sorry," I say to the policeman." Do you smoke?"

"What?" he says.

"Do you have a light?" I put a cigarette in my mouth. He stares at the Marlboros I've just got out of my pocket. Of course. Marlboro – better than money.

"Can I have one of those cigarettes?" he asks. I hold the open pack towards him. The woman stays where she is outside the shack next to the bar. The other policeman comes over.

"What sort of cigarettes are those?" he asks.

"American cigarettes," the first one says.

"*Eeehhhh* – Marlboro. I've heard they are very good," the other one says. I hold the pack towards him. He takes a cigarette, the first one lights it for him.

"Our papers are in order," dad says. He still hasn't opened the back. They don't pay him any attention. They are smoking American cigarettes. I am smoking with them.

"Has the boss returned yet?" the first one asks in a low voice.

"No, not yet," the other one says.

"Keep the pack," I say, holding it out. The first policeman takes it.

"Thanks a lot," number two says.

"You have to open the door to the cargo," number one says.

"Can't we leave before your boss returns?" I ask.

"When you have goods in the car, the boss has to see them," the first policeman says.

"Even if our paperwork is in order?" I ask.

"Papers aren't everything. They may not be right," number two says.

"But American cigarettes are very good," number one says.

"The smoke has a nice spice to it," number two says.

"Dad, I think you just have to give them a little money," I say in Danish and continue in Swahili: "We are in a great hurry – can't we work something out so we can leave sooner?"

"You are going to have to stay until the boss returns," policeman number two says. I don't think they'd want to wait for the boss if we were to give them something, because then the boss might take it. Dad shrugs:

"It's very difficult to give them something when they haven't asked for it directly. Then you might get in trouble for trying to bribe them," he says in Danish.

"If you help us, so we can get going, we'll help you – then we'll help each other," I say.

"How can you help us?" the first policeman says. "We're standing here in the sun and we don't even have a cigarette to smoke."

"Wait," I say and go to the passenger side of the car, root around in the bag in front of my seat. Dad comes over to me.

"What are you doing?" he asks.

"Give me some money," I say. He hands me a handful of banknotes, about what a field worker would make in two months. I pull out the carton of Marlboro I nicked yesterday when we were packing – I've only taken two packs from it. Policeman number two comes over so he can see what I'm doing behind the open door. He sees me stuffing banknotes into the carton where the missing packs were. He holds out his hand to receive it. I hold it against my stomach. "Is that alright?" I ask, looking at him questioningly. He looks over at number one. "Dad, I think it's working," I say in Danish. Policeman number two goes over to number one, speaks to him, returns to me. I look over at number one. His face is inscrutable. He nods faintly, turns his back and goes towards the bar and the shed and the policewoman.

"It's alright," number two says. I hand him the present. Dad starts getting in behind the wheel. I sit on the passenger seat. Dad closes his door and starts the engine. Policeman number two runs over to his buddy, who raises the bar with a wooden face, and as we drive past him, he cracks a wide smile – they both wave; it's a good day for smoking cigarettes.

"Christ, that's disgusting," Dad says. "I hate that shit."

"I think it went alright," I say.

"Where did those cigarettes come from?" he asks.

"Thorleif's cigarettes."

"Well, what do you know?" he says.

"Always handy for breaking the ice," I say.

"You're becoming too much of an African," Dad says. But he's grinning. I'm grinning too.

At T.P.C. Mum is upset.

"Do you know what John's been getting up to?" she asks as soon as we step through the door.

"No – what's happened?" Dad asks.

"John's chasing ladies in town at night with that Jonas chap while Katriina is at home with the girls."

"Where did you hear that?" Dad asks. Rogarth told me the same story, but who does Mum talk to who would tell her that kind of thing?

"Miriam told me when she was drunk – which she is most of the time," Mum says.

"Right," Dad says.

"And the next day when I tried to talk about it, she denied it completely and said that John was the perfect husband."

"Right," Dad says.

"Surely that's not good," Mum says.

"No," Dad says.

"But . . ." Mum says but stops.

"What do you want me to do about it?" Dad asks. Mum is standing in the middle of the sitting room as tense as a tightly drawn wire, her hands bunched up in fists.

"Just . . . do something!" she shouts and walks down the corridor, slamming the bedroom door. Dad looks at me.

"Could you take yourself off for an hour or two, do you think?" he asks. I hold my hands up in front of me:

"I'm out of here," I say and leave.

Marcus

AALBORG

I now have two white children to look after. Solja and Rebekka – my new daughter. She has been carried around on my arm from the moment she was born. And now Rebekka is one year old, so her mother thinks it's fine to run to the club while the negro does the dirty work. When Rebekka shits her nappy, she totters after her parents, but they disappear, flee, hide. It's a European nappy – her *pupu* doesn't fall out when she runs, because there are elastic bands to keep it on her arse, but it feels nasty to her, and when she comes close, you can smell it. She comes to me. I prepare the warm water, take off her pooey nappy, fold it around her shit, get rid of it, wash her bottom and put on a new nappy, and I smile and don't pull any unpleasant faces at the shitty smell, because children notice these things, and she can't help making *pupu*.

I fetch the European milk, which doesn't come from Katriina's *titi* but is kept in bottles in the fridge, and I heat it so that it'll run down Rebekka easily. And recently the work with Rebekka has become extra difficult. A poisonous snake almost bit the Knudsen baby at T.P.C., so now I must follow like a shadow when Rebekka trains her little legs on the lawn, because the white grown-ups can't stand in the sun like that – black Marcus was made for it.

And they leave me with the kids in the evening. Maybe Katriina would like to stay at home with the children, but if Jonas is out alone, then who knows what he might get up to?

I put on the music, every night: Zaire Rock, soul, reggae. I dance with Rebekka in my arms and at the same time I teach Solja. "You must move your hips like they are on ball bearings," I say, showing her the African way. Solja becomes very good at it, and from birth Rebekka's every movement is African – when they grow up white men will find them very exciting and dangerous.

But at night I am bored almost to death; I can't play music because the kids are asleep, and I must be able to hear my white daughter if she's thirsty during the night. But I am also thirsty, so I go to the larder with Katriina's key. The Carlsberg has been drunk, and the brewery in Arusha is on a break because they are out of bottle caps. I discover that the bottles of strong spirits have been marked with a needle or scratched on the label to mark how much had been drunk. So I take a glass, fill it and scratch the label to mark how much I've drunk: a new mark. And they have a special kind of alcohol – schnapps – it's called Aalborg. A transparent, clear *gongo* – it smells very good. I drink it, get high, and I sleep like a log for two-three hours. And when the alcohol effect wears off, I hear *beep-beep-beep-beep*. They are back, the guard opens the gate, it's perhaps three a.m.

Jonas comes out into the kitchen. He stares at me. Goes out into the larder. Lifts the bottles.

"Something's missing," he says, staring at me.

"I don't know. What is in those bottles? No, I'm afraid to drink that sort of dangerous stuff." I gibber like a parrot; pretend to be stupid because the white man loves to think about the negro's stupidity.

I have made new marks on the labels, which match the contents in the bottles, but it diminishes too quickly. So I start pouring water into them when I've had a drink.

I heat milk, I change pooey nappies, I carry Rebekka on my arm, I brush the children's teeth. The parents take off on weeknights as well. Really, what else would they do? You have a sawmill in the forest; people are working, things are working out for you in town, you have people working well for you. You don't have to do anything – it's sheer holiday, nothing but drink. So I don't think there's anything wrong with my drinking just a little bit to get to sleep. It's good.

CHEESE

My situation gives me opportunities to taste new joys in life. When you are constantly shopping for other people, their money moves through your pocket, and sometimes a little bit of it is left there with the lint.

I invite Rosie to Liberty in the city centre on Saturday night. *Eeehhh*, the sound is good, they have flashing lights in all the colours, a large dance floor. Alwyn is at the bar, bragging. He has finished I.S.M. I've already heard it from Phantom – Alwyn's exams were very poor. But that doesn't matter when you have a rich Chagga father.

"Me and my little brother are going for training at a dairy in Denmark which is part of an aid project that provides education for Tanzanians," Alwyn says.

"Will you be back to produce exciting cheeses from your father's cattle on West Kilimanjaro?" I ask.

"Cheese?" Alwyn says. "I'm not a farmer. While I'm in Denmark, I will get better business opportunities – see if I don't."

"And what about Africafé for Mika?" I ask. "Do you want that export to continue while you're away?"

"Yes, Gaspar might be round with a few more tins – you just send them," Alwyn says. And I hurry away from him, because when Rosie hears all that talk about Europe, Alwyn instantly becomes more interesting than me, even though I've paid her entrance fee.

Christian

"That John – he's a violent man," Mum says. She's just come back from the T.P.C. sick bay and has taken Annemette in her arms.

"What?" Dad says. "Has he beaten Miriam?"

"No," Mum says. "I've just sewn eight stitches in the scalp of a mechanic who'd been beaten with a metal pipe," Mum says.

"By John?" Dad asks.

"Yes," Mum says.

"Did he say that – the worker?" Dad asks.

"No, but his wife who was just standing there, screaming – she said it," Mum says.

"In Swahili?" Dad asks because Mum only speaks a few words of Swahili. She gives him a look:

"Yes, but the doctor translated it for me, and he didn't sound surprised," Mum says. Dad looks at her for a moment.

"I'll talk to him about it," he says.

"Yes, you will," Mum says.

But there's no time. That night we go over to eat at the messroom. John and Miriam are sitting at a table with Léon Wauters from Simba Farm. There are several tables free, but Mum heads straight for the one next to theirs and greets them politely. We order our food. It's all perfectly nice, but I can feel that Mum is about to explode. She addresses Léon:

"So, how do you treat your workers up at the farm?" she asks in an everyday tone of voice.

"Well enough, I think," Léon says.

"Do you beat them?" Mum says, innocently.

"Of course not!" Léon says.

"The negroes work better, you know, when they're beaten," Mum says.

"What do you mean?" Léon asks.

"Our field workers are beaten all the time. Today there was one who was beaten with a metal pipe," Mum says.

"Tell your wife to calm down, will you?" John says to Dad.

"I'm right here," Mum says to John. "And I don't need to calm down at all."

Dad speaks to her in Danish:

"Kirsten, please don't."

"You know what, I'm going to," she says in Danish and continues in English to John: "You are a sick, perverted sadist." Miriam and John get up.

"You'd better get that dog on a lead," John tells Dad as he gets up to leave. Dad sighs.

"John's a swine," Mum says to Léon in English.

"Did he beat a worker with a metal pipe?" Léon asks.

"Eight stitches in the scalp," Mum says. "I stitched the man up myself."

"But that's terrible," Léon says.

"Yes," Dad says. "But I don't know what to do about it."

"But you have to complain to the management," Léon says, looking at Mum who says:

"Yes, I think so too." I look at Léon. Is he sitting there telling her exactly what she wants to hear, or what is this?

Finally school starts. I see her in the hall:

"Samantha – hi," I say, smiling. She's looking good.

"I'm pissed off," she says and walks on. I'm left standing, staring after her wriggling arse. What should I do? I go to the library. Shakila is sitting at a desk, reading. She's making notes on a pad and sticking her pencil into her big afro as she reads and pulling it out when there's something she wants to underline. She is unbelievably beautiful. I'd like to say something to her, but I don't know what. I find Jarno, and we go out into the cornfield behind the dining hall and smoke.

The next day I have to go with Dad to Simba Farm on West Kilimanjaro to fetch rye flour from Léon Wauters. I go over and look at Annemette, who is lying on the sofa, paddling away at the air with her stubby little legs.

"Say hello to him from me and tell him to come out and play golf with us soon," Mum says. I go over to the factory area to pick Dad up. He has taken the car to pick up a sack of sugar to give to Léon. All the staff do it – their cars are never checked by the guard, and sugar is in short supply. When you need other things that are in short supply – such as car tyres, butter, ice cream – Tanzanian Monopoly money just doesn't cut it – you have to be able to offer something in exchange.

Emmanuel has told me that the workers at the factory are given twenty kilos of sugar every month on top of their salary. They sell it or trade it for other goods. The field workers don't get any sugar. They just have to chew on the sugar cane to get the sweet juice so they don't notice how hungry they are. In the mornings they have corn porridge, and in the evenings they have corn porridge – lunch doesn't exist.

I catch Dad in the packing department.

"Did you get the sugar?" I ask.

"Yes, that's all taken care of," Dad says.

"You're stealing from the Tanzanian state," I say, just to hear what he has to say for himself. Dad points:

"See that mechanical arm reaching out across the conveyor belt?" he asks.

"Yes," I say.

"It registers how many sacks pass on the conveyor belt towards the storerooms. Sometimes they lift that arm and let a number of sacks pass without being counted. They go on the lorry as well. Everyone's in on it. The packing department, the guard at the gate, the lorry driver – anyone and everyone," Dad says.

"And you," I say.

"Yes, I know. It's not good, is it?" Dad says.

We drive into Moshi, out to Sanya Juu and then on towards West Kilimanjaro. It's only 110 kilometres from Moshi, but the dirt road is like brown soap because it rained last night.

We deliver our sugar and get a couple of sacks of rye flour which we take back to Moshi – there's a Chagga just north of the school who has a mill where he can process it for us. Afterwards we drive over to the Larssons' to give them some of it. Marcus is at home.

Marcus

MATCHES

"Can I please stay here until tonight?" Christian asks his father.

"No," bwana Knudsen says. "I don't have time to come and pick you up."

"He can stay until tomorrow, that's no problem," Katriina says. "I spoke to Kirsten on the phone – she was thinking of coming round for a visit."

"Oh, alright then," bwana Knudsen says. So Christian stays, and I cook for the entire family – except for Jonas who isn't home.

"We'll go to the cinema," I tell Katriina cautiously, so no-one will hear it. But Solja comes out on the veranda when she sees us walking down the drive.

"If you're going to the cinema, I want to come too," she says.

"We're just going for a walk," I say.

"You're going to the cinema – I know it," Solja says in Swedish.

"Leave the boys alone," Katriina says, also in Swedish.

"It's not fair," Solja says.

We watch the film – lots going on: fights and car chases. When we come back, there's no rocking car on the back road. The Land Cruiser and a Land Rover from the Nordic Project are outside the house, and Katriina and Jonas are in the sitting room with a Norwegian man called Thorleif – they're drinking Carlsberg. We enter the house through the kitchen door and stop at the entrance to the sitting room.

"Katriina," I say, and she gets up and comes over.

"They're thieves, the lot of them," Jonas tells Thorleif.

"Of course they are," Thorleif says. "We have everything: a big house, two cars, five employees, children in an expensive school, we drink beer, have stereos, go to restaurants, we go on holidays. I picture myself in Norway: if in my city there's a hundred Arabs in extravagant mansions with gilded limousines, and I have to wash their dirty underwear, and there are dollar bills everywhere in the house – I would put a couple of them in my pocket." Thorleif nods and drinks from his beer – he's drunk.

"If they were as good at working as they are at stealing, things would be looking up in Africa," Jonas says.

"Negroes are like those Kibo matches," Thorleif says. "You strike them, and they light up and flash and splutter as the sulphur burns off, and right away the flame goes out before it even reaches the wood. There's no connection between head and body."

Katriina looks at me and at the men.

"Never mind them, they're drunk," she says.

"We'll take a few cushions from one of the chairs. Then Christian can sleep in my room," I say.

"O.K.," Katriina says. Solja comes into the sitting room in her nightie.

"You're being noisy," she says. Katriina turns, looking surprised.

"Aren't you asleep, darling?" she asks.

"No. Because you were being noisy," Solja says. Katriina sighs.

"Goodnight," I say.

Christian

The next day Mum arrives to spend the day with Katriina and Tita. Mum has brought *mama* Nasira so there's always someone watching Annemette. After the incident with the snake, she doesn't want the kid to be let out of sight.

We leave at five-thirty in order to be home before it's dark. I am on the passenger seat, and *mama* Nasira is in the back with Annemette on her lap. On the T.P.C. road the lorries slug their way forwards while clouds of black diesel fumes billow from their exhaust pipes. Darkness falls. The last of the locomotives have broken down, so all the sugar must now be transported across the country by lorry. Mum overtakes them as they come.

In the distance a bike or motorbike appears around one of the soft bends in the road.

"Oh no," Mum says and accelerates to overtake the lorry up ahead. The vehicle coming in the other direction is fast approaching. I squint.

"It's a car," I say. "It's missing one of its headlights." Mum is only halfway through overtaking – it's not just a lorry we're passing; it has an articulated trailer, but you can't see that from behind in the dark. The car coming towards us is now fully visible – a Land Rover.

"There's no time," Mum says, braking hard. The Land Rover blinks its single headlight, but it doesn't seem like it's slowing down. Mum pulls to the right, out into the verge, while braking hard, but she steers out too far. A crash. Metal against concrete. The seatbelt presses against my chest. We're not moving. Awkward angle. One front wheel is in the main irrigation canal, which runs parallel to this stretch of the road. The Land Rover whizzes past. The articulated lorry fades into the distance. Mum turns her head, blood on her forehead. "Annemette," she says. I turn around. *Mama* Nasira looks down at the child in her arms and starts screaming and shaking her – her head bobs unnaturally on her neck. "*Ngoja ngoja,*" Mum says in a shrill, breaking voice – wait, wait.

"Keep the child still. Don't do anything," I say in Swahili as Mum crawls between the seats into the back, wiping the blood off her face so that it doesn't pour into her eyes. She lifts Annemette carefully with a hand under her neck and head. Mum's face – which she keeps close to Annemette's – is deadly pale.

"No, no, no," she says. "No." *Mama* Nasira starts howling shrilly, slapping her forehead. Mum starts screaming. Loudly, crazily. She's holding Annemette out in front of her, looking at her, her face distorted. And she's screaming. *Mama* Nasira reaches a hand out towards Mum. Mum slaps it away hard. "*Toka!*" she says – get lost. *Mama* Nasira gets out of the car, still slapping her face while speaking in a shrill voice, although I can't understand what she's saying. I have cigarettes and matches in my pocket. I need a cigarette. I know I can't light one now. But I need one.

Shauri ya Mungu – God's will. That's what the locals say. There's no talk of police or problems for the *aya*. It was the white lady herself who tried to overtake when there wasn't enough room to. The white lady who drove the car into the ditch. Mum has been given a sedative by the doctor at T.P.C.'s sickbay. *Mama* Nasira has been admitted with a broken shoulder. Dad moves about in jolts – pale, with vacant eyes, muttering. He speaks on the phone to Denmark, drives into town to sort out transportation and tickets for us. I don't know what I should be doing. Mum is walking around on the golf course. She's not playing – hasn't brought her clubs. They all stop playing when they see her. I sit in the garden, smoke cigarettes. Rogarth doesn't come over. Nanna doesn't either. No-one says anything about whether I should go to school or not go to school. I stay at home. I can't understand why they want to bury Annemette in Denmark. She lived here, she died here. It would be fitting, I think. But I don't say anything. I don't feel like going to the messroom to eat. There's no food. I go to the workers' canteen and order chicken and chips. A few people come past my table and shake hands.

"*Pole sana*," they say – they feel sorry for me.

"*Asante*," I say. They nod and leave. My golf caddie, Emmanuel, comes over.

"*Pole sana*," he says.

"*Asante*," I say – thank you. A young girl comes over and puts the plate on the table. "Sit down," I tell Emmanuel. "Eat." He sits. We share the food. I give him a cigarette. We smoke.

"It's terrible about those lorry drivers," Emmanuel. "Drunk on *gongo* all the time."

"*Tsk*," I say.

Dad comes home in Thorleif's Land Rover. In the back is a small coffin made of painted wood.

"Jonas had it made," Dad says. Mum doesn't say anything. Dad looks at me: "Tomorrow morning, first thing, I'll go in to K.C.M.C. to pick up Annemette and take her to the airport. I need to bring the officials so that everything is done right. Katriina will be here at seven to get you and your mum and take you there."

"O.K.," I say, nodding. We're flying to Denmark to bury her.

Marcus

MAKU

The little Knudsen baby Annemette has died in a traffic accident, so all the family has gone back to Denmark to put her into the ground. Rebekka has started walking on her short legs, and she wants to play outside, but little Annemette was close to receiving the snake's kiss in the T.P.C. garden, so now Rebekka must be watched closely. Katriina keeps her inside the house.

"Mmmm . . ." Rebekka says inside the house.

"Oh, Jonas, do come," Katriina shouts. In the kitchen I stop chopping vegetables. I can hear Jonas' chair scraping against the veranda. He goes into the sitting room.

"She's starting to say 'mama'," Katriina says happily.

"Mmmm . . ." Rebekka says. "Maku." No-one says anything.

"No," Katriina says, her voice is as thick as corn porridge.

"Bugger," Jonas says. Rebekka chirrups:

"Maku, maku, maku." Marcus. That's me. I put the knife down quietly on the chopping board and sneak out the back door, down to my own room. Maku. My white daughter is saying my name. There are tears in my eyes.

The following week they don't go to the club, they won't have me inside the house, they change her pooey nappies themselves. When they don't know that when I'm in the kitchen to get food, I can hear them practising:

"Can you say 'mama', darling? Mama, mama, mama?" Katriina says.

"Maku," Rebekka says.

Christian

"I want her to be put in a different coffin," Mum says as we fly into Kastrup.

"Why?" Dad asks.

"I don't want her to be buried in a coffin made by Jonas," Mum says. Dad is silent for a few moments.

"O.K.," he says. I'm standing at the baggage carousel, looking at Mum. She's chain-smoking and seems completely empty.

"You get our things together," she tells me and walks stiffly towards the toilets. Dad is standing with someone from the Foreign Ministry –

Annemette's coffin must be transferred from the plane to a hearse, which will take it to Køge. Our luggage arrives. I walk through customs with Mum.

"Kirsten," a tall man in a suit calls. My uncle Jørgen, Dad's older brother, who works in the Home Office. He gives Mum an awkward hug, says a few words, takes our bags, carrying them quickly to his Mercedes in the car park.

It's summer. He takes us back to his large flat in Østerbro. "I am going to have to get back to the office. Will you be alright?" he asks. Mum doesn't say anything.

"Yes," I say.

He leaves.

"I never did like him," Mum says. I light a cigarette. Mum stares out of the window. I go into the kitchen and get myself something to eat, drink some coffee. After an hour Dad arrives in a taxi.

"We can go down to the undertaker's in Køge tomorrow morning," Dad says. Mum doesn't say anything. He goes over and puts his arms around her. "Don't," she says. "I'm going out." She leaves the flat. Dad sighs.

"I don't know what to do," he says.

"I need some new trousers," I say. "For the funeral."

"Yes," Dad says, digging in his pockets for money, handing me a few large notes.

"Don't you want to come?" I ask.

"No, I have to be here when your mum comes back." He finds a map in the phonebook, pulls out the page, marks where we are and where I must go. Finally I get out – breathe – I follow the map. It's strange being in Denmark, but I don't care. I just can't be around those two. Is there something wrong with me, when I can't even feel that Annemette is dead? What do they expect me to do? How am I supposed to look? I just have to say nothing – wait for it to pass. The sun is shining. I buy a pair of jeans, some sunglasses, a black shirt and dark leather shoes. Smoke cigarettes and drink Coke in a park until I have to go back.

We have a large guestroom in Uncle Jørgen's flat. Mum sobs at night. Dad comforts her. "Go and lie down on the sofa," he tells me. I go into the sitting room, look out over the city lights – the inner-city lakes. Open a window and smoke. Fall asleep.

The next morning we go to Køge. There are several family members at the church – I can't remember their names. Shake hands, my face an unmoving mask. Mum cries as she sees the coffin – which is a different one from before. She cries all the way through the service. I help carry Annemette out to the hearse. She is to be cremated. We step out of church. Mum is howling shrilly behind me. I turn my head.

"I'm sorry, I'm sorry," she screams and falls to her knees on the paving. I blush. Mum's little sister Lene grabs Mum's arm and Uncle Jørgen comes over and helps lift her up.

"Pull yourself together, Kirsten," he says in a low voice.

"Let go of me," she scolds, pulling her arm out of his grasp. The coffin is put in the back of the hearse, and Dad goes over and takes Mum's hand. Tears are slowly running down her face, dripping from her chin. I need a cigarette. Everyone goes over to the parish hall, where a spread of coffee and cake has been laid out. Mum's sister Lene comes over and stands next to me.

"It's just awful," she says, shaking her head. I simply nod, hoping it'll be enough.

"I'm just going . . ." I say as we reach the door and point indistinctly towards the cemetery and leave her. Lean against a stile. Put on my sunglasses. Light a cigarette. What do they want from me? She was very young. She is dead. It's sad, but . . . I really can't feel it that much. Is something the matter with me? It's only a few minutes before Dad comes towards me.

"Are you alright?" he asks. I shrug – looking at the ground. I don't know if I'm alright. "We're leaving, Christian," Dad says. "Your mum . . ." he starts, but leaves the unfinished sentence hanging in the air, turns and walks towards the car park. Mum is in the passenger seat of Uncle Jørgen's car with her face in her hands. Uncle Jørgen isn't there. Dad gets in behind the wheel; I sit in the back. We drive towards Copenhagen. No-one says a word the whole time. Mum and Dad leave the flat to me and go for a walk together.

We spend two excruciating days in Copenhagen, with Dad flitting around trying to change our flights so we can get back quickly; Mum sits staring vacantly into thin air, and I walk around the city lakes, smoking cigarettes until I taste green slime on my tongue.

Back at T.P.C. We arrived yesterday. Mum is congealing on the sofa. Back straight, legs crossed. She's staring vacantly ahead of her. It's very quiet. I want to say something, but the words die in my mouth. In my room I take out my schoolbooks, find a maths assignment that I don't understand. Take the book into the sitting room and sit down next to her on the sofa.

"Mum, can you help me with this?" I ask, sitting next to her and showing her the book. She looks at the book, at me – as if she doesn't recognize me. Turn her eyes back towards the empty room.

"I don't know," she says. I'm sitting right next to her. If I just get up again and leave, it'll seem all wrong. But what can I say to her? That Annemette is dead, that it's sad, but . . . I'm alive. I lift my arm and put it round her awkwardly. She is as stiff as a board. Doesn't even react. I lift my arm again. Get up. Go to my room, light a cigarette, do the maths assignments. No-one has said anything about my going to school tomorrow, but I can't wait any longer.

I try to be cool as I walk down the corridor past the classrooms. It's very strange. Nanna didn't say anything in the car coming in, other than: "Hi." Rogarth didn't say anything either. Jarno is lounging up against a wall.

"Hey, you," he says.

"How're things?" I ask.

"You didn't miss anything," he says. Not a word about my little sister. Who is dead. The bell goes. The lesson gets underway. Something about the 1973 oil crisis, the O.P.E.C. countries, car-free Sundays in Europe. What's the point of us knowing that? At break I hang around outside. Try to look dismissive. Shakila is standing some way off, looking at me. I wish she would come over, but I don't know what I would say to her if she did. The bell goes again. Someone grabs my arm.

"Come here," a voice says. I turn my head. Samantha is standing next to me.

"Aren't you coming?" Gretchen, a quiet German girl, says – Samantha and her share a room.

"I just need to do something with Christian," Samantha says, and Gretchen turns her eyes heavenwards as Samantha pulls me along, round the corner, down behind the classrooms and towards the trees. We disappear among them – no teacher has time to see us. Samantha stops. "Are you alright?" she asks. I shrug, look away. "*Tsk*," she says. "Your little sister – that was very sad." I nod, there's a lump in my throat. Samantha lights a cigarette and, putting her arm around my shoulder, hands it to me. "Smoke," she says. I take the cigarette and suck on it. She squeezes my shoulder. "But we're still here, man. We are. We're no way over," she says. I nod and blow out smoke, try to smile at her. "So, it's like that, is it?" she says, putting her arms around me. I start crying. "There, there. It's O.K.," Samantha says. "You'll get over it."

At the house silence is so thick you could cut it with a knife. John comes round with Miriam to ask if we want to come along to some hot springs southwest of T.P.C. that weekend.

"Sit down," Dad says. "I'll fix you a drink." They sit down – Mum is there.

"It's good to have you back," Miriam says.

"How have you been?" Mum asks.

"Oh, you know," John says. "Miriam plays golf, and I empty the bottles." Dad smiles a strained smile.

"A not unfamiliar division of labour," he says. Mum gets up, walking across the sitting room and down the hall. Dad shakes his head. "She's going through a very difficult time," he says.

"We'd better leave," John says, emptying his glass. Miriam puts hers down.

"Do let us know if there's anything we can do," she says. They go out to their car. Dad pours himself another gin and tonic and drops into his easy chair.

"Why can't she just . . . ?" he says, waving his hand aimlessly. Takes a gulp of his drink. Looks at me. "We have to go on living," he says, nodding slowly. Looks into his glass. Takes another gulp. Sighs. Lights a cigarette. I go round to the back of the house. Light a cigarette.

The next morning *mama* Nasira returns. She knocks on the front door. The bandages on her broken shoulder are gone. Mum looks through the glass of the door with a scared look on her face and turns to me:

"You have to tell her to leave, Christian. I can't bear to see her." Mum walks quickly out of the sitting room, down the corridor. I open the door.

"*Pole*," *mama* Nasira says when I open. I thank her and say:

"There's no more work here."

"I just came to see *mama*," she says.

"*Mama* is not feeling well," I say.

"*Pole*," she says.

"Thank you."

Mum allows the house to become cluttered. Goes for long walks during the day. Dad asks the gardener whether he knows a cook or a house girl.

"My niece," Benjamin says. "She is very diligent. I can bring her over tomorrow."

"Alright," Dad says. The next day Benjamin brings a seventeen-year-old girl from his village on Nyumba ya Mungu – God's House – the dammed-up lake south of T.P.C. The girl's name is Irene. She'll be living in the other room in the servants' quarters.

"You'll have to show her where everything is," Dad says and goes over to his office. Mum is nowhere to be seen – she might be on the golf course. I show Irene around the house. The laundry basket, washing powder.

"*Mama* will be sure to teach you how to use the washing machine," I tell her – we have a semi-automatic one, and I don't know how it works. I show her the ironing board, the iron, buckets, soap.

"It's fine," she says – somewhat nervously, I think – and gets started on the washing-up.

"Have you been a house girl before?" I ask.

"I've helped out at home," she says. First job – no wonder she's nervous; she has helped out in a hut made of wattle and mud without electricity or running water. And now she's in the house of some white people who have just lost their daughter. It goes with saying that Irene has heard about the traffic accident from Benjamin.

I go into the sitting room, where Mum is standing staring out of the window.

"Who is that?" she asks in a singsong voice without looking at me.

"The new house girl. Irene. Benjamin's niece. She has to be told what to do."

"So tell her," Mum says.

"What about shopping?" I say, because while there are local markets at T.P.C. they're not as good as the market in Moshi.

"I'll do the shopping in Moshi," Mum says. "From now on." Then she turns, walks down the corridor, into the bedroom.

In the evening we eat in the messroom. Afterwards I go to my room and shut the door. I can't hear the folks. The fridge is opened, I think. Footsteps. Otherwise nothing. I do my prep, but I have a hard time concentrating. Then I hear the veranda doors being opened.

"Why are you sitting out here?" Mum says, now outside.

"What do you want me to do?" Dad asks.

"But you're just . . . you're always drinking," Mum says, her voice tearful.

"I'm not always drinking," Dad says. "I just have one drink."

"Your getting drunk doesn't help," she says.

"I'm not drunk," he says.

"You can't pretend it didn't happen," she says.

"I'm not."

"You can't even talk about it – about . . ." Mum stops. She's crying.

"Annemette," Dad says. "She's dead."

"You're just drunk," Mum says.

"You try saying her name," Dad says.

"I can't talk to you when you're like this," Mum says.

"It was an accident, Kirsten. It wasn't your fault," Dad says.

"You're a monster," Mum says.

"Annemette," Dad says. "Annemette is dead." Mum goes back inside. Not long after, she leaves. "Where are you going?" The car door slams. The car starts, drives off. It's the first times she's driven since Annemette died.

I've been playing football with the lads and must hurry back for a shower. I hope Dad remembers that I need a lift to school tonight. I see Léon standing outside the house with Mum. They've been playing golf.

"Léon will give you a lift to school," Mum says, smiling. For the first time since forever.

"Irene?" I call.

"She's not here," Mum says.

"Where is she?" I ask.

"I've given her the day off," Mum says.

"But did she iron my shirt?" I ask.

"No," Mum says.

"Why the hell not?"

"I told her she could just go," Mum says.

"And what about my shirt?" I ask.

"Put on a T-shirt instead," Mum giggles. She doesn't get wound up. Doesn't get hysterical. She giggles in an odd way. I shower, get dressed, go out on the veranda.

"Right then," I say. Léon gets up. My mum gets up. He kisses her cheek.

"Don't be a stranger," she tells Léon, suddenly very collected and alright – I don't get it.

"I won't," Léon says. We drive off in his old, scarred Land Rover.

"How are you?" Léon asks.

"Fine," I say.

"I mean . . . your family? After everything . . ." he says without actually saying the words. Annemette died.

"We're hanging in there," I say.

"Your mum and dad – are they . . . ?" he says.

"What?"

"Are they coping?" he asks.

"Yes," I say and nothing further. I don't bloody know, do I? Coping? They bloody well have to. What the hell is he on about?

At the party Nanna is still peeved because I tried to pull her top off in her room. She wants to dance with me, but won't slow-dance, which is the only thing I know how to do. I hate dancing – I have no idea what to do with any of my limbs. I don't have the balls to ask Samantha to dance. She dances with the older pupils because she knows them all from school in Arusha. First with a white bloke called Mick, and later a big Indian bloke called Savio. I stare at Shakila – the smooth black skin, the plaits, breasts, thighs. She smiles at me. The D.J. plays a slow song, and suddenly I go over and ask her to dance with me. We're dancing, and my heart is pounding in my chest. Annemette's death is what makes the difference – I get that. It makes me interesting. It makes me not care, which in turn makes me bold. Shakila takes my hand, and we go outside in the dark. She takes my face in her hands and kisses me. Heaven. Our lips part and Shakila's tongue plays in my mouth; I can feel the softness of her breasts. Our teeth bump, and we pull back, smiling in the dark. I light a cigarette, which we share. But I have no idea what to say to her. No idea at all.

That Monday I can't figure out how to connect with her, because the world is so sodding bright, and on the Tuesday she comes over to me at lunch.

"This isn't working, Christian," she says.

"O.K.," I say. Feel like an outcast. Is it my fault Annemette died? I don't talk to anyone at school. I can't say anything. What can I say? It seems like people are avoiding me. Except for Samantha, who comes over and puts her arm through mine. It makes me feel warm inside.

"You and me, we're going down to the river," she says.

"Why?"

"To smoke, you dimwit," she whispers.

"Too right," I say. We go down to the river. Talk about ordinary school stuff; stupid teachers, too much prep. We sit on the riverbank, where we can't be seen by anyone but the goatherds.

We smoke without speaking. Samantha looks straight ahead. I peep at her – the smooth tanned skin of her arms, the breasts under her tight top.

"Things didn't work out . . . with Shakila?" she says.

"No," I say. What can I say?

"That's a shame," Samantha says.

"Yes," I say.

"What went wrong?" she asks.

"I don't know," I say.

"You're too shy," Samantha says. I get up and walk a bit further down the slope. Shy. As if I didn't know. I ought to put a hand on Samantha's thigh right now, but I'm afraid to. I shrug and gesture towards the river.

"Oh, fuck it," I say loudly and talk to the river because I can't look at Samantha when I say it. "I just can't . . . bollocks – talk to her. Because she is so damn . . . bright and beautiful." Behind me Samantha laughs.

"And has such huge tits," she says.

"Yes, that too," I say laughing. "Shit," I add, because I was almost too afraid to touch her. It was only when Shakila took my hand and put it on her breast. And it was amazing. I go back and sit down. I had no handle on that shit at all.

"It'll be fine," Samantha says.

"You really think so?" I ask.

"I really don't know," Samantha says.

When I get home I go into the kitchen to take some cold water from the fridge .

"Hi," Irene says.

"Hi. You alright?" I ask in Swahili – Irene doesn't speak English. I have been here for more than a year – my Swahili is quite good.

"I don't know what to do," Irene says.

"Didn't *mama* say anything?" I ask.

"No. She went shopping in Moshi, and then she went out again. Perhaps to the golf course."

"Alright," I say. "I'll try to find out."

Not long after Mum returns and I go into the sitting room. Irene follows and waits at the door.

"Irene would like to know what madam wants her to do," I say in Danish. "It's her first job as a house girl." Irene is right behind me, eager to please. Mum turns around and looks at us.

"Then you tell her. You have to help out a little in this . . ." Mum stops, holds up both hands in front of her face, her shoulders shake, she turns around and goes back into the bedroom. Crying. I turn around and look at Irene, who looks frightened.

"*Njoo*," I say – come. We go out into the kitchen. "Sit down," I say. We sit at the little dining table. I tell her: in the morning she must make coffee, toast bread, cut mango and papaya, lay the table. Irene looks heartbroken. "What is it?" I ask.

"But . . ." she says, sighing. "What goes on the table?"

"Butter, cheese, jam, juice." I stop, I have seen Emmanuel's house – one of the slave hovels on the plantation; his father is a field worker. They have electricity but no fridge. They have running water, but it comes out of a tap at the side of the building, and their toilet is a hole in the ground. Irene comes from a fishing village – huts made of wattle and mud with a dirt floor. There's no electricity, even though they live close to the hydroelectric station – the electricity from the dam is sent into Moshi.

I get up. It's late in the afternoon. "I'm going to make breakfast, then you can see how it's done," I say and take the things from the fridge. Lay the table, brew the coffee. Explain that when *mama* brings fruit home it must be rinsed in a chlorine solution to remove bacteria and D.D.T. residues, so it doesn't upset your stomach. I am about to show her how to cut a mango to make it easy to eat with a spoon.

"I know about that," she says. I tell her how to make juice with passion fruit and oranges; how much fruit and how much water. And how to fill the bathtub and the bucket with water so we have some in case it's turned off. She must pour water into the water filter, and the filtered water must be poured into bottles and put in the fridge. Then I move on to cleaning. Sweep the floors, dust. The semi-automatic washing machine I can't explain.

"My parents will do the washing," I say.

"I'll just wash it by hand," Irene says. "No problem. But what about lunch?" she asks.

"My mum makes lunch," I say. "Don't worry about that. Just help out."

Mum doesn't make lunch. She doesn't do the washing. She goes to the market to shop, and it takes the better part of a day. And then she plays golf.

"*Tsk*," Irene says when she opens the bag of plain flour from the market. Our shipment from Denmark ran out, so Mum went and bought some more.

"What?" I ask.

"Weevils," Irene says. I go over and look. The weevils scamper about. It's no use sieving the flour– they're so small they fall through the netting of the sieve. Your options are simple: buy flour without weevils, and you know that the sacks have been drenched in D.D.T. Mum doesn't want to do that – "It's stored in the body. It makes you sterile," she says. I'm in favour of flour with weevils. They're here after all, and we'll be eating them. The weevils have lived on flour. They are made of flour. But they also give the bread a musty aftertaste. And if you don't kill them, they breed until in the end there is no flour left – just weevils. The longer you hold off on baking the bread, the more animal the bread becomes – inedible for vegetarians.

"You have to freeze it," I say. "Then the *dudus* die."

*

That night I have a snoregasm. I might have dreamt about Irene. I don't want to throw my underpants in the laundry, because she might see the dried stain. I rinse them in the bathroom and dry them in my room.

One day Mum gives me a pile of clothes.

"Give them to Irene," she says. "I don't wear them anymore." I go down and knock on Irene's door.

"It's for you," I say. It makes her very happy. She'll have something to wear on Sunday when she goes to T.P.C.'s church.

"Leave it," Irene says if I try to clear something off the table. Whenever my parents are there, she waits on them hand and foot. One afternoon I go into the sitting room barefoot. No-one else is home. Irene is lounging on the sofa, leafing through a magazine, *Alt for damerne*. I lean against the door. She sees me. Jumps up.

"*Hamma shida*," I say. "*Wazee hawapo*," – the folks aren't home. She leans back in the sofa sceptically. I go towards the kitchen.

"Do you need anything?" she asks.

"No," I say, taking a Coke from the fridge. Open it and put it on a tray with a glass which I fill with ice and a slice of lemon. Take it to her. "*Karibu mama*," I say – there you are, ma'am. Irene laughs, thanks me. When I'm standing close to her, I am standing in the scent of the coconuts from the oil she puts in her hair.

"Could we have some music, please?" she says like a customer at a bar.

"One moment, ma'am," I say and go over and put some on. I take my cigarette pack out of my pocket, holding it out. "Would you like to smoke?" I ask. Irene shrugs. I go out into the kitchen. She follows me.

"Not outside," she says as I go through the back door.

"Why not?"

"My uncle might see," she says. We share a cigarette in the kitchen.

"You're a good girl," I say. She smiles.

"You," she says. "You're a naughty boy." I think we're having the same thoughts.

Saturday afternoon I come home, and Irene is washing an enormous pile of clothes in a tub. Mum hasn't shown Irene how to use the washing machine. And Irene can't work out how to ask Dad, because when he's at home he is either drunk or asleep. And when Mum finally is home, she locks herself in the guestroom. They don't sleep in the same room anymore.

"I will tell my mum, I promise," I say. Irene is standing with her back to me – her bottom bobs up and down as she works the laundry energetically in the tub.

"*Eeehhh*," Irene says and nothing further.

"That she must either wash the clothes herself or teach you to use the washing machine," I add.

"*Eeehhh*," Irene says. She sounds as though she's about to cry. I look at her. She stands up. Holds one arm up across her eyes, so I can't see them. Soapy foam is dripping from her hand. She dries her eyes with her arm, looks at the floor, her breath catches.

"What's wrong?" I ask.

"But . . ." she starts, then sighs. "I was supposed to go home today. With a *matatu*, earlier, back to my village. But there's been no-one around I could ask for permission. *Tsk*." Now she looks angry.

"I'll see what I can do," I say.

"It's too late now – there won't be another *matatu* today." Irene bends over and continues washing. I check the rooms. No-one's home. Go to the messroom and find Dad – he's quite drunk.

"Irene would like to go home to see her parents today. She wants to know if it's O.K.?" I say.

"Yes, of course," Dad says.

"There won't be another *matatu*, so I'll ask John if I can borrow his motorbike and take her – it's a ten-kilometre drive," I say – it's one of the villages on the western side of Nyumba ya Mungu.

"That's fine," Dad says. Luckily John's at home. "Yes," he says. "The tank's almost full." I leap up, kick-start it, drive to the house, stop out front, go inside.

"Irene," I say. "We leave when you're ready."

"Really?" she says.

"Yes," I say. And then she hugs me, quickly, before letting go and half running towards the kitchen door to go to her room – get her things. Not long after we're off. Irene has a scarf around her hair and a *kanga* wrapped around my mum's denim skirt. I don't go fast because in Tanzania ladies ride side-saddle – they won't have the motorbike between their legs. But the dirt road is uneven and there are deep tyre tracks. When she sits the way she's sitting, we're off balance, and she has to put one arm around me to hang on. We arrive at the roadblock that marks the end of the cultivated part of T.P.C.'s lands.

"Where are you going?" the guard asks.

"I am the girl's taxi driver – she is going to her village," I say. He smiles.

"Will you be back this way?" he asks.

"Yes," I say. "Before it's dark." We drive on, the road gets worse.

"Stop for a minute," Irene says. I stop. She gets off. "The road is very bad," she says. "I can't sit like that." The fishermen have their cornfields on the roadside, but the plants are crippled by the saline soil. Irene pulls up her *kanga* and her skirt, straddling the motorbike behind me. "Now we can go," she says. I increase the speed, and we approach the lake. Irene's hands are on my hips, I can feel her against my back. "It's very close," she says. "You have to stop." Irene gets off. I wonder if she wants to walk that last stretch, so she won't arrive behind a *mzungu*? Or perhaps she's embarrassed by her home. But all she does is unwrap the dusty *kanga* and wipe the dust off her calves and ankles, before tucking the it away into her bag. "Now then," she says and gets up, side-saddle-style. "Let's go." A few hundred metres further on we meet the first little children, who run next to the motorbike shouting: "Irene, Irene." Geese, ducks, chickens and Tanzanian sheep with fat tails go about amidst the houses. She points towards the family's hut. Wattle and mud and a thatched roof. Outside a large, elderly woman is grinding flour by banging a long stick onto the kernels at the bottom of a hollowed-out tree trunk. A little naked child is secured to her back, wrapped up in a *kanga*. She stands up. The woman must be Irene's mother. I stop the motorbike.

"*Shikamoo, mama*," I say.

"*Marahaba*," she says.

"The last *matatu* had gone, so the boy in the family took me home," Irene says quickly.

"That's nice," the *mama* says. It's so late in the afternoon that the light has become gentle. In the distance Kibo's crown has appeared between the clouds. When the sun is no longer baking hot, no mist rises from the rainforest and the mountain is fully visible. All the contours are hazy because in the dry season the air is thick with a fine dust. A one-legged boy of about twelve comes limping on crutches towards Irene.

"That's my little brother," she says.

167

"What happened?" I ask.

"The crocodile took it," he says.

"I can make tea," the *mama* says. I would like some tea, but Irene quickly says:

"You have to leave now. Otherwise you won't be back before it's dark." And she's right.

"Safe trip," the *mama* says. I drive off, my body feeling light. It's almost dark by the time I reach T.P.C. I return the motorbike to John and walk back to the house.

"I don't want you riding that motorbike, Christian," Mum says.

"Dad told me it was alright," I say. She turns towards Dad.

"I don't think it's alright at all," Mum says and looks back at me. "Neither of us thinks so," she adds. I shrug, walk past her into the sitting room, towards the kitchen.

"But we can't stop him, just because . . ." Dad starts.

"Just because what?" Mum shouts.

"You know what I mean. He has to have a life."

"Yes," she shouts. "He has to have a life. Not riding around out here in the sticks." She's crying again. I don't have to look to know that my dad is in his chair, immobile.

"We can't just lock him up," he says. He's not so immobile he can't take a sip of his drink. Mum scoffs.

"It was lucky we got that shipment of booze, so you can drown yourself," she says.

"Yes," Dad says. "It was." I sit down on the back stairs with a Coke. Light a smoke. Why must they be such sad losers?

Marcus

THE SPIRIT OF ILLNESS

As I switch off the engine to roll the last stretch down the drive, I hear Rebekka's cries piercing the air. Women's wailing comes from the house as well – it can't be Katriina, because the car is gone. I throw the motorbike down on the veranda and run into the house. Josephina is in front of the bed with the woman from next door – I push them aside and look at Rebekka: pale, swollen and oddly grey in the face.

"It's the evil spirit," Josephina shouts – tears are running down her face, her eyes are wide. She's afraid. She's holding a tray made of woven banana leaves – usually used for rinsing rice. Round the back edge she has stuck in four chicken feathers: two black, two white. I bend over Rebekka, who falls quiet, silently sobs. It's her allergy – she has probably eaten cashew nuts, which she isn't supposed to have.

Josephina starts waving the tray back and forth over Rebekka's head, muttering spells against evil spirits in the old Chagga tongue, which I can hardly understand. Every time she waves the tray back and forth with one hand, she uses the other to tap on the inside of the tray with a small hand-held broom made of palm leaves that have been sliced finely lengthwise and gathered into a bunch.

"Stop it," I shout, grabbing hold of the hand with the tray.

"But I'm helping her – otherwise she'll die," Josephina shouts in Swahili. I slap her, because Rebekka understands what she's saying.

"She won't die. She's just eaten something she's allergic to." I look at Rebekka – they've smeared ash all over her face. "Did you eat anything at playgroup today?"

"We had some cake," she mutters. I turn towards Josephina.

"Why is there ash on her face?"

"It protects her from evil spirits."

"It's very good," the woman from next door says. She's the one who fetched her local powder when she saw Rebekka – bought from the traditional pharmacists down by the bus station. "It draws the evil spirit of illness out of the child."

I quickly send the woman away while thanking her – the crazy bitch was just trying to help – and she presses the bag with the rest of the powder into my hand. I tell Josephina to wash the powder off Rebekka and remove the chicken feathers – the Larssons would fire her on the spot if they knew. And then I get the pills and give one to Rebekka. Josephina is standing by, telling me that Rebekka must have an *injection*. People believe in spirits or the Lord, and if scientific medicine is to work, it must come in an injection – pills are cheating. A doctor at K.C.M.C. injects stupid patients with saline solutions and right away they feel better. And Josephina is a Christian lady, but if you ask for help from God and He doesn't help, you have to make do with the old ways – witchcraft from the bush.

Christian

At break I go up to Kijana. Outside there's an area with benches where the people with smoking permits are allowed to sit. People without smoking permits aren't allowed. Savio, Mick and some of the other older pupils are there. I sit down.

"I didn't think you had a smoking permit," Mick says.

"Nope," I say, lighting a Dunhill – Mum left a pack lying about.

"Dunhill," Savio says. I hand him the pack.

"Smoke?" I ask and light up.

"Alright," Savio says, taking one and passing the pack on to Mick. Mr Thompson, the Deputy Head, walks past.

"Christian," he says, 'you don't have a smoking permit, do you?"

"Are you sure?" I ask.

"Come along," Thompson says and turns, starts walking towards his office. I dump my cigarette on the ground, tread on it, get up.

"Keep the pack," I say to no-one in particular and start walking after Thompson.

"Cheers," Savio says.

Sent down for a week for smoking. The folks don't speak to me – they hardly did before, so it doesn't much matter. I'm snuggled up in bed. Hear the car start and drive off. I hear the sound of the ironing board being flipped open and not long after I hear music from the sitting room. Stevie Wonder: "Hotter than July". Put on my clothes and walk down the corridor. The ironing board is there, next to the laundry basket, but no-one's using it. Reach the sitting room: Irene is dancing in the middle of the floor. Her rotating hips, her vibrating arse, her bobbing tits. She sees me and stops.

"Christian," she says and looks at the floor with her head tilted – smiling ever so faintly. Then she moves over to turn off the music.

"Keep it on," I say and go out onto the floor. "You dance well – perhaps you can teach me." I raise my arms, shuffle my feet, snap my fingers.

"I have to do the ironing," she says.

"First we play a little," I say. In Swahili the word for dancing is the same as the word for playing – cheza. She looks out of the window to see where the gardener is.

"No. He can see us," she says. "Why aren't you at school?"

"Because I've been wicked," I say. "So what if he can see us?"

"Then he'll speak ill of me. Wicked how?" she asks, and I remember the daughter of one of my dad's local business partners at T.P.C.; he said his daughter had been sent home from school because she had been wicked – it meant that she was pregnant.

"I was caught smoking cigarettes – that's all," I say.

"*Tsk tsk*." Irene shakes her head. "Let me make you some toast." She goes to the kitchen. When I've eaten, I light a cigarette. She shakes her head at me – can't help smiling. I hand it to her. "Enough!" she says. But she takes it, inhales. I shake my head:

"*Tsk tsk*," I say, getting up.

I arrive home to find a note on the table. Mum and Dad have gone to Moshi Club to play golf. It seems I wasn't invited. Perhaps that's part of my punishment for smoking. Irene arrives to make corn porridge for the dogs and some coffee for the guard.

"I'll make the coffee," I say. "Then we can play afterwards."

"No – I don't want to."

"All you have to do is teach me – just a little."

"No – I'll get in trouble."

"Do you want me to go through life dancing like a white man with a big stick up my arse?" She grins.

"Alright then – just a little. Mind you, no trouble!"

"We're just going to play," I say. And we dance. She shows me: the arse must rotate. I have a hard time at school dances – I don't know how; I have no idea what to do with my arms, my legs, my body, anything. She laughs at me.

We dance several nights. We laugh together. The folks have started going to Moshi Club most evenings, driving to the Larssons' at night. Suddenly they can't understand why I don't want to go. "I'm reading," I say. I'm getting better – everything rotates when I take to the floor. Then one night she doesn't want to dance.

"No," she says. "No more."

"Why not?" She looks angry.

"The guard saw it."

"And so what?"

"That's not good."

"Why?" She sighs.

"He goes to the bars and says I've been bad with the white boy."

"Damn him," I say. "I'll bloody well have him fired."

"No, please don't. Don't do anything – it'll just make it worse."

"But . . . we're just dancing," I say.

"He's an old fool," she says.

"I've agreed to teach Danish at the school," Mum says. I look at her. "No, you don't have to come if you think it would be so very terrible to have me for your teacher."

"Good," I say. The next day I see her in the corridors. She doesn't spot me, so I make myself scarce. Mum being at school is odd. She's a teacher – part of the enemy in a way.

"She's not half bad," Nanna tells me – she has started taking Mum's class. And Mrs Harrison comes up next to me in the hall.

"Your mother is a remarkable woman, Christian," she says. "You should be very proud of her." I should? Our house is a tip, but when she's at school, she looks as if she's on top of things.

"You're hardly ever home these days," Dad says to her one night.

"What can I say? It's just nice to meet new people and not just the usual T.P.C. lot," Mum says. She's meeting teachers – how nice can that be?

The next day, after a trip to Moshi, Dad comes into my room and speaks to me in a low voice:

"Now you have a smoking permit," he says.

"Alright!" I say.

"But don't breathe a word about it to your mum," he says.

"It's a deal," I say. "Thanks."

The house smells of freshly baked rye bread. We're sitting at the dining table. Mum has been to see Léon at Simba Farm to pick up some rye flour.

"It's an amazing life he's got up there," she says. "Lovely climate, enormous vegetable garden, the forest – it seems the colonialists were on to something after all. And he's nice to his staff – teaches them things." Dad sits there, cutting up his meat, staring at it.

"It can't be all great," he says.

"It's a lovely place, of course it is," Mum says, looking out of the window as she chews her food. Then she smiles – turning her head towards me: "And he's got motorbikes."

"So?" I say.

"Well. You like motorbikes so much."

"Yes," I say. "But you won't even let me ride John's."

"Yes, but you could ride around up there. There's hardly any traffic."

"What's the use when this is where we live?" I say.

"Oh, it's only if . . . if we were to go there for a visit one day," Mum says. Dad gets up from the table and goes to get his cigarettes. Mum doesn't say anything more.

"Thank you – that was lovely," I say and leave the table as quick as I can.

Marcus

FROST BURST

It's like a car crash in a bottle. They're having the Knudsens round for a Christmas party. Katriina knocks on my door. In her hand she's holding the expensive schnapps, Aalborg, but the bottle has broken – full of ice. She looks at me.

"What happened to it?" I ask.

"I put it in the freezer."

"But you can't put it into the freezer – wet things expand in the frost," I say, because I've tried it with cans of Carlsberg when they were warm. You forget about them, and they become pillars of ice with a metal skin.

"Yes, if there's a lot of water in them – but when it's got a high alcohol content, it can't freeze."

"*Eeehhhh*," I say, looking down.

"So someone has drunk from this bottle and filled it up with water," she says.

"That is very bad," I say, shaking my head.

"You mustn't drink, Marcus," she says.

"No," I say.

"We have enough people drinking in the house as it is."

"Yes," I say. "What about . . . Jonas?" I ask.

"I'll tell him I dropped it on the floor."

"Thank you," I say.

Christian

The Larssons are celebrating Solja's birthday today, and we've been asked to come round in the afternoon – Dad, Mum and me, all of us.

That morning Léon arrives at our house in an old American military jeep that he uses for hunting. It's completely open, but with a sturdy metal frame right behind the front seats, so you don't break your neck if the car flips over. Dad is at work, but apparently Léon and Mum have arranged to play a round this morning. Perhaps her mood is improving. They don't ask me if I want to come, and there's no-one I can play football with before noon, so I go over to Nanna's. There's no-one home, so I swim laps until I'm bored with it. I go back home.

"Christian," Irene calls from the kitchen. "*Njoo kunisaidie!*" – come and help me.

"*Kufanya kitu gani?*" I ask – help you do what?

"*Mama* said to have lunch ready, but I don't know what to do," Irene says. "Does she want me to grill meat or what?"

"Didn't she say anything?" I ask.

"No, just lunch for four, and then they left."

"*Tsk,*" I say. I show her how to make a green salad.

"What about an omelette?" Irene asks.

"Yes, that'd be fine," I say and lay the table. "I'm going out for a smoke before they come back," I say. Irene smiles.

"Thanks for helping me, Christian. You're a real friend," she says.

"You're welcome," I say and slap her arse on my way to the back door.

"Enough!" she says and tries to smack me with her spatula, but I'm already gone. "*Tsk,*" she says. "*Wewe ni mshenzi kabisa*" – you're completely mad.

"Mad about you," I say through the door.

"*Toka!*" Irene says – get lost. I smoke. Léon and Mum return, and some time later Dad does as well. We have lunch. They drink beer, and afterwards they have coffee. Soon it's time to go to Moshi.

"Can I ride with you?" I ask Léon, because I've never been in a Jeep like that.

"Yes, of course," he says, putting his arm around my shoulder. We get up, and he shoots off down the road, but not long after he kills the speed again.

"Christian," he says above the wind, "I want to ask you something."

"What?" I say.

"It's a hypothetical situation," he says. "Do you know what that means?"

"Yes," I say.

"Good," he says, looking straight ahead. "What do you think one should do if you fall in love with a woman who is married and has children, if you yourself are divorced and living alone. What would be the right thing to do?"

"Errr," I say. "That would depend on her, I suppose . . . I mean, who are we talking about here?" I'm almost shouting so he can hear me above the wind.

"I mean," he says, swallowing, looking at me, then back at the road, clearing his throat, taking a deep breath. "You know, it's . . . please don't tell anyone," he says.

"No, no – don't worry," I say.

"Katriina," he says. Katriina? I mean . . . Jonas is a bastard, but Katriina and Léon? I'm having a hard time imagining it. The big farmer and hunter with the little helpless woman who's got slightly too fat and whose tits have started to sag. Katriina's lovely, no doubt about it, but . . . Well, what do I know? "No, but, do you think it's . . . wrong. I mean, if you . . . pursue a married woman?" he continues.

"I wouldn't know. I'm not old enough," I say. We cover some distance in silence. Soon we're approaching Moshi.

"You promise you won't tell anyone, yes?" Léon says.

"Yes, absolutely," I say.

And we arrive at the Larssons'. Solja's happy; there are buns and cake and hot cocoa, and coffee and balloons and a few of her classmates and several grown-ups and a treasure hunt in the garden set up by Katriina – who insists I join in, even though I'm too old for that sort of thing. But O.K. And I look at Katriina. With Léon – it makes no sense. *She* might, but I can't see him being mad about her. Later there's pizzas and lasagne from *mama* Androli's. We sit around the sitting room and on the veranda. I keep an eye on Léon and Katriina. I can't see anything going on between them. Léon is sitting next to my mum, talking about golf, laughing. He's bloody good at hiding it. And I can't feel any vibes coming from Katriina either when she comes into the sitting room to ask Dad if he would lend her a hand in the kitchen. She doesn't even try to get Léon on her own. Léon and Katriina – I don't think so.

1983

Marcus

MAMA FRIEND'S GUESTHOUSE

There is an upturn in international relations. In town Phantom tells me that Asko has rented a house some way out on Uru Road and that he has installed Chantelle in it so he can visit her whenever he feels like it.

Madness has also spread the other way round. I meet Christian in town. He's very quiet. I bring him home with me.

"I'd like some coffee," he says, so we go into the kitchen. Katriina hears us coming and comes out to greet him.

"Oh hi, Christian," she says.

"Hi," he says, but without looking up. And now it is Katriina who is quiet. I give Christian the cup with the coffee, and right away he digs into his pocket, lights a cigarette. Katriina doesn't say anything about his smoking. She doesn't ask about his parents. She is silent towards Christian, but when none of the Knudsen family members are around, the talk with the other *wazungu* is like a swarm of bees about how Léon Wauters is pumping *mama* Knudsen at Mama Friend's Guesthouse in Soweto, while *bwana* Knudsen is living inside a gin bottle at T.P.C.

THE SWEDISH TEACHER

Rebekka teaches me perfect Swedish – we learned it together from the very beginning. She has been carried around on my arm from the moment she was born. If the parents are home in the evening, I go to my ghetto, because then I have a night off. Jonas doesn't want to see me in the house.

"Sleep at Marcus'," I hear from the house, and I look out of the window. She struggles down the kitchen stairs and totters across the lawn in her nappy, while Katriina stands at the kitchen door shouting that Rebekka is on her way. She lies on my bed chatting away, until she falls asleep with Burning Spear on the tape recorder. Late at night Jonas comes down to get her when she's asleep. He says no more than "Hi" at the most before lifting her up, muttering to her in Swedish that she's going to her own bed now.

"Why not you school?" she asks in her baby Swahili when I stay at home.

"The school fees haven't been paid," I say, even though I know that Aunt Elna has sent money for this year. Then Rebekka goes to the house and says that I can't go to school because the money wasn't paid, and that she feels sorry for me because I want to go to school. Later she totters down to sleep and hands me an envelope:

"Money for school." Then she curls up by my pillow, and I ask her if the music's too loud.

"A little," she says. And I tell her that Stevie Wonder's blind, but that he can play anyway – because I am recording a tape of "Hotter than July", and Stevie sings, "*Though the world's full of problems, they couldn't touch us if they tried,*" but she's already asleep. And I sit there recording for the longest time and writing the names of the songs on the cardboard from the cassette cases – that way I make a little money from each tape. And finally – late at night – Jonas comes down and asks if she's asleep, and I say, "Yes, she's been sleeping for a long time."

Christian

"What's up?" I ask Nanna, because she's being really strange these days. But at least today she doesn't mind walking home with me from the T.P.C. car. Perhaps it's because they'll be moving to Denmark soon. She keeps asking me if I'm "O.K.".

"Yes," I say. "Why wouldn't I be?"

"Oh. I was just thinking that . . ."

"What?"

"About your parents . . ."

"What about my parents?"

"You know . . ."

"I know *what?*" I ask.

"It's just . . . They say that . . . I mean, your mum is never home. She's . . . They say she's always in town."

"Why shouldn't she go into town?" I ask.

"I don't know. It was just that my parents were talking about it – I heard them. But then they didn't say anything else, when they saw that I was there. I have to go," she says and goes inside, shutting the door behind her.

It's true. Mum is always driving into town. Even on the days when she's not teaching Danish at school.

"I have to go in to get a few things," she says, and then she's not back until right before sundown. "I went absolutely everywhere," Mum says, somewhat fidgety. "But I just couldn't find any toilet roll." Dad just grunts, stares at his plate without really eating anything and goes to the messroom every night to drink beer. Then he goes on a business trip to Dar.

At school Nanna comes over to me.

"Is your mum ill?" she asks.

"No. Why?" I ask.

"Her class has been cancelled the last two times," Nanna says.

"I'm damned if I know why," I say. After school we're picked up by the T.P.C. car.

"Can you ask your mum if she'll be there next time?" Nanna says outside our drive.

"Will do," I say. There's a Land Rover I don't know in the driveway, and Léon Wauters is sitting on the veranda with Mum. They're drinking beer.

"You know, Léon just popped by with some rye flour for us. And flowers," Mum says, smiling. There's an enormous bouquet in a vase on the dining table. "You'll have to sort yourself out, if you want something to eat," she says quickly. "I've given the house girl the day off."

"Why did you do that?" I ask.

"She should have some time off now and then, don't you think?" Mum says. I go inside, get some bread and cold cuts. On a whim I go and look into the folks' bedroom. It looks normal – the bed is made.

I go over to play football. Léon's Land Rover is gone when I return, but Dad is back and I can hear them rowing. I want to go closer to eavesdrop, but Dad sees me. "Christian," he calls from the sitting room. I go in, and they both vanish down the corridor towards their rooms – the bedroom and the guestroom.

"Why did you leave the room?" I ask.

"We're having a few . . . problems," Dad says.

"Is it anything to do with me?" I ask him.

"No," he says, and I hear the doors close behind them. I sit down in the sitting room.

Dad leaves to go to a three-day meeting with the government office in Dar. They must evaluate the interim transfer of key jobs at T.P.C. to local staff. Production is plummeting and petty theft is on the rise. "T.P.C is going native," as Dad puts it.

I come home from school to find Léon on the veranda with Mum.

"We're going out for a round of golf soon," she says. "But it's still too hot."

Doesn't that man have a job to do? Some flowers to pick? If he arrives here right after lunch, it's pretty bleeding obvious that it'll be a few hours before you can play golf without getting fried.

I go inside. She's given Irene the day off again. I get myself something to eat. I have an empty pack of cigarettes in my pocket, so I lift the lid off the rubbish bin and lift up the top layer to put it away discreetly. A condom. There's a condom in the bin. But, really, it could be one my dad has used, I think. Except, he hasn't been home for two days – and the bin is emptied every day, to stop it stinking in the heat. What a . . . *Eeew*. At least she isn't so screwed up she's trying to have his baby. I can hear them go to the golf course. I go and look at the double bed. It's perfectly made. But then she is sleeping in the guestroom. I open the door. Yes, her bed has been made too, but not perfectly like Irene does it. The bedspread seems a bit sloppy at the headboard – not stretched to military standards and forced down behind the frame the way it usually is. *Eeew*, fucking *eeew*. I go out. Consider going to Nanna's, but what would I do there? Then I realize she must have known for a long time but was too scared to tell me. Then everyone . . . everyone must have known – at school as well. I walk past the factory and towards Moshi. Get myself a ride with a diesel tanker. Go to Marcus'.

"My mum's shagging the flower farmer from West Kilimanjaro," I say.

"*Tsk*," Marcus says – but he doesn't seem to be surprised. Everyone knows. We don't talk about it. Katriina saw me coming. Right before it gets dark, she comes down to Marcus' ghetto.

"Your mum's looking for you," Katriina says.

"So?" I say.

"Marcus, you're going to have to take Christian home," she says.

"O.K.," Marcus says. I shrug. We drive. Mum is angry.

"You can't just take off like that," she shouts.

"I don't want to talk to you," I say.

"You have to talk to me. I'm your mother," she says.

"And?" I say.

"And that means you have to listen to what I say," she says.

"Really?" I say. "So it's not enough I have to listen to the things you do?"

"What things do I do?" she says.

"The fact that you're . . . running around," I say. My voice almost breaks.

"Running around how?" Mum asks. She seems fidgety.

"With your boyfriend," I say.

"My . . . ?"

"Your boyfriend," I say again. Mum turns her back on me.

"What sort of nonsense is this?" she says.

"It's all over town," I shout. "How you're shagging Léon Wauters." She turns around, takes two steps towards me, slaps my face, holds her hands to her mouth, stares.

"No!" she says.

"*Tsk*," I say and, turning away quickly, get the hell out of there.

Marcus

BANANA LICKER

Tonight I have to wait on tables at the Larsson house. "Marcus," Katriina calls. "You can bring in the pudding now." I carry the cake and the coffee to the table. *Bwana* D'Souza is here with his taciturn little wife, and John and Miriam as well. And *bwana* and *mama* Knudsen too – but no Christian.

"Oh, how pretty," *mama* Knudsen says about the cake, which was bought at *mama* Androli's.

Bwana Knudsen touches my arm.

"Marcus," he says in a low voice. "Can you get me a banana?"

"Yes," I say.

"Don't you want some cake?" Katriina asks.

"Thank you, no," *bwana* Knudsen says – his voice is wet, he has drunk a great deal of beer. In the kitchen I put a small bunch of bananas on a plate with a knife, in case he needs one to peel his banana. Carry the plate to the table. Katriina is pouring coffee, and *mama* Knudsen is speaking to John:

"We buy our rye flour from Léon Wauters. You know, the man who grows flowers on West Kilimanjaro and sells the seeds to a Dutch company? Us Danes, we need our rye bread."

"Does he still live up there all alone?" John says, squinting, and his wife Miriam sends him a warning look.

"Well, yes, he does," *mama* Knudsen says.

I go out towards the kitchen but stop in the hall right around the corner, leaning my back against the wall – listen to their conversation, hanker for a cigarette. It's not my life I'm listening to – it's theirs. But their life determines the quality of mine. *Mama* Knudsen continues speaking to John:

"And I was given a large slab of ostrich meat as well. You know – the ostriches raid his fields, and then he shoots them."

"You do realize it's illegal to shoot ostriches?" John asks.

"Well, yes, but he does have to make a living, and he has an arrangement with the local police, who say it's fine," *mama* Knudsen says.

"Corruption," John says.

"Of course that's not corruption," *mama* Knudsen says. I take the second lot of thermoses with hot water for tea and coffee from the counter and carry them in. *Bwana* Knudsen is holding a banana in his hand, staring at it as he peels it with slow and steady movements. He starts licking it. Long, steady pulls, letting his tongue play with it, sliding it around the tip of the banana before opening his mouth and taking in the whole banana, pulling it out again with his lips locked around it. *Mama* Knudsen has stopped talking. Everyone is silent. *Mama* Knudsen scolds him:

"Don't play with your food, Niels." He removes the banana from his mouth.

"Remind you of anything, does it?" he asks, staring at her. She doesn't say anything. He holds the banana up in front of him. "What do you think it looks like?" he asks.

"A wet banana," John says.

"Really?" *bwana* Knudsen says and takes a big bite.

"You've got something in your beard," *mama* Knudsen says.

"Yes, there's always a little smut that needs to be cleaned off when you've eaten the fruit," he says.

"You swine," she says. Gets up and leaves. I can hear the car door opening, slamming shut. No-one else moves. In all likelihood *bwana*

Knudsen has the car keys. He takes the last bite of the banana, wipes his mouth with the napkin and, getting up, makes a quick bow.

"Thank you for a lovely evening," he says before leaving the table, going outside. The car starts, drives off.

Christian

The folks have gone off to a dinner at the Larssons'. I didn't want to go – sit there bored off my tits at the table in that bizarre vibe while they drink, shoot their mouths off and just generally act weird. No. I listen to Eddy Grant, eat a sandwich and smoke cigarettes. Wait. I want to go to the servants' quarters, to Irene. But it's no good – the gardener is at home. Doesn't she have something to do in the house? Shit. I smoke another cigarette. I get a bloody hard-on every time I think about her. I try to read a book. The Eddy Grant tape runs out – the cicadas are making an ear-splitting racket.

The back door opens. I turn off the cassette. She comes into the sitting room with a basket full of clean laundry.

"Hi, Irene," I say. "How are you?"

"Not bad," she says. "What's that music?"

"Eddy Grant – 'Electric Avenue'."

"It's nice," she says, setting up the ironing board. She's wearing a denim skirt, one of Mum's hand-me-downs, and a top that's tight around her breasts. Bare feet. She irons. I light a cigarette. The hiss of the sulphur makes her turn.

"Christian!" she says. "You're not allowed to smoke."

"Never mind, they won't be back for ages." I get up and go over to her, holding out the cigarette. She giggles, looks towards the garden – the curtains haven't been drawn on the garden door, so the guard may see us if he passes. Of course she's allowed to smoke – no-one can tell her not to – but she would get a bad reputation. I stand very close to her, put my hand on her hip. She slaps it away.

"Uh-uhhh," she says, making a sharply disapproving *tsk* sound with her mouth as she tries to look through the veranda door. Hands me back the cigarette, grabs the iron.

"I really like you," I say, putting my hand on her arse. She doesn't move. I caress it. She turns around and slaps at me, but I have enough time to jump out of the way, laughing.

"Enough! Don't do that." She irons. I sit there watching her. Bollocks.

"Why do you keep looking at me?" Irene asks.

"I think you are very beautiful," I say.

"*Tsk*," she giggles, shaking her head.

"I want to kiss you," I say.

"Enough!" she says. When she's finished the ironing, she takes the laundry and walks down the corridor to my parents' bedroom. I follow – my shorts are like a tent. With my hand in my pocket I try to position my cock so that the belt and the waistband of my trousers press it against my stomach. The curtains are drawn here. She has opened the wardrobe and is putting the clothes on the shelves. I stand behind her, put my arms around her waist – she can feel my cock. It's electric.

"I need you." She tries to twist out of my embrace, laughing.

"I'm working," she says. I kiss the back of her neck. She turns around and pushes me off, looking down at my shorts. "Uh-uhhh," she says. "What is that?"

"That's because I like you." I reach out and touch her stomach through the fabric of her top – she's not wearing a bra. She's still looking at the tent of my shorts. I take her hand and guide it towards my groin.

"No! Stop that trouble," she says, pulling back her hand.

"It's not dangerous," I say and put her hand back.

"You're mad," she whispers but allows me to guide her hand to my cock. She lets me press her hand against it and when I let go, she keeps her hand there. Slowly she folds her fingers around it, clutching it through the fabric, and all the while she is looking in wonderment at her hand, my groin. But then she looks towards the closed curtains, lets go of my cock and crosses her arms in front of her body.

"The guard might see," she says, even though she knows he's in his shed. I go over to the door and turn off the light, so there's only a faint glow from the corridor. She follows me and tries to brush past, but I take two steps to block her – there's only a tiny distance between us. She is standing quite still, and I can see that she is looking towards my groin, even though it's almost completely dark. The double bed stands beside us. I touch her breast gently through the fabric, move my other hand in to touch her stomach. Her skin is warm and soft. Up towards her breast. She pushes my hand out from under her top, giggling. I open my belt, the button, the zipper, so the shorts fall to my bare feet. Take her hand slowly and put it on my cock outside my underpants. She lets me. We're standing stock-still. Until she pulls at the elastic carefully, so my cock juts out, and she lets go, making a small sound, taking half a step back. My cock is standing to attention before her, and I push my underpants down around my hips.

"Why is it like that?" she says.

"What?"

"Like a stick," she says.

"Because I like you."

She puts her hand around my cock, and my legs feel so weak I have to sit down on the edge of the bed with an arm behind me for support. She sits to my left, a bit sideways, so she can see it in the dim light.

"You are very, very lovely, Irene," I say. "I love you." I reach my arm out and gently lift her top. I can see, can feel the lower parts of her breasts.

"Do you like my titi?" she asks – teasing me a little, I think.

"Yes." My voice is hoarse. She lifts up her top so her breasts are free – they look both soft and firm at the same time. In the dim light from the corridor I see the bluish-purple nipple – caress it with my hand. Her hand is lying still on my cock; pressing it. I lean down my face towards her breasts to kiss them.

"Stop it! I don't want that." She pushes my head away but allows me to touch her breasts again. She lets go of my cock and takes my balls lightly in her hand, squeezing them gently, lifting them up a little as if weighing them. Lets go and grabs my cock again. Doesn't move her hand but squeezes it. I stare at my hand on her breasts – how I wish I could have the lights on. Stare at her face, which is as concentrated as mine. Caress the nipple, press down on it lightly.

"Mmmm," she says quietly. I move my hand down to her knee, let it slide up under the fabric of her skirt.

"Don't make trouble," she says, distinctly, but without moving, but all the same I take my hand from her thigh and clasp the hand that is holding my cock.

"Do like this," I say and start guiding her hand slowly up and down.

"Why?"

"It's nice." She does it. I moan faintly. She looks at my face and then back at my cock again.

"Do it fast." She speeds up. It's amazing. I try to hold back. Lean back with my arms pressed against the bed. Her hand on my cock. Her breasts bobbing. I come.

"Ahhh!?" she says, yanking back her hand as my sperm sprays from my cock and out onto the floor. She pulls away on the bed, making her breasts vibrate abruptly.

"Ohhh," I say. "*Safi kabisa*" – super nice. She giggles.

"You're mad," she whispers and gets up, pulling her top down over her breasts.

"You are very lovely," I say. She walks down the corridor, and I hear the back door open and shut. I go out to the toilet and fetch toilet paper, wipe off my cock, wipe the sperm off the floor, put my shorts back on, close the wardrobe, smooth the bedspread, go into the sitting room and fold up the ironing board – put it away with the iron. My cock is hard again. I wish she were here. Go to the bathroom and wank. I last much longer this time; think about her breasts, her rounded arse, her thighs, I want her to touch me again. I come. Then I go out and get myself a beer from the fridge and replace it with a lukewarm one from the larder. I sit down on the kitchen stairs and smoke a cigarette, drink the beer, look down towards her window where a faint light is shining behind the curtain.

My body feels light – not just from the beer and the cigarettes, but simply . . . soaring. And tired. I lock up. Go to bed. Think about Irene. And do it once more.

Wake up. The door? It was the veranda door slamming. That means the folks are home. I feel good inside – even if my head's a bit heavy from the beer I had. A quick, hectic think – did I manage to remove all trace, the evidence. I did. Lie still and listen, because there are no voices, but somehow I can tell that it's Mum walking around. But that's all. I get out of bed and open the door a little. She has gone into their bedroom and is clattering about in the wardrobe.

"Oh drat," she says – there's a tinge of hysteria to her voice. I go over and lean against the door. She's standing with her back to me, going through the desk drawer. On the bed is an open suitcase with clothes bunged into it higgledy-piggledy.

"What are you doing?" I ask. She spins around.

"Oh!" she says. "You startled me." I can see she's been crying.

"What's happened?" I ask. "Where's Dad?"

"I . . ." she starts, looks at me. She stops. Turns her back on me and starts going through the drawer in a more methodical way. "I can't live with your dad anymore. I have to get out."

"What are you talking about?" Her back starts shaking. Should I go over and put a hand on it? I won't. "Are you two splitting up?" I ask. Somehow she gets a grip on herself. The shaking stops. She stands with her back to me, both palms resting on the desk, then turns around and looks me in the eye.

"He drives me round the bend. I have to get out." I shrug. Give her a hard stare:

"But where is he?" She goes to the suitcase on the bed, starts closing it. Doesn't look at me.

"He'll be back soon," she says. And that's it. I ought to ask, What about me? But I don't, because I know the answer: indifference – she doesn't know. I go into the sitting room and sit on the sofa with my feet on the coffee table. After a while she comes in with a holdall slung over her shoulder and a suitcase in her hand. She puts the bag down, lays a folded piece of paper on the dining table and places the vase on top of it. Looks briefly, nervously at me. She stands stock-still, staring at the veranda door. I don't say anything, don't move a muscle.

"I'm sorry, Christian," she says. I don't answer. She starts coming towards me. I don't budge. She stands in front of me – about to lean down to hug me.

"Don't," I say. She stands up.

"It's not my fault," she says – tears are running down her cheeks.

"Yes, it is," I say. She turns and goes over to get her things.

"You don't understand." She looks around the sitting room – her face is vacant. Goes abruptly to the sideboard and takes the frame with Annemette's picture, stuffing it into her holdall. She looks over at me. "I'll call you tomorrow," she says. I look at her, let my cheeks fill with air and exhale, shaking my head. "Goodbye, Christian," she says and opens the door.

"You're being stupid," I say. And then she's gone, and a sob wells up into my throat. I swallow it, get up – go out into the bathroom and splash water on my face. She takes the picture of the dead child and lets me sit like a turd on the sofa. I hear the car starting, driving off. Go out

189

on the veranda, light a cigarette. The guard comes over. Why can't he just mind his own business?

"Where did *mama* go?" he asks.

"I don't know," I say. I go back inside. Sit on the sofa. Remember the note. How could I forget? Sit there a while, staring at it. It's not for me. I don't want to read it. But . . . get up and move stiffly to the table. Unfold the note:

"Dearest Niels. I can't stand it any longer. You won't speak to me about Annemette. It has broken my heart – seeing you like that as well. You are ruining yourself. You won't help us move on. I feel like you hate me. I can't do it anymore. I'm going home. Look after Christian. Love, Kirsten."

How banal. Broken her heart. Sick. I put the note back the way it was. Sit back down again.

I wake up. Sit up on the sofa. "Guard – come." Dad's voice from outside. I hear the gate opening. I rub my face. There he is.

"Where's your mum?" His face and clothes and hands are black with soot.

"What happened?" I ask. He makes a dismissive gesture.

"Your mum?" he repeats.

"She's gone," I say, pointing towards the dining table. "There's a note. What happened?" He goes over and reads the note.

"Oh bugger, bugger, bugger," he mutters, holding it up, looking at me questioningly.

"Too right," I say. "I've read it." He is visibly drunk but sufficiently upset to try to ignore it. "What happened?" I ask again.

"We were on our way home. She drove off when I stopped for a tinkle." I don't say anything. He looks down on his soiled clothes. "Well, of course then I had to jump aboard one of the sugar trains to get here." The plantation trains go all night, and the sugar canes are covered in soot – you set light to the fields before harvesting the sugar to chase away snakes and other creepy-crawlies and to remove the sharp outer leaves, which can cut deep gashes in the field workers' skin. Dad hasn't answered my question.

"But what happened?" He sighs.

"We had a row. I thought she was just punishing me with a walk home." He goes to the phone, starts making calls. "I am going to have to borrow a car so we can go after her. There was hardly any petrol in the tank."

He gets hold of Nanna's dad. It's two-thirty in the morning. "Let's get going then," he says when he puts the phone down.

"I'm not going anywhere."

"Errrr . . ." he says and stops. "Christian," he says, "you have to help me . . . persuade her to come home." But I can't help him do that, can I? She doesn't seem to think we have a home.

"No," I say. "She didn't take me." He looks at me for a little while. I want to tell him that I sat right here and saw her – how she took the picture of Annemette and left me where I was. But I don't say it . . .

"I'm going," he says without moving.

"Where to?" I ask.

"To Dar, of course," he says.

"You might want to go the other way – to West Kilimanjaro," I say.

"Why . . . ?" he starts but, again, stops, goes towards the door. I go to bed. Fall asleep as day breaks.

When I wake up sometime before noon, I can see our car parked outside. The house is quiet. I tiptoe down the corridor. The bedroom door is closed. I think I can hear faint voices. In the kitchen I boil water for coffee and make toast. I eat. Irene enters. I smile at her, reach out for her. She dodges me, slaps me over the back of my head.

"Enough!" she says.

"I love you," I whisper.

"Couldn't you get me a pair of sneakers – good ones like the ones you have?"

"Why?" I ask.

"As a present," she says and looks into my eyes with surprise.

"Do mine fit you?" I ask.

"Yes," she says. I get up and fetch them for her.

"Thanks," she says, kicking off her flip-flops and putting on the shoes.

"You're welcome," I say. At the other end of the house my parents' bedroom door is opened. "See you," I say to Irene, who quickly picks up her flip-flops and slips out of the door. She has probably heard from the security guard that the whites were acting up last night.

My dad comes into the kitchen.

"Christian. Do you think you could think of something to do today? I mean . . . Your mum and I need to talk."

"Sure thing."

"Do we have a deal?"

"I'll be out of your hair in just a tick," I say.

"Do you need money?" he asks. I don't really, but say yes and he gives me some more.

"I need some new sneakers," I say.

"What happened to the ones you have?" he asks.

"They don't fit anymore – I've given them to Irene."

"Oh," he says. "Well then, we'll just order some new ones for you."

"Alright then," I say. He leaves again. I have another cup of coffee. Smoke a cigarette I find lying about in the kitchen. Find another pair of sneakers, worn-out ones, and go over to borrow John's motorbike. Fetch Rogarth. We go towards Kahe and down to the river. Go for a swim even though there might be crocodiles – it's so rare to see them and we've hired a Maasai boy to keep an eye out. We go over to one of the field workers' villages to buy fizzy drinks at the kiosk. It's a Sunday – loads of workers are sitting there drinking *mbege*. I offer cigarettes to the ones I know; two years ago they had time to play football in the afternoon – now they're slaves in the fields. When I go home in the late afternoon, I see Nanna lying by the swimming pool. I turn off my engine and roll over to the bougainvillaea hedge. She comes over to me.

"Hi, Christian," she says.

"Hi," I say.

"Are you alright?" she says. I shrug, looking down. Now her dad comes out on the terrace, crosses the lawn. Nanna sighs. I turn my key and flip out the kick-start.

"So, Christian, what an awful . . ." His voice is drowned out by the noise from the engine. Nanna gives him an angry look and then looks at me.

"Are you coming to school tomorrow?" she shouts. I shake my head and release the clutch – dust and gravel spin from my wheel. I return the motorbike to John. Go home.

I go to the servants' quarters. Irene isn't there. I go back to the house. The folks don't say anything when they see me.

"What are you doing?" I ask.

"Nothing," Dad says.

"We're sitting, talking about how . . ." Mum says. "Perhaps you should sit down with us."

"No," I say. "I'm going to the messroom for supper."

I turn my back on them and leave. As I approach the messroom, I think about Nanna's dad, Bent. He might be there. Dad called him last night and borrowed his car so he could go looking for Mum. And Bent likes making people feel uncomfortable. I change direction. Go to the canteen where the locals eat. Buy Coke, fried chicken, chips.

Mum is nowhere to be seen when I return. Dad is in the sitting room, listening to classical music. He doesn't see me.

"Goodnight," I say.

"Errr, goodnight, Christian," he says. He listens to music late into the night. He drinks. The next morning he doesn't get up. I go over and take the T.P.C. car to school.

"I thought you weren't coming," Nanna says. I shrug. What can I say? "My dad's an idiot," she says.

"Yes," I say. He isn't the only one.

When I come home from school, there's no-one in the house. Dad has left a note saying he won't be back from the office until late. The afternoon passes and there's no sign of Mum. The gardener has been given the day off to visit his wife, who is ill, in one of the villages.

From the kitchen I see Irene, her *kanga* wrapped around her and a towel in her hand, go through the door at the gable end of the servants' quarters. That's where their toilet and shower is. I go through the garden. I can't see anyone around. The shower's on. I go up the stairs. The lock on the door is broken. My cock is poking out. I silently undress and get in with Irene. She is standing bent over in the shower with her back to me and I can see . . . everything. The round, dark arse, the strong thighs, her waist, her plump arms, her breasts vibrating as she scrubs energetically at her calves.

"Ohhh," she says, holding her hands up before her when she turns and sees me. But I have just enough time to see the black bush between her legs.

"Irene," I say and take a step towards her, so I'm under the water as well. She takes a step back and raises her arms. She hits me. Hard. Several times.

193

"Enough!" she says. "Get lost. You're mad." She hisses it in a low voice, probably because she knows there is no-one around who could hear us. I shield myself, try to grab her. She keeps hitting me. I manage to press her arms to her sides, pull them behind her back, so I can draw her towards me. My cock is hard against her wet stomach, her breasts press against my chest. She's standing still, her arms relax, her head is down. Water is pouring down over us. I realize she is crying. I let go of her arms – feel terrible.

"I'm sorry," I say, smoothing down her hair. She's crying more intensely now. My erection has gone.

"You can't come in here," she says. "It's not right."

"I'm sorry," I say. "I like you very much." I step away from her, go over to my clothes.

"Here," she says. I turn around and she throws me her towel. I dry myself quickly. Pull on my clothes.

"I'm sorry," I say again.

"I won't have you do it – understand?" Irene's voice is hard.

"I understand," I say.

"I'm serious," she says.

"I promise I won't do it again," I say and leave.

I have got used to having my supper at the workers' canteen. I sit and chat with the friends I used to play football with. These days they're working in the fields. I offer them a few of Mum's Dunhill cigarettes or Dad's Princes. The car isn't there when I get back. There's no note about where they've got to. I go down to the servants' quarters. I knock. Irene doesn't answer.

"She's gone for a visit," Benjamin says from his room.

"What happened at the house?" I ask.

"What do you mean?" he asks – he doesn't want to be mixed up in it.

"I mean, did they have any visitors today?"

"There was a man in a Land Rover earlier. The one who plays golf," he says. And bangs my mum.

"Did my mum leave with him?" I ask.

"I don't know," he says. "I went out to visit someone." That's not true. He would never leave the house when there are people in it.

I sit down on the veranda and smoke a cigarette in the twilight. Irene comes walking up the drive in my sneakers – she's had them cleaned; they look brand new.

"Gorgeous shoes," I say when she walks past the veranda.

"Yes," she says, smiling faintly.

"Gorgeous shoes for a gorgeous girl."

"Tsk," she says. I go inside. Do my prep. Eat a few sandwiches. By the time I go to bed, there's still no-one else in the house.

In the morning the house is empty – their beds haven't been slept in. Should I be worried? Irene makes me coffee.

"Thanks," I say. We share a cigarette. She doesn't ask any questions – she's worked it out; our home is disintegrating. We sit across from each other at the small kitchen table, drinking coffee, smoking cigarettes – the new lord and lady of the house. Irene looks at the cheap wristwatch Mum has given her.

"Time you were off," she says.

"Yes," I say and go to the roundabout at the entrance to the staff's residential area and get in the car to be taken to school.

The folks' car is parked outside the house when I return in the afternoon. Dad is on the sofa in the sitting room, drinking whisky.

"Your mum's left," he says – his voice is addled with drink.

"Right," I say. I don't ask any questions.

"Simba Farm," he says.

"You guys are out of your heads," I say. He makes no comment. I go outside. To the workers' canteen. Rogarth shows up – he doesn't normally come here.

"Christian," he says.

"Yes," I say.

"What happened – it's really weird," he says, shaking his head.

"What did happen?" I ask.

"Yesterday," Rogarth says. "At your house."

"What happened at my house?"

"Don't you know?" Rogarth says.

"Nothing happened after I got home from school. I was the only one there."

"That man . . ." Rogarth starts but then stops.

"What man?" I say.

"The one from Simba Farm," Rogarth says.

"Léon Wauters," I say.

"Yes. He came and picked your mother up at the house."

"Right," I say, nodding. "Yes, I did notice she wasn't around anymore."

Dad has called in sick. He is constantly drunk but tries to hide it from me. I don't get to hang around the house with Irene, and I can't go down to the servants' quarters in case Benjamin hears something. When I try to put my arms around her in the kitchen, she slaps me.

"*Bwana* is here," she whispers angrily. I masturbate all the time, thinking about her. And about Nanna. And Shakila. And Samantha.

The phone rings. I go over and pick it up.

"Yes?" I say.

"Christian, it's me," my mum says at the other end.

"*Tsk*," I say. Hang up.

"Who was it?" Dad says.

"Wrong number," I say.

The looks I get at school. Of course it was all happening before I found out . . . People have known for a long time, but no-one said anything to me. Perhaps they thought I knew all about it and was just ignoring it. But now I know and have to act like nothing's wrong, and I feel sick. She can't be so stupid she didn't realize she would be found out. That people would talk. White man and white woman arrive at a cheap local guesthouse during the day and with no luggage – it's so fucking blatant.

Samantha comes across me lounging about in the hall, leaning against the wall. She squints at me.

"Can you take it?" she asks.

"What?"

"The pressure," she says. I sneer and shake my head, digging my hands further into my pockets. She leans against the wall next to me. "Parents," she says. "Good for precisely fuck-all."

"Too right," I say.

I am sitting in the girls' toilet, smoking a cigarette during a citizenship class. They won't look for me here, not in a million years – the only risk is that a girl might smell the smoke and squeal on me. I flush the butt and get up. As I round the corner, I see Mum standing outside the classroom talking to another teacher in hushed tones. I turn on my heel and hurry back round the corner – stand there eavesdropping.

"Alright, thanks," Mum says. She's been told that I'm in the toilet – comes this way. What is she thinking? Has she gone completely mental? I quickly disappear behind the building, off the school grounds, down to the river. Sit down and smoke another cigarette. It makes me feel dizzy. She's come asking after me. Everyone in my class has seen her. Everyone knows what she's done. What should I do now? My bag is in the classroom. I stay away until after the last lesson, waiting for the bell to ring – as soon as the teacher is out of the class, I go over.

"There you are, man," Jarno says.

"Yep, here I am," I say.

"She left again, your mum," he says.

"Tsk," I say and go in to get my bag and out to the T.P.C. car.

"Your mum came to the school," Nanna says. "Did you see her?" I glare at her. "Sorry," she says, looking down.

Of course I'm not meant to hear it. He's raging drunk. I wake up because the veranda door slams shut. He crashes into the furniture, curses. A glass is broken. It sounds as if he is muttering to himself. I get out of bed quietly and go over to open the door. I can see a strip of light from under the sitting room door. And then he speaks loudly in English: "I need to speak to my wife. Get her." What's going on? Has he gone mad? "She's my wife," Dad says in English. "I need to speak to her now, you stupid fuck. We have a son. We need to talk." His words are slurred. There's silence. "Kirsten, is that you?" Dad asks. It seems Mum has come to the phone at Simba Farm. Dad mumbles something I can't hear. And then I hear him loud and clear. It makes me shiver – his voice drips with contempt: "Annemette?" he says. "I don't believe she was my daughter. You slept around while I was away. You are a despicable woman. Oh!" he says. "Well, I'll be damned." I can hear him hanging up, muttering to himself. And then I hear him sobbing. It sounds awful. He snivels and mutters and sobs. I can't bear it. I close my door carefully. Light a cigarette. Stand at the window. After a few minutes I can hear him snoring. I go into the sitting room. He is sitting on the sofa, his back straight, head tilted back, mouth open. There is broken glass on the floor. I am cold. Turn around. Go back to bed.

Marcus

WHITE RAIN

I give her a thorough-once over. When Tita has been on the sunbed in the sun, the white skin becomes like a chicken on the barbecue; if I pull off her yellow bikini bottom, it looks like she's wearing knickers made of cream. The customs are very different. You would never see a Tanzanian woman go into the sun voluntarily – she would turn black as coal, blue-black, and everyone would think of her as a field worker who hadn't risen from her peasant life.

I work well as Tita's replacement husband, but Asko gives her a problem of a mental nature:

"Why do those women want to be with him?" Tita asks. We're sitting on the small patio, where they've put up a shower next to their sauna with a wooden floor and a wooden wall surrounding it. It's late in the afternoon – the house girl has been given the day off, and the gardener has been sent into town to buy dog food. Asko has gone to Mwanza with Jonas, and Tita has got out the Carlsberg.

"It's not like they don't know he's married to me," she says.

"Yes, they know, but the rain falls on them when he so much as speaks to them – they've already risen a step on the ladder. Something good is bound to happen," I say.

"What sort of rain?" Tita asks.

"Presents. They go with him in the big car, go to restaurants, eat fine food, drink bottled beer. Rain is constantly pouring from the *mzungu* – the harvest will be incredible. He gives them money for a dress or to help with their rent, and—" Tita cuts me short:

"Do you think he does?"

"Of course he does."

"But are they . . . whores?"

"No, they are girls who hope the *mzungu* will take them with him to Europe. A sort of trade-off – their beauty in return for the ticket."

"I just don't understand how they can think that," Tita says. "Those girls."

"The main reason is their poverty. And their ignorance. Not a good combination. When they see the coloured man – the white man – then their first thought is that now they'll be very rich, that now they'll have a lovely house. Now they'll go to Europe. Now all their family will be rich. Now they'll live as well as in Heaven. That's how it is. She'll go to Europe, and she can help her family in Tanzania."

"But that's so naïve," Tita says.

"She's younger, and she can satisfy him, and she knows he'll drop his wife like a stone. During sex the black girl will be miraculous. She will perform plenty of miracles for the white man, so he'll completely leave his wife; so he'll think his wife is useless. When the poor ones do it to achieve something, they perform a total sexual hypnosis. And the white man will be totally bewitched. He'll forget his home." Even before she speaks, I know I've revealed too much.

"You're saying . . . Am I not sexy?" Tita asks.

"Oh yes – very. To me you're the most wonderful woman ever."

"Can't I perform miracles? Like the black girls?"

"You have to understand . . ." I start, then pause to think a little, because our talk about the black berries might make my white berry dry out. Is white love really that different? Was it something else entirely when Katriina caught Jonas, son of the white forest king? I tell her the truth: "In most Tanzanian tribes, girls are sent off to their father's sister when they start bleeding from their flower, so she can teach them how to be a woman."

"And? What does that mean?" Tita asks.

"The girl is taught how to live as a woman with a man. How to treat him. How to have sex with the man, where to touch him and how; when the man would prefer it, how to treat him in general, how to make him nice food, all that stuff. If the man treats her badly, she must still receive him. The man is king."

"And what if he doesn't bring her to Europe?"

"Then she must suffer – her investment failed. She must try again if she isn't too old and worn by then."

"That's so . . . cynical," Tita says. The African woman sees her papaya as a commodity, a plot of land; it's her commodity to sell – if a rich man wants to buy it, she'll let him have her plot of land to plough and sow his seed in. "I just don't understand . . ." Tita snivels. "Why doesn't he love me anymore – am I ugly?"

I thought we were going to go to the sauna and be wicked in the white flower, but Tita is sad.

I want a love – my own colour, my own age, so it doesn't feel like doing a job, but like a game for children.

Christian

Nanna comes over in the afternoon. I don't say very much. She's got something she wants to say, I think, but I doubt it can be anything good. So instead I focus on trying to get her top off. I've managed the feat once before.

"Stop that, will you!" she says and pushes me off.

"I thought that was what you had come for," I say. She shakes her long dark hair out of her eyes.

"Have you talked to . . . ?" she begins. I don't say anything. "Your . . . mum?" she says.

"No," I say. Strictly speaking it's true. She called – I hung up.

"But . . ."

"I don't want to talk to her – she left."

"Will you stay here?"

"Me and my dad?"

"Yes?"

"I would think so, yes," I say.

"Oh. It was only that . . ."

"Only what?"

"It's just that . . . My dad was talking about how Mærsk . . . Mærsk don't like it when these things happen."

"These things, what things?" I say. Feeling tired. "For fuck's sake, people get divorced all the time."

"I don't know," Nanna says. She leaves not long after. Dad comes home. He calls Simba Farm. His face is one big, constant tic, even before the line connects. I go to my room so I won't hear their conversation.

"Christian," he calls, "your mum wants to speak to you."

"I don't want to talk to her," I call back.

"Come on," he shouts.

"No!" I can hear them talking a while longer before it goes quiet.

I wake up. I'm going to West Kilimanjaro today. Going to see Mum. Tell her a thing or two. Tell her what? It's grey outside – the light will come soon. I get up, put on my clothes, go outside and smoke in the cool morning air.

On Rombo Avenue I tell the driver to stop. He asks me why, but does it nonetheless.

I walk up through the corn stubble and climb through the fence. Knock on Marcus' door. He opens.

"We're just leaving," he says. Katriina is taking the kids to school, and Jonas is asleep. Marcus hands me Solja's swimming goggles. "To stop the dust from getting in your eyes. The dirt road is very dusty north of Sanya Juu."

We set off. Cool wind in the early morning. In Sanya Juu we stop and go to a café to have tea with hot milk and cane sugar. Peel our hardboiled eggs. I have told Marcus my mum is up here. He knew already – he has probably known much longer than I have. I focus on the flakes of eggshell that fall from my fingers onto the Formica table with its millions of microscopic scratches.

"Marcus," I say. "Why doesn't anyone say anything about my mum and that farmer?"

"Who would they say it to?" Marcus asks.

"To me," I say.

"They can't say it to you," Marcus says.

"Why not?" I ask.

"It would be like hitting you," Marcus says.

I don't say anything. We're off again. Marcus stops at the exit to Tilotanga – the gate to Simba Farm is a few hundred metres further down.

"I'll wait here," he says.

"Alright," I say – he's got his interests to look out for. I get off and push the swimming goggles up in my forehead, brushing the dust off my face. My spit is rusty red – my mouth tastes like mud. I stroll the last few hundred metres down the road and turn right, through the gate. Nod at the guard, cross the courtyard, where a load of European agricultural machines are parked, surrounded by a multitude of barns, workshops and garages. I go through the opening in the fence which surrounds the main house and round to the back door by the large vegetable garden.

"*Mama yoko wapi?*" I ask the cook through the open kitchen window. He says she's in the garden. I go round the house and into the garden, but at first glance I can't see her. On the veranda there's a table with two glasses and an earthenware jug. I go up the steps. There's a round piece of finely woven tulle around the jug to keep the insects out, with beads sewn around the edge to weigh it down. And there are my mum's Dunhill cigarettes, her gold lighter, her sunglasses. I look out over the garden. She's on her knees in front of a flowerbed at the far end of the garden, with her back to me; khaki shorts, pale blue man's shirt tied in a knot around her middle, a large straw hat on her head with a white band tied round the crown. I go over. My steps make no sound on the well-tended lawn. I stop, get my cigarettes out of my pocket – can no longer remember what it was I wanted to say. The pack makes a faint noise as I shake one out. I sense her turning at the sound, but I don't look up.

"Christian?" she says, eyes fixed on my forehead. I remember the swimming goggles – I leave them where they are and get a match out, strike it, suck down smoke. "What are you doing?" she asks – now there's befuddlement, a touch of confusion, even a hint of reproach in her voice. I look up and exhale smoke.

"I'm smoking," I say.

"But . . ." she says and then stops, starts getting up. "You're all dusty, you know," she says, taking a step towards me, raising her hand to my face. I take a step back:

"Don't ever come to my school again," I say. Mum stops.

"Why not?" she asks.

"Everyone knows," I say.

"But I . . ." she says.

"My friends, my teachers – everyone. They've known for ages."

"I . . . I'm so sorry," Mum says.

"Who are you, really?" I ask.

"What do you mean?"

"Are you Baroness Blixen or something?" She takes a deep breath and sighs. Then she takes a quick breath, holding for it for a fraction of a second, sorting through the words she's about to say to me. I know the attitude; now she wants to step up to the plate as a mother, as an adult – well, too bloody late. I take the opportunity to turn away.

"Christian?" she says. I go out of the garden, out into the yard, down to the gate and onto the road, walk past the flower fields, smoking my cigarette. Smoke billows behind me; I don't turn my head. No-one calls to me; no-one comes after me. I reach Marcus. I look into the motor-bike's side mirror. Rusty-red face, white circles around the eyes, and the swimming goggles like two sawn-off horns on my forehead.

"Let's be off," I say. He starts the engine; I get up behind him, we're moving. Gone.

*

I have just enough time to shower and change into fresh clothes before Dad comes home from work. I don't tell him I've seen Mum. He's stone-cold sober and has something to tell me:

"I've applied for a job in Moshi," he says.

"Why?" I ask.

"I'm fed up with this whole Mærsk business," he says.

"What about Esplanaden?" I ask. I though his plan was to return and work at the head office.

"Would you like to move back to Denmark?" he asks.

"Nope. Absolutely not," I say. The mess he's made of his marriage will not go down well at Mærsk, and what would he do with me if he were to be posted abroad again?

"There's a job with D.A.N.I.D.A., working with the Nordic Project," Dad says. "Consultancy for the co-ops on the mountain."

"Aren't they the ones Thorleif works for?" I ask.

"As a matter of fact it's Thorleif's job I've applied for – his wife has gone back to Norway and now he wants to go home as well, as soon as he's trained up the new man on the job," Dad says.

"Will we be living in Moshi then?"

"If I get the job – yes," Dad says.

"That's fine by me. But I would like to have a motorbike so I can get around on my own and don't have to always wait around for you to be able to take me."

"We'll work that out," Dad says and turns away.

"What about Mum?" I ask.

"I don't know – you'll have to ask her yourself," he says and looks down at his hands, which he keeps busy with a cigarette and a lighter.

I sit down by my desk and try to do prep. Try not to think about Irene's breasts. Her breasts. Dad has gone to the messroom – to drink, probably. Should I go over to Nanna's for a swim? But she just lies there on her sunbed in her baby blue synthetic bikini with her arse sticking out. An arse that's so bloody precious it must be treated like a piece of fine china – be washed, wiped down and put on display in a cabinet; only look, no touching mind! Almost no touching. And her dad is a tosser.

As twilight falls, I start to get hungry. Go over to the messroom. The guard hasn't arrived yet. That means I have to go down to Irene and tell her I'm leaving, so she can keep an eye on the house. Her door is a little ajar.

"Irene?" I call.

"Eh?" she says.

"I'm going over to the messroom," I say. "The guard isn't here yet."

"O.K.," she says. That's all. I go there. Dad is nowhere to be seen – his car isn't either.

Miriam is there.

"Where are your parents?" she asks.

"I don't know," I say. Miriam must be hitting the bottle pretty hard, if my parents' situation hasn't sunk in yet. I have barbecued chicken and a Coke. I walk back to the house. Sit on the veranda and smoke. The guard has arrived. Go to the sitting room – turn on the stereo. I can hear Irene coming through the kitchen door to make the guard some coffee – get him his dinner. She comes down the hall, leans against the door.

"What sort of music is that?" she asks.

"Bob Marley," I say.

"I like it," she says. "Where is *bwana*?"

"I don't know." She walks through the sitting room and stops where the bedroom corridor starts. I follow her with my eyes – I can't help it.

"Come," she says. I get up. She sits on my bed. I sit down next to her. Feel her breasts through her top. She puts her hand on my cock. Lifts her top up over her breasts with the other hand. I start opening my trousers – she helps me. When my cock is out, she takes hold of my foreskin with her thumb and forefinger.

"Why is it like that?" she asks.

"What do you mean?" I say. She puts the side of her hand next to it.

"*Kata hapa*," she says – cut here – making a sawing motion against the foreskin. She's a Muslim. Perhaps she expects all boys to be circumcised. I pull my foreskin back. My bell-end is throbbing with blood. She wanks me until I come.

"Thank you," I say. The kettle starts whistling in the kitchen. She pulls down her top and goes to deal with it. I clean up after myself, wash my hands. Lie down on my bed and stare at the ceiling.

Nanna gives me an odd look in the car going to I.S.M. in the morning.

"What is it?" I ask.

"Nothing," she says, looking out of the window. She hasn't said a full sentence to me in days. Perhaps she's thrilled I've stopped chasing her. I can't fight that top any longer. When the holiday starts a few weeks from now, she'll move back to Denmark. But by then I will already have moved to Moshi with Dad. At school the day drags by, and when we return home, she gives me that odd look again. I look at her and smile because it's so weird. She looks away.

"Why don't you come over tonight?" she asks.

"I could do that," I say.

Her parents aren't there when I arrive. I ask her where they are.

"In Moshi, at a party," Nanna says.

"Alright," I say and hand her a Kim Wilde tape that I had Jarno make for me, because I thought it might help me in my endeavours against her top.

"Thanks," Nanna says and puts it on. "Would you like a beer?"

"Thanks," I say. "If you're having one."

"I'm having a gin and tonic," she says.

"Then I'll have one of those as well," I say. She goes into the kitchen and mixes our drinks, leaving me alone with Kim Wilde. I feel nervous. Go out onto the veranda and light a cigarette. She comes back.

"You can smoke inside if you like," she says. We sit down on the sofa.

"Cheers," I say. "Good luck in Denmark."

"Good luck in Moshi," she says. She drinks quickly. Soon her glass is empty. Then she gets up and goes down the dark hall towards her room without saying anything. I empty my glass. Should I smoke another cigarette?

"Christian?" Nanna's voice from down the hall.

"Yes?" I say.

"Won't you come here?"

"Alright," I say. Get up. Walk down the corridor. In the light from the sitting room I can see that her door is open. But the room is dark. There's music playing. She must be able to see me silhouetted in the doorway.

"Don't put on the light," she says from the bed. "Come here." I cross the floor slowly. She's lying in her bed under the duvet. I sit on the edge of the bed. Put a hand on her cheek. Kiss her. Feel her naked shoulder. "Come down to me," she says. I get up and rip off my clothes. All my clothes. This is it. Lie down next to her carefully. She's naked. Except for her knickers. I kiss her. Kiss her breasts, her stomach. Move further down.

"Don't do that," Nanna says.

"I want to," I say, kissing her inner thighs. I've read about how you do it in a Harold Robbins novel. I pull of her knickers and put my face between her legs. Now she's not asking me to stop. Afterwards I lie down next to her. Kiss her breasts, her neck, her mouth. "You're beautiful," I say. She touches my balls very gingerly. My cock. Then she grabs onto it hard and starts pulling at it.

"No, not like that," I say.

"I have a rubber here," she says and reaches down under her bed, gives it to me. It's difficult to put it on in the dark. Nanna giggles.

"One moment," I say – there: it's on. "O.K.," I say. She doesn't say anything now. I touch her stomach, move my hand down, and one of my fingers slides in. She's wet.

"What should I do?" she asks.

"Is it your first time?" I whisper.

"Yes," she says. I don't tell her it's my first time as well – I have read about it.

"Sit down on top of me," I say. She does it. But I'm outside. "You must help me in," I say. She lifts a little, guides her hand down, takes hold of my cock and guides me in. It's amazing. I touch the breasts above me. It's amazing. Much better than I thought.

Marcus

SAWMILLS

It happens when I'm in the middle of my final exams – equipment starts arriving from Sweden to be transported to West Kilimanjaro. D'Souza is the secret advisor to Jonas in all matters relating to Tanzanian authorities.

"You must start at the F.I.T.I. forestry school on Monday," Jonas says when I get my results.

I have done my homework and got good grades, even though I have also had to run around like a rabbit for the Larsson family and F.I.T.I. and everyone else when I was supposed to be at school – and all of it without being paid so much as a shilling. And now the white man wants to put me in a school that will take me to a forest somewhere to cut down timber like an idiot.

After a couple of weeks I put it Jonas directly:

"I don't want to have anything to do with the things you work with, because I don't understand forestry machinery and timber production. I want to stay in school some more." That's what I say, but all the while I'm thinking: No way my black arse is going to freeze in some forest on West Kilimanjaro – it's going to Sweden to be an attraction in the white country.

BOYFRIEND–GIRLFRIEND

I lie and say I'm going to visit my family, and instead I go to an expensive party at Nechi's house. His older brother's job as boss at the Police Academy opens all sorts of coffers to the family to dip their long trunks into. All my friends are there. Beautiful Rosie and her quiet friend Claire, Edson the Acrobat and Big Man Ibrahim from Swahilitown. We have a big *ngoma*, and suddenly I have two tongues in my mouth – Rosie's and my own. She even lets me feel the holy of holies.

"Now we're boyfriend and girlfriend," Rosie says.

"Yes," I say. "I love you very much."

Christian

"Go outside. Play some golf," Dad says when I ask if I should help pack up our things at T.P.C. In the bedroom there are two large cardboard boxes full of Mum's things. I wonder if she'll be down to pick them up. I haven't seen her since I stood, all mussed up, with swimming goggles pushed up onto my forehead, at Simba Farm. The clothes would fit Irene.

I do a round of the golf course with Rogarth. Lose. Give Emmanuel all the money I have as tip. Go back to the house. Now there's a Nordic Project Land Rover parked outside, and Dad is lugging boxes and bags into it with Thorleif.

"So, are you ready for the big city then, Christian?" he asks.

"Absolutely," I say. I'm looking forward to it. Moshi. It'll be cool. I go into the house.

"I think I have everything," Dad says. I take a quick look through the bedrooms. The two cardboard boxes are still there – closed. It seems we're not taking them.

"What's going to happen with those boxes?" I ask. Dad shrugs:

"It's . . . I don't know," he says and goes outside.

"Irene," I call.

"What?" she says.

"Come." Unfortunately Irene isn't coming to Moshi. The Mærsk man who takes over Dad's job will be down with his wife and two children. They'll inherit her. She'll be a very well-dressed house girl.

Dad is outside, chatting to the guard. He gives him some money, and then we're off.

The house in Moshi is an old villa in the colonial style, situated where the road forks between the city centre and my school – not far from Uhuru Hotel. I get a large room, and we inherit a friendly, elderly cook called Juliaz from the previous owners. Yes. I'm looking forward to living in Moshi.

I get to know Sharif from the school football team. A striker. His parents emigrated from Yemen and live in Mwanza. Sharif is staying with his uncle. He has thick, longish, shiny black hair. Nimble. The girls love him. Finnish Katja in particular, who's got the best breasts at school. Sharif is picked up by a younger uncle after football practice, and they give me a lift down Lema Road to the corner of Kilimanjaro Road where they live.

"Come round sometime. I live right where the road forks," I say, pointing. "You can come by for supper any time."

"You do know I'm Muslim? I don't eat pork," he says.

"We don't always eat pork, you know," I say.

"No, no," he says. It takes a while but one Saturday afternoon he shows up. I can hear him calling from the road:

"Christian? You there?"

"Yes," I shout.

Juliaz has gone home. He comes in the mornings and makes a hot meal for our lunch. We do our own supper.

"Can Sharif stay for supper?" I ask the old man.

"Yes, of course," he says, getting up from his chair, putting his *Economist* down. I don't know what he had planned to make for supper, but now he kicks into action.

"Is your dad going to be cooking?" Sharif asks sceptically.

"He does know how to," I say. "The cook's gone home."

"In Denmark – does the man cook?" Sharif asks.

"Your cook's a man, isn't he?" I say.

"Yes, but he's a cook," Sharif says.

"Come on," I say and go into the kitchen. The old man is kneading dough.

"Sharif is a Muslim," I say in English.

"Don't worry," Dad says, looking at Sharif. "We're not having pork." Dad starts telling Sharif how – back in the day – people used to pickle pig's trotters in Denmark. "My grandmother used to make them for me. Barbaric, don't you think?" Dad smiles. Sharif laughs.

Saturday afternoon Marcus takes me with him down to the Y.M.C.A. There's a kiddie disco. His girlfriend Rosie is there with her friend Claire. Music is playing in the large sports hall where they sometimes have boxing practice.

"Let's dance," Marcus says and moves his body to the rhythm without lifting his feet.

"Yes," Rosie says and looks at me. "You can dance with Claire."

"I'm white – I can't dance," I say, even though I learned with Irene at T.P.C. – but I've never danced in front of other people.

"Everyone can dance," Marcus says. "It's like walking, but at the same time you think about a naked woman, and suddenly you're walking in a sexy way – that's dancing."

"Enough!" Rosie says, slapping him. Claire doesn't do anything. The sun is shining outside. It's very light in here. Rosie starts dancing to one side of the room. Marcus is moving without moving. Claire gives me a look and I don't know what it means. Then Marcus takes Rosie's hand, says something; they come over and take my hands and Claire's and pull us out onto the floor. O.K., I'll give it a go. I feel stiff, angular, awkward. Stupid. I'm like my dad. I'll be up against the wall in any room where there's dancing. I'll try to start a conversation with anyone and everyone, male, or ugly, or both – just to seem busy, so I look like I know what I'm doing.

Marcus can surrender to the music like he's dreaming his way into it – it's not an act. I've seen it in the residential areas at T.P.C. – the children dance from when they are very young. When I move, I'm constantly thinking about how it looks to others. Marcus comes over to me:

"Your hips," he says. "They have to feel like they're on ball bearings; up, down, round everywhere." He's moving. I can't.

"I'm too white," I say in Swahili. Rosie dances over to me. Puts her hands on my hips, tries to move them around. I think about how it looks – look round. The only white man in the room. A couple of the girls are laughing. Are they looking at me?

"I can't do this," I say, but Rosie doesn't let go. She moves me round with her hands, while shifting me about with her own pelvis. And I think about her naked. I move with her. Later we sit, drinking Cokes and smoking cigarettes in the café. Irene did teach me something. Perhaps I can dance like a white negro.

The summer holiday is only a couple of days away. We're having supper. I do my prep. Peer into the sitting room:

"I'm going to down to see Marcus," I say.

"O.K.," Dad says. "Don't be home late. Tomorrow's the last day before the holidays."

"Righto," I say and am out of there. A short walk and I am in Marcus' room behind the Larssons' house. We listen to Black Uhuru, smoke cigarettes until it's time for me to go home.

"I'll walk you," Marcus says.

"There's no need," I say.

"Yes, it's dangerous if I don't," he says.

"Relax. There's street lights all the way."

"Yes – big problem. Anyone can see your colour under those lights," Marcus says. We go up the narrow path to Kilimanjaro Road and say goodnight at the top. Marcus waits for me to turn up the drive before leaving. The dogs don't bark. They know my steps by now and run to greet me silently. I look towards the niche in the servants' quarters, but I can't see Zaidi, the night guard. Perhaps he's doing his rounds. I go through the front door. The lights are on, but it's very quiet. Down the hall, opening the sitting-room door. Dad is lying on the sofa, his eyes closed and his mouth open. There's a glass with a little golden fluid on the coffee table: whisky. But something's not right. I look towards the veranda door, which has been left open to let in a bit of air, but the net screen . . . it's been cut, and a large triangle of it is hanging down. I look around. "Dad," I say. The large Sony shortwave radio has gone, but the B. & O. stereo is still there. "Dad," I say again, shaking his shoulder. He opens his eyes.

"What?" he says.

"The radio has gone." He sits up.

"What?" he says. Looks around.

"The netting," I say.

"I'll be damned," he says. "Where is Zaidi?"

"I couldn't see him when I got in." Dad gets up, goes to the net screen, puts his hand through the hole.

"Zaidi?" he shouts. The dogs come running, wagging their tails. Dad turns around, looks at the coffee table. "My whisky and tobacco pouch are gone," he says.

"Let's go outside for a look," I say.

"Yes," he says. We go outside and walk round the house. Wake up Phillippo the gardener.

"Zaidi was here when I went to bed," he says.

"Drat," Dad says.

"What?" I say.

"Yes, well, the dogs didn't start barking, so it must have been Zaidi," he says.

"Yes, of course it was," I say. "He must have seen you were asleep, cut open the netting and snuck in. If you had woken up, he could always say that he came to wake you because there were thieves outside." Dad looks at me.

"If I'd woken up, he would probably have given me a once-over with his *panga*," he says. He might be right. People say that Africans are excessively brutal when they're startled. There are stories of people who have pulled over at night because someone had left a felled tree across the road. They're butchered with *pangas* and their cars are nicked. There are stories of households that receive visits from robbers with lorries – they take everything, empty the whole house. Dad has told me that if that were to happen, we must immediately sit down in the corner and close our eyes, facing the wall, so we don't see them. We must tell them they are welcome to take it all. That way we won't get the chop. But there are always stories. If the old man were like the more paranoid whites, I'd never be allowed outside after dark. He has made me promise that if I run into thieves at night, I'll hand over my jeans, jacket and sneakers and walk home naked.

We go into the sitting room again.

"It's strange that he didn't take stereo," Dad says, looking at his B. & O.

"He can't have known what it was," I say. "When Marcus saw it, he thought it was a European Makonde."

Last day of school. Samantha comes out of a classroom. She's holding the strap of her shoulder bag in her hand and pulling it after her across the concrete decking.

"Samantha," Mr Harrison says behind her. She stops. Stands still without turning. Doesn't answer. "You should carry that bag properly." She turns, slowly.

"How do you carry it properly?"

"Pick it up," Mr Harrison says.

"That's for me to decide. It's my bag," she says.

"But it's the school's books," Mr Harrison says.

"Are you sure?" Samantha says.

"Do you actually want to be sent to the Headmaster?" Mr Harrison asks. Samantha shrugs. What will she do now? What will he do? She stands still, waiting. Mr Harrison looks impatient. He'd like nothing so much as a cup of coffee and a cigarette in the teachers' lounge. Break time is vanishing like sand between his fingers. Samantha is not in any way bothered. She's got all the time in the world. She goes to the toilets to smoke during lessons. It's hardly the most interesting confrontation in the world, but it's the best we've got at the moment. Fifteen or so pupils are watching developments, while keeping well clear. Then a smile spreads over Mr Harrison's face. He goes over to Samantha, takes the strap from her hand, lifts it over her head and positions her arm so her hand is resting on the bag – which hangs down with the strap between her breasts. Beautiful. "There," Mr Harrison says and pats Samantha's shoulder before hurrying towards the teachers' lounge without a backwards glace. Samantha stands there a moment. Then she grabs the strap, lifts it over her head and lowers the bag onto the concrete decking.

"Samantha," Gretchen says, shaking her head.

"Would you carry a mangy dog like that?" Samantha asks and starts walking again, dragging the bag behind her. A Norwegian chap from her class goes up behind her and gives the bag a hard kick, laughs as it swings up into the wall.

"Idiot," Samantha says and swings the bag hard. The Norwegian chap jumps out of the way, so Samantha misses her mark, but she steams on, letting it twirl full circle above her head before it slams into the Norwegian bloke's neck.

"Samantha!" Mr Thompson's voice. Everyone freezes. Samantha turns her head towards it. "My office. Now!" Thompson jerks his head. "You too," he tells the Norwegian, who straight away starts moaning. I want to hug her. Samantha shrugs and goes towards the office. She drags the bag behind her across the concrete decking. I'd like to talk to her – say any old nonsense. But I can't. Annemette's death and the mess my parents have made – it all adds up to my being an outsider at school. The only thing I've got is football. And now it's the summer holidays, and Dad's working, so I'll be on my own. Luckily, there's always Marcus.

Marcus

THE PILL

Christian and *bwana* Knudsen have moved to Moshi, not far from the Larsson house. It's holidays at I.S.M., so all the kids are home. *Bwana* Knudsen practically lives at the bar at Moshi Club, and Christian comes to visit me in the evenings. We listen to music and smoke cigarettes. I do dance practice with my white daughters; Christian plays Ludo with Solja – being a babysitter isn't nearly as tedious now.

But even though it's holiday, I have a lot of work, because Asko has gone to Finland to negotiate with F.I.N.I.D.A., the Finnish equivalent of S.I.D.A. And once again Tita's plug is acting up. She picks me up from the Larssons' in her big Mercedes-Benz.

"Do you have all your tools?" she asks before we get into the car. Even without tools I can fix her problem, because the remedy lives in my trousers. Tita has given the house girl the day off, and the gardener has been sent into town. She takes me into her bedroom and undresses me. I open the drawer to put on a sock.

"There's no need," Tita says. "I'm on the pill." Usually Tita wants to be on top, but today she's on her back, very quiet and concentrated – almost a crazy look in her eyes. I shoot my load, and she holds me fast with her legs. "You must stay inside me," she says. Her eyes are leaky. *Tsk*, this work is confusing me. A few minutes later the limp pump can be pulled out of the flower, and Tita brings me a large gin and tonic – my reward. "I'm going to take you home now," she says. But her car goes the wrong way. She drives down Uru Road until she stops and points out a house.

"That's where Asko's whore lives," she says. "He pays her rent, so he can come and visit her whenever he wants." I don't say anything – it's no news to me. Tita turns the car and takes me home.

DANCING TO THE DRUMS

Alwyn started exporting spiritual Africafé to Mika in Finland before he himself was sent to dairy school in Denmark to learn how to make cheese for the black man. Now he's back. But his little brother stayed in Denmark and married the daughter of a man who invented a kind of cheese wrapped in plastic called Lillebror – Little Brother – which tastes like foul air – I've tasted it at the Larssons'. I hear that Alwyn will be running a disco at Liberty. He has rented a ghetto in town behind the Air Tanzania offices at Clock Tower. I go there. Alwyn is wearing the smart clothes; he's got girls like flies around him – he's got it all; a stereo with powerful speakers and unbelievable music on L.P.: Peter Tosh, Bob Marley, Burning Spear, Pablo Gad, Black Uhuru, Linton Kwesi Johnson, Pablo Moses, Gregory Isaacs. Even a big fridge with a freezer and a T.V. set and a video machine. Phantom has come as well to admire the abundance. Alwyn has grown long dreadlocks.

"Welcome home," I say.

"Marcus," Alwyn says. My eyes are bright with envy. "Would you like a Coke?" Alwyn asks and goes to the fridge. I am hypnotized by the stereo.

"How did you make enough money to buy it?" I ask. He comes over and stands next to me and we let the nice sound wash over us. Alwyn says, loud enough for everyone to hear:

"I taught African tribal dance."

"Get out of here," I say.

"It's true. At community college. Just I shake my black arse, the white girls go crazy. Loads of money and pale papaya."

"But you don't know how to drum," I say.

"I beat the drum, primitive-style, like a barbaric negro, and shouted at the top of my voice in Swahili – they thought it was great," Alwyn says with a big grin. It's fantastic. I can go to Europe as well – to Sweden – if Jonas Larsson opens his heart and gives me the chance.

"So are you going to make cheese now?" I ask.

"Cheese? No, I can't be bothered with that work," Alwyn says. *Eeehhh*, his father will be angry.

"Why didn't you marry a white girl?" I ask.

"It's too cold up there. You could climb into a fridge, shut the door, live there. The fridge would be warmer than Europe. It's like a freezer. It'll turn you into an ice cube."

We have pilaf delivered from a street kitchen round the corner.

"Go to Coffee House and get us a taxi," Alwyn tells Phantom, who runs off at once. Alwyn goes inside and takes the stereo apart. The taxi arrives. Phantom helps load the stereo into the car. I lend a hand as well. And then Alwyn drives off to Liberty. No room for me or Phantom – we have to walk on our legs.

"Damned rich-boy," Phantom says.

"Yes," I say. We help Alwyn carry his decks inside, set it up – just to touch those fine machines is a pleasure. And we get free access to the disco. Alwyn is up there in the glass cage, playing the crisp music. The girls are flies around a fresh cowpat. Alwyn gives us beers – the big man. Late at night we pack up, carry things out to the taxi. The decks can't be left at Liberty – they'd be gone before morning. Alwyn pays for an extra taxi with room for the girl he has chosen, and for us, so we can help him carry his decks into his ghetto. When we are done, Phantom lights a stick of *bhangi*, which we share while the girl waits for Alwyn in his bed. Alwyn grabs his pump through the fabric of his trousers:

"White women can't make love like a Chagga girl," he says and, grinning, hands the spliff back to Phantom and says goodnight, shooing us out. We're left on the street as he goes to the girl in his bed.

Christian

Marcus takes me into town on the back of his motorbike and introduces me to Phantom – a Rasta guy who has a tiny kiosk at the entrance to the market.

"Do you have dollars?" Phantom asks.

"No," I say.

"I can give you a good price," he says.

"Yes, but I haven't got any," I say.

"Phantom knows everything about the black market," Marcus says.

"How about *bhangi*?" I ask, because my dad has talked about how he smoked *bhangi* with John one night, and he'd like to try it again, he just doesn't know where to get it. Phantom raises his eyebrows.

"*Bhangi*?" he asks.

"Yes," I say.

"You haven't got any dollars, I haven't got any *bhangi*," Phantom says. I leave with Marcus.

"What do you want with *bhangi*?" he asks.

"It's for my dad. He'd like to try it, and I thought I'd give it to him as a present."

"Alright," Marcus says. "I'll get you some."

The next time I see him, he gives me a cigarette pack with four spliffs. I go home and wrap it up in some gift paper and give it to my dad. He unwraps it.

"What am I supposed to do with these?" he asks.

"You said you'd like to try it," I say. "So I got you some."

"How?" he asks. I shrug.

"Down at the market," I say.

When the old man isn't in, I go in and trawl through his drawers. I find an envelope with quite a bit of U.K. money. I take a few of the smaller banknotes. Go down to Phantom.

"Will these do?" I ask.

"Yes, they're fine," he says and explains the black market currency exchange rates to me – gives me a load of shillings. I don't know if he's fair. I will have to look into it. But now I have money to burn – loads of it.

Sharif is still in town. He bests me at squash at Moshi Club. We have to play through the worst heat of the day, at two, because we are considered children – we can't get a game at the squash court when it's cooler. We sweat. Afterwards we sit in the spectators' seats, drinking passion-fruit juice and smoking cigarettes. We have the place to ourselves until around four.

"You can come have supper with us if you like," Sharif says.

"I'd like that," I say.

I write a note to the old man and go over to Sharif's late in the afternoon. Shake hands with his uncles and aunts.

"*Salaam aleikum*," I say.

"*Aleikum salaam*," they say.

We go to Sharif's room at the back of the house. He has a wardrobe, a bed, a small desk, a dining-room chair and an easy chair. There's a Koran on his bedside table.

"Do you read it?" I ask.

"Yes, a little bit every day."

"Can we smoke?" I ask.

"Wait until it's dark. Then we can go to the bottom of the garden."

"O.K.," I say.

We're called to dinner. The youngest girl in the family ladles out chicken soup for the men – the oldest is served first. The soup is eaten with a spoon – there's no other cutlery. On the table are bowls of basmati rice, a thick beef stew, a spicy vegetable dish, a plate of chapattis.

"You have to learn how to eat with your hand," the youngest uncle tells me. Sharif grins. His uncle shows me how. "You'll get the hang of it," he says.

"Alright," I say, feeling awkward, because my hand is covered in sauce.

"Time to wash your hands," he says, patting my back. Sharif laughs at me.

"*Mwarabu*," he says. We go out for a smoke. The cook calls to us, and we have cinnamon tea with milk and sugar before I go home.

I'm hanging out by the school swimming pool. It's mostly kids with their mothers. I'm bored silly. Wish the holidays were over. Sharif has gone off in one of his uncle's lorries to see his parents in Mwanza.

"I'm bored," I tell Dad at night.

"I'm afraid I can't take any holiday now, because Thorleif will be going home soon and we have to finish the handover," Dad says. I shrug. He gives me an odd look. "You could visit your mum," he says.

"Are you going to make me?" I ask.

"No," he says. "But she did call."

"She'll have to make it up to me first," I say. Dad shakes his head in despair.

"Do you want me to tell her that?" he asks and raises his shoulders as if to say he's giving up, but he can't help smiling.

"I can tell her that myself," I say.

"Are you going to call her then?" he asks.

"No," I say.

"What then?"

"She's the one who has to apologize – I'm not going to do anything," I say.

Early next morning I am sitting drinking coffee in the kitchen when a car honks outside. I get up and go outside. Mum is getting out of a Land Rover – Léon is behind the wheel.

"Hi, Christian," she says, wringing her hands as she takes a few steps towards me.

"What do you want?" I ask. She sends a quick look back at Léon.

"We wanted to ask you if you'd like to come up to the first cabin."

"With you guys?" I ask.

"Yes," Mum says.

"With that guy?" I ask, nodding towards Léon.

"Christian, come on. Don't be like that," Mum says.

"Not on your life," I say and go inside. If she follows me, I'm going to ask her to leave – it's not her house. But the Land Rover starts and drives off.

Dad hands me a small, folded-up piece of tartan cardboard.

"There you are," he says. I open it.

"A driver's licence," I say.

"You do realize you are only sixteen, don't you?" Dad says.

"Yes," I say, smiling at him. It's for a motorbike. He's bribed a policeman. According to the licence I'm eighteen.

"So, you'll be careful," Dad says.

"But . . . what will I drive?" I ask.

"John knows some Germans outside Arusha who have a motorbike for sale. We'll go see them tomorrow," Dad says.

The next morning we drive to Mountain Lodge on the south slopes of Mount Meru – a small, upscale hotel. The seller turns out to be Mick from school, who is going to Germany and needs to get some cash together.

It's a Spanish bike – a Bultaco 350cc. Red.

"Be careful on the throttle," Mick says. "It's quite fierce."

"I will," I say and get up on it. Dad pays and we drive back – him in the car, and me on the motorbike. You can't get crash helmets in Tanzania.

Wind in my hair. It's fabulous. I make sure not to give in to the temptation of overtaking Dad in the car. The rules for my bike are laid down that night. I'm only allowed to drive it during the day. And only to park it in safe places like at school, at Moshi Club, and with friends who have guards.

The next day Marcus introduces me to a motorbike mechanic right across from Liberty on Station Road.

"Don't take your motorbike out at night. All the robbers will be waiting for you in the dark," the mechanic says. "Including me." He grins.

"What does your father think?" Marcus asks.

"If you don't want to come, I'll just go myself," I tell him. I want to go to Liberty – the leading disco in town – to see what it's like. "I've got money to pay for us," I add, because I haven't yet spent the money from currency exchange Phantom sorted for me.

"Alright then," Marcus says. Rosie comes over, and we go there together. I'm the only white person there – that goes without saying. I go to the bar and buy us beers. I go out and dance with Rosie. The D.J. is a former I.S.M. pupil who was sent to Denmark to be trained at a dairy. Alwyn – that's his name. Marcus takes me to the D.J. cage right under the ceiling.

"With a stereo like that I could do quite well for myself, just doing discos around town and running a recording shop making cassettes for people," Marcus says.

"Really?" I say, because the stereo is alright but nothing special.

"Yes," Marcus says. We go back down. More beers. Rosie pulls me out onto the floor. The girls sit in pairs at tables along the back wall; they smile and laugh because the white boy is dancing with the black girl. I'm laughing as well. A young girl looks at me, I think. I look at her. I wish I had the guts to go up to her and ask her to dance. I don't. I drink more beer.

"We'd better get home," Marcus says. I have enough money for a taxi, so Marcus and Rosie get out on the way, and I sneak into the house. A strip of light is visible under the door. I'm not so late home. It's the holidays. Strange that he isn't at the club getting drunk. I open the door slightly and peer in. The smell of burning weed – *bhangi!* – Dad is stoned. He squints.

"Good evening," he says.

"Hi," I say. "Just thought I'd say goodnight." The room is thick with smoke, and the spliff crackles in his hand.

"Come on in," he says.

"I'm tired."

"Come on in and let me look at you," he says. I open the door a little more.

"No, I really do have to get some sleep." I don't want to come too close, because then he might smell beer on me.

"You look like your mother," he says.

"I don't look like her," I say.

"You have her eyes," he says.

"But what they see is very different," I say.

"Somehow I don't think so," Dad says.

"You're wrong," I say and shut the door. I go to bed. Lie down. I'm dizzy with fatigue. The bed starts spinning. My stomach. Everything is spinning. I try to hold it still. No, must . . . vomit is coming into my throat. I only just manage to get my legs out of bed, and as they hit the floor, I lean over and puke – a cascade. Stop. Going towards the door, I retch again. Open the door, am sick in the corridor just outside the toilet. Stagger in and raise the toilet seat. All that's left now is spit and spasms. Reel out into the corridor. Good job the floor is concrete. The sitting-room door opens, light spills into the hall. Dad stands in the doorway, looking at me.

"I'll get a bucket and a rag," he says and goes towards the kitchen. I stay where I am. Listen to the tap running in the kitchen. He returns. Puts the bucket of steaming water down – a rag is floating around in it. "Wipe it off," he says, gesturing with his hand, before turning on his heel and going back to the sitting room, closing the door behind him. I slide to my knees, wring out the rag, wipe up the sick, allow it to dissolve in the water in the bucket, wring out the rag again. More sick is welling into my mouth – overpowering, there was more. That too must be wiped up – all the way back to bed. The sick trail. Empty the bucket into the loo, spit. Dump the rag in the laundry basket. Squirt a bit of toothpaste on my finger and put it in my mouth, working it round with my tongue. Rinse with water. Spit out toothpaste slime into the basin, feel the taste of gall at the back of my throat – it itches. Let my hand run along the wall as I go back towards my room. The sitting-room door opens. Dad looks, nods. "Sleep tight," he says. I continue back to my bed. Keel over.

Marcus

MUHAMMAD ALI

"But can I not go for training in Sweden later, then?" I ask Jonas on the veranda. "After that I could do a good job for you on the project in Moshi."

"Sweden?" he says. "You said you wanted to go to school, and my aunt Elna is willing to help pay the fees. But you're Tanzanian, so you'll go to school in Tanzania."

"But schools here are no good," I say.

"If you do very well at school, I may be able to get you some work with the project afterwards," Jonas says. Katriina comes out to us:

"You still have your room here – we're not chasing you off," she says.

"But you have to go now," Jonas says. "We don't need you tonight."

I go to my ghetto. Tsk – I'm eighteen years old and have completed school with fairly good grades from Kibo Secondary School – I need to move on in life. But now they want to put me out to pasture in the useless Tanzanian high school.

Christian comes to my door, while the smooth Swedish ABBA music pours from the house.

"Let's get out of here," I say. We walk to the city centre in the dark. I am hungry. Outside the ABC Theatre we buy Tanzanian hotdogs – yams grilled over charcoal. "I need to talk to the D.J. from Liberty," I say, and we go to Alwyn's ghetto. Eeehhh – the T.V. set is on with a video.

"Sit down," Alwyn says – he likes having people round, because how can materialism give great confidence unless poor people watch it with envy? I swallow the lump that is my pride:

"Do you need an extra man for your work at Liberty and the recording business?" I ask.

"No," he says and smiles nastily. Christian is already sitting in front of the television. The video machine is playing an old boxing match. The one where Muhammad Ali beats up George Foreman in Zaire, 1974.

The Congolese side with Ali – Foreman is beaten. We walk back in the dark.

Christian

Dad throws a farewell dinner for Thorleif. He's invited an Icelandic couple and their daughter who have come up from Iringa – the man works for Nordic Project as well. The daughter's called Sif. She's eighteen months younger than me and has come to enrol at I.SM. as a boarder in the year below me. Sif is tiny, with very black hair, a very white face and small, pretty features. Except for her eyes, which are large and dark.

"What's the school like?" the Icelandic mother asks.

"It's fine," I say, looking at Sif, who's huddled in the corner. "Don't worry. People are nice."

"Alright," she says.

"Now at least you know Christian," her father says. "Then he can give you a hand if you need any help. Can't you, Christian?" Does he want me to be his daughter's minder?

"Yes, of course," I say. Then the grown-ups start talking politics. And I try to tell her a bit about school. She doesn't ask me anything, just nods a bit. So I tell her anything and everything I can think of.

"I just need to pop outside for a minute," I say after dinner, because I have a feeling the Icelanders will give Dad a hard time if they see me smoking. They're already giving him a once-over for his conservative political views.

"Where are you going?" Sif's mum asks.

"To water the dog," I say.

"I'll come with you," Sif says.

Once outside I go round the back of the house and light a cigarette. Hand it to her.

"Care for a smoke?" I ask.

"No, thank you," she says. That's the extent of our conversation. Not long after the Icelanders leave to go to Hotel Marangu, where they're staying the night before going up to the first cabin tomorrow.

"I'll see you at school," Sif says.

"Yes, see you," I say.

"Showed you, didn't they?" Thorleif says to Dad.

"Yes, they were a bit sanctimonious, weren't they?" Dad says. I light a cigarette, take a large gulp from Dad's glass. He raises his eyebrows but doesn't say anything.

"Originally they came down to work for Action Aid, before he got that new job," Thorleif says.

"That goes a long way towards explaining things," Dad says.

"At first they meant to live like the locals, no cook, no nothing. These days they drink whisky from Ostermann like the rest of us," Thorleif says.

"What made them change their mind?" I ask.

"The absurdity of it all," Thorleif says. "Sif is going to be boarding at I.S.M. now – the fees alone would feed an entire village. And that money counts as part of what we call our aid to Tanzania. When you have to accept that you're part of the aid industry, you might as well wash away the nasty taste with whisky." Thorleif raises his glass. "Cheers," he says.

Year Ten. The teachers give us loads of prep from day one. I see Sif in the hall, but I don't go over and talk to her. That Friday there's a party at school to mark the start of the academic year.

"So, do you still have the hots for Shakila?" Samantha asks.

"Shut up, will you?" I say. I have the hots even more for Samantha, but I don't know what angle to work. Stefano dances with her. Later Samantha dances with Savio, while Stefano stands around moping. She seems to be making him jealous on purpose. Panos would like to dance with Truddi, who comes up to me and says:

"So, Christian, are you going to ask me to dance? Or are you afraid?" And so I dance with her, even though I think she's a slag. And Panos is ticked off. But he gets a grip and asks Diana to dance, because Diana is Truddi's best friend, and Panos will do anything to get close to Truddi. I watch the others out of the corner of my eye. After dancing with Irene and getting in more practice with Marcus and Claire and Rosie at the Y.M.C.A., I move pretty well. I see Sif huddled up against the wall with a friend. She's looking at me. I look away. Soon after, the party ends. The boarders must go back to their houses. The day pupils must go to the car park to be picked up.

I smoke a cigarette with Panos and Jarno under the banana palms behind the dining hall. Panos is quiet.

"Shit," is all he says.

"Too right," is all I say. Jarno is famous for saying nothing at all. The local cigarettes are terrible; the tobacco has been sprayed with D.D.T. and is packed so loosely that the cigarette will smoke itself if you forget to inhale for a second. Jarno stubs his out against the face of his watch – classy.

Marcus

LUTHERAN PRISON

I go to high school at Makumira, a Lutheran boarding school near Arusha. I get support from Aunt Elna, and at school there is an elderly English lady I met when I lived with the Reverend. I was christened a Catholic, but who can tell the difference? They'll look after me. I think Jonas prays I have left the family even though I still have my ghetto behind the house.

I am the young pupil who becomes slave to the older pupil. His room: I must clean it. His clothes: I must wash them. His shoes: I must polish them while he sits drinking *gongo* and smoking *bhangi* at the local hangout. I do everything he asks, so he won't beat me hard. I am afraid. One day in dining hall, I see my neighbour from the dormitory covered in blood, because he wouldn't obey. I am not used to living like that, like a whipped dog. Right away I run to the English lady and tell her everything I've seen; I don't want to stay at school.

In Moshi I explain it to the Larssons.

"O.K.," Jonas says. "If you can't handle going to school, you'll have to work for the project, and later you might even get to go to the sawmill school in Sweden."

"Yes," I say. But Jonas doesn't work for F.I.T.I, the forestry school, anymore. The portable sawmills have opened in West Kilimanjaro. I must work in the office in Moshi, which will deal with marketing, accounts and administration. Jonas has rented a logging site at the plywood factory in Boma la Mbuzi, not far from Pasua – that's where the house will be built. But it's not ready yet.

Once again I am stranded in the Larsson house. They want me to look after Solja and Rebekka and organize the house with guards and gardeners. Katriina doesn't like giving orders, and Jonas still speaks Swahili like a deaf man. He's away a lot as well, because he goes to Dar and Mbeya with Asko – they go to look at other people's sawmills.

It's up to me to wake Solja up in the morning, make her packed lunch, take her to school, get the gardener to work, go to the market and get food for everyone's mouths, pump Tita's papaya in every break I have, prepare dinner and food for the dog and coffee for the guard – everything.

DOGSBODY

After a while I start working for the project, attending to the stockroom – looking after spare parts and work wear. Everything comes from Sweden, so I make sure we have burglar-proof facilities built, complete with shelves and big padlocks.

A few days later everyone from administration goes into town for a meeting at F.I.T.I. Asko, who is now in charge, speaks about how some of us will be sent to Sweden later on to learn things. Everyone would like to be the one to go.

"But it won't be until later, when the project is running smoothly – we'll need to have a number of people trained up so they can take over our jobs when we go home. We're talking training in Tanzania, but also in Sweden."

The casual labourers live up on West Kilimanjaro. For a while we spend our time building a village for them. We're constantly having to get building materials – windowpanes, nails, screws and rafter fittings. I can find all that in Moshi and Arusha, but sheet metal for the roofs is hard to come by; the project tries to procure them from Sweden, but it's too expensive so we get them from Kenya instead. In principle the border's closed, which means we have to go through all sorts of bureaucracy. My work is split between Moshi and West Kilimanjaro. I make sure things are running smoothly in West Kili – I go there on my motorbike three or four times a week. Find out what they need, find the goods in Moshi, transport them there – chains for chainsaws or new driving belts for the sawmills – the main saw is pulled by a belt drive from a SCANIA diesel engine which once used to run a lorry in Sweden and now lives in a patched-up wooden shed in Tanzania. The casual labourers are paid every two weeks. There is an accountant in the office in Moshi, but to save expenses I take the money with me on my visits. It's a secret between me and the office – all the bandits think the money is sent in a project car. Then suddenly, there I am on my motorbike with loads of money for the workers.

Afterwards the workers ask me for favours – one of them needs painkillers, another needs a lotion for his wife's eczema, a third has a watch whose arms have stopped moving. I must fix it all in Moshi. Or there might be a question concerning the business. My role is key. How can a forest worker talk to his Swedish boss, when the boss is in Moshi Club nursing his beer? The foreman of the casual labourers, *bwana* Omary, comes to me:

"You must speak to *bwana* Larsson. We're told to wear car-tyre sandals while the Tretorn boots the Swedes sent us are being sold in Arusha."

"I will be your advocate to *bwana* Larsson," I say. Omary has more problems:

"The forest boss says we must trim the branches with an axe and a saw as if we were still in colonial days, because the boss has sold the petrol for the chainsaws," he says.

"This is very wrong," I say. "I will say it right into the Swedish ear when I get back." Omary is satisfied, because the Swede can condemn the living to death, and Marcus is a small stick that can be used to knock on fate's door.

I go on living in my ghetto all that time. At West Kili they have a shortwave radio so they can call on Jonas if their problem is serious. Sometimes I have to get up at four or five and get myself to West Kili – almost 110 kilometres. The road is dreadful – you almost have to make your own way. When the rain comes, it's hell.

One good thing: I have been almost part of the family: used as a nanny, a gardener, a worker, gigolo to their friend, everything – but not a penny for my pocket. Now I'm paid.

CAREER MOVE

Finally one night I'm not working, so I take Rosie on the back of my motorbike to visit my former classmates at Nechi's family home. Edson the Acrobat sits with his head in his hands and can hardly speak to us.

"What's happened to him?" I ask Nechi.

"Edson has been wicked with a girl, so now she's big-bellied, and he's being forced to marry her," Nechi says.

Edson shakes his head and looks at Rosie, who he used to chase:

"Now Rosie has captured my old friend Marcus, who is on his way to Europe with the Swedish ticket, perhaps with Rosie in his hand luggage. And I am stranded with the G.M.'s wicked secretary from TanScan – tsk. And I can't even afford the rent."

"If you plant a seed when you make trouble, you have to tend the plant," Rosie says. I don't say anything because I don't like this talk of Sweden in Rosie's ear – she'll be very demanding. I change the subject:

"Has Big Man Ibrahim found work after school?" I ask. Tiny tar-black Vicky has the answer:

"He's working for his uncle. If anyone owes his uncle money, Ibrahim goes and shakes them up a bit," Vicky says. "How about you? How are you doing?" she asks.

"We might go on holiday to Dar es Salaam soon," Rosie says. "But right now Marcus is very busy with his sawmill project."

Ah, this Rosie is very quick to dream. Only her friend Claire doesn't say anything – her family is very poor, so she works as a house girl for an Australian family.

FURNITURE FACTORY

The sawmills on West Kilimanjaro make good money, and the project is expanded through the purchase of a building close to the Kibo Match plant – Imara Furniture Factory, right on Karanga River, the machinery is absolute rubbish. It was nationalized at the beginning of the 1970s and has been run to the ground. The only things working are the walls, the roof and the concrete floor. The Swedes order machinery to make furniture, and after several months it arrives; the furniture production begins slowly with staff trained at F.I.T.I. Things are going well. We even export shelves to a big company in Sweden called IKEA. Other furniture is sold to ambassadors in Dar. Lots of orders.

BAOBAB THIGHS

"Today *mama* Mtawali, our G.M.'s wife will be here," Jonas says at the office. Right away I am alert. The G.M. is the General Manager – the boss to the bosses – and his wife is a very influential person. "She owns a furniture factory not far from Mwanza – I want you to help her," Jonas says.

"What do you want me to do?" I ask at once.

"She needs ideas for new furniture – designs."

"But the G.M.'s wife is our competitor. Why should we help her?" I ask.

"We're an aid project – so it's only right that we should help her private initiative," Jonas says – I suspect he has a shady agreement with the G.M. over all that money that – according to the paperwork – is spent on educating workers but which in reality lives in Jonas' own pocket.

It's a big old *mama* who arrives at the office.

"I want brochures on all the furniture you produce, and pictures of other Western furniture to get new ideas. You must put together a folder for me."

"No problem," I say.

"Do you know where I live?" she asks.

"Yes – I know the house," I say.

"Just come round and drop it off when you're done."

I start putting together pictures and drawings from our office, and at the Larsson house I cut out pictures from old Ostermann catalogues and Scandinavian magazines and different furniture catalogues and paste them onto cardboard. I put together a pretty folder, because the old *mama* is the G.M.'s wife – a powerful woman. When it's done, I go to her office in town.

"No," she says. "You must take it to my home, to my house." She doesn't even look at the folder.

"But why?" I ask.

"If the folder is in the office, someone will just take it. So you must bring it round to my house tonight."

"Yes, ma'am," I say, but it doesn't seem right. She's here, she's got a car, and I'm here with the folder. She could just take it home with her. I haven't got time tonight. "I could take it there now," I say.

"No," she says. "You must bring it round at nine and explain it all to me then. I haven't got time now. Then I'll tell my husband what a good job you've done." Her husband is the G.M. of all of S.I.D.A.'s sawmill projects in Tanzania. He's always in Dar es Salaam or Mwanza, never at home with his wife; she is old, she is fat. The G.M. is a *bwana mkubwa* with secretaries at the office who must go with him to towns where no-one knows him. The secretaries must help him with his paperwork at the restaurant, in the bar, in the hotel room.

At nine I go to her house, feeling nervous.

"Sit down," she says, pointing at the sofa and calling to the house girl. A relief – there's someone else here. The house girl brings us beer. "You can go to your room now," the old *mama* tells her. "I won't be needing you again." The old *mama* sits down next to me on the sofa, close, and leafs through the folder. Her thighs are large baobab trees in her tight dress. *Titi* like giant watermelons. Big paunch. Now I am even more nervous. "This is very good, your work. You are very good. If you do even better now, I will tell my husband you've been a big help to me." Now I am the fly in the spider's web. "You must have another beer," she says and gets up to fetch it herself. I drink while trying to talk about furniture. "You must have another beer," she says. As she walks towards the kitchen, her big arse wobbles. "You're a good boy," she says as she sit her big arse down next to me. She takes my hand and puts it on her thigh. "Do you like me?" she asks.

"Yes," I say. "You're a wonderful woman." Because I don't want to lose my job. So I let my hand run up the baobab thigh. "I like a woman who isn't just a stick. A woman like you where you can go on touching the lovely thighs, the plump breasts, the gorgeous bottom."

"*Ahhh,*" she moans and rubs my pump through the fabric of my trousers. And my pump is alive, filled with beer, even though I want it to be dead. "But you must go now," she says. "We can't be together here." I get up quickly; thank the Lord for the house girl – she might suspect us, and Moshi is only a small town. "But anytime you're in trouble, you just call me – this is my number." She gives me the number, and I hurry home. I'm already in trouble. I don't want to call. And I've heard of this problem before. *Bwana mkubwa* is married with children. And his wife – now she's old, she's fat, and he doesn't feel she gives him satisfaction. He is powerful and has money, but he can't divorce her, because that would give him a bad name. He runs around with his secretary. Or he buys *malaya* when he's away on business. His wife is in their hometown; she can't go to bars in their local area to look for men. There are male *malaya* as well, but she will lose her good reputation if people see that she is a bitch in heat. And she too misses the satisfaction. She must find another way – one that won't be noticed.

REPORTING

I stop my motorbike outside the veranda, ready for the interrogation. Jonas has been woken by the sound of the motorbike. The Swede has been very busy with life at Moshi Club. Now he grunts and rubs his eyes to get the old beer out. It's time for me to inform against all the negroes on the project who have acted against the Swedish world order on West Kili. The questions rain down on me: did the shipment of timber arrive?

Was the furniture collected and paid for? Did you get the wood glue? Did the head of accounts show up at work? Did he stay all day?

"Yes?" I say. How would I know? – I was only there three hours. The pay is not enough to live on – it's just a spice for the potatoes you must get from somewhere else. I was running all over town attending to my own business – recording cassettes, selling Carlsberg beer to wealthy Indians and pumping Tita – very frightening; I think there's a bump on her tummy.

Christian

Samantha and Tazim come by my place one Saturday – they've missed the school's pick-up. Tazim is nervous. I think she may have been crying.

"Could you give us a lift up to school?" Samantha asks.

"Yes, sure thing," I say. "But one at a time. Who wants to go first?"

"Tazim," Samantha says. I start the motorbike. Tazim gets up on the back.

"Back in a tick," I say to Samantha and then we're off.

"Drive safe," Tazim says.

"No," I say and go so fast she screams. But it's also so fast she has to hold on to me. I can feel her breasts against my back. Tazim is from Goa, Catholic – not like the other Indians. She has boyfriends, doesn't care about race. When I stop at the school car park, she leaps off and slaps my shoulder.

"I told you to drive safe," she says.

"You're very welcome," I say, smiling.

"Tsk," she says, smiling. Walks off. She has a very pretty bottom. I race home, turning the motorbike in the yard. Samantha is sitting in one of the chairs right outside the front door.

"Do you want a lift?" I ask.

"I'm in no hurry," Samantha says, staying right where she is.

"O.K.," I say. Brilliant. I flip down the kickstand and get off. "Can I get you anything?" I ask.

"Cigarettes and whisky," Samantha says. I laugh.

"The old man locks the bar cabinet, but cigarettes I can manage. Coke?"

"Yes," Samantha says. I go inside. She follows me, stands behind me when I open the fridge. It just so happens I promised Sif I'd come up to school to see her, but she never says anything. She just wants to walk with me to Mboya's at Kishari to buy fizzy drinks. I can kiss her – snog her. But every word must be wrung out of her.

"I want to see your room," Samantha says.

"Alright," I say, handing her a Coke and leading her down the corridor. Juliaz is in the sitting room, ironing. Samantha pops her head through the door and says hello. He asks if we'd like something to eat. "Are you hungry?" I ask Samantha.

"Always," she says.

"Yes, we'd like something to eat, please," I say in Swahili – as much as anything to show Samantha that my Swahili is good. I'm not as damned white as I look. She's lived here since she was three. We go to my room. I put on some music. Eddy Grant, which always reminds me of Irene. "Cigarettes," I say, pointing. "Help yourself." They're Marlboro. Samantha sits down on the bed, lights one.

"Mmmmm," she says, leaning back until she's lying flat on her back, taking a big drag, making her breasts rise. She looks up at the ceiling – I look at her breasts as she expels smoke rings. "They're nice, these Marlboro," Samantha says. I don't say anything. What should I say? That she looks good when she smokes? "Where are your parents?" she asks. I don't say anything. She must know only too bloody well that my mum's done a runner and is fucking Léon Wauters. She watches as I speed-smoke the cigarettes. Perhaps it's just as well to get it out there?

"My mum's playing at being a colonialist at a Dutch farmer's on West Kilimanjaro, and my dad is drinking."w

"Did your mum ... move out?" Samantha asks. Maybe she didn't hear. I take one final drag and go to the table.

"Yes. She's done a runner," I say, squashing the cigarette in the ashtray. "She thinks she ... What the hell do I know? I suppose she thinks that farmer is more ... something ... than my dad. More ... human. Or just more of a man."

"Is he?" Samantha asks.

"How would I know?" I say. "I'm seventeen years old."

"Has your dad gone native then?" Samantha asks.

"Gone native?" I ask.

"Started chasing black women?" Samantha asks. I shrug:

"I don't know," I say. Does it even matter? I can hear the old man's Land Rover in the drive. He brakes hard, turns off the engine, slams the door. I start counting out loud: "One, two, three, four, five . . ." The front door slams open, and he yells:

"How many times do I have to tell you not to park that sodding motorbike in the middle of the yard? One day I'll bloody well run it over."

"Translate," Samantha says. I translate for her as he comes down the corridor and opens the door. Then he sees Samantha lying on the bed. Dad doesn't know what to do next.

"Hello," he says, taking two steps into the room, shaking her hand. "Niels," he says. Samantha raises her upper body from the bed, shakes his hand.

"Cut out the shouting, will you?" I say in Danish. He gives me a look. Samantha puts out her cigarette. She doesn't have a smoking permit, and the old man is on the board, but he doesn't know whether she has one or not. He is too hungover to pay attention to such details.

"*Karibuni chakula*," Juliaz says in the hall – please eat.

"Would you like to stay for lunch?" Dad asks Samantha.

"Of course she's staying," I say.

Conversation is laboured. Something about school. Dad asks about their hotel in Tanga, and I'm afraid he'll make a fool of himself – insult Samantha by asking if the staff have improved. And she might tell the old man that her dad shags all the waitresses and ask him if he too has gone native. We eat quickly and take off. Samantha's hands are on my hips, lightly. We approach Lema Road. If we go to school, I'll be stuck with Sif for the rest of the afternoon. And if she sees me arriving with Samantha, it'll be one mopey Sif I'll have to contend with.

"Want to go to Moshi Club?" Samantha shouts. I slow down, stopping at the T-junction where Lema Road veers off to the right.

"You know, I really don't," I say. "Any minute now my dad will be going there to get plastered."

"But can't we go for a ride, then?" Samantha asks.

"Alright," I say and drive past the exit to Moshi Club and down across the old iron bridge over Karanga River. On the other side I rev up, so Samantha clasps her fingers over my stomach to stay in her seat. The air rips at us – it's cool. I drive past the back of Karanga Prison and onwards. The tarmac road is narrow but quite good. We drive past a gang of convicts in washed-out white overalls with a few guards. They're working on the road. If we continue for long enough, we'll hit the road north to West Kilimanjaro where my mum is living with that colonialist of hers. After a few kilometres we reach a village. I stop outside a kiosk.

"Have you got any money?" Samantha asks.

"Yes," I say.

"You've always got money," she says.

"I steal it from the old man," I say.

"Aren't you worried he'll find out?" Samantha asks.

"No, he's too hungover. I steal a little foreign currency he's got lying about," I say, paying for our fizzy drinks. Offer Samantha a cigarette. We smoke in silence.

"They're not even here," I say.

"Who?" Samantha asks.

"My parents," I say. "The . . . whites. It's got nothing to do with Africa. They move between their houses, their jobs, their clubs and the homes of the other white people. If someone really pushes the boat out, they go to the market with their cook or their gardener in tow, so he can lug their shopping back to their car."

"What's wrong with that?" Samantha asks.

"It's . . . They're in Africa – they know fuck-all about the Africans," I say.

"Do you think they're missing out on something?" Samantha asks.

"Yes, well . . ." I say.

"What?" Samantha says. Perhaps she's right.

"They might as well stay at home, then," I say.

"No, because they live like kings," Samantha says.

"Yes, but then it's really got nothing to do with aid for Africa, has it" I say. Samantha doesn't say anything.

"Have you . . . seen your mum?" she asks.

"I went up there – Marcus took me," I say.

"And?"

"She's a white farmer's wife these days. Super-colonialist. She's really going for it," I say and light another cigarette, so I won't have to say anything else – just smoke. Samantha doesn't say anything about her parents. I sit with my elbows resting on my knees so I can't see her. I call it like I see it:

"All of a sudden you discover your parents are idiots."

"Yes," Samantha says. "I don't bloody well want to be like that when I grow up – I'd rather not grow up, then."

"Yes," I say.

"Drag me all the way down here as a baby, and now they start talking about sending me to England. Do you want to go to Denmark?" she asks.

"I don't know, actually," I say.

"Hard to know what it'd be like, isn't it?" she says.

"Cold," I say.

"Yes," Samantha says. I turn my head and smile at her:

"Shall we?" I ask.

"Absolutely," she says. I hold on with my hands over her stomach, which is soft and warm, and I can feel the muscles right underneath. Samantha really goes for it – we're flying over the potholes in the road.

Marcus

PARASITES

Aunt Elna comes down for another visit. I almost miss her. Right away they pop her into the car with the children and go off on a long safari to Ngorongoro and Serengeti. But before she returns to Sweden she puts the question to me:

"What are your plans for the future, Marcus?"

What can I say?

She asks the Larssons while I am standing there:

"What have you planned to do for Marcus?

"He might be sent to Sweden for further education," Jonas says. "The project has a number of facilities."

"When will you send him?" Aunt Elna asks.

"That depends on Marcus. First he has to prove through his work that he is ready."

Prove? I have raised his children for two and a half years. You can't do anything for that long without proving your worth. If you live as a farmer for two and a half years and fail to reap any harvest, you'd be better offer digging yourself into the ground. But Jonas doesn't want to send me to Sweden. Then who would look after his children while he pumps in Majengo and drinks at Moshi Club?

The vibes I get from Jonas aren't good. He knows I understand everything about his activities outside the marriage bed. But he needs me as his secret spy in the project while he plays the field in Majengo. And I need him so I can live in my ghetto and inch my way closer to the plane to Sweden. The trap is perfect. We're going round in a ring – leaching off each other.

I am caught in another net as well. One Saturday *mama* G.M. orders me to be at Hotel Tanzanite at nine, room eighteen. I have to tell the Larssons the age-old lie: "My uncle in Arusha is sick and on his deathbed." I drive off to the ugliest job I have ever had to face, and I can't even speak the words. Horror.

THE PRICE OF LOVE
"Let's take the project car and go to Dar es Salaam on a mini-break," Rosie says. I know it's impossible, but I lie to her, even though it's wrong. I so dream of her pretty papaya that I can't help it.

"Yes, I'll check when that might be possible." The right answer. Five minutes later we are naked like children in bed. After making trouble we cuddle.

"You must have your own house soon," Rosie says. "It's not right that you should live like a house boy when you work so hard for the project."

"Yes," I say. *Tsk.* Nothing but problems.

THE HOLY SPIRIT
Tita comes round in her car. "Hi, Tita," I say.

"Hi, Marcus," she says, but goes straight to the house to see Katriina. I sneak round to the other side, to the window. Tita is crying.

"But that's lovely. I didn't think you were trying anymore," Katriina says.

"But, I don't even know . . ." Tita says.

"Perhaps it's the Holy Ghost?" Katriina asks. Tita laughs through her tears. The Holy Ghost? A chill comes over me, because I remember. How I pulled the pump out and the sock was drooping around the base. But I removed it quickly without saying anything to Tita, because we don't talk – we just pump. And I remember Tita speaking about the pill when she wanted me to pump and spray with no sock on. The Holy Ghost is Marcus Garvey Dread. Black Star Line.

"What are you going to do?" Katriina asks.

"You know, I don't even know if I want to have a child with him now, because he . . . he chases other women." Katriina doesn't say anything for a bit.

"Yes, men are terrible, but so long as it's not completely out of control, I suppose you just have to live with it," she says.

"I find that really hard," Tita says.

"But we live lovely lives here, don't we?" Katriina says. She's in that trap herself – two children and the life of a queen in Africa. What are her options if she rebels? "But . . ." Katriina says and stops. "Could it be someone other than Asko?"

"It might be," Tita says in a low voice.

"No! Who?" Katriina asks, giggling like a schoolgirl. Tita sighs.

"I don't want to mix you up in it as well," she says. Is Tita running around like a bitch in heat? Perhaps it's not me then.

GANGBANGERS

The G.M. is in Moshi to visit the project and see his family. As usual the phones aren't working.

"Marcus," he says, "you must go and tell my family I have arrived, so they can come pick me up." I do it. Damnation! If the G.M. discovers that I am his wife's gigolo, I am dead. He'll divorce his wife quietly; no-one will know why because the wife will not want to have her own disturbed randiness known. But I know everything – I will have to be removed. At the house I drive up to the veranda – two of her lazy children are sitting about doing nothing. *Tsk*, one of them is older than me – as a baby he drank from *mama* G.M.'s *titi*, and now she's forcing me to swing in them like a crazed monkey.

Mama comes out of the house on her baobab legs.

"What?" she says from the top of the stairs. I tell her the message. To her I am nothing but air, or perhaps a fly. She doesn't say thank you or give me a message to take back. She just tells her son he must go and pick up his father. Deranged.

My work is done for the day, so I go past the Y.M.C.A. to pick up Rosie from catering school, where she is learning how to run a hotel. I say hello to my former classmate Big Man Ibrahim, who has borrowed a car from his uncle – the car, in combination with fizzy drinks, is intended to impress a girl who is on the same course as Rosie. "We'll take my car and go to Liberty," he tells the girl. "Or I can take you home to your parents in my car." The whole time he's sitting playing with his car keys, so you can't help but imagine he's got a really big pump between his legs. We go outside and Rosie sits on the back of my bike – it's almost eight, and we're going to the Larsson house to find exciting food that might impress her. After the Y.M.C.A. gate we take a right up Kilimanjaro Road. At the bend on Uru Road we see felled trees on the road. Thieves, I think and hit the brakes; I must stop, I must turn; I must get us out of there. The street lights are dead – they have killed them with a stone's throw as a preparation for the robbery. You can't see what's at the side of the road. As I brake, the thieves pour from the shrubs with *pangas* and long sticks. A big stone hits me on my chest. They will do for us. *Eeehhhh*, we fly to one side and the motorbike to another. There's the pain of falling from trees, and the sound of the motorbike scraping over the tarmac.

"Thieves, thieves, thieves!" Rosie screams.

"Let's get out of here," a man shouts. We hear the motorbike starting again – before we have even got up it races off with two of the guys. The others disappear back into the shrubbery. Me and Rosie, we're hurt, have been struck down, badly. But we can stand. No bones broken. Can limp back to the Y.M.C.A. to seek help. Ibrahim is there. We get into his uncle's pick-up truck, start pursuing the motorbike. Ibrahim is driving ludicrously fast. But did the motorbike go straight on or up Sokoine Road or out into the bush? No-one can be sure. At the police station we report the assault, the robbery.

Ibrahim takes me back to my ghetto. Oh terror – my door has been broken open. My Boombox is gone. And my good Swedish T-shirts. Who can have done it? Is it Edson the Acrobat, who needs money for his rent now that he's got my G.M.'s secretary pregnant?

I can hardly walk, but the next day I go to the office – tell them of the unhappy events.

"How can you prove you didn't take it yourself?" the G.M. asks.

"There are witnesses," I say. "I reported it to the police at once."

"Those witnesses – are they people you know?"

"Yes. My girlfriend and a friend."

"They may be in league with you – then you sell the project's motor-bike and share the money." I lift up my shirt and show him the wound from the stone, the mark from the stick. "Perhaps your friends beat you to make it look real. I need proof from the police." Now I can lose my job and must also pay for the motorbike or go to prison. So I go to the police, feeling very frightened, because the police can beat you even if you're not the thief. You have lost your motorbike, and then you must pay the police to tell everyone that it is so, there really were thieves. The police go and search my ghetto – no motorbike there.

But fortunately the same thing has happened to three or four other motorbikes recently – or something similar; it even happened to a white ex-pat from K.C.M.C., so the police know it's going on. They take me back to the project and explain at the office that the stolen motorbikes are sold in Merelani out behind the airport where they dig for tanzanite. The violet gems are only found in this one place on earth. The chaps who deal in stones have cash there. Jonas is in the office. He says: "Then you must do a search."

"We haven't got any cars that can go to Merelani – the road there is very bad," the police say. Jonas lends them a car from the project, and a driver. "We haven't got any petrol," the police say.

"I'll fill the tank," Jonas says. The police ask me:

"Would you be able to recognize the motorbike?"

"Yes," I say.

"We'll take you to look for it tomorrow."

The next morning we leave early; there are two plainclothes officers in the car carrying guns, because there is no government, no police, no nothing out there – just savagery. From the airport we take the dirt road towards the village of Merelani a few kilometres from the mining area at the foot of the Blue Mountains. On the way we stop with the district police who have an outpost in the middle of nowhere. We ask for their help. They let us have a police officer in uniform, but once we reach Merelani he refuses to leave the car because savages have guns as well – anything could happen. There are motorbikes everywhere. Our policemen have to hide their guns in the car so as not to attract attention. The two plainclothes officers, unarmed, go with me between the sheds and the houses in the bandits' lair – the notorious area where so many motorbikes are parked. We go to the garages where they repair them and the ground bleeds with oil. The machines all look the same; you lose your vehicle one day – the next day it's a hodgepodge of parts. They take parts from one machine to use for another. Swap fuel tanks, seats, lights – all the things you're used to looking at have been mixed up. So we have no success. Luckily I don't get into more trouble, because the police told the G.M. all the stories about motorbike hijackings. But I have to stay in bed for a week with sore ankle and knees the size of balloons. Rosie didn't get badly hurt. She comes to my room:

"I have an internship at Mount Meru Hotel in Arusha," she says.

"Congratulations," I say. Mount Meru is very posh, a tall house built by Danes in a strict, European style. Rosie is perfect for the reception – *mzungu* tourists can feast their eyes on her black beauty. "I'll come to Arusha and visit you all the time," I say.

"No," Rosie says. "Don't come visit me."

"Why not?"

"I am moving on now – we're over."

"Why?" I ask.

"You're not a boss or on your way to Europe. You're just a babysitter," she says and leaves. Tsk, that girl is cold. This misfortune and trouble with the G.M. and the police have shown her where I'm really at; Marcus – nothing but a tiny louse.

I lie in bed for a few days with swollen knees, and then I limp on, because even though my body is in agony, life is work and work must go on. Now I ride a different project motorbike. I wonder if Jonas is upset that the motorbike was stolen? No, it belonged to S.I.D.A. – it didn't cost him anything. Nechi tells me Rosie is fooling around with a bloke called Dickson – his father owns tanzanite mines in Merelani, and Dickson has lots of money.

Christian

R.E. – we skive off. Samantha takes me down to the school's old swimming pool behind Karibu hall. The small pool's concrete walls have cracked and the bottom is covered in soil, leaves, weeds. I'd like to say something about the situation at home, but how do you begin? We sit down with our legs dangling over the edge.

"What are your parents like?" I ask.

"Why?" Samantha says.

"Well, it's just . . . you know, your dad's got the hotel, but . . . What about your mum? Is she alright?"

"Parents," Samantha says. "They'll all restaurant, cash box, hotel, shuttle service and endless blithering."

"But what does your mum do?"

"Who cares what she does? She lives in Tanga, half a day's journey from here. Suits me just fine. Where's that cigarette?" I get our one cigarette out. There's a shortage of them these days. It's undignified to speak about parents at school. I mean, we're not kids anymore; we're just stuck with those parents for a little while yet. And Samantha's lucky. She boards. She doesn't have to see them every day. I light the cigarette and hand it to her. We're both listening for footsteps; there's a footpath from the teachers' houses and up past the old swimming pool to school, but the ground is covered in old eucalyptus leaves, so you can hear people coming from a long way away.

"Fancy a recycled puff?" Samantha asks.

"A what?"

"Come here," she says and grabs on to my neck. "Open your mouth." I open my mouth. "Smoke tunnel," she says, blowing smoke into my mouth – almost like a kiss. I breathe in the smoke. She guides her parted lips onto mine. Both tongues are in my mouth. "You're not half bad at that," she says. She takes another drag. "Come again," she says. She blows her smoke into me. I try to kiss her. "Stop it. For fuck's sakes, I'm trying to smoke here," she says. But then she kisses me again, hard, with her tongue in my mouth. "Cop a feel," she says, putting her hand on her breast. I caress it.

"Mmmm," I say, leaning forward, licking her neck. She giggles. I am rock hard. She moves my hand to her naked thigh; I start moving it towards the inner thigh – closer to her cunt. She pushes it off.

"We're friends," she says, handing me what's left of the cigarette, getting up. "I'm going back." She looks down on me. I suck hard at the cigarette. Can't get up right now. Something between a snort and a titter escapes her. She shrugs, and then she's gone. I smoke the cigarette all the way to the filter; green slime on my tongue, dizzy.

"You have to meet with your mum," Dad says.

"No," I say.

"She calls me twice a week and tells me to speak with you, so the two of you can meet," he says.

"I notice she didn't take me when she left T.P.C.," I say.

"Would you have liked to go?" Dad asks.

"She didn't even ask – I noticed that," I say.

"But did you want to go?" he asks.

"No, but I think she should have asked."

"She knew you wouldn't want to go," Dad says.

"Tsk," I say, because I need an explanation – from him, from her, from anyone. But I don't get anything. She took the picture of Annemette with her. I know that Dad noticed that. So did I.

Samantha and I are smoking down behind the changing rooms at the swimming pool – it's completely dark because there's a power cut. We have to be ready to stub out the cigarette if it comes back. She's standing very close to me – it's probably only so she can find my hand to pass me the cigarette. She likes toying with my feelings. I'm not sure what to do. I take a drag.

"Smoke tunnel?" Samantha says.

"Samantha. I'm not sure . . ." I start, but then stop. Take another drag. I only just manage to take the cigarette out of my mouth, then Samantha's in front of me, taking hold of me – her lips against mine. We're kissing. I don't want to blow smoke into her. I turn away my head and exhale the smoke, guide my lips back to hers. Our tongues. Blood roaring in my ears.

"Come," Samantha says. She pulls me through the door into the boys' shower room. I touch her stomach, feel her hands on my hips. She isn't like Nanna, I think. Pull up her top. Yes. Lean forwards, kiss her nipples. "Here," Samantha says, taking my hand and guiding it up between her legs under the skirt. This is crazy. Her knickers are wet. I pull up her skirt, squat down in front of her, and with my tongue out I guide my face in between her legs – finding the wet spot, slippery like a mussel. Samantha's fingers come down to my face, right above my tongue. "Right there," she says. "Your tongue." And I move my tongue up, let it ram into her. She musses up my hair.

"Come here," she says. I get up. Her hands are at my trousers, my cock juts out. "Inside me," she says. I bend my knees a little, Samantha spreads her legs and grabs onto my cock, guiding me inside her. Slick, tight, warm.

"Uhhhhhnnn." The sound seems to come from me as I slide in.

Footsteps? We both stiffen.

"Shhh," Samantha whispers. I slip out of her, my wet cock feels the cold and goes limp. Is anyone coming? Samantha lowers her leg.

"Who's there?" someone says from the doorway. The voice is that of a grown-up, a teacher. We don't say anything. I quickly pull up my trousers, while Samantha pulls down her skirt and smooths down her top.

"You, guard," the teacher calls. "Come here with your torch." The voice is no longer coming from the doorway – he must have gone over to the guard. Samantha whispers in my ear:

"Go into one of the cubicles." The toilets are right across from the entrance – the shower room is to the right of it. If I slip out of the front door, the teacher will see me. And even if I run and he doesn't have time to see that it's me, he'll still find Samantha alone in the boys' shower room. My legs almost collapse under me, but I hurry into the nearest of the two cubicles. Fortunately the door is open and the hinges don't squeak.

"Light, here please," the teacher says from outside. No light appears.

"It's not working." That must be the guard speaking.

"Give it to me," the teacher says.

"Now it works," the guard says, and I can see the cone of light dance through the crack under the toilet door. I take a deep breath, exhale quietly so they won't hear me. Step up onto the toilet seat. Stand there. Tell myself to keep calm, but my face feels stiff and my limbs drained of all strength. I hear footsteps.

"Can't a girl pee in peace?" That's Samantha's voice from right outside my cubicle. "Don't do that," she says. Has he grabbed her?

"Why didn't you answer when I called?" the teacher asks.

"I was having a pee," Samantha says. "It's a private matter." I can see the light shining under the door again. The teacher is bound to check out the shower room. And the toilet cubicles.

"Why are you in the boys' toilet?" the teacher asks.

"The girls' toilets were busy," Samantha says. Christ, she's one quick thinker.

"No," he says. "I've just been there."

"Wow, they've been quick about it," Samantha says. "Did you need to pee as well?" She's stalling – hoping something will come up so he won't find me. I raise my arms and catch onto the upper edges of the brick walls. There's no ceiling in the shower room, and the walls are only about two metres tall. I can reach the top easily when I stand on the toilet seat. The question is if I can lift myself up. My arms are trembling. Relax. I have to do this – that way there's a chance.

"Don't be cheeky," the teacher says just outside.

"I'm not being cheeky," Samantha says.

"You came from inside the shower room – I saw that," he says.

"I was peeing down the drain," Samantha says. "Anyway it's past my bedtime."

"You're not going anywhere," he says, and his footsteps approach as the dancing of the torchlight from under the door intensifies. It feels unreal. Now Samantha speaks to the guard in Swahili:

"The sick white man fancies me like mad," she says. The guard doesn't answer. The light disappears.

"What did you say?" the teacher asks – I can hear he's turned around. I tense my muscles, the tremor in my arms disappears. I lift myself up, manage to put a foot up above the door and the other all the way up on the edge of the wall.

"I'm speaking to the guard in Swahili. We're in Tanzania. Don't you speak the language?" Samantha asks.

"Watch it," the teacher says and pushes open the door to the toilet cubicle next to mine. I manage to push my foot in over the edge into the shower room and use the leg to pull myself up and over, letting go of the top of the wall with one hand and catching on to the rafter, which I can just make out in the flicker of the torchlight, pulling myself over so I'm straddling the wall. I only just have time to pull the leg that was dangling into the cubicle up as the door opens, and the light shines in below where I was standing a moment ago. I hold my breath. He flicks up the torch and the light approaches, but glides past me. He didn't look up. I lift up my other foot. He must have already turned his head. Light shines into the shower room. One of my feet scrapes against the top of the wall.

"What?" the teacher says and turns – the torchlight dances some more.

"I don't know," Samantha says – now the sound comes from the shower-room door. She's worked it out – is blocking the door. I grab on to the rafter with both hands, so my body is released from the top of the wall almost without a sound, lower my body with my arms and let go, landing on the toilet floor, as the teacher directs the torch at the rafters in the shower room. I slip through the half-open toilet door and out of the building, past the guard and into the night. I run round the house. Stop to catch my breath. My legs are shaking. I sweat all over. What can I do? Samantha will be in trouble now. But . . . what can he prove, that teacher? That she was in there? Big deal. It dawns on me.

"Samantha," I call. "What's going on?" I start walking back round the building.

"Can I go now?" Samantha asks. "That's my boyfriend calling."

"You're not going anywhere," the teacher says. He comes out just as I'm coming round the corner. Of course! It's that French bloke, Voeckler.

"What took you so long?" I ask.

"He won't let me leave," she says.

"Why not? What's going on?"

"Don't get clever with me," Voeckler says.

"Clever?" I say. "I'm going home – I was just trying to say goodbye to Samantha."

"You two have been . . . naughty," Voeckler says.

"You wouldn't believe how naughty," Samantha says. Why doesn't she just shut up? I give a laboured smirk. Voeckler comes all the way over to me.

"You smell of smoke," he says.

"I smoke," I say.

"You haven't got a smoking permit," he says.

"As a matter of fact, yes, I do," I say.

"You're to leave school premises right now," he says.

"Why?" I ask.

"Because I say so – otherwise you can report to the Headmaster tomorrow morning." Voeckler turns back to Samantha. "And you're coming inside," he says, taking hold of her upper arm.

"Don't touch me," Samantha hisses and tries to pull her arm out of his grasp. He doesn't let go. I should do something.

"Off you go," he says, pulling at her. Out of the darkness more students appear – they line up to watch the spectacle. Voeckler shines his torch at them.

"What's going on here?" Panos asks, appearing at my shoulder.

"Let go of me. You're sick," Samantha shouts – she starts crying. "All you want to do is to feel me up. All the girls say you're always ogling them in class."

"What?" Voeckler says, letting go of her arm.

"Hmmm," I say, nodding.

"It's true," Panos says. Voeckler takes two steps away from Samantha. I suddenly see that Gretchen is here as well – she's looking at me, and her face is all funny. Voeckler shines the light at Samantha and me and Panos. Samantha's shoulders are shaking – it seems very real, but I don't know if she's acting or not.

"Everyone, inside. Otherwise you can all go see the Headmaster tomorrow morning," Voeckler says and point his torch straight at me: "And you – get out of here right now." I shrug.

"See you," I say and walk away, as Tazim shows up next to Samantha and puts her arm around her shoulders. I should have done something. But what could I do? It would have made no difference. I should have done something anyway.

The next day Samantha is back in school. I find her during the lunch break. She seems miffed.

"Want to go down to the old swimming pool for a smoke?" I ask. She shrugs but comes nonetheless. She doesn't say anything about yesterday. About what happened. About what happened later. I don't know what to say. As soon as we're out of sight, I light a cigarette and hand it to her, put my arm around her hip, try to pull her close.

"No, but . . . I don't really want to," Samantha says.

"But . . . I thought that . . ." I say.

"No, it was just that . . ." Samantha says, but I've already turned to go. I could cry. I should have done something. Yesterday. I should have said something. Not just let myself be sent away. And now it's just . . . Now she thinks I'm weak. I am. I was. Wrong. Not enough. Not up to it. Fuck, why can't I . . . ?

Samantha. And Sif! I see her in the hall. She comes my way. I stand still, frozen. She always makes me feel guilty – I can't live up to her expectations. She sees me. Turns around and disappears, almost running.

I talk to Panos. But I don't tell him I licked her between her legs – that I was inside her.

"Why did she kiss me when she wants nothing to do with me?" I ask.

"Beats me," he says. "You know she likes to get a rise out of people."

"Perhaps," I say.

"Listen, I'll try to talk to her about it," he says.

"No, don't do that," I say. "If she thinks I'm a tosser, that's what she thinks."

"Nah, she doesn't think that," Panos says.

A couple of days pass. I don't want to go looking for Samantha. Well, I do, but I force myself not to. And I feel seriously guilty about Sif. It's my fault she's upset. I see Samantha a couple of times further down the hall or crossing the playground. I also see Sif and call to her, but she walks away from me hugging her bag to her chest. A French boy whose name I don't know comes over to me. I think he's in Sif's class.

"If you speak to her again, I'll thrash you," he says.

"Is that so?" I say.

I'm playing badminton with Masuma in Karibu Hall. Samantha comes into the hall during the match. I don't look at her and win by a long shot, because I'm so pissed off with myself. Afterwards I go outside and sit down on a bench. Samantha comes over and sits down next to me.

"You like me," she says.

"Yes," I say, looking straight ahead. I'm afraid to say anything else.

"But we're friends, Christian. We can't be together," she says.

"Then why did you take . . ." I start but stop. Why did she take my cock in her hand and put it up her cunt? Why did she stick her tongue into my mouth? I didn't ask her to do that, and now she's pissing on me.

"But," Samantha says, sighing, "I need a man."

I don't say anything. Stare right ahead.

"Not a boy," she says. I get up and leave. I could kill her right now.

Marcus

SWEDISH HEARTS

A guest arrives from Sweden. The man has been here before – Andreas – the old friend from Jonas' youth, who has become a journalist. Andreas drinks a lot and chases any and all women, regardless. But the whole family goes on safari in Arusha National Park, and Katriina is happy. And Andreas goes with Jonas to F.I.T.I. and the plywood factory and up to all the portable sawmills on West Kilimanjaro. Andreas takes pictures and writes on a typewriter.

"These are stories for the Swedish newspapers," Jonas says, but I don't believe it. But two weeks after Andreas has left, the newspapers arrive in the post.

Katriina drinks gin and translates the newspaper to me: "Jonas Larsson – the amazing Swede who teaches the negro how to fell the trees in the forest".

Andreas writes about the Swedish king of the Tanzanian forests – a giant among men, a great teacher, full of self-sacrifice and idealism. A true philanthropist – friend of the negro. With his own two hands Jonas has established an amazing project. The Swedish newspaper leads you to understand that the Swedish nation is one big, throbbing heart which helps all the other colours of the human race who cannot help themselves.

KICKBACK

A man must be independent, otherwise he is a boy. For the longest time, I made no money. Now I receive a salary, and I can save. No expenses for a house or food, no girlfriend and no wickedness after hours. I must save my salary for investments. Even my clothes are old rags, handed down to me from Jonas or Mika or anyone. And juice for my motorbike is paid for by the project cash box. I'm going to build a kiosk so I can have my job and at the same time be an independent man with a firm grasp on life. But there's no arguing with the numbers. It will be two years before I have enough money to pay for a building, a fridge, stock, everything. It's not working.

I start my own financing. When I am buying goods for the project, I drive round to the different *wahindi* merchants and drive a hard bargain. I play them against one another:

"How can you ask that much? I've been to Patel's on Aga Khan Road, and he will give me the same amount, the same quality, but for twenty per cent less."

In the end when I have negotiated the lowest price possible, I make my proposal to the merchant:

"I want you to make out the invoice for ten per cent more when you write the receipt." I look straight into the man's eye. He doesn't blink.

"And what's in it for me?" he says.

"We split it – five for you, five for me." The merchant writes the receipt like I told him. I get money from the project; ninety per cent covers the price we agreed on. The last ten per cent is a kickback – we go halves.

What's wrong with that? We've got to help each other. My bargaining has already lowered the price for the project considerably – shouldn't I get a bonus in return for my efforts? And the project is run by the Swedish government to help the negro. The Swedes are rich.

Shouldn't I receive some small help? I do a good job, am constantly on the go, and they keep me down in the dust like a dog. And do you think my eyes don't see it? A friend from Sweden comes down for a free holiday and writes to the Swedish papers about all the amazing things Jonas has done. Do you believe that to be true? No – that is one friend lending the other a hand. We must help each other. If my work is nothing but sacrifice, and no help comes back my way, then I must help myself.

Money for my investment is steadily growing, and soon I have enough to begin. I can buy boards from West Kilimanjaro at a friendly price, organized through a deal with the foreman of the casual labourers and a driver – who will say that his lorry has broken down for the time he spends taking planks round to my place. At F.I.T.I. I find a carpenter. It used to be just a dream inside my head, but now the kiosk is rising from the dust on Nechi's family's land; they live close to the Larssons' in a colonial villa on Kilimanjaro Road right across from the Police Academy – if I buy the guards a free fizzy drink now and then, they won't mind keeping an eye on my kiosk as well, and I'll have plenty of customers, and it'll be a real earner for me. I could also record cassettes in the kiosk, but my big Boombox has been stolen and the tape heads in my little tape recorder are dying, so as far as a life in music goes I am at a complete standstill. And it's not good for the kiosk if you can't play music.

My money has all been spent, so my stock is limited. And I have to go to my mother against my will:

"Give me my youngest brother to man the kiosk," I say.

"What will you pay me for him?" she says. We negotiate, and it ends up being very little. But she has to agree, because she has a husband who spends every shilling he can get his hands on on drink. And I must feed my little brother so at his least his belly is full.

The kiosk gets me a little extra money, so if the other workers or the accountant see me drinking a beer, it's not strange; they know I have other sources of income. But man doesn't live on beer alone, he needs a woman as well – not just for love but so he has a competent partner in building his life. I miss Tita – the activities in her garden have suddenly stopped, because a seed grows inside her. Who planted that seed? Is it a cocoa fruit?

DRAPES OF FLAP

Fourth beer at Hotel Saba Saba in Arusha. It's Saturday. The *mama* came into the office yesterday: "Go there tomorrow afternoon at two. Here is money for food and transport, and to pay for the room." She gave me an envelope. I'm a total *basha* – the young man who pumps an old hag. I just hope I have time to get drunk first.

She comes in. Sits down. We say hello. She takes a folder of papers from her bag. Opens it, leafs through it and points as if we're in an important business conference. "What number room are you in?" she asks.

"337," I say.

"When you've finished your drink, you'll say goodbye and go there."

"Yes," I say. We leaf through the folder. I drink up. Go there, quite drunk. I don't know what will happen next. I pull the curtains and sit on the bed. It's almost dark, and I can close my eyes as well. Here she comes; an assault on the senses. Soon my clothes are off. I'm drowning in old flesh, lumpy and strange like that of a sick elephant. A man almost can't find the papaya, because it's hidden behind drapes of hanging flab which have long jagged burn marks everywhere – they shine brightly, and I'm thinking "what's that?" *Eeehhh* – they're stretch marks, because the fat grew so much inside her it stretched the skin so wide it almost split.

Lots of screaming from the old *mama*. The beer is in my pump, so it's straight, but it's very difficult because I'm without joy. It's exactly like sleeping with your own mother. Nasty.

SICK NEGRO

As soon as I come home, there's more screaming:

"No, you have to stay at home," Solja shouts.

"We'll be home soon, and after all Marcus is here now," Katriina says.

"It's not fair. You're being stupid," Solja screams and her screaming launches Rebekka into howling.

"Fuck," Jonas mutters and turns on me: "Where have you been all day?" he asks.

"With a mechanic in Arusha who put new cables in a chainsaw because the mouse had chewed them over," I say. Jonas doesn't know anything about his new project, because he never goes anywhere but Moshi Club. There was no chainsaw, only a sick old elephant-*mama*, and

I feel rotten all over my body and only want a shower. Jonas gives Solja an angry stare, and Katriina and Rebekka and I get angry stares as well. He'd rather beat us.

"We have to leave," Jonas says and goes outside. Rebekka wails like an ambulance, and Solja howls with her arms around her mother's hips.

"Can't we stay in tonight?" Katriina says.

"No, they mustn't be allowed to bully us," Jonas says and continues out to the car, gets in, starts the engine. Katriina looks miserable. I pick Rebekka up from the floor.

"Give them a bath, Marcus," Katriina says. Solja's going to a birthday party tomorrow, and she can't show up in a week's worth of grime like a pig. I go over and put a hand on Solja's shoulder, as she sobs and hangs on to her mother. "Let go, sweetheart," Katriina says. And Solja lets go, looks up at her bad mother and says:

"Stupid Mummy."

"We won't be long," Katriina says.

"You're never home," Solja says. White people don't beat their children. They comfort their children, so they won't be afraid of the world. They talk to their children about everything. But not in this family. The parents go to the club and come home drunk while shouting madly at each other. And the father smokes *bhangi* and behaves oddly.

The car drives off. I go to the bathroom, but there's no water in the taps and no water in the buckets either, because the slave has been to Arusha to pump for the preservation of his job. I have to go to the ghetto, where Josephina has filled our buckets. Carry two buckets to the kitchen and heat the water. Take the children to the bathroom and wash them. Solja can wash herself, but Rebekka needs help. She stares at me:

"Marcus," she says. "You smell funny." Then we hear the sound of the car outside. Solja smiles in the bathtub: "It's my parents," she says. But is it her parents? The door opens, but no-one speaks, there's only the sound of footsteps. Jonas opens the bathroom door with eyes that are red from *bhangi* and a mouth that smells of beer.

"WHAT ARE YOU DOING TO MY CHILDREN, YOU SICK NEGRO?" And he pushes me, and my back slams into the basin and the children scream, and he beats me with his fists – I hold my arms in front of my face. His aim is poor, because there's so much *bhangi* inside him. Right now I could ruin all my chances of a good life. Take his head in my hands and crush him.

"Daddy – stop!" Rebekka shouts.

"Quiet," he says. "Get lost!" he shouts at me. And I have to go. Leave my girls to the devil.

Christian

The old man's gone to a meeting. Or he's gone to Moshi Club to get drunk. He never even mentions my mum anymore. She doesn't call, and he doesn't say anything about how I ought to go see her. It's weird that. She hasn't shown up since she came here with Léon to get me to come to the first cabin. And the old man gets drunk. Not stinking drunk, but just sufficiently addled to be a pain to have to listen to. I'm in my bed reading when he comes home from the club. He can see the strip of light under the door and comes in.

"Did you do your prep?" he asks.

"Yes, yes," I say.

"You have to understand, Christian, that you'll never be really good at anything unless you make an effort at school," he says, trying to instil diligence in me, but the whole thing drowns in his beer-breath. What's he really good at? Being a fool? I'll admit, he does that rather well.

"I've done my sodding prep," I say.

"Doing it isn't enough. You have to understand it as well," he says.

"Goodnight," I say. He takes a breath, planning to say something else, but gives up, sighing.

"Goodnight," he says, closing the door. At work he tries to gain respect by growing a beard. Tanzanian men don't grow beards until very late in life, and they don't go grey until they are really old. The old man is forty-five and has loads of grey hair already. People think he's old, wise. Now all he needs is a gargantuan paunch, and he'll be a proper *bwana mkubwa*.

Luckily I spend a lot of time home alone, because part of his job is going round to all the smallholders on the mountain to teach them about accountancy and finances. Sometimes he stays at a guesthouse so he won't have to drive all the way there and back the same day on the lousy roads.

I am stranded in the house after school, because the accelerator cable for the motorbike is bust, and I need someone with a Land Rover to take it down to the mechanic.

Juliaz comes to say goodbye. Every day he takes a nap on Phillippo the gardener's bed before biking home – out along the eastern slope and quite a long stretch up the mountain – on an old, heavy China bike. He bikes here and back every day even though there's an empty room in the servants' quarters. But he's an old man, so he doesn't want to take off too early, because then his wife, Flora, who is responsible for the running of the smallholding and the livestock, will put him to work.

It starts to grow dark. There's tension in the air, and then it happens: the sound of the first heavy drops hitting the vegetation. I run out into the garden. The drops make me shiver as they splash heavily against my skin. The rain beats the dust into the ground, and the wet soil gives off a spicy scent. The temperature drops suddenly, all the vegetation is rinsed clean leaving the leaves shiny and bright. Reddish-brown water spills out of a defunct drainpipe, and there's a sound like machine-gun fire from the neighbour's sheet-metal roof. I step out of the rain onto the veranda, wet through, light a cigarette; the tobacco tastes noticeably better when warm smoke is inhaled into lungs in air that is cool and clear. Boiling hot black coffee, I think, and run into the kitchen, putting on the electric kettle, making myself a cup. Then it hits me – I run into the sitting room and quickly flick through the L.P.s, finding Gabriel Fauré's Requiem. The music spills into the air, as cars pass outside, their windscreen wipers pulsating, not a grain of dust rising from the road. The short rains have begun.

"Christian," someone says at the front door. It's Marcus. I go over and open it. He is wet through. A stream of reddish-brown muddy water runs down the drive, and the croaking of frogs mixes with Fauré's strings and the song of the cicadas.

"Come in," I say. "I'll find you some dry clothes."

"You're listening to wild music," Marcus says, laughing.

"What are you doing here?"

"I haven't seen you in a few days – I thought perhaps you were ill," he says. We get Marcus into some dry clothes and sit down in the sitting room. The rain continues.

"It's bloody cold in here," I say.

"I'll light the fire," Marcus says. All the old colonial houses have a fire-place. Marcus scrunches up newspapers and puts on twigs. In no time at all the fire is roaring.

"What do you want to listen to?" I ask and go to the B. & O. Hi-Fi.

"Can I work it?" Marcus asks.

"Yes, of course," I say.

"Where do I press?" he asks. I show him. "I like those electronics," he says.

"How are things with Rosie?" I ask.

"Rosie has gone to Arusha," Marcus says. "We're not together anymore."

"Oh. I'm sorry to hear that," I say.

"She was a greedy girl," Marcus says. "Have you got yourself a girlfriend up at that school of yours?"

"No, not really," I say. "Let's make some popcorn." We go into the kitchen, make popcorn and tea, return to the sitting room and listen to Eddie Grant – on full whack. Smoke cigarettes. "When will the Larssons send you to Sweden for your training?" I ask.

"*Tsk*, I don't know," Marcus says. "He talks about Sweden to everyone on the project, but no-one gets sent there." Marcus goes over and turns the record. "You see, if I were in Sweden I could get a stereo like the one Alwyn's got at Liberty. Then I could build a good business and take care of myself."

"That'd be good," I say.

"Isn't your father coming home?" he asks.

"I don't think so. He might have gone to the club," I say.

"Do you think I could take some old copies of *The Economist*?" Marcus asks and points at a stack which has been left in the basket of kindling.

"Yes, of course. What do you want do with them?" I ask.

"All my life has been in Tanzania. I like to read about the world so I'm prepared for Europe."

Marcus

THE COLONIALIST ON THE MOUNTAIN
That morning Jonas calls to me from the house.

"You must go round to Simba Farm and deliver a letter," he says and gives it to me. "You must bring back an answer – a simple yes or no. And then you must cut some fresh eucalyptus branches and bring them back for the sauna tonight." *Wazungu* like the smell of eucalyptus while they're sweating.

First to the office at the plywood factory in Boma la Mbuzi to pick up the payroll and small spare parts. Then west from Moshi, taking a right at Bomamombo and on towards Sanya Juu on narrow, potholed tarmac roads. The temperature drops, and it becomes a dirt road which gives my kidneys a pummelling. After a long time the wheat fields come to an end, and then: forest. I drive past Simba Farm – I have to go to the project first.

Finally I see the tall fence. I stop in the yard with its workshop and stockroom made out of two containers, and two of the portable sawmills among sawdust and planks. Behind the yard are the workers' houses – made of wood in the Swedish style.

My entire body is tired; my limbs are almost asleep. We have a small diesel generator for making electricity, but it's only ever turned on when *mzungu* Gösta is here. The office shed is built on the foundations of an old colonial farm. I deliver the spare parts to the stockroom and walk the short distance to the small village by the Londorossi gate to Kilimanjaro National Park. It's 2,250 metres high.

I find myself a wooden shack where I can get a Coke and some rice with a meaty stew. Almost everyone has come here from Mbeya to work in the forest and grow potatoes.

In the morning the place is damp, misty, cold, foggy even. We're surrounded by clouds. People don't wash up here – it's too cold. Everyone smells of wood fire. Children in rags from head to toe, with snot pouring from their noses, as they push loads of firewood on heavy wooden wheelbarrows.

The food isn't good. I hurry back to the office shed and pay the two hundred casual labourers their wages. Then I smoke a stick of *bhangi* to rouse my energy. Drive down, out of the forest and over to Simba Farm to deliver that letter.

"I have a letter for *bwana* Wauters," I tell the guard.

"I'll give it to him," he says.

"No, I must deliver it myself, because his reply must come with me to Moshi." Now I can get inside and see how the colonialist lives.

"He's inside the house," the guard says. I go from the yard into the house through a gate of bougainvillaea. Behind the house there's an enormous vegetable garden; perfect – no weeds, but onions, chives, an avocado tree, a hazel tree, plums, all sorts of cabbage, carrots, peas, potatoes, strawberries, green peppers, lettuces, aubergines. There's a garden shed where the gardener sits, tending a fire under a water tank. The gardener pumps the water into a different tank, which sits in a tall iron structure so that it can run into the house and shower hot water onto the colonialist.

I knock on the back door. The cook will take the letter. No. Then I have to go round the house, because *bwana* is on the veranda – I would have liked to go through the house; from the back door alone I can see leopard hides, Zanzibar chests, buffalo horns, a big basket full of ostrich eggs.

In front of the house, the garden is like a park. There's a small pool as well. *Bwana* Wauters sits in his khaki clothes behind a desk laden with papers. He looks serious.

"*Shikamoo mzee*," I say. Give him the letter. He opens it and reads. How can he have lived here all alone without a woman to be his hot water bottle at night? Maybe I can't see the woman, because he uses Jonas trickery – disguises her as a house girl. And now he's stolen *mama* Knudsen. The farmer has colonized her – now he's cultivating her garden as well. But I can't see *mama* Knudsen anywhere either.

"Yes. You can tell Jonas we'll be there tomorrow night," he says. So it was a sauna invitation.

"May I cut some eucalyptus branches from your trees for the sauna?" I ask, because I won't do it without his permission – he might even shoot me for it and say that I was stealing his flowers. He says yes. "May I also take one of the red flowers from the field for our garden in Moshi?"

"An opium poppy? It won't survive the heat of Moshi," he says. "But you're welcome to try. Plant it in the shade and water it twice a day."

In the yard I smoke a cigarette before I mount my motorbike. Up here there's a large fence around the yard and all the buildings for the European agricultural machinery – meanwhile the negro must till the soil with a pick just to feed himself. And what was I offered at the colonialist's? Not so much as a drop. I look out over his land. All those flower fields south of the farm that create seeds for the European gardens. Further to the south and west are fields of hops and wheat which *bwana* Wauters grows for the brewery in Arusha. And all the way down I can see the lowlands where the Maasai walk in the dust behind their cattle and goats. A movement catches my eye – a horse with a rider and two large dogs following it. *Eeehhhh* – *mama* Knudsen; she's adopted the colonial lifestyle. If she sees me here she'll ask questions about Christian – Marcus will become a wire between two telephones that don't connect. Quickly I start my machine and whizz off.

I stop on the long drive, which has eucalyptus trees on either side, cut off a few branches and tie them onto my luggage rack. On the field you can see the plant he called an opium poppy. A pretty red flower with delicate petals – very erotic. And reaching out and up from the middle of the flower: a seedpod as big as a baby's fist or a light bulb. He grows them for companies in Europe that use the seedpod for flower decorations. I've brought some wet newspaper to tuck around the roots and a plastic bag to wrap all the way around, and I stash the plant under my jacket. I drive very carefully so it won't die, but it starts to grow dark, and I go faster. Two sticks of bhangi inside me by now. I may as well die with chameleon eyes from the wind which whips the tears away.

As soon as I'm back, I plant it. Jonas and Katriina come down and look on with interest. "Ooh dear, an opium poppy," Katriina says. They are very shocked by it. Why?

TYRES

The next day I must carry firewood for the sauna shed, empty the oven of old ashes, sweep the ground. Tonight Léon and mama Knudsen will come for an evening in the sauna. Christian might be here as well. The boy often comes to my ghetto at night to relax for a bit while his father drowns his sorrows in whisky. Must I now attend to these confused whites and their family feud? No, I refuse flatly – on this occasion I will play the negro's trick: be stupid, deaf, blind, dumb. I will be a boon to the confirmation of their prejudices.

And Christian does come – he takes the back way across the empty lot, through the fence. We smoke cigarettes and listen to the old Marley L.P. "Chances Are" – very Rock'n'Roll. And Christian goes pale inside my shed when he hears his mother's tinkling laughter from the sauna. His eyes are enough to frighten me, but his mouth doesn't say a word – only action; he gets up.

"What are you doing?" I ask. No reply. He goes outside. I can't go, because I am tied up by baby Rebekka, asleep on my bed. I can only watch as Christian goes into the house through the back door and comes out with a carving fork which goes right into the tyres of Léon Wauters' car – all four of them, flat. Christian takes the fork back inside, comes out and disappears through the hole in the fence. That boy's behaviour – like a stupid negro from the slums; you tread on his emotions – his reaction is not diplomatic, but violent and destructive. And Marcus can only wait for the big trouble. I step outside when Léon and Jonas call for the guard.

"It was Christian who did it," I say. "He came to see me and heard his mother – and then he went straight into the kitchen for the carving fork."

"Why didn't you stop him?" Jonas asks.

"I thought he was going to say hello to his mother," I say.

"Why didn't you call out?" Léon asks.

"I didn't see him – I was in my room with baby Rebekka. When I looked out of my window, the fork was already in the tyres."

"Then why the hell didn't you come get me?" Léon steps close to me.

"Why?" I ask. Léon Wauters slaps my face – PAH – a total colonialist.

"Léon," mama Knudsen says. Léon doesn't answer her, comes all close to my face.

"I could talk to the boy," he says. Perhaps the colonialist also wants to use his hand to talk to his girlfriend's son.

"What are you doing?" mama Knudsen says to Léon, but he doesn't react to her words. I give my opinion:

"The tyres were already flat – if you talk to Christian, that's not going to help how he feels," I say. Léon Wauters raises his hand.

"Stop it," Katriina says and put her hand on his arm. "We don't hit people in this house."

"Why not? He's asking for it," Jonas says. I look around. Mama Knudsen is walking towards the gate, her arms wrapped around herself.

"Oh, shit," Léon says looking after her, but he doesn't move.

"Why don't you go after her?" Katriina asks.

"She needs to blow off some steam first," Léon says.

"Let's get a beer," Jonas says and goes back towards the sauna. Léon follows him. Katriina shakes her head, watching the colonialists go back to the pleasures of the bottle.

"Marcus," Katriina says, "I'm sorry about that. Can't you ... Can't you try to find mama Knudsen – she can't go about on the streets alone at night."

"Do you want me to bring her back here?" I ask.

"No, but if you could take her wherever she wants to go," Katriina says. But where can you take someone who doesn't know where they want to go?

"Alright," I say. "Rebekka."

"Rebekka?" Katriina asks.

"She's asleep in my room," I say.

"Oh god, yes! – I'll get her. I'm sorry, I'd forgotten about that," she says. I go down there – Katriina follows me. I take my jacket, my cigarettes, money, keys. Katriina lifts Rebekka up from my bed and steps outside. I lock my door.

"When I have taken *mama* Knudsen wherever, I won't be back," I say.

"Why not? What do you mean?" Katriina whispers with Rebekka on her arm.

"I am tired of being the negro who is beaten by the colonialist. I am going to sleep somewhere else," I say.

"Marcus – I'm so sorry," Katriina says.

"I'm going," I say and walk towards the motorbike, start it and drive slowly out to Kilimanjaro Road and towards Christian's house. Where is *mama* Knudsen going? To *bwana* Knudsen and his son's house – the people she had left behind? No, she's lost in the night. Or past the house and towards Uhuru Hotel? But that is a godly hostel – could you come there in drunkenness at night? I can't see her on the roadside all the way to Uhuru Hotel, even though everything is lit by the lampposts the regional commissioner had put up to light his evening jog. I turn around. *Mama* Knudsen can be clever as well. She thinks that Léon will come looking for her at Uhuru Hotel. I whizz the other way, almost as far as Sokoine Drive, and see the white lady walking in the dark far onto the verge. I stop. She turns, hunched over – afraid of the negroman who has stopped for her. "It's me. Marcus," I say.

"Marcus – ohhhh, I'm so sorry that . . ." *mama* Knudsen starts.

"Come on. I'll give you a lift," I say.

"I don't want to go back," she says.

"I'll take you wherever you want to go," I say. "You can stay at the Y.M.C.A.," I say.

"He'll look for me there," she says. "I need to think." I'm thinking: where can you put the white lady? Can she stay at *mabwana makubwa's* bonking house, K.N.C.U., in the city centre? No. Moshi Hotel? No – he'll look there as well.

"Do you know anyone who can put you up for the night?" I ask.

"No," she says.

"Have you got any money?" I ask.

"I forgot to bring it," she says, and the tears start. Oh, this incompetence.

"Get up on the back," I say. Most of all I want to take her straight to Mama Friend's Guesthouse where she began her adultery with *bwana* Wauters, but I can't be so cruel. "You'll go to the bad place in Swahilitown," I say. "Shukran Hotel – he won't look for you there." She sits up on the bike like a man – the engine between her legs. I go – right through the city centre to the scarred tarmac on the other side of the market. The poor part of town. Shukran Hotel. I stop, dig into my pocket. Hand her my money. She doesn't take it.

"Won't you come in with me?" she asks.

"In? With you?" I say. Does she share Tita's madness?

"Just until I have signed in," says *mama* Knudsen. She's afraid.

"Alright," I say and step into the reception with her. The receptionist is being difficult in order to make the biggest possible profit:

"I need to see the Tanzanian residence permit if the woman is to stay here," he says.

"Stop that nonsense," I say. "This lady is on the run from trouble, so she must have the room for the night. Name your price." He says the white price. I say the black. We cut and carve at a deal, squeezing each other until we meet in the middle. I pay and hand *mama* Knudsen almost all the money I have left.

"You'll get it back, I promise. From Katriina," she says.

"*Tsk*," I say. "It doesn't matter about the money. They do a good breakfast here, and afterwards you can find your own way."

"You won't tell Christian about this, will you?" she asks. I look at her. *Eeehhhh*, the logic of liars – you can get so immersed in a lie that all you see is your own confusion.

"I won't say anything. Personally, I'm not even interested in your problems," I say and leave. And where will I sleep tonight now almost all my money has been taken by the white lady? *Tsk*, I'll end up in a guesthouse in Marengo where I must take the motorbike into my room, and lie fully dressed on the sheet, dreaming horrible dreams – the wickedness of the mattress collected through dirty pumping penetrates right into my body.

TEARS OF THE SUFFERING

One night when I'm babysitting, Tita arrives at the Larsson house in her Mercedes. The girls are already asleep. I go out onto the veranda.

"Hello, Tita," I say. "They're not at home. They might be at Moshi Club." Tita has turned off the engine, her window is wound down, but she is very quiet. Only the ember of her cigarette seems alive. "What is it?" I say and walk over to the car. Up close I can see that her cheeks are wet with tears. I lean over and put my hand on her neck – I can see the bump on her stomach in the moonlight. "What is the matter?" I ask quietly. Tita swallows.

"I'm so scared," she says.

"What are you scared of?" I ask and rub her neck – it is like steel.

"The baby scares me," Tita says.

"Why?" I ask. Tita shrugs. "Is it Asko's baby?" I ask.

"Yes," Tita says, patting my arm. "Don't worry, it's not yours." I am sad and relieved all at once.

OPIUM EXPLOSSION

The interest of all the guests in my opium poppy makes me think. I conduct research. Make sure to be early to pick up Solja from school, park my motorbike and walk to the school building.

"Stop, stop. Where are you going?" calls the *mama* in the office behind the Venetian blinds.

"I am here to pick up Solja Larsson. But I'm a bit early."

"You must stay in the car park. You have no business on school premises," she says, sounding very cross and pointing to the car park.

"I just need to look up something in a dictionary," I say.

"No," she says.

"*Tsk*," I say and walk on while she yells and sputters in her office. But I'm already in the library, looking in a dictionary for the letter O – opium – a hard-core drug. The picture of the baby fist and the erotic flower. You can make incisions in the seedpod, and it will bleed. The blood can be scraped off and eaten as a drug and it will result in a devout vision. You can also cut seedpods into pieces and make tea from them – get high. A hand lands on my shoulder.

"You're not allowed in here," the owner of the hand says. I look at the hand. It's black.

"It's not right for one African to keep another African in ignorance. We must know we can fight for emancipation," I say.

"But first you must go to the car park," the man says.

"*Tsk*," I say and go out to my motorbike, wait. As soon as I have taken Solja home, Katriina says that Tita has new problems with her electrical sockets. Marcus must come and fix it. *Eeehhh*, right away I go to the festivities – a sort of slavery I almost look forward to. It's not till that night that I see my poppy has died – the heat of the lowlands has killed it.

The next time I'm up at West Kili I stay until dusk and drive to the bottom of one of Léon's flower fields, where he can't see the thief to shoot him. And I harvest the seedpods quickly – snip, snip, into my bag and off to Moshi. First chance I get, when the Larssons are at the club and the children are asleep, I cut the seedpods into pieces and boil them in water – the taste is nasty in my mouth, but with sugar I can take it. And then I'm off on a space rocket. I get out my cassette with Jimi Hendrix the American witch doctor: "Crosstown Traffic". A pleasure in my body and an explosion in my head, travelling to all places and through time with crazy colours.

BLACK BLOOD

BOOM, BOOM, BOOM, BOOM. "Marcus, Marcus!" *BOOM, BOOM, BOOM.* My dream is shattered, the ghetto door shakes. The night is completely dark, but noisy – pouring rain.

"What?" I shout.

"*Bwana* wants you to come to the house, right away – there's been an accident on West Kili," the guard says.

"I'm coming," I say, looking at my watch. It's five. They take timber to Moshi at night – a Swedish Valmet tractor pulls the two-wheeled transporters. The night is best because there's less traffic, but also because cool air is good for the engines. I pull on my trousers, slip my feet into my boots, grab my raincoat. There's always an escort car – if something like an engine failure occurs, the car goes to the nearest phone or back up to the shortwave radio. Or if they're closer to Moshi, they come here and wake me up, and then I must go and drag the mechanics from their beds; the escort car takes them to the transporters – and I follow them on my motorbike to organize everything and in case spare parts are needed urgently; perhaps in Arusha, perhaps in Moshi.

I go to the house. The driver of the escort car is standing in the rain, looking frightened. Jonas is on the veranda.

"You must go to West Kili," he says.

"Is it the tractor?" I ask the man from the escort car. He shakes his head, doesn't say anything.

"A woman is stuck in the timber," Jonas says. "The police are on their way, so you must go now – quickly." The driver of the transporter also uses it as a taxi to make a bit more money for himself, even though he's not allowed to – it's not a taxi company. But what is he to do? He has to make a living. It's dangerous. The women from West Kili sit on top of the timber in the dark with their vegetables, going to the market in Moshi. If the entire load of timber shifts, people can slip down between them and get stuck.

"But what do you want me to do?" I ask.

"You must take care of it. I haven't got time. Then you'll call me and tell me what's happened," Jonas says and turns to go back inside.

"What about money?" I ask. He stops and looks at me.

"For what?"

"The palm greasing – bribes?"

"The project can't be held accountable just because the driver did something illegal." He goes inside. I walk towards the escort car.

"You'll have to take your motorbike," the driver says nervously.

"Why?" He nods towards the escort car. I look inside it – there's a young woman.

"I'm going to K.C.M.C.," he says. "Her foot was crushed between the logs." I bend down to the car. She is young.

"I am very sorry, sister," I say.

"Thank you," she says. And what sort of treatment will she be getting at K.C.M.C. without money? Why doesn't Jonas have the decency to give her money for a doctor They will cut off he foot with a round saw – she will limp around on crutches until she dies, marry the worst man in the village, end up in eternal Babylon because of the merest coincidence.

"Wait here," I say and run to the ghetto. Put on my jumper under my raincoat, cigarettes and matches in my pocket, grab my stash – I can't afford it, but there has to be a little. Run to the car, reach a hand in to the girl. "For the doctor," I say.

"Thank you," she says.

"For fuck's sake, get a move on, will you?" Jonas shouts from the sitting room. I see off the escort car, don't say anything, unlock my motorbike, check the fuel level, start. The rain is whipping my face. Out to Sanja, up towards Londoroki. A long way. The tarmac runs out. The motorbike skids and slips in the mud. Finally, there are headlights – *eeehhh*, the police. I stop by the side of the road. A child is screaming next to the police car where a group of woman are standing, wailing; they must be the other passengers from the wheeled transporter. The foreman of the casual labourers, *bwana* Omary, is standing with a policeman in the light from the tractor. I can see that the timber has slid out at the front end of the first wheeled transporter. Omary must have been in the escort car.

"It's better if we wait for the crane. Then we can lift the boards carefully," Omary tells the policeman – in the forest there's a tractor with a crane which is used for lifting logs up onto the transporters so they can be taken to the sawmill.

"No," the policeman says. "She could die. We can't wait." Rain is pouring down, and my boots slush in volcanic mud as I walk towards them.

"*Shikamoo mzee*," I say to them, one at a time.

"*Bwana Jonas ikwa wapi?*" Omary asks. I tell him Jonas couldn't come.

"And who might you be?" the policeman asks angrily.

"He works at the project office," Omary explains.

"What can you do here?" the policeman asks.

"If there's anything I can do to help . . ." I begin, but stop.

"Madness," the policeman says. I catch sight of the driver, who is sitting on the side of the road with his head in his hands. I walk towards him. "Stay away from him," the policeman says, and the driver raises his head – his lip is bleeding; he will be beaten many times today.

"Marcus," Omary says, "we must loosen the chains." I go with him all the way over to the wheeled transporter. Coming down this mountain road during the rains with at least twenty tons worth of wood on your arse. Madness. The transporter is made of axles with small, fat wheels, carrying an iron frame with iron lintels and holes for sticking iron rods horizontally down along the sides, so the planks don't topple off; finally there are three iron chains wrapped around the cargo to hold everything together when the transporter is shaken by potholes on the road. They're always overloaded. Tonight, one of the chains has snapped, and the planks have bent the front metal rod like a piece of wire. They are thick, straight pieces of timber, two men are barely enough to shift one plank, and the policeman is too important to lift anything so lowly as wood. And the load is completely held together by the two remaining chains – we can't pull the planks out one by one to make room around the trapped woman.

We crawl up behind the tractor, so I can see . . . *eeehhhh* – between the planks, great big eyes, white all the way round in the middle of a face slick with sweat and rain – I can only tell it's a woman because I know it; otherwise all I'd see was fear. An entire load has fallen onto her. It covers everything up to her stomach.

"We'll get you out," Omary says. "Help is on its way." The woman hears him but doesn't answer – she's paralysed. Omary shows with his hand where we are to go. The child is still screaming over by the police car. He pulls me away a little, whispers: "It's her child, screaming – she managed to lift it off her back just in time."

"What should we do?" I ask.

"We have to loosen the chains. The police won't wait for the crane. Have you brought money?" He's thinking about the greasing.

"No money." The other women move closer now – one of them is carrying the screaming child.

"My baby. My baby. I want to see my baby," the woman screams from the transporter.

"You have to step back – it might be dangerous," Omary says. The policeman comes over.

"Do it now," he tells us before shooing the women off.

"You'll get up on the back of the tractor and get ready to help when I loosen the next chain," Omary says, wiping the water from his face with his hand.

"Do you think it can be done?" I ask.

"It's in God's hands," Omary says. I crawl up onto the tractor, forcing myself to look at the frightened animal the woman has become.

"My child," she whispers. I have no answer. I stand on the edge of the transporter, to the front of the load, leaning forward, catching the woman's hands.

"It'll be alright," I tell her, but where will that be? In hell?

"Ready," Omary's voice says from the side of the trailer. Water splashes against my raincoat. My are eyes locked firmly on the woman's. The scraping of metal against wood as Omary starts turning the middle chain clamp on the side of the transporter – he too is in danger of becoming buried under planks, because the load is lying at an angle out over the edge. He turns, and there's a creaking sound – perhaps a movement? The creaking sound intensifies. The woman's eyes. Her hands are crushing my knuckles, the planks shift, bend the next iron rod as easily as anything, tumble out to the right of the woman with a creaking sound, and Omary jumps out of reach. The planks to the left of the woman follow suit – there's room now; they shift faintly towards her, move just a hand's breadth, and she opens her mouth, squeezes my hands hard and her grip slackens. She stares in surprise, blood bubbling into her mouth, her head falling limply to one side, hitting a plank with a dull sound. I step down, looking at Omary, shaking my head. The policeman approaches – I go towards him – can see the women staring back at me silently.

"What?" the policeman says. I shake my head. The women see it and launch into a joint wail; some of them beat their breast, others slap their faces. I go towards Omary – the policeman follows. He is grumpy; all I can do without money is pass my cigarettes around. I think about the girl in the escort car – her foot; it may already have been sawn off at K.C.M.C., but at least she's alive. Jonas doesn't understand anything; his unwillingness to pay the police for their trouble – their standing in the rain – one day they may pay him back in kind: they owe him a problem. Now Omary will have to take the woman's body to K.C.M.C. when the escort car returns. I must go to West Kili to tell the tractor driver's wife the news; her husband is going to prison. And to the dead woman's husband – her relatives must come and get the baby. And I must track down the family of the girl with the crushed foot. Dawn is breaking. From a distance we can hear the crane come rattling down the mountain. Perhaps it can take the other women back – I don't think they'll go to the market today.

All in a day's work for the *wazungu*; the driver is going to Karanga Prison, and his wife and children will starve. A casual labourer is now a widower, his child lost its mother. No-one complains about the *mzungu*. "*Eeehhh*," they say on West Kili: "Jonas is a god. He is a great forester in Sweden, and now he's come here to teach us everything. He will make us rich." Who is rich? The young girl – now without her foot?

Late in the day I return home. My mouth can take no food, even though my stomach is empty, tied up in a knot. I look at the bread and my hand, which must carry food to my mouth. The woman's mouth is in my mind. The blood; first bubbling, spilling over the white teeth, onto the lip, down across her chin; thick, warm, dying. The only thing I seem to be able to get down me is coffee. Black on the outside; black on the inside. The coffee unties the knot inside me, until I can be sick on the ground.

Christian

I am sitting in my room. Hear a car. Go to the bathroom and look out of the window. It's a taxi. My mum. Why would she come here? And in a taxi of all things?

My dad goes out. I stay indoors.

"Is Christian here?" she asks.

"No," he says, even though he knows I am. Why would he say that? I'm pretty sure he knows I'm here. But of course the motorbike has been sent off for repairs. I wonder if he's forgotten and thinks I've taken off.

"I'd like to see him," she says.

"I don't think he wants to visit Simba Farm," Dad says.

"I don't live there," Mum says. "Not anymore."

"Oh, did something happen? Where do you live now?" Dad asks.

"I'm staying at Uhuru Hotel."

"But . . ." Dad starts and then stops. He puts his hands into his pockets; they're moving towards the chairs just outside the front door. I can't see them from the window anymore.

"Have you . . . met someone?" she asks.

"No," Dad says.

"He's my son too," Mum says. "Christian," she adds as if there could be any doubt. "Where is he?"

"He noticed you didn't take him with you when you left T.P.C. That's what he keeps saying. Over and over: 'I noticed.'" Dad's laugh sounds resigned. I can hear it in his voice – he's sat down – he hasn't offered her anything to drink.

"How would I have been able to take him – there?" Mum says. He doesn't answer that.

"Are we getting a divorce?" he says.

"What does Christian say?" she asks.

"What do you care?" he asks.

"Thanks," she says. "I'd like to know."

"He has no respect for either of us."

"What about himself – does he respect himself?"

"In his own way, I think," Dad says.

"Well, tell me about it. But is that enough?"

"It . . . Isn't that something we taught him?"

"Yes, perhaps it is," she says. "I'm flying back the day after tomorrow."

"It didn't work out?" Dad asks.

It's a little while before she answers.

"I just needed you to talk to me about it," she says, and her voice is thick. She sobs. "Annemette," she says.

"I couldn't," Dad says. She's crying. I think he's holding her. Comforting her. "Do you want to try?" Dad asks. At least that's what I think he's saying. How can he even ask her that?

"No," she says. "I can't live here. I want to go home." For a long time neither of them says anything. He doesn't say he wants to come home with her. I don't want to go home. I am home.

"Tell Christian I'm staying at Uhuru Hotel. I'd like to see him before I leave."

"Would you like me to take you to the airport?" Dad asks. The most henpecked husband ever. She doesn't answer. I hope she's shaking her head. Done with Léon Wauters – maybe he too liked blackcurrants. Marcus says that black fruit has the sweetest juice.

"You have to," Dad says.

"It feels wrong," I say "She's the one who left." Dad looks away:

"Annemette."

"All the same," I say.

"We would have got divorced if Annemette hadn't come along," he says.

"She didn't ask me if I wanted to come with her when she left T.P.C. I noticed that," I say.

"Would you have liked to go?" Dad asks.

"That's not the point. The point is she didn't give me the choice," I say.

"She'd be happy to take you back to Denmark, if you'd like," Dad says.

"Denmark?"

"It's up to you," Dad says." I promise I won't twist your arm."

"What's up to me?"

"Whether you want to live here or go to Denmark and live with your mum," he says.

"That's up to me?"

"Yes," Dad says.

"I see," I say. Dad sighs:

"You'll go and say goodbye to her. You know you have to. It's not up for discussion. And don't try to cheat your way out of it. I'll go and ask her if you've been there."

"It doesn't feel right," I say. He lowers his head and looks at me from under his brows. "Yes, yes," I say.

I get up, patting my pockets to make sure I have cigarettes and a lighter, then I go to the door.

"Are you going there now?" Dad asks.

"Yep," I say.

I walk – chain-smoking all the way to Uhuru Hotel, get the room number at reception, find the door and stand outside, lighting another cigarette. My arm feels like wood as I knock on the door. She opens.

"Christian," she says, throwing a quick look over her shoulder. Her things spread out across the bed; souvenirs and clothes. The picture of Annemette is on the bedside table. "Come in," Mum says and opens the door wide. "Or do you want to go somewhere and get a fizzy drink?" I stay where I am. It makes her nervous. "Did your dad tell you, you can come and live with me in Denmark if you want?" she says quickly. I point at the bedside table, the picture:

"You took a picture of Annemette and left me and Dad at T.P.C. You can take that picture to Denmark," I say and turn around. There are tears threatening to spill over, but I hold them back.

Christmas break is a sorry affair. Christmas Eve Dad throws a dinner for Jonas and Katriina and their girls. No-one says anything much at the table. Me and Solja go to my room and play Ludo until Rebekka becomes hysterical: "I want to go home to Marcus," she screams. Solja sends acerbic smiles across the Ludo board until they call for her and go home. Dad shakes his head.

"What?" I ask.

"Isn't that odd? The kid wanted to go home to her nanny," Dad says.

"It's not that odd, really," I say. "He talks to her."

"No, perhaps it isn't," Dad says.

New Year's Eve we go to a theme party at Miriam and John's. I drink three glasses of punch, smoke ten cigarettes, am sick and go to sleep on the back seat of the car, like my first evening in Tanzania three years ago.

1984

The holidays are over, and Dad has abandoned his ban against my riding the motorbike at night – I'll be seventeen in three months, so I'm expected to be responsible.

Prep is almost over for the boarders. I'm watching a game of table tennis on the veranda at Kiongozi House. Sif comes over and stands next to me. It's been a long time since I've spent any time with her, because she never says anything, and I don't know what to do. There's a haunted look in her eyes.

"Hi, Christian," she says.

"Hi," I say. "Are you O.K.?" She shrugs. I've heard from Dad that her parents are worried that Sif might not be happy at school. And Dad asked me to look out for her a bit. How do you do that when she's a mute?

"Do you have a smoke?" she asks.

"I didn't think you smoked."

"Well, I do," she says. I look round, sneak one into a loose fist and give it to her. "I haven't got a light," she says. "Can we go somewhere and smoke?" she asks.

"Where?" I say.

"I thought you'd know all the spots around here," she says.

"I do," I say and start walking. Sif follows me. I decide to go down behind the furthest block of classroom. Not the safest place, but in the dark all the good places are taken by lovers, and I don't particularly want to bump into Samantha or Shakila or . . . anyone, really. I stand with my back against the wall, light my cigarette, smoke. Hand it to Sif, who has gone very quiet. She takes a drag, coughs violently.

"I'm sorry," she says.

"You don't have much practice smoking, do you?" I say.

"I smoke," she says, handing me the cigarette and standing right in front of me. "I'm so sorry about you and your family," she says. What? "Families suck," Sif says.

"What are you talking about?" I say. Now she's standing so close we're almost touching. She stands on her tiptoes and kisses me lightly on the mouth. I throw away my cigarette and press my tongue into her mouth, squeeze her little tits, grab her buttocks, press my pelvis against hers.

"I love you, Christian," she says – her voice almost breaking. I don't say anything. "I love you," she repeats.

"You're lovely," I say – I have to say something when we're not kissing, and while I get my hand up her thighs. She pushes it off.

"I want you," I say.

"It's too soon – not like that," she says. I catch her hand and put it on my cock.

"Do it, Sif," I say.

"What do you want me to do?" she whispers. I open my trousers, show her how. She does it.

Mrs Harrison gives me detention for not answering her questions in lessons. Jarno gets it for being noisy. After school we're made to dig dirt out of the concrete trenches that run along the school's drive so they're ready for the long rains. Samantha arrives in a taxi. She stops and looks at us.

"How's it going?" she asks. I won't answer.

"How does it look like it's going?" Jarno asks. I look at her – I loathe myself for doing it, because she won't go out with me.

"Tsk," I say, spitting. Get on with my digging.

"What did you do?" Samantha asks. Jarno looks at me, but I don't say anything.

"Christian keeps saying: 'I don't know – I don't care,' whenever Mrs Harrison asks him anything. It drives her round the bend," Jarno says.

"And you?" Samantha asks.

"Behind with my homework," Jarno says.

"What about your clothes?" Samantha asks. We're wearing white T-shirts, blue jeans.

"That's our look," Jarno says. "The Carlsberg Twins." That's what some of the boys call us, because I nick Carlsberg from home for me and Jarno. It's better that we drink it than if Dad does.

"Jarno, Christian," Samantha says. "See you."

"Alright," Jarno says and starts filling the wheelbarrow. I don't say anything.

"See you, Christian," she says again. I don't say anything. Look at her. "O.K.?" she says.

"O.K.," I say – I can't help smiling at her. Tits. Thrust the shovel into the caked mud at the bottom of the trench.

Friday night there's a party at school. I'm lounging against the wall. Staring at Shakila and doing my damnedest not to look at Samantha. She's been going out with Stefano; I don't think she is anymore, but I don't stand a chance anyway. I start walking and Sif appears next to me.

"I'm sorry," I say. "But I have to go home. My stomach's gippy."

"I'll walk you," Sif says. So I kiss her for a bit and say goodbye. She goes back, and I squat in the darkness, light a cigarette. I see a couple approaching, and I hide the ember in the curve of my hand. It's Samantha and Baltazar. They smoke and talk, but I can't hear what they're saying. I'm pretty sure she's tossing him off. He moans. Yes, she is. I can't bear it. Finally they go back to the party, so I can get up and leave without being heard. I ride my motorbike home. Go to bed. Can't sleep.

Marcus

STRANGE STICK

I meet little Vicky outside the kiosk. She used to be a year below me in school. Her father is the Deputy Commissioner at the Police Academy. Vicky's skin is almost blue, and her eyes are vivacious and tell a story of what might happen. The motorbike I'm riding is an attraction. So is the kiosk. And when I give Vicky fizzy drinks for free, she behaves like a cuddly kitten with me.

"What is it you do at the company?" Vicky asks.

"What company?" I ask.

"The *wazungu* company," Vicky says. "The one who has started the sawmills on West Kilimanjaro." *Eeehhhh*, she sees me as a boss in TanScan and a part of the white family, just like Rosie did until she learnt the truth. Vicky is very set on a relationship. And I lie as fast as a sports car because the attraction is strong.

"I am head of the purchasing department," I say, and we're already on the road to nakedness.

What sort of life is this? At work I have to lie about important negotiations in town so that I can sneak away and see Tita. Asko doesn't want her to send the cook and gardener home in the afternoon, so now we're at Mama Friend's Guesthouse in Soweto – the same place *mama* Knudsen used for her trouble with Léon Wauters. But our trouble is different, because Tita's tummy is big. Who is in there?

"Isn't it dangerous?" I ask.

"No," Tita says. "Not if you take me from behind."

Staili ya mbwa – doggy style. I am the he-dog, and Tita is Lille Gubben on her knees with her big tummy and pretty breasts hanging down. The little baby is lying in the dark without even knowing its own colour, and suddenly it's knocked over the head with a strange stick – a big headache. Tita's crying. I stop.

"I'm sorry. Am I hurting you?"

"No, no – don't stop – ohhh," she cries. Strange customs. Fast work. And back to the office. Home to mind the children. And when the adults are at the club, and the children are asleep – I can finally relax. But no.

"Marcus?" the guard calls. "There's someone to see you." I get up from my relaxation. Vicky! She's got something. And she's ready to give it away. Soon we are in the Swedes' bedroom, the bush before my eyes. *Eeehhhh* – Vicky is a dark jungle with a flower as red as blood. Now I am the gardener to that flower, and the jungle becomes a rainforest.

The next day I have to smoke a stick of *bhangi* – drink two quick beers before I am tossed liked a hollowed-out tree trunk on a stormy ocean – *mama* G.M.; everything is rocking until I feel sick and almost drown in the fat old sea.

Christian

"So, is she up for it, your little girl?" Samantha asks.

"What are you talking about?" I say.

"Sif. Is she up for it?"

"Wouldn't you like to know?" I say.

"I would, but she's not talking to me," Samantha says. "Maybe she thinks I'm going to try something on with you." Sif definitely thinks I've got the hots for Samantha. As it happens she's perfectly right.

"Sif's cool," I say.

"I suppose she does what you tell her to," Samantha says.

"It's not like I have to make her," I say.

"Carnal urges," Samantha says and wriggles off.

There's no music at Liberty tonight – the stereo is bust.

"Let's go to Kilimanjaro Hotel," Marcus says and points across the street. Scratchy Zaire Rock is surging from the old single-storey building across from Liberty. They cater to the slightly older clientele – the ones who can't afford the prices at Moshi Hotel. We go over, up the steps and into the large, dark room. I can see a bar and a D.J. behind a desk. A load of fat old men in tatty suits and ladies bulging with excess flesh, not as young as they once were. They drag their feet rhythmically across the scarred concrete floor, their arses bouncing as they dance with the fat men.

"Quite different, isn't it?" I tell Marcus.

"A pumping station," he says and heads towards the bar.

"What do you mean?" I ask. He points – an open door. In front of it are two men with a small cash box. Through the door I can see a gallery which runs along the outside of a low building out back with lots of closed doors leading into what I think must be very small rooms.

"Those are the bonking rooms," Marcus says. "You pay to hire them. How long will you need? Five minutes? Ten? Perhaps you're slow and need a full quarter of an hour." He orders beer for the both of us from the bulging bar *mama*. I take a long sip.

"Are they *malaya*, all of them?" I ask.

"Some of them are amateurs. They'll pump in return for a beer, but they might also charge you money."

"But they're so old," I say.

"They're cheap, because they are so old," Marcus says. "But some men like old meat."

"Why?"

"Lots of experience. And less mockery if the man is useless. And lots of fatty bulges for the man to explore like an adventurer in the mountains."

Liberty is better. Even though there's no music, at least there are young people. Fingers press into my upper arm, hard. I look down. Marcus' hand.

"Christian," he says. I look at his face, but he's looking towards a corner of the room. I follow his eyes. My dad. He's at a round table with

Jonas, Asko and John. And three black whores. I put my beer down on the bar.

Perhaps he's just been waiting for my mum to leave. Or perhaps it's racism. When I was little, he was stationed several places in the Far East. Perhaps it was more appealing with a yellow, rice-run fucking-machine? I wonder what my mum got up to when she was a nurse-anaesthetist in Køge? Fancy a game of doctors and nurses? I don't even know who these people are – my parents.

"We're leaving," I say and start moving in a semicircle across the floor, so that I can put a number of dancing bodies between myself and the table in the corner. I sense that Marcus is right behind me. We reach the back stairs. I stop, light a cigarette feverishly. Look to the side and see Marcus there. Nod towards Liberty and start walking down the steps.

"Christian?" My dad's voice. Behind me. I stop, turn around. He's standing at the top of the stairs looking at me. His face seems muddled. He doesn't say anything.

"It's a black outlook, isn't it?" I say. He grins. For the first time in two months. It doesn't look pretty. He stops abruptly.

"Yes," he says. I turn around and continue towards Liberty. Marcus catches up with me.

"Your dad's still there," he says.

"Right," I say.

"Your dad went back inside," Marcus says.

I don't say anything. We sit down at the bar. I get absolutely hammered, and Marcus drags me into a taxi.

The next morning I wake up in his bed. Dad isn't there when I get back. When he arrives late in the afternoon, he's brought Thorleif along and pretends nothing's happened. How is it possible to be that daft?

Marcus

PORN SAFARI

She wants the light on to see the young pump in the rottenness. Oh horror. Almost every Saturday I must go to Arusha to be made dirty. Three sticks of *bhangi* are required to face this Babylon and four Safari beers to fill the pump so it stands in hypocrisy.

The old *mama* pushes my head: "You must suck on the bean." She is so old she's got grey dreadlocks between her baobab trees, full of dust and mites – it's so bad I'm almost sick as I make my way down towards the papaya of rottenness. *Eeehhhh* – what is that? A very potent *Kalles Kaviar* for my birthday treat – as sour as rotting fish. Yes, really – 27 February, 1984. It's my nineteenth birthday today, and I am celebrating it in hell.

What can I do? I'm pumping for my life. Money on the bedside table when she's gone. What's to be done? I can understand why the G.M. would rather pump Edson's wife – yes, really; he's been doing it for a long time, she is a secretary at TanScan and very *chiki-chiki*. Edson doesn't know it yet, and it's embarrassing to tell him – it would be an insult.

Mama calls the office: "Next weekend I have a meeting in Arusha. I am staying at Mount Meru Hotel. The meeting will be finished in the evening – you must be there by eleven." That's when my planning starts.

Saturday: The meeting ends with a large dinner. She has already had many beers before eleven. I only pump her once before she's sound asleep, making noises like an elephant. I put on all the lights. Pull the blankets off her, spread the baobab trees to open the papaya. And I work like a kitchen whisk making mash; finally the pump vomits white seed that falls on the barren ground. Right away I take the camera hanging from the noose around my neck. I have rented it for good money from the Indian at the photo stall on the market. I push my pump in to the camera's frame – a dollop of white seed on the tip, more white seed in the dreadlocks of the papaya, her *titi* are balloons with stretch marks on them, tumbling down to either side of the mattress, and the *mama* – the G.M.'s wife – her face satisfied and relaxed like that of the sweetest grandmother. I am on a photo safari – I shoot an entire roll of film: my slack pump on her half-open mouth, my finger in her papaya, my hand on the balloon. Bob Marley as a photographer – that's me: *Emancipate Yourself*. Job done. I go and have a shower. Luckily Rosie isn't in reception to see *malaya*-Marcus leaving work. I find a bar up on the high street. Sleep at a guesthouse with bedbugs. I can't have the film developed in Moshi – the Indian would look at the pictures to check the quality. The police would be summoned. They would imprison me for indecency and start blackmailing *mama* G.M. themselves. The film is sent off to Finland by express post the next morning.

"Why were you not there in the morning?" the *mama* says on the phone. "I wasn't done with you. If you don't behave, I'll tell my husband you were drunk and tried to pump me when you came to our house with that folder about the furniture."

"I'm sorry," I whisper down the phone. "The next time I'll give you my best love."

"I hope so for your sake, little man. Otherwise I will ruin you."

The trip to the post office is pure excitement; will the box contain my declaration of freedom? *Eeehhh*, finally. Mika's letter is very surprised: "Everyone at the photo shop thinks I am an absolute psychopath," he writes.

She's like a lion when I give her the present. I run from the hotel room, shouting: "There are many copies. I have hidden them with my friends. If I die, they will be sent to your husband by special delivery." It's not true. The copies are hidden in the Larsson house, and the negatives are at the kiosk, but dangerous men can be hired for pennies. That Monday she comes to the office.

"This is a special meeting," she tells my assistant. "You can't be here."

"How much?" she asks when the assistant has left.

"They're not for sale," I answer.

"You know my husband will have you killed if he sees them, and I tell him it's you."

"Yes. But you'll also be killed, or divorced, if he sees them; *mzee* G.M. will see to it that you lose everything."

"What do you want?" she asks.

"I want you to leave me alone."

"You were crazy about pumping me as well."

"No, I was crazy about not losing my job, so I wouldn't have to starve, and you threatened me and said I could lose my job if I didn't do as you wished."

"You're a sick man," the *mama* says.

"Just remember that the photos will be delivered even if I die – it makes no difference."

She gets up and leaves.

All that bother just to live a normal life.

JEALOUSY

Even though I am done working as a *basha* for *mama* G.M., there is still Tita. It's an odd sort of trap, because I've also got Vicky who says:

"Why don't we take the car and go to Arusha – we could go to the good disco there?"

"We can take the motorbike," I say, because when I tell that I'm not allowed to drive the car, it'll be obvious that I'm not a boss at TanScan.

"You can buy a car," she says. *Tsk*, her father mustn't see us together, because then there'll be trouble – I'm too small a man for his divine daughter. But she too is a slave to materialist thoughts. If I can't drive her in a car, I'm not allowed to drive her in bed. And Tita sees me driving with Vicky on the back of my motorbike.

"Who's that?" she asks.

"Just a friend from my schooldays," I say. Tita goes quiet. Now she'll punish me by not opening her flower for a party. But is that a punishment? I am like a casual labourer, but I never get any pay. Lovemaking should be a juice, but to me it's become a drought, because I have crazy women on all sides, sucking me dry.

The Larsson family are going to Hotel Tanzanite to enjoy the weekend, but Tita doesn't go with them, even though that was the plan. She says she is ill and comes straight to me for treatment. Josephina and the gardener have the day off, so the treatment takes place in the house – just my luck. Vicky comes to the house while I'm pumping the white flower, and I hear her calling my name down by my ghetto, so I have enough time to pull on my clothes and go out on the veranda.

"Whose car is that?" Vicky asks, pointing at Tita's car in the drive.

"Oh, that's just the Finnish lady, Tita. She is here to pick up some things," I say. But Vicky is suspicious, because Tita looks very ruffled when she comes out of the sitting room without anything in her hands and gets into the car. The situation can only be remedied by fool-ishness:

"I have decided to buy a car – I have started looking for one," I say. And right away Vicky is a cuddly kitten once more, but I don't want her nakedness, because the smell of the white lady's lovemaking is all over my body.

Christian

Samantha makes herself pass out. She squats and hyperventilates. Two Norwegians from her set stand by, ready to catch her – Svein and Rune. She gets up, her eyes lose focus, and she falls as she passes out. They catch her and lay her flat on the ground while Rune gropes her breast.

"Damn it, don't do that," I say.

"She's fainted," he says. Samantha opens her eyes.

"Cut it out," she says. "Who was that groping my tits?" She looks up at me.

"Hey, don't look at me," I say. Svein and Rune give me angry looks.

"I know it wasn't you, Christian. You think it's wrong. It's one of those damned glue-sniffers," Samantha says.

"We didn't do anything," Svein says. "All we did was catch you." Rune titters.

"Rune," Samantha says. "You're a big baby. The only time in your entire life you'll be completely covered in cunt-juice – do you know when will that be?" She gets up.

"Next weekend in Arusha," Rune says. "Black cunt."

"Not bloody likely," Samantha says. "You'll have to make do with the time your mummy squeezed you out."

Svein laughs.

"Shut it," Rune says. She starts hyperventilating again. I turn around and walk off. She's grotesque. I wish it were me touching her breasts. But not while she's out.

I go through the old man's drawers and pockets. Find money. Go down to see Marcus.

"Want to go for a drink?"

"Yes," he says. And we're off. "Liberty?" he asks.

"No, a bar," I say. "One without white people."

"Majengo," he says, showing the way. Dirt roads, small grotty buildings, loads of bars. We sit down. I order. Beer and Konyagi. I want to get drunk.

"How are things at the house?" Marcus asks.

"Off kilter," I say. He smiles.

"*Tsk*," he says. Life is crazy.

"We're animals," I say. "Monkeys."

"Crazy monkeys," Marcus says. We empty our glasses. I call on the bar *mama*. Order more.

"You can come borrow my stereo if you like," I say, because he's talked about it several times.

"Thanks," he says. "I'd like that." We drink in silence while I look around. Young women in revealing clothes and seedy-looking *mabwana makubwa*.

"What sort of girls are they?" I ask him in Swedish, which no-one else understands.

"They're whores," he says.

"All of them?" I ask.

"The three ones over at that table are of that kind," he says.

"But . . . how do you do it?" I ask.

"Which one of them do you want?" Marcus asks.

"The small one with the big breasts," I say.

"Have you got money?" he asks.

"Yes," I say and tell him how much I've got. Marcus waves at the serving lady.

"Three beers for that table," he says in Swahili, pointing at the girls' table. She gets the beer. Marcus goes over, speaks with them. The small one with the large breasts and the hard, pretty face takes her beer and her glass and comes over to our table. The two other girls look on.

"Hi," she says to me.

"How much is the soap money?" Marcus asks her in Swahili. I have no idea what he's talking about. I'm drunk – want to touch her, naked. Get inside. She names a figure. "That's a lot," Marcus says.

"It's because he's coloured," the girl says. Coloured? Because I'm white – to her that's coloured. Marcus tells me in Swedish how much I must pay for the room and how much to give the girl afterwards.

"Go with her now," he says.

"Where is it?" I ask him in English. The girl gets up.

"It's just around the corner," she says. We get up. The two girls at the table titter.

"Keep an eye on my motorbike," I say.

"Of course," Marcus says. The girl takes my hand, we walk down a dark dirt road and in through a door where a man is sitting at a table under a faint light bulb. I give him what Marcus said.

"Give me more," he says.

"No," I say. "That's enough." He shrugs and looks away. I am coloured – white. I give him another note.

"O.K.," he says and gives me a key. I follow her down the corridor, into the room. It's dark here.

"What's your name?" I ask.

"It doesn't matter," she says.

"No, tell me your name."

"Scola," she says and lights a candle. It's still dark. She doesn't ask me what my name is.

"Scola," I say and slip into her darkness. I like it there.

"Thanks," I tell her afterwards and give her the money and then a little more.

"No problem – I'll see you around," she says.

I go back to Marcus. The two other girls have gone now. Marcus calls for beer. We drink. I can't start the motorbike when it's time to go home. Marcus takes the handlebars from me, but he can't find the lights. I lean forwards and try to turn them on; the motorbike wobbles, he brakes. We almost fall over, but manage to get our feet on the ground before we do. Put the lights on. Drive home to his ghetto. I put the chain around the motorbike while trying to smoke a cigarette. I am very tired. I am drunk.

For the first time in weeks I feel fine.

Marcus

DREAMING ABOUT CARS

Freedom can't rise from the dust. In these hard times let us pray to His Royal Majesty Haile Selassie. I have my job and my kiosk and am saving money and am going to try to buy a second-hand car that I can lease to one of the city's legendary taxi drivers – some of them have a reputation for looking after your car and handing over the agreed sum every day. But red tape still rules: I can apply to the authorities for a permit allowing me to buy a car from the government-owned T.M.C. – Tanzania Motor Corporation. The price is right, but the greasing to queue-jump is steep. I need to get more money and go to Dar myself to research the market.

"Can't we go to Dar on a holiday?" Vicky asks for the third time.

"I can't afford to," I say for the third time.

"But the kiosk is making good money," Vicky says.

"Yes, but that money must be spent on building up stock so it can make enough for a living, and I won't have to be dependent on *wazungu*."

"But you did talk about going to Dar to look at a car," Vicky says – she wants me to be a boss with a car and a slave in the kiosk attending to every practicality. Vicky could work in the shop and we'd make more, because the shop boy always steals a little, and Nechi's relatives always steal a little as well. His sisters-in-law go out to the boy, who says: "You're not supposed to take the things without paying – Marcus says so." And the sisters-in-law say: "The kiosk is on our property – if we can't have a little flour and some fizzy drinks, he can take it somewhere else."

Vicky wants the good life, served up to her on a platter. But to be honest, I would like to go to the capital to look for a car and to see the sights. I organize things at the project; suddenly I'm required to travel to Dar es Salaam to look for some very special hinges for an important order of cupboard doors. Vicky is only seventeen years old, but she lies to her family about visiting an older cousin in Dar es Salaam, and the cousin is in on the deception.

We take the bus to Dar and stay there for a week. I have rented a cabin by Upanga. It's amazing; all alone with a naughty girl day and night, no control. We have a lovely time together. In the day I look at cars, and in the evenings we groove and dance at the discos, and in the middle of the night we spend two or three hours on sexuality. God knows we're not children. Now my Vicky is a good girl, and we walk along the beach together, and all the time she keeps me close to her bosom. Until it's time to go home.

"I had looked forward to going home in a car," she says as we stand sweating in the sun at the bus station. All that talk about a car is making me weary. We get back, and at the kiosk I can't find my Stevie Wonder tapes, which I gave to the boy so he could play them to the customers. The stock is gone from the shelves and there's almost no money in the till. My Walkman has gone from the ghetto even though I always lock it. Vicky comes to the kiosk to be given Cokes, but she doesn't come to my ghetto anymore, and I won't beg for lovemaking – a man must drive his car into her papaya before she's happy.

A few days later I meet Phantom in town.

"Are you in trouble?" he asks.

"What do you mean?"

"Money trouble?"

"Always, yes. Why do you ask?"

"Vicky came to me to sell your Walkman," Phantom says.

"Oh that," I say. "I just didn't want it anymore."

The next day Vicky comes to the kiosk wearing new clothes.

"Have you got a Coke for me, Marcus?" she asks, leaning in across the desk so I get a peek at her *titi*. I say:

PAH. Right to her face. "Get lost." A bad business. Not a lady. But it clears the air – I see it in her eyes: the materialist lady is a leech as well; her love is false, the papaya is only opened to the man who gives her presents.

My work situation improves. I am busy with West Kili and the kiosk. No girls hanging on to me – I spend my own money in my own way. Building my life, while Vicky becomes a lady at the bars; beer and money and you're in there. A complete, great *malaya*.

GET UP

I can attract any woman I want, until she sees through the deception. First it was Rosie, then Vicky. They think I am a part of the *wazungu* family, with a nice house, a motorbike, an important job. But when I don't give them presents, the attraction fades. They discover the chain around my neck; Marcus is colonized– just a doormat for white people to wipe the muck off their shoes. Yes, Rosie was very beautiful, and Vicky was wild and from a good family. But that kind of girl will run away from me. I need a girl of a different kind of quality.

Not far from the Larssons' there's an Australian family; Dr Strangler with his wife and children. Strangler is a family man – not chasing women all night. Strangler's house girl, Claire, is Rosie's quiet friend from our schooldays. Back then my eyes were blind to her, but now she's grown like a panther – lithe and beautiful. Every day I see her walking on the street. I say hello and ask if she'd like a lift. Almond-shaped eyes, full lips, *titi* that are small the way I like them, pert bottom, and her legs . . . they go on all day. She sits behind on the motorbike like a lady; the machine isn't between her legs – she keeps them together on the same side.

"Would you like to drink a Coke?" I ask.

"Yes," she says. We go to my kiosk and sit down on a bench in the shade.

"Get up," I say. She gets up from the bench. "Sit down," I say, and she sits, looking confused. "Why do you get up?" I ask her.

"You told me to get up . . ."

"Yes, but if I told you to take off your dress, would you do that as well?"

"No! Of course not. What are you saying?"

"But why didn't you ask me why I wanted you to get up?" I ask.

"I don't know."

"When you ask me why I want something, then we're having a conversation. But if you just do whatever I tell you, then it doesn't matter – then you're just a parrot," I say.

"But why did you tell me to get up if you didn't want me to?" she asks with her head held high like a queen.

"I just want you to do what you want to do, and not what people tell you."

"Well, now I want to sit here and drink my Coke, and then I want to go home."

"O.K.," I say.

"Good," she says. We drink our Cokes in silence for a while. Then she lifts her head and looks me straight into the eyes: "You're always so busy showing off, like a *bwana mkubwa* with your kiosk and your motorbike. But you're just a small fish working for *wazungu*, like me."

"Yes," I say.

BASTARD CHILD

I go to a bar with Edson, who is now the driver for a *bwana mkubwa* at K.N.C.U. Edson's wife is still working as a secretary at TanScan. Still going on business trips with the G.M. Now child number two has arrived, and Edson gets very drunk.

"That child looks nothing like me," Edson says. "I say to her: 'Whose child is that?' But she says it looks like her great-grandfather or an uncle. I say: 'Show me pictures of them.' She says: 'They didn't have a camera.' But the child – that ugly little boy – he looks exactly like your G.M."

And now Edson is crying into his beer. They think too much about sex in this country. Edson himself knows that game – he picks up *malaya* and brings them to the great man at K.N.C.U. When a poor married woman sees that there are problems in the family, she has to take action herself. She may even pump strangers to provide for her own husband and children. Edson is shaking with despair. This country has no power to light the darkness, no radio, no television, no books. Only ignorance. And pumping.

The rest of the world is very different. I know it. I am always borrowing multiple copies of *The Economist* from *bwana* Knudsen once he's done reading them – a very serious magazine. To understand the message you must be stone-cold sober. I read about things we don't know in Tanzania. There is insane wealth beyond all reason. And they write without mincing matters that Nyerere's African socialism has failed. If I said that out loud on the street, I would soon be a guest of Karanga Prison.

PACK OF THIEVES

Things keep disappearing from my shop, and I can't be there all the time to keep an eye it – I have to work. In the end I can hardly buy stock with the money that comes in. I complain – they steal too much and kill the future.

"It's not your kiosk," Nechi's older brother says.

"It is mine," I say. "I have paid for it – I bought the stock."

"Yes, but the kiosk is on my property, so that makes it my kiosk. I don't know why you put it here."

"You told me it was fine, because I'm Nechi's friend. And you have taken plenty of things in my kiosk without paying a single shilling."

"But of course, it's our kiosk as well. Now we must look at the accounts, because we must have half the earnings," he says. Nechi doesn't say anything – he's only the little brother. I go straight in and pack up all the most expensive items in the kiosk, get a taxi, load the things into it while Nechi's family look on from behind their curtains. The kiosk is as heavy as all hell – how can I have it moved? And I'm afraid that they'll take it apart and steal the rest of the stock. And Nechi's brother is with the police. If I don't move fast, he could do anything. Right away I go to Musa Engineer and sell him my fridge. Hire a carpenter from F.I.T.I. and ask for the Valmet tractor to come with a transporter from West Kili. I don't sleep.

The next day we go to the kiosk. It's broken open – empty; the stock has gone. I go to the house. Nechi's sister-in-law is at the door:

"You're not coming in here – it's not your house," she says.

"You've taken my stock," I say.

"If you try anything funny, I'll scream for the police," she says. Across the road at the Police Academy gate two police recruits are on duty in the guard shed, carrying guns – they would come running over to gain a little goodwill from their instructor – Nechi's older brother. I pretend to walk away, but sneak round to the back of the house, look in through the window, *eeehhhh* – there are all my goods, stacked up on the sitting-room floor.

Right away me and the carpenter set to work dismantling the kiosk – taking it to the Larssons', stacking it as boards and planks on the ground behind my ghetto. The dream has come apart, torn to bits; I am without a fridge, without stock, screwed over. Nechi comes to my ghetto, very guilt-ridden.

"I am terribly sorry they have done that to you," he says. "You must tell me if there's anything I can do."

"Have you got money?" I ask.

"No," Nechi says.

And my very last money is taken by Edson. Providing for the child with the G.M.'s face makes him angry. He looks at his wife, he looks at the child, and all he sees is her deception.

Late one evening he comes to my door and his eyes are wild.

"You have to help me," he says. "I have to get out of here."

"What happened?" I ask, but then I see the strong acrobat's hands with knuckles like minced meat. Edson is shaking.

"She said . . . She said I'm not a man. And she brings home expensive things she would never be able to buy on her salary. Where do those things come from? They're presents from the G.M., because he uses her as a field to be ploughed."

"Is she alive?" I ask and look from the mince on his hands to his wild face.

"Yes," he says, looking at his hands. "Only her face is ruined." So I give him money to escape. "Once I have begun my new life in Dar es Salaam, I will write you a letter. You will have your money back." And I wave goodbye to my money as he goes into the night.

FUTURE

I speak to Claire about my problems. She looks at me coldly.

"You expect other people to build your life for you. Nechi's family must help you; *wazungu* must help you. If you want to build your life, you must help yourself," she says. I am almost struck dumb, because you never hear a girl in Tanzania speak directly to a boy like that. Claire looks down: "I'm sorry I'm speaking like that to you."

"You're right," I say. "But if you and I were together, we could help each other as well."

"All you want is to go to Europe and live in the white country. I have heard about those plans from Rosie," Claire says.

"No, I don't want to live there. Europe is like a fridge. The plan is to go to Sweden on a course where I could learn things and buy decks for a professional disco in Moshi. Then I could build a good future in Tanzania. With you," I tell her.

"You just want to be wicked and make trouble with all the girls," Claire says. She's heard of all the wicked pumping – with Rosie, with Vicky. "But I'm a good Christian girl," Claire says.

"I know – that's why I like you. I don't want to be wicked with you," I say. Because I think Claire is clever – not greedy. And God is great with her – He stands in the way of nakedness. I can wait, because all that nakedness – I've learned that it's hard work.

"You can be my friend, but if you want to be my husband, you must take me to church," Claire says.

DOLLAR

Tita comes to visit Katriina. Jonas is at the club with the children. Tita's tummy is like a great big ball – ready to explode. Who lives inside it? I go to the kitchen to prepare some food. Tita comes out to me.

"I'm going to Finland tomorrow," she says.

"Why?" I ask.

"I want to be there while . . . and have the baby.'"

"That's a good idea," I say. "Good luck."

"Thanks," she says and hands me an envelope. "That's for you. It's not very much, but it's all I've got."

"Thank you," I say and am about to open it, but she puts a hand on my arm.

"No," she says. "You can open it later. And don't tell anyone."

"O.K."

"Goodbye," she says.

"Goodbye," I say. And I go to my ghetto, open the envelope. Dollars. Lots of dollars. Three hundred – an amazing fortune. All night I don't sleep – I'm thinking. A hundred dollars could resurrect the kiosk, buy stock, get the business up and running. The kiosk could be put on the empty lot behind the Larsson house. The guard could keep an eye on it at night, if I give him just a small present. Claire's little sister could man it during the day. Two hundred dollars would be just enough to buy the smallest Pioneer Boombox from Ostermann so I can listen to music and record cassettes once again, if I also use Solja's little Philips tape recorder when she's sleeping at night.

The next morning I am at Phantom's kiosk at the market with my hundred dollars.

"I don't know anyone who can exchange that much money on the black market," he says.

"Just go to Musa Engineer. You ask for the black-market rates – eight times those of the bank – he'll be happy to buy." I give him a note with the figures.

"Why don't you go to Musa Engineer yourself?"

"Because he knows the *wazungu* I work for. He'll tell them I've got dollars, and they'll think I've stolen it, even though it's money I got in Arusha," I say.

"Alright," Phantom says and we agree on what his share is to be. No problems. I get shillings by the boatload.

And a private conversation with Katriina without Jonas around: she agrees – she'll take my two hundred dollars and order the Boombox in my name from Ostermann and ask D'Souza to get it smoothly through customs at the airport.

LIGHTS IN THE NIGHT
The white people have a party and get insanely drunk. I go out into the garden to watch. They are bathed in the light of paraffin lamps on the veranda while I myself am standing in darkness. *Tsk.* Men groping wives – reaching out hands, pulling at *titi.* Gösta staggers up the drive, almost falling over. I go over to him.

"Do you want me to help you get home?" I ask.

"*Dra år helvete,*" he says – go to hell – pushing me off as he looks away. His voice is thick, and there are tears on his cheeks. He gets into his car and drives it at such an off angle that he hits one of the concrete gate-posts. One of the headlights is completely smashed. But Gösta is wild, refuses to stop, he reverses a bit and tries again, finds the opening this time and wobbles down the road.

I walk on and look at the foreign mores; see movement at the back of the garden, close to the hole in the hedge, leading out to the kiosk. Sneak closer. *Eeehhhh* – a white man's arse pumping up and down, and under him is Stina – Gösta's wife. And the man is fat, his arse is the colour of dirty milk. Asko's arse pumping light into the night. And Stina's pretty to look at, but why would she do this to her husband? And why isn't my arse going up and down on top of Tita? It's well suited to the night. But my arse has done it already, and now Tita is in Finland with a bellyful of baby, and I can only wait in trepidation for the result.

THE PROMISE OF AUSTRALIA

Claire starts coming round to visit me in the late afternoon. When she walks past the main house, Jonas puts down whatever he's doing and goes to the window to follow her with his eyes. Katriina comes into the sitting room and looks at him. "Who was that?" she asks.

"Claire – Marcus' girlfriend," Jonas says.

"Why are you staring at her like that?"

"Oh well – I just wasn't sure it was her."

"Hmmm," Katriina says.

My thoughts about Claire are ungodly as well, but Claire's mother is very godly, so Claire doesn't want to be wicked and make trouble – not even if I put on a sock.

One day Claire comes down and tells me that Jonas has asked her if she'd like to go to Stereo Bar one night, just for a Coke and a bite to eat. "He would come and pick me up on the corner of my street, or I could get money for a taxi. He also asked me if there was anything else he could do for me; if I was short on money for anything, help me make ends meet. Why would he ask me that?" I point at her papaya. She's shifting from one foot to the other.

"He wants that," I say.

"But . . . what's he thinking? Katriina would kill me. And he's so old – and he eats dirt. That's so disgusting."

"Yes," I say.

The Strangler family has a lot of guests. A doctor from Australia arrives, one *bwana* Strangler used to go to school with. Claire comes over to me in the evening when her duties as a house girl are over. "He says he wants to take me to Australia with him – the guest does," she says.

"Do you believe him?" I ask.

"He said so."

"Did he say it to anyone else?"

"No, he said it to me."

"Did anyone else hear him saying it?"

"No, *bwana* was at work, and *mama* had gone to pick up the children from school, but the guest had stayed at home to rest."

"Why do you think he would want to take you to Australia?"

"He likes me – he said so. That I'm a good girl."

"But why would he take you to Australia – it's expensive."

"I don't know."

"Did he not ask you if you wanted to go out with him?"

"He told me that when they came back from safari, we could do something together."

"Wasn't it just last night he arrived?"

"The evening of the day before yesterday."

"So he's known you for a day and a half, and now he wants to take you to Australia."

"Well . . . I thought it was a bit odd as well," Claire says. I point:

"It's that again," I say.

"You think so?"

"Yes, in a few days – maybe tomorrow – he'll touch you."

"But . . . I don't want him to."

"Then you'd better tell him."

"But don't you think he'll tell *bwana* Strangler?"

"No, because then *bwana* Strangler would be angry. He doesn't want his guests to treat the house girl like a *malaya*."

"A *malaya*?"

"He's white – you're black and very beautiful. He'd like it out." I point at it again. "He'd even pay for it."

"But I wouldn't do anything as dirty as that," Claire says.

"I don't blame him for wanting to. I'm sure it's very nice."

"Stop it!" Claire says.

"I don't think I'll be able to stop myself once I've tried it." She slaps at me, I grab her around the waist and pull her onto my lap. She holds her arms in against her chest and smiles, embarrassed. "Don't worry," I say. "I'd like to try it as well, but I won't take you to Australia."

"I don't mind," Claire says. "What would I do in Australia anyway?"

I'm fond of Claire. And now she's happy to kiss me. But God sits like a great rock on my path to paradise. I thought I was tired of the nakedness. But my hard work with Tita and *mama* G.M. is over. I am getting no juice from Rosie or Vicky. It's only Claire that visits me in my ghetto and sits there on her chair with her legs crossed. She's Pentecostal; must I say "I do" at the altar before I can even lay a finger on her?

CHOCOLATE

I come home from work and go to the house to see if we are low on food, because then I must go shopping. Jonas comes right into the kitchen and points at me:

"Get out!" he says.

What?

"But we don't even know if it was him," Katriina pleads in Swedish from the sitting room.

"Right now!" Jonas says and points at the door. I leave. What's going on? If it's me? I haven't done anything wrong for a long time. Maybe I've taken a beer, a sip of gin – nothing more. I wait in my ghetto – hear them driving off. Katriina in the car with the kids, Jonas on his motorbike. But at the gate, they go in separate directions – the car goes towards the club, the motorbike towards the city. Later Katriina returns with the kids.

"They need to be fed," she says and leaves again. She's in a strange mood, it seems. Solja goes into their bedroom, where she's not normally allowed. I go to the door.

"What are you doing in there?" I ask.

"There's something you need to see," she says, rummaging through the drawers. I go to the kitchen and work on the food, while Rebekka sits on the floor, drumming with a wooden spoon on a pot. Solja comes out and hands me some pictures. "They arrived in the post today," she says. And I look. There's Tita in a hospital bed, and the baby is a piece of chocolate in her arms. I stare at it and shiver. He might even murder me – Asko. Does he know?

No-one says anything to me. The next morning Jonas still isn't back. It's only when I've got Solja ready for school that Katriina fills me in.

"Marcus, you must stay away from Asko. He is very mad at you."

"Why?" I ask, because she doesn't know that I've seen the pictures of the chocolate baby.

"Just do as I say," she says. And I'm scared as all hell when I leave my ghetto.

I can't stay in Moshi. I could stay at West Kili – sleep in a shack like a dog. Perhaps my motorbike will break down up there, and I can call home on the radio and say I'm stranded. I take the back way out. Disappear for a few days.

FALSE CIGARETTES

"Just come home," Katriina says on the radio. "Nothing's going to happen. Asko has gone to Dar es Salaam for a few days for the project."

"Are you sure?" I ask.

"Yes, yes," she says. "And your stereo has arrived from Ostermann." My Pioneer Boombox – my payment for spraying in the white garden. At five I drive into Moshi – do I have to change nappies, cook, do all the practical things for the white family? I want to listen to sound of my new machine.

BURNING SPEARS

It's already starting to grow dark. I drive up and sneak my motorbike back along the side of the road against the one-way traffic on Kawawa Street – that way I can whizz up Arusha Road at full speed until I come to the roundabout and get back quickly to relax with my glorious Boombox. Right before I reach the intersection, some idiot tries to push me out onto the verge, so I almost run into two bikes on the corner, but I dodge them and turn up Arusha Road in my own lane. But what do I see? An oncoming Land Rover – very fast. It changes direction, comes right at me – I see the white man behind the wheel: Asko! he doesn't like chocolate. I hear a BANG as if someone's fired a gun at me. Am I shot? There's a burning spear in my leg, like a very quick fire. That's all I feel. And then I am like a superfast aeroplane in the sky. And I crash by the roadside; there is a post that is meant to hold the sign with the street name, but the sign has gone. I am flying when, *dufffff*, I hit the top of the post with my stomach at such a speed that I fold over the top of it, but it stops my flight and makes me drop to the floor of the world, and I see the motorbike skid out with sparks over the road, and it's like a bow, bent at the middle, bleeding petrol from the fuel tank, utterly wrecked. I fall down into the ditch – the big, deep concrete one that runs beside the road to collect water during the rains. It's supposed to be covered by a concrete barrier so you don't run your car into it at night, but it's never in order. I'm lying at bottom of the ditch and can't really move. I look down at myself; it's like my leg has been taken apart by an axe. Not broken. Crushed and split and cut open as if with a maul and an axe. Blood and bits of bone rain out into the ditch, pulverized, right above the ankle. My foot is only connected to my shin by the Achilles tendon – the only thing that connects it to the body – otherwise it would have flown away completely. I take . . . I'm wearing leathers, Swedish, with a zip down the side, and I'm pulling at my sock, pulling my leg together so it's not split open. I am lying with a crowd of people around me, squawking like a parrot:

"Help. Call an ambulance." And they jump into the ditch to examine me. Not to see what has happened or to find out who I am. They're checking my pockets. One of them takes my cigarettes, the other my money, a third my watch. They would even take my boots if they weren't full of blood and meat and bone. "You're crazy – what are you doing?" Two boys try to take my motorbike – you can't even pull it down the street, and it's too heavy to be carried. Luckily Ibrahim passes in his uncle's pick-up and stops to check out the spectacle in the ditch. The thieves have scurried off. Now it's just me and the spectators along the edge. Asko is there – his face content:

"You've dented my bumper – you're going to pay for it," he says with a nasty smile. I look round at the spectators.

"You saw that the *mzungu* swerved to hit me – to kill me with his car. You must tell the police," I shout. They don't say anything; everyone looks at Asko. Have I got money to pay for them seeing it? No, the money has been taken out of my pocket. But the *mzungu* – perhaps he'll pay them for seeing me drive in the wrong lane?

Ibrahim leaps into the ditch; he lifts me up and into the pick-up, my motorbike up into the back – he is very strong. Ibrahim takes me to Mawenzi Hospital right around the corner. The blood is like a great big water tap from my leg. The doctors examine the wound, and they are frightened. They stop the water tap with a knot. Everyone comes and looks and is appalled. What should they do? My leg is almost shattered. I'm alive and I can see my own bones with my eyes; people are not meant to be able to do that; I see bone from one leg and the other is fine.

They get an ambulance and take me to K.C.M.C. because the staff there have a firmer grasp on the science of making people better; right from the start they put drops of water into me from a plastic bag and through a needle into my arm, while the doctors prepare for the operation. I am there, fully conscious. All the time.

Katriina arrives with Solja, who is crying like my leg – water from a tap. Ibrahim has fetched them for me, so they can ensure my survival.

"How did it happen, Marcus?" Katriina asks – she knows it was Asko, but was it on purpose? She wishes the answer to be a no, but my eyes, they tell her yes – that's my payment for Tita's chocolate baby, with his compliments.

"I'll talk to the doctors and see to it that you have the best of everything," Katriina says.

DYING FOOT

Where am I? I am strapped down, and one of my legs is a bloody disaster in a sort of frame on the bed – a box so the leg isn't shaken if I move my thigh. Katriina appears with the *mzungu* doctor who was midwife to little Rebekka.

"We have stopped the bleeding and taken out all bone fragments – otherwise they'll cause infection," he says and explains that they can't put a cast on the open wound. It's going to have to heal up first. The bones that are left are in the box, not connected but in the right order.

"But . . . where is the pain?" I ask.

"You were given chemicals so you couldn't feel it while we did the work on your leg," Dr Freeman says.

So I lie there until the next day – I am given more chemicals to force the pain out – I still can't feel anything. Nothing. My body is fine, no grazes on my skin, no injuries – only my leg; the foot is almost on its way into the grave.

The foot is only a foot now, with no leg to work with – a foot of no importance. Life – we only get one shot. Asko is a wealthy man – dangerous. He could even pay other men to kill me in the hospital; he could go to the Indians – they can help him.

THE SHOCK

Tears spring from Rebekka's eyes when she sees me. Solja is very quiet. Katriina says: "I have spoken to the consultant surgeon, *mzee* Kinabo. We're getting money from the project to pay for your medicine – don't worry."

Katriina must have put the most serious kind of pressure on Jonas to make him help me. Perhaps she threatened to take his daughters all the way to Sweden, where his family might also say that, yes, as a married man Jonas is a disaster.

"What does Jonas say?" I ask.

"Jonas has talked to the doctor as well because he is building a house for himself and needs timber." Jonas can promise him timber and furniture, for free or perhaps just at a reduced price. Then the doctor will give me special treatment. Of course the doctor is meant to treat people for free, but his salary is low, and a doctor is an important man – many obligations to his family, wife, children, nieces, nephews, cousins, brothers, parents – almost everyone in the village will want to use his wallet.

Katriina goes out to find Dr Freeman, who helped Rebekka out of her belly and into the world – he must keep an eye on me.

"Are you well?" I ask the children.

"You're almost dead," Rebekka says, crying.

"They're fighting nonstop at home," Solja says.

"Why's that?" I ask.

"Asko is very angry with you," Solja says.

"Why?"

"Because Tita's baby is like chocolate. That means it's a black man who made it." Solja looks at me. "Is it yours?" she asks.

"I don't know." She thinks for a bit:

"If you don't know, that means it . . ." she says and stops, looks away, thinks for a while before she continues: "Asko is angry with Mum, and Jonas is angry with her too."

"Why are they angry with your mother?"

"Because Mum was always sending you down to help Tita with stuff," Solja says. Rebekka has stopped crying. Solja goes on: "But then Mum said: 'How was I to know she was fucking him? We don't even know if it was him.'"

This Solja, just twelve years old, and already she understands all the monstrosities that go on around her. And baby Rebekka is also witness to the destruction – not even three years old.

Katriina returns to the sickroom. She tells Solja to take Rebekka outside – they must go to the inner courtyard and get some fresh air, wait for her there. Katriina sits down in the chair and sighs, shaking her head.

"Have the police been here yet?" Katriina asks

"No," I say.

"But surely they must look into the accident," she says.

"No," I say. She looks at me.

"Why not?"

"If you can pay, the police give you no trouble," I say. Asko has paid them – he could even get them to say that I must replace his bumper, because my body has dented it.

I myself could pay some men to beat up Asko, but I can't afford to have him killed – it's expensive when the man is white. And I need my money to survive at K.C.M.C. What am I to do?

As soon as Katriina has left, Claire comes.

"Hi, Marcus," she says, smiling. It leaves me with tears in my eyes. "You will be well again," Claire says and wipes the tears from my cheek. "Don't worry."

"You're a good girl," I say. "I'm very glad you're here." We talk to each other very affectionately, and I'm thinking that Claire's God is very troublesome when it comes to sexuality, but he makes a good girl with genuine feelings for her man. Soon Claire has to leave.

"You must bring me a little money from my kiosk, so I have some to grease the nurses," I say. Claire looks away from me. "What?" I say.

"The kiosk was robbed by the Larsson guard. He's gone missing," Claire says. These disasters pack a heavy punch.

BARBARIAN
Forty hours after the surgery. That evening my stomach inflates. Faster, faster. Big. There are no grazes on my skin. Big, big, big. And I am medicated, violently powerful drugs. I am infected with inflammation. They don't know why. They do tests. Perhaps my appendix is pierced through.

It must come out. Into the operating room. My head hurts like all hell, and I can't breathe. Then I am given oxygen from a mask and more chemicals to make me sleep, and then they cut out my appendix.

Now I wake up without my appendix, and at the same time the pains in my leg arrive – it feels like it's in boiling oil.

"Is it possible to have it taken off?" But I don't want it taken off. I want to have my leg with the foot on it. And I am constantly in and out of the operating room, where they pick more bone fragments out of the wound. It stinks worse than shit. Rotting. The wound – it's a dead body. Have you ever been to a morgue? If you go into the morgue, and there hasn't been any electricity for a week – the way that stinks – my leg stinks like that.

Katriina comes down.

"The police say it was your fault," she says.

"What about . . . Asko?" I ask.

"He says . . ." Katriina stops. I'm waiting. "He says he hopes you die. I just can't bear it. He ought to be in prison."

"I'm scared he might get someone to kill me," I say.

"Yes," Katriina says. And I have an idea, because the white people see themselves as guests in the black land, as helpers of the black people. As teachers and instructors in how to live the right way. The white embassies don't like it if the white teacher lives like a barbarian when the negro can see him.

"Asko has his black woman in a house on Uru Road. He has bought a house for her and pays for everything so he can come and pump her whenever he likes."

"A woman? Who he's . . . paying?"

"Yes, like an expensive *malaya* – with Asko as her only customer. Chantelle. She lives on Uru Road, right next to Gadaffi Bar."

"Why are you telling me this?" Katriina asks.

"The embassy doesn't like it when Finnish guests in Tanzania live a scandalous lifestyle with multiple wives like a Maasai – they might even send them home."

"Yes," Katriina says, looking pensive.

DEADLY HELP
I am ill, almost dying, but Claire comes back to the hospital to visit me. That's a great joy, because she has been the cause of more fear. Will she

disappear now that I am broken? But her love is from the heart – she doesn't let me down.

Nechi is staying with me at the hospital. When you can't walk yourself, you must have someone who can fetch help when you're at death's door. And someone has to bring you food from the outside. You can't eat the food they give you at K.C.M.C. – if you're ill already, it will kill you. Nechi gets my food every day from the Larssons'. Katriina has told Josephina to prepare it, and she does a good job. Nechi's helpfulness is his way of making it up to me, because he feels guilty that his family stole from my kiosk; their thieving is now helping save my life.

"You must go to the doctor and to the head nurse," I tell Nechi. He knows the system. Nechi arranges to meet the doctor at a bar at a certain time. "How are you?" Nechi will ask. "Not well at all. There's no money at K.C.M.C.," the doctor will say. Nechi will buy him beer and give him an envelope full of money. Nechi will say: "This is a present for you." The head nurse: Nechi will visit her bringing a present – it could be anything: a chicken, a goat. When people are hungry, they have no time for ethics.

"But how will we be able to afford a goat?" Claire asks.

"Nechi must take my Boombox and sell it in town," I say. If I am dead, I won't hear anything but worms gnawing at my ear anyway.

The hospital is full of corrupt scavengers. The consultant surgeon decides which of the nurses get the good and simple jobs at the hospital. And oddly enough all the pretty nurses get the best jobs, even if they're as useless as a brick without a wall. The doctor pumps them, even on the hospital's time.

Luckily my doctor is *mzee* Kinabo – a godly African from the same Pentecostal church as Claire – and the *mzungu* doctor Freeman is working with him, and those two aren't of the pumping tribe.

I discover that the hospital offers some pleasures in life, because here I am free of that Swedish despot. I am the most important spy in the whole of his forest empire, but do we see this Jonas visit his devoted slave at K.C.M.C.? Not at all. Yes, I know everything about this man's infidelity – everything about his abuse of the aid from the Swedish people to the black man, his abuse of *bhangi* and alcohol – and of people.

"You little shit." What? My eyes are shut. I was asleep. Now I open them to the man who eats dirt. Jonas has his evil face close to mine. He speaks in a low voice so no-one will hear: "I can have you killed as easily as anything. If you give me any more trouble, I will kick your stinking black arse out into the gutter."

"Yes," I say, feeling very frightened.

"Does that hurt?" he says and pokes a straight finger right into my stomach. I scream. "Good," he says and leaves, as the nurse comes running to see what sort of pain produces such animal cries. The pain of a life in crisis.

DEAD BODY

Finally my leg gets that special cast bandage; they put on the white stuff. It's like cassava, like concrete. When it's wrapped around my leg it dries up and goes hard like a brick. But they left made an opening so the nurses can get in and remove the pus every day. And every week I must go to the operating room, have the cast taken off; the *mzungu* is busy rearranging my bones to make the leg straight again the way it's meant to be.

Solja comes straight from school on her own legs to see me.

"Asko has been sent home to Finland," she says. That's a relief. I have had a chocolate baby with his wife, but he has lost his job, lost his money, had his opportunities for enjoying the miraculous sexuality of a black woman obliterated.

"Why was he sent home?" I ask.

"Because he had a black wife at the same time he was married to Tita – that's illegal," Solja says. "Gösta's wife has left as well – they're getting a divorce."

"How are things at home?" I ask. She looks upset.

"They're always arguing. Dad says Tita was bad because she had a baby with a black man. But Mum says that doesn't give Asko the right to kill you. And Rebękka can't sleep at night, because she's so scared all the time. And Mum's angry, and Dad is almost never at home – not even at night. And he's drunk all the time, and weird."

I don't say anything. What can I say? That it will be alright? I don't even believe it myself. Solja waits for my reply, but I don't say anything. "Do you think my parents are going to get divorced as well?" she asks.

"I don't know," I say.

"I think they are," she says.

ARSE ON FIRE

The bacteria reproduce so quickly in my leg that it could kill me. So I have to take almost the strongest antibiotic you could ever find. It must be bought in town, and I must take a lot of it, and I must pay for it myself. Otherwise they are going to have to take off my foot. They give me the antibiotic as shots – the sort where the doctor pokes you so badly with the needle the pain can make you jump up even if you're missing one leg. They have to tie me to the bed. It burns. Burning spears in my arse. Like taking red-hot charcoal or a blowtorch to your skin. The more the doctor presses the injection syringe; the more I feel it. A totally toxic thing. They can hear my creams throughout the whole hospital, so they start putting antibiotics into the water that drips into my arm instead. Every drop that falls – it's like fire. It comes into my arm. It drips: ta, ta, ta. Straight into my arse is more painful. But in my arm – it goes on for hours. Three hours, and I have it every day for two weeks. I can feel the antibiotics moving through my blood, sweeping along with the flow. All over. Burning stuff on my inside. My hair falls out all over my body – now I am bald.

MOSQUITO KILLER

I've been in bed at K.C.M.C. for three weeks. Perhaps I can be let out in six weeks; Jah is making sure I get better. Claire comes round with a parcel: "Aunt Elna has sent you some shoes." I open the box – they're Eccos. She writes: "A little something to keep you going once you're back on your feet." I try on a shoe on the right side of my hospital bed – it's amazing, built to last. "It'll be fine," Claire says, because tears well into my eyes. Two shoes are too many for just one foot.

The box from Aunt Elna also contains T-shirts and three pairs of underpants. Claire takes the things back to her ghetto, because here everything will be stolen by the nurses once they have medicated me to sleep.

When no-one's around I just look at my leg to cry. I pretend to be asleep, but I'm constantly crying. A headache like madness. I wonder what will happen? Will my walk be the walk of a limping man?

"I can't give you more than six tablets," mzee Kinabo says.

"But I've got money for them," I say, because I must pay for the tablets – if not, they won't give me anything for the pain.

"If I give you more, the chemicals will ruin your body," Kinabo says.

"But it hurts so, so much," I say, crying because my body has already been ruined by pain.

Big Man Ibrahim comes to visit.

"Bring me the most powerful painkillers – my head's exploding," I tell him. Ibrahim feels very sorry for me.

The next afternoon he comes back and gives me the pills without speaking to my doctor. Touching anything without your doctor's permission is forbidden. I am desperate and eat the pills like sweets. It helps me. The pain goes away, and I can eat my dinner. Because now I'm no longer in the Intensive Care Unit but in an ordinary sickroom. The wound from my appendix has healed, and I have started eating. All the time I'm thinking: will I walk again? Every time the pain is screaming in my flesh, I beat it down with pills from the city. A mosquito comes and sucks from my stomach. I don't need a mosquito net any longer – the drugs kill it right away, so it dies with its trunk still inside me.

At midnight I vomit blood. Blood, continuously. I feel like I must use the toilet; there's blood when I do. Then there's blood from my mouth, blood from my arse. Everything is blood, blood. And I'm looking at it – my blood bursting out of me, taking my life with it as a passenger. And there's no pain in my stomach. The pain's in my head. Insane headache. I'm thinking: this is it – I'm dying.

I go straight to Intensive Care.

A nurse brings me a large bowl of ice cubes and puts it on my bed.

"Eat," *mzee* Kinabo says.

"Why?"

"Something's not right with your intestines – either your small or your large intestine. The ice can stop the bleeding from the wound inside you." I start chewing. "Don't chew," he says. "Suck it." I keep swallowing. They take my temperature and starting warming the outside of my stomach with a fan heater, otherwise I'll freeze to death. They have to help me with oxygen from a mask. At the same time, I have to keep on eating ice cubes.

I can still feel, I can still talk – no problem.

"Count back from ten," *mzee* Kinabo says, and I start:

"Ten, nine, eight, seven . . ." They're looking at watches and all sorts of machinery all around me. And then I can't count anymore, and afterwards I don't know where I am – at all. I can't open my eyes – only hear things.

Can't speak for a long time. It's because of the chemicals – Babylonian they are. But after a long time I return.

"It was sheer luck – you surviving," *mzee* Kinabo says. "When we had done everything, and after we had closed up your stomach, we couldn't bring you round – wake you up, as it were." All the places they might put a drip into me had been ruined – the skin and the muscles hardened by the destruction of the needles. "We had to use the last option, from the neck rather than the hands or the arms." The operation lasted almost three hours. Three hours just to fix the things inside me. It's not difficult to cut away the thing and put it back together – the problem is that other organs are starting to fail. "Putting it back together when you're dead – that's no use, is it?" the doctor says with a big laugh.

"But what was it you cut away?"

"We've taken out a section of your stomach and sewn it back together and removed bits of your intestines because they were completely shot," he says.

"Why did you do that? You should have asked me – I don't want to be without my intestines – I need it."

"If we hadn't done it, you'd be dead. You've created that illness yourself," he says, very angry. I created chemical juice in my stomach with too many thoughts. Gastric acid. The juice is meant to aid digestion, but not too much of it. That stuff gives you ulcers. A product of stress. I had created a very large wound in my stomach, in my intestines. I had destroyed myself completely. My head was about to burst, but my head was only a sign something else was very wrong. And I overdosed on the painkillers. Completely. The more I overdosed, the more I made that juice; it's a double poison. The wound exploded.

"Your intestines and stomach will be disrupted for a very, very long time. It is going to cause you a great deal of trouble," *mzee* Kinabo says.

I have to say goodbye to Nechi. His family have got him a scholarship at the university in Canada. His older brother is now the deputy boss at the Police Academy, so now he meets the Minister of Justice and scratches his back. And the Minister likes it; right away he throws the family a bone – a scholarship for the little brother. Who will bring me my food? Nechi has been my salvation – but now K.C.M.C. might kill me.

GIFTS OF BLOOD

The casual labourers on West Kilimanjaro have heard of the new disaster in my stomach. We are friends. Almost thirty of them come to K.C.M.C. to donate blood for me. I cry: their love flows right into my veins. Jonas will never understand it. You don't just give your help in return for payment, but because it gives you spiritual satisfaction and sets you apart from the animal – makes you human.

The blood bank gives a report to the doctors: this number of people have donated that amount of blood to go into Marcus. That's good because in Tanzania blood causes many problems – sometimes it's all wrong, full of diseases making the transfusion risky. Are you dying because you run dry, or are you dying because the new blood brings a fresh disease? And they haven't got proper machines to check and process the blood.

Me, I've had almost twenty litres of blood. And at first I looked at the pack of blood, and I could read the name of the man, and I didn't know him. Was he full of diseases from the bush? Now I am given blood from men I assume are living right. But what do I know of how they spend their nights?

That Sunday I receive a visit in Intensive Care from *bwana* Omary. He tells me of Jonas' reaction:

"Right away he said: 'Everyone who went to Moshi will be docked a day's pay.' And I said: 'But we went there to save your employee, Marcus. He was drying up.' And Jonas said: 'The workers are paid to fell trees – not to give blood. Marcus has brought his problems on himself.'"

Omary shakes his head at this Jonas, who is always so blind to the bigger picture if it takes even a small effort on his part. The Swedes sent him to Tanzania to help, but Jonas doesn't just fell trees – he fells people as well.

Christian

The old man is pissed off with me, because I was caught smoking at school outside the designated areas. It's that eternal refrain: "Only stupid people get caught." And with him on the disciplinary board . . . He's made sure I can't run a tab at Moshi Club, so when I play squash I either dehydrate or have to drink water from the tap, which means shitting like a fountain a few hours later. Or steal a bit of cash from his pockets. He himself has a tab. Beer and whisky. I go through his pockets.

My motorbike is stranded as well – it's impossible to get any petrol these days. The Nordic Project employs people to wait parked outside petrol stations all night long in case a tanker should arrive.

I go up to K.C.M.C. to visit Marcus. The road winds through the doctors' residential area – detached houses with large gardens, all the same style, built at the same time as the hospital. It's easy to see that there are Western doctors in some of the houses – those gardens are tended by gardeners. The Africans don't care about that sort of thing. Sweat seeps through the back of my T-shirt. Sun digs into my skull – the hottest time of the day. I reach the hospital and go inside. The air is cool but reeks of disease and disinfectants. The last time I saw Marcus, he was almost in a coma and was delirious. Katriina says he can speak now; he's in I.C.U. – they've cut out some of his intestines, and if he gets an infection, he might die.

A nurse points me the general direction. I go into the room – like a dormitory; metal beds on either side. A few people look at me without any obvious interest. I can't see him – am about to leave.

"Welcome to Death's waiting room," a voice says. I look. Marcus? A greyish-black man who looks like he's been locked up in a K.Z. Camp gives me a lazy stare. His eyes are shining faintly, dull and dark in the sunken face. I look around. It's him. Did they forget to remove the dead? I go over. Concentrate on Marcus. He tries to smile, but all I can see is his skull trying to escape his body and break free; on his bald scalp a single vein is throbbing. He tries to sit up in bed, wincing and moaning.

"Where's your hair?" I ask.

"It fell out," he says.

"Crikey," I say. Marcus doesn't say anything. What can he say? "Is it true?" I ask. He looks at me. What am I asking him? "That you had a baby with Tita?" I add.

"Yes," he says. "I pumped some black colour into the white flesh."

"She's old," I say. Even though I too have thought about her. Loads of times.

"Very *chiki-chiki*," Marcus says with the glimmer of a smile.

"Is it true that Asko had a woman living in a house so he could visit her whenever he wanted?" I ask.

"Yes," Marcus says. "Down on Uru Road. Chantelle. A very good *malaya*."

"Does Jonas have one as well?" I ask.

"Jonas doesn't want to spend that much money on something black. He just pumps in the back of his Land Cruiser – you saw it yourself."

"But . . ." I say and stop.

"All the white men do it. Except your father, perhaps. He hasn't gone into that dark night. Not yet." Marcus grins faintly. Stares up at the ceiling.

That afternoon I go through Dad's pockets and find quite a lot of shillings. In the evening I tell him I'm meeting Sharif at the cinema. I tuck the banknotes into my sock, and then I go down to Majengo – most of the way you can't see because there's no stars and moon isn't out, but I make it all the way to the bars. My heart is pounding so hard I think I'm going to be sick. She's sitting at a table with a tall, skinny girl. It's still early, so there's not a lot of people out yet. I cross the dirt road. The skinny girl makes a sign at Scola, who turns around so I can see her large breasts and her skinny body. She smiles like a cat.

"Hi, *mzungu* – did you miss me?" she asks.

"Come," I say – my voice sounds croaky. She gets up lazily and comes towards me. "Come," I say again and start walking towards the guesthouse.

"Wait," she says with a hand on my arm. "How much money have you got?" she asks. I tell her. "We can go somewhere better," she says.

"Yes," I say. She takes my hand and leads me to a different guesthouse – less run-down. I give her the money for the room. She gets a key, and we go in. Scola quickly pulls off all her clothes and stands in front of me.

"Give me the money," she says and holds out her hand. I hold the notes towards her – she puts them away in her clothes and lies down on the bed

"Come and taste me, *mzungu* boy," she says, spreading her legs.

Marcus

CHAINSAW

My leg is still a scandal – not properly put together. They're always opening it up to have a look. And what I feel most of all is that it would be better to run away when they're going to open the cast. They open it with a machine; something like a circular saw, and the doctor cuts through the plaster, following the skin. And I know that if he … just one centimetre too deep, and it'll go right into me. And the terrible thing about it is that it's an old model – it's noisy. It's like felling a tree with a chainsaw. It's shaking. Oh, it is bad.

SPARE-PART ARSE

They start giving me skin grafts. That means they take skin from my arse and move it down to my leg. The piece may be four inches long and two inches wide. Over and over they take it from my arse. They take a large strip because the part that takes root on the leg that might only be half the piece, and the other half might rot because my arse-skin doesn't want to live close to my foot. I can see my arse-skin put down there – half of it is rotting, and then it's taken away; now they need more and I've hardly got any arse left.

"You won't ever smile at that arse again – it's completely ruined," I tell Claire.

"Who cares about your arse – so long as you can walk."

LETTERS FROM EUROPE

Solja comes to my sickbed while Katriina talks to Dr Freeman – quietly and up close. Solja has brought letters from Sweden and Finland – Aunt Elna and Mika. First I open the one from the old *mama*. Ohhh – she has become ill with cancer. Two years ago they removed one of her breasts. Now the doctor's telling her: "You are ill; you must sort out your affairs." She writes to me: "I am dying, Marcus. I will make sure you will be alright in the future." Included in the letter is information about a Swedish bank account in my name and papers I must sign and return so they will recognize me. There's hardly any money in the account, but that's because we have to go through complicated European procedures to ensure that I really am Marcus. "The money will be there later," Aunt Elna writes. The old *mama* has embraced me as part of her family. She paid for my fees and everything when I was in school. And Jonas thought I didn't know.

Mika writes that he wants to come down for a visit while the Larssons are in Sweden on summer holiday. He writes: "If you buy tanzanite, I will pay you for them in dollars when I come down." His idea is a good one, but right now I can't move at all.

CHARLIE CHAPLIN

Finally the wound starts to heal, and I can no longer see bone – only arse-skin. They put on a full cast from my hip to my toes. My leg feels heavy. And the air is close when it escapes at my hip where the cast opens. The heat is tripled under the plaster. The smell is tripled too. And the itch – after two weeks the itch under the plaster starts. I try talking to it, ask it to stop: "Please?!" Plaster for four weeks and then the cast is taken off, and a new one put on for four more weeks. They have to clean the leg and examine it constantly with X-rays.

"Your leg is pointing in the wrong direction, so you'll get a foot sticking out like Charlie Chaplin," *mzee* Kinabo says. You can tell he's a Pentecostal: "Nerves and bones must be arranged by God, in the manner He intended – not by man. So when the bones grow back together in the wrong way, you'll be in pain for the rest of your life."

"So what now?" I ask.

"We are going to have to take you to the operating room and break the bones again. To arrange them right."

I have to stay at the hospital for another month. My body is disappearing. I feel full, but the doctor says I'm starving.

I can feel everything that happens to the food from the moment I swallow it until it leaves my arsehole, every process, its passage through a particular piece of intestine, past a bit of scar tissue – it's all as clear to me as when other people are touched by human hand.

After two weeks I get up and try to walk using crutches. My stomach has a migraine when I move. Perhaps my cast will come off in two months – they say I will be able to walk again.

THE PENTECOSTAL PUMP

My healing progresses. I do exercises with my upper body because I am weak from lying down. They take me to physiotherapy – lessons between iron bars; I walk forwards and back five times, sweating enormously. Really? Is that me? Later I move with a walker. At night I can't sleep. I get up to practise my walker-walk down the empty corridors. I can go everywhere in the hospital. The Israelis built it well – lots of galleries, inner courtyards, an airy structure. And yet the air is still full of disinfectant, disease, medication and rotting flesh.

ZION

"It was sheer luck that you survived," *mzee* Kinabo says. I have been his lab rat; breaking me apart and trying to make me survive. Katriina has come to pick me up. The cast is only on my foot and ankle now, and I've got my crutches. It's a joy to come outside and feel the air and the sun, and to just stand and breathe the air without the stench of disinfectant and rot. I get into the car. That Toyota is my Zion Train, and she starts it – it hums and shakes; it comes to life. The air pours in through the windows, and the sun lights up the world which has the scent of petrol and detergent from Katriina's clothes, the clean smell of woman, dust, man's joy in life, a very great joy.

"We're getting a fizzy drink," Katriina says, so we go to a kiosk by one of the nurses' colleges. I sit, with the car door open, and she gets us a Coke. And then I see the chimney of the K.C.M.C. morgue; it's meant to be white like the rest of the hospital, but it's caked in soot – black. The dead are there on the chimney – it was meant to be me, or at least my leg should have been burnt in there, but I'm taking it all home with me. All I'm missing is a bit of stomach, a bit of intestine – nothing much.

But the world never tires of shitting on the little guy. I go home with all the bones in my leg connected, but what is my ghetto like? Robbed by thieves: my clothes, many of my tapes, the jacket I had, and even the amazing new underpants from Aunt Elna – all three pairs. Who did it? Must I go and pull people's trousers down to find the thief? I can't even walk. And if I go to the police – useless. I have lost my things. They are gone. The police will only write up a report, and they won't even bother to come and see how it was done. And I'm poor – I've got no insurance.

"I didn't want to tell you," Claire says. "You would have had even more to worry about then."

"It doesn't matter," I say. Claire has been good. On the door there is an enormous padlock like in a prison – I lock if I so much as go to the toilet. I have to sneak into the big house if I want to listen to a single beat, because the new Boombox was sold to pay for medicine. My room is almost empty, and I have to put my nose back to the grindstone to fix the problem myself. I miss my music and my wonderful underpants. But I'll fight on, because just to be alive is amazing, thanks and praise be to Jah. My ghetto is without music, but full of joy.

*

Solja comes down to see me. "When we go back to Sweden, we're buying a boat," she says proudly and shows me a Swedish magazine with pictures of big, gorgeous boats.

"Aren't they very expensive?" I ask.

"I don't know. Dad says we can afford it." She's almost skipping for joy, up and down. "Then we'll go sailing whenever we're home on holiday." Where does all that money come from? When they're at the club, I limp to the house and root through Jonas' papers. I find bank statements from Sweden; his account is full of money. It's impossible that his salary could be that high – are the funds in his account the S.I.D.A. money that was meant to be spent on training locals but never was, because no negro is ever sent to Sweden for training? I'm sure that money from the project is flowing into Jonas' account – now the S.I.D.A. money will take the shape of a boat on the Swedish sea.

That night Claire comes to my room in a very pretty dress. She's standing at my desk and reading the notes from the doctors, and her bottom is sticking out in such an amazing way that I am almost about to explode after all that time in the sickbed. I curse that Pentecostal church to hell. But then a miracle happens – Claire turns around with tears in her eyes and jumps into my bed and kisses me and talks and mutters:

"I am so happy you've come back to me." And God's blessing comes to me straight through her hand – she fiddles with the button and the zipper – *eeehhh*. She goes like a train – Zion Train.

BOOMBOX

I get mail. A letter from Tita. Not a word about the chocolate baby. Only that she's heard about my disaster, and that she wants to give me whatever small help she can. Wrapped in tinfoil are two hundred-dollar banknotes. The white lady trying to pay for her dark conscience.

Right away I order a new Pioneer Boombox with Katriina's assistance and a telex to Ostermann in Denmark. It must come super quick to Kilimanjaro International Airport and be helped into the country by *bwana* D'Souza.

Phantom comes to see my cadaver. "Liberty has shut down its disco. Alwyn's loudspeakers are bust," he says, grinning.

"His father will help him again," I say.

"No, no," Phantom grins. "His father won't help him anymore. First he put Alwyn through I.S.M. – very expensive, and he only has poor grades to show for it. Then he sent Alwyn to Europe to learn about the cheese business, but Alwyn came back and said he was a Rasta and a D.J. Now his father says: "Enough. I will pay your salary if you make cheese – otherwise you're on your own.'" Phantom is laughing so hard he slaps his thighs. I'm laughing too.

"Did he start making cheese then?" I ask.

"No, now he makes a living from his recording shop – he can still make tapes even though his speakers are dead – the work is done through headphones. But he's poor. No more taxis, the girls are gone. Back to the corn porridge." It's true. At night he was a D.J. at Liberty, during the day he recorded cassettes, because he has a lot of good music.

I could do that job, but I don't have any decks; these days I'm using Solja's little Philips tape recorder , which she lent me because she knows I love music, even though I've hardly got anything good to listen to. I need music. To be led and guided by Jah.

"Just imagine what an easy life Alwyn has led," I say.

"No," Phantom says. "That boy doesn't know who he is, what he is, is he black or white? – Chagga or Rasta? The International School ruined him by sowing great confusion in his soul."

I know that confusion.

TO HELL

I soon call D'Souza to ask where the Boombox is. It was sent straight to the airport with K.L.M. He says it isn't coming. Someone stole it on the way. I have to send an insurance claim to Ostermann in Denmark. I do it by telex: a letter might be delayed by as much as six months – and that's before it even leaves Tanzania. So I spend money on a taxi and on a telex and everything – lots of communication back and forth. "The stereo has been delivered," they say. "And where is my receipt for delivery?" is my question. In the end I succeed; they acknowledge that I have a claim on them for two hundred dollars. But I feel it clearly: they think I've cheated them. I don't order the Boombox again. Right now I have to wait for my circumstances to stabilize, and when the Larssons are in Sweden I can use their stereo to make a bit of money by recording tapes.

"You have to eat," Claire says, pointing at my plate, almost untouched – food she made especially for me. She hides her face in her hands and weeps.

"I am stuffed," I say, because I am feeling sick. "I need a beer."

"You have to eat food as well," Claire says. "Otherwise you'll die." Ibrahim gives me a hard look.

"Go and limp about a bit – get the food settled in your stomach. And then you eat a bit more," he says. I do a few circles, take a few more spoonfuls, but mostly I just toy with the food on the plate. In my stomach the food is compressed, but there might be little holes in between – better if I pour some beer on top that can trickle into the holes – beer gives extra nutrition as well.

Money is a big problem. The kiosk is empty. I talk to Jonas about compensation for the wages I lost. All he has to say to the office is that the accident took place during working hours. As a worker I'm insured through the company with a local company. It won't cost Jonas anything. I can buy a new stock for the kiosk – rise from the dust.

"You weren't working," Jonas says. "You're always taking the project motorbike for your own purposes."

"Yes, it was work. Because the company's insurance has already paid for the dead motorbike. If I wasn't working, then I would have stolen the motorbike, and then I'd have to pay for it and go to prison."

"It was after working hours," Jonas says. "We've turned a blind eye to your wrecking the motorbike."

"I was fetching cigarettes for your wife," I say.

"Fetching cigarettes isn't your job," Jonas says.

"When the G.M. says I must wash his private car, I wash it as part of my job, because otherwise I have no job," I say, standing up to this man and speaking my mind for the first time, straight to his face and into his ear. Jonas grins as he shakes his head.

"Go away," he says.

Katriina is my salvation. She comes to my ghetto and gives me a few shillings.

"Don't tell Jonas," she says.

"Of course not."

ZAIRE

I start preparations on Mika's behalf. I ask around to learn about the tanzanite stone – prices and quality control. There is a *mzee* with many properties in Shanty Town who lives off mining in Merelani. A clever old Chagga – very hard. I find his son – Dickson, the man Rosie was fooling around with.

Dickson and I come to an understanding. We take his pick-up the way to Merelani, through the village with its bars and garages for motorbikes and onwards up the bumpy road to the mining area, which is called Zaire, because everyone hopes they'll find wealth in the ground, just like in the nation of barbarity in the West.

We buy stones straight from the miners for cash – it's cheaper than if there's a middleman involved. I write to Mika that he can stay here, but that he must me help first. Mika must bring a lot of L.P.s down on the plane with him. I need good music, so I can sit with my weird leg and my ruined arse and record cassettes.

BABYLON

The Larssons have gone to Sweden, and I am alone in the empty house: no children, no food. Katriina did give me a little money so I can buy dog food – corn porridge and rotting meat; must I share it with the dog, or should I eat grass like a zebra in the national park?

I take a taxi to the TanScan office to get money.

"Hello, Marcus. Still in one piece, I see," the accountant says. I just stare at the office girl. The pump is so very hungry, even though Claire has been working it hard.

"What happened about that motorbike?" I ask.

"We got a new one through S.I.D.A. – it was insured. No problems," the accountant says.

"What about the insurance for my injury?" I ask.

"Well, all your medication that was paid for by S.I.D.A. – no problems there either."

"But what about my accident? It was an occupational injury. I must receive compensation. Four months without pay. Stomach ruined, leg ruined, arse ruined – forever."

"Jonas says you weren't working when it happened."

"I was fetching cigarettes for the wife of the project boss on a project motorbike. If I wasn't working, I should have been reported for stealing

315

the bike, and then the police would have come and taken me to prison, even without my leg they would have, and I would have been fired and they would have insisted on being reimbursed."

"I don't know about all that," the accountant says. "You'll have to talk to Jonas about it."

"What about my pay for those months?"

"You haven't been working – how can we pay you?"

"I almost died, and now I'm starving."

"You have to talk to Jonas." But Jonas has gone to Sweden for a three-month summer holiday to sail on the waters in the boat of corruption and be far from the negro. The happiness of the Babylonians is made from the tears of the suffering.

Luckily two guests from Sweden come down to stay in the house. I advise them on Africa and eat their food. There's one bloke who is young and very friendly. He takes me out in the evenings, or he buys drinks and we sit on the veranda. We talk, drink, eat. I get drunk very quickly, because my stomach doesn't have room for food and my weight is low – I'm nothing but skin and bones; the muscles walked off while I was at K.C.M.C.

"You have to ride the motorbike now," the bloke says.

"But I've got plaster and crutches."

"It doesn't matter. You can sit on the back with your leg sticking out. If you don't, you'll never ride one again."

And we do it. I am very frightened.

At home I practise using my crutches. God is at hand, because I have survived my operations. But it remains to be seen whether my foot will cooperate with my leg.

"You have to believe," Claire says. It's not easy. I limp to the garage – on the floor is the motorbike I crashed on, bent like a bow – finished, the end. In the corner there's another of the old, worn Yamaha bikes. I have to believe. I start my work. Sit on a stool with my leg stretched out in front of me. Take the bikes apart – completely. Screw things together and clean things, tighten, make repairs. Two corpses put together to make one living machine. It runs alright.

I limp around and look through the house. Find little *bhangi* sticks in odd places; banknotes – dollars – tucked behind bookshelves, papers, bank statements with large figures, all of it belonging to Jonas – much more than he can have made from S.I.D.A. And I find the picture of my chocolate baby. Is it a boy or a girl? – I don't know. But it's my baby. I take the picture to my ghetto along with a nice one of Tita.

I came close to death, but now I'm alive. My pump is stiff. All the time. It's been asleep for a long time and misses the activities in its white garden. But Claire comes to me; black roses will bloom as well.

THE ETHICS OF CORRUPTION

My training is working. I am moving forward now, using only one crutch. After four weeks I go to the hospital to have the cast changed. But the doctor from the Pentecostal church won't see me:

"Your *mzungu* promised me a load of timber for my house," *mzee* Kinabo says. "That's why you have two legs now. But the timber hasn't been delivered." I apologize.

"But I have to have the cast taken off," I say.

"Then you'll have to give me my timber," he says. But I can't get timber when I'm not working. The ethics of bribery have been disrupted by Jonas, but he doesn't care. The white man is nothing but a tourist; if he is taken ill, he'll go to Sweden. If trouble breaks out in Tanzania, the military aircraft from Europe will land on T.P.C.'s golf course and pick up all the Scandinavians and fly them home without so much as a scratch. I crutch about at K.C.M.C., broken everywhere and getting nothing but frowns from *mzee* Kinabo. But I then find Dr Jackson, the American intern. He changes the cast.

"In a couple of weeks when you're moving about a bit more easily, you can go to work with the cast still on – that's the best way to get started," he says.

Christian

The old man's face is one big tic as he speaks on the phone. Now his right eye blinks, now his left; the corners of his mouth twitch, he bites his lower lip, and there's a nerve on the side of his neck which is pulsing. Something's up. At the same time he is bobbing his foot up and down, scratching his shins, pulling at his moustache. He lights a cigarette and puts it down in the ashtray, his jaw milling from side to side, and then grabs the pack, shakes out a fresh one, lights it and puffs away while the first is lit and smoking in the ashtray.

"That's that settled, then," he says. "That's quite alright. No, that's fine, fine. No problem," he says. I go over and take the abandoned cigarette from the ashtray. The old man looks up at me, perplexed, and then down at the cigarette in his hand. Shakes his head quickly and abruptly, as if cleaning the cobwebs. "No really, I'm completely on top of what he's doing," he says, blinking repeatedly – pressing his eyes shut and opening them wide, sucking hard at the cigarette, so it burns hot and goes limp. "Yes, I will," he says. "Goodbye." He puts down the phone. "Your mum sends her love," he says.

"I bet," I say.

Last day before the summer holidays. Samantha comes over all of a sudden and hugs me:

"You take care up there – do you hear?"

"Yes, ma'am," I say. "You too, down here." She gives me a wet kiss on the cheek, lets go of me and slaps my arse before wriggling away.

I ask Sharif if he wants to go for a game of squash in the afternoon, because my plane isn't until tomorrow, and I'm in no hurry to get home.

"I can't. I have to say goodbye to Katja," he says.

"But her parents have already picked her up," I say.

"My parents are coming as well. We're going to the mosque together," he says. Fuck. Then what am I to do? Go home with my report card looking the way it does? – not until the old man has had a few drinks. He's asked some people round tonight, so irrigation should be guaranteed. I go home when it's growing dark. There are a few cars outside. The first of the guests have arrived. I go inside. Dinner is on the large dining table in the kitchen – a buffet. There's something in the oven, being kept warm. I can hear them in the sitting room. I go in and straight over to Dad, give him my report card. His guests are colleagues from the Nordic Project as well as people from school, among them my English teacher.

"Proficiency," Dad says and takes the report card. Everyone goes quiet. He opens it, checks the numbers, reads the teachers' notes for each subject. All eyes are on him. It's not appalling – except for the few classes where I've hit rock bottom, pretty much dug myself into a hole. I stand next to him, without saying anything; trying to read his expression. He finishes the little leaflet and leafs back through it, stops, clears his throat, looks up and reads the R.E. teacher's note in a steady voice:

"Attendance: random. Grade: No grade is possible as he has completed no work. It's sad to reflect that someone – in his own words – believes that reggae music should be mankind's ultimate spiritual influence. If he hadn't been so sure he knew it all, he might have benefitted from the lessons." Dad looks up. Strained laughter erupts from across the room. He pats my shoulder. "Oh well," he says. "We've never been a particularly superstitious family."

I get an aisle seat on the plane – if I turn my head, I can see Katja sitting behind me in a window seat. We take off – her face is turned to the windowpane – one last glimpse of Africa – she's going home to Finland. I think she's snivelling. I lean in across the man next to me – a shrivelled Indian on his way to see his family in England. Through the window I can see West Kilimanjaro approaching. Sometimes they circle round Kibo so the tourists can look down into the crater. But we're quite badly delayed as it is, so the pilot flies due north. We've already ascended quite a bit, but I can follow the road up, see the forest behind, and there, to the west of the forest: Simba Farm. Barns and workshops around the yard. The main house and the guesthouse, the neon green lawn and the flowerbeds. On one side of the lawn I can even see a tiny pale blue square – the swimming pool – and a pale speck swimming across it. Could it be the colonialist who fucked my mum? And now I'm going home to see her. Because I'm the only child she's got.

We reach our flight level. I go to the back to use the toilet. Truddi's sitting nearby, being sick into a bag. I realize the bar is open. I press the button, order beer and salted almonds over and over. In the end I fall asleep. Fly through broken glass and blood – crash to the ground and . . . wake up. Look out onto a patchwork of sharply defined fields, farms, forests – there's not a single patch of wilderness in all of northern Europe. The approach to Schiphol Airport, Amsterdam. We're spending the night at the Sheraton – I'm on a connecting flight to Copenhagen early tomorrow morning. Here it's full of businessmen, stewardesses, swanky suitcases, sleek lino, shining bright signs, perfume. Each and every surface is even, consistent, clean. No cracks, weeds, stones or dust. The tarmac is like a billiard table, finished with a straight edge where the pavement begins – completely even, no gaps, holes, or broken concrete. And there are street lamps – all the bulbs work. The cars are clean, noiseless, no exhaust fumes. Science fiction. A bus takes us to the hotel. The receptionists stare. Businessmen in their suits and a bunch of I.S.M. pupils in worn jeans and faded T-shirts, wearing car-tyre sandals or worn-out sneakers. Keys are distributed. A few of us stand there, milling about. Katja is in the group. Disoriented by jetlag even though it's nearly the same the time zone. Europe is plain weird.

"This way, ladies and gentlemen," an efficient receptionist says, striding ahead to lead the ragamuffins out of the reception area. We fall in behind him. I almost stumble on the deep pile of the carpet. The beer I had on the plane has evaporated while I slept. I am on the ground floor – the receptionist points at a door and continues down the hall with Katja in tow.

"See you," she says with a faint hand gesture.

"Yes," I say. The room I enter is organized madness. The bathroom! Little soaps and bottles of shampoo. I strip down. So much hot water comes out of the tap that I almost drown. The towels are soft, bordering on the impossible. I wrap one around me. Brush my teeth – the tooth-paste foams like mad. Open the sliding door. So bizarre it almost makes me dizzy. What is that? The lawn outside – I step on it; as even as an industrial carpet. Uniform – no dry patches, no weeds. Odd. There are . . . birds. The birds are singing. No cicadas. It's still light even though it's evening – it must be eight. I look at the planes landing and taking off in the distance. Things work. The grass tickles my feet. I look back towards the room, see the open door, see the curtains move in the room next to mine. Was that Katja? I look down at myself. Tanned, with a towel around my waist, standing on the lawn – a savage. A jolt shakes me: I have to lock the door or I'll be robbed by people from the street. But no, there are no people here, only the perversely new and clean cars passing by in a steady stream, noiseless and finely tuned so no diesel fumes seep out. No-one has the presence of mind to steal here. I go back inside, grab a Coke from the minibar, take my pack of Sportsmans. No. I put my clothes on, go to reception for cigarettes. The old man's given me a few foreign banknotes he had knocking about. I exchange them for Dutch coins with the receptionist. Draw a pack of Lucky Strike from an automat with countless labels and lights inside it. IT'S TOASTED, it says on the pack. I light up. The cigarettes are much more tightly packed – they taste better, the draw is more even. Probably not as much D.D.T. either, which is what the Greeks around Iringa use. New guests arrive at reception – a host of gentlemen in suits. They speak German. Two men are staring at me. I look down at myself. My sneakers are tatty. I go to the bar.

"You're too young," the man says.

"I'm not too young," I say.

"Then you'll have to bring your passport," the man says.

"*Tsk*," I say. In reception I wonder if I can ask what room Katja is in. But I can't bring myself to do it. I could also just knock on the next door – I think it was her. I stop in front of it, but I don't knock. Go into my own room, kick off my sneakers and take my Coke with me out on the lawn. It's getting dark now. I light another cigarette. A faint hissing sound. A sliding door? I turn around. Katja.

"Hi," I say. "Feel that grass." She sneers but comes outside. "Take off your shoes," I say – surprising myself. She throws her shoes into her room and giggles as she walks on the grass.

"Have you got a cigarette for me?" she asks.

"Yes, of course. American. Lucky Strike," I say. She comes over. It's too dark for me to see her face. She takes one. I light a match for her – it lights her up as well. She looks as if she's been crying. Sharif's girl – but not anymore, I suppose.

"Mmmm," she says. "Did you get them at the airport?"

"The reception," I say. "There's an automat. And a bar."

"Did you go to the bar?" she asks.

"No," I lie.

"Will you go with me?" she asks.

"Absolutely." We go in through our rooms. Put on our shoes on the way.

"Europe," I say. "Will you order?" I ask and hold out some cash to Katja.

"I've got money," she says and goes to the bar. I sit down at a table behind some large plants that look like they might be made of plastic. Katja brings us two beers. We toast. The bartender comes over.

"You're not old enough," he tells me.

"Yes," I say. Katja smiles.

"I've told you once," the bartender says.

"Why do you bother?" I ask and I really do want to know.

"I'm going to have to ask you to leave," he says.

"Let's just go," Katja says and gets up. I take both our beers in my hand.

"They're staying here," the man says.

"No," I say and go round the table in the opposite direction, walking towards reception. The man considers for the briefest moment – perhaps he'll try to pull the bottles from my grasp, but there are more people in the bar – the altercation would disrupt the organized civilities. We go through the reception down the hall. "There's a minibar as well," I tell Katja, who is walking ahead of me – short legs, tight arse, blonde hair.

"Let's go to my room," she says. Once there we open the door onto the lawn. It's dark now. We turn on the T.V., open the minibar. Drink beer.

"What time are you leaving?" I ask. She's getting on the same plane as me, first to Copenhagen and then on to Helsinki. Katja calls reception and asks for a wake-up call the next morning. We turn off the T.V. Sit on the bed smoking cigarettes. Katja fetches two mini bottles of gin from the fridge. We toast. She takes her Walkman and puts it on. Puts the headphones on the bed and turns up the volume.

"If only we had a spliff – a little *bhangi*," Katja says.

"That'd be wicked," I say.

"Did you bring some?" she asks.

"My dad found it when he went through my luggage last night," I say. Bob Marley's singing.

"Oh. I'll miss the parties," Katja says. She picks up the headphones, looks at me. "We can share," she says and pulls them wide open, leaning over against me so our cheeks rest against each other, putting one headphone against her own ear, one against mine. Bob's singing. When the song ends, she turns it off and puts the headphones down on the bedspread again. The room is almost dark now.

"I've always really liked you," I say – very nervous, but sufficiently drunk. Katja's a year older than me.

"You have?"

"Yes." I don't know what else to say. There's a pause.

"I didn't want to go," Katja says.

"Why not?"

She doesn't say anything.

"Are you going to stay in Finland?" I ask.

"Yes," she says and snivels, just once. I put an arm around her shoulder.

"It'll be alright," I say, even though . . . I'm not really sure that's true.

"I don't know . . . anyone there."

"You'll meet people. You'll come and visit us all in Tanzania." The things I'm saying – perhaps I sound daft, so I stop. "I'm going to . . ." Once again I stop myself. I was going to say I would write to her. But I don't think that's true. We don't say anything. Katja lights a cigarette, hands it to me, I smoke and hand it back. She sighs. Puts it out.

"Kiss me," she says in the dark. I find her face. We kiss. It's amazing. She starts crying. We hold each other. It's very sad. We kiss again, with her tears, and she smiles through her tears as we kiss. "I didn't know you liked me," she whispers.

"You're very beautiful," I whisper and touch her stomach. She pulls off her top. I touch her breasts, kiss them, and . . . we do it – all the way. It's . . . amazing. Divine.

The phone wakes us.

"Katja," I say.

"Yes," she says. Smiling faintly.

"Thanks."

"You're welcome. I'll meet you down in the restaurant. For breakfast," she says and goes into the shower. I'd like to join her under that shower. Go into my own room. A quick shower, get my things together, return the key, go into the restaurant. Katja's at a table with Truddi and Norwegian Øystein. I grab myself some food.

"Good morning," I say and sit down. Katja acts like nothing's happened. We take the bus to the airport. On the plane we're sitting quite some way apart.

In Copenhagen we all go to the baggage carousel. I go over and stand next to Katja.

"Are you alright?" she asks.

"Yes," I say. "How about you?"

"I'm . . . not alright," Katja says.

"I miss you already," I say.

"I know," Katja says. We don't say anything as the luggage moves past us, round and round. My bag arrives. I let it pass. The next time it comes round I take it and put it down. The carousel keeps going. "Have you got anything else?" Katja asks.

"No," I say.

"Why don't you go then?"

"I'm waiting for you," I say.

"I want you to go," she says. "I have a plane to catch." I don't say anything, don't move. Truddi and øystein are standing a little way off. Katja gets in front of me, takes my face in her hands, looks me in the eye, asks: "Can you feel the emptiness?"

I look down at my feet.

"I'm going to kiss you, and then you'll go," she says.

I look at my feet, swallow.

"O.K.?"

I nod. She kisses me. I hold her. Tight. Until she lets go. Turns away. I bend down for my bag. Leave. Breathe deeply.

Marcus

BORED OFF MY ARSE

When I was fifteen, Mika showed me how young white people get drunk and then walk back using lampposts to support their bodies as they spew sick. That was four years ago. Now Mika has grown hair on his chin and chews dirt like Jonas Larsson. Mika speaks without stuttering and stammering now, but his words are still a mess.

I pick him up at the airport with Ibrahim's help and his uncle's pick-up. And on the way back to Moshi Mika's mouth speaks of nothing but *bhangi*, Konyagi, Alwyn, tanzanite stones, *malaya*, Africafé, zebra meat. Mika stays in the Larsson house, sleeps in the Larsson bed. There's just the two of us – Josephina is on holiday in her village. Mika opens the fridge.

"What the hell – is there no food?"

"There's no money," I say. He sees three of the project's motorbikes in the garage, chained together with a heavy chain and a padlock.

"It'll be easier if I have my own motorbike. Where are the keys?" he asks.

"Jonas has taken them to Sweden," I lie, because I don't want to deal with the trouble if the white boy has an accident or gets a motorbike stolen – I would prefer to be told off by Jonas for not giving Mika a key.

In the evening Mika and Alwyn meet at Stereo Bar.

"You're coming too," Mika tells me. "You'll never be well if you just sit here." So we take a taxi into town. I limp into Stereo Bar. Just one beer and I already feel drunk. Mika looks at the waitress:

"When I see a black woman with a flat arse, I feel sorry for her; it's evolutionary injustice," he says in Swedish. But Stereo Bar has *malaya* he can look at as well. They wear skirts or tight trousers – their arses rippling voluptuously. "Those arses jump right at my face," Mika says. "It's almost frightening."

"What are you afraid of?" I ask.

"Of how much I want to climb into that arse." I don't tell him it's the arse of a *malaya* – he knows that.

"I don't like it," I say. "They stuff a kilo's worth of corn porridge into that arse every day, just to make it big – it's too much. I prefer *chiki-chiki*."

"I like pumping a big arse," Mika says.

I don't say anything else.

"Have a look at that one," he says, nodding. A *malaya* as big as *mama* G.M. "I want to stuff an entire bunch of bananas up her cunt and yank it in and out so they squelch past the lips and slap against her when I ram them back up again. I want to twist the bananas around inside her like I was tightening the bolts of a wheel."

I don't say anything. Mika is madness. Alwyn arrives. They start whispering about tanzanite stones and Africafé.

"I'm going home," I say.

"Alright," Mika says.

"You have to give me money for a taxi," I say. He looks at me for a bit, before he gets out the money, hands it to me, and right away he's back to talking to Alwyn, so low I can't hear it. Alwyn sends me a brief smile, sneering. The *mzungu* is his now. I limp out. Go home.

TAUT FLESH

I have put the kettle on to make coffee when I hear the moans. It's coming from the master bedroom. I go over, the door is ajar. *Eeehhh*. The fat *malaya* is sitting on Mika's face, jumping up and down. Is a face a horse to be ridden? A banana is sticking out of her arse, and her *titi* . . . it's so strange; one of them is an enormous saggy tit, but a pale sisal rope has been wound tightly around the other, and the nipple sticks out at the very front in the midst of a round piece of taut flesh. And she sees me. I think she would feel embarrassed, but no. She grins at me and grinds her papaya down on Mika's face as if she were grinding flour with a stone – he might even drown. I tiptoe back to the kitchen.

I hear Mika sending the woman away and going into the shower. In the kitchen he pours himself a cup of coffee and then throws himself on the sofa. He is very hungover.

Later Alwyn comes to pick him up. It's clear what's going on – Alwyn has told him all sorts of dirt about me, just to reap the benefits for himself. I can't go with them, because I only have one leg. Alwyn has taken my market. Mika moves into Alwyn's house in the city centre. The next day Mika comes walking back on his own two legs.

"Damn it if he didn't want me to pay to live in his stinking craphole."

"If you're going to live here, there'll be no more *malaya* in the house," I say.

"What do you care?" he says.

"I do care – they've got diseases in the blood."

A few days later Gösta comes round to the house with a black lady in his car. Not a *malaya* – a lady.

"It was terrible what Asko did to you," he says.

"Yes," I say, but there's no mention of Asko pumping Gösta's wife on the Larssons' lawn – perhaps he doesn't know that I saw it. Afterwards the wife went home, and they got divorced. Now Gösta is going native. He introduces the black lady. She is from a good Chagga family that owns many small businesses around the country.

"We're getting married," Gösta says.

"Congratulations," I say. "That's the right way to do it."

"Yes," he says. "You can only be married to one person at a time."

"Can I offer you anything?" I ask. "Or did you need something for the project?"

"I just need to pick up a motorbike," Gösta says. I show him where the keys are. The lady invites me to come visit them in Old Moshi. She drives the car – an efficient lady; the right kind of Chagga, not like lazy, degenerate dirt in the gutter. Gösta rides the motorbike. The white man with the good black woman – the perfect partnership; he gets the foreign currency, and she's got the connections, knows all the tricks for building a solid business – the good life.

HIGH FIDELITY

Mika dreams tanzanite stones and ivory – everything that is exotic, expensive, illegal; he wants to take it back to Finland and make a profit. Alwyn is willing, but he can't do what Mika wants, so now Mika is coming to me. I get hold of some stones through Dickson. We do a deal and agree on how much money Mika must deposit in my bank account in Finland in return for the tanzanite. I don't see a risk of Mika cheating me, because he knows that would lead to all the truths about him going straight into Katriina's ears and from there to his relatives in his own, cold country.

Mika is getting ready to leave. He must fly to Sweden first and then take a boat to Finland.

"The stones you can carry through customs yourself – they're small," I say. "Are you taking *bhangi* back?"

"Yes, of course I am," Mika says.

"Then you must put it into the post and send it, because it's dangerous to carry it through customs here in Tanzania. You could go straight to Karanga Prison. And in Sweden they have special ways of finding you out."

"O.K. I'll get Gaspar to pack it in tins of Africafé and post them."

"You must take these to Finland," I tell Mika and hand him the envelope with the few dollars I have and a letter with the name and address of my bank in Sweden and the number of the account that Aunt Elna set up for me. "You can transfer the money from your own account in Finland," I say.

"Yes. I'll do it as soon as I get back," Mika says. I don't trust him, but there isn't enough money in that envelope that it would be worth stealing it and losing Marcus the Mule who is always sprinting to the post office with his tins of Africafé. With money in my Swedish account, I can buy decks straight from Ostermann without needing the help of *wazungu*. The dollars in the envelope and my claim for two hundred dollars from Ostermann for the Boombox that never arrived; soon I'll be able to order a proper high-fidelity stereo and take over the market for recording tapes. No-one goes to Alwyn anymore – his recordings sound like the whispering of the wind in a cornfield.

Ostermann will send the date and flight information to me by telex, and I'll go to the airport and bribe the customs officer myself – no more nonsense with D'Souza.

Mika returns to Europe. I don't hear anything. I wait two weeks before I send a telex to my Swedish bank to ask for a statement – it's void, they say. What's going on?

TINS OF COFFEE

Mika is gone, and the fear that he may have robbed me makes the acid bubble in my stomach.

Stop it, I tell myself. Here I am – the same problems as always, but I'm facing them on my own two feet. The Larssons are still in Sweden, so there's no food to eat, but at least I was free from the white madness for a while. They'll be back in a week. Mika gave me a camera before he left. When I get the good stereo, I can play at weddings and be the wedding photographer at the same time. Once more I go to the post office and send a telex to my Swedish bank. They reply that the account is void. The sweat breaks out all over my body, cold, cold – it's so bad I'm shaking. Is it fraud? I wish Mika would write to me and tell me what's going on, if only on a piece of toilet paper.

When I get back, Gösta is sitting on the veranda, waiting. He shows me the newspaper he's got in his hand.

"That Mika really is an idiot," he says. There's a picture of Mika – the headline says something about coffee tins.

"What does it say?" I ask. Gösta shakes his head and starts translating: Mika was caught at the Swedish customs with tins of Africafé full of *bhanghi* and tanzanite stones sewn into his jean jacket. The idiot didn't do as we agreed. The paper also says that the coffee tins would have got safely through customs because they had been sealed at the factory. He was found out because one of the customs dogs smelt something in his luggage. What was it? Zebra meat and leopard skins. Damned imbecile alcoholic. He was probably completely wasted after the flight. Paulo must have got the meat for him. And that striped donkey doesn't even taste good compared to roast impala.

"What's going to happen to him?" I ask.

"He's been fined and sent to prison," Gösta says.

"How much is the fine?" I ask.

"The equivalent of three thousand dollars." I may as well wave goodbye now to the eensy-weensy eighty-three dollars in the envelope. I play my part, but he ruins everything. With enough experience of Jonas – I ought to know better. Jah Rastafari tells us not to be in touch with people like that. Mika is in prison. He will be in prison for two years. And the Larssons' tiny SHARP double tape recorder already has problems with the tape heads – it's worn out by dirty old cassettes – damp and dusty. I'm broke and can't make any money. There's just the two hundred dollars I am owed by Ostermann – my last cup of water in the desert.

Christian

I have a ticket all the way through to Aalborg. Mum is at the airport with her little sister, Lene. I've promised Dad I'd behave. I walk towards them.

"You're so tanned," Lene says.

"Hi, Christian," Mum says and gives me an awkward hug.

"Hi," I say. We drive up to a summerhouse they're renting in Grønhøj. I go down to the wide beach for a smoke. The sun is shining, the waves are big. We have Danish meals with lots of salami, herring, liver pate. There are Danish newspapers; the cigarettes are fabulous.

"I'm waiting to hear from Médecins sans Frontières," Mum says. She's renting a flat in Copenhagen and works at Rigshospitalet, but they are starving in Ethiopia and she wants to go.

"I don't understand that you're not afraid," Lene – who is also a nurse – says. Lene's husband is a lawyer called Torben – they don't have any children. He comes up to the summerhouse, and we have yet another large Danish lunch. We take the car into Aalborg and walk around. White people, houses that look like they have just had a good wash, streets that have been swept, order and conformity. I can't breathe.

"Why do you want to go with Médecins sans Frontières?" I ask.

"I want to get out and see the world," Mum says. She did see some of the world. But she didn't like it and she ran away. She's my mum, and I just don't get what's got into her. Now she just wants to be something else, and this holiday feels like a duty more than anything. Nothing is said about . . . it.

Fortunately Mum gets the go-ahead. I get the ferry to Oslo and meet up with a bunch of people from I.S.M. At least we can speak in English and about things that matter. Africa. Katja was supposed to be there, but she isn't. Shit. Four days of heavy drinking with Jarno and a bunch of Norwegians. Back to Denmark. Stay in a room in Lene and Torben's basement in Hasseris for about a week. Shop for clothes and shoes and music. I can't wait to get back.

Train to Copenhagen and a bus to Kastrup Airport. On the way to the departure hall I ignore a red light at a zebra crossing. A police car pulls up next to me – the officer in the passenger seat winds down his window.

"Do you think red lights don't apply to you?" he asks.

"Excuse me," I say. "I don't speak Danish."

"Oh hell," he says and turns to his partner. "I can't be bothered. Just go." They drive on. Idiots.

First I fly to Schiphol, where I have a stopover. I ask at the information desk: "The time on my ticket, is that local time or is it G.M.T?"

"Local time," the lady says. O.K., then. I have three and a half hours to kill. Sit down with a cup of coffee and some cigarettes. Smoke – first one, then another. A girl comes running down the corridor. Solja?

"Solja!" I shout. She turns her head but keeps running:

"Hurry up," she shouts. "They're closing the gate in a minute." She disappears. I get up, grab my bag, drop my cigarette, run after her. Reach the desk.

"You're very late," the steward says.

"Yes," I say. "Very, very late."

I see Solja again when I board the plane.

"Hi," I say. "Where have you been?" She's grown breasts over the holiday.

"With my Aunt Elna," she says.

"Alone?"

"No, but my parents flew back a week ago."

"How are they?" I say. And realize that she probably doesn't know half of what I know about her parents and how they're doing.

"I don't know," she says.

Marcus

MENTAL CRUTCH

"It's your fault," Jonas tells me. I don't want to say anything, because that would be like accusing a friend, even though he's not a good friend.

"I don't know anything about Mika's smuggling." Even you, Jonas, would have taken those tins of coffee with you on a plane for Mika if he had asked you, because they were sealed.

"Mika wouldn't have known where to get *bhangi* and zebra meat – you must have helped him."

"No," I say. "I could hardly walk while he was here. He hung around with his old friends from I.S.M."

Jonas arranges for me to start work again right away. I am picked up by a car from the office every morning. He needs me there to be his spy, while he himself is at Moshi Club.

Working helps. I gain weight and lose many of the worries in my head that lead to acid in my stomach. I'm working on my crutches; registering the stock, filing. Desk work. I have my leg stretched out on a stool, trying to act like I'm O.K.

Two weeks before my last and final visit to K.C.M.C. – something happens: I'm going home from work. I go to the car, sit down. "Where is your crutch?" the driver asks. I've forgotten it – now my only need for a crutch is in my head. It's time to walk for myself.

EAT THE DISAPPOINTMENT
"We've had photos developed in Sweden," Solja says in the house one evening when her parents have gone to their drunkenness in the club. "Come and see." We sit on the sofa. I have Rebekka in my arms. There are a lot of pretty pictures taken in Moshi and on West Kili and at the forestry school. There is even one of me lying like a dead man at K.C.M.C. I'm smiling because I'm still alive. And ... *eeehhhh*, a children's birthday party at the D'Souzas – right there in his sitting room: my Pioneer Boombox. It wasn't lost in transit, but stolen and imprisoned by the greedy man from Goa – the good machine must play bad music to thieves and bandits. D'Souza has enough money to grease the police, so I would be wasting my time trying to get justice. I am the little man, so I must swallow the disappointment, the rage, the grief, the feeling of being cheated and abused over and over. And I must do it quickly and then forget, because otherwise the acid in my stomach will bubble up and cause a wound that could put me in my grave.

DEAD SKIN
They remove the cast for the last time. A shock. Am I an Indian? My leg has the same colour as a tortoise shell – pale brown. And it's shit, just shit. It looks like the leg is dead. It doesn't belong to me. One side is a

331

leg, the other is a stick. No muscles. A stick that someone's taken a *panga* to, seeing the leg as a tree to be felled. *Eeehhh*, I'm crying.

"What sort of shit is that? Is that a leg or what?" I ask.

"It's a leg," Claire says. "The foot moves." And it's true – a tiny tremor. The muscles are almost dead after four months of no activity. We go home. I wash my leg properly, and what happens when you go to the sauna happens here – my arse-skin doesn't stick properly to my leg; it falls off like wet, thin paper, bit by bit – and it stinks. *Ehhh*. I walk around with a stick, because my leg is as thin as a stick. I am used to having the plaster for protection. My brain says: I have to have two sticks on the left side. I walk very slowly up stairs. My entire brain is in my leg. I am only my leg. If anyone moves something in the vicinity of my foot, it becomes almost electric – moves far away so nothing touches it. Scared like all hell.

Mika writes to me: "It will be a while before I get back on my feet and can pay you back your eighty-three dollars. But I will – I promise." Dreams. Why should I reply to the thief when he's already fleeced me? It'll only prolong my discomfort.

BEER DRIP

If I don't eat, I will die – when I do eat, there is trouble. My intestines are too short and too narrow, and my stomach has shrunk. I haven't eaten properly for a long time – I've mostly subsisted on fluids. And I keep eating little things – everything inside must expand first, even though the food is good for my body. I should eat a little all the time, all day long. I should eat, walk a little, eat a bit more, allow it to settle until I can top it up with some more. But I can't afford to do that – I'm working. So I have to spend a lot of time and money on food. I can't go about carrying a bag of food from home all the time – the food would be old and cold and lacking in flavour: I refuse to eat it just to avoid being in pain. So I have a beer instead. That makes it worse because the beer takes my appetite, but it also has the energy from the wheat which made it. A beer can be almost like eating a slice of bread, just poured into your body through the throat like a special, very tasty nutritional drip.

THE ILLNESS

Katriina calls me. "What did Mika do when he was here?"

"I don't know very much about it, because I couldn't walk on my leg then."

"But . . . did he go out a lot?"

"Yes, he drank a lot and smoked a lot of *bhangi*."

"Who with?"

"He went to bars with his old friends from I.S.M."

"But did he . . . go with girls?" I don't want to tell Katriina how Mika pumped the fat *malaya* in her bed.

"I don't know – my leg couldn't go to the bar, and I wasn't being paid, so I didn't have money for beer and trouble."

"Marcus! Did he go with girls?"

"Yes. Yes, he went with all the girls you can buy for money. The cheap girls from the bars. The price of two beers will buy him the right to pump for twenty minutes."

Katriina shakes her head.

"He is sick," she says.

"The devil of alcohol is inside him," I say, shaking my head like a sad man.

"No, he is sick now – in prison. He's got . . . the new disease," she says.

"*Eeehhhh*," I say – H.I.V. / A.I.D.S. In Tanzania we cannot speak openly about these things, but I have read about the disastrous disease in the *Economists* I borrow from *bwana* Knudsen. Mika was drunk, stupid, pumped without a sock. Fetched the tainted blood from the girl into his own body.

"*Pole sana*," I say.

THE MARRIAGE COUNSELLOR

Christian comes to my ghetto. *Bwana* Knudsen isn't afraid of negroes at night – he lets his son walk on the street like a goat. He has brought lots of good cassettes from Europe as presents for me.

"You have to hear this – 'Biko' by Peter Gabriel," he says. But Christian also has Stevie Wonder, Rufus and Chaka, Gregory Isaacs, Steve Kekana, Cool & the Gang, L.K.J., Third World, Herbie Hancock, Eddy Grant, Earth, Wind & Fire. Even though the tapes are played on Solja's ridiculous baby machine, the harmonies are a miracle in my ghetto.

I walk Christian home – when you arrive at their house, it's the exact opposite of the lifestyle at the Larssons'. There's no screaming or scary atmosphere; *bwana* Knudsen is reading a book or a newspaper or listening to the B.B.C. on the radio, and he is serious and knows

333

everything and doesn't pump house girls and secretaries, and even though he drinks too much, he minds his job.

The Larsson house still carries on in its Babylonian style. The next day the phone isn't working, so Katriina drives to the club to find *bwana* Knudsen. She wants him to come down and talk to Jonas. By the time *bwana* Knudsen arrives, Jonas has gone to the club, so it's just Knudsen and Katriina. I am helping Solja with her maths homework at the dining table, while the grown-ups talk on the veranda.

"It's never getting better – I may as well get divorced," Katriina says.

"Give it some time. Give it a chance," *bwana* Knudsen says. "You have to really try." He is wrong, because something that doesn't work can be repaired, but if it doesn't work at all, it's better to get rid of it and get a new one. And I still see the red Land Cruiser on the dark roads at night, and the motor isn't going, but the car is moving like a tree shaken by a storm.

LAST WILL AND TESTAMENT

Rebekka is sitting outside my ghetto, crying, when I come home from work. "Aunt Elna is dead," she says. Ohhh – sad. I comfort her. A telegram has arrived. Solja comes down to see me.

"Dad is furious," she says.

"Is it because Aunt Elna is dead?" I ask – how can you be angry when you're meant to be sad?

"Yes – something about her will," Solja says. *Eeehhhh* – her will; what does it say about my future?

Two days later; Jonas calls me to the house. There's no-one else at home.

"You're mentioned in Aunt Elna's will. You and Josephina. I have received information from the lawyer in Sweden. You must write a letter to him so that he knows you're the right person. And then you must write one for Josephina. Then I'll send the letters to Sweden, and you can have the legacy she left you."

"How much is it?" I ask.

"I don't know," he says. I dare to ask again:

"How can you not know?" He gives me his evil eye.

"Because the will won't be shown to me until the lawyer has located all the people mentioned. So you better write those letters – otherwise nothing's going to happen."

"What should I write?" I ask. He tells me the words that will work on the lawyer, and I write them down exactly as he says.

A SACK OF POTATOES

Again I am called to the house, as a maths teacher for Solja. Perhaps her parents are unable to put two and two together? Their lives are like that; two adults and two children, but the result is never satisfaction. On the veranda the Swedish language is spoken straight out, so that their daughter can hear as well:

"Won't you stay at home?" Katriina asks.

"At home?" Jonas says. "Why would I want to stay at home? All I ever get here is nagging."

"But we never . . . spend any time together. Can't we just . . . you know, cosy up? Go to bed early?"

"To bed? You want me to get into bed with you?" he asks.

"I might do."

"In that case I really think you should lose some weight. You look like a sack of potatoes."

"What?" Katriina says.

"You look like . . . I don't know what. Rebekka is three years old, and you're still . . . huge. Do you think I want to get into bed with that?"

Katriina is crying now.

"That's not fair. It's your children I've had."

"That's no reason to look like that. You don't work all day. Why don't you do something about it?"

"I do – but it's hard."

"There are lots of young girls here who are still fit. And they're not always nagging," Jonas says. Katriina screams in Swedish so fast I can't understand what she's saying. Jonas goes outside and gets on his motorbike.

COOL DOWN

I've waited a long time. Now I ask Jonas, with Katriina there to witness it:

"Did you hear from Aunt Elna's lawyer?"

"You need to relax, Marcus," Jonas says. "These things won't be completely settled for another year – then we'll be allowed to distribute the inheritance."

"A year? *Eeehhhh*, that's bad."

"What's the problem, Marcus?" Katriina asks. I tell her about the empty kiosk – I need things to put inside it.

"How much do you need?" Katriina asks.

"Enough to buy a fridge and stock. Then I can start saving, put away money for a finding a house so I can get married – I'm almost twenty."

But already Jonas is scolding in Swedish:

"We don't have to give him any money – he'll have to wait."

Two days later: Katriina tells me they've made a deal. I can go to Musa Engineer and ask for the money, because Musa owes them money for some things he's bought from the Larssons. I do it right away; the country has no fridges for sale, so I have to buy a freezer if I want things to be cold. And I start to build up the stock. When the kiosk gets up and running, and I get a reliable boy from the village to man it, I can use the rest of my inheritance to pay a boss at Co-operative College – buy real exam papers that say I know how to do things, get myself a good job in administration. I can build a future with that inheritance.

Right away the freezer gives me problems. Claire puts fizzy drinks into it and forgets to takes them out, so the bottles break like that time when all the strangeness started and I always needed a liquid sleeping pill and topped up the bottle with water to hide my theft.

"I'm very sorry," Claire says. The trouble is that bottles are expensive and almost impossible to get. If you can't return an empty bottle to the fizzy drinks factory, you can't buy a full one.

REVOLVER

I'm sweeping the house; the broom hits something under the bed. *Eeehhh* – it's a revolver, a small one. A girly thing, but loaded and ready to kill. Not even in a box. White man's madness. Who does he want to shoot? I discover that it goes with him when he goes out after dark, when the negro is black as night and the white man shines like a diamond in the darkness, ready to be grabbed by the robber.

Christian

Home again. School starts tomorrow. I kick-start my Bultaco – it feels great. Tear down to Phantom at the market and pick up a few sticks of *bhangi*, and then on to Marcus. Dad's Land Rover is parked outside. He's sitting on the veranda with Katriina. I stop.

"Hi, Katriina," I say. Solja and Rebekka are nowhere to be seen. Nor are Jonas or Marcus.

"Grab yourself a Coke from the fridge," she says. I get one and come back.

"What are you doing?" I ask.

"We're talking about Miriam," Katriina says. "She's gone back to her parents' farm in Kenya, because she's ill, but no-one knows what's wrong with her."

"Maybe he's passed something on to her which he picked up from one of his many women," Dad says. Has he forgotten I saw him sitting with John and Jonas at Kilimanjaro Hotel, surrounded by women?

"It would be just like him to get syphilis and pass it on to Miriam," Katriina says, shaking her head.

"Did you hear about Rogarth?" Dad asks, looking at me.

"What about him?" I ask, because it's been a long time since I've really talked to Rogarth. It petered out when we moved away from T.P.C. just over a year ago.

"His dad's been sent to Karanga Prison, so you probably won't be seeing him at school again," Dad says.

"What a pity," I says. "Did he steal too much sugar?"

"Can you really steal too much of anything in Tanzania?" Katriina asks.

"No," Dad says. "But it seems he didn't see the point of sharing with the other thieves."

"Then where is Rogarth's family now?" I ask.

"Not at T.P.C. – and no-one there knew where they'd moved to," Dad says.

"Right. I'll be off again. Will you be home later?" I ask.

"I'm waiting for Jonas," Dad says. "I need to talk to him about something." I shrug. Get up and kick-start the motorbike, wave at them and set off. Odd to find him sitting there with Katriina waiting for Jonas.

School's on again. Samantha comes to the house one afternoon.

"I got done for drinking," she says.

"When?" I ask.

"Yesterday," she says.

"Are you out?"

"They're meeting later today. They'll let me know tomorrow."

"What do you think?" I ask. Samantha smiles.

"I called Minna a despotic whore from hell and slapped Truddi. I think I'm out." Minna is Samantha's houseboss in Kiongozi.

"Out for good?" I ask. Samantha shrugs.

"Hair of the dog, what do you say?" she says.

"It'll have to be with Coke in it. My dad might come home," I say.

"I don't mind," Samantha says. And I add:

"But he's probably going to the school."

"Is he still on the board?" Samantha asks.

"Yep."

"You must have been a blot on his reputation," she says. We drink our Coke-coloured beers, smoke cigarettes. The old man's car stops outside. He comes inside.

"Hi, Samantha," he says.

"Hi, *mzee*," she says, and he smiles. He turns to me and says in Danish:

"I've been called to a emergency board meeting at school. Something about someone who's been misbehaving?" He raises his eyebrows and looks at me. I hold up my hands defensively. "You'll have to sort out supper for yourself," he says and adds, to Samantha: "See you later."

"Yes, bye," she says, looking at me.

"He didn't know who the meeting was going to be about," I say.

"As long as I can drink the man's beer, I don't much care," she says and takes another one of my cigarettes, her thighs resting invitingly on the seat of the chair.

"Damn it, Christian," the old man says when he returns.

"What?"

"You know . . ." he says and stops. Starts again: "You might have said something. She was sitting right there." He points to the chair where Samantha's glorious thighs rested not three hours ago.

"Would it have made any difference?" I ask.

"No," he says. "Suspension. Two weeks."

"Everyone does it," I say.

"Everyone does what?"

"Smokes, even though they haven't got a permit. Drinks, smokes *bhangi*, fucks – and you can't even *get* a permit for that."

"But not everyone gets drunk and calls their houseboss every name under the sun and slaps their roommates."

"Samantha's got personality."

Juliaz puts a plate of food for the guard in the fridge before he bikes home late in afternoon – too late for the *mama* Flora to put him to work. The old man is away on business in Mwanza. He has started doing more work as a travelling consultant for the Nordic Project. So I must give the guard his dinner and make him coffee. He always wants more sugar. I must cook corn porridge for the dogs and mix it with scraps of offal.

I have no money and I've been through all Dad's pockets – nothing. There's petrol in town, but I can't pay for it, so I've not got wheels either – I'll have to go in the Larssons' car in the morning.

Friday. There's no party at school. I drink gin and smoke cigarettes. On the Saturday I open my school bag and take out my books, but that's as far as I get – before long I'm back on the veranda smoking cigarettes. I ought to do something, but I can't be bothered. I'm bored.

Late in the afternoon Marcus arrives in a taxi. He seems agitated.

"The management at the Police Academy are having a small party tonight, but the man who was going to play music has cancelled. I can get the job, if I can get some decks," he says.

"And can you?" I ask. He points at Dad's B. & O. stereo.

"If I can borrow the Makonde stereo," he says.

"What about the Larssons?" I ask.

"Jonas says no," Marcus says.

"I . . . I'm not sure," I say.

"We'll be taking it in a police car both there and back," he says.

"I'd have to be there," I say.

"Yes, of course," Marcus says and grins.

At eight he shows up in a car with a policeman. I have already packed up the stereo. We drive to the Police Academy's canteen and set it up. It's a bit stilted – too many uniforms, too much fine dining. We play some quiet soul. But then as soon as dinner is over and the lights are dimmed, it becomes warm and meaty. People are sweating on the floor. We turn up the volume – Donna Summer, Stevie Wonder, the Beatles, ABBA.

"Good work, boys," the Police Commissioner says, passing us beers. We play Zaire Rock, and the room is on fire.

"You see – the disco business in Tanzania is very accessible. There are hardly any stereos that can play loud music, so when you've got one the money flies right into your pockets."

"Yes," I say. Late that night we're taken home by a drunk policeman. Take the stereo inside.

"Let's grab a beer," I say.

"Yes," Marcus says and sends the policeman away. We get beers from the fridge.

"This is the life," I say.

"It could be our life. We just have to get the decks," Marcus says.

"That would be so cool," I say.

"It's possible," Marcus says.

Marcus

FRAUD

The machinery at the furniture factory breaks down, even though it's only just arrived from Europe. The mechanic has gone missing; first he went to Sweden to be trained for six months and now – after just two months back – he's gone. His family have moved; no-one knows where. But I know he's working at the furniture factory in Mbeya, which is owned by the G.M.'s wife. One more is there at the moment, but apart from those two no-one has been to Sweden. The project has a consultant in Sweden who purchases all the things you can't get here. When the two mechanics were due to leave, TanScan's head office fixed their paperwork – visa and tickets. They put them on the plane and everything was arranged in Sweden. The consultant met them at the airport. He had sorted out accommodation for them, training facilities – everything. But only for the two mechanics. Not for me.

"You must really make a push to go to Sweden and receive training," the G.M. says. "Otherwise you won't know anything when the Swedes leave, and the project might collapse. We have to learn how to fend for ourselves." Perhaps the G.M. thinks more about getting qualified people for his sawmill and his furniture factory which is nominally his wife's, so he won't run into problems from African socialism, because at heart he is a complete private capitalist.

We ask about training but nothing happens. The man in Sweden and the Swedes here, they are the same – they have a deal. They tell S.I.D.A.

the negro has been trained, even though he's never been taught how to use a screwdriver but only how to swing his hammer. And to fake expenses they arrange to cart us around Tanzania in a double-cabin Toyota Hilux – they drag us round to Mbeya, Iringa, Mufindi – and they make a great big report: "We took fifteen people on a training journey, we spent two hundred thousand Swedish kronor." But you can't cheat me like that – I don't want to go to Mbeya; I don't want to go to Iringa; it's the same as Moshi. You can send the fools – I'm staying here. If it's real training, then send me to Sweden. I can wriggle my ruined black arse at night and be a gift to the Swedish women.

When an evaluation mission arrives from S.I.D.A., the Swedes in the project make sure the G.M. is off on a trip abroad, so he can't personally present his complaints. The trip is a big bonus for the G.M. – he will get his subsistence allowance in foreign currency, which he'll be able to exchange at black-market rates in Tanzania. So he decides to go. Let little lice fend for themselves in the dust. The G.M. thinks first about number one.

I ask Gösta – he at least is afraid of how an evaluation might judge him, so he sends the stockroom manager and his assistant and six mechanics to Sweden for a month. But there was enough money to send a great many people there for two years. For our part – the sawmill workers – it's Jonas' decision: not a single person is sent. My beat-up arse is only allowed to wriggle in Tanzania without an attentive audience of Swedish girls who would like to tame the black mamba. The money is being spent – I see it in the accounts. But where does it go?

GODLESS

Josephina's eyes flash. She's in her room in our ghetto, flinging her things into cases and bags.

"*Shenzi*," she says – madness.

"What happened?" I ask.

"The whites are mad," she says.

"But what happened?" I ask.

"I don't want to talk about such matters," Josephina says. *Eeehhhh* – she has seen something bad in the family. I must take her and all her belongings in the Land Cruiser all the way to her daughter's house.

"Josephina is leaving," I tell Katriina. "I need to borrow the car to take her."

"Yes," Katriina says.

"What happened?" I ask.

"Nothing," Katriina says, but without meeting my eyes. In the car Josephina says:

"Those *wazungu* are godless. The man is godless, and the woman is godless. The children . . . I feel very sorry for the children." That's all she'll say, so I must use the methods of the house slave.

When I return from Josephina's village, I go inside to check on the sheets – they have been changed, so where is the answer? In the laundry basket. Someone made trouble in that bed, and it wasn't Jonas, because he never pumps white meat anymore. Josephina is a woman; she can accept the waywardness of the man, because all women know that men are useless in that way. But when the woman in the house is being satanic as well; that's just too much.

Who did it with Katriina? I ought to know everything about my rulers, otherwise the slave is like a car manoeuvring without a steering wheel. But we're in the third world; do you suppose Josephina has a phone in her mud hut, so I can call her and ask? The new problem is mine: we have no house girl.

"How about Dr Strangler's house girl?" Jonas says.

"But we can't steal Dr Strangler's staff," Katriina says. "Marcus, you'll have to try and find us a new one."

JUNGLE PATH

There is an unpleasant atmosphere in the house. I consider going to visit the witch doctor to get a juice or a powder to pour into Jonas' coffee to change him from a wild dog into a lamb. *Tsk*, so much trouble from those people, and I have problems of my own. I go to Jonas.

"Could I have the last part of my inheritance from Aunt Elna so I can build up my stock? Then you can deduct it when the inheritance comes."

"The inheritance is finished," he says. "You've already had your money. It's over. There won't be any more."

And now I understand that the letter I wrote to the Swedish solicitor was a document that enabled Jonas to get the money for himself. I don't know how much. I just wrote like a fool, and now I'll never know how much of a fool. Yes, I can, if I want to. Because I have Aunt Elna's address. If I write anything, any letter at all, it'll be passed straight to her solicitor, because she doesn't receive post in her grave. I know that much. But I also know that if I do it it'll be even more of a mess. Jonas will start all sorts of trouble for me. Perhaps, if I'm lucky, I would get the money eventually. But until then I would be without a roof and a floor, without transport, without work, without even corn porridge and spinach. Jonas knows a lot of people around here – I could even be killed.

Josephina shows up at the house one day where the Swedes are not home.

"What's happening with the inheritance?" she asks. What can I say? Josephina has received some, but is there more?

"I don't know," I say and ask Josephina straight out:

"Why did you leave us? What was the problem?"

"I won't speak about such matters," Josephina says and leaves.

When Katriina comes home, I ask her about the inheritance again.

"I don't know," she says.

"How about Josephina – has she got all the money she was due?" I ask.

"I don't think she'll get any more," Katriina says.

"But have we got all the money the will said we were due?" I ask.

"Marcus!" Katriina says. "Leave well alone."

I go to Josephina, who is living with her daughter in the village.

"I don't think we'll get any more money. I think he's cheating us," I say. Josephina's eyes are open.

"The *mzungu* is satanic," she says. I drive back.

No more inheritance money in sight. But Jonas can't kill my dreams. I had put my faith in the great stereo for playing discos at Moshi Hotel, meeting posh people, the dignified life. But a small axe can fell a large tree. Right away I order the world's smallest Boombox from Ostermann. I pay with the money I have had in my Ostermann account since D'Souza stole my Boombox for himself. The Boombox must be sent direct by plane. But I can't use D'Souza to get the machine through customs again – perhaps he'll steal this new one as well and give it to his son. I drive to the airport myself and locate the boss of the customs officers and question him. Yes, it is possible to grease a narrow path through the jungle of regulations and taxes, so the Boombox will slide smoothly all the way to my door.

GOD'S CLEANING SERVICE

No cook or house girl around to do the washing-up, the laundry, wash the floors – I am working myself to the bone. Under normal circumstances the white people inherit each other's house girls, but none of the whites are going home at the moment. Or the gardener brings his cousin who needs a job. But the gardener likes his pretty cousin – he doesn't want her in a job like this.

"Do you know anyone, Marcus?" Katriina asks.

"No, not for this kind of job," I say. Does she think I would expose anyone I know to Jonas' madness? Sometimes girls come right up to the veranda, asking for work. Katriina employs the first one she sees – young, but not too pretty. I show her around. There is an enormous pile of laundry. She washes it in the bathtub, because the Larssons' washing machine is dead. She hangs the laundry on the clothesline and washes all the floors, wipes away the dust. She takes in the clothes and folds them.

The next day Katriina calls me. I go into the house. She and the house girl are standing in the bathroom in front of the big laundry basket.

"I don't understand why she hasn't washed everything. She refuses it do it," Katriina says. I ask the house girl.

"I can't wash the man's private things," she says.

"What?" I say.

"I'm not allowed to wash them."

"Why not?" I ask, but the answer is obvious – she's a born-again Christian; the man's underwear is dangerous. I explain it to Katriina, who shakes her head.

"We're going to have to hold on to her until we find someone else," Katriina says and washes the underwear herself; hangs them on the clothesline with all the other clothes. When I come home, the house girl has taken in all the other clothes, ironed them and put them away. Jonas' underpants are still there. She's not allowed to touch them, even though they've been cleansed of all drippings from the man's pump. The Larssons are at the club. I take the underpants in, fold them and put them away without ironing them – perhaps a larva from a mango fly can drill its way

344

into Jonas' arse and turn his flesh to painful shit. In the evening they have people round. The house girl comes early the next morning. I am lying relaxed in my bed, happy not to have to deal with the untidy home.

"Marcus!" Jonas shouts from the house. I have to run. "What the hell is the matter with her?" he says, gesturing with his hand. The house girl is standing tall and proud in the recently cleaned sitting room. The coffee table is weird. The ashtrays have gone, the tonic bottles, the rubbish from peanuts and cigarette packs. Only beer bottles and glasses remain. I ask her.

"I'm not allowed to touch the godlessness," she says. I explain it to Jonas.

"*Toka!*" he tells the house girl – get lost. She turns around and goes straight to the bedroom. I have to get out my own money, pay her for three days' worth of godly cleaning, and remove the bottles and glasses and do the dishes myself.

TROUBLESOME TRUTHS

Solja is big now – twelve years old – and that presents a new problem. She might start asking grown-up questions: "Why are they always going to the club at night? Why is Mum sad? Why is Dad being weird?" I can answer with a loving and protective lie, or I can tell her a truth that would pull the rug I'm standing on from under me – in an instant.

The truth has already created new troubles. At K.C.M.C. I was pumped full of drugs and croaked like a frog about Asko and his *malaya*. Katriina's mind has swapped the names: not Asko, but Jonas. Now she's taking her own little liberties.

"You must stay home with Rebekka this morning. I have some errands to run after I've taken Solja to school." From a life of leisure the woman suddenly starts running errands two mornings a week and coming home empty-handed but with rosy cheeks and a big, bright smile. Josephina and God's house girl are but memories now, so the house is a tip, and I am running far behind with my work – everyone's complaining in my ear.

Another morning of Katriina's errands with me stranded at home. The phone rings. From I.S.M. There are problems with Solja, who has beaten another pupil to a pulp, but where are the parents? I have to pick her up on my motorbike. I go to the office, where Solja is sitting, looking very sad.

"I only want to be picked up by my parents," she tells the headmaster when she sees me.

We are working with simple equations – even I can work them out. She's making trouble to get her parents' attention. And when I think back to the time around Rebekka's birth, I can work out where Katriina's errands are taking her.

"Then let's go out and find your parents," I tell Solja. She walks behind me silently. Sits behind me on the motorbike. I go straight to the K.C.M.C. residential area and over to one of the houses. The Larssons' car is parked outside. I stop in the drive and toot the horn before switching off the engine.

"That's our car," Solja says.

"Dr Freeman's house," I say. "Rebekka's midwife."

"What's she doing here?"

"You'll have to ask her that yourself," I say as the front door is opened; Katriina comes out with her hair all tousled.

STEREO DEATH CERTIFICATE

The Boombox arrives at the airport. Marvellous harmony. When your road forward in life is blocked, you have to take the back way. Ostermann offers a six-month warranty in case the stereo is broken in transit. I take the receipt and the warranty all the way, 220 kilometres – to an authorized Pioneer workshop in Nairobi – the nearest one. Officially the border is closed, but there are markets in no-man's-land at all the border crossings I take the bus to Rongai, enter no-man's-land and go out the other side. A negro on one side of the border looks the same as a negro on the other side of the border, and they speak the same language. The customs officers only do random checks. And how do I carry the stereo that was broken in transit? I don't bring it – how would you transport a stereo by bus all way from Moshi to Nairobi without being robbed? And after all, it's completely broken, because it must have fallen off the plane and hit the ground. At the Pioneer workshop in Nairobi I explain that the stereo was pulverized.

"But where is it?" the man says.

"Here are the papers," I say, handing them to him. They're folded up. "Take a good look."

"One moment," the man says and goes into the back of the shop. He finds his gift among the papers. He hands me them back along with his authorized note for Ostermann – the stereo is dead. And I receive another credit note from Ostermann, who must be quite fed up with that Marcus who is not completely bust after all. And the stereo is there in Moshi – it's working well. I've got my sound back.

THREATS

"What if they send an evaluation mission – then what do we do?" Gösta asks on the veranda, sounding almost hysterical.

"They won't," Jonas says. "And if they do, the embassy staff understand that it takes a few bribes here and there to get anything to run smoothly in Tanzania." I'm standing at a little distance washing the car while keeping my eye on Gösta. He's shaking his head.

"I'm not talking about the embassy. I'm talking about an evaluation mission from Sweden. I don't think they'll be too thrilled with the level of corruption. And particularly not when it's our machinery that keeps breaking down even though it's supposedly only two years old. We were the ones who bought it."

"Relax, will you?" Jonas says – but his voice is less confident than before. "It'll be fine." But it isn't fine, because Andreas wrote a false truth in the newspaper, which made the Swedish people happy because their countryman was helping the negro with Swedish money, given with a warm heart. Now the Swedish hearts might discover that it was a scam. They might be out for blood – who is guilty?

REFUGEE CAMP

The room next to mine is empty now God's own house girl has been sent away, but not for long – it becomes a refugee camp. One of the teachers from I.S.M. comes to talk to Katriina.

"We can't seem to get hold of Niels Knudsen," the man says.

"No, I believe he has gone to Dodoma for a project meeting," Katriina says. "What's wrong?"

"Well, you see . . . Christian came to school drunk, so we've suspended him for two weeks. But we're not entirely happy about him being home alone, and we don't really know what to do with him," the man says.

"Oh dear," Katriina says.

"We mean to hold off on the suspension until his father is back, so he'll still be coming to school. But we still don't feel happy about him being alone in the house. So I just wondered if you knew anyone close to Niels who might be able to take Christian in for a few days?"

"But of course. He can stay here," Katriina says.

"Please don't feel obliged – we can probably find some other solution," the man says.

"No, I'm happy to have him. Where is he now?" Katriina says.

"He's at home," the man says.

"Alright, I'll have him picked up," Katriina says.

"I'm very grateful," the man says. "I'll drive round and tell him on my way back."

Katriina says we must make a bed for Christian in the empty room in the ghetto, because there's no room for him in the house. I think it's because she doesn't want Christian to see what really goes in there. She sends me to pick him up. He comes from a family where a war between man and wife led to dissolution. Now he must go to a house where that same war is raging. I find him outside with a cigarette and a Coke.

"Hello, neighbour," he says with a grin.

"Were you drunk in the morning?" I ask.

"No. I was stoned in the street outside school one night while there was a party inside," Christian says. "In my opinion that's my own business." The attitude of a sullen child – tsk.

"So what now?" I ask. He shrugs. We drive down to my place. The Larssons have gone to the club, the whole family. We go down to a local restaurant in the city centre. Drink beer and eat. Later we smoke a stick before bedtime.

The next day I take the naughty boy to school.

Christian

Dad is away on business. There's a party at Killeen tonight – the boarding house for the oldest girls, a few hundred metres from the school itself. I don't want to go. Samantha treats me like I don't exist, even though she hasn't got a boyfriend. I can't take it. Sit in the sitting room and down a large gin and tonic. And another one. Go outside and kick-start the motorbike, whizz up Lema Road in the dark – the wind tears at me. Turn down Shanty Town Road and stop at the fence that surrounds Kilele, flicking down the kickstand. Samantha comes to the fence – she's heard the motorbike.

"Hi, Samantha," I say. "Fancy a little *bhangi*?" I go over to the fence and stick the end of a spliff through the wire. A Finnish teacher comes out of the gate towards me.

"Christian, I'm going to have to ask you to leave school premises right now. Monday morning at eight you report to Owen's office," he says.

"Hey, you can't tell me what to do. I'm a man on the street, smoking my own weed. I'm a private person. You have no rights over me." I take another drag, sucking it deep into my lungs while I look the teacher in the eye, blowing smoke in his direction. The teacher comes towards me. I raise my right hand and bunch it into a fist so the ember of the spliff shows between my index and middle fingers. "If you hit me, I'll hit you," I say. The teacher stops. I laugh at him, put the spliff in my mouth, get up on the motorbike and whizz off down the street. How stupid was that?

Monday. I'm suspended from school, but the sentence is postponed because they've discovered I'm living on my own in the house while Dad travels around and evaluates the different branches of the Nordic Project. At Kilimanjaro the project has been phased out – it's not working anyway; corruption is rife among the co-ops, and the farmers are never paid for the crops, so they've stopped growing anything beyond what they need for themselves, or they smuggle their produce into Kenya. The plan is for Dad to be a sort of flying lawman. He goes to the various unions and implements new accountancy methods that track the money more effectively, making cheating more difficult. The local bosses tell him there has to be room for some cheating, because if it isn't built into the system, the system will be sabotaged from day one.

The school has talked Katriina into letting me stay with them until they can get hold of Dad. I'm staying in Marcus' ghetto – there's an empty room there, because the house girl absconded. And why did she leave? I assume it's because Jonas fondled her rather more than Katriina could stomach.

It's too much hassle. I'm no longer allowed to ride my motorbike to school, because they can't have all sorts of irresponsible brats zooming about when there are kids around.

Katriina and Jonas bicker and fight whenever he's in, but then he hardly ever is.

Marcus

SOLJA'S SICK

The screaming in that house grows day by day. I can hear it from my ghetto. They have supper. The voices grow louder. Katriina: "I want a divorce. I'm taking the children home. I'm going to tell the embassy you're just here for the black whores, and you're stealing S.I.D.A.'s money – you'll be fired. And you'll never get another job in Sweden because you're too lazy. All you do is drink and smoke dope and cheat and fuck." Solja comes out onto the veranda. She goes over and sits in the car.

"What the hell are you doing?" Jonas shouts from inside the house. Solja slams the car door. She's got the key, starts the car. Jonas sprints out after her. She's already driving, speeding up; he has to jump aside to avoid being hit. Tries to grab a door handle, but the doors are locked, and Solja is on her way through the open gate, pressing the horn and stepping on the accelerator, as the car spurts quickly down the road. Off into the dusk. "*Jävla skit*," Jonas shouts – damned shit. I'm at the back door of the house – hungry. "*Jag åker för at hitta Solja*," Jonas says – I'm going out to find Solja – and goes over to his motorbike. It's not Solja he's going after, but the escape of beer, *bhangi* and *malaya*.

I walk into town to find Solja. The Peugeot is parked outside Stereo Bar; yes, Solja is inside with her friends. A Sikh boy from school. *Mwarabu-coco* from Swahilitown. She's drunk. Twelve years old. But the bartender can't tell the ages of *wazungu*, and she's already got *titi* – she can easily pass for a grown-up.

"Let's get home," I say.

"Bring us four Safari," Solja calls to the bartender and looks at me. "You must have a beer, Marcus." Her friends are silent. I see Chantelle sitting at the bar, looking down at me. Asko's kept woman. "It will rain on me," she thought when she caught Asko in her net. What happened to her? She's stuck in a house she can't afford. She's got a small stereo, fancy clothes, fancy furniture – all of it paid for by Asko, because her miracles flooded his brain. Then he was sent home.

The waitress brings us our beer.

"You know everything that's going on," Solja says to me in Swedish.

"*Jag vet inte*," I say – I don't know.

"Isn't that Asko's whore sitting there?" Solja asks.

"Yes, that's her," I say.

"What's she doing now?" Solja asks.

"She's hunting."

"For what?"

"A man with money to spend."

"Perhaps she can trap my dad," Solja says and starts to laugh; her laughter is nasty, and she gets up to go the toilet in the backyard – dark and dirty.

"Go with her," I tell the *mwarabu-coco*. "You wait for her and bring her back inside."

"O.K.," he says.

"She's not feeling well," the Sikh says.

"Don't worry about it," I say. "She'll be alright." And now Chantelle is getting up – her eyes locked onto mine. She sways across the floor, standing with her legs spread at the end of the table, leaning forwards on both hands so her large *titi* bob up and down close to our glasses and bottles.

"Marcus," she says.

"What can I do for you?" I ask.

"I need to talk to you," she says.

"What about? I ask. Chantelle sends the Sikh boy a quick look – he mustn't hear what she's about to say.

"Business. You can come to my house tomorrow."

"I'll try to make it," I say, just as Solja comes back with wet eyes and looks at Chantelle.

"Did you pump my dad?" Solja asks in street Swahili.

"*Tsk* – that child is bad," Chantelle says and walks back to the bar with dignity. Maybe she has. Maybe the Sikh boy's father has gone to Chantelle. I don't know. I don't care. I call for the waitress and pay the bill, even though Solja is mad at me for wanting to go home. But I grab her arm hard, pull the key from her pocket and drag her into the car. Now she's sobbing; she's collapsed completely, and right after the roundabout the girl's stomach does a flip and she's sick – it run's down the outside of the car. Twelve years old – *tsk*.

CHANTELLE'S POVERTY

"We're moving house, and the other house is already full of stuff, so I want to sell a few things," Chantelle says, with a sweeping gesture round the room. Furniture, a stereo, an electric fan – everything Asko bought for her. Chantelle isn't moving, but she doesn't want to be honest. Materialism has got into her blood.

"I haven't got the money for these kinds of things," I say.

"But you might know someone who does. If you do the work of selling the things, I will pay you a share of the profit. Myself – I haven't got the time for that work," Chantelle says. Eeeeehhh – the question is not one of time – these objects only have a market with the *wahindi*, and how could Chantelle come to their door like a saleswoman? The Indian men may have pumped her, and the Indian women would beat her from their door with brooms so everyone can see what she's really selling.

"Alright," I say. "Let me take the stereo – I'll see what I can get for it."

"No – not like that. You'll find a buyer and bring him here. When the price has been negotiated, I will give you ten per cent." Chantelle doesn't want to be cheated. And I must even bring *wahindi* through her door, so that they can see that in this house one might pump discreetly.

"I have my own job already. If I am to be your salesman, I want thirty per cent."

"Thirty per cent? – *tsk* – you're mad," Chantelle says. Yes. But she's mad as well. She should have asked around about Asko: "Where does this man come from, what is his background, what is he, what is he do?" She doesn't have that kind of experience, so she can't see the reality of the situation. Hope is enough to keep the system going. She'll end up ruined. It's already getting hard to capture the big fish; her family will soon be back to nothing, the sandcastle will collapse in no time. Poorer than ever before. There's a house girl in the kitchen, and Chantelle's daughter is at boarding school in Arusha; Chantelle is pumping so her child can get ahead in life. I look at her. She's already started drinking, even though it's still light. And in the light I can see that she too is getting older.

"Thirty per cent, I say. She gets up and comes over to me. Sits on the armrest with her perfectly shaped thighs and her bottom pressing against my shoulder and arm and body.

"If we say twenty per cent, I could also help you with your needs," she says. I get up and take two steps back.

"Thirty," I say. Chantelle sighs.

"Alright," she says.

SHERIFF REBEKKA

I come out of my ghetto and see the guard running like a gazelle up the drive, out of the gate, down the road. What? Rebekka is on the veranda, grinning. In her hand – the revolver. The guard knows there's a real gun in the house – I told him myself. Rebekka doesn't know what she's doing. I hurry over to her, grabbing on to it with my hand, pointing it upwards as I shout: "Let go!" She is very frightened. And because I grab her hand so hard, she screams, tightening her grip, pulling the trigger. *PAW* – a large bang. Broken tiles fall on her head like a hard rain. Rebekka is crying – a three-year-old gunman. "You mustn't EVER touch that," I tell her. But how can she not touch it when her father leaves it out like a toy?

I tell Katriina. She goes as pale as flour, but doesn't say anything. The next day the revolver is nowhere to be found, but the glove compartment of the Peugeot is now locked.

Everything is tense. Jonas has run out of dirt to put in his mouth. And he doesn't like cigarettes. They make him cough like hell. And *bhangi* doesn't have nicotine.

The project is not doing well. Normally he wants me to spy on everyone and give him a report. But at the moment he doesn't even ask me. I direct my attentions to Gösta, who wants the project to survive because he has married his Chagga woman. I ask him:

"Is there something else I can do for you?" Gösta turns the espionage on its head:

"What does Jonas get up to?" he asks, and I tell him everything I know.

Christian

"Your dad's here," Panos tells me during break.

"Where?" I ask.

"I saw him heading into the office," Panos says. "Are you ready for a serious talking-to?"

"Like you wouldn't believe," I say. During the next lesson the secretary comes and tells me to go with her to the office.

"Tsk, tsk, tsk," Diana says. Jarno gives me the thumbs-up. I follow the secret-ary's enormous arse into Owen's office. Dad is there.

"You're bloody stupid, you are, Christian," he says in Danish.

"It's a hereditary condition," I say.

"Sit down," Owen says. I do. He continues: "Right now, we've agreed that you're going to be boarding from now on since your father is travelling so often. So, as of Sunday, you'll be a boarder. You'll be moving into Kijana, sharing with Böhmer. We realize you've had a . . . rough time, so we're prepared to overlook this latest incident, but even the slightest misbehaviour on your part during the rest of your time in Year Eleven, and you'll be out. Permanently." Owen stares at me.

"Yes, sir," I say.

"Good," he says and looks down at the papers on his desk. Corruption is the only word for it. I ought to be sent down for at least two weeks – perhaps sent away permanently. My dad's on the board and does a good job for them, and he'd probably leave if he no longer had at a child at school. The fig leaf is my having had a rough time because my little sister is dead and my mum cheated and left – everyone knows about it. Owen looks up again. "That was all, I think," he says. "You'll report to Sally at Kijana on Sunday at four." We get up. I leave the room. Dad exchanges a few remarks with Owen. Then he too comes out.

"So, that was the deal, was it?" I say to him. He walks right past me into the car park.

"You and me – we're not on speaking terms," he says.

I go back to class.

"Are you out?" Jarno asks.

"In," I says. "At Kijana from Sunday."

"O.K.," Jarno says.

"Be quiet," the teacher says.

Böhmer is a German neurotic who wears tight, pale canvas trousers, tightfitting long-sleeved shirts buttoned up all the way up, polished half-boots and carries a briefcase. His newly made bed would be a cause for much rejoicing in any German military camp, and you're not allowed to touch anything on his side of the room. But he smokes *bhangi* every night, rolled up in cigarette papers he buys from a Norwegian bloke.

"Put a towel under the door," he says.

"You do it," I say.

"You want to smoke or not?" he asks with his brows raised. I haven't got any myself.

354

"Alright," I say and press my towel under the door so neither the light nor the smoke can get out. Afterwards the room gets a few spritzes of mosquito spray, and then we go to sleep.

Friday night we're taken to the cinema. I've started going out with Sif again, even though we barely speak. I sit and smoke in the cinema so I don't have to kiss her.

On the Saturday we're taken into town in the school's pick-up truck and unloaded by Clock Tower roundabout so we can do some shopping, go to the post office, that sort of thing.

I want to go down to the veranda bar at Liberty with Jarno.

"But why?" Sif says.

"I want a beer," I say.

"That's just stupid," Sif says.

"In that case I'm stupid," I say and walk after Jarno. Liberty. A nice place. Just off the main road, hidden behind a large bougainvillaea. We're sitting under the lean-to and can see who is coming from a long way off. Samantha shows up, bums a cigarette.

"How about it, Christian – she up for it?"

"Who?"

"Sif?"

"She's cool," I say. We have a couple of beers and hide the smell with cigarettes and Big-G chewing gum. No drunkenness, just the good life.

Saturday night there's a party in the dining hall.

"What if Sally shows up?" Sif says when I pull her towards my room in Kijana – I've arranged with Böhmer that he'll stay away.

"Relax," I say. "If we keep the lights off, she'll think we're at the party." Once back in my room I get Sif out of her top, kiss her breasts, put my hand down to her cunt and get a finger inside her. She pushes my hand away. I can't see her face. "What's the matter?" I say.

"You'd much rather be with Samantha," she says.

"We're friends," I say. "Me and Samantha. Is there a law against a bloke being friends with a girl?"

"You fancy her," Sif says.

"No," I say. "I fancy you. Cop a feel," I say, taking her hand, putting it on my cock.

"Don't do that," she says.

"I fancy you something rotten," I say. Someone knocks on the door. We go silent. "The party is over in fifteen minutes," someone says. It's Sally. "By then I want Kijana cleared of anyone who doesn't belong here." Right, so she's smarter than she looks.

"I don't want to go out with you anymore," Sif says the next day. I go to the music room and bang on the drums.

Marcus

THE PERFECT HOUSE GIRL

God's own house girl is gone, and I don't want to wash any more of Jonas' underpants – who knows all the ways they might be contagious? Phantom has a cousin, Sia – she's perfect. I pick her up on the motorbike and take her home – when I know Jonas is out. I show Katriina the perfect house girl. Sia is short, her head as round as a ball, her teeth are bad, her *titi* sag, her arse is huge – Sia looks so odd that just looking at her makes you feel happy and want to smile and laugh. Katriina falls in love on the spot.

"Who's that?" Jonas asks when he comes home.

"Isn't she just lovely?" Katriina says. "That's Sia – our new house girl." Jonas merely grunts. The phone rings. He picks up, talks for a long time, sounds furious – I can't hear the exact words from the kitchen. Then Jonas slams down the phone.

"Damn that Erland Lundgren," he says, and my ears are like the elephant's. Lundgren is the new man at the embassy in Dar es Salaam. He's S.I.D.A.'s new project coordinator and travels around to see all the S.I.D.A. projects in Tanzania. He doesn't think Jonas is amazing. Lundgren thinks the portable sawmills look old; have they bought old junk in Sweden for the price of new machinery? Where are all the skilled workers that have been on courses in Sweden? Many questions, and the answers to them are all illegal. "I need that job in Nicaragua," Jonas says.

"But I don't want to go to Nicaragua," Katriina says. "The kids will go mad if we move from one place to another all the time. And Solja is finally doing better at school again."

"Who says you'd be going?" Jonas says.

"What do you mean?"

"Perhaps it's better if you just went back to Sweden," Jonas says.

"Then you could get yourself some Latina whores," Katriina says in a calm voice.

AIR TOTAL CONFUSION

There are no screws to be had for love or money in Moshi, Arusha, or anywhere else in northern Tanzania. All the parts for bed, tables, and chairs are ready to be assembled at Imara Furniture Factory, but gluing the bits together isn't going to produce good furniture.

"You'll have to come with me to Dar to look for screws," says the G.M., who is going to meet with Erland Lundgren to answer questions about poor machinery, deficits, lack of training. A single bank statement from Jonas would explain it all, and I know where to find them. But do I want to shoot myself in the foot or just find the screws for the furniture?

"Alright," I say. "What time does the car leave?"

"We're flying this afternoon," he says. Flying? I don't fly – I'm not in that league – it will be my first time. I go to the airport like another piece of the G.M.'s luggage. We're flying with Air Tanzania Corporation – a.k.a. Air Total Confusion. We are at the airport early, because sometimes the planes are delayed, but at other times they leave early, or the President takes the plane all alone to go off and have tea with the dictator of a neighbouring nation, and then you'll just have go home and wait a week. It takes the trains four days to reach Dar, and on the bus you're lucky if you get to your destination alive; the driver falls asleep and the brakes don't work. I go outside the airport terminal and smoke a stick of *bhangi* – if I'm to fly through the air, I'll need a little help to take off.

It's late in the evening. Finally the plane is ready, but we're refused at the gate.

"I confirmed the tickets this morning with Minji in Moshi," the G.M. says to the man at the desk.

"You're not on the passenger list," the man says – he insists until he's given money.

We land in Dar at once and are picked up at the airport in a double cab pick-up, and I – little louse that I am – sit in the back. We drive to a guesthouse, but they're full. We start to go from place to place, but they're all full. The big tourist resorts are the only ones with rooms available. We go to Embassy Hotel – posh, very posh.

"This is my boy," the G.M. says, pointing at me. "He must have a room. Send the bill to the project." No cockroach nest for me – I'm at the biggest tourist resort there is. I sit there in my room, not quite believing my luck. Life should be like this always. There's a fridge in my room with beer and everything. No cockroaches, no mosquitos. There's no T.V., so I just stare at the fridge until, by the morning, it's empty. I get up and put on sunglasses to hide how tired my eyes are.

"You look tired, Marcus," the G.M. says.

"You know, yesterday we travelled so far I can barely see a thing." But I find the screws – no problem. Black Star Line – now it's flying.

BLACK AS PITCH

They're both at home, on the veranda. I'm sitting on the stairs by the kitchen door, smoking a cigarette. The children are with friends. *Bwana* Knudsen arrives in his Land Rover and gets out. His hair went very grey after his little daughter died – he is now *mzee*.

"So what's up?" *bwana* Knudsen says.

"What?" Jonas says.

"Didn't you . . . ?" *bwana* Knudsen begins.

"We have to talk," Katriina says to Jonas.

"What? What about?"

"I've asked Niels to come to help us talk to each other. About the things that are going on."

"You did *what*?"

"I thought you knew," *bwana* Knudsen says to Jonas.

"We have to, otherwise I'm going home," Katriina says. Jonas sighs.

"Let's go inside," *bwana* Knudsen says.

"I don't believe it," Jonas says. "This is completely . . ." Katriina cuts him short:

"You think I'm blind," Katriina says. "I know you're sleeping with the secretary from Imara . . ." Jonas cuts her off:

"You know fuck-all."

"People see you everywhere," Katriina says.

"See me everywhere? What are you talking about?" Jonas sneers. Katriina continues:

"Moshi Hotel, Stereo Bar, Kilimanjaro Hotel, Mama Friend's Guesthouse – always with your black whore."

"Listen," *bwana* Knudsen. "You have to talk one at a time. No interrupting each other."

"But . . ." Jonas begins.

"Stop," Knudsen says. Jonas is silent. I imagine him lighting a cigarette while Knudsen lights his pipe and large clouds of smoke billow to the sky. "Alright," Knudsen says. "So, what do you say, Jonas?"

"Do you really think you're the right person to counsel other people about their marriages?" Jonas asks.

"Jonas!" Katriina says.

"What?" he says.

"They lost their child," Katriina hisses.

"It's not my marriage we're discussing right now," Knudsen says.

"The man in the glass house is throwing stones," Jonas says.

"It seems we're all living in glass houses," Knudsen says.

"Stop it, will you?" Katriina says. "I'm going to get us some coffee, and then we have to talk about us, Jonas. You and me. About what we must do. And the children."

I'm sitting with my back against the door and can hear her in the kitchen until she goes into the sitting room. Then I sneak straight in and down the corridor on my bare feet. Yes, eavesdropping is my speciality, because it's my life they're talking about as well. I peek round the corner. Katriina takes the milk jug and pours some into her cup. Then she asks Jonas:

"Would you like some milk in your coffee, darling?"

"No," Jonas says.

"Oh no, you take it black these days, don't you? Pitch black," Katriina says. Jonas doesn't say anything. Katriina looks at Knudsen: "When we were still in Sweden, Jonas liked his coffee milky and white, but down here in Tanzania he wants it black. Milk?" Katriina asks and holds the jug over Knudsen's cup.

"Yes, please," Knudsen says, a bit baffled.

They talk back and forth, and Jonas is constantly lying. Katriina's lying as well. In the end Knudsen stops them: "This is going nowhere. You each have to do a bit of thinking. You each have to make up your minds what it is you want. One of you should take the car and the kids and go away for a while. Then we can all meet again in a week."

"What good would that do?" Katriina asks.

"You have two children," Knudsen says. "If you go home to Sweden, then . . . It's important to think things through carefully."

"Alright, then I'll go tomorrow," Katriina says.

Once *bwana* Knudsen has left, Sia goes up to the house to work. A little while later Katriina leaves to pick up the children. An hour later Sia returns to the ghetto.

"That *mzungu* is mad," she says.

"What happened?" I ask.

"*Tsk*. There I was, doing the ironing, and all the time he's sitting in his chair staring at me with a very hungry look in his eyes." Sia shakes her head. Even Sia's sagging *titi* – Jonas wants to swing in them.

The next day Katriina drives off with the children. *Bwana* Knudsen comes round in the afternoon, but Jonas is too stoned to talk with him.

Sia goes to the house and prepares pilaf. I go to help out.

"I won't go in to lay the table – not when *mama* isn't here," Sia says, so I take the plate, the cutlery and the glass – go to the table.

"Dinner's ready in a minute," I say. "Pilaf."

"I don't want that kind of food," Jonas says. I remove everything. We plate up for the guard and go back down to our ghetto, and Claire comes, and we eat. Afterwards Sia takes the plates and goes to the kitchen to do the washing-up, and I try to get close to Claire, but the Pentecostal church gets in the way and she goes home. After only a few minutes Sia returns.

"He is *shenzi*," she says – mad.

"What did he do?" I ask.

"*Tsk*. There I was, at the sink, and then he comes towards me with a hard stick against my arse, grabbing my *titi*." Sia isn't upset or scared. Just angry.

"What did you do?" I ask. Sia smiles.

"I hit him where it hurts a man the most."

"*Eeehhhh*," I say. Sia leaves through the hole in the hedge and goes to sleep at a friend's until Katriina is back.

Later *bwana* D'Souza and John from T.P.C. arrive. They drink sundowners on the veranda, and I see John chewing like a cow – on the table there's a large paper bag of *mirungi* – the fresh green leaves Somalis and Arabs chew to get high and stay awake. When you take it, you can drink like a fish in water – perhaps it's a replacement for dirt in the mouth. Jonas puts old bottles on the lawn near the empty lot. *PAW!* The revolver. They're playing with the deadly weapon. *PAW, PAW.* A stray bullet can fly onto the neighbouring lot and kill a man or a chicken. Perhaps a goat. No-one can go against the white man. If he hits someone, he can pay for it. Even if he kills. The police and the judges want to have comfortable lives as well. An accident can be paid for. Perhaps that goat was really a thief on his way into the grounds to steal the white man's stereo. I scamper over the fence right behind my ghetto, so the building shields me from the shooting. I disappear far away and sleep in a guesthouse until the next day.

The next night the same madness begins afresh. Now a fire in the sauna is required, and food must be fetched from *mama* Androli's, and there must be beer in the fridge. When I have done those duties, I am told: "Go away." From my ghetto I can hear the laughter from the small patio outside the sauna where you shower or sit with a beer before going back inside the oven once more. Madness. Then there is a giant roar like I have only heard from the largest lions in Serengeti. But it's the roar of *bwana* D'Souza. I run to the sauna. D'Souza is standing naked and odd-looking in the shower with his enormous paunch hanging down almost past his pump, and now he hardly has sideburns or hair – his chest and arms and neck and head are red, and he is roaring.

Jonas is sitting on the bench outside, completely wasted with *bhangi* and *mirungi* and Konyagi.

"Has he gone mad?" Jonas asks.

"He poured a full glass of vodka on the stones. Flashover," John says. "Marcus – get all the ice cubes in the freezer," he says. Now I understand – that trick Mika showed me. You pour vodka on the stones of the sauna oven so you can inhale the alcohol fumes and get drunk fast in a stoned sort of way. But you have to be careful, otherwise the vodka becomes a sea of flames.

WARM BONNET
I am Marcus – a stupid little trailer that just goes in whatever direction the white driver directs his wheel. To me life is like a prison – oppression. People should wish for other people to be independent, but the Swedes are in favour of slavery. I just have to be cool and calm and wear

the mask of hypocrisy, follow the rules of the fools, obey their orders until I am ready to see myself off.

The next morning my alarm clock goes off early so I can help kick my little girls into action. I go into the kitchen and see Jonas sleeping on the sofa in the sitting room. I wake up the girls and go to the kitchen and get out the juice, start on the toast. The veranda door opens; I look out of the window. It's Katriina in her bathrobe. She goes out to the Land Cruiser, puts her hand on the bonnet. On her face the message is clear: it's still warm – he got in very late from his pumping.

But Sia is good – she works well, so I don't have to do everything at the house and on West Kili. She comes to my door.

"Marcus, I have been accepted at the Police Academy," she says, grinning.

"Ohhh, congratulations," I say – very sad, but also happy for her wonderful future. A police officer, maybe in traffic; lots of palm greasing, which will make her very wealthy. Is she not lucky? To get away from the misery of being a daily, to get away from the insanity of the *wazungu*. Sia took the job as a daily only for security in case her application for the Police Academy was rejected. Now I get the job of finding a new house girl.

Sia is paid by Katriina and leaves. Right away Katriina goes around the house, takes all the money and packs Rebekka into the scuffed car. "I'll pick Solja up from school and then we'll go to Hotel Tanzanite," she says as she leaves.

EXODUS: SWEDEN

Gösta is happy with my work for the project and sees me as a valuable link between the black and the white – I understand both worlds and can manoeuvre in both directions.

"Marcus, I will make sure you go on a course in Sweden the next time it comes up," he says.

"Really?!" I am almost shouting, grabbing his hand: "That would make me very happy. I will always do a good job for you," I say.

"I know, Marcus. You deserve to go to Sweden," Gösta says.

"But what about Jonas?" I ask.

"Jonas has let you wait for far too long. It's my decision, and I have told him as much."

"Thank you. Thank you," I say. "When am I flying out?"

"The whole thing must be organized and approved first, but things should fall into place within a few months," Gösta says.

Ohhh, wonderful miracle. I am dreaming with my eyes open. I am going to be seeing the western world – quite amazing. Do you think I'll be sitting on a school bench in Sweden? Yes, perhaps a little. But I will be moving around, and I will talk to all the Swedes like a colourful parrot. Even though my arse-skin has been harvested till hardly anything was left, I will swing that arse for all the Swedish girls to see – perhaps I might even marry one, so I'll never have to return to this Tanzanian Babylon. They will experience the miraculous lovemaking of the black man – absolutely insane.

BUMPING HEADS

Katriina comes home from Hotel Tanzanite with the kids after dark. They get out of the car – all except for Katriina who calls from the driver's seat:

"Marcus, would you make them some dinner, please?"

"But, Mum, where are you going?" Rebekka asks.

"I'll be right back," she says and drives off. I go into the kitchen and put on some rice, start frying the chicken in peanut oil. A loud crash of metal and glass from outside. I run to the hole in the fence, through the cornfield to the back road. Katriina has climbed out of the red Peugeot, which has rammed into the back of the Land Cruiser. Jonas is shouting from the front door:

"You crazy bitch . . ." and more words like that. The crazy bitch is lying in the back of the Land Cruiser. She was hurt in the collision and is scared of getting out. Katriina doesn't look at Jonas, nor at me. She walks right past me, into the corn, up towards the hole in the fence. I follow her.

"Marcus," Jonas shouts. I stop.

"What?" I say with my back turned.

"You have to drive the car home," he says. I shrug. Go over and get into the Peugeot – a sound of scraping metal as I back it away from of the Land Cruiser. The headlights are dead. I drive it home. Katriina is sobbing in the bathroom. Rebekka is very frightened. I go into the kitchen. Solja is standing at the cooker, turning the pieces of chicken in the hot oil.

"Don't worry," she says. "It hasn't burnt."

FIRE

Now I've found myself a reliable boy to man the kiosk, and I've talked to Claire. She says: "If you can get us a house, I will move in with you." I tell her that's good – we can get on in life together and keep each other warm in bed. But tsk, she wants to get married. God must lie in our bed with us – in fact He must lie between us.

Everyone has their worries. Two days before the evaluation mission from Sweden comes to inspect the whole project: all the Imara workers have just been given the day off. Jonas is working in the furniture factory's office. The guard is sitting on his chair outside in the shade. Jonas comes out and talks to him, offers him a cigarette, gives him light; that's never happened before in the history of the world. They have a cosy chat about the guard's family and fields. But what is that? Smoke? Is that fire? Oooohhhh, it's a fire in the factory hall right next to the office – the machinery is ruined and all the paperwork burns; files with accounts and statements detailing the felling, transport, production, sales, everything – a burning flame has taken all that up into the air and into nothingness. How can you tell me that the machinery was bad from the day it was bought? They are bad because of the fire. And the accounts show that we had to spend a fortune building roads on West Kilimanjaro to even get close to those trees. It says so in the accounts that were burnt.

"How could that happen?" the policeman asks.

"Sometimes the workers don't follow the rules about not smoking in the factory," Jonas says.

"The workers had already gone home," the policeman says.

"Yes, but an ember can smoulder for a long time in the sawdust without anyone being able to see it, and suddenly the flames spring up," Jonas says.

"But the entire floor had just been swept clear of sawdust," the policeman says and points around the room.

"I think there may have been a pile of it over there, right outside the office," Jonas says and points to the wet, burnt-out side of the factory hall where it's impossible to tell whatever may or may not have been.

"Perhaps I should take the workers down to the station – they may be able to tell me whether there was sawdust there," the policeman says. And the song and dance continues until Jonas pays up.

"It's lucky I was here when it happened," he tells them. "Otherwise everything would be gone."

But what will the evaluation mission make of the burnt accounts? Jonas doesn't say anything – my journey to Sweden isn't graced with so much as a word either? Is it in jeopardy? Perhaps he doesn't know about the plan. I go over to Gösta's new house.

"S.I.D.A. haven't given us the verdict yet," Gösta says.

"But you said I was going to Sweden," I say.

"It's not looking good, Marcus," Gösta says and shakes his head.

BOOMERANG

Tsk, this chaos. S.I.D.A. refuse to give more money to the project – it was meant to be funding itself by now. The *wazungu* have options: if they want to, they can buy into the company with their own money – make it a joint venture. After twenty-five years of incompetent hell the Tanzanian government understands that it's not up to running of any kind of business. It means to start privatizing a few companies, and TanScan is going to be a pilot project. It's up to Jonas and Gösta: can they produce enough timber and furniture to give themselves a good salary?

"We're buying in. We can't go back to Sweden," Katriina says. But Jonas has spent the money from S.I.D.A. on crap machinery and his private sailboat, and now he realizes that the knife which cut his slice of cake is a boomerang that is coming back at him. He's been cheating the whole time. The recorded expenses were never real; he bought old machinery in Sweden. So now, if they want to buy in, they'll have to do so according to the values stated in the false documentation they themselves gave to S.I.D.A. And Jonas doesn't want to accept that. It says in the papers that the equipment is new, but he knows it's very worn. First it was used in Sweden until it was on its last legs, and then it was used in Tanzania. The equipment is on the verge of total breakdown. A fraud, nothing but lies. Gösta comes over and is very agitated when he speaks with Jonas:

"How are we going to be able to pay that much for that pile of rubbish?" he asks.

"We can't," Jonas says. "I've applied for a new job in Nicaragua." Gösta is scared; will he be able to get a new job when all the scam is discovered? He has married a Chagga woman from a family of businessmen. Here in Tanzania that woman has a function – if Gösta must go home to

Sweden, she will only be a heavy passenger. And he too will be lost, because he has got used to lording it about in Tanzania.

"I will make them an offer," Gösta says. "Do you want in?"

"No," Jonas says.

Two weeks later the answer arrives. The government doesn't understand Gösta's offer; according to the paperwork the equipment is worth at least ten times more – even if one does take depreciation because of heavy use into account. But the equipment is worthless. Now the Swedes are stuck like passengers on the back seat of their own idiocy and greed. And I'm stuck with them, ready to be driven off the cliff, as I wave goodbye to Sweden. But I am smiling – it's a joy to see their terrible confusion.

At the same time *bwana* Knudsen starts to come round the house in the afternoons when Jonas has gone to the club's bar. Solja is seeing friends, and Rebekka is given into my care.

"I don't want to be disturbed this afternoon," Katriina tells me. Does she think I don't understand how these sums work? I too need to reap what advantages I can, and Katriina is careless with her security. She thinks the sound of a car or a motorbike will always alert her before she is found out. But I tiptoe about on my negro feet with Rebekka in my arms, because the little girl always sleeps for an hour in the heat of the afternoon. When I reach the house I am careful and make no noise at the door. I move through the kitchen with Rebekka's heavy breathing against my neck. And in the sitting room I see what I came to see. Katriina is on the sofa in the sitting room, her bottom pointing out at me and underneath her *bwana* Knudsen has his hands on her *titi*, while they exchange lots of spittle. Knudsen has lost his wife – now he's trying to catch a new one, and he prefers white flowers.

"Errr," Knudsen says. Katriina turns around.

"Don't come in here," she says and she quickly gathers her shirt around her and her face goes red.

"There are a lot of mosquitos in my room. They're eating up Rebekka in her sleep," I whisper as Katriina moves away from Knudsen and stands up. Of course my room has no mosquitos.

"Marcus, you can't . . ." Knudsen begins but stops.

"You won't say anything, will you?" Katriina whispers. I go through the sitting room towards the girls' room as I answer her:

"People have rights. If one person is allowed to, then the other is as well," I say.

"Promise?" Katriina says, in a low voice because Rebekka has started muttering in her sleep. I whisper my answer:

"Do you think I would say anything to your mad husband that could mean I would lose touch with my little girls?"

Katriina smiles.

DEAF ISSA

Sia comes to my kiosk with an old man.

"He's a good cook," Sia says.

"What sort of food can you make, *mzee* Issa?" I ask – twice, because Issa's ears have been worn out by his long life; hardly anything enters them.

"Arabic, Indian, English," he says.

"You're hired," I say and give Sia and Issa soft drinks. I arrange with Issa the time he must come to the kiosk – then we can go and pick up his things, and he can become my deaf neighbour.

"Where has he worked until now?" I ask Sia.

"With *wahindi*. But now they think he's got too old because he can't manage all the cooking and laundry, ironing and cleaning for an entire family," she says. It's the same number of jobs that the Larssons need done, but the Indians require perfection from early morning to late at night – if Issa can make a nice dinner, he will work well at the Larsson house, because he won't have to listen to all their shit.

"Do you remember that doctor you told me fancied the *mzungu* lady?" Sia asks.

"Dr Freeman?"

"Yes," Sia says and smiles. "Now he's fooling around with your old girlfriend Vicky."

"What?" I say. "I thought that man was afraid of the dark." Sia grins:

"Yes, but now he has had a peculiar job at the Police Academy and has seen the black gardens." Sia tells me that Dr Freeman was hired to conduct medicals on all the Police Academy recruits. The problem is that the pumps drip because the cheap bargirls in the local area carry bestial diseases in their papayas. And the boys at the Police Academy pick up these diseases and give them to the female recruits.

"Did he check the girls as well?" I ask.

"Yes, all the recruits," Sia says. I point: "Did he study the flower in that garden as well?" Sia holds her hand up to cover her mouth and giggles – she nods.

"Eeehhhh," I say. "But Vicky is no recruit."

"No, but the Commissioner invited the doctor for dinner after his great garden-safari. And now he's seen so many black snakes and red flowers in the curly bushes, he is hungry for Vicky – and she performs miracles for him."

"Yes," I say. "I know her miracles."

I return to the Larsson house and right away the life crisis threatens. Jonas is on the veranda and waves me over:

"I don't want you here anymore," he says. "You can start looking for a new place to stay."

What's this? I was on my way to Sweden on my Gösta ticket. I have just found a wonderful deaf cook. And now the despot threatens me with a life on the streets.

Christian

Flambéed pancakes for pudding and Irish coffee. The Larssons' new cook is a brilliant old man. They're celebrating Dad's fiftieth birthday. I think Katriina is feeling sorry for him because he's alone. I sneak outside to grab an Irish coffee from the tray before they're carried in from the kitchen. Go outside, drink it there – smoke a cigarette. I'm sooo tired; on weekend leave from my new status as a boarder. Absurd – Dad is living in a big house a mile from school, and I'm forced to live under a prison regime at I.S.M. I eat crap food, other people decide what I can and cannot do – I have been robbed of my civil liberties.

"Christian," Katriina calls from the veranda, "won't you come to the sauna with us?" I go round the corner of the house.

"No," I call back. Can see my dad standing there with Katriina.

"He doesn't like to look at old people naked," Dad says.

"You're not old," Katriina says and hugs him. He puts his arms around her. For just a tad too long perhaps. And he's not exactly right. I would like to see Katriina naked – her breasts may sag a little, but they're very beautiful. I think the old man may have a touch of the hots for her – probably after all those times when he's gone to counsel them to get

Jonas to give up his black women. I go to the kitchen and ask Marcus if I can go and lie down on his bed.

"Did the whisky make you tired?" He grins.

"Yes, I'm a bit befuddled," I say. He gives me the key. I go down. Old *bwana* Issa is sitting outside, smoking. I wish him goodnight as peals of laughter echo from the sauna. Go in and lie down on Marcus' bed. Fall asleep.

Marcus

BLOODY HAND

It's late. Dr Freeman and *bwana* D'Souza and the others have already left the festivities.

I am doing the washing-up while the whites drink outside – *bwana* Issa has already gone to bed; he can't handle so much work. Katriina comes in through the back door. Her eyes are wild:

"Marcus, you have to help me."

"What's happened?" I ask.

"Jonas fell over in the sauna," Katriina says.

"Is he hurt?" I ask.

"No, no, no," Katriina says very quickly, wipes something from her eyes. "He's asleep. He's drunk." She walks across the lawn to the sauna. I can't see *bwana* Knudsen anywhere, but his Land Rover is still there. Katriina opens the door to the sauna. There's a faint light coming from the gaps in the oven where the fire is raging – very hot. On the floor I can see the body – Jonas.

"Is there any light? I can get a lamp," I say.

"No," Katriina says sharply. "No lamp."

"Do you want him carried into the house?" I ask.

"No, onto the bench," Katriina says. Her voice is very strange.

"We can carry him to the house," I say.

"No, I don't want my girls to see him . . . like that," she says.

"Alright," I say and grab onto him by the shoulders, and as I touch him I feel that yes, the despot is alive. He grunts. Katriina takes hold of his legs. Jonas is wet with sweat; he almost slips out of my hands. We unload him onto the bench, like a sack of rice. Katriina is sobbing. "Is something the matter?" I ask. She whispers in a wet voice:

"I am tired of living like this," she says.

"Yes," I say and go outside, holding the door for Katriina and leaving it open.

"Close the door," she says.

"But it's very hot in there," I say.

"It's good for him to sweat," she says. And I think that when you sweat a lot after drinking, your body dries out and your headache becomes twice as bad. I close the door tightly.

"I will lock the kitchen door," I say, making my way across the lawn.

"Thanks, Marcus," Katriina says.

I go in to make sure the cooker is turned off, the fridge door shut, and the door locked so the guard can't sneak in at night and steal from the house. I can hear Katriina talking in the sitting room:

"Niels, you must leave now," she says – using *bwana* Knudsen's first name.

"Where is Christian?" he asks.

"I think he's fallen asleep in the servants' quarters, but you can't be here now," Katriina says.

"Alright," *bwana* Knudsen says and I hear the veranda door open. Myself, I reach for the fridge door to take a Carlsberg for a sleeping pill. Eeehhh, my hand is red. Blood? I sniff it, feel it – yes, it is blood. Where does it come from? Perhaps Jonas didn't fall down in drunkenness, but someone hit him with a bit of wood until he fainted? Or with a rock? Should I go over and see how he's doing? No, I'll let the despot suffer. I look out through the kitchen door – *bwana* Knudsen is walking on his drunken legs towards my ghetto to fetch his son. I scrub my hands to be rid of the filth.

Christian

Someone's shaking me. What? My dad.

"Christian, Christian," he says.

"Mmmmm."

"We have to go," he says.

"Why?"

"The party's over – it's time we went home." I wake up; I can smell the cigar fumes on his clothes and beer from his mouth.

"Why don't you just crash on the sofa?" I ask sleepily.

"No, we have to go home. I don't want to be here tomorrow morning."

"What do you mean?"

"I don't want to wake up here."

"You're far too drunk to drive," I say, squinting at my watch. It's just after five – it'll be light soon.

"I can drive," he says. I swing my legs over the side of the bed, get up. Look at him. His skin is pallid – exhausted.

"Alright," I say and wonder where Marcus is. I grab his key and we leave the servants' quarters – I put the padlock on Marcus' door before following the old man round the corner of the building. His legs are already wobbly, but he seems quite collected. "Has everyone gone to bed?" I ask.

"I think so," he says and continues towards the Land Rover.

"Have you seen Marcus?" I ask. "I have to give him his key."

"I don't know," the old man says. I run up to the veranda – the door is open. Go into the sitting room, but there's no-one there. Go down the hall and look into the bedroom where Solja and Rebekka sleep in their double bed. Katriina and Jonas are nowhere to be seen. Look in on the children's room. No-one. Hear the Land Rover being started as I go the other way, to the kitchen. Marcus is there, drinking a Carlsberg. His face is carved in ivory, his eyes cold.

"Hey," I say. "What's up?" He doesn't say anything. Takes another gulp. Watches me. I hold out his key. "Good job I found you – your key." He takes it. "What, err . . . Did something happen?" He shrugs.

"I'm tired," he says.

"But where the hell are Jonas and Katriina?" I ask.

"I think . . ." he begins but stops, looks at me for a long time. "I think he's sleeping outside in the sauna," he says at last. Outside the house I can hear the gears of the Land Rover grinding – Dad is far too drunk.

"I've got to dash," I say. Marcus nods. "See you," I say. "Goodnight."

"Goodnight," he says. I run outside. It seems the old man has got it into gear after all and is reversing – the back of the Land Rover fells two small trees right next to the house before he manages to brake.

"Dad!" I say and run over to the Land Rover.

"Oops," he says.

"Let me drive. I can pick up the motorbike tomorrow," I say.

"Alright," he says and scooches over. I get in behind the wheel. The guard has opened the gate and is standing silently next to it, waiting. We drive off in the false dawn. The old man is completely silent.

"So. Fifty years," I say. "How was the party?"

"Very nice," he says. That's all.

"Very nice," I say. He turns his head and looks at me.

"I had too much to drink," he says. "I fell asleep on the sofa."

"These things happen," I say.

Marcus

COOL SKIN

There's a knock on my door early in the morning. I hear Rebekka crying right outside, and Solja's voice:

"Marcus, Marcus, there's something wrong with Mum," she shouts. I jump out of bed, rip open the door.

"What?" I ask.

"Dad's passed out in the sauna," Solja says – very pale and frightened. Rebekka is wailing like an ambulance, and I pick her up – run to the house through the kitchen door. Issa is standing at the sink, wringing his hands. Already he's got pancakes and freshly squeezed juice ready. Katriina is in the sitting room, rocking back and forth like a madwoman, beating her thighs with her fists.

"What is it?" I say harshly.

"Jonas," she says without looking me in the eye.

"Where is he?" I ask. She doesn't answer. "Is he in the sauna?" I ask. She doesn't answer. Solja is standing like a white stick in the room, and Rebekka is hysterical in my arms. I speak very sharply: "Solja – come here," I say and go towards the kitchen with Rebekka. Once there I stop, put Rebekka down on the floor. "You will keep your sister here," I tell Solja. She swallows and nods and her chin wobbles. I run out of the sitting room, out the back door and into the sauna.

The man is lying on the bench, as dead as a pig at the butcher's. I feel his arm – no pulse and his skin is cool. I run back to the house, grab Katriina by the shoulders, look her in the face. "You must call Gösta, and then you must call the police and tell them you've got a dead man here."

"Can't you do it?" she mutters.

"No," I say, grabbing the phone to make the call and holding it to her ear. There's no connection. "The line's dead," I say. "I'm going to go over to Gösta to tell him the news and send him over and then I'll go right to the police and tell them as well. Do you hear me?" Katriina nods. I go over and stand in front of her. "You have to get up now and be strong for your little girls," I say. She looks at me:

"It wasn't my fault, Marcus," she says.

"Get up and go and have breakfast with the girls," I say. Katriina gets up, and I leap onto the motorbike and race down to Gösta, explain the situation – he gets into his car and drives to Katriina while I race on to the police.

"The white *mama* found her husband dead when she woke up this morning," I say.

"You must show us the way," they say and two men follow me in a car to the house. Solja and Rebekka are gone – Gösta has taken them to his house.

"I found him dead when I woke up this morning," Katriina says, points at the sauna shed. Old Issa has had the good sense to vanish from sight. The two police officers are very confused. Right away one of them leaves to fetch more senior officers.

"Should I be doing anything?" I ask the other officer.

"Don't say a word," he says. We wait. I'm sweating in fear – when a murder has been committed, you need a murderer. Who will they pick? Katriina smokes cigarettes and looks vacantly ahead. A new police officer arrives with more ornaments on his uniform.

"Arrest him," he says, pointing at me.

"I didn't do it," I croak as they slam on handcuffs and drag me straight to the police station. Their logic is black and white. The dead man was white; the black man must have done it.

They throw me into a cell. They beat me with garden hoses – *eeeehhh*.

"What have you done? What have you seen?"

"I haven't seen anything." *PAH*.

"How can you not have seen anything? You live there – you know everything about them. You were going to steal their things."

"We found a large stereo in your room – you stole it from them."

Satan in his hell couldn't scare me more than these guys do, because I have heard of their methods: the cold baths, drowning, beating the soles of your feet, so you can never walk again.

"That's one I was given – you can ask the *mama* in the house about it." *PAH*. Now they take me to the tub. A room with a sort of concrete bathtub. Full of cold water. I have heard about this: they put you into it. They leave you there. You're not allowed to get up. All the day you must lie there, and all night. You become as sick as a dog, shivering, can't walk or stand or think. You'll admit anything and everything – the things you didn't do as well as the ones you did.

They push me in – they almost drown me.

"You wanted the white *mama*. She paid you. Her lover paid you to do it."

I croak like a frog about Dr Freeman – he's the one who wants the white *mama*.

"Don't finger the innocent," the policeman says and drowns me again. He pulls me up my the ears – almost yanks them off my head. "You did it yourself," he says. Already my skin is like a raisin. They let me lie for two hours until my skin starts to die – now it's pale, almost grey. Then they come in and start beating me.

Christian

The old man's still asleep when I wake up. I go to the kitchen. Sunday – Juliaz's day off. Make toast, fry up some bacon and eggs, put on the kettle for coffee. I want it all. Eat while I read Ian Fleming's *Thunderball*. The I.S.M. library is full of this sort of stuff. When people go home, they take all their proper books. But excess luggage is expensive, so they all give their pulp fiction to the school library. I make myself another cup of coffee. Sit down in the shade outside. My head feels a bit heavy – must be that Irish coffee I had at the Larssons'.

I can hear a car and go outside. It's Gösta. He was at the party last night as well and seems tense when he gets out.

"Is your dad up?" he asks.

"Not yet," I say. "Do you need him?"

"I'd better wake him up," Gösta says and goes towards the house.

"Has something happened?" I ask.

He stops with his hand on the doorknob.

"Jonas is dead," he says and goes inside.

"Dead," I say, following him. "How?" Gösta continues down the hall towards the sitting room.

"Katriina found him in the sauna this morning.."

"How?" I ask.

"I don't know," Gösta says and opens the bedroom door. I follow him, but he holds a hand up against my chest.

"Go outside, Christian. I'll tell him." Then he closes the door. I stand there for a moment, wondering about eavesdropping, but I feel I'm not that kind of person. I go down the hall, lighting a cigarette. After a while I hear the old man going to the bathroom and Gösta in the kitchen, fiddling with the electric kettle. I finish my cigarette and am putting it out as I hear the old man coming into the kitchen – I go back inside to join them. Dad is sitting with a cup of coffee, ashen-faced.

"You have to eat something," Gösta says. The old man chews a slice of toast. Eats a banana. Looks at me.

"We're going down to Katriina's to see if there's anything we can do," he says.

"I'll come with you," I say.

"No," he says.

"But my motorbike is there."

"You can pick it up later."

"I'm bloody well going to need it, aren't I," I say.

"Later," he says and gives me a look that shuts me up. Should I give him the key and ask Marcus to take it up here, so I can find out what's really going on? But the old man gets up stiffly and goes to the bathroom – we can hear him being sick. Gösta drinks his coffee and raises his eyebrows just once. When he returns, he smells of toothpaste. He points at me.

"You stay here until I come back," he says. I nod. "I mean it," he says.

"Alright, alright," I say.

Marcus

THE GOOD KIND OF EVIL

PAH, PAH, PAH . . . The blows are raining down on the knobbly skin on my back where my father butchered me with his belt during my child-hood. They rain down on my reunited leg, my harvested arse. The police have lifted me out of the bathtub so they won't get wet as they beat me. Fear of death opens my arsehole, and shit runs out of me.

"You little swine," a policeman says, kicking my back. I try to roll away from my executioners – the concrete floor is wet with piss and blood and shit, all of it mine. The policemen just laugh. When one of them is tired, he takes a break and smokes a cigarette until they change over again, so their strength is always up. They grab onto me and throw me back into the bathtub.

"In a little while we'll get our tools out, and then you'll be singing like a parrot," one of them says. Even a life in Karanga Prison would be better than this death cell. I squeal like a baby:

"Will you stop if I say it was me?"

*

My salvation comes in the form of another police officer. There seems no end to the distinctions on his uniform – he is an important man.

"Why are you beating this man?" he asks.

"He might have killed the *mzungu* in the hot house, or else he knows something. But he refuses to say."

"Leave. I will speak with him."

"Yes, sir," they say and leave.

"So, the murdering *mzungu* is dead – hmmm." *Eeehhh*, it's the policeman from the accident on West Kilimanjaro – when the *mama* was crushed between the logs.

"*Shikamoo mzee*," I croak. He offers me a cigarette. I lift my arm out of the water to take it, but my hand is shaking badly. "Wait," he says and lights the cigarette – placing it between my lips: the best cigarette of my life.

"Did you do it?" he asks.

"No, no, *mzee*. He died in the special Swedish sweat lodge – sauna, they call it. He was in there all night at a very high temperature. In the morning he was dead."

"Why was he in there?" the policeman says.

"He drank a lot of *pombe* – he probably fell asleep," I say.

"Yes, that *mzungu* was fond of *pombe*, fond of *malaya*, fond of the colonial lifestyle," the policeman says.

"Yes, *mzee*," I say.

"And the *mama*?" he asks.

"The *mama* is alright. Now she's alone with two children."

"She'll have to go home to her own country. And you? Are you still working for the sawmill project?"

"Yes – these days I work mostly at the Imara Furniture Factory."

"*Eeeeehhhh*," he says. "I'll get a car to take you home."

"Thank you, *mzee*," I say. He leaves. They lift me out of the water because my body can't do it alone. They wrap me in a blanket, take me home. They're the same men who beat me. At the gate of the house I can't get out of the car, so they drag me – dump me like a carcass by the side of the read

KAMIKAZE
The guard helps me to the veranda and tells me Katriina and the girls are at Gösta's house. The body has been taken to the morgue at K.C.M.C. In my ghetto I change into dry clothes and take all my blankets with me,

sitting like an old Chagga in an easy chair on the veranda. Old Issa has returned – he brings me a large plateful of lovely biryani. I eat and regain some of my strength.

A smile breaks out on my face. Why? I was arrested by the police, and all the *wazungu* left the house. And yet I return alive and my Boombox is still in its place in the ghetto – it hasn't even been stolen. Is this the age of miracles?

Soon my saviour from the police arrives, and in a Land Rover behind him are *bwana* Knudsen and Gösta.

"*Shikamoo mzee*," I say to the policeman. He doesn't want to talk to me. He goes to the sweat lodge, carrying papers in his hand. *Bwana* Knudsen and Gösta follow him, and I get up on legs that still tremble so I might know what fate may bring.

"It was in here she found him," Gösta says, pointing inside the sauna. The police officer looks at his papers:

"It says here that *bwana* Larsson was lying on that bench there?" he says as if it's a question.

"You know, I wasn't actually here. It was his wife who found him," Gösta says.

"But you had been at the party earlier in the evening?"

"Yes, but I had gone home." The police officer turns from Gösta to *bwana* Knudsen.

"But you were here."

Bwana Knudsen clears his voice:

"Yes, I was at the party, but I didn't see him towards the end of the evening. I thought he had gone to bed."

"Was he drunk?" the police officer asks.

"Yes," *bwana* Knudsen says.

"Someone hit him," the policeman says.

"What?" *bwana* Knudsen says.

"He fell," Gösta says. "He was drunk. He must have fallen over, his head hit the oven."

"You told me you had gone home. I didn't say anything about his head," the policeman says, his eyebrows raised.

"No," Gösta says. "But his wife said he had a wound in his head and that there was blood in his hair, so he must have fallen."

"I'm not sure he fell," the police officer says.

"Why not?" Gösta asks.

"How could he fall in such a way he would land on a bench inside a shed?"

"What do you mean?" *bwana* Knudsen asks. The police officer looks at the police report in his hand:

"It says here he was lying on the bench. People only ever fall down. Not even a white man becomes an aeroplane when he dies."

"Perhaps he staggered over and lay down on the bench after he hit his head," Gösta says. "Or his wife lifted him up when she found him."

"She has given evidence saying she didn't touch the body," the police officer says.

Gösta looks at *bwana* Knudsen in confusion.

"Did they take pictures?" *bwana* Knudsen says quickly in a strange sort of Swedish.

"No," Gösta says in Swedish.

"Then they can't prove he was lying on the bench," Knudsen says to Gösta.

"A black policeman will state it in court," Gösta tells Knudsen.

"Then we'll just say that the police lifted the body up later in order to be able to blackmail us," Knudsen says.

"And then the judge will ask for his palm to be greased," Gösta says. "I think it'll be cheaper to pay this one right now."

The police officer laughs:

"The dead man doesn't become an aeroplane just because you two talk in a strange language," he says.

"Who would benefit from killing him?" Gösta says – in English once more. The police officer shrugs:

"There might be another man who likes the woman and wants her husband out of the way – it's not uncommon." Gösta shakes his head:

"Now the woman has two children and no husband. She'll have to go back to Europe where she doesn't even have a house," Gösta says.

"But I have to put it in the report. I'm not sure the man fell. He may have been hit," the policeman says. Knudsen's shirt is soaked with sweat. Yes, feel the fear.

"And then what will happen?" Gösta asks.

"Then the judge will have to weigh the evidence," the policeman says. The dance has begun.

"His wife is a widow now – with two children. It would give her a lot of problems in Europe if someone thought her husband was murdered,"

Gösta says. The police officer shrugs. "How can we help you solve this case?" Gösta asks.

"Life in Tanzania is hard," the policeman says. "Let's go into the shade." They all go round the house and towards the veranda door. "Don't disturb us now," the policeman tells me. I limp down to my ghetto on my raisin legs and keep an eye on the veranda. They come out again. The policeman goes to his car. I go to the veranda. *Bwana* Knudsen sees me coming, so he speaks in his strange Swedish:

"How much did you have to give him?" he asks Gösta.

Gösta names a figure – a nice big year's salary.

"Did you carry that much on you?" *bwana* Knudsen asks.

"Yes, my wife explained how it works."

"You'll get it back – I will get it for you," *bwana* Knudsen says.

"You don't have to," Gösta says.

"Yes – I wouldn't want you to . . ." *bwana* Knudsen begins. Gösta cuts him short:

"You can give me half."

"I just don't want Katriina to hear about it," Knudsen says.

"Exactly," Gösta says. "It's bad enough as it is."

Me, all I think about is Sweden. Is this death a blessing or a curse on my pilgrimage?

Christian

It's late afternoon when the old man gets back.

"What's happening down there?" I ask.

"You can go down and get it now, but don't disturb anyone."

"Get what?"

"The motorbike."

"But what about Katriina, the children?"

"They . . ." the old man stops, shrugs resignedly.

"What about Jonas?"

"Well. The police have been there all afternoon. Jonas' body will remain at K.C.M.C. until the police let Katriina take it home."

"Is she going to go home?"

"Yes. She's going home to bury him," Dad says.

"Will she be back?"

"I don't know."

"What do the police say?" I ask.

"You know . . ." the old man says with a sigh. "Marcus was arrested."
He looks at me.

"Marcus!?" I say.

"Yes. He's been released now. But it's just . . . They want to be seen to
be doing something."

"But . . . surely it was an accident, wasn't it?" I say.

"They have to 'investigate'."

"That's bloody stupid, that is."

"Just . . . go and get it if you want. Or do it later. I'm going out to Gösta's
to help organize . . . things."

When I get there Marcus is sitting on a chair outside the servants'
quarters. His skin seems grey and his face is bruised.

"But what happened to Jonas?" I ask.

"I don't know," Marcus says.

"But you were here, weren't you?!" I say.

"I was in the house," Marcus says. "I don't know what happened in
the sauna."

"What's going to happen now?" I ask.

"I don't know," Marcus says. I sit down. We smoke cigarettes. Marcus
leans back his head and shuts his eyes.

"I'm going to have to dash," I say. "The boarders have to be back by now."

"O.K.," he says without opening his eyes.

"O.K.," I say. "See you." I drive back to the house and park the motorbike. Dad is on the sofa, staring vacantly out into the room. "You're
going to have to give me a lift up to school," I say. "They won't let me
take my bike up there."

"Alright," he says. "You drive."

"I don't think they'll like that either," I say. Dad sighs.

"They'll live," he says. In the car he's silent, stares out of the window.

"It's just ridiculous, you being in the house and me boarding just
around the corner."

"That's a situation of your own making," he says.

Marcus

GRAVE ROBBER

I get my beat-up body on the motorbike and get together a few carpenters, paying them with money Gösta has given me to stay up all night

long and make a beautiful coffin out of wood from West Kilimanjaro for the dead boss. And I too am there all night, overseeing the construction of Jonas' last residence.

What happened at that party? I was busy clearing things away in the kitchen and washing up when all the *wazungu* had moved to the sauna. Katriina went to get me to lift Jonas up, with his head all damp with blood, and *bwana* Knudsen was there as well – he was in the sitting room. We carried Jonas. He was breathing. I got blood on my hand. But what had gone before? The question remains: was it murder?

I ask Katriina straight out:

"What happened to Jonas?"

"Africa drove him mad," she says.

"But what happened to him that night?"

"I don't know," Katriina says.

"He had hurt his head," I say. Katriina looks shocked, but regains her composure.

"He must have fallen and hit his head against the oven," she says and looks away from me, snivelling. "We didn't see it when we picked him up because it was so dark."

The next few days *bwana* Knudsen comes to help Katriina. Dr Freeman comes as well. I watch their circus act – it's like lions in the Serengeti. Jonas is dead, and the others fight for their rights to the lioness, who is thinking about her cubs. How can she best ensure their future?

Also D'Souza comes to spread his poison.

"Perhaps it was you who murdered him," he says, straight out, just like that.

"Where is my motive?" I ask.

"He was going to kick you out," D'Souza says. Katriina is surprised:

"He was?" she asks.

"Yes," D'Souza says. "Jonas suspected Marcus of stealing the project's funds."

"Do you think I would kill a man to be allowed to live in there?" I ask, pointing at my ghetto.

"I'll be talking to the police about you," D'Souza says.

"Stop that nonsense," Katriina says. "Marcus did nothing wrong."

*

I pick up the coffin with *bwana* Knudsen and drive to K.C.M.C. But we can't have the body, because a lot of paperwork and phone calls to the embassy and the airline must be done first. The next day there is no plane, so it isn't until the day after that the body is put in the coffin – a devilish experience. I take it to the airport myself in the Land Cruiser in which the body used to pump *malaya* when it was still alive. Gösta and Knudsen take Katriina and the girls there.

"We'll be back in a few weeks," Katriina tells me.

"What will happen then?" I ask.

"I don't know," Katriina says. Solja is standing by, looking grumpy, while Rebekka clings to my legs and screams when she is pulled away by her mother.

I wave at the aeroplane that will carry the dead *mzungu* to his Swedish hole in the ground. And then right away I rush over to Rombo Avenue, and do a great search of the house. It doesn't take me long to find the revolver. Should I sell it? No, it is devilry. But there has to be a place . . . the paranoid man was always hiding things. I find *bhangi* in three places. A picture of his boat hangs on the wall – behind glass and in a frame. I take it down, take everything apart. Behind the picture is two pieces of cardboard and between those – *eeehhh*, enough money for a fresh start, dollars. I take every bit of it and close up the picture, putting it back together nicely, hanging it on the wall. A grave robber, that's me.

Issa slobs into the sitting room.

"*Eeehhh*, what will I do now? *Bwana* is dead, and *mama* has gone to Europe?"

"She will be back, so you must just stay in your job," I say. "You will be paid."

"Would you like something to eat?" Issa asks. I say yes please, and he goes to the kitchen. His food is always sheer perfection.

"Marcus?" The voice comes from outside – it's Christian. I go out on the veranda. "Did they get off alright?" Christian asks.

"Yes. Ugh! – that Jonas. He stank," I say.

"Stank?"

"Yes. The cold storage plant at K.C.M.C. has broken down completely. Normally in Tanzania we bury the body very quickly. But Jonas, he lies there for three days in the morgue, just stewing. He stank like a carcass on the roadside – rotten."

"What about Katriina and the kids?" Christian asks.

"They'll be back in a week or two – to sort out things here. So I don't really know anything. They'll probably have to move back to Sweden. Katriina doesn't have a job or enough money to go on living here." I smile.

"Why are you smiling?" Christian asks. I don't want to tell him it's because I've got dollars in my pocket.

"I'm glad the crazy *mzungu* is dead," I say.

"But what about you?" Christian asks.

"I'm alive. I've got my job."

"Do you think you can go on living here?"

"I don't know. I may be sent away," I say. Jonas did get one thing right; the timing of his death – the year is almost out, and my white girls can go back with his body to Sweden and celebrate Christmas with snow the way they always wanted to.

VULTURES

The *wazungu* women come round to ask about Katriina. Dr Freeman comes round – he's going back to Australia and wanted to say goodbye. He's taking Vicky with him on the plane. *Bwana* Knudsen doesn't come round. Perhaps he's afraid of me. What will happen next? Katriina said she would be back to pack up and sort things out. And Solja must finish the school year. But then what will happen?

A handsome woman comes to the house. I am sitting on the veranda.

"Where is *bwana* Larsson?" she asks.

"He is dead," I say.

"Dead?" She looks shocked. "He promised me he would . . ." she starts but stops, walks away. He had promised her money for the rent, a ticket to Sweden – all the lies I know so well.

The man who has bought some of the Larssons' things still has six instalments left to pay. His business is doing badly, so he arranged to delay payment for a few months. And now he's in the papers for doing evil, encouraged by the witch doctor in his village: "You need to acquire new power to create success for your business – you must pump your daughter right away; if she is pure, the power of her virginity will give you a great success.'

But the man's wife doesn't like that superstition – she goes right to the police, and he is put in prison. Then she comes to the Larsson house with her brothers soon after Jonas has died and is on his rotten way to the Swedish soil, demanding that I give her what she is owed.

"They're not yours until all the payments have been made," I say.

"We have paid enough," one of the brothers says. "We will take our things now."

"That can't be done. The things must be given to the man who has paid for them. Where is he?" I ask.

"He is finished," one of the brothers says.

"If I can't have the things, I want my money back," the *mama* says.

"Where are the papers? The contract which shows how much your husband paid before he went to prison?" I ask.

"*Tsk*," one of the brothers says. "Where is the dead *mzungu*'s wife, so we can talk to her?"

"She'll be back in two weeks. You'll have to return then," I say. "I am only guarding the house."

"You're a little man," the other brother says. "We could take those things ourselves – see if you can stop us." Straightaway I call to the guard:

"Run to the Police Academy and tell them we have problems with thieves here." The oldest brother points at me.

"When we meet you in the dark, we'll do for you." They walk away. I run straight down to my saviour – the policeman who got me out of the cold bath. Using the stolen dollars I grease him into talking to the wife and her brothers, so they will keep quiet. My policeman smiles: "Even in death that *mzungu* is a good man to know."

1985

Marcus

SEIZED

One day when I come home from work, Katriina is sitting on the veranda, drinking gin and tonic. I say hello.

"Have a drink," she says – I can hear she's had quite a few already.

"Where are the girls?" I ask and my sweat is cold – did she leave them in Sweden?

"With their friends until tomorrow."

"When are you travelling back to Sweden?"

"I don't know," Katriina says. "I've got Jonas' salary from S.I.D.A. for the next six months – I need to think about what to do after that."

"It'll be lovely for you to move back to Sweden," I say. She shakes her head.

"Even if I get myself a job, what am I to do about Rebekka? She's so young and her Swedish is so poor? She doesn't like Sweden. Two children, no money, no place to stay."

"Can't you sell the big ship and buy a small house?" I ask.

"The boat has been seized by the police because Jonas stole S.I.D.A.'s money," she says and looks at me questioningly.

"Yes," I say.

"Do you have any *bhangi*?" I shake my head. "Then go get some more tonic," she says and grabs the gin bottle from the table.

Christian

Exams approach. Next year I will be in the top year. I take it easy – I'm sick of being stranded at school. There aren't that many exams at the end of Year Eleven, and as for grades, well, who cares? I just have to make sure I'm not booted out. Perhaps it might be good to get out of here – go home to Denmark. Get my own life.

I've moved down to board with the rest of the oldest students at Kishari. Panos comes round, and we go over to Jarno and Salomon's window to ask if they want to go out and play football.

"What are you doing?" I ask.

"We just need a smoke first," Salomon says. He's Ethiopian, son of the ambassador, a Rasta, totally stoned all the time. He's in Year Twelve and will be off to Dar es Salaam for his revision week soon. Salomon has a big hookah in his room and a brown paper bag full of Arusha-*bhangi*.

"Couldn't you do that later?" Panos asks through the bars and mosquito netting – it's too easy to beat them when they're stoned.

"No. Rastafari must smoke Jah's weed to play the ball Natty Dread style," Salomon says from inside, lighting his pipe. He can't open his mouth without saying things like that. The smoke starts billowing. There's a crackle and a roar inside the hookah – the seeds haven't been removed from the *bhangi*. There's a knock on the door. Me and Panos pull back as the door is opened. We're standing with our backs to the wall on either side of the window.

"Why are you boys using a hookah?" Atkinson – one of the teachers. He's the sort who wouldn't dream of waiting until he's asked to come in when he knocks on a door; I suppose he's hoping to catch someone red-handed in a spot of recreational masturbation. But he's not the brightest banana in the bunch. Salomon answers:

"It makes the smoke cooler on the lungs, plus the water filters out some of the poison – which means we can smoke the cheap tobacco from the market." Salomon explains too much. If Atkinson can't smell it's *bhangi*, then there's no need to explain anything.

"What's that?" Atkinson asks. I can hear the brown paper bag rustling.

"Just more tobacco," Salomon says. Atkinson is standing there, fiddling with the bag.

"I'll take that bag with me," we hear Atkinson saying inside the room.

"You can't take my tobacco," Salomon says. "That's theft."

"I don't know if it's tobacco," Atkinson says. "I'm confiscating it to have it analysed."

Jarno speaks up for the first time:

"Try smoking it."

"I don't smoke," Atkinson says.

"You don't say," Jarno says.

"Then how are you going to analyse it?" Salomon says.

"K.C.M.C. – I'll go there and have it analysed."

"That's not a good idea," Salomon says.

"Maybe you want to tell me it's not tobacco?" Atkinson asks.

"It's a hospital intended to save poor negroes, and you want to waste the doctors' time by having them analyse my cheap tobacco. Tsk," Salomon says. "You'd better speak to Thompson first. He's in charge of the boarders, not you."

"It's not the last you'll hear of this," Atkinson says as he walks out the door.

"Shit," Jarno says.

"You are so fucked," Panos says. Right then Atkinson comes round the corner of the building.

"Don't think I didn't see you," he says.

"We're outside, just enjoying the air," I say.

"You're witnesses," Atkinson says.

"We didn't see anything," Panos says.

"Yes, you did," Atkinson says and walks away. Salomon and Jarno come out and we all go up to play football.

The next morning Salomon, Jarno, Panos and I are called to Thompson's office. Slowly the nature of the problem is revealed to us:

Atkinson didn't go to Thompson or Owen. He went straight up to K.C.M.C. to a local doctor. That means it may now become a police matter, because the *bhangi* has been officially recorded and registered outside the school. The Tanzanian papers frequently print grand appeals to young people about not smoking *bhangi*. And you can't get away with ignoring the country. If word gets out . . . expulsion for Salomon and Jarno; something like that. But what about Salomon, the ambassador's son – can you expel him? What would the ramifications be? There are the other parents to take into account. The daughter of the Minister of the Interior and several other children of *mabwana makubwa* are in the Ethiopian's year.

"Right, let's not get carried away," Thompson says.

"Carried away?" Salomon says. "You're saying we may be kicked out of the country. And you want us not to get carried away? I need witnesses. What is this tobacco you're talking about? I don't know anything about tobacco."

"Take it easy," Thompson says.

"What does Atkinson say?" Jarno asks.

"I'm handling this now," Thompson says, looking at us.

"We were outside, enjoying the sounds of the insects," Panos says. "Me and Christian. I don't understand what we're doing here."

"For now, I'm just going to ask you all to keep mum about this," Thompson says. As if the entire school didn't already know.

"What happens next?" I ask.

"The board meets this afternoon – you'll hear more tomorrow."

Alright then. We leave and go down the hall. Look at each other. Tomorrow. As we do, people approach:

"What did he say? Are you out?" they ask.

"We'll know more tomorrow," we say. The white kids are all fired up:

"If they boot you out, we'll go on strike. We'll boycott exams," they're saying. But not the Indians. They'd be happy to see us gone. To the Indians exams are a matter of life and death. Otherwise they'll be stuck behind some tiny till in Dar es Salaam or Mbeya or some other godforsaken hellhole for the rest of their lives. They have to get out. Good exams can get them a scholarship to Britain, the U.S., Canada or Australia. In their eyes we're just a bunch of spoiled brats.

The next morning we are called to the office. Thompson says:

"This is how it's going to be: Salomon will be allowed to take his exams, but he's not allowed to attend the graduation ceremony. Jarno, you're suspended for two weeks, and the next time you do even the smallest thing, you're out altogether. And you two buffoons," he says, pointing at me and Panos. "Panos, you'll be suspended the next time you do the least thing, and Christian, you'll be out on your ear if anything else happens."

Right. We're in the clear. No problem. But Salomon's classmates – except for the Indians – they all freak out. The hypocrisy is too blatant. There can be no backing down. Revolution.

"Fuck it," they say. "Salomon is our friend. If he's not allowed to attend the graduation, we won't take our exams."

It's a massive problem, because Salomon's supporters are the sons and daughters of Tanzanian hotshots who want to see their children get good grades and get all dressed up at the graduation ceremony. If their children won't take their exams . . . the story might spread, and then the authorities will have to step in.

To me things are simple. I got off scot free, but I'm hanging in there by the finest thread imaginable. But the Ethiopian ambassador is angry with his son, angry with Atkinson, angry with the school. Jarno's dad doesn't care, but his mother takes the bus from Morogoro.

Salomon's year have called a meeting for all the representatives of the upper two years. The Indian pupils don't show – they've gone to their lessons, they're getting their exams. They'll graduate alright, heading off to new lives in the West. Fuck Africa, fuck the Ethiopian, fuck Bob Marley. Jarno is still at risk – if the police get involved, he'll be out. Of the country. His mother gets up:

"I'm Jarno's mother," she says. "Hello."

"Hello," people mutter.

"I didn't think Jarno had a mother," Salomon says. She goes on:

"What is a graduation ceremony, anyway? You'll all meet at the party afterwards. The important thing is that you take your exams. You have to understand that being a loyal friend is fine, but this is breaking the law, and if you make a big song and dance about it by boycotting the exams, all your parents will be asking questions. Your friends here will get into trouble," she says, gesturing towards Jarno and Salomon. "You may all miss out on your graduations, but they could be sent to prison or even be kicked out of the country." Alright, people mutter and nod. I look at Jarno's mum. I'm impressed. Shakila gets up.

"What do you say? Shall we put it to the vote? Hands up all those of you who say we take our exams and participate in graduation so long as Salomon gets his exam papers." No-one puts their hands up. It's more fun to kick up a fuss, but now it just feels a little uncomfortable. "Come on, guys," Shakila says. "We've shown our displeasure, and Jarno's mum would like to keep her son in the country. Plus if he goes, they'll be no-one decent to D.J. at parties." People laugh sheepishly and raise their hands. An overwhelming majority. Jarno is saved by reggae and disco music. Shakila goes over to Jarno: "Your mum's really cool."

Then she walks off. She's pretty cool too.

Saturday afternoon I see Juliaz on his bike at Clock Tower roundabout.

"Juliaz," I call. He stops.

"Ahhh, Christian. *Habari sa siku nyingi?*" – how have I been?

"Good," I say.

"*Mzee* has been well as well," he says.

"Are you looking well after him when he's home?" I ask.

"Yes," Juliaz says. "No problem. The last two weeks he's been working with the co-op in Moshi, so I always have his lunch ready when he comes through the door." Juliaz smiles.

"Does he come home for lunch every day?" I ask.

"Yes, warm lunch every day."

"And *pombe*?" I ask.

"No, no," Juliaz says. "*Mzee* has stopped drinking so much *pombe* since he's become friendly with the nice Swedish *mama* who is alone with her children."

"That's good," I say, and we part. Katriina and Dad. Two weeks he's been at home. That arsehole. Not one word have I had from him. I could have gone home on a weekend leave. Might have slipped into town completely legally with Marcus without getting into trouble. But no, no – he doesn't want to be troubled by his pain-in-the-arse of a son. Annemette is dead, and he's divorced Mum. Jonas died under suspicious circumstances. And now Dad's getting up to something with the dead man's wife. Maybe Dad wants to take her for himself. That's really fucked-up.

Marcus

WAITING ROOM

"The police have called," Katriina says nervously. "They want to see me for a meeting at the station tomorrow. You must come."

"Can't you ask D'Souza? I don't understand their madness," I say, and my sweat is cold, because my body still aches from the torture.

"Please," Katriina says. That woman is helpless.

"I will do it," I say.

The next day we're sitting in the good policeman's office:

"Is everything alright concerning the dead man? Has he been buried in Swedish soil?" he asks in English.

"Yes, thank you," Katriina replies. "There were no problems." The man gives Katriina a searching look.

"Do you speak Swahili?" he asks in Swahili.

"Only a little," Katriina says in Swahili. The police officer starts speaking in my ancestors' tribal language from the mountain – Kichagga; I don't speak it well, but I understand nearly everything. He smiles:

"When I see which man has taken over the widow, it's the murderer I am looking at." I answer him in my broken Kichagga, careful not to provoke him:

"If there was any evidence, the murderer would already be in the courtroom," I say. He raises his forefinger:

"Careful," he says. "In Tanzania a trial can be conducted without evidence."

"What's he saying?" Katriina asks in Swedish.

"Shut up," I tell her in Swedish, and the police officer smiles and speaks to me in Kichagga:

"You understand more than one would suppose at first glance – maybe you know everything."

"I know nothing," I say. "I myself am in crisis because of the *mzungu*'s death."

"I don't like a murder with no murderer. I am watching all you people," he says in Kichagga and gets up, extending his hand to Katriina. "Goodbye," he says in English. She shakes his hand and says goodbye. We go out in the burning sun in front of the police station.

"What did he say?" Katriina asks.

"That we were to watch ourselves," I say,

"Why?" she asks.

"He doesn't like a murder without a murderer."

"But it wasn't a murder," Katriina says shrilly.

"He's keeping his eye on us," I say and go towards the car.

"Should I pay him?" she asks.

"He's already been paid," I say.

"By whom?"

"Gösta and *bwana* Knudsen," I say, opening the door. She's standing by the passenger's side.

"But . . ." she says. I speak to her harshly:

"Why do you think we're allowed to walk around free?" Katriina doesn't answer my question. I get in, start the car.

"What do you mean, he's keeping an eye on us?" she asks.

"I don't know," I say.

"Perhaps I should pay him some more," Katriina says.

"*Tsk*," I say. Myself, I haven't been paid. The body flew to Europe, but where is my ticket? Am I stranded in Tanzania's waiting room forever until my death?

THE WIDOW'S BED

Bwana Knudsen comes round and talks to Katriina almost every night. He picks her and the girls up from Hotel Tanzanite. He takes them on a trip to Ngorongoro. He has dinner at the house and reads a book to my white daughter Rebekka, throws a Frisbee on the lawn with Solja; all the things Jonas never did – *bwana* Knudsen does them. And suddenly one morning when I get up, his Land Rover is parked in the drive, and now I'm the one feeling the bonnet just like Katriina did with Jonas' car in the mornings during the troubles. The bonnet under her hand was warm because Jonas had kept the engine going all night during his pumping. The bonnet under my hand is cold – the engine has been still, but what about *bwana* Knudsen? Has he been kept here running round the widow's bed?

It raises my hopes. If Katriina can catch the fish, my white girls can go on living close to me and I can continue seeing them. I am hoping for that.

Christian comes to my ghetto on Friday night – on the weekends he stays in his father's house.

"I'm going to Liberty. Do you want to come? I've got money," he says.

So we go – Faizal is playing. Christian drinks beer and looks at the young girls.

"Do you like them?" I ask.

"Yes, there are lots of beautiful girls here," he says. I take him up to the D.J. cage. You go through a door next to the bar and take the stairs.

"This is Christian," I say. "He's the one with the good music I gave you on tape."

"Ahhh, Christian," Faizal says. "You're the expert on the good music. I am very pleased with it."

"You play it well," Christian says. "Everyone says you're the best D.J. in Moshi."

"Yes, I can take an empty dance floor and build it up to a big *ngoma*," Faizal says. And it's the truth – the floor is teeming. But I know that Faizal's decks belong to an Arab man who gets big payments from the owner of Liberty – Faizal only gets a small salary from the Arab, but everyone thinks he's the great king, so the girls wriggle on the floor to catch his attention in the D.J. cage.

"The girls are dancing for you," I say.

"Yes, everyone wants my black mamba," Faizal says and looks at Christian. "I've heard about your father. A very hard man. You're from a family of killers."

"What do you mean?" Christian asks.

"It's nothing," I say to Christian.

"He will kill another man if he wants the man's wife," Faizal grins.

"What the hell are you on about?" Christian says.

"You don't know anything, Faizal," I say. Faizal shrugs:

"It's what they tell me," he says.

"What the hell is he on about?" Christian says.

"Come here," I say, pushing Christian towards the stairs. He goes down. I follow. Downstairs to the veranda bar.

"Explain it to me," he says.

"I don't know anything," I say.

"Yes, you do. You know what he was talking about," Christian says.

"Yes," I say. "But it's only spiteful rumours."

"And what do the rumours say?"

"They say that your father killed Jonas to take his place in Katriina's bed."

"And what do you say to that?" Christian asks.

"I don't say anything," I say. "I don't know the truth."

Christian is as white as a sheet.

Christian

Lying on my bed in Kishari, staring at the ceiling. It's far out. A family of killers. We were at the Larssons'. I had an Irish coffee and fell asleep in Marcus' bed. Dad woke me up – we couldn't be there in the morning. He knocked over trees with the Land Rover because he was drunk, so I had to take the wheel and get us home. And the next day he was completely beside himself. But then Gösta had just told him Jonas was dead – I don't know what to believe. And Juliaz said he's getting friendly with Katriina.

How friendly are we talking here? I don't like it. Maybe I should go back to Denmark – get a life of my own.

Marcus

DIRT-EATER

On Wednesday night Christian comes by my ghetto.

"But what about school?" I ask.

"They've let me stay with my dad for a few days," Christian says.

"I thought he'd gone on a safari," I say.

"He came back early," Christian says. We hang out. Later Christian goes back to his father's.

The next day it turns out that I.S.M. is conducting a manhunt. Who are they looking for? Christian. *Bwana* Knudsen isn't at home – Christian just left school without telling anyone. He's kicked out. He will never be welcome there again.

Myself, I have my own agenda. I drive over to Gösta's house.

"How is it going with my travel arrangements to Sweden?" I ask. Gösta sighs:

"Everything has been put on standby, Marcus. The evaluation mission from the Swedish embassy in Dar es Salaam found a lot of irregularities with the project. They suspect Jonas of having withdrawn money from the project account for his own uses and hiding his tracks with false invoices. Now everything must be looked into before anything new can take place," he says, shaking his head sadly. But why should he be sad? He was part of the scam himself, and now he can point a finger at Jonas and say he was the guilty party. *Tsk*, why couldn't this Swedish dirt-eater hold off on his dying until I was on a plane to Europe?

Christian

"You've got yourself kicked out," Dad says. "Permanently. Do you know that?"

"Yes," I say.

"Did you do it on purpose?" Dad asks.

"Good question," I say.

"If you did, you're more stupid than I thought."

"You're too stupid to assess just how stupid I might be."

"What do you imagine is going to happen next?" he asks.

"I don't know," I say.

"Stupid."

"It might be said it was stupid of you to put me in prison," I say.

"In prison?" he asks.

"Boarding school," I say. "It's a fucking prison. And you're bleeding well living here, but I'm not allowed to. You want to conduct your thing with Katriina undisturbed. What is that?"

"None of your business is what it is – we're both adults," Dad says. I look away.

"You can't live here," Dad says the next morning. "I'll be moving to Shinyanga for work."

"No. I'm going to Denmark," I say.

"I'll talk to your mum about what we can do."

"By all means . . . Talk away," I say and drive into town. Smoke *bhangi*, drink beer – same drill that got me booted out of school.

Two weeks Dad has it all sorted:

"You can stay with Lene and Torben in Aalborg."

"Aalborg? Alright," I say.

"They live close to a Sixth Form College, Hasseris Gymnasium, where you can do a full H.F."

"Am I doing a H.F.?" I ask.

"What would you rather do?"

"No, no, H.F. is fine," I say.

"Good," he says and hands me some papers, points at where he wants me to sign. I scribble my signature.

I'm looking forward to going to Denmark. Dad has found out I can get a local flight from Mwanza.

That last night we're sitting on the veranda, smoking dry cigars. The old man is a bit the worse for wear. I look at him in the twilight. Is he capable of killing? I let it out:

"People in Moshi are saying you were the one who knocked Jonas' head against the sauna oven and killed him."

"What . . . ?" Dad says and sits up abruptly. "No," he says, loudly.

"You've got a motive," I say.

"What sort of motive?" he asks.

"Katriina," I say. He looks at me in silence – searchingly, I think, but then it is dark.

"But that's ... insane," he says.

"Is it?" I ask.

"Yes," he says and gets up, shaking his head. He throws the cigar down onto the dusty yard in front of the veranda and goes inside.

Dad drives me to Mwanza – the road is so bad you should wear a body belt to keep your organs in place.

"Christian," Dad says at the airfield, "don't do anything stupid."

"Stupid?" I say. He sighs:

"You know ... you can come down on holiday. In a year, after the first year of H.F. – I'll pay. You know, I ..." he starts but stops. I pat him on the back.

"Right back 'atcha," I say. "See you."

I walk towards the old propeller plane – a DC3. I make a mistake – I turn my head and look to the end of the landing strip. There's some scrunched metal next to the tarmac: another DC3 broken into three pieces.

"What happened?" I ask the man walking next to me. I point.

"Ahhhh," he says, grinning. "It landed like a stone."

The cabin is crammed with people. There's a handful of goats at the back. The plane rattles and shakes as we race down the landing strip, but we take off before hitting the wreck. Everything is leaky – cold air is pulled in as we ascend. Down on the ground I can see bushland all the way to the horizon. Here and there a single dirt road winds between scattered trees and shrubs. I can see a shepherd with his cattle and goats. And a *manyatta* – the characteristic circle of thorns surrounding the mud huts to keep predators out at night. Suddenly we're hanging above Dar with the ocean on the horizon. We have a smooth landing, and four hours later I am on a K.L.M. plane heading towards Schiphol for my connecting flight to Copenhagen. And then on to Aalborg.

Aunt Lene picks me up at the airport.

"Woooow, you're so tanned, Christian," she says.

"Thanks," I say, smiling.

We drive to Hasseris. After Tanzania it looks like Legoland.

"You'll be living down here," Aunt Lene says, showing me the basement. The room has a few tiny windows just beneath the ceiling. There is a utility room with a shower, two hotplates, a small oven. The toilet is at the end of the stairs – it doubles as the guest loo. Perfect – my own ghetto.

"We have to respect each other – am I right?" Torben says.

"Yes, of course," I say. "I won't cause any trouble." Having my own room, and my own entrance through the garage, feels brilliant.

I'll be starting at the sixth-form college in two weeks.

The first few days I have dinner with Lene and Torben.

"But the idea is that eventually – when you've settled in a bit – you can take care of yourself," Lene says. The neighbour comes over – a plump little woman with a slightly anxious look on her face. She has brought a rhubarb tart.

"I'll make us a nice cup of coffee, shall I?" Aunt Lene says. "Yes, and this is my nephew Christian who will be taking classes at Hasseris Gymnasium."

"Are you the one who's been to Africa?" the woman asks, studying me intently.

"Tanzania," I say. "Yes."

"Were they very dark-skinned where you were?" she asks.

"Dark-skinned?" I say.

"As dark as the negroes?" she asks and her eyes are as wide as saucers.

"They were negroes, yes," I say. "That's what they were."

"Were they . . . nice enough?"

"Yes."

"Did you have servants?"

"Yes."

"Did you not have to do anything yourselves then?"

"No," I say, getting up. "Thanks for the coffee."

I walk around, taking in Aalborg – everything is nice and neat. I have to be careful when I cross the street – the cars are coming at me from the wrong direction. The shops have everything. I buy groceries, try my hand at cooking – no servants here. But it feels good to be in control of my own life. I decided I wanted to get away from that mess. I did it. I don't know if Dad had something to do with Jonas' death – it's got nothing to do with me.

Danish cigarettes are amazing. The tobacco is tightly packed and aromatic – the smoke slips smoothly into my lungs. But I have to be careful with money. Mum pays Aunt Lene a little bit every month to let me live with them. And Dad transfers money to me every month so I have something to live on – it's only enough for food and cigarettes and a new L. P. every now and again, but it sort of works.

I go over and look at Hasseris Gymnasium. The building looks like a white cubist rhino.

Marcus

TWO FACES

A Swedish man is sent down as a replacement for Jonas. His name is Harri and he will be new boss of the portable sawmills on the mountain until everything works out with the capitalist joint venture. I often drive to his house and give him messages when the phones are down and he isn't at work because the climate makes his head ache.

On the road there's a good-looking girl – I see her often. "Hi," I say. "Can I give you a lift?"

"Yes, please." Her name is Rhema and she is Harri's neighbour's daughter. "You're welcome to come inside," she says when we're parked outside the gate. Some girls behave like sugar cubes to me because I live with white people. They think I can set up an introduction.

"I have to go to *bwana* Harri," I say.

"Oh yes – you're one of the bosses at the sawmill as well."

"No, I just work in the purchasing department."

"But you do live with the *mzungu* who is the project manager, don't you?"

"Yes, but he's dead, and I was only the babysitter to the white family anyway." Rhema grins and slaps at my arm.

"No, you're joking. You're no babysitter. I've seen you in the project car." She sees me as one of the rich white men that have money. She thinks my life will take me to Europe. So if she catches me, I will take her with me – the same old dream.

"I am just a slave to the *mzungu*," I say. She doesn't believe me.

"*Bwana* Harri – is he project manager?" she asks.

"He is the new boss of the sawmills on West Kilimanjaro."

"Do you think I could find work there?"

"Would you like to work for the sawmills?"

"My father died last month. We need money," she says.

"I will try to ask *bwana* Harri," I say. She embraces me and kisses my cheek.

"Thank you so much," she says, and I think I have to be careful or I'll be the man with two faces – one for each girlfriend, because Claire is still with me, even though God still blocks the path to her garden.

I explain to Harri that the family next door are now living together as an extended family with a grandmother and everything, but that the father has died and they need work.

"The old man in there? I haven't got work for him," Harri says.

"No, the old man is dead. It's the daughter – Rhema – the young girl."

"The daughter? Well she can't work in the forest, but I'll see if there's anything going at the furniture factory."

Rhema becomes my stockroom assistant in Moshi, and she always has a problem. "Could you borrow me a few shilling for my family?" she asks. "My little brother can't go to school, because his uniform is worn to shreds."

In Tanzania primary school is free. The system of using uniforms is British colonialist. It is supposed to ensure that the child from the wealthy family is no better dressed than the child from the poor family. Everyone wears a white shirt, khaki shorts and black shoes. But when hunger gnaws at your stomach, poor people can't get through the school gates, because they have no money for uniforms and nothing to wear but rags.

I give Rhema money for her little brother's uniform, and she promises to pay me back.

"No," I say. It's O.K. – she has no money, so she can't pay me back anyway. Her family are already in danger of losing the house – then they would have to live in a shack in Soweto.

"You can come and visit me," she says. Uhhhhh. She knows I am with Claire. But me and Claire, we argue all the time, because Claire knows the truth.

"You act like a big man with sunglasses and a stereo and a motorbike and beer at the bar, but you don't have your own house, you're just a babysitter to *wazungu*. I want a real man," she says. She was never like this before. Now she won't even speak to me.

BREAK-UP

Christian's departure to Denmark made the difference. From the darkness and into the light come the feelings *bwana* Knudsen has for Katriina. Yes, Knudsen has moved with his job to Shinyanga, but every month he finds an excuse to drive the long way back to pump the widow. And time has not stood still. S.I.D.A. gave Katriina Jonas' salary for six months after his death, but now there's no more salary, and she must leave the government-owned house, because that is only for people who work for Tanzania. Katriina must stand on her own two feet.

"We're moving up into *mama* Androli's guesthouse," Katriina says.

"But will you manage when you're not getting money from S.I.D.A. anymore?" I ask.

"Niels Knudsen has rented it for us," she says. Eeehhh – this woman is a crafty passenger who has got herself a new ride in life.

"But what about Solja's school fees?" I ask, because I know the white people pay for I.S.M. in foreign currency so the school can pay for white teachers.

"They've let me pay in shillings for now," Katriina says.

"Good," I say – the girls will stay on in Tanzania. That's good for my little Rebekka. Soon she'll be four – all her life she's known nothing else. And me as her loving father. Yes, four and a half years I spent on these Swedes. Now I am twenty years old, and my investment has come to nothing.

"Can you help me pack?" Katriina asks.

"But what about Marcus?" Solja asks – she is thirteen and very independent in her thoughts. Katriina sighs:

"I don't know. I hope you can manage," she says.

"It's a disaster for me," I say.

"There's nothing I can do," Katriina says.

"It's not fair," Solja says angrily.

"I can't help it," Katriina says. And what is my reward for long and faithful service? A fridge and a freezer and a worn stereo that doesn't actually work. Now they're mine, and I can sell the freezer. The fridge will help at the kiosk, with cool sodas as the main attraction. The stereo will go to a mechanic when I can afford to repair it.

Bwana Knudsen drives all the way to Moshi to take part in this exodus. The Land Rover is packed with their personal belongings – clothes and kitchen utensils – because the furniture belongs to the government house. Solja refuses to get into the car.

"I want Marcus to come," she says.

"Of course," Rebekka says in Swahili. "Marcus must live in the new house." I am almost in tears. Katriina shakes her head.

"No, Marcus is a grown-up now – he needs a house of his own."

"What?" Rebekka says and starts howling. First her white father dies, and now the black one must go as well. Ah, it's tough to say goodbye to my white daughters. I pick her up and comfort her, but Rebekka is snotty with howling.

"I will come and visit you all the time," I say and smooth down her fine, blonde hair.

"No, no, no," she screams. It's awful. I have to wave goodbye to the car. Katriina takes *mzee* Issa with her – never before has she had such a good cook. Me – the little black trailer – now I have no car to take me anywhere.

DREAMING OF TAXIS

Dreaming about cars makes me go to Dar es Salaam again. I have to buy one – it makes no sense to take a taxi every time I need to get something from the shop; fizzy drinks, corn flour, paraffin, vegetable oil, rice. And I can't bike there and back like a negro – the puzzle of bones in my foot from the accident is no good for that sort of work. The car could also be rented out as a taxi, so I can have an extra income.

I have to think that way, because now I must provide for myself completely. More than three years ago Aunt Elna told me: "Don't expect other people to help you, Marcus. You can't rely on that. You have to do it yourself." The old Swedish *mama* was right.

At the furniture factory I make sure they are short on glue and take the bus to Dar es Salaam at the Swedes' expense, because the project is still running while the Swedish authorities try to work out what all the funds were spent on.

In Dar I take a room at the Y.M.C.A. with Edson – still on the run after beating up his wife for giving birth to a son with her boss' face. I lent him money for his escape – for a year and a half I've needed that money, so Edson must help me. He's stopped doing acrobatics. Now he is as wide as he is tall – a square; that's bodybuilding. He works as a debt collector for a *mhindi* usurer.

We go out.

BEGGING

Rebekka is in my thoughts when I wake up. I miss my little white daughter, so I go up to *mama* Androli's guesthouse to visit Katriina and the girls. The gate is locked.

"Hello?" I call. A gardener comes over.

"What do you want?" he asks.

"I'm here to visit the Swedish family – they're my friends," I say.

"I can't let you in," he says. *Tsk*, I've walked on my legs, and he sees me as a negro come to beg.

"The Swedish *mama* herself invited me to come today. Go and ask her," I say. The gardener calls to Katriina:

"There's a man here who says he is your guest."

There's no sign that the girls are home. Katriina doesn't shout for the gardener to open the gate. She comes down the drive and speaks to me through the bars.

"It's not good – you coming now," she says. "Solja and Rebekka are very confused."

"But I just wanted to say hello," I say.

"They have a hard time understanding what happened. I think it's better if they don't see you for a while," Katriina says.

"O.K., I'll just come back another day," I say.

"You have to wait a while," Katriina says. "I'll let you know when it's O.K."

"Goodbye," I say. *Tsk*, does she think they're her daughters? Those girls are mine in my heart. Four and a half years of my time and affection. Of course they're confused – they're changing fathers more often than their underwear; first they have two – a white and a black. Now the white is dead, and the black must stay away. Instead they have a third father who doesn't even know how to speak Swedish properly. *Tsk*.

CATTLEHOUSE

The Larsson house is taken over by the local guy who now runs F.I.T.I. in the pay of S.I.D.A. "It's my house now – you must move out of the servants' quarters," he says.

"I can't move until I have found a new house," I say. And I have already been looking for four months – without a good house Claire won't be naked with me. My name is on the waiting list at National Housing but very far from the top. Then the new king starts to get tough. When I come home the gate is locked, so I have to go around and through the hole in the fence. He comes out on the veranda:

"I can have you shot as a thief," he says. "I want you out as soon as possible – I want to have cows in that room."

"No – I'm not moving," I say, "because this house belongs to the Tanzanian state. There are two rooms in the servants' quarters – the other one is empty; if you put your cows there, then fine – I'll live next to them, even though I know that it's against the law to have cows in the city; this house was built for people."

I am standing in the kiosk, talking to the boy, counting the stock, looking over the accounts. The music stops, the fridge stops humming. Another power cut. Afterwards I go back to my ghetto through the hole in the fence. There is light again in the house, so power is back, and I turn on my tape recorder. Nothing. What's wrong? I check everything. Finally I look at the wire which I drew myself from the main house like an electrician, through the air and into my ghetto; cut in two. *Eeehhhh*, I'm back in the dark.

Another day he says: "Maybe your things will catch fire when you're not here." And if Claire is standing at the gate wanting to see me: "Marcus? No, he doesn't live here anymore – get off my property." So I use political advantages. I go to the government party's office, and I explain my problems to the man there. He gives me a letter I must take to the F.I.T.I. manager. It says I can live there until I've found a place to move to, and that he's not allowed to lock the gates on me. The gate, the house, everything belongs to the state. And the companies we work for, they too belong to the state. The neighbouring room where Jonas used to make mash: I come home and my neighbours are cows and goats – I'm living like an old-fashioned Chagga on the mountain: one side of the house for the human animal – once side of the house for livestock.

In the evening I go to National Housing's two-storey terraced houses on Uru Road not far from the Y.M.C.A. I go to the bar to speak to the chairman of the housing association. Buying beers in the bar can raise your name right up on the waiting list.

"The man on the ground floor of number seventeen – he's talked about moving back to the mountain," the chairman says. I find *mzee*, ask him out for a beer.

"When are you moving back to your family on the mountain?" I ask.

"I could move tomorrow, but I need furniture for my house in the village," he says. That's how lucky I am.

"I can help you get some very cheap furniture," I say. I buy furniture from Imara at a reduced price without notifying the head office and have it taken to the man's village. At the same time it's up to me to arrange with National Housing that I can take over the flat, so I go to the boss at his office. I show him the letter from the government office – I'm threatened by goats and cattle.

"But your name isn't at the top of the waiting list," he says.

"Maybe the ones at the top will say no, because they don't want to move right now, and then I could help you as well."

"How could you help me?"

"I hear your brother needs timber to finish his new house up in Old Moshi – I could get very cheap timber for him."

"My brother has no money for that," he says.

"I may be able to get it for free for him, because you've been such a good friend to me," I say.

"I'll talk to the people at the top of the list," he says.

I drive to West Kilimanjaro. Occasionally they mislay a load of timber, and then they forget about it. There might even be a lorry which breaks down in the company's service for an entire day while it takes boards to a construction site in Old Moshi. All in all I spend a year's wages on solving these problems, but I solve them using the money I found behind the picture of Jonas' ship. The National Housing official writes a memo saying I can take over number seventeen. I say goodbye to goats and cows and move right in.

Straight away I have the kiosk taken apart and driven down to the residential area and hire a worker to reassemble it across from my door. It's only a little crooked after the transport. Here there'll be lots of customers, but I haven't got any stock – all my money has been spent for furniture, timber and beer. As it is I have to sell the fridge from the Larsson house just to have enough to live on. And who will man the kiosk and steal from me while I am at work at the furniture factory and West Kilimanjaro?

Christian

First day. Induction course. There are loads of pretty girls there. They ask us to tell each other about ourselves: I come from Zealand. My parents work abroad. I'm staying at my aunt's. I don't say anything about Tanzania. I don't really know what to tell people.

First lesson. English. The teacher points at me:

"Do you know what that means?" he asks.

"What?" I ask.

"That thing it says on your T-shirt?" I look down my front. BLACK UHURU – written in the colours of the Ethiopan flag: red, yellow and green on a black background, the letters swathed in white barbed wire.

"It's a reggae band from Jamaica," I answer.

"Yes, but do you know what *uhuru* means in Swahili?"

"No," I lie. I've got an African tan, and I can smell from a hundred feet away that he's worked abroad for Action Aid Denmark, trying to save the negro from the white man.

"Freedom," he says. "Black freedom."

"Right," I say, and he launches into a lecture about reggae and Rastas and colonialism.

I'm constantly listening to reggae. I spend my food money on L.P.s. Eat spaghetti with ketchup.

Mum is in Geneva doing some admin work for Médecins sans Frontières. She calls me to hear how I'm doing. I tell her I need money.

"What are you spending it on?" she asks.

"I need to buy an L.P. now and again, you know," I say.

"Christian," she says.

"It's not my fault you two make so much money I can't apply for student grants."

"Then you'll have to get a part-time job," she says.

Life is full of odd jobs. The first time I wash my clothes, all the whites get a bluish-grey hue and much of the coloured stuff shrinks. Luckily Marcus sends me a package. Garvey Dread is listed as the sender. Tanzanian tea. Inside the package is Arusha-*bhangi* wrapped in cellophane. Plus a begging letter. He needs a tape recorder, or new tape heads for the one he has. He says he's starving to death. I can't help him with that at the moment.

I don't get any letters from Samantha. Nothing from Panos or Jarno either. A postcard from Shakila. She writes that she misses me. She's at the university in Dar now, "studying and working round the clock".

At school I smoke cigarettes and don't say much – it's sort of become my thing. I've taken music as an optional subject.

"I play drums," I say. Steady as a rock. And I can play a reggae rhythm – no-one else can do that. Afterwards some bloke comes over to me. Anders. He plays the bass.

"You're bloody good at that," he says.

"Thanks," I say. I offer him a cigarette. He asks me if I want to go for a drink over the weekend. Yes, definitely – I'd like that. "But I'm a bit strapped for cash," I say.

"Don't worry about it," Anders says.

"Why not?"

"Ways and means," he says.

Thursday he comes up to me at lunch. I haven't got a packed lunch.

"Let's split," he says.

"Alright." I follow him out. "I lived in Africa until this summer," I say. "Four and a half years."

"What?" he says.

I explain.

"Well fuck me," he says. "You're a bit of a dark horse, aren't you? Want to go over to mine and smoke a bone?"

"A bone?" I say.

"Hash," he says. Compressed *bhangi* – I've heard about it.

"Alright," I say. He lives in Skelagergaarden – an estate a couple of hundred metres from the college. We go there. He tells me he's living with his dad, who is on disability benefits.

"His health was ruined by asbestos," Anders says. "He just sits at home, doing puzzles – 3,000 to 4,500 pieces. Once he's completed one, he glues it onto a piece of cardboard and sticks it on the sitting-room wall. Completely hammered on painkillers." We make it to the fourth floor. And true enough: there's the dad in the kitchen with his jigsaw puzzles. Wasted away. We go Anders' room, and he gets his gear out.

"What about your mum?" I ask. He snorts.

"We're all living out here. My mum lives in a flat with my little sister and her new husband and his daughter from his second marriage, while his daughter from his first marriage is living in another flat with her two children and her ex-husband lives in a third flat, and my dad's little sister who – by the by – took my virginity a few years back. She likes them young. She's in another flat three doors down, and she – miracle of miracles – is still married – to my cousin twice removed, but it's simply too complicated to explain. My half-cousin's half-brother Gert is mental and used to live out here as well, but he's in prison now; I'll get back to that. So there we go." The verbal torrent comes to an end, as Anders starts mixing the hash with tobacco.

"And your crazy cousin?"

"My half-cousin's crazy half-brother," Anders corrects me. "He broke into a house in Hasseris to steal, but there was a woman sleeping there, and of course she woke up. And then the idiot goes and rapes her, and afterwards he strangles her and gets scared; he's doped up on all sorts of stuff, obviously. Then he finds some hunting cartridges in the house, and he stuffs them up into her cunt with a few gas lighters, and then he sets the house on fire to remove all traces of his sperm. The woman is . . . well, almost fried. And his greasy little paws left fingerprints all over the back door. Damn me if I didn't get him locked up," Anders finishes and nods to himself, almost done with the spliff.

"How so?" I ask.

"He was wanted. Billed on the radio – the police had already been here when he showed up and wanted to hide in my flat, his half-cousin whom he'd beaten up with a maggoty cat only six months earlier," Anders says and lights the spliff.

"A maggoty cat . . . ?" I say.

"He tied me to a tree down there," Anders says, pointing towards the window, "and then he beat me with a dead cat that was full of maggots. A complete psycho."

"Then how did you get away?"

"He got tired of it – left me there."

"And then you escaped?"

"Some people came by – they untied me."

"What happened to him – your half-cousin?"

"Happened?"

"Yes . . . Wasn't anyone called?"

409

"Who do you call when you've been pummelled with a dead cat?"

"I don't know," I say.

"Someone poured sand into the petrol tank of his moped," Anders says.

"Who?"

"Take a guess."

"But then what about when he was on the run – did you let him in?"

"Yes, sure I did. And he sent me off to get him a few strong beers to wash down his diazepam. So money in my pocket and down to the phone booth to call the coppers – using his cash," Anders says and laughs out loud. "So now he's been sentenced to compulsory treatment and locked up exactly where he belongs."

"Right," I say. Anders is sucking at the spliff. Passes it on. We smoke.

"But your mum's sister took your virginity?" I ask.

"My dad's sister," he says. "She's one beautiful lady, I can tell you that. Big in all the right places."

"How . . . did that happen?"

"Well, she was drunk. And horny," he says, laughing.

We listen to Metallica, and Anders' little sister shows up.

"Get out. I won't have you in here," Anders says.

"Oh, come on," she sneers. Her bubblegum smacks between her jaws, and her lips are sleek with gloss. He throws her out, and the way she wriggles her arse as she walks down the hall is all exaggerated.

"That spliff has knocked me for six. I could use a cup of coffee," I say.

"You're welcome to make yourself a pot. Just . . . help yourself. Don't mind my dad – he never says anything." I go out into the kitchen.

"Hiiiiii," the little sister says. I mention the coffee. "Here, let me help you," she says and stands on her tiptoes to get down the coffee filter, leaning in close and giggling by the worktop. Her name is Linda – she's thirteen. She asks me about all sorts. I tell her a few things – Africa. "Wow," she says. "You're almost a negro."

"Professional negro," I say.

"See you," she says as I leave with the coffee. There'll be no more H.F. for us today.

Back in my basement I am lying on my bed, staring at the ceiling. Lene calls from the ground floor:

"Your dad's on the phone." I run up.

"Hi, Dad," I say.

"Christian," he says, "there's . . . There's something I have to tell you."

"What?"

"I . . . Katriina and I have got married." His voice comes with a satellite echo – the sentences are being chopped up, the ends of the words disappearing.

"Right. O.K.," I say.

"Christian – you have to understand . . . it's not that . . ." Or perhaps he simply can't bring himself to say what it is he wants to say.

"It's not that what?" I ask.

"It's not . . . I mean . . . she's stranded here with the girls. Solja and Rebekka," he says.

"Yes?" I know what the girls are called.

"She doesn't have anything to go home to, and she can't afford to pay the school fees," he says. Did I have something to go home to? I'm starting to doubt it.

"So now I have two half-sisters," I say.

"Yes, but you don't have to . . ." The connection crackles violently. The stratosphere hums.

"It's quite alright, Dad. You do what you do," I say. "But can't you . . . ?" I start. And then the phone's dead in my hand. Fuck. I was going to ask for a bit of money – Dad would have caved because of the situation – the fact that he's just given me a stepmother whose husband died in suspicious circumstances.

I don't hear from Mum. She calls me just once but doesn't say anything. Maybe she doesn't even know that Dad's married Katriina – I don't say anything because it's none of her business.

I miss talking to someone from Tanzania – feel oddly foreign. I think about Nanna – how she took my virginity at T.P.C. before her family went home to Denmark – two and a half years ago. I call her parents and am told Nanna is in her second year of *gymnasiet*. One afternoon it's Nanna herself who picks up.

"I'm in Århus on Friday," I say. "I was wondering if you wanted to meet up?"

"I can't. I've got other plans, and I really haven't got the time," she says.

"Some other time, perhaps," I say.

"Maybe – I don't know," Nanna says. She doesn't ask for my number, or what I'm doing.

"Alright. Bye," I say. Right, so I won't be seeing her, it seems.

Another begging letter from Marcus. I am eating crap food and my trousers have holes in them, but I'm white. Money grows on the trees in Europe, every African knows that. Not a peep from Samantha. Shakila writes to me that Samantha's been ill and away from school, but that she's back again. But they don't speak, because Shakila used to go out with Stefano. I want to see them. Next summer – it'll be here soon, I guess.

In the evening I go to Rock Nielsen with Anders. We look at the girls. I don't know what to say to them, when they're that white and happy. Anders has a little money. He buys us beer. We drink, watch the crowd. Anders hands me a beer glass that is still three-quarters full, gives me a wink. He's exceptionally good at nicking other people's beer from the bar or the tables. We get drunk quickly.

"I'd better stop," he says. "When I'm intoxicated, I cock up and people find me out." We're almost out of cash, so we leave, stroll down the dark pedestrian street.

"How about we just make a dash for it?" I say, thinking about the moped that got us here.

"Yeah, we'll just swing by McDonald's first."

"Are you hungry?" I ask.

"No," he says.

"Then what?"

"I need to see if my sister's there." We reach Nytorv and turn the corner. Linda's standing outside with a friend – they're looking good but a bit overly tarted-up. Linda seems scared when she sees Anders coming towards her. He grabs hold of her. "You little whore," he says, smacking her face.

"Don't, you bastard," Linda's friend screams and beats him with her small fists. I'm standing there – gobsmacked.

"Hey," someone says behind me and a group of three men appear and grab hold of Anders, who gets a punch in the stomach.

"You can't bloody well hit girls," one of the men says.

"Serves you right," Linda yells and runs away, round the corner, with her friend.

"That's my fucking little sister," Anders says. They hit him again, and I step up behind the guy holding Anders' arms. As I pull my arm back, I know that I should be scared, and that it's the alcohol that's making me slam my fist into his kidney – his elbow slams back and up into my face, and I stagger backwards. Anders twists out of their grip and headbutts one of the men. Gang fight. Punches and kicks. The sound of sirens, police surrounding us. We're thrown into the back of a police car. The policeman on the passenger seat turns around and smacks Anders when he tries to say something to me. Down to the station. Interrogated in separate rooms.

"I really don't know," I say, because I don't. In the morning they give us tepid coffee and let us out. Bodies aching – bruised faces.

"I'm sorry about that, mate," Anders says. I shrug. "But bugger it," he says, shaking his head. "She's a burger-whore."

"A what?"

"Burger-whore. They hang out in front of McDonald's late at night, and then men come over and pick them up – take them to their cars or into a back alley, and then the girl blows the guy in return for money for burgers and clothes, make-up, jewellery – that kind of shit. Burger-whore, that's what they're called – fellatio only. As far as I know."

"But fuck it, they're no more than . . . fourteen."

"Thirteen," he says. "Gob's big enough to fit a cock in, though."

Marcus

FROM THE MOUTHS OF BABES

Katriina said she would tell me when I could come for a visit. But she hasn't said anything, and I don't want to wait. Four months it's been since they moved, and I haven't seen the girls at all. I walk there, because I've got no money for petrol, which is very expensive with the supply still so bad. I'm lucky – the gate is open. Katriina's sitting outside, looking slightly frightened.

"Is *bwana* Knudsen at home as well?" I ask.

"He's in Shinyanga, working," she says.

"Will Christian be down for Christmas?" I ask.

"No. Certainly not until next year when the school breaks up for the summer," Katriina says. *Tsk*.

I can hear the girls inside the house. But am I invited in? No. Katriina calls to old Issa, and beer is served to me on the veranda, and the girls stay away.

"How are the girls?" I ask.

"They're well," Katriina says and calls: "Come out and say hello to Marcus, girls."

"MARCUS!" Rebekka shouts and comes flying from inside, hugging me right away and showing me drawings and speed-talking in Swahili and asking me about everything to do with my new house and the kiosk and Claire. A bit later Solja comes out, already almost a stranger – she barely recognizes her African father and holds out her hand like a businessman for me to shake. *Tsk.*

It's lovely, but also sad. I drink up and say goodbye, leave my former family. I hear footsteps behind me. It's Solja. She falls in next to me.

"Hi," I say.

"Have you got a cigarette?" she asks. I hand her my pack and a box of matches. She lights up and gives me back my things.

"Just keep it, but give me one," I say. She shakes a cigarette out of the pack and lights a match for me. Now we both have our smoking sticks. Solja starts walking. We walk together. I can only wait.

"They're being silly," she says. "The grown-ups."

"Silly how?" I ask.

"They have separate rooms, but at night they sneak into each other's rooms, only we're not supposed to know," Solja says.

"You have to understand," I say and stop.

"But they're married now. Did you know that?"

"Who's married now?" I ask.

"My mum and Niels Knudsen."

"Really?"

"*Eeehhh,*" she says.

"But then they should sleep together," I say.

"They say they're only married because then Niels' work will pay for me to go to I.S.M.," Solja says.

"Madness," I say.

"*Tsk,*" Solja says – like a total *mswahili*, and then she drops her cigarette on the road and squashes it with the toe of her shoe.

"Thanks for the cigarettes," she says and turns around – runs back to the house. Children always know what goes on in their homes.

BEGGARY

Once again I write to Christian that I'd like to send things like jewellery and curios to Denmark – he can sell them, and the money can be divided and put into an account that he can set up for me in a Danish bank – not let me down like Mika. In the future I want to be completely independent and act and do business in all sorts of ways to survive. Because I know that now I'm finished with the Larssons everyone is laughing at me and enjoying my suffering.

Claire sees me more and more as a disappointment.

"You must go to your family for help."

"How about your family?" I ask to shut her up, because she only has her godly, impoverished mother and her little sister, who seeks the path to the good life by opening her papaya to any and all *mabwana makubwa*.

"No, your brother," Claire says. "He drives a *matatu* from Moshi to Holili – the drivers on the small buses receive lots of greasing money because they act as go-betweens when passengers need goods smuggled from Kenya through the police blocks on the road to Moshi."

And she is right. My little brother is rising in the world. Can I ask him? No, because I have refused to help my family and have cut myself off from the African safety net where one day you borrow a kilo of corn flour from your brother, and the next day he moves into your house with his four children and his stupid wife, and there's nothing you can do about it, because he's family and you owe him a kilo's worth of flour. I can't feel sorry about that. No, because my entire family will drag me down every time I myself take a step up the ladder. They want be pulled up without having to move a muscle.

"But now – now you could use their help, couldn't you?" Claire says with a stony look.

"No," I say. "We must carry each other and create our own family which really works. You and me." Claire turns her back on me.

"*Tsk*," she says and leaves.

I meet Ibrahim in town.

"Aren't you seeing Claire anymore?" he asks.

"Why are you asking?"

"I see a lot of blokes following her, trying to catch her."

"Where?"

"She goes to Jackson's in a very tight dress that lets everything show," Ibrahim says. Jackson's – dangerous men go there. They chase a lot of different girls, and that makes me scared – they can carry death in their blood. At the Strangler family's house the guard comes to the gate and tells me Claire isn't there. Maybe she'll be there tomorrow. I drive to see Claire's mother in the terrible end of Pasua. And Claire won't see me; her mother tells me to go away.

"But why isn't she at her job with the Strangler family?" I ask.

"The Strangler family is going back to Australia in two days," Claire's mother says.

"In two days?" I say. "But then where will she live and work?"

"She doesn't want to see you anymore," her mother says and shuts the door in my face. What will Claire do without the Strangler family? Why hasn't she said anything? Claire has kept it a secret from me while she's been working on the plan for our church wedding.

Claire won't see me. What can I do? I visit Rhema, and she treats me well, because I got her the job on the project through Harri. But her family is full of problems. First her father died, and now her mother is sick.

"Is it malaria?" I ask.

"I think so," Rhema says. But malaria can never ruin someone that quickly. Perhaps her mother is like an old-fashioned negro from the bush; her husband is dead and now she has chosen to die using only willpower. Rhema won't speak about it. She wants to love me well. She comes to my ghetto every night and opens her papaya to me. And yet the feeling isn't right.

"Why do you want to be with me?" I ask her.

"You've been good to me – I want to give you my love." When I am lying down with Rhema, I think about Claire. Afterwards I am tired, and I want Rhema to leave.

Christian

"Would you like to make a bit of money?" Anders asks.

"How?"

"Moonlighting. Insulate a few houses, lay a few tiles in some drives, that sort of thing."

"I don't know how," I say.

"Doesn't matter," Anders says. "I do."

416

As it happens Anders doesn't know, but his uncle puts us to work and shows us how before leaving us to it. I'm wondering whether that uncle is Anders' dad's little sister's husband – the lady who liked them young and who took Anders virginity in a drunken stupor. But I don't ask.

We are in a big bourgeois villa, carrying bales of Rockwool into the hall and lifting them up through the loft trapdoor. Once up under the roof the sheets of Rockwool have to be laid out on top of the layer that is already there – insulation, to reduce the heating bill. A very white occupation – not particularly African. It's dark and cold up there. We're only allowed to step on the rafters, otherwise we might fall through the ceiling boards, which aren't built to carry anything but insulation. And the insulation that has already been laid down is covered in a thin layer of dust that scratches at your throat, stabs at your skin. Rockwool – granite that has been heated until it's liquid and blown into something like wool, like candyfloss. But it's still rock. Fine hairs of granite that drill their way into your skin. It itches. We sweat, climbing the rafters, laughing, opening the packs of Rockwool and laying them down – you can't have any gaps – the heat would just whizz out.

"It itches like hell," Anders says when his uncle returns.

"You'll get used to it," he says.

"Will it stop once we've showered?" I ask.

"If you switch the water between ice cold and scalding hot a few times, the pores in the skin will open and it'll wash off," he says.

"Lovely," Anders says.

The following day we have to lug flagstones for a drive and a yard at another villa. We skive off from school in order to work. It's hard graft, but they pay us cash in hand. I spend it all on L.P.s – dream about being a D.J. at Liberty in Moshi; living the good life.

I write to Samantha about my thoughts and how I feel about her. I know I'd never be able to say it to her face, but . . . I love her, miss her. I want to kiss her all over. I hesitate for just a moment at the post box. Then I let the letter drop.

I can't go around with Anders all the time, and I don't really know anyone else. I walk around Aalborg with my hands in my pockets. Feel like an outsider. Where should I go? The sky's overcast; I go to the art museum, down through Kildeparken and over to the bus station to play on a cool pinball machine in a greasy spoon. Watch the buses, smoke a few cigarettes. I don't know anyone I could get on a bus for. I've spent my money on music. No-one here will want to buy my tatty jeans, my worn sneakers. I run out of coins, pull up my collar and step outside in the wind. Black ladies. There are two black ladies speaking Swahili outside.

"*Habari gani?*" I ask – how are you.

"*Nini?*" they say – what. They're shocked. I laugh, they laugh, we laugh. "Where did you pick that up?" one of them asks. I tell them. They're originally from the Mwanza area. "You're accent is absolutely perfect," the other one says.

"What are you doing here?" I ask and add. "In Denmark."

"We live here – West Aalborg," one of them says. I introduce myself. Their names are Olivia and Sheila. Sheila is the prettier – lush.

"Are you getting the bus?" I ask.

"No, we were on our way home," Sheila says. "Do you want to come and get a cup of coffee?" We go to the western side of town. We shop for cakes on the way. They're staying in a flat upstairs from a bicycle repairman in Borgergade. We take the back stairs up and step into the kitchen. The door leading in to the rest of the flat is locked.

"We just sit here," Olivia says – Sheila gives her an odd sort of grin. There's a small table with three chairs. They turn on a small tape recorder – Zaire Rock.

"Africafé," I say as Olivia puts the tins on the table.

"Yes, my family sends me tins of it." And then we just sit there in that kitchen, speaking in Swahili, drinking coffee, eating cream cakes, smoking cigarettes, laughing. I ask them again what it is they do.

"Erm, we have Danish boyfriends, see," Sheila says.

"Are you getting married?" I ask.

"No," she says. "We're just here to make a little money, and then we're going home." Alright. I don't ask them how they're going to make that money. There's the sound of steps on the stairs.

"Oh, that'll be my friend," Olivia says. A bloke in a blue boiler suit with greasy hands comes through the door. The bicycle repairman.

"Hi," he says. "How are you?" In English.

"Fine," they say. "This is Christian from Tanzania," Sheila informs him.

"Hi," I say. He takes a cup of coffee and asks what I did in Tanzania. I tell him. We chat for a while, while the penny drops all the way to the bottom – slowly. And it gets there, finally, and I think, yes, of course, why didn't you see it before? The bike guy is their pimp – perhaps he's come up to see if they're working? I've heard that there's a pub on the east side of Aalborg called Gøglerbåden, where there are always black whores to be had. They might be there at night. Now is either their free time or they're working off the clock. The man is very nice, has a cup of coffee, smokes a cigarette, asks me what I get up to, leaves again.

"Right, well, I'm going to have to get home. I have homework to do," I say.

"Yes, studying is important," Olivia says, while Sheila scribbles on a piece of paper and hands it to me.

"Come and have coffee with us again sometime," she says. "You just have to call first and check that we're not busy."

"Thanks," I say. And she gives me a naughty smile, and I want to stay – go with her through that closed door. We could lie on that bed.

I come out of the front door, stand on the street. The taste of Africafé in my mouth and the memory of Zaire Rock jars with the cold rain which is blown into my face by the wind. I push my hands into my pockets and start walking towards the harbour. The sound of Zaire Rock and reggae – I almost can't take it, because . . . it's so grey here. Even though it still gets dark later than in Tanzania, the sun has no force here – it just hangs limply in the sky. No-one talks, no-one smiles, everyone just rushes about in their own grey way. When I reach the feedstuff dealerships, I turn away from the harbour, go into town and into the central library where it's warm. Go over to the boxes of cartoons and come out with five Blueberry books – sit down and read until I get hungry. I immediately turn off the pedestrian street to avoid the crowds – down the smaller streets. Gøglerbåden it says on a sign, a corner building – the bar with all the black whores. How fucking gross is that, coming to Denmark and having to fuck fat, liver-paté-coloured pigs? I hurry on. I never call them, even though I think of Sheila when I am lying with my hands under the duvet. And about Samantha, Shakila, Irene.

Marcus

THE CONCRETE JUNGLE

Christian doesn't answer my letters – not with so much as a single word. What the hell on earth can have happened? I need to know how things are going with him and his life in Denmark. Does he have a girl already? Is there money for a tape recorder so I can make a living? I can send anything in exchange – Tanzanian shillings are no better than toilet paper, but I can buy jewellery and Makonde and coffee and cashew nuts and batik – everything done by the book, so it can be sold in Denmark.

And I send packages from Garvey Dread with *bhangi* hidden in packs of teas; Tanzanian Tea Blend, Brooke Bond Tea. The *bhangi* is stuffed into the middle of the packages, wrapped in very thin cling film; there is tea above, below and to the sides, so no customs officials can smell the weed. The smoke can lift him up, move him to Africa; he can perform a thanksgiving and a prayer. But if the customs officers find it, he'll know nothing – it's arrived by mistake, he doesn't know any Garvey Dread, the man who sent it must be mad! I can't understand why he doesn't write – I'm sitting here with an ache in my arse waiting for a reply. I hope he's alright, and that if anything is wrong he will tell me, so we can understand and learn about each other. I am sorry to play the victim, but the family is rich – Christian must help me.

CONFUSION

I drink beer and whisky at Stereo Bar because Claire has been sharp in my ear about building a steady future. A man is leaning against the bar by my side.

"Now we see the murderer clearly," he says. I squint. Who is this man?

"Which murderer?" I ask.

"Of the *mzungu* in the sweat lodge. Now the murderer has taken over the dead man's widow," the man says. It's the police chief in civilian clothes.

"No, no," I say. "The death was an accident." The policeman laughs, and I hurry out. My white girls are still here in Tanzania. If anyone asks too many questions about Jonas' death, it could be dangerous.

I go for another visit. Solja is in the garden with her dog, Lille Gubben.

"Solja," I call. She comes to the gate, smiling.

"Marcus," she says, smiling as she opens the gate. "How are you?"

"Everything is well and good," I say, because I don't want to trouble her with adult problems. "Is Rebekka home?" I ask.

"Sorry, no. She's at a birthday party, but Mum will be back soon," Solja says and fetches a Coke for me. We sit on the veranda and talk very comfortably. She is a good daughter.

Then Katriina comes home, and Solja goes into the house.

"I don't think you should come here so often," Katriina says.

"It's only the second time," I say.

"Solja is very confused," Katriina says.

"I think she seems very well," I say.

"It's something I notice. I'm her mother," Katriina – who has never been a mother to the child the way I have – says.

"That confusion isn't because of me," I say.

"I want you to leave now," Katriina says. *Tsk*.

THE TO-DO

Rhema has vanished from work, and her house is empty. I hear that her mother is dead now as well, and that Rhema has moved to a shack in Soweto with her old grandmother and her little brother.

At work Gösta and Harri come to the stockroom.

"The stockroom on West Kili is one big mess," Harri tells me. "You're not minding it properly."

"We need a storeroom assistant on West Kili," Gösta says.

"Rhema will have to move up there," Harri says, giving me an angry look. *Eeehhhh*, he's given Rhema a job, but I'm the one eating papaya while Harri is in the forest. Now he wants some action. "We've already got a room ready for her," he says. Has Rhema been told that Harri is married and has two children in Sweden? He'll never give her that ticket. But maybe he thinks he will.

My life is moving at the Tanzanian pace. Every time I buy something for the project, I need a healthy kickback. Every time something goes missing from the project, I swear I know nothing about it, even as I'm selling it in town.

I drive to the mountain with the payroll for the casual labourers and oil for the chainsaws. Rhema is there. She tells me what they need for the stockroom.

"Where is Harri?" I ask.

"He had to go to Mbeya," Rhema says.

The next time I meet Harri on West Kilimanjaro, he quickly goes very red:

"Why the hell didn't you get the right oil?" he says, though I know I did. "You're very bad at your job. You're constantly going into town to get things instead of coming here to work, and you do it just to relax." So he steals my new girlfriend under false pretences, and now he starts hating me because I was there before him. Maybe I did a better job of filling the papaya? *Wazungu* think that *waafrika* have very large weapons between their legs, just like our women have large arses – that one thing steals their sleep and replaces it with worry.

Rhema doesn't say anything. Harri is the great white hope.

THREATS

Bwana Knudsen arrives in his Land Rover and stops outside my house.

"You mustn't go and see the girls so often," he says. "Katriina doesn't like it." I stare at him, completely shocked.

"I'm only trying to help you," I say. "When I meet the police chief in a bar in Moshi, he tells me straight out that when you see who's lying in the widow's bed, you're looking the murderer."

"But that's just not true," *bwana* Knudsen says, and his face goes red.

"Are you sure?" I ask.

"If you think that's true, you go to the police – I won't hear another word of that nonsense," he says.

"I don't want anything from you," I say. "But why can't I visit the family? It's my family too."

"It's not your family. And where is the proof of these allegations concerning Jonas? There isn't any," *bwana* Knudsen says angrily.

"The proof is inside us – impossible to see," I say.

"Stay away from us," he says and gets into his car, drives off.

WITCHCRAFT

In Moshi Claire comes to my house. "I am pregnant," she says.

"You've been running around with other men," I say.

"It's yours," she says. "I haven't been with anyone else." Claire can't lie because her God is always listening.

"But you say you hate me."

"No," Claire says. "I don't know. I've just felt . . . weird. So confused inside. It's like it's all exploding."

"Will you move into my house?" I ask.

"No, first you must marry me."

"I don't want to be married," I say. "We're not from the same church."

"Then you'll have to change your church. My church has the right faith," Claire says. That's her mother talking out of her mouth.

"My church is every bit as good as yours," I say.

"I hate you," Claire says and from that moment there's no more talking. Claire is on top of me on the sofa, almost naked, and she's tearing at my clothes to get my body out.

"You must do it now," she says, like she's possessed by spirits. Her talk is Christian, but her methods are right out of the bush – witchcraft in the name of Jesus. Never before has she been like this. Afterwards I ask her again:

"Will you move in?"

"I am staying with my mother until I've had the baby," she says, straightening her dress and fixing her hair. "I don't know what I'll do."

KUKU

All the money I've managed to scrape together goes on stocking the kiosk. But who will look after it?

I go to see my mother.

"Give me my oldest little sister, and I'll look after her," I say. My mother is angry with me, but agrees because she's got serious problems herself. My oldest little sister is called Ida and she knows her sums. I put her in the kiosk. Life becomes odd. I have a terraced house, but I sleep in the kiosk, so things won't be stolen. Ida sleeps in the terraced house. But she is good. In return for nothing more than food and board, she works in the kiosk from dawn till dusk. Late in the afternoon she takes a break from the kiosk while she prepares our supper.

Claire is a great worry in my head. Must she have our baby and let her godly mother look after it, while she herself goes to work as a house girl? The child will be forced into the hazy confusion of religion from its earliest infancy. I must fix everything and persuade Claire to move in.

As soon as I have sorted the kiosk out, I divert a carload of low-grade timber from West Kilimanjaro and use my very last shillings on hiring workers to build a chicken coop in my garden. I need more income to buy currency, so I can get decks and run the recording shop and a big disco.

I learned the alphabet at school, and reading gives me the edge. The co-op runs a store that sells fodder and medicine for livestock, and they give you a booklet that tells you everything about rearing chickens.

It takes two months. I get them when they are tiny from a poultry breeder – two to four days old. In the beginning I keep them inside the house, in the room below the stairs. Even if you don't believe in God, you'll be on your knees every night in that critical period for the young chicks: "Oh God, please let the electricity plant run all night without interruption – otherwise disaster will strike." The chickens are under heat; one week under a six-hundred-watt light bulb, one week below a three-hundred-watt bulb. The stench of the chicken shit fills every room, gets in my clothes – foul, a terrible life. Then, after two weeks, out into the shed and drop the power to two hundred watts. Six weeks in the shed, with the light always on – then they eat all the time. Lights on. Eating. I can sell them after eight weeks instead of waiting for three months. I give them chicken feed with different types of corn, chemicals, vitamins, calcium, salt – all of it mixed with ground-up fish bones and tiny fish. At first very finely ground, later a little coarser.

After two weeks I inoculate the chickens by putting antibiotic chemicals in their water. Two weeks later I do it with a different medicine. The poultry breeder has given me instructions: if their immune system is weak, they get *dawa ya kuku* – a local chicken medicine made from crushed aloe leaves mixed with water. It doesn't taste very nice, so I start by giving them fodder mixed with *pili-pili kichaa* – which means insanity pepper – tiny little chillies, about a centimetre long. When the chickens get sufficiently hungry, they eat the burning fodder, and by then the water has been removed and replaced with the aloe juice, so their insane thirst makes them drink the unpleasant fluid. Their immune systems reach peak condition in no time. There are people who say that *wazungu* women smear *dawa ya kuku* on their faces to get lovely baby-skin, but I've never seen it. The chickens grow, ready for the barbecue. Maybe I get an order from a hotel: I must deliver by morning – fifty chickens. I go to the day labourers and tell them: "Tomorrow morning at five – come, I've got fifty." I pay a small advance. They come and start the work, build a bonfire in my garden with a big tub on it, boiling water. They kill the chicken, drop it in the water, pull it out, pull off the feathers – the smell is enough to make you sick – they clean the bird. Wrap it in a plastic bag and tie a knot. At eight, when they've got fifty, into a taxi – straight to the hotel, or the supermarket or wherever.

GUILTY

Claire comes to my door one afternoon.

"I need money for the doctor," she says.

"I haven't got any," I say.

"You've got me big-bellied. Now you must help." I scrape together whatever money I've got. At the same time my old dirty father comes walking up to the kiosk.

"Take your things," he tells little sister Ida. "We're leaving."

"I have to help Marcus," she says.

"No. We don't know any Marcus," my father says.

"But . . . he's my brother," Ida says.

"I have no son called Marcus, so he can't be your brother," my father says.

"But Mother said . . ." Ida begins, but the hand stops her: *PAH* – right in her face. I run from my veranda to the kiosk.

"Don't you hit her, you old idiot," I say. He tries to hit me. I grab his hand in mid-air, bend it back until he cowers and pulls away.

"You have kidnapped my daughter," he says. "When I have fetched the police, you will go to Karanga Prison." Yes, may be right about that.

"Get your things," I tell Ida. She does it and leaves with my dirty father, tears running from her eyes.

"*Tsk*," Claire says. "You people are like that place where you come from."

"What do you mean?" I ask.

"Your family – you're from the Serengeti. Not people – wild animals." She leaves with my money. No money and no-one to man the kiosk.

Phantom comes by in the evening and buys me a beer.

"Alwyn has shut up his recording shop. His machines are bust," Phantom says. Then there's only one left in town, down by the bus station, and all his music is on cassettes, so the sound is dirty – when the rain pours down, the moisture gets in everywhere, and the tape reels inside the cassettes rise like dough with too much yeast. If you have a C90 cassette in a tropical climate, the tape reels can move towards each other and in the end they can't go round. His sound is shite. I look over at the Larssons' broken-down stereo, which I inherited after long and faithful service, but I haven't got the money to pay for the repair. I ought to be ready now – the market is open to me, but I haven't got the decks and still there's no post from Denmark.

FOOD AND AGRICULTURE ORGANIZATION

The next time I come to West Kilimanjaro, I find Rhema crying. "I'm pregnant," she says.

"Then you have to talk to your *mzungu*," I say.

"He won't speak to me. He has gone to Dar es Salaam."

"Then the police will have to speak to him when your chocolate baby arrives."

"But . . . it's not his. He's used the sock every time." *Eeehhhh*, it's true. You only get pregnant by the *mzungu* man when he chooses it – he is stingy with his seed. I have sown – now I must harvest problems: shit, screams and starvation.

"You went to the *mzungu*," I say. "Now I'm back with Claire."

"But you got me pregnant."

"Claire is pregnant as well," I say.

"No! What am I to do?" Rhema asks. What am I to do for that matter?

A letter arrives from Mika in Finland after a year's silence. Now out of prison and still alive – maybe A.I.D.S. was just a lie. "I am out and free," he writes. "Don't be in touch, because they're keeping an eye out for every movement, every contact. Stay away from me." And this from the guy who owes me more than two thousand dollars – all wasted on the fine for his *bhangi* and zebra meat. I'll won't be seeing him again. Dreams. I have to stop dealing with that sort of person. Never again will I contact this Mika, who starting abusing drugs in Moshi and was flushed back to Finland like a turd, and then returned to destroy my life.

CATCH-22

African socialism has been dead for a long time. Now the carcass stinks like a hyena, and we must give the market economy a shot. Imara Furniture Factory becomes a joint venture with Indians and Swedes as the private partners with a fifty-one per cent stake and the

Tanzanian state with the remaining forty-nine. Gösta is allowed to be a partner because after Jonas died all the corruption that came to light was blamed on the evil dead man. Harri goes home, and the company gets a different flavour. Rhema has already been kicked home to her grandmother in Soweto, because my seed is growing in her stomach. The next thing I know, I'm being accused by the head accountant:

"You're ripping off the project – you keep the money for yourself," he says.

"No, that's not true," I say. The accountant himself is interested in my job as a purchasing agent; he wants to buy things cheaply from the *wahindi* in town and make out the amount to be very large – then they can split the difference and keep it as a kickback. The accountant speaks to Gösta:

"Marcus always has money. I see him in town every night, drinking beer. Where does he get the money? From Imara's kitty, that's where." I shake my head:

"I make money from my kiosk and my chicken farm as well," I say. "Everyone knows I work hard on my businesses on the side." The accountant raises his voice:

"That chicken farm was built with timber stolen on West Kilimanjaro. Where is your receipt for it?" he asks.

"No," I say. "I bought my timber from the sawmill at Rongai." That's West Kilimanjaro's big competitor.

"You always lie," the accountant says. "You say you've bought diesel, but we can't find that diesel." But Gösta argues in my favour:

"Marcus has done a good job for me, and he knows where to get everything. If I order screws, Marcus gets the right screws. I want to keep him."

"I can't run our accountancy department if you have a man employed to steal from my kitty. Perhaps you want all thefts that occur here to be reported straight to the government office?" the accountant says with an evil eye; he knows something of the Swede's dirty linen. Gösta is frightened – I see it. Perhaps Gösta himself has his trunk in the kitty, because now he's learning all the Tanzanian methods from his clever Chagga wife.

"Marcus," Gösta says, "you'll have to go up and work at West Kilimanjaro counting logs and boards, and managing the stockroom."

"I can't live that far away," I say. "I can only go there and go back the same day, because if something goes wrong inside me, I have to be close to K.C.M.C. and the doctors."

"Now you're just lying," the accountant says.

"You'll have to bring a letter from your doctor," Gösta says – he doesn't want to oppose the accountant, because new winds are blowing and they may blow the truth of Gösta's thieving from the accountant's mouth to the ears of the government office.

That night I find my surgeon in a bar and buy him beer to get proof; he gives me a letter. I go back and give the accountant the letter.

"You're fired," the accountant says.

"What?"

"This letter just proves that you can't do your job – your body isn't strong enough."

"What about my severance package?" I ask.

"We'll send it to you," he says. I go out and am about to get on the motorbike. The accountant has followed me.

"The motorbike must stay here," he says. "It belongs to the project."

"No, it's mine," I say. This motorbike is one I put together myself from two wrecks that had been written off by the project – I managed to create a living machine from them.

"I'll call the police," he says.

"You do that," I say and drive straight to see Gösta in Shanty Town – the house where he lives with his clever Chagga wife.

DOCTORS OF DEATH

"I can't do anything right now," Gösta says. "Since it became a joint venture I don't have very much of a say in things. You'll have to return the motorbike to the project office. But I will try to get your job back." I look at this man who once promised me a journey to Sweden. I am not in Sweden, but this Swede is in Tanzania and has got himself a lovely Chagga woman, – tsk. But I have read in The Economist about the special doctors who examined the piles of dead people after the fall of Idi Amin's regime in Uganda. I drill like a machine into Gösta's conscience:

"In Europe they have doctors who can read about the death struggle like from an open book; was the head hit before the body died? How long from the blow until the body was dead? And when you think about the investigation, where the Tanzanian Commissioner says that the body can't wing its way onto the bench – then what is your result? The dead body hit its head before it died. Was it a fall or a blow? We don't know. But the negro helped the wife make that body wing its way onto the bench in the sweat lodge. The negro was there."

"That investigation is closed," Gösta says.

"I can make a lot of noise," I say.

"You can't do anything," he says.

"The Tanzanian police chief has been bought and paid for, yes. And the judge will demand both a Mercedes and a marble palace to re-open the investigation. But if the Europeans hear this information, they will ask: should the dead body's wife have called a doctor? And their answer will be yes."

"Wait here," Gösta says. After a few minutes he comes out with a piece of paper that proves that the motorbike is mine, was bought from the project by him two years ago. I put the paper in my pocket – later I will show it to the police to disprove the claims of the accountant.

"When will you have that ticket for Sweden for me?" I ask Gösta and smile.

"Watch it," he says and smiles as well. We both laugh, and I drive on in my life.

When I am in town, I ask Ibrahim if he's seen Claire.

"She's very big now," he says. "But there is trouble."

"Trouble how?" I ask.

"Rhema is going to the witch doctor to kill you."

"I don't believe in those ghosts and voodoo," I say.

"No, but it makes Claire very nervous," Ibrahim says.

Now I must deal with Claire's family. There is a godly mother, and a useless sister who thinks of nothing but catching a *bwana mkubwa* in her net so she herself can live a life of glorious indolence.

"I went to church with Claire this morning," the mother says. Does she expect an answer? I don't say anything. "It's not easy for Claire to go to church now," she says. Not easy? *Eehhh*, because of her tummy. No-one at church has ever seen her get married – and yet she is sitting with a large seed inside her. She has been wicked.

I look at that mother-in-law intently, speaking slowly and clearly:

"A great many men may have planted that seed in your daughter. The seed only becomes mine if I say it is mine. Otherwise you can keep your daughter and have an extra mouth to feed." She doesn't say anything. Claire comes in.

"Would you like a cup of tea, Marcus?" she asks. I nod. "How much sugar do you take, Marcus?"

"Three," I say. She ladles sugar into the cup with her spoon and stirs, like a good woman would for her husband. Staying with her mother has shown her the light: the mother drives her mad. She cannot stay here; her relationship with me must be rebuilt with sweetness. Step one: sugar in my tea.

"I will go on living with my mother, at least until after the baby is born," Claire says. We are in touch again, but still stumble across rocky ground, even though she wants my caresses as soon as we're alone – the peculiarities of women ...

TEARS

At Kibo Coffee House I see Katriina sitting alone at a table with a glass of iced coffee. I go over to her, sit down across from her and set the tears to work:

"I miss seeing Solja and Rebekka so much. They were with me for four and a half years, and now they're gone. And I have a daughter in Finland I've never seen. It'll be Christmas soon. I need to give them a present." Katriina sighs:

"Then come visit us," she says.

"I will never mention it again," I say.

"Jonas?" she says.

"Who?" I say. "I've never heard of the man."

MTOTO MSWAHILI

I buy sweets and two fun T-shirts in town before driving out to Katriina and the girls. Solja is at school all afternoon, but my white daughter is at home. Rebekka – a total *mswahili* to the eye. The way she walks, lazily and rhythmically. How she moves her eyes and smiles, but if you press her for an answer and demand something from her – she can totally pull down blinds behind her eyes, so they go flat and empty like a negro who is fed up with some tiresome white person.

Katriina serves Coke to me on the veranda and watches Rebekka as she plays with her Lego.

"I'm glad she won't remember very much," Katriina says.

"And Solja?" I ask.

"Solja is very angry," Katriina says.

"But she's also very strong," I say. "She will be alright."

"But what about you, Marcus?" Katriina says and looks straight at me. "You don't have to get every woman pregnant, do you?" she says and laughs. I shake my head:

"Those women are very erotic – I completely forget to think," I say. Katriina enters the house. How much can she help? She used to be on Jonas' ticket – now she's on *bwana* Knudsen's; it's better, but she still doesn't have financial independence. Katriina returns:

"That's all I've got," she says, handing me an envelope.

"Thank you," and say and leave. Dollars – even with my own few dollars it's far from enough to buy a new stereo, but nevertheless it will help towards repairing the old one. That same day I go to the Indians and exchange it on the black market, take a bus to the best Hi-Fi mechanic in Arusha and hand over the dead machines. Soon the recording shop will be up and running again, and the life-giving music will play in my ghetto.

ENTICING ILLNESS

I'm sitting outside with my coffee, and sunglasses covering my red *bhangi*-eyes. A young woman comes through the front garden. When I look into her eyes, I think sexual thoughts – *eeehhh*, all the things I would do with her that would take my hangover away.

"I am your brother's wife," she says. "He needs your help." She tells me that he was caught smuggling at the Holili border and the goods were seized, so now he must pay a large fine to get out of prison.

"Your husband's a fool," I say. "The police only confiscate things if you haven't greased them as you should."

"Yes, but as a family we must help each other," she says and looks straight through my sunglasses. "If you help me, then I'll help you – we can help each other. Maybe your house needs cleaning? Maybe I should make your bed, so that it becomes nice? I can do that right now."

I can't even get up to offer her a cup of tea, my trousers would be like a tent. She is naughty in the dirty way – dangerous to the man. As if she's carrying lots of diseases in her, and all you want is to catch them for yourself. But the entire neighbourhood is watching: Marcus is a man who is living on his own and who has two pregnant girlfriends in town, and here comes a lonely woman – he invites her right in and shuts the door. Everyone would know. No. It's impossible.

"I haven't got the money to help," I say.

"*Tsk*," she says. "You've got a house, a kiosk – no wife or children. You're rich. If you won't help, that's just evil." She turns and leaves; it's lovely to watch, but sad that she goes. Yes, it's true that I could help, but am I my brother's keeper?

1986

Christian

I get a letter from Samantha – I can tell from the postmark that it's been a long time coming. I rip it open. She writes that she wants to die – she writes that to me. She hates her life. She misses me. She hates school. She doesn't want to go to Europe – Britain, where her mum is. She can't stay at school in Moshi. Her dad's an arse. Everything is shit. And there I am – in a basement in Hasseris. Fuck. We should be together. We should be in charge of our own lives. Imagine all the things we could do . . . I write back to her at once: that I'll be down this summer; that I'm thinking about how to launch a business in Tanzania; that she's gorgeous; that she must hang in there, not take any crap from anyone, not be sad – because she's better than all of them.

We set up a band at school – me, Anders and a girl called Marianne. She sings and plays the keyboard. Other than that she doesn't say much – brainy, I think. She's got a great arse. We have trouble getting a guitarist who knows how to play a reggae rhythm. "You're too white," Anders tells the ones who audition and adds a "tsk" which he's picked up from me. Marianne sings well. School's alright. I almost get all the prep done I should, but it is a drag. Still no word from Samantha. I write to Panos and ask him about it, but he doesn't answer either. I write to Jarno, but he just sends a postcard with the words: "I am in exam hell. Afterwards I'll be at the Norad Guesthouse. Feel free to stop by."

There's a party at the school. I am stoned when I arrive with Anders. We lounge against the bar next to the dance floor. They're playing rock, and Anders gets into it. I look at the girls. Pointless; nothing in their life is the least troublesome – their greatest pain is not having the money to buy a new shirt when they want it. Then Bob comes out of the loud-speakers. I leave the bar, stand at the edge of the dance floor and let him flow into me. I half close my eyes so I can't see all the white people. Someone comes over.

"You call that dancing?" Anders says, grabbing my shoulders, grinning. I look at the white people – several of them are watching me. Marianne comes over.

"Hi," she says.

"Did you see it? Christian is dancing like a bloody negro," Anders asks.

"Far out," I say.

"I think you dance well," she says. I don't say anything. "Want to dance?" she asks.

"Alright," I say.

Monday, around noon, we go back to hers. Her parents are at work. She asks me about Africa. I talk about Stone Age communities who have no contact with the surrounding world because of the impassable geography. All the energy that is expended on survival in a tough climate. The diseases. The poor soil. No scriptural culture. Colonialism and the slave trade. The attempts to bring Africa two thousand years into the future which have led to a society that doesn't work at all, due to tribal nepotism and corruption. Not enough people with further education – no stable governmental institutions. The continent needs an age of enlightenment, a folk high-school movement, a political reformation. In Tanzania they have a co-operative movement, but it was wrecked by top-down African socialism, centralism, the planned economy. The E.E.C.'s subsidies for European farmers combined with high tariffs against African products:

"So the only things Africa is capable of producing more cheaply than us are the things we won't buy from them," I say. "Rice, corn, cotton, sugar." The sound of my dad's voice rolls through my head; the sound of whisky – but it's just talk, that's all. "I have to see your room," I say after a pause.

"Why?" she asks.

"I just do," I say and go up the stairs. The bed has been made. I lie down on it. She's standing at the door. I reach out my hand. She doesn't move. "Come," I say. She comes over. She is . . . pale. Oddly white. We make out. Gradually we become naked. I close my eyes and think about Samantha as I come inside her. We shower and go downstairs again because I fancy a cup of coffee.

She starts questioning me about Africa. She wants to go down and work for the U.N. after she's finished school.

"It's just so unfair. I mean . . . we've got everything, and we don't want to help even though they're starving to death," Marianne says. I laugh. "Why are you laughing?" she asks.

"What do you want me to do? Cry?" I ask.

"It just seems . . . unnatural. That you're laughing." I laugh even more.

"It seems sick, doesn't it?" I ask. Marianne looks at me.

"Yes," she says. I think of the roaring laughter at the prostitutes' place over the bicycle-repair shop.

"That's what people do in Africa. Laugh at fate so it doesn't crush them," I say.

"You're not African," Marianne says.

"I'm not as white as I seem."

Marianne and I are together that winter. I learn to say what she wants to hear so I can get laid. Winter turns to spring. She is busy with her exams. I talk to Dad on the phone. He's going to transfer money so I can buy a ticket to Dar es Salaam. Marianne is looking into becoming a nanny in England – to improve her language skills and save up money for her trip to Africa.

"Are you going there as well when you've finished your second year?" she asks. Which is just another way of asking if we're going to be there together when she returns from England? But I don't want her tagging along – I want to go down and see Samantha.

"I don't know if that's a good idea," I say. "I'm just going down to see my friends. It's very different from what you want to do."

"Are you going to decide whether I can go to Africa?" Marianne asks.

"No, no. It's your life," I say. "But I have no plans to save Africa, because it can't be done."

"But surely we can make a difference," Marianne says.

"No, you can't," I say. "You can make sure you feel better about your guilt about being white."

"If everyone was like you, the world would be a truly ugly place," Marianne says.

"Did the Africans ask for your help?" I ask.

"They need help," Marianne says.

"You're just doing it for your own sake," I say.

"You don't mean that," she says.

"As a matter of fact, I do."

Marcus

FACE TO FACE

With love and praise through Jah's love. The destruction approaches – terror in our hearts. But *bwana* Knudsen says Christian will be down this summer. Ohhh, I hope he can help me.

Finally a letter arrives with some good cassettes. But there is confusion about when he will arrive in Tanzania – he explains his problems with money, the family, school, girls; the white country isn't working for him. But I trust the stereo will work; the letter shows how much he appreciates his native friend. My idea of exporting goods from Tanzania to Denmark isn't mentioned. But he will be down soon – we can discuss it face to face.

I immediately write back asking him to buy three pairs of underpants for me if he can – medium size. I am going about nearly naked. Well, I am so poor that I ask for everything – old shirts and trousers he doesn't use – the tailors in town can refit them for me. Perhaps he can send it by surface post – by ship – that's cheap. Or maybe a friend of his has some? I am in a life crisis – I hope he realizes and understands.

THE PARADE OF HARDSHIPS

Now I have to get the kiosk in perfect working order, because my severance package hasn't arrived.

I miss Claire. To help out around the house as well. Not because Claire must make my dinner – I won't eat corn porridge. But when Claire isn't living here, I can't have a house girl, because then people would think we were godless, and that would mean I would have no customers for the kiosk. So I have to pay far too much for a Christian neighbour's wife to do the cleaning and washing, and that arrangement gives me a lot of trouble – I have to hide my tin of *bhangi* in the garden every time she comes to work. And her son keeps an eye on my house every time I run an errand so thieves don't empty it; in return I give them free chickens.

I take the bus to Holili to buy a few luxury goods for the kiosk straight from the smugglers on the border. It's cheaper than buying them in Moshi. When my bag is full and my purse is empty, I catch sight of Sia. Now she's no longer fun, because she's wearing her police uniform – everything she says is the law, so I must smile at her like a cautious child.

"Marcus," she says, sounding happy. "I hear the crazy Swedish man is dead."

"Yes, he's in the ground now," I say. We talk of the crazy Swedish days and how life goes on. Sia smiles – she's got a house, she's got a husband, she's got a baby. If you're a police officer close to the border, the smuggling pours a flood of money right into your pocket. I ask about my brother.

"Your brother was a not a good smuggler," Sia says.

"You know him?"

"Yes, I was the one who caught him."

"What was the problem?"

"Your brother won't abide by the rules for greasing."

"But greasing is illegal," I say.

"So is smuggling," Sia says.

"He smuggles in order to make a living," I say.

"And I have to be greased to make mine," Sia says.

"But how will his family cope now?" I ask. Sia looks surprised:

"But he's already out," she says and tells me the family sold all their possessions to pay the court. Now he's working as a bus driver on the route to Dar es Salaam. I tell Sia goodbye. In the bus home I think how the police force has given Sia great happiness – I should have taken that path in life. When you live in corrupt countries, you're better off on the side that gets greased than the side that does the greasing.

BUSH RELIGION

One day a boy comes to my kiosk, sent by Claire's mother.

"You must come at once. Your daughter is born in Pasua." I shut the kiosk at once, and we go in a taxi to the house.

"There is some problem with the mother," he says. "She's talking about a witch who has cast a spell on the baby." We arrive at the rooms. Claire is lying in the bed, her mother is in the chair with my daughter on her arm. The mother doesn't even say hello but speaks very quickly:

"Rhema was the first person to visit yesterday – the day after Claire had the baby. Rhema fetched the bottled milk from the kitchen when Claire couldn't see her," the mother says. She is Pentecostal, but now she also believes in the primitive religion. Claire whimpers from the bed:

"Why did she come to my house? It was early yesterday morning, the first day I'm back from the clinic with our baby. And I don't know this Rhema, even though she is . . . big-bellied. It's witchcraft," Claire says. Of course she knows that Rhema is pregnant by me, and who she is, but they've only ever spoken hypocritically to each other. And now it's mystery and spirits and evil eyes. I go over and look at the baby, which is amazingly pretty. I say to Claire:

"It's superstition – bush religion. The baby is fine. You being here as a ball and chain on your mother's leg serves no purpose. As soon as you can get out of bed, you must come to Uru Road and take over the running of the kiosk, so you can be in charge of the money. Then we can make money for the child." And the next day Claire comes to run the shop with the baby on her back like a Chagga in the field, and I go into town and get baby oil, rice, corn flour, fizzy drinks, chewing gum, matches, soap, candles, paraffin and everything you can possibly sell.

That's how it goes for a week – Claire works in the kiosk next to my terraced house and goes back to her mother's place in the evening, and I sleep without sounds or caresses. It's stupid. We haven't yet got over our problems.

"Take the child and yourself and all your things and move here. This is a much better area. Much safer, and you can live here with me."

That's how it starts. At first Claire sleeps on the sofa, but she doesn't like the sofa. She wants leather furniture – that's what fashion requires: big, round and bulging furniture you sink into. Loads of foam covered in brown leather. I have my pale wooden furniture from Imara – Swedish style. It's perfectly good and it's been bought and paid for.

"That wood is ugly," she says.

"No, because I want you, soft girl, in the house with me and the hard wood." She is shocked. But one day she moves to the Swedish bed.

Claire can't work very much in the kiosk, because the baby sees her as its cow, and in the kiosk she can't have her titi out behind the till. We are in Moshi – not in the jungle. So I lose income. That's why it's very important that the recording shop works well – I have functioning machines, but I need to promote my business, and I need all the new music. My old tapes are worn and ruined by dust from the dry season and moisture from the long rains.

THE SHACKLES OF COLONIALISM

I go back to Imara Furniture Factory to demand my severance package.

"You're not a well man," the head of accounts says. "We don't owe you anything."

I write a letter to State House about how these people refuse to pay me according to my rights – all they do is kick me. I get a letter telling me to come to State House and see a particular official.

"You must come back in two or three months. In the meantime I will find out how to solve your problem," he says. Two or three months? I might die of starvation before then. And there's no money to sweeten my wait. The state is co-owner of Imara, and now one part of the state must punish another part of the state. Can you imagine a man's hand hitting his own head as a punishment for being guilty of stupidity?

I'm still waiting when I hear that Gösta has got the job as M.D. for the new TanScan, running the furniture factory and the sawmills. If I continue with my complaint, I will also be pointing the finger at Gösta. So I give up. For his sake and for mine – he can see I need a job. He knows me. We've been together all this time. And he knows I haven't been paid. And he's the boss of the Moshi department and the ones in Mwanza and Mbeya. With all those options he can offer me something to do, some job or other. The accountant who took my job as a purchasing agent has been thrown in Karanga Prison because his fingers were far too long. But even though Jonas' body is rotting in the ground, it's also rotting in the air around me, and no-one likes it when that stench reaches their nose.

Christian

One day when I come home from school there's a letter. From Samantha. Finally. I rip it open:

"I bailed on school. But I don't think it makes any difference to my future, because I'm going to train to be a beautician, which is just a maker-upper, but it sounds more impressive, don't you think? You know, I'm completely wasted, and tonight I'm going to this totally posh Scandinavian party at the yacht club, and I hope I'll have fun. Never use a girl just for her body, O.K.? Remember that. My love life is in full flower, but I doubt you would approve because he's old enough to be my dad, but he's so kind, and maybe he does represent a sort of father figure.

Don't be mad with me – I don't know why, but I'm feeling really guilty about it. You know what I mean? Anyway, it's a really odd relationship, you see, the guy is thirty-eight years old, and he's a guest in my dad's house. He has been for about a month now, and we've just discovered this really powerful bond between us – it's more like a friendship than a sexual relationship, but it's also quite risky, because he's a friend of my dad's, and my sister is living here in Dar as well, so it's quite secretive, you understand, and that makes it an adventurous relationship. You see what I'm trying to say?"

Shit. And she must have been so stoned she forgot to put a return address. I can write to Baobab Hotel in Tanga, but who knows if they'll forward it? I have to get down there. Soon. It's spring. We sit our exams. Marianne takes her final exams and has pretty much given up on me. I'm not bothered. Soon I'll be flying to Dar es Salaam.

Marcus

HUNDRED-YEAR-OLD COALMINER

The baby screams and shits; the chickens under the stairs shriek and shit, the customers shout for service in the kiosk, so Claire has to pull her teat from the babe's mouth and rush out and sell fizzy drinks and rush back into the house and pop the teat back into the babe's mouth so it doesn't wail like an unending ambulance siren in the house. I am looking for a new job, but I haven't got any judges to plead my case, so I must help myself. There's no money for petrol for the motorbike, so I go around on a rented bike like a negro in the sun to pick up supplies: flour, rice, fizzy drinks, soap, cooking oil, knick-knacks, sweets, pens, light bulbs, arse wipes, batteries and everything. And I must get chicken feed and mind the birds, so they can grow large enough for slaughter. And when the evening comes and decent folk may sleep, I can get on with my orders for recorded cassettes. I sit in the chair, nodding, and my hungry babe is like an alarm clock, waking up and wanting to be fed, alerting me to turn the tape so I can make my few coins. The biggest problem of course is that I am running on old music – no access to anything new. My face looks terrible – as exhausted as a hundred-year-old coalminer's. And it doesn't make enough money. How can people know I've got a recording shop when it's hidden in an ordinary house outside the city centre, one that doesn't even have a sign? I have my regular customers, but to everyone else I am a big secret.

I have to take the chance on the old Larsson stereo. I tell anyone and everyone: "I can play at your parties – I can even take pictures of the party in the prettiest colours, so you'll have beautiful memories of the day." I take the stereo to small birthday parties around town in a taxi, and then, finally, I'm asked to play at a wedding dinner at Moshi Hotel. Now I can become famous.

The party's getting going. "Turn it up," they say. And I turn it up and up, and my stomach is in knots, because the amplifier is but a small one. Then the toastmaster comes over:

"Give me the microphone," he says. And I just have to say:

"Please speak loudly." There is no microphone. In order to create a sensation and lure people in, you have to have a microphone, so the speaker can feel important; you need a strobe lamp to get the flashing lights people like. I haven't got those things. What am I to do?

THE HOUSE OF EVIL

An old woman comes to my house. I invite her in. "Rhema has given birth to your son," she says – it's Rhema's grandmother. If this were her village Rhema's father or brothers might have come – they could force me to marry her, even kill me. But Rhema lives in Soweto and has no-one but her little brother and her grandmother. "You must look after them," she says. Claire has got the house girl to man the kiosk. Claire comes in and says hello. I say:

"Rhema has been with many men – she has even lain with a *mzungu* on West Kilimanjaro."

"The baby is as black as you are, with a Chagga nose and a Chagga mouth. And you know – back then she was only with you."

"She can't live here – there is already one woman in the house, and we have had our baby."

"Rhema is your responsibility," her grandmother says. I say:

"It's impossible to live with two women in one house – you can only love one, or one of them will kill you."

"You'll go to hell if you don't accept responsibility for your child," Rhema's grandmother says. "Evil will live in your house."

Maybe it was my child Rhema gave birth to, but only a judge can determine it and decide what I must pay. Rhema doesn't have money for a judge, and I won't run in the direction pointed out to me by a witch.

Christian

Taxi to the Norad Guesthouse where Jarno's waiting. We go straight to a bar. Kilimanjaro Hotel. It's the afternoon. Hot. I'm sweating. Mental jetlag even though I'm in the same time zone. Aeroflot was noisy and stank of old dirt and cheap industrial disinfectant; wooden toilet seats smeared with a lumpy black oil paint. We drink. I go out to take a slash in the urinal. There are no naphthalene balls because there are none to be had for love nor money. Tropical style: my piss splashes over slices of fresh lemon. And – wonder of wonders – there's liquid soap. I pump it out into my palm, open the tap and . . . no water. Try the other tap. Nothing. Shit. My hand is covered in soap. Go into a toilet cubicle. No loo paper to wipe off the soap. I look down: brown calcium deposits inside of the toilet bowl, but clean water at the bottom. I put my hand down there. Shake it in the water, which foams with the soap, until the skin of my hand feels tight and firm when I run my fingertips across it. I flush, holding my hand under the water that springs from the front back of the toilet. Now the cistern is empty. Clean hands. Welcome to Africa.

After a few beers we take a taxi to Msasani and swim in Oyster Bay.

"Have you seen Samantha recently?" I ask.

"It hasn't been that long," Jarno says.

"What does she get up to these days?"

"I don't know, Christian," he says. "I haven't really spoken to her."

"But did you . . . fall out?"

"No, no, I just don't really know who she hangs out with. It certainly isn't me," he says. I leave it at that.

That night we go to the drive-in cinema with Diana, who was in Samantha's year at I.S.M. I feel like tiny insects are swarming around under my skin, which vibrates with heat – sunburn. We get drunk on Konyagi and Coke. At four I wake up sneezing with a running nose. The next day I've got water-filled blisters on the back of my neck and my scalp. My skin breaks when I touch it. The fluid runs out. The skin flakes dry up and flake off.

Jarno's mother calls from Morogoro and tells him that the Finnish embassy are looking for him; something about him being late in reporting for military service and now there's an arrest order for him in Finland. So now he must go and speak to the ambassador, otherwise he'll be put away as soon as he sets foot on Finnish soil. Jarno laughs:

"They'll be using me as cannon fodder when the Russians come." He drives over. This afternoon we're going to the yacht club. Loads of time to kill. I get a phonebook and find the number for Shakila's dad's hospital – I know she works for him in her spare time. Dial the number.

"I have to help out at the hospital until two," Shakila says and gives me the address. It's not far. I can come pick her up. I drink more Africafé. Smoke cigarettes. Take a shower that removes the dead skin and the blisters from my back.

Stroll to the hospital. A couple of well-tended one-storey buildings – room for about twenty patients. Shakila comes running out of the building, stops.

"Christian," she says.

"Hi," I say and walk up to her. Peck each other on the cheeks without our bodies touching.

I ask her if she's looking forward to uni.

"I've been kicked out," Shakila.

"How?" I ask. "I didn't think you'd started yet."

"Yes, I started last year, but now they've kicked me out."

"Why?"

"Because of my dad," Shakila says and explains that her dad – the famous consultant surgeon in the country – used to work at the university until he quit and set up his own private hospital. So his former colleagues are more than a little envious. And they were the ones who were supposed to be teaching Shakila. "So they got back at me by kicking me out."

"Can you get in somewhere else?" I ask.

"My dad is arranging something – so I can go abroad, perhaps," she says.

"Have you seen Samantha recently?" I ask, looking at her. Her eyes are hidden, but her face changes, she turns away and looks out across the ocean.

"Things aren't going well for Samantha," Shakila says.

"How . . . not well?"

"She's in bad company," she says.

"But what does she do?"

"I don't know. I think she'll be going to England soon," Shakila says.

"Did you hear anything about what it is she gets up to?" I ask. Of course she has – she's just too decent to speak ill of other people. She'd rather not say anything. And she knows I like Samantha.

"She . . . She's been ill for a while. And now all she does is go to parties all the time – she doesn't seem to care what people say about her. Here, let me have a cigarette." I hand Shakila the pack and light one for her. If Samantha doesn't care what people are saying about her that means she's deliberately doing everything in her power to make them speak ill of her. There can be no other explanation. And she sent me those letters – one saying she wanted to die and one saying she was sleeping with an older man.

"Do you know where Samantha's staying?" I ask.

"No. Perhaps at her sister, Alison's. She married the K.L.M. boss in Dar – they've got a place around here. But you'll see them at the yacht club, I would think."

"O.K.," I say.

"Or talk to Mick," Shakila says.

"Mick from Arusha? Who dropped out of school right before his exams?"

"Yes. He's the manager of a large garage in Kariakoo, owned by a Brit from Zambia."

"But . . ." I start and then stop.

"But what?" Shakila asks.

"Samantha. What happened to her? I've hardly heard from her in a year," I lie.

"I don't get Samantha," Shakila says. "She's had every opportunity in life, but she ruins it for herself with bad behaviour, just so people will notice her. I think it's stupid. Very stupid." Shakila shakes her head. "*Tsk*," she says.

I spend the next day pottering around the city centre. Later I go out to the yacht club. I've been put down as Jarno's younger brother so I can get in on his parents' "up-country" membership.

I order chicken and chips and a Coke. Eat. Look around. Spot a woman with a baby. The woman looks like Samantha but older. Beautiful. It might be the big sister, Alison. I go over to her.

"Excuse me, are you Samantha's big sister?"

"Why?" she asks.

"My name is Christian – I'm here on holiday from Denmark. I went to school with her until a year ago," I explain. She smiles.

"Christian," she says. "Yes, I've heard about you. I'm Alison." She holds out her hand.

"I've certainly heard about you as well," I say and smile at her. She invites me to join her.

"How is she?" I ask.

"She's been ill," Alison says. "And then there was all that to-do with school, but she's alright now. It won't be long before she'll go home to our mum in England." The baby whimpers, and Alison nurses it, so I can see the plump, milk-filled breasts – the same genetic make-up as Samantha's. Afterwards the baby falls asleep and a nanny materializes and takes the sleeping infant off for a stroll. Alison starts asking me about what I do in Denmark, but then suddenly Samantha and Jarno come to the table. Samantha's face seems stiff behind her sunglasses and cigarette. I hug her, ask her how's she doing. Tell her about things that happened in Denmark. Samantha doesn't say very much. She drinks her Coke, smokes, smiles and laughs – relaxed or standoffish, I can't quite tell which.

"Do you want to go swimming?" I ask, gesturing towards the beach.

"Nah, I'm knackered," Samantha says.

"Oh. Alright," I say.

"You know what?" Alison says. "We're having a garden party and a barbecue in two days to celebrate the baby, and you're all invited. Samantha will be there, and you'll meet a chap called Victor. His wife is in England at the moment – she's heavily pregnant and the baby is due any day now."

"Thanks," I say. Jarno nods. Samantha asks what time it is, and I tell her.

"I am going to have to dash," she says. "I'm meeting someone."

"How do we meet?" I ask her. "Where are you staying?"

"Can't we just meet up at that garden party?"

"How about tomorrow?" I ask.

"I can't. I've got plans," Samantha says. Alison gives her a look, but she doesn't say anything.

"I might stop by the Norad Guesthouse tomorrow," Samantha says.

"Alright," I say.

"We bloody well can't sit indoors all day and wait for you to maybe show up," Jarno says.

"I'll stop round before noon, O.K.?" Samantha tells him.

"Yes, O.K.," he says. "Now how the hell am I going to get back?" Jarno says, because he got to the club on the back of Samantha's motorbike. Why doesn't she ask me to go with her?

"I'll give you a lift back, both of you," Alison says. "That way I can show you where we live. It's on the way."

"See you later," Samantha says. She turns her back on us and raises her arm in farewell, and then she's gone.

When Alison takes us back, she gives us her phone number.

The next morning we sit and wait for Samantha, but she doesn't show.

"I simply can't be arsed," Jarno says and heads off to the beach. I didn't ask Alison where Samantha lives, because she was supposed to come today. And I didn't ask for Samantha's phone number either. I call Alison, get Samantha's number and call her.

"Oh God, I'm really sorry, I forgot I had a doctor's appointment," she says. "But I'll see you at the party tomorrow. I'm going to have to dash now. Bye."

The phone beeps in my hand.

I go to Kariakoo and find the garage where Shakila said Mick works. There's a yard with cars in various stages of disrepair, a large lean-to casting shade over the five cars that are being worked on, and lastly, a small office and stockroom. The mechanics are locals and Mick is standing in front of two lorries, talking to a tall, sinewy man with greying hair and scarred forearms. He is wearing dark khaki clothing.

"Hi, Mick," I say.

"Hold on a tick," Mick says. "I just need to finish this." I go over and stand under the lean-to. Mick discusses something with the man, they laugh, shake hands, and the man gets into a lorry with a silent African man in camouflage.

"You're Christian, aren't you?" Mick says and comes towards me.

"Yes, that's me."

"I remember you," Mick says and shakes hands. "A friend of Samantha's."

"Yes," I say.

"That's the man himself – Samantha's dad," Mick says, pointing at the lorry, which is now driving through the gate.

"O.K.," I say. "How did he come by all those scars?"

"You don't know?" Mick asks.

"No."

"Oh. I would have thought Samantha would have told you. He's a mercenary, former S.A.S. – special forces. Fought with them in the Far East and on the Arab Peninsula.

"Really?"

"Yes."

"Is he still . . . ?"

"A mercenary? Absolutely," Mick says.

"Where . . . does he fight?"

"Every African war in the past twenty years – at least all the ones that paid well."

"Why the hell didn't she tell me?" I say.

"I don't know," Mick says. "What could she say? That her dad kills negroes for other negroes? – not really cool, is it?"

"I can't believe he hasn't been killed."

"I can," Mick says.

"Yes?" I say.

"Yes. He keeps his African soldiers in front of him, so they're the ones who get killed – he only gets injured. How else would he be paid?"

"Does he have African soldiers who work for him?"

"The local soldiers he's hired to fight the war with. He trains them and . . . I don't think he actually leads them in battle – he directs them. They're not paid proper wages, so they may as well be killed," Mick says.

"So that's what he does – he's a mercenary."

"Yes, I mean – he's a businessman. He's got a few businesses here and there."

"The hotel," I say.

"Yes, the hotel in Tanga, although it looks like they'll take that from him."

"Why?"

"The government – the Tanzanians – believe he was involved in a scheme to topple the powers that be in the Seychelles."

"Was he?"

"I don't bloody know."

"What does he do now? Is he in Dar – with Samantha, I mean?"

"No, he's working. Something in Congo. Training guards for some mines." Mick laughs, adds: "That's an awful lot you don't know – that's probably why Samantha likes you." There's something terrible in his face as he speaks.

"Yes, but I can't seem to find her – see her," I say.

"That's probably also because she likes you."

"What do you mean?" I ask. Mick sighs.

"She's in deep shit."

"Everyone says that," I say. "What sort of shit?"

"Too much partying, too much powdering of her nose," Mick says, tapping the side of his nose with his index finger.

"But . . ." I start and am on the cusp of asking him why he doesn't help her. But just then I realize that perhaps he likes her. That she's maybe pushed him away too. That maybe he has the same feeling inside that I do and that I'm doing my best to hide. "But why doesn't anyone help her? Her sister, or her dad?"

"Or you," Mick says.

"I can't find her," I say. Mick lights a cigarette, hands the pack towards me, holds the match to my cigarette.

"You can't help someone who doesn't want to be helped," he says.

"But what happened to her?" I ask.

"Lots of trouble – something involving some guys who got in a fight about her. Then she was ill for a while, and then an Indian chap in her year offended her, and she beat him up with a chair and was expelled," Mick says. "At least that's what I hear, because I don't see her these days."

Samantha isn't at her sister's when I arrive at the garden party with Jarno. We're wearing our Carlsberg Twins uniform: white T-shirt, blue jeans, but holding Heinekens in our hands because Alison's husband is Dutch. I down the beer quickly, grab a new one.

"I'm sure she'll be here soon," Alison says to me. Their dad is there. Standing at the barbecue, jovial, downing his beer. And a girl I remember from school – Angela. I am introduced to Alison's husband, Frans, who seems nice. Not long after I can hear a motorbike in the drive, and a moment later Samantha comes round the corner of the house, followed by a powerful blond man with cold blue eyes who must be in his late thirties. Samantha says the briefest of hellos.

"I just have to take a look," she says and goes over and looks at the baby lying in its cot, exchanges a few words with her dad. She doesn't introduce us to the man she's with. I assume she is fucking him. Alison brings him over to us.

"This is Victor," she says. "He works with my dad. And this . . ." she says to Victor. "This is Jarno and Christian, who went to school with Samantha at I.S.M." He shakes our hands, squeezing them rather too hard – pathetic loser. I finish my beer, take a new one and go over to Samantha.

"He's a lot like your dad, isn't he?" I say, nodding at Victor.

"No," Samantha says. "They're nothing like each other."

"He could be your dad," I say.

"But he isn't," Samantha says. "And he couldn't be. He would have had to start really early for that." Victor is standing with Angela at the bar, grinning. Samantha goes over to them. Angela puts her arm around her shoulders and guides her towards the far end of the garden. Angela speaks in a low voice as they walk. I follow them with my eyes and can see that Samantha shaking Angela's arm off her shoulder and stepping away from her, sneering. I stand next to Victor and say:

"So, what are you doing in Tanzania?" He answers with something or other, and – out of the corner of my eye – I sense that Samantha is approaching.

"When is your wife coming down?" I ask.

"I don't know," he says. "The baby is due the day after tomorrow, but she might not have it until a little later." Samantha steers away from us, goes straight into the house and disappears. I look round. Alison is in there as well with her baby. I think about going inside, but I can't. It's starting to get dark. We eat with our plates in our laps. The meat is nice. Samantha comes out again with Alison, whose husband goes over to her with a plate of food, kisses her. Samantha sits down with me and Jarno and starts bullshitting about this one time when we almost got caught at the school gates after a night on the town. Her eyes seem odd. Then a phone rings in the house. Frans goes inside to pick up. Calls to Victor, who goes inside. Frans comes out.

"That was Victor's sister-in-law from the hospital. Mary is having the baby as we speak" Frans says.

"That's amazing," Victor shouts into the phone in the sitting room. "Call me as soon as anything happens." He comes out, grabs a beer. "Cheers, everybody," he shouts into the garden. "I'm having a baby." Everyone raises their glasses and bottles. Except for Samantha. She lights a cigarette. I look at her. She looks at her dad, who gives her a hard stare back. She gets up. Goes to the bottom of the garden. Stands with her back to the party. I go after her.

"Are you O.K.?" I ask.

"No," she says.

"What are you going to do?"

"I don't know. I don't care. I'll think of something. What do you want me to say?"

"Something that isn't completely inane," I say. I've never spoken to her like that before – or to anyone. Except for my parents.

"Everyone's lecturing me. Everyone," Samantha says. "Now you are too. I just can't be bothered." I don't say anything. "*Tsk*," she says. It's so utterly sad. I shrug.

"It's so fucked up," I say and go further into the dark garden. Samantha follows me. My eyes tear up. She puts her arm around me.

"No, don't do that," I say, pushing her away. She doesn't mean it anyway. She's just playing me. She hugs me again.

"Stop it," I say, twisting out of her arms, even though they are wonderful arms. "You've . . ." I start. Swallow my spit. Continue: "You're just using . . ." I gesture towards her – her body. The smooth skin of her arms, the pert tits, her waist, the luscious arse. "That's the only thing you know how to do," I say.

"Just, come off it," Jarno says Sunday morning.

"What?" I say.

"Samantha," he says. "She's fucked up."

"What the hell sort of a thing is that to say? We're friends. Samantha is my friend. You're her friend. She's our friend," I say.

"I don't think friendship is what's on your mind," Jarno says.

"Fuck you," I say and smoke on.

Sometime later Shakila shows up.

"Do you want to come for a swim?" she asks.

"I don't know," I say.

"I'm too tired," Jarno says.

"Oh, come on," Shakila says. "I've come all this way to see you."

"Alright then," I say and get my cigarettes and lighter, put on my sunglasses, go inside and put on swimming trunks under my shorts. We stroll through the residential neighbourhood to Oyster Bay. I don't say anything, even though I really like Shakila. But it's just so sad that I can't . . . think of anything to say.

"What's wrong, Christian?" she asks. I light a new cigarette.

"We went to a party at Samantha's big sister's the day before yesterday," I say and tell her about the party, about Victor.

"She's going through a rough patch," Shakila says.

"But, why?" I ask.

"She . . ." Shakila says but stops, puts a hand on my arm. She looks me in the eye. "You can't tell anyone, Christian," she says. "It's illegal for me to tell you."

"O.K.," I say, nodding.

"She had an abortion last year."

"Who?" I say.

"Samantha."

"No."

"Yes. My dad told me," she says. Shakila's dad – the doctor.

"But who . . . ?"

"I don't know, but it's been very hard on her. She's had a very rough time."

"Yes, but it's not likely to help that she's having an affair with a man who's old enough to be her dad and who's married," I say and start walking, blinking with my eyes behind the sunglasses to hold back the tears. I wonder who the dad was? Was it Stefano? Was it Baltazar, Mick, Victor? I can't bear thinking about it.

We continue walking in silence until we reach the beach.

"Last one in is a tosser," Shakila says and starts pulling off her T-shirt. I quickly kick off my shoes. We dash into the waves. Swim, play tag. Shakila is beautiful. I have to stop thinking about Samantha.

"We need to get out and have a smoke," I say, and we stride through the breakers and only just have time to throw ourselves onto the sand before Samantha arrives on her motorbike with Jarno on the back. Shakila gives me a serious look. They tumble down on the sand next to us. Samantha looks at me:

"Are you going to be in Dar your whole vacation?" she asks.

"No, I'm going to Shinyanga to see my dad, or if not I'm meeting him in Moshi," I say.

"How about you, Shakila?" Samantha asks. Shakila smiles.

"University in Cuba," she answers.

"Did you get that scholarship then?" I ask.

"Yes. My dad performed the Cuban ambassador's hernia operation and got him a particularly cheap summerhouse in Pangani. They play golf together," Shakila says, smiling.

"But that's great news," Jarno says.

"It's quite common," Shakila says. "If Canada offers Tanzania twenty university places as development aid, you'll have all the Secretary of Education's best friends lining up at the airport, waving goodbye to their kids. And the Secretary will have all sorts of juicy bones to gnaw on." She shrugs.

"Why the hell does everyone want to leave?" Samantha asks.

"We want to leave," Shakila says, "because God has forgotten Africa."

"What are you going to do, Christian?" she asks.

"What do you mean?" I say.

"Are you going home and back to school, or are you staying here, and what on earth are you going to live on?" Samantha asks.

"I've got one year of school left. I might train to be a diving instructor in Denmark and then start a diving centre for the tourists here in Dar or somewhere along the coast," I say.

"You won't get any customers," Samantha says. "We had one in Tanga, but Tanga and Moshi are both too far from the northern tourist route – it just won't work. People who want to dive go to Mombasa or the Seychelles."

"I've also thought about setting up a disco in Moshi," I say.

"You haven't got a stereo," Samantha says.

"I could get one in Denmark. I'm just looking into my options, and then I can have it sent down and start in a year," I say. Samantha doesn't say anything. If she's in England, we can meet there or in Denmark. But I can't suggest it, because she acts like she'd rather see the back of me.

"When are you going to England?" I ask.

"I don't know if I am going to go," Samantha says. "What do you have planned for the next few days?" she asks, even though it's obvious that she couldn't care less.

"I'm going to swim," I say and get up and go into the water. Shakila and Jarno follow. Samantha stays on the beach, lighting a cigarette. We splash each other. Shakila rises wet and luminously black from the water, rolling on the seabed so that the fine grains of sand make her skin white in large patches.

"Do you like it?" she asks.

"What?" I say.

"If I were white?"

"No, damn it – get it off." I go over and grab her, starting to drag her towards the edge of the water. She slips out of my grasp.

"Is it because I'm black that you like me?" she asks.

"I like you the way you are," I say. "Black is beautiful." I throw Samantha a look. Her face is an unmoveable mask – her eyes hidden behind her sunglasses. I want to go over and hold her. At the same time I want to spit at her.

Jarno catches the plane to Finland – he's going back to do his spot of national service. We've arranged to meet somewhere in Scandinavia this winter. I've spoken to Dad. He's arranged for me to stay with some Norwegians in Valhalla for a few days. Then I must take a bus to Moshi and stay with Katriina and the girls until he comes back in a week or so. After that we're going on safari. Shakila is busy preparing for her move to Cuba. Samantha . . . I don't know how to get hold of her, and if she doesn't want to see me, it doesn't really matter. I don't get it. I call Alison and leave the address and the phone number for the house in Valhalla; tell her to let Samantha know.

I potter about. Hang out on the beach. Swim and run, lie in the sun, smoke cigarettes and drink Coke. Jarno has gone. Samantha . . . I am looking forward to Moshi – hanging out with Marcus. Maybe I should just go there as soon as possible. I haven't got that much money left anyway. I walk back to Valhalla, sweating like a cow in the sun. The area is fenced-off; there are guards at the gate. I go to the house, which is completely Scandinavian in style. Sit down in the cool sitting room. The Norwegians are at work. They have no children. The house girl roots around the kitchen. I drink another Coke, go to the guestroom, lie on the bed, smoke. The doorbell rings. I can hear the house girl going to open the door. I get up from the bed and walk down the corridor. Samantha!

"Hi there," she says. "I just need to use your toilet." She rushes past me. I can hear her flushing, washing her hands. I go to the fridge and take out two cans of Carlsberg.

"Do you want a drink?" I ask when she comes out.

"I have to leave straightaway – the taxi's waiting outside," Samantha says, gesturing towards the road.

"Oh. But I thought . . ." I start but stop.

"I have to pack and stuff. I simply can't stay, Christian," she says. I stand still and look at her. "I'm sorry," she says. Right. Good for you. Sod off and die. "But I'm having dinner with my dad tonight, before he's taking me to the airport. You could come and have dinner with us . . . ?" she says.

"Do you think he'll think that's a good idea?" I ask.

"No, but he's already given me a piece of his mind. Go on – that way he won't have to repeat it all."

"O.K.," I say.

"Oyster Bay Hotel, eight o'clock." She comes over and hugs me, kisses my cheek. I don't lift my arms. Stand still. Am cold inside. "I'll see you at eight," she says and goes out to her taxi.

Samantha's dad, Douglas, is sitting at a table. I go over to him.

"Hello," I say.

"Hello. What are you doing here?" he asks.

"Samantha invited me," I say.

"Oh, alright. She isn't here yet," he says. "Christian, was it?"

"Yes," I say. He starts questioning me about what I do in Denmark. What my parents do. I tell him about the situation: that I'm going to visit my dad and his new wife in Moshi.

"Oh, your parents are separated as well?" he says. "Yes, I'm going to have to send Samantha back to her mother in England. I don't know what to do with her here."

I don't know what to say to that. Does he think Samantha knows what she's going to do with herself in England? Her dad laughs:

"Yes, that's what she asks me as well." We drink a beer, smoke. Samantha's dad looks at his watch. "Bollocks," he says, getting up. "That's what she always does," he explains. "We going to have to go out and find her." We go out to his Land Rover. "She's at Alison's," he says.

But when we get to Alison and Frans' house, there's no-one there. The guard says they're at the yacht club, but that Samantha wasn't in the car when they left.

"Right," Douglas says. "Shit. Then perhaps she's gone to my house to pick up a few things. She lived there until recently – now one of my partners is staying there." He drives quickly and doesn't say anything else. We both of us smoke. When we get to the house, the gate is opened by an old guard.

"*Shikamoo mzee*," Douglas says to him and asks whether he's seen Samantha.

"No, not today."

"Could she be in the house?" Douglas asks.

"I don't think so. There was a lady who hurried out a little while ago – she was crying. And then *bwana* Victor rushed out with a bag and left on the motorbike. I think he went after the lady. It's too late for a lady to walk alone in the dark like a dog."

"A white lady?" Douglas asks.

"Yes."

"But you haven't seen Samantha?"

"No, but she could be here. I only just arrived. My daughter was here earlier."

"Then ask her if Samantha was here," Douglas says impatiently.

"But she's gone out to drink *mbege*," the old man says, looking at the ground.

"Alright," Douglas says and stops the engine. We get out, go towards the entrance. Douglas grabs the doorknob. The door is locked. He gets a bunch of keys out of his jacket, unlocks the door, enters. I follow him through the kitchen; almost bump into his back when he stops in the sitting room. "Samantha," he says – his voice is thick. I look past him – my body jolts. Samantha. On the sofa. Blood from her eyes, her nose, her ears. She is sitting stock-still. Her eyes frozen in red. The blood is dark – dried on her cheeks, neck, her vest, knickers. Her hands are idle, rusty red. There are bloodstains on the sofa as if she's lain down before sitting up. There's white powder spread across the coffee table in front of her. A rolled up banknote. Douglas moves over to his daughter and feels for her pulse. Of course she hasn't got one. Her life has dried up in her veins, has run out with all the blood. I am sick. "Close the door," Douglas says. I close it. Douglas squats down, strokes Samantha's cheek, looks into her red eyes. "Samantha," he says, shaking his head faintly. Cigarette smoke; I've got a lit cigarette in my hand. Put it to my mouth. Douglas has got up. He removes the coffee table, looks at the sisal rug underneath it. He goes to the bedroom, returns with a sheet. Douglas grabs the sisal rug, pulls it to one side, puts the sheet on the floor and lays the rug on top – Samantha's deathbed. He lifts her, puts her down. Rolls the rug up around her like a cocoon. The cigarette burns my fingers. I let go of it. Stand frozen in the doorway. Douglas is standing in front of me – his mouth is moving without sound. He slaps me. "Help me carry her." I move. Lift. Samantha is heavy. The guard opens the back door of the Land Rover. "Get in," Douglas says. I get in. He stands, talking to the guard. Gets in behind the wheel. "Where are you staying?" he asks.

"Valhalla," I say. He drives. Samantha is lying behind us, wrapped in a rug and a sheet, dead.

We arrive. They let us through the gate – we're white. "Which number?" he asks. The sound of his voice is very distant.

"Thirty-eight," I say.

Douglas stops out front.

"Get your things," he says. I go inside. Tell the Norwegians I've got a lift to Moshi. Throw my things into my bag, go out, get in the car. We drive. Out of town. "Once we've buried her, I will take you to Morogoro. You can get a bus to Moshi from there. If anyone asks you, you just tell them . . . Just tell them the truth," he says. What is the truth? The car leaves the road and drives into the bush, stops. Dogs barks in the distance. We dig a hole using shovels from the back of the Land Rover. "It has to be deeper, otherwise the dogs will get to her," Samantha's dad says. Doesn't he realize they've already got her? We put her down. I pray to God as we put earth over her. God doesn't listen. Afterwards we stand still by the filled grave. "I promise you I will kill him, Samantha," Douglas mutters.

We're driving. All the way I stare out of the window into the darkness.

The next morning we reach Morogoro. Douglas steers the car along potholed roads and to the front of a dirty brick building, Paradise Guesthouse. He brakes and lets the engine run idle. I nod curtly, grab the pack of Winston cigarettes from the dashboard and get out. He drives off. The door into reception is closed, so I sit down in an easy chair on the porch. Smoke cigarettes. Not long after the Portuguese owner shows up. She seems worn out. A refugee from the Angolan War of Independence. Gives me a key. I find the room in the wing at the back. It's got a concrete floor, a ceiling made of cardboard sheets painted white and bare, dirty yellow walls. The mosquito netting in front of the windows is full of holes, dust. The windowsills are dirty, and the same goes for the bars and the mouldering curtains. The foam mattress has collapsed in the middle. I can feel every slat of the bed against my back. An empty socket hangs from a bit of wire from the ceiling. Another empty socket sticks out from the wall above the bed. I lie on my bed and stare at the ceiling. Get up and go to the bathroom, where water drips from the joints in the drainpipe from the sink. The towel is frayed and has a nondescript colour, but it smells faintly of detergent. Finally the shadows start to get long. I find an Indian restaurant. Have something to eat. Drink beer and Konyagi. Go back to Paradise Guesthouse.

I've had enough to drink to knock me out. I sit up in the chair and smoke a Sportsman – the fortieth today . . . Stub it out in a black chipped china ashtray which advertises Black & White Scottish whisky. Open another pack in the dark. Force myself to smoke another and another. Lie down again. I sweat with the sheet covering me and am cold when I take it off.

The next morning I scale the mountain.

The road deteriorates the higher I get. At one point it splits into two – the one to the right goes towards the Telegraph House close to the top. I take the left one towards Morningside. The road is coming apart, and by the end it's nothing more than a footpath. Jarno told me that only ten years ago you could go all the way in a 4x4. The hillside almost hides the view as I work my way towards the top of the ravine that leads you on the final stretch to Morningside. And as I step around a corner, I find the building in front of me. A brick house on a tableland surrounded by greenery. On the knoll above I can see a clump of enormous cypresses standing oddly detached and majestic against the sky. I reach the building from 1911. It's still standing, but it does seem a bit more dilapidated than when I was last here.

I sit for a while, feeling sick inside. Then I take the steep climb up to the tall cypresses. From there I can see to the edge of the rainforest, which has moved a bit further off than last time. The ground is tilled to the last inch. I would like to stand at the fringes, in the cool darkness amidst the heavy greenery. I start making my way over. A footpath winds its way here and there, across a small brook which runs from the rainforest and down past Morningside. There are fields of sweetcorn and savoy cabbage aplenty.

I can't see anyone about, until I catch sight of a young man who waves down at me from the edge of the forest above me. "*Njoo*," he calls. "*Karibu sana*." He wants me to come. I am very welcome. He stands above the field and the brook next to a low hut made from sticks, with a roof made from palm leaves. A short distance away there's a small hut – his bog. I clamber on my hands and feet across the boundary between the field and the rainforest.

"*Mambo. Vipi?*" I ask in street Swahili – hi, how are you?

"*Poa*," he says smiling, holding out his hand so I can slap the palm of his hand – he's well. We grin at each other.

"Is that your *shamba*?" I ask.

"Yes," he says, gesturing with his arm, describing the extent of his land – an acre or so. "I've cleared the land myself, so I can grow things. Cabbage, sweetcorn, beans, tomatoes, carrots. Soon I will grow passion fruit," he says. I compliment him on his fields. They look good even though they're illegal. He has cleared a patch of rainforest that's designated as a natural amenity. What is he supposed to do? The rest of the land is taken by other people. He's trying to make a living.

"Come and sit in the shade," he says. "Rest a while." At the gable end of the house he has extended the roof so it casts shade over a small patio with two narrow, short wooden benches and a little table made of roughly cut boards. I have to bend to get into my seat. He smiles and sits down. Right inside the hut's doorway there is a small fireplace with an aluminium boiler so he can prepare corn porridge or beans. The hut itself has a plank bed with a layer of dried grass and a few blankets. The walls have been insulated with fodder sacks to keep the cold and the wind and the dew out. It gets cold up here at night. I tell him my name, where I am from and ask him his name.

"Johnny Costa Winston," he says. I smile, repeat his name. Cool. I get a pen out of my pocket and my pack of Sportsmans – write his name on it and hold it over, so he can read.

"Like this?" I ask.

"Yes," he says. I didn't want to ask him to write it – if he didn't know how, it would embarrass him.

"Would you like a cigarette?" I ask. He nods. I root in my pockets. Have I got more? Yes. The scrunched-up pack of Winstons I took from the car before I got out. "Winston," I say. We laugh, slap hands. I offer him one – he becomes solemn.

"United States," he says and smokes with a rapt look on his face. "*Safi kabisa.*" Sooo good. I get out my last pack of peanuts, offer him some – it's all I've got.

I tell him I am on holiday from my school in Europe and am going to visit my dad who works for *ushirika* – the co-op. "Do you live here?" I ask.

"When I work on the mountain, I sleep here. Otherwise I live in the village a bit further down the mountain."

Johnny Costa Winston's wife is called Jane and is twenty-four. He himself is twenty-five. Right now she's in town, selling vegetables. Their son is called France and is five years old. Sometimes Winston visits them in the village, sometimes she comes up to the little hut. The water in the stream on his land is good for drinking, for washing, for watering. He makes a little bit of charcoal for his own family.

"Isn't that illegal?" I ask.

"Yes," he says, laughing out loud. I look around and catch sight of the small *bhangi* plants that grow along the walls of the hut.

"What are those?" I ask, pointing. We laugh.

"Would you like some?" he asks.

"No, thanks. Not right now," I say. "They're quite small, your plants."

"Yes," Winston says.

"Have you got more?"

"They're all over," Winston says with a sweeping gesture, and we slap hands again.

"Do you smoke a pipe?" I ask.

"No, I roll," Winston says and makes a rolling motion with his fingers, looking questioningly at me.

"In a newspaper?" I ask.

"No," Winston says and gives me an odd look. "*Kitabu,*" he says. Book.

He digs a small plastic bag out of the side pocket of his worn combat trousers. He is going to show me the finest possession he has. Along with the plastic bag comes a small book in a black binder. His rolling paper – it's got pages missing.

"You *bwana*," I say, laughing. "You're smoking God's book – am I right?" The New Testament. He slaps his thighs.

"That's absolutely right," he says and hands me the book. The Gospel of Matthew has already gone up in smoke. Now he's working his way through Mark.

"It's a good book to be smoking," I say.

"Yes," he says. "The paper is better than newspaper."

That night I sit down outside Paradise Guesthouse and smoke Winston's spliff – rolled in the Gospels. Afterwards I lie on the bed and listen to the night. I can hear Samantha underground; the sound of her flesh disintegrating.

"You look pale," Katriina says. "Are you ill?"

"I might have caught malaria," I lie. That'll have to explain my appearance – I look like a chemo patient.

"Have you seen Marcus?" she asks – slightly nervously, I think.

"No, I'm just not up for it right now. I'll wait a little," I say.

"Oh, alright. I think he's doing not too badly," she says. "I don't know where to put you," Katriina says. "I mean, the sitting room isn't that great when you sleep in later than the girls." I'm sitting on the sofa with a Coke. Solja is at school, swimming, because the pool remains open even though the holidays have started. Rebekka is with a friend. It's a typical, poorly thought-out colonial house – two bedrooms; the girls have the one, Katriina's got the other.

"What about the servants' quarters?" I ask. That would suit me just fine – I don't feel like talking to anyone.

"Yes, that's no problem at all. Issa is staying in one room, but we just use the other for storage. I'm sure the things could be put in the garage instead." Issa is their cook now; Juliaz got the boot when Dad shacked up with Katriina.

"Is there a bed?" I ask. Because I'm exhausted.

"No," Katriina says. "But we've got a spare mattress." She sounds doubtful – so am I. A mattress on the floor – cockroaches, maybe even rats, spiders.

"I'll see if I can work something out," I say. Go to the servants' quarters at the end of the garden and take a look. There are two large aluminium crates from Ostermann on the floor. They're about thigh-high. The lid is big enough to support the width of the mattress but not the length. I find a few boards in the garage that can be used to bridge the gap between the two crates – I tape the boards in place to stop them shifting on the smooth aluminium. It feels good. I mean, not . . . Samantha is everywhere. I communicate with the dead. She's not happy. I'm not happy either.

One of the Ostermann crates is heavy and locked. I find a jemmy and take the padlock off. Inside is a lot of papers about F.I.T.I. and Imara Furniture Factory, TanScan, West Kilimanjaro, the portable sawmills; Jonas' things. I lift a stack of papers – underneath is a plastic box, which I open. A revolver. Marcus once told me Jonas had a gun. There's a box of bullets as well. I take the weapon out carefully. It's got faint traces of rust. I open the cylinder. It's not loaded. I put it back in the crate with the papers on top. Then I finish my bed. Lie down on it and stare at the ceiling. Now what? Dad will arrive from Shinyanga in a few days. He works with the cotton union S.H.I.R.E.C.U. up there, but is hoping to get work in Moshi again, because it's so much lovelier here and Katriina would rather not move and let Solja board at the school, even though she is fourteen years old. I assume D.A.N.I.D.A. has been paying her school fees since Dad married Katriina,

What am I to do? Maybe we're going on safari once the old man gets here – I don't know. I'm not up to it.

I go to bed early. I masturbate; think about Marianne – it does nothing for me. Sif. Irene. Shakila. Nothing happens. I try not to, but in the end I do think about her – the dead one. It's terrible. It works. I will kill Victor.

Marcus

AFRICA VICTORIOUS
Is Christian coming or isn't he? I drive to Katriina and *bwana* Knudsen's house several times and am told: "No, he is in Dar – we don't know when he's coming." Then one day Katriina comes in her Nissan Patrol right to my ghetto and says:

"Christian is here." I crane my neck to see if he's in the car. Katriina shakes her head. "I don't know where he is," she says. "Maybe . . . I think he might be ill."

"Ill?" I say. "Is it malaria?"

"No – he's tired and . . . I don't know. Can you come round?"

"Yes," I say. "Is he there now?"

"No," Katriina says. "I don't know where he is."

"I'll come tonight," I say. Katriina drives off. Ill? But when I arrive, he isn't there. No-one knows where he is.

"Perhaps he's at the club playing golf," Solja says.

"It's dark," I say.

"He might be hanging out at a bar."

I drive my motorbike towards Moshi Club in the dark, slowly, keeping an eye on the roadside where the cowherds drive their cattle to the abattoir in Pasua. And there he is, like a goat in the night.

"Christian," I call and drive up in front of him and turn off my engine. "Welcome back. I've been looking for you."

"Hi, Marcus," he says and gives me an oddly tired smile.

"How are you?" I ask. He gives me a slanted look, shrugs, looks away.

"Let's go to Uhuru Hotel and get a fizzy drink," he says. I kick-start the engine. He gets on the back, and I can smell *bhangi* from his clothes. He dances an odd sort of dance. He has a smouldering anger covered by a completely empty sort of sadness – it's a very white feeling, and I don't know how to speak to it. So I just tell him things – everything that's happened. It's late, and Uhuru Hotel is closing.

"What should we do now?" I ask.

"I don't know," Christian says.

"We could go down to my new ghetto – there's a bar not far away. And Claire is at her mother's with our daughter."

"Alright," Christian says. "I just need to grab a jumper from the house." We go there.

I turn off the engine, because I'd like to go inside. Has Christian brought good things from Denmark? He goes towards the servants' quarters, turns around once we're halfway there and grins at me:

"Yes, now I live in a ghetto, just like you," he says.

"You live in there?"

464

"Yes," he says. I follow him. He's living in one room, like a gardener, with a mattress on crates.

"Don't you have any music?" I ask.

"It's in the house." Yes, of course, otherwise it would get stolen. Christian grabs a jumper, puts the padlock back on the door. "Let's go," he says.

"Shouldn't you tell Katriina where you are?"

"I'm damned if I know," Christian says and tells the guard: "*Mimi nitakaa nyumbani ya Marcus mpaka kesho*" – that he's staying with me until tomorrow. We drive to my house. I pull the motorbike into the sitting room and lock it. We go to the small bar round the corner from my house. At a table are four *mabwana makubwa* – otherwise the place is empty.

"Have you got any Zaire Rock?" Christian asks at the bar. The barmaid says she doesn't. Christian orders drinks and sits down. "I've got quite good at playing the drums," he says. "I'd like to play in a band here."

"In Moshi?" I ask. "We only have live music at church, but even that is rare."

"At the hotels in Arusha," Christian says. The girl brings our beer and Konyagi.

"Have you been ill?" I ask, because Christian isn't looking well.

"No, I'm just not feeling . . . I'm tired," he says. I ask why and he tells me about Denmark – he doesn't like it.

"Did you get some girls?"

"Yes, I had one. She talked a lot about coming to Africa, but . . . I don't know."

"But you still have one year of school left?"

"I'm sick of school," he says. "But fuck that. Let's get some more to drink . . ." And Christian slips into Swedish: "*Och så åke hem til dig och röka en liten ting*," – and then go back to yours and smoke a wee thing. He calls to the waitress for more beer, more Konyaki.

"Natty Dread Rides Again," I say, because it's great that he's finally come and that we're seeing each other after more than a year, despite all life's turbulence.

WARTIME MEMORIES
On the Saturday we go to the big kiosk in the middle of the National Housing township – this place also works as a bar at night, and they play nice Zaire Rock.

"Is Liberty still the best disco in town?" Christian asks.

"No, that would be Moshi Hotel," I say.

"Let's go down and check it out," Christian says.

"O.K.," I say, even though the city centre isn't nice.

"It's great to be back," he says. But I don't like it anymore. Today the girls are half naked. The *malaya* are now as plentiful as the grass on the plain. Everyone out on the town – something's not right with them. We should go out to the countryside, be with people at an old-fashioned *ngoma*. The party should be like a juice. Feeling the people. Today that juice is rotten. The girls are dogs – they're not human. If you're a man looking for her caresses, when you try to put on your raincoat to keep your seed under control she might even rip it, because when you're naked with lust she's the catcher and you're the fly. Rhema … a flycatcher. Eehhh – I have to drink strong *gongo* tonight to flush my twofold baby problems out of my head.

The night also sees another confrontation with my failure. Who do I see at Moshi Hotel? Nechi. My former classmate, whose family stole from my kiosk when it was placed on their land across from the Police Academy. Nechi, who brought me Josephina's special meals while I lay dying at K.C.M.C. Nechi, whose family's corruption got him a scholarship at a Canadian school for journalism. Now he is back in a big way.

"I am a *Daily News* correspondent in the Kilimanjaro region," he says. His clothes are good, his potbelly growing, the girls flock around him – he is very quick and smooth in the art of verbal deception. Now party bosses will grease his fist to make him write like a blind man, and his life will be the lushest of treats.

"See you later, Marcus," he says quickly and leaves me in my dump. I could have gone to Europe and built a solid foundation. But my Swedish sponsors gave me empty promises with a cloven tongue. Now I am left to pin my hopes on a white boy.

Christian

"I hate it," I tell my dad. "I'm not going back."

"Christian," he sighs, "just finish it, then you can come back down here – travel for a year; I'll pay for the ticket – I promise. But getting started on an education is important."

"But I don't know what I want to do," I say.

"It doesn't matter much what education you get, as long as you get one. You can always use it for something later," Dad says.

"Do you even hear what I'm saying?" I say. "I hate it there. I hate living at Aunt Lene's. School sucks. Aalborg is a load of old bollocks. I hate it."

"What do you want me to do about it?" he says. "Maybe you should apply for an apprenticeship?"

"As what?" I ask.

"What would you like?"

"I don't bloody know, do I?"

"You were the one who got yourself kicked out of I.S.M.," he says.

"Yes, because you put me in prison as a boarder, even though you lived here," I say.

"Let me remind you of the historical facts," Dad says. "Whenever I was away with work, you went to such excesses at school that they forced me to make you a boarder – either that or you were out on your ear."

"Yes, and then I became a boarder and was out on my ear."

"That was your own doing," he says.

"Not to my mind it wasn't," I say.

"You're nineteen years old, Christian. If you want to behave like a baby, be my guest. But I really can't be bothered to listen to it." He gets up and goes into the house.

During dinner we try to be civilized.

"How about Jarno?" Dad asks. "What's he doing in Finland?"

"Armed forces," I say. "They have obligatory national service."

"How does he like it?" Dad asks.

"He's not thrilled."

"But you're exempt from military service, aren't you?" Dad asks.

"As if I didn't bloody well tell you. Don't you even remember?"

"Yes, yes," he says, chewing his food. Goes back for seconds. We eat in silence for a while, then he speaks again: "Did you see Samantha in Dar?" I swallow my spit – make up a hurried lie:

"No," I say. "She's gone back to England."

I will kill Victor.

467

Marcus

GREAT ATTRACTION

Christian's been on safari with his dad, Katriina and the girls. When they return, they tell me Christian is in Arusha. But after a while Phantom tells me one day that he's seen the white boy in town, so I drive over to *bwana* Knudsen's house. Christian is sitting outside.

"Where is your music?" I ask.

"In the sitting room," Christian says. No-one else is in the house. I go straight into the sitting room – *eeehhhh*, L.P.s and cassettes like you wouldn't believe; many of them, exciting, new, vibrant.

"With this music and just a record player and a good tape recorder you could start the best recording shop in town. Everyone would flock to it, because this music – it's never been heard in Moshi before."

"Really?" Christian says. And I explain it to him – I paint a glowing picture, money rolling into our pockets.

"You could rent a shop in town and put just one loudspeaker out on the street – it would be a great attraction." I don't mention the money for the shop. The seed must be put into the ground – now I will have to see if Christian can believe the idea is amazing.

"Hmmm," Christian says.

"If you come down once you've finished school, we could create a good business which could earn us both a living. If you leave the music behind, I can even make money for the two of us while you finish school. Then I will have got money together for the start-up of a real disco business when you get back. Then all we need is some good decks."

"Hmmm," Christian says. "What sort of decks do you need for playing at local discos?" I explain it to him.

"And Claire's sister Patricia has told me that their church has a good guitarist who knows how to play in the Zaire style," I say.

The day before he flies back, his music lands in my ghetto.

"You can't lend the records to anyone. They must stay here – in your house," he says. "No-one but you can touch them."

"Yes," I say.

HOLOCAUST

Early morning and I am up, pouring water into buckets and taking them to the chicken shed in the back garden. The house girl could do it, but does she understand how to ensure the chicken's wellbeing? No. There have been problems with upset stomachs and slow growth, so Marcus the Chicken Farmer must be alert. And what meets the farmer's eye when he opens the door. Holocaust. Chickens in heaps, still, limp – death and destruction – only the faintest twitch of nerves here and there. No, no, no, no, no. Straight from my eyes, a great flood – tsk, I can't take any more problems right now. Must we starve? I go towards the back door of the house and can hear the house girl clattering in the kitchen.

"*Toka!* – *nenda kulala*," I say in an ugly voice before opening the door. She mustn't see me as a whining woman. The house girl hurries away, but Claire has heard the shouting and comes into the kitchen with our baby on her arm.

"What's wrong?" she whispers and holds my head in her hands.

"It's no good. I can't do it anymore."

"What happened?" she asks.

"The chickens – they are dead."

"All of them?"

I nod.

"*Pole*," she says, stroking my old head. She doesn't ask what we're going to do. That's my problem – I am the man. It's time to think. Hard thoughts. That's the African life – before a stone can become a sculpture, it must be beaten many times.

"Get me cigarettes," I say. The house girl fetches them. "Bring me coffee." She brings me coffee. "I need an omelette." She makes me an omelette, which I eat a bit of, and coffee with lots of sugar, and a cigarette follows the first one, and then one more.

There are no answers. The recording shop has done well on Christian's new music. Everyone I know has bought cassettes from me – even Faizal the D.J., although that may be unfortunate next year when Christian comes down to learn that Faizal has the good new music. My hope is that Marcus & Christian Ltd will be the new disco kings in town. Now the recording shop's flow of customers has run dry, because I'm totally invisible in my house on Uru Road.

Claire makes the house girl man the kiosk, even though she can barely count. Claire comes in and pours me another cup of coffee, putting sugar in it, stirring it in.

"I've had a thought," she says, sitting down.

"*Eeehhhh*," I say. No-one must hear us. It's the man who must think. If the woman starts thinking, then what need is there for a man?

"Do you want to hear it?" Claire asks. I look at her. She looks unhappy – she fears for our future.

"Yes," I say.

"If you were to rent a small shop in town, you could run the recording shop there, and I could sell clothes out the front."

"Then who would mind the baby?" I ask.

"My mother and sister – they could help me. It could be second-hand clothes from the market in Kiborloni. My mother could wash and repair them. The wealthy women from the city centre don't want to be seen in Kiborloni. And once we've made a profit, we could get in nice clothes from the dressmakers in Zanzibar," Claire says.

"Going to Zanzibar is expensive," I say.

"I could take the bus to Dar es Salaam and sail over cheaply and buy the expensive dresses. And bags and some jewellery and scarves – all of it at good prices. If we can get a small shop, I could sell things in town."

"How would we get such a shop?" I ask, sighing. But Claire has already found it, on Rengua Road, right between Stereo Bar and ABC Theatre. There's even a small square out in front. You can have tables and chairs and a fridge full of fizzy drinks that people can buy and if you have a loudspeaker out in front you can play all the most enticing music to make people order cassettes of music – lots of business then.

I don't ask her how we will finance the rent for the shop. That's not her problem. And it's true that Claire could do it – she knows how to strike a deal and her clothes have always been very *chiki-chiki*.

And now I have to do something I don't want to. I get up, go into my room, open the petrol tank of the motorbike, shake it. Yes, there's a little bit left. I pull it out of the bedroom and outside, put on my sunglasses and drive to Zahra's restaurant – very run-down, but good Indian food. Next to it is a small printer's shop, owned by the fat son of Musa Engineer. I just sit outside with a cup of coffee and a cigarette, because Musa's son always asks me when he sees me. Now he comes out:

"How much do you want for that motorbike of yours, Marcus?" he asks. I name my price.

"Really?" he says. "That's far too much."

"No, that's the right price. You can have it if you've got the money for me in an hour." He goes right into the shop and comes out with the money. We sign the paperwork. I walk away. Done with wheels. A goat on the street. I walk to National Housing Commission office that deals with the city centre. The small shop next to Stereo Bar is still empty. Right away I rent it and go up to examine conditions. Very dirty, but there's a nice bit of security in the shape of a sturdy door and a rolling grille you can lock at night. A lick of paint, and it'll be fine. Slowly I walk back on my feet to give Claire the news. As soon as she sees me walking on my feet, she gets nervous.

"What happened to the motorbike?" she asks.

"I sold it and rented the shop," I say.

Claire is very careful how she treats me that day.

Christian

It's just not possible. I simply can't get out of bed and over to Hasseris Gymnasium. I've got no money. I discover that I can nick cognac from the corner shop. Hasseris – theft is so alien to them that they don't pay any attention. I put on my large coat, stick a bottle in each of the inside pockets. Then I can spend my money on cigarettes instead. I pull a sickie. I get a letter. The school demands a doctor's letter.

Anders pops round.

"What's going on, Christian?" he asks.

"I can't be arsed anymore," I say.

"They'll give you the boot," he says.

"Yes," I say. And sure enough a week later a letter arrives telling me to come to a meeting with the Headmaster. I go down to social services. Take a number. Sit down on a chair. Look at the other losers, look down at the lino floor. Wait. A lady comes out of a door, calls: "Christian Knudsen?" I go in.

"Hello," I say. We sit down. I tell it like it is. No more H.F., no job, no money. "I'm going to have to go on the dole."

"But shouldn't you be getting an education?" she asks.

"No," I answer. "I'm useless at the whole school thing."

"What about your parents – can't they help you?"

"My parents?" I ask.

"Yes?"

"Erm, I'm not in touch with my mum. She works for Médecins sans Frontières in Geneva. If you want to call her, go ahead." I gesture toward the phone on the lady's desk.

"What's her number?" the social worker asks.

"I haven't got it," I say. "You'll have to ask directory enquiries." She stares at me.

"How about your dad, then?" she asks.

"He lives in Shinyanga," I say.

"Where?"

"Shinyanga in Tanzania."

"What does he do?"

"Works for D.A.N.I.D.A. – the Foreign Office. Aid."

"How does he feel about you leaving school?" she asks.

"I don't know," I say.

"But . . ." she says, looking bewildered.

"I can't afford to call him," I say. "I haven't got a phone. Plus it's almost impossible to get through – your best shot is in the middle of the night, but that just ticks him off. But if you'd like his number, you're welcome to try," I say.

"Couldn't you write to him?"

"I could, but it might take the letter weeks to get there, if it ever does."

"But . . . aren't you in touch at all?" the lady asks.

"Listen . . . why do you think I'm here, while he is in Africa, and my mum is in Geneva? It's probably because they don't really care a whole fucking lot, don't you think?"

"And you have no income at all?" she asks.

"No," I say.

The social worker puts some papers in front of me – hands me a pen. I sign a statement in which I solemnly declare to have no other income. They give me money. I go up to the Job Centre and am listed with them: unemployed. They give out a card which I must go in to have stamped every two weeks. Alright then. One week later I get the letter from school telling me that unless I start showing up, I am no longer a student.

*

Anders has got us some more moonlighting – insulation with glass wool again – splinters in my fingers.

"There's a party at the school on Friday," he says. "Do you want to come?"

"I'd like to steal the two big loudspeakers and the mixing desk with the amplifier in the music room," I say.

"You would?" Anders says. "You pop them through the window – easy-peasy."

"Yes," I say. "But I need someone to stand on the other side and grab them. And someone to help me carry them off. And I'm not sure about the alarm either," I say.

"How would you get into the music room?" Anders asks, grinning. He wants to be sure I've got a handle on it. I don't.

"Don't you think it'll be unlocked when there's a party? They'll be using the stereo from the room, won't they?" I say.

"No," Anders says. "But I've got a master key."

"You do?"

"I nicked one from the caretaker's station."

"Alright." I nod. He's crafty. "Then what about the alarm – those metal wires over the windows?"

"They disconnect it for parties," Anders says. "If they didn't, it would go off all the time. With that many students larking about, opening doors that are meant to be closed – it's not going to be a problem."

"But would you help me?" I ask. "Take the stuff outside the window."

"Yes, of course. Definitely. And you'll be the one outside. You're too suspect. They haven't seen you for weeks, and suddenly you're strolling round the halls at a school party. I'll hand you the stuff and help you get it out of there."

"Cool, Anders," I say. "I really appreciate that."

"But," he says.

"But what?"

"What do you need it for? Are you going to set up a rehearsal space or what?"

"I'm going to Tanzania," I say.

"Seriously?"

"Yes." I tell him my plan. A recording shop and disco with Marcus in Moshi.

"Would you be able to live on that?" Anders asks.

"Yes. Rent a small house, mind my own business – the good life."

"I'll come visit," Anders says and lets me into his plan. I mustn't sign off at social services. You're only called down for an interview every three months. You have to stop by the Job Centre every two weeks, but Anders could do that in my name. If I were to leave right after a meeting with social services, I could claim dole for three months, while I was gone. Anders could take it out on my behalf, keep a third for himself and exchange the rest for travellers' cheques and send it to me in Moshi.

"What do you need your third for?" I ask.

"Save it for my plane ticket," Anders says.

"If you do this," I say, "I will pay all your expenses while you're there – that's no problem."

"Deal," Anders says.

It all works out smoothly. Anders lifts the things to the windowsill – I'm outside receiving them. Carry the mixer, a tape recorder, a turntable and the two loudspeakers to a bush at the very back of the school grounds. Wait until four-thirty and then set to work – bike over, lift the mixing desk up onto my baggage carrier, strap it in place and pull my bike home. It shakes under the weight. Push the mixer in under my bed. Four more trips to take home the rest. Now I've got the gear. All I need is to get it to Tanzania.

Rock Café in Jomfru Ane Gade. I've lost Anders. I'm pretty well plastered and don't want to be here. Go outside. The night is cold. Hard, white faces. Made-up with empty eyes, sudden movements. Hunting for something. What? I slip between them, up the pedestrian street. Don't feel like going to sleep. Cross Nytorv and go down Algade, which is empty. I've never been there – Gøglerbåden. I'll have a single beer, see the place, then go home. The room is dark, crowded, warm. Fat, pale men. A large, black bar *mama*. A few black girls at the tables; there's a small stage – empty. At the end of the bar a girl with her back turned to me is practically rubbing herself against a white man with a beer gut. The girl's shorts are so tiny her arse seems about to bust the seams. I sit down on a barstool and order a beer in Swahili. The bar *mama* laughs. She asks where I learned the language. I explain. She herself is from Entebbe in Uganda, married to the owner of the bar.

"*Njoo*," the bar *mama* calls to the girl at the end of the bar – come.

"Christian," the girl says. "Mr Africafé." I turn on the barstool. Sheila from the bus station. Her eyes swim a bit, she raises her arms above her head, walks towards me with swaying movements, starts dancing in front of me, right between my legs, so that her thighs are rubbing up against mine, her breasts rubbing against my jumper.

"What do you want to do tonight, baby?" she asks in Swahili.

"I want to drink my beer," I say.

"Is that all you want to do?" she asks, turning around so that her pert arse rubs against my crotch. She looks at me over her shoulder while the ball bearings in her hips rotate. What happens, happens. Another black girl has got up on the small stage and is writhing – taking off bits of clothing. Sheila turns to face me again. I look at her purple lips, her dark cleavage, look into her eyes – big, black almonds.

"Would you like a beer?" I ask. Now she's got her hands on my knees, my thighs.

"I only drink champagne," she says, giving me a saucy smile – mocking me, I think. "Shall we have champagne tonight, Mr Africafé?" she asks. I want to fuck her. I can't afford champagne. She lets her hand slide up my thigh, up to my crotch. "Mmmm," she says when she feels how hard I am. She smiles lazily at me, massages me with her hand through the fabric, leaning forwards towards me. Speaks in English: "Do you want to fuck me?" Is that a question?

"I'm sorry, but I can't," I say.

"Haven't you got any money?" she asks.

"No," I say.

"Money is important," she says.

Marcus

UHURU'S PRISON

My brother's dirty wife is sitting in our living room like a weeping angel with her young child. Claire has served tea.

"What's going on?" I ask.

"Your brother is in prison," Claire says and pulls me into the kitchen. "Your brother came home from Dar es Salaam and found her in bed with another man," she whispers. "And your brother beat that man, hard. Slammed his head against the floor, many times. So now that man is dead, and your brother is in prison in Rombo."

"What is it you want?" I ask my sister-in-law, and at the same time I think that I too would like to pump her now my brother is out of the way. It's lucky that Claire is here to save me from all the diseases that dirty woman is tempting me with.

"I need money for the palm greasing, so he can get out of the tough prison in Rombo and be sent to Karanga instead."

"It doesn't matter," I say. "Your husband may as well die in Rombo as in Karanga."

"Marcus!" Claire says.

"You have no heart," my sister-in-law says.

"Yes, like you. But I'm neither a killer nor a whore."

"*Marcus!*" Claire says.

"Why must we pay? We didn't pump her," I say.

"She is the mother of your brother's child," Claire says. I point at the baby:

"Do you really think that's my brother's daughter? When every dog in Holili has lain with the bitch he takes for a wife?"

"I don't know," Claire says, looking down.

I don't go to the container bar not far from our house, because my tab is already too long. I go up to the big bar in the Co-operative College area. And I know that Claire is giving the whore money so she can go back to the village and live out her life in shame.

Many hours later I come home to Claire. I look at the baby, who is waving her arms and legs in the air.

"Her name will be Rebekka," I say – my white daughter's name.

"Alright," Claire says. "That's a good Christian name." In Soweto I have another child – a little boy. Two children by two women. And number three in Finland with Tita. My *uhuru* after my accident has just become another kind of prison.

Christian

"Can Katriina pick my things up at the airport? – get them through customs?" I ask Dad for the second time across the crackling satellite connection from my aunt's sitting room in Hasseris to my dad's house in Shinyanga. Aunt Lene is out shopping this afternoon, so I'm taking advantage of their phone.

"Christian," he says, "please wait until this summer. Then I promise I will pay for the ticket."

"I've bought the ticket," I say. With money from the dole. I don't tell him that.

"But you will go back and finish that *H.F.*?" he says.

"I don't know," I mutter. The satellite starts chopping at his sentences – the ends disappear, there are dropouts, echo, delays, audio haze.

"... harder to start an education the longer you ... to regret ... a proper education ... that it's exactly the right ... use it for something else later."

"Is there anyone I can stay a few nights with in Dar?" I ask, because Aeroflot doesn't fly to Moshi, and I can't afford K.L.M.

"Ingemar," Dad says. He has to repeat the number three times before I've got it down. Ingemar, an old Swede whose family has gone back home. He lives out on Msani.

"Will you stop by?" I ask.

"... your mum ... be right ... act in that way when ..."

"I can't hear what you're saying," I tell him. "The satellite is fucked." His voice comes from far away through crackles and hums, chopped into bits.

"... don't belong in Tanzania ... Mick told ... that Samantha is dead ... is meaningless."

"Can Katriina pick up my things at the airport and get them through customs?" I ask him again.

"No," he says.

"Dad, I can't hear what you're saying anymore," I say into the phone. "I will stay in Dar for a week or so, and if you're not there, I'll see you in Moshi." I disconnect, exhale slowly, go to the basement and speed-smoke two cigarettes.

That night my aunt calls down to me:

"Marianne's on the phone from Cambridge." Of course Aunt Lene has already told her that I'm in, so there's no getting out of it, even though I'm not actually missing her. We went out last year, but it seems like ages ago. I go upstairs and pick up the phone in the open kitchen; Aunt Lene is there cooking – I can hardly ask her to get lost.

"Hi," I say.

"Hi, it's me," Marianne says. "How are you?"

"I'm alright," I say, turning my back on my aunt.

"Are you going down to Tanzania for Christmas?"

"Yes," I say. "That's the plan."

"I was really looking forward to spending some time with you," she says.

"I do have to go, you know."

"When will you be back?" she asks.

"I don't know."

"What do you mean?"

"That I don't know."

"But . . . what about school?"

"What about it?" I say. "I've quit." She doesn't say anything for a moment, then she says:

"I've thought about quitting here as well and going travelling instead. I've been looking into some U.N. camps in East Africa."

"I wouldn't know anything about those," I say.

"No, no, but then we could see each other. We could visit each other when we were both there," she says.

"I suppose," I say. I can feel my aunt looking at me.

"Are you . . . alright, Christian?" Marianne asks. It sets me off laughing.

"You know what? I think I am," I say. She's already got the address and phone number for Moshi from last summer. I just have to hope she doesn't come down in the end. "I don't know that your going is such a good idea," I say.

"What's happened?" she asks. "Are you seeing someone else?"

"No, I just don't know that it's such a good idea."

"I want to work for the U.N. – a refugee camp or an orphanage," Marianne says. "I don't think it'll kill you to get a visit from me." She adds a goodbye before hanging up. Afterwards she cries; I just know it – she's that white. There isn't a lot of Samantha in her. But then, perhaps I will have got a band up and running before she stops by. She's got a good voice, Marianne.

Later comes an even more strained conversation with my mum, who calls from Geneva and stresses that she is "so disappointed".

It turns out I can't afford to send the decks down by plane anyway – they're too heavy. I borrow my uncle's car and drive the stolen goods over to Anders' place. I can leave them there until I get money for the freight. I leave with a small stack of L.P.s and a few bits of gear: a used but good amplifier as well as the units for building a fair set of loudspeakers. Marcus has a tape recorder and a record player. At least we can play music.

Msasani peninsula in Dar es Salaam – where the wealthy people live. I leave Ingemar's house and go past Alison and Frans'. Through the hedge I can see that they have gone. The garden looks like a desert. Africans have moved in. Then I go over to Diana, who used to board with Samantha at school. They're so European – they have a gardener and everything. She is back from Canada, where she's studying, and of course her dad lives in a large villa on Msasani. Diana is the only person I know in Dar. Shakila is in Cuba, Jarno in Finland. Everyone's gone.

Sitting on the veranda with Diana while the house girl serves coffee and juice feels odd. We were never friends, but it's nice to see her.

"What about Sharif?" I ask. "Is he in Tanzania?"

"*Tsk*," Diana says. "He's become a complete fanatic."

"A fanatic?"

"Muslim. When he came back from Dubai, he had grown a mullah-beard and had started wearing Muslim get-up. When I met him, he wouldn't even shake hands."

"What do you mean?" I ask.

"He wouldn't touch a woman's hand – *my* hand."

At the hospital I meet Shakila's little brother, Valentine: "Is Shakila coming home for the holidays?"

"No, she's not coming home. She'll go to our mother in the U.S. for her holiday."

"And you?" I ask.

"I'm on my way to the States myself," Valentine says.

"Will they let you in?"

"I will put myself at Uncle Sam's disposal – the military. After five years I'll get automatic citizenship," Valentine says.

"By then you might be dead," I say.

"There's always a risk," Valentine says.

"Do you think Shakila will return to Tanzania after she gets her education?" I ask.

"No. Cuba is just for her basic training. I think she'll go to Chicago and live with our mother and specialize."

"Brain drain," I say.

"No," Valentine says. "Evolution."

Can I be bothered to search out Sharif when he won't shake hands with women? No. I take a nightbus to Moshi – the roads are appalling, and it's almost impossible to get new tyres, so they prefer to drive by night, because hot tarmac takes a toll on the road when the vehicles are overloaded, and they always are. The bus clatters into Moshi early in the morning. I take a taxi from the bus station. Drive up to the house, move into the servants' quarters. Solja and Rebekka have already been sent off to school and kindergarten. Katriina doesn't say very much to me.

"*Shikamoo mzee*," I say to old Issa – he has already put out some breakfast for me. I eat, sleep a few hours. Wake up perplexed. What's the next step? I just need to settle in before I speak with Marcus. I go inside the house, find the old man's golf clubs and slop over to Moshi Club. What should be my priority? Getting a band together? If Marianne comes down, she could sing in it; she'll get herself a job working with children or refugees – she'll get tired of it soon enough. Or should I play at small disco nights with my decks, while Marcus records copies of my L.P.s onto tapes. But Marcus also has Claire and the kid and the kiosk – maybe I should find someone else to help me.

"Have you brought sweets from Sweden?" Rebekka asks when she sees me.

"No," I say. When Solja comes home from school, she comes to the servants' quarters.

"There's a letter for you," she says, holding it out.

"When did it get here?" I ask. It's from Anders; my dole money changed into travellers' cheques after he's taken his cut – our scam is working.

"Have you got any Princes?" Solja asks.

"You can have a pack," I say and hand her the cigarettes. She's grown very beautiful. Solja tucks the pack into her front pocket and pulls her top out of the waistband to hide the bulge.

"Thanks," she says, turns and leaves. I'm on my own. I've got a bagful of L.P.s and cassettes as well as my Luxman amplifier and units for building loudspeakers. I've got my large decks ready to be sent down from Denmark. Time to see how the land lies.

Marcus

WALKING LIKE GOATS

My ruined flesh, all my scar tissue, itches like an anthill in my foot and ankle. But I walk all the way to Katriina's house, because Christian has come.

"Oh. I didn't hear the motorbike," Christian says.

"The motorbike is gone," I say.

"Has it been stolen?" Christian asks.

"No, I sold it."

"Why the hell did you do that?" Christian asks.

"To get money for food," I say.

"You could have borrowed some," he says.

"From whom?"

"Me."

"You weren't around," I say.

"Will we have to walk then, whenever we're going anywhere?" Christian asks.

"Like goats," I say.

"Solja says you've set up a recording shop," he says.

"Yes, right next to Stereo Bar."

"Do you leave my music there at night?" he asks.

"No, I take everything home with me every day," I lie – I did it for the first time today when Solja told me Christian had arrived. "Have you brought decks?"

"A good amplifier and some powerful loudspeakers – but the cases must be built first." He shows me the things and gives me a drawing. I have to arrange for a carpenter from Imara Furniture Factory to build the cases for the loudspeakers and an electronics man to fit the cables – and behind the cardboard of the loudspeakers the box must be filled with kapok like a sofa cushion.

"Yes," Christian says. And it's a good thing he's here, because the recording shop has ground to a halt. Every student with money to spare has already bought all the music I've got.

"When are you flying back?" I ask.

"Flying back?" Christian says.

"Back to Denmark?" I say.

"I'm staying here."

481

"But don't you have six months left of Danish school?"

"I've left school."

"So what will you do?" I ask.

"Live here. I think my Danish girlfriend might come down as well. She sings – I'd like to start a proper band," Christian says.

"But school's important," I say.

"School can bloody well wait," Christian says. My thought was that I would use the music and the decks while he was away. Make some money until next summer and at the same time Christian could perhaps get some decks that would be big enough to use at Liberty or Moshi Hotel.

"But if you put off school, you might never finish it," I say.

"You sound like my fucking dad," Christian says. I don't say anything. The white people can get anything when they want it – so they appreciate nothing. But now I begin to understand Christian's idea – he wants to put together a band that can play in Arusha with a white girl as the draw. He doesn't want to go to Denmark, but to stay in Tanzania and make money. Should I put a stop to his idea when it might also lift me up?

"You said you knew a guitarist?" Christian says.

"Yes."

"Could you set up a meeting with him?"

"Tomorrow," I say.

"Tomorrow . . ." Christian says. "I might have to go to Dar to meet with my dad. But let's go grab a beer," he says.

"Can't we wait until Katriina and the girls are back," I say, because I'd like to say hello to them.

"No, let's get going."

TANZANITE

We go to my local container bar. It's been set up in a large metal container of the sort they put on the ships that sail to Europe. A big metal hatch has been put in one side. The hatch can be opened, and you can look in and see how the container has been turned into a kiosk with all sorts of goods and a fridge. Outside there's a covered concrete decking – even during the rains you can sit there at night and be completely dry. I could make money from alcohol in my own kiosk, but Claire says harshly: "If you sell so much as one beer – I am done with

482

you." The sanctity of God. My kiosk is like a sweetshop for children, but I also attract the godly women who refuse to buy their flour and oil from Dickson, because he also makes a great living from the godless drink, and his customers make a racket at night.

Dickson is sitting outside. I introduce Christian, even though I don't want him talking to this man, who asks him right away:

"Are you interested in stones? Tanzanite? Or diamonds from Shinyanga? I can get them." Beers are served to us by the girl who runs the kiosk. She puts them on the table with an arrogant look – as if she's above it all. Her features are small and pretty, but her eyes are hard. And I see the white boy already being seized from two sides: into his ear comes the talk of precious stones, and for his eyes there is the girl with small firm breasts, narrow waist, strong thighs, fabulous round arse. Africa's witchcraft.

"Dickson was in the mines in Merelani," I say.

"Five years," Dickson says, nodding. "Down that fucking hole for five years, digging, digging, digging until I hit my seam. And five years isn't even that long."

"Were you in the mine itself?" Christian asks.

"Yes," Dickson says, nodding. "In the dark, deep underground. Dust everywhere, hardly any air. Ate corn porridge and beans – lived in the dark until I hit tanzanite – a big find."

"And then you quit?"

"Yes." Dickson nods, a sweep of his arm: the container with the kiosk and the bar, the big American pick-up. "Now I am a businessman."

"Have you got other businesses?" Christian asks.

"I've got two *matatu* on the Marangu–Moshi and Holili–Moshi routes."

"Then you're not going out there again – to the mines?" Christian asks.

"No, no. Five years! Enough is enough. You can die out there. It's hot down there – you sweat until your clothes are so wet they drip. You work at night, through the day. In the pit there is no night, no reason to stop, nothing else to do except sleep a few hours and continue. You're not there for fun, but to hit the big time. Then you can pump, drink and forget." Already Dickson's got his hook deep into my white boy.

"But then you hit a big seam, or what?" Christian asks – completely caught in the web of lies.

"*Eeehhh*, yes. Lots of money. The first six months was one long party. Every night – a party." Dickson stands up, grabbing his pump with his hand, lifting it with the fabric of his trousers. "Every day, *eeehhh*, a new girl. I pumped a hundred, maybe more."

"Not girls – *malaya*," I say.

"*Tsk*. Not *malaya*," Dickson says, shaking his head. "Young girls; big arses, big thighs, small *titi* – very *chiki-chiki*." Dickson dances a little on the spot, sits down again. "Now I've got my bar, my *matatu*, my American car with a good stereo – two thousand watt," he says.

"*Tsk*, two thousand," I say.

"It says so on the loudspeakers," Dickson says. I don't want to correct him sharply. Now Christian too can hear the exaggeration; two thousand watt – Dickson's innards would turn to mush.

"We need to smoke a wee thing," Christian says in Swedish, so Dickson can't understand him. We finish our drinks and get up. Dickson says:

"But let me know if you want to buy stones – I can get them at a cheap rate." As we walk, I explain how things really are to Christian:

"Dickson lies. His father owns five mines and Dickson has never dug so much as a spadeful; all he's ever done is beat the poor guys who do the work for no pay – only for food and the hope of hitting the jackpot."

"No pay?"

"No – they don't get paid. They are fed, and if they hit a seam, they get a cut."

"That's not much," Christian says.

"It is if they hit one. It can set you up for life. You can buy several houses, new cars, everything."

"And pump."

"Yes, Dickson pumps everything. Even the girl who works the kiosk."

"But . . . she's not very old."

"No. Just a girl from the village. She lives in Dickson's house. He pumps her. If she doesn't want to, she can get lost – he'll find someone else for the job."

Luckily Claire and the baby are with her mother – they wanted to fix up some clothes tonight. We can smoke our stick without my woman nagging.

Christian

I sleep in. Marcus is sitting drinking coffee.

"Hi. You sleep alright?" I ask.

"Yes. Would you like a fried egg?" Marcus asks. He needs only call the house girl, and she'll start bustling about in the kitchen.

"No, thanks." I make myself a cup of Africafé and eat a peanut-butter sandwich. My head feels a bit heavy, but otherwise I feel good.

"Shall we go down and take a look at the shop?" Marcus asks.

"Yes. Just let me go to the loo first." Africafé does that to me every time – my stomach hasn't yet recalibrated to cope with the bacteria here. I ask whether they have toothbrushes at the kiosk. Marcus calls through the window, a lad comes running. Marcus sends him back for a toothbrush. The lad brings it over, hands it to me while his other hand holds onto the hand with the toothbrush – a traditional a way of showing that he isn't carrying a weapon.

Claire comes round with their daughter Rebekka hanging in a *kanga* on her back. We say hello. I ask about Rebekka.

"She's been ill, but now she's almost ten months old and growing well," Claire says, smiling. And then she speaks to Marcus. I listen. My Swahili is rusty, but gradually it awakens. Claire needs money to buy stock for the kiosk, which is placed right across from their flat on the ground level of the terraced house. She wants to shop for vegetable oil, rice, corn flour and fizzy drinks – all of them heavy, so they must be taken back in a taxi.

Marcus and I stroll down towards town. It's twelve-thirty, and the sun is cooking us alive. We walk towards Clock Tower roundabout, passing Coffee House and go up Rengua Road into the Christian part of town. Marcus' shop is called Roots Rock, and the name is painted in large red and black letters vertically down the shop front. The shop is squeezed in between Stereo Bar and one of the two cinemas in town – ABC Theatre – which has closed down. Across the street is the head office for the government-owned electricity company, Tanesco. Under the lean-to in front of the shop is a fridge with fizzy drinks, secured by a small padlock, and there is a fenced-in veranda with green plants in rusty twenty-litre vegetable-oil containers. The veranda is really a stretch of pavement that Marcus has appropriated; his neighbour – Stereo Bar – has done the same thing.

Marcus opens the padlock on the sliding grille and after that the double-door. He lifts out two small tables and two tatty sunshades to let us in. The room itself is a narrow sliver of space, some four by two and a half metres, with a small niche of two square metres to the left of the entrance, where a stack of plastic chairs for the veranda has been placed. Inside there's an old Pioneer stereo and a DUX record player, a couple of AIWA loudspeakers, a nice collection of L.P.s and a load of cassettes. On the walls I recognize a couple of Bob Marley posters I have sent him.

"Aren't you afraid to leave your things in the shop?" I ask. It would be a simple thing to cut off the padlock with a bolt cutter and clear the room, not to mention the fridge outside.

"Tanesco has guards that patrol all night – we stay friendly with them. That way nothing happens."

I turn on the stereo and put on an L.P. – the sound isn't actually bad, but the stereo can't play very loud at all, so it's no good for discos. Marcus has a small set of loudspeakers, which he puts out on the pavement when the shop is open. With my new L.P.s we could get the recording shop into full swing, if only we could get a decent tape recorder – perhaps I can borrow my dad's.

There are a few wooden racks and some boxes of clothes in the shop as well.

"What's that?" I ask.

"Claire's sister Patricia sells some clothes and fizzy drinks from the fridge," Marcus says.

"Where is she?" I ask.

"She runs on African time," Marcus says. But just then she arrives. Patricia is beautiful. She smiles at me, grins. Marcus ignores her, then says something to her very quickly which I don't manage to pick up. She starts lugging the wooden racks out under a large tree outside. Then she hangs up the clothes – long trousers, polo shirts, long-sleeved shirts, socks, boxers.

"Are the clothes second-hand?" I ask Marcus.

"They're from the European aid organizations. Claire's mother buys them at the market in Kiborloni and fixes them up and washes them. Then we sell them to the snobs in town."

"Isn't it supposed to be handed out for free?" I ask.

"Nothing in life is for free," Marcus says.

We go over to a *mama*'s to eat – it's in a former garage behind Tanesco. A yard with a tall lean-to over the oil-stained concrete decking.

We sit down at an empty table. The girl who serves us is small with a slightly square face – powerful jaw, a very pretty nose, almond-shaped eyes and a mouth whose lips are full without being too big – they are amazingly sharply drawn. She touches something inside me, the way her pert breasts jut out under her top, her powerful buttocks rippling under a long, tight, leopard-print nylon skirt – I think she's amazing; she looks at me. We order and are served our fish.

The girl comes to our table.

"Is the food satisfactory?" she asks.

"Yes, it's very nice," I say. She laughs.

"You speak Swahili," she says.

"This *mzungu* has been here before," Marcus says.

"I don't speak very much," I say.

"That's good," the girl says. Marcus looks at her:

"Which part of the fish is the tastiest?" he asks.

"It's all tasty," she says.

"No," Marcus says. "There has to be a part of the fish which tastes better than the other parts."

"No," she says, "because it's all the same fish."

"But what about you," Marcus says. "Isn't there a part of you that is just a little bit tastier than the rest?" She hesitates a little.

"Yes," she says.

"Which part is that then?" Marcus asks. She looks into the distance. Then she makes a vague gesture past her lap, as she smiles:

"This bit," she says, and then we giggle, all three of us, and I look at her and we start laughing and she turns, walks away – the way she walks so slowly is just amazing. She sits down and some time later she looks at me. She doesn't lower her eyes when I meet them – in the end I am the one to look away, but soon after I am looking at her again. We finish our food.

"Come," Marcus tells the girl. She comes over. "What's your name?" he asks.

"Rachel," she says. I pay her for the food and tip her nicely.

"Keep the change," I say.

"Thank you," she says.

"What do you think of my *mzungu*?" Marcus asks.

"I don't know," Rachel says.

"Oh, go on," Marcus says. She looks down and smiles. She raises her face:

"I like him," she says and looks into my eyes as she turns away. Then she walks away from the table.

I laugh.

"You're the limit," I tell Marcus.

"That girl is lovely," Marcus says. She reminds me of Irene, only more intense. And more beautiful than Shakila. The way she walks, stands, the parts of her body that . . . stick out.

I go down to Marcus' and have a cup of Africafé while he gets ready. It's a pretty, chubby little baby Claire's had. We go out into the night – we're going into town to check out the discos.

"We can get a taxi at the Y.M.C.A.," Marcus says.

"Why don't we just walk?" I say, because we're early, and I like walking around Moshi at night, because it's so dark even though you're in a city – almost no streetlights.

"It's not safe," Marcus says.

"Do people get mugged?"

"Sometimes."

"It happens all over the world. Has it got worse?"

"Yes," Marcus says. "If you walk in Majengo, they'll rape even a man at night. But arses are for things to come out of, not for sticking things into." Majengo is a suburb slightly to the east of Moshi which has grown to become almost a part of town – lots of brothels, open sewers and shoddy one-level housing fashioned from unburned brick.

"Yes, but we're not going into Majengo," I say. And we walk. It's a question of attitude with Marcus as well – we must get a taxi – I must pay for it. And for the entrance. We must drink beer in the bar – O.K. I am white – hence I have money. But I don't have all that much of it – enough to give me a brief respite. And everyone sees me as a walking wallet that must be opened or dragged to the altar. When I lived here, I was still just a boy, a passenger with my dad; everyone knew I didn't have money. We met as equals. Hung out because we wanted to. Now everyone wants a ride with the white man.

The soft powdered dust over sun-baked soil. The smell of dry plants. Velvety darkness against my skin. I like it.

"Did you know that Rogarth from T.P.C. is at Moshi Hotel?" Marcus asks.

"Rogarth? No. I've lost touch. I thought he was abroad, studying."

"When wealthy parents are destroyed, the child suffers."

"Did his parents go bust?"

"Yes," Marcus says and tells me that Rogarth's dad was imprisoned for corruption in 1985 – right after I was kicked out of school.

From some distance I can make out Rogarth's wiry figure leaning against the door on the Moshi Hotel's veranda. He is wearing black polished shoes, dark gabardine trousers and a tightfitting purple nylon shirt. His hands are in his pockets, one leg is bent at the knee so the sole of his shoe rests against the wall behind him, giving him a relaxed air. But once I come closer I can see that his clothes aren't all that new, his hair unkempt – not like he used to be. And the relaxed air about him doesn't fit with his face, the skin stretched tight across his skull – a face of hard shining surfaces.

"Rogarth," I say. He turns his head. Gives me a cool look that turns to surprise and then his face lights up.

"Christian!" He pushes off the wall, spreads his arms, smiles broadly, hugs me tight, pats my back. But I have enough time to catch the haunted look in his eyes.

"How are things?" I ask as he grabs onto a few of my fingers. Holds them while we speak – African style.

"Fine. Everything's fine," he says. "What are you doing here?"

"I've come down to see my dad. And Marcus. And now you."

"Good, good. For how long?"

"I don't know."

"We should get together some time," Rogarth says. "Maybe tomorrow." His eyes flick up the road; a car arrives, turning into one of the parking booths in front of the hotel.

"Of course," I say. "But how about you? What are you doing these days?"

"Are you coming in?" Rogarth asks and points behind him at Moshi Hotel. I nod. "Good," he says. "Then I'll see you there later. Right now I have to deal with a few things." He lets go of my hand and walks towards the man from the car – early forties, suit, short and fat. A businessman or a civil servant – corrupt.

"Let's go inside," Marcus says as I hear Rogarth greeting the man:

"*Shikamoo mzee*. Is there anything I can do for you tonight?"

I pay for the two of us at the top of the stairs. We stroll onto the veranda, which is filling up nicely. The doors to the right, leading into the bar and the dance floor, are open, the music is pulsating out – the sound is decent, not the scratchy loudspeakers you hear in the smaller bars. We find a table outside, and a waitress comes over, takes our order and brings the beer soon after. Rogarth comes up the stairs with the fat man. They go inside together.

"Rogarth is a dogsbody now," Marcus says. "He's been working for the big man for a little while. The man can't be seen to approach a *malaya*; he is a respectable man, happily married, serious. *Bwana mkubwa* pays the boy's entrance fee – buys him a few beers over the course of the evening. The boy is supposed to flit in and out and keep an eye on the big man's car – he doesn't trust the guards. And the boy must make sure the waiters jump to attention every time the big man feels thirsty. He will send the boy over to some girls. '*Bwana mkubwa* over here would like to buy you a beer.' If the answer is yes, we're in business. Maybe the boy will tell them which of them it is that has roused *bwana mkubwa*'s appetite, or maybe the girls will have to compete – maybe *bwana mkubwa* wants two *malaya* – who knows?

"Once *bwana mkubwa* has deliberated, the boy goes over to the chosen *malaya* and tells her that *bwana mkubwa* is leaving at such and such an hour. How would that suit the girl? That works well for me, she says if she is willing. All that remains is to settle the question of soap money."

"Soap money?" I say, as I see Rogarth call a waitress over with new beers for the two girls.

"When you talk about it, you call it soap money. The girl must have it as a token of gratitude, so that she can wash afterwards."

"And then they get out of here and pump," I say as I watch Rogarth speaking to the girl who shook her arse.

I wave the bar girl over, order three beers so that there is one ready for Rogarth. Marcus goes to the toilet. He will probably drink a Konyagi at the bar before he comes back, bought with his own money. At this table he expects me to pay for everything. Now I notice the girls watching me. I avoid eye contact – it's unpleasant to be watched like that.

"Christian," Rogarth says. He's standing next to me.

"Hey," I say, gesticulating. "Have a seat. I've bought you a beer." I take out my Danish cigarette pack from my pocket, tossing it onto the table in front of him. "Have a Prince."

"Ohhh, Prince," Rogarth says. "I remember those." He digs out a cigarette, sniffs it, lights it, inhales deeply. "Not like the Tanzanian D.D.T. tobacco," he says.

Marcus gets up and leaves. To get more Konyagi, I imagine. Rogarth looks after him:

"Tsk," he says. "Marcus has become so much more of a drunk since you left." Sitting with Rogarth is nice. We speak about football, golf, old times at T.P.C. – everything. We talk about tanzanite; I tell him about Dickson and say that I would like to take a trip to Zaire. Rogarth warns me: it's dangerous. He's not constantly touching me for a beer, looking for the way to my wallet.

Katriina pops her head into the servants' quarters. It's midmorning. I'm not up yet.

"Your girlfriend called last night," she says.

"Who?" I ask.

"Marianne," she says. "How many have you got?"

"I don't think she's my girlfriend," I say.

"Really? That's the impression she gave me," Katriina says. "And she'll be here in two weeks."

"Bugger," I say.

"Why would you say that?" Katriina asks.

"I haven't seen her in six months, and now she wants to show up out of the blue." I sit up in bed.

"I think she is applying for some U.N. work," Katriina says.

"I think I'd better call her," I say.

"Sounds like it," Katriina says and leaves. A little while later the car drives off, and I'm alone in the house. Except for Issa, who serves me breakfast. Afterwards I call Marianne's number in England, but she's gone back to Denmark. I call her parents in Hasseris but I can't get a connection. Fuck. Why the hell didn't I just tell her I didn't want her here? – that I want her to stay away.

*

I don't eat enough, because it's so hot, and I'm always on the go to get a feel for the situation: which bars have a dance floor big enough for a disco, and are the owners even interested? – would they share the profit? – are they reasonable? I had two slices of fluffy white bread with peanut butter this morning and of course coffee and a cigarette, and then I had a bit of passion fruit and carrot juice in Swahilitown – at Shrukran Hotel, which is run by some Somalis – good food, cheap, a place to hang out. But now it's one-thirty, and *mamas'* kitchens close at two. I'd prefer to eat at the *mama*'s behind the shop, because she's got good chapatti, tasty, loose basmati rice cooked with grated coconut, a nice sauce with beef. But my eyes would rather eat at the one behind Tanesco, even though the food isn't good at all. I spot Rogarth sitting at a table, but stop and have a look around. Yes, Rachel is here. Today she's wearing pinstriped gabardine trousers and a black top and flip-flops. She looks cool. Sexy.

"How are you, sister?" I ask when she sees me, and she smiles, happy and shy all at once. I order – she is busy serving the other customers. Sit down with Rogarth, who has almost finished his lunch. Rachel brings my food – the only thing left is pilaf, or corn porridge and beans, which I simply can't be bothered to eat.

"There you are," she says.

"Thanks," I say. She stays where she is, looking at me.

"Do you like him?" Rogarth asks.

"I might," Rachel says and walks away. Rogarth grins. He's got things to do, but we arrange to meet up later. I'd like to talk to him about the disco business – where he sees the best opportunities. I eat. It's after closing time, and Rachel gets her plateful of whatever is left. She goes to the furthest table, which is in the shade of a tree in the yard. She sits down to eat. Marcus has told me Rachel comes from the Tanga region on the coast – he can tell from her dialect. That's where all the most well-behaved and hardworking girls come from, he says. They get the waitressing jobs in Moshi, even though there are plenty of poor Moshi girls who need work. I light my cigarette, pay the *mama* and go over to Rachel's table. She's sitting at an angle at the table with her feet up on another chair. She's eating – rice and beans, mostly – and I put one hand on the back of her chair, leaning forward.

"Why are you sitting over here, when I'm sitting over there?" I ask.

"I don't know," she says. "I think I probably just wanted to sit alone."

"Do you mind if I sit down?"

"No."

"That's good," I say, sitting down. "Where do you live?" I ask.

"In Majengo," she says. The sleazy suburb where Rogarth also lives.

"With your family?" I ask.

"With my aunt and her daughter."

"Do you dance?" I ask.

"Yes," Rachel says.

"Liberty is open again – are you going there this weekend?"

"Is that the place on the other side of the roundabout?" she asks.

"Yes," I say.

"I don't know," she says. And I stop myself.

"I not really sure either," I say. "I may be going to Arusha, so I might not be there until Saturday." And it's true, but it's also . . . she's just waiting for me to ask her where she lives; whether I could come and pick her up. Then she'd say alright. And then we'd go there together. We'd dance. Then . . . the consequences are huge, and Marianne . . . Marianne will be landing any day.

That morning my palms are sweaty as I call Mountain Lodge outside Arusha – owned and run by Mick's mum. A woman picks up and speaks English with a faint Danish accent. Her name is Sofie.

"Are you Danish?" I ask.

"No, I'm from Greenland," she says in Danish.

"Alright. Hi. My name is Christian and I'm looking for Mick – we were at I.S.M. together," I say. She tells me Mick will be back later that afternoon. I go down to Arusha Road and wait for a bus. They're already full when they leave the bus station, and then you just cram more people in along the way. I stand up all the way, but it's better than sitting with an old Maasai woman on your lap and smelling of cow dung, snuff and dried blood all day.

Near enough to Mountain Lodge I get off and start walking up the dirt road between the tall trees. It's an old coffee farm from 1911 that has been converted into a luxury hotel. I can hear the river not far from the road. Walk a few miles up through fields of coffee plants until I pass the lodge's trout farm and reach the two-storey main building.

"Christian?" I look up. On the balcony is a dark-haired young woman with Greenlandic features.

"Sofie?" I say.

"Yes. Hi. Come in, sit down. Mick isn't back yet."

We sit down on the veranda. The waiter serves juice and coffee.

"Ohhh, Princes," she says when I offer her a cigarette. "Have you got Danish salami in your pocket?" she asks and smiles naughtily. I blush.

"No, not really," I say.

"Pity. Anyway, I'm married to Pierre – Mick's older brother." She tells me how she travelled down through Africa with a former French foreign legionnaire in the mid-1970s, and was then sprogged up by Pierre in Nairobi.

"And now I am a colonialist – much nicer than being colonized," she says.

"Colonized?" I ask.

"Greenland," she says.

"Fair point," I say.

Sofie shows me round. The main house with a large dining-cum-sitting room with an enormous fireplace for the guests. The family's own apartments upstairs. A row of whitewashed bungalows in the lush garden. The trout pond. The stable. The garage with the vehicles used by the safari company; it's almost empty because most of them are in use. They've got it all going for them – and it's working.

A little while later Mick shows up. He looks pensive when he sees me.

"It's been a while," he says.

"Yes," I say – slightly nervous.

"You buried Samantha," he says.

"Yes," I croak – the lump fills my throat – burning hot, sickened, dry. Does anyone else know?

"How do you know?" I ask.

"Her dad told me what had happened, but in a fairly disjointed way. He was drunk. What did happen?" he asks.

It's hard. I stumble through. I'm crying.

"She took the easy way out," he says.

"I don't think it was easy," I say.

"No, but she sure as hell didn't make our lives easier by bailing on us," Mick says. I don't say anything. He shakes his head. "A lot of us cared about her," he says. "If she were here right now, I would give her a big kick up the backside."

I swallow the lump.

"I wish she'd told me about . . . all that with her dad," I say.

"If she had, you would have helped her? You would have saved her, is that it?" Mick asks and looks at me with raised eyebrows.

I don't say anything.

"You can't help people who don't want to be helped," Mick says. I light a new cigarette.

"What happened to Alison and Frans?" I ask, even though that isn't what I want to know.

"Moved to Thailand," Mick says. "Away from . . . it all."

"And Douglas?" I ask.

"Gone missing in Congo," Mick says.

"Victor?"

"Congo," Mick says.

"Missing?" I ask.

"No, alive."

"*Tsk*," I say. The question was asked, but the answer wasn't what I wanted.

"Anyway. Let's get a beer," Mick says and calls the waiter. He asks what I do. I tell him about the recording shop, the discos, Marcus.

"Yes," Mick says. "I remember him from Moshi. Lots of good music." Mick has quit the job he had in Moshi – these days he works for his mum arranging high-end safaris for wealthy Americans and Japanese.

"But Pierre and I don't see eye to eye," he says. Sofie grins at him. "So I'll be setting up my own garage in Arusha soon – fixing up cars for the safari companies."

I tell him I'm looking to buy a motorbike.

"Have you got dollars?" Mick asks.

"Travellers' cheques," I say. Mick gets up.

"Come with me," he says. It turns out he's got five Spanish Bultaco bikes. A few of them he's cannibalized to use as spare parts for the others.

"Where did you get them?" I ask.

"I bought them from Oxfam. They had this project where they went round everywhere on Kilimanjaro and Mount Meru and advised smallholders on how to grow coffee. But then the world market crashed, and they closed up shop." He sells me a 250cc, which runs very nicely.

"Do you remember Savio?" Mick asks.

"Indian, from Goa?"

"Yes, that's the one. He runs a tanzanite mine in Merelani Hills. You should go and see it, man," Mick says.

"Does he sell stones?" I ask.

"He's reasonable," Mick says and gives me Savio's phone number.

"Alright then," I say. "I'd better get going if I want to be back before dark."

"Yes," Mick says. "I'd ask you to stay the night, but I've got some work to do. Stop by some other time."

The motorbike is an amazing ride – such power, great road grip. I reach my destination as dusk falls. I leave the motorbike inside the servants' quarters – I need to get a proper chain which can be wound through the front tyre as well before I use it in town.

Marcus

UHURU NI KAZI

I go to Katriina's house to pick up Christian. Rebekka is at home, but it's been a while since we lived together in the house of madness – a year and a half – and she is gradually forgetting her black father. To her heart Marcus has become a distant acquaintance, almost a stranger. *Eeehhhh*, it's sad.

Christian has bought a Bultaco motorbike from Mick in Arusha. I remember that guy from when he went to I.S.M. and bought cassettes from me. His skin is white, but the man is a total amalgamation – he knows all the ways, both the white systems and the black wilderness. Mick is a second-generation *mzungu* in Tanzania.

And Christian's got enough money for a motorbike – yes. But how much money has he got after that?

My life crisis continues. Rhema from Soweto comes right to Roots Rock with my little son on her arm – she is hungry:

"Now you've got a white partner who is making you rich, you can afford to give me something" she says.

"He's not making me rich. We're collaborating on a small business venture," I say.

"Ahhh – you always have your lies as an excuse for being stingy. But I was never stingy when it came to giving you a hot dessert whenever you came to West Kilimanjaro," Rhema says, holding out the little boy. "And now you won't even recognize your own son. Tsk." She leaves the shop, very angry and proud and disappointed.

In the evening I go with Christian to the disco at Liberty.

"Alwyn is back on the decks. Do you remember him from school?"

"Was he the one who sold loads of *bhangi* to your friend Mika in the old days?" Christian asks.

"Yes, that's the one," I say. We pass between flowerbeds over Arusha roundabout with its small tower in the middle. At the top of the tower is a sculpture of an arm carrying the torch of liberty – Uhuru Torch. On the side of the tower are slogans from our one and only party: LIBERTY AND LABOUR and OUR POLICY IS AGRICULTURE. But the agricultural policy is insane. People armed with picks who have never seen a tractor. Is that supposed to be liberty?

Christian

"You can hear already how bad it sounds," Marcus says as we walk through the wide hall with doors leading into offices no-one wants to rent. The loudspeakers at Liberty crackle from the strain; it sounds like the cardboard membranes may have knocked themselves out of place or are falling apart. We reach the passage to the toilets and the kitchen on the left. If you go further ahead, there is yet another door, and behind it is a long series of small bonking rooms. But we step out into the yard behind the door on the left and stand under a narrow strip of open sky right by the wooden building – an old warehouse – which takes up the entire yard; that's Liberty. You enter at the very end of one side. A long room with high ceilings and a concrete floor; all the way down both long sides are barred outlets right under the ceiling to let air in. Table and chairs have been placed along the walls. To the left of the entrance is a passage to an interior staircase leading up to the D.J. room, which is situated above the bar. There's a small glass enclosure built out into the room, just above the bar – almost like a bridge – so the D.J can see how the music is working on the crowd. There's a big crowd, but I can't see Rachel.

"Come on," Marcus says and opens the door to the staircase. "But don't tell him you're planning to go into the disco business." We go up the stairs to see Alwyn.

"So," Alwyn says, "you've come back to Tanzania."

"Yes," I say. "Denmark isn't hot enough for me."

"Yes, don't I know it? Like a fridge it was," Alwyn says. "So you're the one who's brought down all that good music for Marcus."

"Yes, I'm the one."

"Then what will you do in Tanzania?" he asks.

"I'm not sure. Right now I'm visiting my family."

"Are you interested in stones? Tanzanite? Diamonds from Shinyanga?" Alwyn asks.

"No, thanks," I say. We go back down.

"A powerful amplifier, a few good record players, some good loud-speakers – then we could take it over or make a better disco somewhere in town," Marcus says. He's right. Those decks are on their last legs. The clientele is poor, and the entrance fee is cheap. Moshi Hotel was better, more expensive. But with our music and my decks I have in Denmark, we can knock them for six.

I buy us beer, and we sit down at a table next to the bar.

I go for a piss. The stench in the urinal almost makes me retch. I rinse my hands under the tap, but there's no soap. Just as I come out, I see Rachel coming out of the ladies' room.

"You came," she says and flings her arms around me. I put my arms around her.

"Yes," I say. "Hi." She holds my hand and asks me if Marcus is here as well. "Yes," I say. "We're sitting right through there." She looks around nervously.

"I'm sitting with someone," she says. "I'll see you later."

"Alright," I say. She lets go of my hand and goes back inside. I follow her to a table, where she's sitting with a well-built guy of my own age. He's got a nice watch, good clothes, decent shoes – but none of that says anything about who he is. He can easily share a scummy room with several others and own only two sets of clothes: his Sunday best, which he is wearing now, and his workaday wear. Perhaps he's her boyfriend. She sits down on a chair. I lean down so they can hear me. "Good evening," I say to him, holding out my hand. He looks at the hand and then up at me.

"I know what you want," he says. "All you want is to fuck my girl-friend. That's what you whites are like."

"What?" I say, smiling. "No, I don't. Just relax."

"Don't be like that," Rachel tells him. He keeps at it. He is right.

"You really are mistaken," I say. Rachel looks embarrassed. I point towards our table. "I'm right over there with Marcus if you want to come over and say hi." Then I leave.

Why the hell would Rachel be with a fool like that? I should have told her I would pick her up today, bring her here; it's my own fault, but . . . I can't bloody well . . . Bugger! And then a sodding whore comes over. Rachel's sweet, she works for a *mama*. She could be a whore as well, but she doesn't hang out at the bars trying to catch a big man. She makes an honest living. But Marianne will be down soon. Bugger!

Marcus

JUJU

Ibrahim comes over one night, sits on the sofa, wringing his hands.

"Big problem," he says.

"What's wrong?" I ask. Ibrahim sends a quick look at Claire before he answers:

"It's Rhema. She is in financial trouble, so she's taking a bad way out," Ibrahim says.

"What does she do?" Claire asks.

"She goes to the bars in Soweto," Ibrahim says.

"What about the boy?" I ask.

"The boy is left with his grandmother while Rhema tries to catch herself a fish," Ibrahim says.

"*Tsk*, if she catches a disease, my son will have to live with that crazy grandmother," I say.

"Not if you get papers from the court saying you're the father," Ibrahim says. I don't say what those papers cost; every month, year after year, there's a payment to Rhema for having my name on those papers.

"Would you do it?" Claire asks.

"We can't afford to do it," I say.

"It's a bad situation," Claire says. "We must all help each other. I'll go talk to Rhema tomorrow."

The next day Claire is quite wound up when she returns:

"Rhema's grandmother is a witch. She put juju on our baby. Have a look." Claire holds out our little Rebekka. She looks fine.

"Nothing's wrong," I say. "Try not to have those old-fashioned thoughts."

"Rhema's grandmother took her into the kitchen to give her some milk. Now her stomach's upset." She's right. The baby's ill. Now she's screaming like a stereo and doesn't sleep for two days, and nor do we. The baby shits, vomits, dries up. Claire is constantly feeding her sugar water on a spoon; the only thing the baby can keep down. We take her to a doctor, who checks things and tries everything. And at K.C.M.C. the doctors won't lift a finger until their palms have been greased. Money is flying out of my pocket.

Christian comes over on his motorbike at night. He could drive Katriina's Nissan Patrol, but he must have that motorbike as well, just for fun. I tell him of our problem with the baby. "Poor kid," he says, looking at Rebekka, who is nothing but a pile of sticks with skin stretched over it, with horrible breath. Claire is so unhappy.

"It's Rhema's *juju*," Claire says. And it's true. Ibrahim tells me Rhema uses insanely aggressive words because Claire lives with me. That means Rhema can never live here. Her ploy, getting herself pumped up on my seed, was meant to be her ticket away from the poor life with the crazy grandmother in Soweto, but the gamble backfired. And now Rhema and Claire have created evil thoughts against each other. Claire goes to church, but I also find powder from the witch doctor strewn around the corners of the house. In Soweto they say that Rhema's grandmother is a witch and makes Rhema do those things. The baby is dried out and thin, and we are worn thin with fatigue. The stench of illness is everywhere.

EUROPEAN DREAMS

I have told Christian to be careful with the local girls who have no schooling or proper families and who all see Christian as the fattest of fish. But he flirts with all the girls in the shops – not the right kind.

"Do you think you can go into town and find a woman with feelings? Never. These girls have feelings for you? Feelings are only one day, half a day, a minute? No. That's the European dream. As an example – for your edification – take that Rachel from the *mama*'s behind Tanesco – exactly the kind of girl I mean." The truth is glaringly obvious, and the white boy becomes very huffy.

"Marcus, give it a rest. There is no fucking European dream. I live here. She knows that. You seem to think that every girl is a *malaya*, except for Claire, who is so sanctimonious you're bleeding well sick of it yourself. You say Claire's sister will become a *malaya* if you don't help her. And at the same time Claire is trying to get me to take an interest in her. You people are just the limit."

Christian

I've got a deal with Shukran Hotel, and now I've got my first small disco in Swahilitown on the other side of the market. At first there's not a lot of people because they have to pay an entrance fee – people gather outside on the pavement, listen. Is the music any good? My back is sweaty. Come in, you fuckers. And then it happens. Everyone comes to the door, pays, comes in, buys drinks, talks to the D.J. – me. What sort of music have I got? All of it. Have I got Gregory Isaacs? Absolutely! It's working. The owner is pleased. I meet a guy called Big Man Ibrahim, who is just a great guy – it turns he went to school with Marcus years ago. He teaches karate at the C.C.M. building. Ibrahim grabs my hand and holds it up before me.

"I can turn it into a deadly weapon," he says, laughing.

Kilimanjaro International Airport, Sunday morning, hungover. I feel odd about Marianne coming down. We were only together during the first half of the first year of H.F. in Hasseris – it seems like a different life. I don't really know what she's doing here – what it is she has in mind. I am standing on the roof terrace of the airport with Katriina and Solja, and we see the K.L.M. plane come to a halt. Marianne gets out. In a way I fancy her, but the thought of having to have a conversation with her makes me feel very tired.

1987

Marcus

MARIANNE

"Marianne." That's the name of Christian's Danish girlfriend. Sweet.

"So now you're here to see your boyfriend's second country," I say.

"Yes," she says. "Plus I needed to get away." She says she used to go with Christian in Denmark, and then he disappeared from school and came to Africa. She herself has finished school and wants to experience the world. That's why she's come to Africa at her own expense.

"She's a singer," Christian says. "She's very good." He looks over at Marianne: "Sing to him."

"No," she says, smiling.

"Oh, go on." She sings:

"*She likes to party – feeling fine.*" A very professional style. "But I'm going to try and find some work," she says. "Perhaps something in a U.N. refugee camp." Christian's eyes go vacant – now he's thinking. Of his secret plan for her. He wants to set up a band. He's the drummer, and I've introduced him to the good guitarist who plays at church and knows the Zaire style, and to the bass player as well – a political refugee from Burundi. The real draw is going to be the white girl in front who sings and shakes her bottom, so the black man can dream about a white night. They've already had a few rehearsals since Marianne arrived, but Christian never tells her – she doesn't know about his plan. Maybe he doesn't believe in it himself, because the guitarist won't do anything that displeases God. What matters most is Sunday morning in church and that means he can't be at Hotel Saba Saba in Arusha on a Saturday night.

Christian has plans for stones as well. He talks about the mining area in Merelani all the time – the blue stones, tanzanite. His thoughts are like Mika's: about things that are illegal, making a quick fortune. Once again I mention my idea of exporting to Denmark; things that are legal – souvenirs, arts and crafts.

"It's not easy," Christian says.

"Why not?" I ask. Christian sighs:

"In Europe there are all sorts of systems. Customs, taxes, papers and permits that have to be in order. I don't know anything about those things."

"You could learn," I say.

"Maybe I'll decide to stay here," Christian says.

"We could get a business partner in Denmark. One of your friends," I say.

"My friends are no good for that sort of thing," he says. "But perhaps we should try buying some tanzanites and selling them in Europe."

"You can get those in Arusha," I say.

"No, in the mining area, out at Zaire, so we get them really cheap – Savio can help us," Christian says.

"You mustn't go there – they'll kill you," I say.

"It probably won't be as bad as all that," Christian says.

"It's very dangerous," I say.

"*Tsk*," Christian says – he thinks he knows Africa, even though he's never gone hungry.

NASTY ADVERTISEMENT

Christian is nothing but work, because in Tanzania he is like a baby who doesn't know how to walk by himself – he thinks he understands everything, but he doesn't know the ways. Yes, he's got himself that deal with Shukran Hotel – small disco nights. But what it takes to make it big – he is blind to that.

"You need a disco permit," I say. "Otherwise you might get in trouble with the police." I take him with me to the town council. The price for a permit is the same as for three beers in the bar.

"How about taxes?" Christian asks.

"No taxes," I say. "It's a small business, one night at a time. The taxman only looks at you if you're a big cheese."

"And when I pay people wages?" he asks.

"Cash in hand – no paper, nothing." Yes, the white boy needs me to find a path through the black wilderness.

Christian brings the Bob Marley L.P. "Uprising", which has a picture of a black man with dreadlocks rising from his oppression with the mountains and the sun in the background – very powerful. "We'll just add our name," he says. "Then it'll say Rebel Rock Sound System – Uprising, and then the time and place."

"No, no, no," I say. "If you put up the picture – three seconds later it's gone – something appealing to put on the wall in someone's home. The picture must be dull and only have words with information about the disco."

We print the posters and drive around on the motorbike, putting them up all over town, taping them onto shop windows and pinning them to trees.

SLUM STYLE

Now I am locked in the cold iron chains at the bottom of the ship, like on the cover of Bob Marley's "Survival" L.P. But my ship isn't sailing to the great life in the U.S. – my ship is a shop, Roots Rock, where I must record cassettes and be a daily advertisement for our disco business. My ship is going nowhere while Christian goes everywhere to meet people, making plans, setting up deals. Me, I don't know anything about those deals, even though I am his partner in the business. *Eeehhhh*, that's a problem. He has a disco night at Shukran Hotel, but I can't be there, because baby Rebekka is still as ill as anything. And at Shukran Hotel he meets all those thieving *mwaswahili* people – poor Muslim immigrants from the coast – and they will take him away from me. Christian starts taking karate lessons in the C.C.M. building and meets Ibrahim the teacher and several boys from Swahilitown, who are drawn by the art of fighting. They are very interested in the disco business and in the white boy, so they come to my shop during the day to meet him. They don't want tapes recorded – just to lounge about in the chairs and drink Coke until the white boy arrives, and they have many propositions for him and want to help him with everything. There's Khalid, Abdullah, who is dangerous, Rogarth, who thinks he is very clever, and Firestone, who is a dirty little piece of market dust and stutters like Mika did back in the day.

Gulzar knows Christian from I.S.M. and speaks straight to his face inside the shop:

"You must be careful about these guys, Christian. They'll steal the shirt off your back when you look away – they're all thieves," Gulzar says.

"I don't think they are," Christian says.

"Yes, they're bums, thieves."

"Everyone has their good sides and their bad sides," Christian says.

"Some people only have bad sides," Gulzar says. "They'll steal whatever you've got." Outside on the veranda I can hear Khalid:

"*Tsk*," he says because he understands English reasonably well and hears Gulzar talking. Christian says:

"They're just young kids who need something to do to earn a bit of cash. Not everyone has a dad who can foot the bill." Outside Khalid laughs and translates in a low voice to Firestone. Gulzar is upset:

"When you spend time with them, you too will be considered part of the slum," he says. "It ruins your image."

"Being with them is my image," Christian says.

Christian

I finally get hold of Savio on the phone.

"Fuck, yes. Come on out," he says. I ask him how. He can give me a ride, but then he can't promise me when I'll be able to get back.

"I have a motorbike," he says.

"I don't know," he says. "You'd better come with me. The place isn't safe if you don't know it." He suggests I get on a bus to Arusha the next morning.

"Then what happens if something comes up and you can't leave?" I ask because I know how it goes in Africa.

"I'm not an African," Savio says, slightly coldly.

"Fair enough," I say, and we arrange a meet-up.

The next morning I'm sitting on the bus being taken through the flat country where the Maasai let the zebu cattle and the goats graze. Mount Meru is visible in the distance and towards the south the Blue Mountains. The tanzanite deposits are found under a wide, flat valley in the Merelani Hills.

I get off at the exit to the airport. Drink tea from a wooden shack while I keep an eye out for Savio. Not long after he arrives in a beat-up Land Rover without a back seat.

"Are you ready for the wild west?" he asks. I jump in and we drive towards the airport, the wide street framed by trees on either side. Savio has a picture of the Virgin Mary, cut out of a magazine and glued onto a small wooden sheet. Screwed on to his dashboard.

Behind the front seats are wooden crates and diesel tanks; there's a long black plastic tube there as well.

"What's that back there?" I ask.

"Explosives and detonators. Diesel for the generator, which runs the compressor that pumps air into the mine. And a new bit of piping because the mineshafts have grown as long as hell." Right before the barrier leading to the airport terminal, we turn right down a shoddy dirt road. "Just over ten miles to the village," Savio says.

"Everyone tells me it's dangerous out here," I say.

"Yes, well, the village isn't so bad. It's about five kilometres from Zaire. Everyone hopes to find wealth like in Zaire. They're ready to do whatever it takes. In the mining area it really is dangerous. If you enter another man's mine, he will shoot you and bury you, and no-one will ever be the wiser," Savio says, grinning. Alright, I think; Tanzania – people get a kick out of scaring the white man.

The sandy road winds in a south-westerly direction through rocky ground, thorns, acacia trees. It's not a road but simply the track most cars have elected to use. The white hangar building of the airport disappears behind us, and further ahead I can see that the landscape becomes a bit more lush, with more trees, because the Blue Mountains break the clouds and make them yield their water.

We pass a police station, right in the middle of nowhere.

"That's as far as the police go," Savio says.

"Don't they come to the village?" Savio shakes his head:

"No. If you go there in a police uniform, you're as good as dead. And you've got no say. One man may shoot another man in front of a police officer and say: 'Fuck you, what are you going to do about it? I'll just shoot you as well. If you want to stay alive, you keep your mouth shut. You didn't see anything. Go back to your office.' If there's a big problem out here, the Field Force Unit comes out – the army specialists. But things have to be a right mess before they come." Mick has told me what it is Savio does out here, but I want to hear his own version.

"What is it you do?"

"Right-hand man for a mine-owner. My job is to make sure the miners don't make off with his stones."

"How so?" He holds open his khaki jacket so I can see the holster – the revolver in it.

"Whenever there's an explosion I have to go down and see if we've got anything. I have to be ready. Climb down the pit with Little Miss .44 in my hand, pick up the stones; back away so no-one lands a pickaxe in my back, move up the ladder, into the car and take them away."

"Would they really . . . ?"

"Hey," he says. "I do right by my men. They know if they screw me over, I will shoot them. Bury them down there. But otherwise I treat them like human beings. Sometimes I even give them meat." I don't say anything for a while.

"Do you own a share of the mine then?" I ask.

"No – it belongs to an Arab in Arusha."

"But couldn't you just make yourself scarce if you hit the big time?" I ask. If the owner is in Arusha – it would take him a while to find out about it.

"He could have me killed," Savio says. "It's cheap in this country."

"But you could go abroad?" I say.

"If I stole enough from him, he would find me there as well. The Arabs have a certain penchant for vengeance. But . . . what the hell would I do abroad anyway? Not my kind of thing."

"You could go to Europe," I say.

"I've been to Europe. Miserable place."

"Why do you think that?"

"The people – they're incapable of relaxing. It's like they're in a hurry to arrive at their deaths."

"What's it like working out here – as a miner, I mean?" I ask.

"Tsk," Savio says. "The mine shafts are deep and not terribly safe. They're always collapsing. If there's a neighbouring mine, you're done for. The guys who climb into the pit are hungry. A lot of kids work there as well; we call them njokas – snakes – ten to twelve years old. In the narrowest and most dangerous cracks they can slither in with their torches to see if there's evidence of a seam. Dig with their hands. Hard work."

We reach the village; shacks of wattle and daub, small mud-built houses with peeling plaster, wooden sheds with tin roofs. Everything higgledy-piggledy. Loads of motorbike garages. I've heard about them. Stolen motorbikes from Moshi and Arusha are taken out here to be sold cash in hand. The mechanics mix and match the bikes; swapping fuel tanks, seats, mudguards, mirrors. In less than an hour they're unrecognizable.

"This is where the miners spend their money, if they make any. So you can have anything you fancy, round the clock."

"Anything?"

"I didn't say it would be any good," Savio says. A baby is squatting outside a house, shitting on the ground; there's rubbish everywhere. No plumbing. No running water. A mess of electrical wiring hanging between tilting telephone poles. Bars fenced in with barbed wire and improvised board walls. People with rotting teeth. Everything off kilter and dirty. Mules and goats rooting through rubbish heaps; other heaps set on fire along the roadside. We stop in front of a bar. I get out and can hear the crackling music – the stereo is on its last legs. We go inside and buy fizzy drinks. Savio introduces me to the owner, who doesn't waste any time when he hears I do discos in Moshi.

"We could work something out," he says. "You could come here."

"Which days are best?" I ask.

"Every day is the same as the next," he says.

"Alright," I say. "When I'm ready, I'll come and we can arrange something and put up some posters around the place. Advertise."

"Sounds good," the man says.

We get out to the car, drive to the mining area. Young chaps in smart clothes and sunglasses pass us in both directions on big off-road motorbikes. Maasai as well in traditional dress – their bodies wrapped in a dusty cloth the colour of blood, their hair plaited with glass beads and styled with mud.

"They're middlemen," Savio says. "Buy small stones from the miners and sell them to buyers in the village who take them out into the world."

The Land Rover struggles up the bumpy track. Tall thin dust devils move restlessly across the lowlands in the heat. We come up over a hilltop, and the valley opens out in front of us – practically no vegetation, rubble everywhere, small shacks. The soil is covered everywhere by glittering, glistening quartz.

"There's no system," Savio says. "You put up your fence and dig a pit. You need between sixty and a hundred workers. You need timber."

"For shoring?"

"For the ladders. We don't use shoring; the rock is solid – mostly."

We reach the mine. There's not much to be seen. A fence around it, a wooden shack, a pit into the earth under a lean-to. Everybody's in there, digging.

Savio calls his right-hand man, Conte, who gives me a hard hat with a torch on it. I am nervous.

"Don't worry," Savio says. "He will only show you the safe shafts with the solid roofs." Yes, but I remember what he said: if one of the neighbouring mines sets off an explosion too close to our shaft, the whole thing could come crashing down around our ears. Everyone steps aside as I climb down the steps anxiously. The rungs are slick with use, wide and difficult to grab hold of – they're set too far apart. My arms soon get tired; I can feel lactic acid building in my muscles. I hold on tight as my foot searches for the next rung on the ladder. The miners are all as slender as dancers, no excess fatty deposits to weigh them down. I'm sweating. The darkness becomes complete, the air death and heat, a stench of sweat and piss and smoke and grime. We pass people dragging sacks of rubble towards the ladder. The sounds of hammering and tapping float up from the bottom of the pit. I crab onwards right behind Conte. Here and there the mineshaft descends steeply – we're moving on all fours through the low-ceilinged shafts with the uneven rock tearing at our palms and the air stinking: heavy, hot, full of dust. The cone of light from my miner's lamp sweeps over sweaty black backs, matte with dust. It seems completely normal and at the same time utterly dreamlike. Some of them are holding hammers and chisels, tapping out holes in the rock.

"For fuses," Conte says. Others are filling rubble into fodder sacks. They greet us, smile, back to work.

I am glad when I get out. Conte shows me some small raw stones that look like matte coloured glass – not the deep purple hue I have seen in the jewellery shops in Arusha. "They must be treated with heat before the right colour emerges," he says.

Savio calls me. It's late. We drive back to the village, where we will spend the night at a guesthouse.

We sit down in the bar and, before we turn in, we agree a price for the handful of uncut tanzanite stones Savio wants to sell me. I have my doubts about the authenticity of the paperwork.

The next day I've arranged to meet Savio at the mine. Savio has meat and vegetables in his car, rice, cooking oil, flour for chapatti, Indian cakes from Arusha, three cases of beer, several bottles of Konyagi. I've got my ghettoblaster and cassettes.

"I will prepare you a very nice meal," the cook at the mines says and immediately news of the feast spreads like wildfire among the young boys who empty the rubble sacks, down the ladder and the shafts. People are working their arses off.

"Other mine-owners think I'm a fool," Savio says. "But if you were to chop the hands off any of my boys, they would use their teeth to dig out stones for me."

"Rebel Rock," one of the workers says. A rumour that we spoke about playing music last night at the bar has already travelled here. They all speak at once. Look forward to it.

Fragile fences surround many of the mineshafts. I ask Savio whether the mine-owners help each other. He laughs.

"My neighbour over there," he says, pointing. "She is three hundred pounds of pure filth. The only woman in Zaire. I don't think she *can* be raped – she's simply too fat. But yes, we have a secret agreement to help each other if any one of us gets into trouble with our workers."

When the darkness falls, the workers are called out. They wash their hands and faces in a big tub of water, chatter and laugh in low voices. I play a heavy dub. Food is served on aluminium plates. Everyone eats with their hands. Beer is shared around, with the very young boys as well – the snakes – they don't make any distinction. Afterwards there's tea and cakes. Everyone is smiling. Savio has a snake pass a pack of cigarettes around.

Savio goes round pouring a small glug of Konyagi into everyone's coffee mugs. We have built a small fire from twigs. Some people sit around smoking, but not cigarettes – the smell of *bhangi* wafts towards me.

"When you take *gongo* with *bhangi*, the spirit of the blue stones enters you, and you can feel the path of the seam when you're standing at the bottom of the pit," Savio says. The guys grin.

"That's true," one of the guys says. "If you give us *gongo* every day, we promise to make you rich."

"You're mad," Savio says.

"It's true," the guy says, laughing with a wet sound from a long way down his throat – it passes into a nasty cough, and he hawks and spits.

The generator has been switched off so we can enjoy the silence, an abundance of stars above us. The ghettoblaster loses momentum – the batteries are spent. I turn it off.

"The *mama* has fallen down the shaft." The voice comes from across the fence. Everyone around the bonfire stiffens – looks at Savio, who places a hand on the ground next to him, ready to jump up. He sits stock-still listening into the night.

"Is she dead?" another one shouts.

"I don't know," the first one shouts. Savio gets up, shooting a look at his right-hand man, Conte.

"Everyone stay here," he says in a low voice to the guys around the bonfire. He looks at me – speaks in English: "You come with me. Stay close. This is not a safe place to be right now." He moves quickly towards the gate. I get up as fast as I can, follow him. Conte has already gone over to unlock the smaller opening set into one of the doors of the gate. The revolver in Savio's hand glistens dully as he slides his big body through the door. We lumber together through the darkness to the fence that surrounds the neighbouring mine. We are just round the corner from their gate. It's a starry night, so I can see Savio clearly as he lifts his hand to silence us. We listen:

"... many stones ..." "... the big seam ..." "... still breathing ..." "... she'll be dead soon ..." The sound of feet moving across the rubble. Savio makes another sign. We move to the gate. Savio tries it – it's locked. We move a bit further along the fence. He shoves his revolver into its holster. Without saying a word Conte gives Savio a leg-up, and Savio signals for me to follow him. We both go over the fence. Savio has already gone over to some empty oil drums which he lifts over to the fence. I quickly join him. He climbs onto one and points at the other. I must give it to him. He pushes it over; the rumble from its impact is infernal. I look around feverishly. Conte gets up on the drum – leaps over the fence. We all squat in the darkness half hidden behind a load of boards – probably for building ladders. The covered pit is clear to see in the starlight. From the wooden shed, the monotonous sound of the generator running the compressor. Savio pulls up the leg of his trousers to reveal a small pistol in an ankle-holster. He hands Conte the gun and speaks to him, quickly and in a low voice. There are no workers in sight – everyone has rushed down into the mine to harvest stones.

"Who are you?" Savio hisses into the darkness. Only then do I see the man cowering on the ground not far from us. In the starlight the fence is casting a shadow over him.

"It's me, the cook," the man says, getting up so the light falls on him.

"What happened?" Savio asks.

"The *mama* wanted to go down to see the find," the cook.

"She bloody well can't get down," Savio says.

"No," the cook says. "She fell."

"Is she dead?" Savio asks.

"I don't think so."

"And Makamba?" Savio asks.

"He's down there," the cook says.

"Helping her?"

"I don't know," the cook says.

"Stay here," Savio says and lumbers over to the pit, disappearing from sight. We wait. Some time later he returns, comes over to us.

"What's going on?" I whisper.

"They're fucking her."

"Fucking her?" I ask. Savio laughs briefly and nastily:

"Africa," he says. "It's a punishment."

A few boys come out of the shaft. Savio signals that we must hide and be silent. The boys run to the gate, which is locked. They fetch picks and smash the locks.

"We have sent *mama* to hell," one of them says.

"Yes, we gave her a taste of our love."

"Now the snakes will grow inside her and torture her in eternity." Finally they can push open the gate and slip out.

"What are we doing?" I whisper.

"We're waiting for the *mama*'s right-hand man," Savio says. There's an edge to his voice, intense anger mixed with sheer hatred and a dull indifference. I am struck dumb. We wait. A few more boys dash past us, out. A few more appear – move towards the wooden shack which must be the *mama*'s house.

"Get lost," Savio shouts to them. They stop in their tracks and then quickly run towards the gate, out. We wait for quite some time.

I can feel Savio growing tense beside me. Look towards the pit. A grown man emerges, bigger than the boys who have run away.

"Makamba," Savio says loudly and gets up, his revolver in his hand. The man stops. "Where is the *mama*?" Savio asks.

"She fell down the ladder. She is dead."

"And who protects her mine?"

"They were going to kill me – the workers, the snakes," the man whimpers. "You have to help me protect it."

"You don't look dead," Savio says.

The man doesn't say anything.

"Where is your weapon?" Savio asks.

"Moses has it," the man says.

Savio points the gun at him, his arm straight. The man runs. Savio shoots. The man falls. Savio goes over to him. I stay where I am. I'm shaking. I can see Savio going through the man's pockets and then his boots where he finds something worth keeping. Conte puts his hand on my shoulder.

"Come," he says and we move forwards. Savio gets up. The man is lying on the ground, groaning. A wet sound.

"You stand over there," Savio tells Conte and points to the wooden shack. "If anyone approaches the house, you send them away. If they refuse to go, you shoot them."

"Why?" Conte asks. I think he'd rather go down into the mine.

"Some of the boys might return once they've thought it over; when they've become frightened in a different way. They will try to blow up the pit to hide the *mama*'s body. The explosives are in the house. Take these stones," Savio says and hands Conte some shapeless lumps – Conte nods. They must be stones taken from the boots of the man he shot.

"I will shoot anyone who comes out," Conte says. Savio points, and Conte moves over to the shed. I can still hear the wet rhythmic sounds of the wounded man's breathing.

"Why must Conte wait there?" I ask.

"If the mine is blown up while we're down there, we will die. Then none of us will make our harvest," Savio says.

"Harvest?" I ask.

"Let's get going," Savio says.

"What are we doing?" I ask.

"Going into the pit. I need to see it," he says.

"I don't want to go down."

516

"You have to."

"Can't I stay here?" I ask.

"It's not safe now."

"Can't I stay with Conte now? I don't want to go there."

"Conte isn't safe now. You're my responsibility and I'm going down there," Savio says. "You're coming with me." He pulls his revolver out of his shoulder holster behind his open shirt. We tiptoe over to the pit. I look down into the dark hole. Can see a faint glimmer of light a long way down. Savio starts climbing down. My shirt is glued to my back.

"Why must we go down?" I ask desperately.

"Don't you want to be rich?" Savio asks and continues nimbly. I start climbing after him. I'm afraid to follow him, but I'm also afraid to stay up there with Conte. We climb through an eternity of darkness.

"Don't worry," Savio says. "We're almost at the bottom." He pulls a small powerful torch out of his trouser pocket. He's had it all along. He shines the light down: big fat legs, naked, spread on the rocky ground. Between the flab of the thighs the obscene cunt – torn open, beat up. He lets the light travel towards her face; she is damp – dust and dirt caked to her skin in splotches. Some of the dust has dried to a thin membrane – cracked. Her flowery dress and underwear are ripped from her body, letting her breasts droop heavily to either side – enormous fields of stretchmarks glimmer palely against the darker skin. Her neck – a red open wound. Violated. Dead. My throat contracts. Savio steps down past her. Holds his revolver and the small torch in the same hand. Bent over, almost on my hands and knees, I move close behind him – it's hot down here, stinking of sweat and smoke. I hear a groan. Savio stops. His torchlight hits a man lying on his front; the back of his worn shirt is dark and wet. Savio pulls away the fabric. A hole in his back. Someone's put a pickaxe in him.

Savio bends down over the man:

"Shirazi?" he asks.

"Savio," the man says faintly and lifts his arm a little. Savio stares further ahead into the darkness. "I can't feel my legs," the man says.

"What happened?" Savio asks.

"Moses," the man whispers. Moses? "Help me, Savio," he says – more loudly now. If there are more people here, they'll hear him. Savio beats him over the head with the revolver, the man's head tilts back – slams into the ground with a dull sound. He doesn't move.

"What a mess," Savio says. He shines on something in his hand – a compass. We move ahead, past other tunnels. How can he know which direction we're going?

"Do you know the way?" I whisper – my voice thick.

"The newest pit," he says curtly. Apparently he can tell which it is.

"Has everyone gone up?" I ask.

"No, they're here – in the tunnels," he says. In the other shafts – waiting for us to move past them; then they'll climb up to Conte . . . or? We approach a fork in the shaft. I hear a crunching sound ahead. Savio stops, switches off his torch and holds on to me with his other hand. The only sound I can hear is the hiss from the black plastic tube that slithers down the shaft – pumping air into the mine.

"Savio," someone shouts. "*Toka!*" Get lost. Savio laughs, raises his hand and fires a shot – the sound is overpowering in the tight corridor.

"Try and make me, Moses," he calls back and pulls me with him through the darkness until we have passed the tunnels, and Savio lights his torch again, looks at the compass and says: "Come quickly now. We must go and see the find."

"Why?" My clothes are drenched with sweat – a fetid stench from my body, my hands shaking out of my control. I can tell from Savio's voice that he's smiling.

"The seam is close to my mine," he says. "I know exactly where we are." It's not his mine, I think; neither this one nor the other. But I have a distinct feeling that doesn't matter – his hand carries the gun: the law. He will dig his way from the find to his own shaft. But that means that . . . he's going to blow up this shaft, He scrambles ahead quickly. The tunnel narrows and finishes suddenly in a pile of rubble – I had imagined an opening, a larger space. Savio shines the light on the shapeless walls, the floor, the ceiling. I see the matte, glasslike crystal gleaming dully around us. It goes quiet. What? The constant hiss from the plastic pipe has stopped. Someone must have turned off the compressor. "And that's it for the generator," Savio says and bends down, rooting through the rubble with his hand, putting a few bits into his pocket. He clears his voice, spits. "We'll run out of oxygen soon," he says. "We've got to get out of here."

"What about the other men?" I ask. Savio smiles.

"Moses – the one who called at us – he's tough as old boots. Get moving." Savio dashes back along the corridor. He's seen what he came to see. I crawl behind him silently, feeling a lump of tears grow in my throat. It seems much further now. I am out of breath. The darkness is almost complete now because Savio is covering the torch with his hand. Why is he doing that? I haven't got enough air to ask. My hands are aching, my knees, elbows, the top of my head slams against the ceiling – I feel something wet in my hair – blood. Savio stops so suddenly I almost slam into him.

"Shhh," he says and turns off the torch completely, finds my neck with his hand and pulls me close, speaking into my ear under his breath. "You hurry ahead past that tunnel – I'll be right behind you." He gives me shove. I do it. POW – a shot; the sound is paralysing in the low-ceilinged shaft. I throw myself down – have passed the tunnel. Am I hit? No. I hear a faint movement behind me. I turn my head. PAW-PAW . . . PAW. The flash from the muzzle lights up Savio, who is taking cover around a corner, shooting into the tunnel. As soon as the revolver is silent, everything is pitch black once more. There's a scraping sound. Savio lunges ahead. PAW-PAW-PAW-PAW – the shots come from the tunnel.

"AHHHRRRRGGHHH," Savio shouts as he collapses right next to me. "Fuck," he says. He crabs onwards – I follow him. He lights the torch. His trouser leg is wet with blood. "Here," he says, handing me the revolver. "If you hear anything, you shoot." Savio rips off his shirt, puts the torch into his mouth, tears the shirt into strips and ties a strip tightly around his thigh. His hairy stomach bulges out over the waistband, but nothing about him feels heavy. "The revolver," he says. I hand it to him. "You go ahead – quickly now." He turns off the torch, sends a shot behind us. The torch is off, so you can't see us from behind. I hear Savio groaning with pain. Crawl on, my palms feel rough; the shaft bends; a light appears behind me – Savio has turned the torch back on, because the twists of the shaft keep us covered. "Stop," he says. I stop, and he crawls towards me. "You shine the light," he says and gives me the torch. I see that the revolver is once again in his shoulder holster. Right away he moves on. I feel lightheaded. Maybe I'm about to pass out because the air is so thin. We reach the injured man – Shirazi – he is conscious again. Savio stops next to him, pulls out the revolver from its holster, places the muzzle at the back of the man's head. Savio speaks to him:

"I am shooting you, because you're paralysed, Shirazi. Have a good trip," he says and pulls the trigger.

"AAHHHHRRRGGHHH." The scream is from my throat. Involuntary. I am sick. Savio moves ahead, the torch is in my hand, and I can't help shining the light as I crab along the furthest wall to get past the exploded skull, get away. Finally we reach the *mama*'s absurd corpse. The air is better here. The ladder. Savio moves upwards at a steady pace; his wounded leg is hanging free as he moves his hands up a step and pulls up his body with his arms, groaning heavily until he can rest his good leg on a step further up and move his hands up a step, one by one. Groaning rhythmically, upwards. Savio's back is glistening wet with sweat in the flickering light of the torch. Drops hit me, sobs stick in my throat, lactic acid builds up in my muscles. Below us . . . I am numb . . . Savio has thought of everything; the man who fired those shots – he could come to the shaft, climb after us, shoot up – it would be me who would take the bullet. Savio has stopped on a small ledge.

"Hand me the torch and climb on," he says. I give it to him, and he puts it in his mouth. I climb past him, quickly – upwards. Savio shoots down – one shot. Has he got more? I climb on, thinking only about the next step. And the one after that. The next one. When I look up, all I see is the ladder and the darkness, the glimpse of the shapeless sides of the pit lit by Savio's torch below me. Step by step. Up into the world. My world. Finally I can see a paler splotch above me. Sweat pours into my eyes, down my neck, over my ribs. One foot slips, hangs without support, my palms are slipping, wet on the worn rungs – too much sweat. I press my free foot against the wall of the pit, let go of the rung with one hand so my arm can reach in and hold onto the rung below. Hang there for a bit; I can feel that my arms will start cramping soon – try to control my breathing. Hold on with one arm, still one foot on a rung. Guide the other hand down until they are both on the same rung. Remove my foot from the wall slowly, allow it to find its way back to the rung and the other foot. Regain my composure. Wipe my palms carefully, first one, then the other on my damp trousers. Light from the torch flickers around me.

"Get a move on," Savio says below me. I start climbing automatically, one arm, one leg, upwards. Finally I'm out and can crawl on my hands and feet on the ground for the final few metres where the pit begins with big shapeless steps. Savio laughs in a low voice as he limps past me and towards the shed. I roll onto my back. Breathe heavily. The air is amazing. Stare out under the lean-to at the stars. The stars. The sky. The world. I crab backwards further away from the pit until I sit up – am absurdly afraid the pit might suck me into it, into its darkness. I look around feverishly to see where Savio is. A sound from the pit makes me throw myself down on the ground. I look over – sense movement, a field of darkness denser than the night – then it's gone. Savio returns – stands about, fiddling with something in his hands. Explosives. If he's out, he can kill us – the man whose name is Moses. What can I do? Maybe I imagined it. Maybe he's out of ammunition. I get up carefully.

"The one you shot – shall we throw him into the pit before you blow it up?" I ask. Oddly matter of fact now. The mama's right-hand man is still on the ground, his breathing has an odd bubbling sound.

"People have to see that he's dead," Savio says. "Go over to the car." I move slowly, my limbs stiff from lactic acid. Legs made of tough, wet wood.

Conte has opened the bonnet of the mama's Land Rover to start it. Sounds from outside the fence.

"Get lost," people are shouting in Swahili. Conte looks at me as I stumble towards the car.

"They're not as scared as they were," he says. "Now they will kill us to get to it." A shot is heard outside.

"Get lost – this isn't your mine." More people are shouting now. Cold sweat is running down my back. Savio comes running towards us.

"Get behind the wheel," he tells Conte, who obeys.

"The man is still alive. Aren't you afraid to leave him there? He will tell them you did it," I say.

"We're coming in," people are shouting from outside.

"He'll be dead in a minute," Savio says, his head under the bonnet, working with the cables in his hands.

"You don't know that," I say.

"Get in the car," he says as he stands waiting with a cable in each hand – holding them a short distance apart, as if waiting for something.

"He might survive," I say.

"I have shot animals through the chest before," Savio says. "You can tell from the sound of his breathing that his lungs are flooding with blood." There's the sound of an enormous boom from the pit. An explosion followed by the rattle of rocks. At that very moment Savio puts his hands together, the cables; the engine starts. I jump onto the back seat. Savio is standing by the door, a lighter in his hand – a stick in his other hand, the sound of a fuse being lit. Dynamite. He throws the stick towards the gate where the voices are coming from, and jumps into the passenger seat. He sits ready with his revolver in his hand, the window is wound down. Conte gets the car in gear. The explosion from the gate; big, brief, followed by a rain of rubble slamming into the ground. Conte reverses, brakes, changes gear and steps on the accelerator, and then we're flying at the fence. Wood splinters, we crash through, out between the rubble heaps that sparkle in the headlights. We tear past Savio's mine, over to the tracks – heading towards the village.

Savio puts on his seatbelt. His pulls his belt from his trousers and ties it around his thigh, cursing under his breath in Portuguese. We drive without saying anything until we approach Merelani Township.

"That *mama* was a cunt," Conte says suddenly.

"Yes," Savio says. "Those boys deserved everything they managed to get out of there."

"Why did you shoot her right-hand man?" I ask. Savio turns around and looks at me:

"He stole her stones." And Savio stole his, but I don't mention it.

"But she was dead," I say. Savio turns back and faces the direction we're heading in, speaking over the noise of the engine:

"People expect miners to steal; of course they do – they're not paid. Mine steal as well. But a right-hand man – you have to be able to trust him; otherwise you're dead. He is paid for his loyalty."

"You can't buy loyalty," I say.

"No. That's why I shot him," Savio says. I don't say anything, I don't understand it at all. "I'm a right-hand man as well," he says. "I had to kill him in order to keep my job. Keep people's faith in me. Now I have to get to her find. Then I can quit." I'm still shaking – can't stop. Conte turns and looks at me. He laughs.

"The *mzungu* isn't up for Zaire," he says to Savio. We drive for a while in silence. Savio digs into his pocket. He turns around in his seat, holding a small shapeless rock towards me:

"There you are," he says. "Want to join the business?" I shake my head. "Take it – it's yours," he says. I take the stone. Feel its surface, bruised, grainy glass.

Savio sits, looking relaxed, saying:

"When God created the world, He endowed Africa with such a wonderful wealth of natural resources that the angels protested: 'Why must they have so much?' God laughed at the angels: 'Don't worry,' He said. 'Just wait until you see the people I'm going to put there.'" Conte laughs.

"*Kweli*," he says – true.

We drive right through the village, on to the airport and up to the main road, where they set me down so I can catch a bus at first light. Savio needs to go see a doctor he knows in Arusha.

"Are you alright?" he asks.

"Yes," I say.

"Africa," he says, shrugging – smiling. "Just let me know if you want to buy some stones."

"Bye," I say as Conte gets the Land Rover into gear – they're off.

My plan of starting a band with Marianne as the lead singer is dead before it gets off the ground. The guitarist is too godly to play to people who drink, and they are the only ones I can find. I'm glad I never got round to telling Marianne about it.

We shagged like bunnies the first few days. We went with Katriina and the girls to Tarangire National Park and to Hotel Tanzanite in Arusha. We went up to the first cabin on the mountain. And then we went back again and shagged like bunnies. But now we've stopped, and that's all we've got in common. She comes back and wants to talk:

"What if I can get work in a U.N. refugee camp out west – would you come with me?" she asks. I didn't even know there were U.N. refugee camps in Tanzania. But there's always some sort of trouble between tribes and governments in Burundi, Rwanda, Uganda, Congo.

"I didn't come here to work in a refugee camp, you know," I say. "To me that seems like slum tourism with a fig leaf."

"You can't be serious," Marianne says.

"I am," I say.

"But surely we've got the means, Christian. It's right that we help out," she says. I understand what it is she means by saying 'means'. I think I understand it better than she does herself. We've got organizational skills – we can make things work.

"What is it you want to save the poor negroes from?" I ask.

"From starving to death. I want to help them return to their homes," she says. They'll be butchered if they return home – they're refugees precisely because they want to survive. Who does she think she is?

"We're in their home," I say. "Africa. That's how they live. You can't change it one way or the other."

"Of course I can . . . People can make a difference. The U.N. can actively protect the refugees that decide to go back. And I'd like to be a part of that."

"Mother Teresa," I say. "Ankle deep in shit. Typhoid, malaria, bilharziasis, worms, malnourishment, genocide, *juju*-crap – that's right up your alley, is it?"

"What is it you do?" Marianne sneers: "Play reggae to them – what good does that do?"

"More than the U.N.," I say and go outside, start the motorbike, drive down to Majengo, go to a bar, have a beer. Christ Almighty, she is so white.

The next day I go to the *mama*'s behind Tanesco at lunch. Rachel isn't there. I ask the girl serving.

"*Mimi sijui*," she says – I don't know. I ask the *mama*.

"*Huyo Rachel, sio mzuri – mimi sijui yoko wapi*," she says: That Rachel is no good – I don't know where she is.

"Tsk," I say.

Marcus

TAX GOAT

The T. R. A. man comes to Roots Rock. Tanzania Revenue Authority – the tax devil.

"A Coke," he says, and Patricia leaps like a flea. My world is too small for taxes, but with the kiosk on Uru Road and the recording shop here and Patricia with her second-hand clothes out the front – it starts sticking in the taxman's eye. I quickly invite him into the yard, serve him beer and *nyama choma*.

"We must settle how much tax you need to pay," he says.

"My turnover is very small," I say.

"Show me the books," he says.

"My turnover is too small for books," I say.

"You could go to prison for not having books," he says.

"I do have books, but I keep them at home," I say.

"Then you must go and get them," he says.

"I can't very well leave the shop right now," I say. "But I could bring them to your house tonight."

"What do I need your books for in my own home?" he says.

"I would give you a small present in return for troubling you in your own home," I say.

"How small would that present be?" he says.

"The size of three chickens – ready for the pot," I say.

"No, it will be the size of a goat," he says and looks me right in the eye as he gives me the address. The rest of the day I am a man who runs around to buy a goat, and in the evening I am a man who pays an extra steep price for taking a goat in a taxi all the way to Kiborloni, where the taxman has built his house – lots of room for presents on his farm, which is full of chickens, goats and stinky pigs.

Christian

First I go to Kibo Coffee House. Sit there chain-smoking, drinking iced coffee. I need to get more business. We don't make enough money, and I've got nowhere with Savio and the tanzanite stones. I need money to pay to ship the decks from Hasseris Gymnasium. If I don't, this is never going to work. And I need a place to live. Katriina's hospitality has worn thin. They have that saying in Swahili as well: after three days your guests start to smell. She hasn't said anything, but . . . Of course she agrees with my dad that I should be in Denmark, getting an education. And now I've got Marianne nagging me. We must save the negroes from themselves – bullshit. Right now everything feels a bit too much. I drink up, pay. Go up towards Roots Rock.

Rachel! Rachel is sitting in a chair next to the fridge outside the shop. She gets up when she sees me. She smiles.

"Hi, what are you doing here?" she asks. "I thought you had gone." She's holding my hand. Holding lightly with a few fingers – Tanzanian style when you speak man to man. But it's rare that girls do it.

"I'm coming to see you," I say, looking her up and down. She laughs. "I hope I didn't get you into too much trouble with your boyfriend," I say.

"My boyfriend?" she says. "What do you mean?"

"When I met you at Liberty that night," I say.

"Oh." She looks down at the pavement, a bit embarrassed, I think. "No, he's not my boyfriend. I don't have a boyfriend." She smiles at me.

"Good," I say, looking at her hand. Her nails are golden brown. I let my fingers run over them. "What's that?" I ask.

"Henna tattoo," she says.

"How do you do it?"

"It's a bark which you make into a powder, and then you mix the powder with tea until it becomes moist, and leave it on your nails for a little while."

"It's *mwafrika* nail polish," I say. She giggles and lifts my hands, tracing patterns on my palm with a finger.

"You can use it to make patterns on your palm and on your fingers as well, like the Indians do," she says. And just then I see Katriina drive up in her Nissan Patrol – Marianne is on the passenger side. Rachel doesn't know about Marianne – unless she's heard I've been around town with a white girl. But that could have been my sister or someone else entirely.

"I'll see you," I tell Rachel, letting go of her hand and going over to the car, which has stopped at the roadside. Katriina isn't looking at me, isn't saying anything. The car isn't moving, but Marianne isn't getting out either. She too is looking straight ahead. I open the door. Marianne gets out slowly, closing it as she leans down and says, "See you," through the open window, and Katriina drives off. Then Marianne walks down towards Clock Tower roundabout without so much as looking at me.

"What?" I say, going after her.

"I saw you, you know," she says.

"Saw who?" I ask.

"You and . . . that girl."

"Her name is Rachel," I say. "She's someone I know."

"Yes, I rather think you do."

"What's that supposed to mean?"

"I saw you holding her hand."

"Listen," I say, "down here even the men hold hands when they walk together and stand about talking. It's not some kind of foreplay."

"Yes," she says. "And the women hold hands too, but not the men with the women."

"Sometimes they do – it happens," I say.

"Yes, so I see," she says.

Marcus

THE FAKE TOURIST

The immigration people come to my shop. "Where is that *mzungu*?" the man asks.

"The *mzungu*? I think he is with his father and the family," I say.

"No, he works with you – when will he be here?" the man asks.

"No, no, no, he doesn't work here. He is just a guest at his father's. And he is my guest as well. And his father is here – he works for the Nordic Project. They have lived here for many years."

"But the young *mzungu* isn't a real tourist," the man says. The lady explains:

"We see him here every morning, every noon, every night. He comes in his car, delivers boxes, picks up boxes. That's a business." The immigration office is right over on Boma Road – the staff have the lunches at the same *mama* as Christian. They see him as a walking cash cow. How much will he pay to make them forget his transgression?

"No, he's just my friend," I say. "He lends me his L.P.s so I can work better and pay my own way."

"You're lying," the man says. "And you won't benefit from the *mzungu*. You're a loser yourself. And he must pay taxes."

"No, no, no, no. He is a visitor. He is here on a tourist visa."

"We're keeping an eye on you," the lady says, and they leave.

EUROPEAN LOVE

Christian is going to the mountain to play a disco at a wedding. But I can't go anywhere because my daughter is a sack of skin and bones. I can only sit in Roots Rock, record cassettes for *wazungu* children at I.S.M. and question Christian's integrity. His white girlfriend, Marianne, comes through the door.

"How are you?" I ask.

"Alright," she says, buying Cokes for herself and me. She sits down, smokes a lot of cigarettes, fidgets.

"Do you like it here?" I ask. She smokes her cigarette, sighs, looks at me, says:

"What is it Christian's mixed up in? What is it he wants? In life . . . just tell me straight out – you know him." And I am in her position myself, but I tell her she must wait, that he will make it work, get it right.

"Give it a chance," I say. But she comes right back at me:

"There's a girl he's in love with. I can see it in his eyes; I know him – he wants her. I can feel it when we make love."

That girl is Rachel – the waitress from the *mama*'s. And I know Marianne is speaking the truth. What can I say? Christian is a hungry fish, and the black girl uses good bait. And Christian thinks he's an African who understands things. The *mswahili* girl is a *malaya* – just a different kind: the one you don't think is a *malaya*; she's the greatest *malaya* of all.

And now this *mzungu* comes – he drives a big car, and no-one can tell it belongs to his father, and he's got a hundred dollars in his pocket – now he's waving it around in Tanzania and it's worth a fortune in shillings. The black girl is looking for a ticket. Rachel can do anything for him. Marianne is so sad she's almost in tears. Watching her eyes is almost like seeing Katriina in the old days of Jonas Larsson's pumping factory.

Christian

She's got almost shoulder-length hair; the frizz has been combed out but her hair hasn't been straightened – she probably can't afford to. She wears it up like the black Americans she's seen in films. Sometimes she puts Vaseline in it to make it shiny. But I've also seen her wearing cornrows. If she hasn't had her hair done, she wears a red baseball cap the wrong way around or a bandana. Her tops always have very short sleeves – a few of them have buttons down the front, a collar. I've also seen her with a *kanga* wrapped around her waist, but most of the time she wears trousers – all sorts of trousers: jeans, linen trousers, dark pinstriped gabardine trousers. On her feet, flip-flops or pretty leather sandals with beaded embroidery, probably given to her by her brother before he died. She probably also has a pair of high heels to wear to church on Sundays. Earrings, a necklace made of dark glass beads, two simple bracelets on her right arm, no watch. Rachel wears nail polish, peeling just a little – a dark pink, on her toes as well. Her nails are long, strongly curved and thick. She has a sturdy build, a strong face – powerful jawline, a wide mouth with lips that are full without being voluptuous, a delicate nose, slanted cat's eyes that are alive and quick and suddenly go lazy in the most erotic way. Her arms are strong, her hands – not too big although the fingers are muscular – are strong as well. Her breasts are large and pert; they jiggle under her top. She has a waist, but she isn't like a

Coca-Cola bottle – she's too strong for that. Her arse is pert as well, without being wide, and her buttocks tip from side to side when she walks. Her thighs are strong and soft at the same time, her shins are powerful, her feet short and wide. She's not stout, there isn't an ounce of fat on her – it's all muscle. Rachel is a proper *mswahili*.

She speaks to lots of men. That's how it has to be when you sell people fizzy drinks from a fridge outside the shop. They have to drink it then and there, because they can't take the bottle away; so they hang around and chat. I am hanging around, chatting.

"Where are you from?" I ask.

"Galambo, out on the coast, not far from Tanga," she says. "I am *mswahili*."

"Are you a Muslim then?" I ask.

"*Mkristo*," she says. "Like you." I drink quite a few fizzy drinks outside that shop.

Marcus' daughter, Rebekka, is very ill. Thin, dehydrated, drained. He once told me he had been with lots of women after he survived the accident and his stay at K.C.M.C. He says the doctors can't find anything wrong with his daughter. I think it's a lie. I'm sure it's A.I.D.S., but he would never tell me because the disease is a huge taboo.

"Have you had an H.I.V. test done?" I ask.

"*Tsk*," Marcus says. "Every test has been done on that little girl – they can't find anything wrong with her." It might not be true. If people have relatives with the disease, they hide them at home and say it's malaria, because that can kill you as well if you're unlucky. But in any event it means that Marcus can't help me on the nights I play at Shukran Hotel. I can't do it alone. The owner insists that I show up with a man who can separate the wheat from the chaff at the door and accept people's entrance fees. Rogarth steps in. He would rather be with me than run around for *mabwana makubwa* at Moshi Hotel.

Sometime during the morning I step into the servants' quarters at Katriina's. My room. Marianne is still here; sitting at the small desk reading through some papers, writing notes, her hair pulled into a tight ponytail – like a schoolmistress.

"Hi," I say. She doesn't turn around, only says:

"Where have you been?"

"You weren't there," I say.

"You were working. I don't have time to sit and watch you admiringly while you flip records."

"It was Saturday night – I thought we were going out," I say.

"It's not me you want to go out with," Marianne says without turning round and facing me.

"What are you talking about?" I ask.

"You're like . . . like that Jonas." I told her about Jonas, about Katriina, my mum and dad – all of that – when we met and got to know each other at Hasseris Gymnasium.

"How am I like Jonas?" I ask. Now she turns around in her chair, her eyes are swollen. She's been crying. She's ugly.

"Do you think I'm a fool? I talk to people like you do – while you go around doing your . . . job. Jonas was having it off with everyone except Katriina, because he wanted them young and black."

"Yes," I say. "He was. I'm starting to think perhaps the man had a point."

"Did you meet your little friend?" Marianne says.

"No," I say. "Rachel, that's her name. No, I didn't."

"Really. Well, she came round yesterday afternoon," Marianne says.

"Right," I say.

"Issa sent her away. Do you know what he says about her?" Marianne asks.

"No, but I'm sure you'd like to tell me," I say.

"He says she's a bad girl who is only interested in money," Marianne says.

"Yes," I say. "Even though old Issa is black and half deaf, his head is still so colonialized he thinks being white is better than being black."

There's a toxic atmosphere the rest of the day, until the evening when we go to the golf course and smoke a spliff. When we get back, she wants to fuck. And I lick her cunt, stick a finger up her arse, suck her nipples, lick her ears, her neck, tell her she's gorgeous, that I'm crazy about her – all that rot. I don't have to count; not once does she touch me. I might as well have sex with a cardboard box that's been standing outside in the rain.

Monday night I drive down to the C.C.M. building at Clock Tower roundabout. Big Man Ibrahim teaches his karate class every weeknight from seven till nine.

"Are you ready to rumble?" he says.

"I just came to meet the people you were talking about," I say.

"You'll work out with us," he says and goes over to stand facing the twelve or fourteen youngsters, starting to belch out orders.

"I'm Khalid," one of the blokes says. "If you don't work out with us, he'll never speak to you again." I work out. Sweat is pouring from us. Afterwards Ibrahim grins at me and calls over a guy called Abdullah. I am introduced. Abdullah is almost as big as Ibrahim. I ask him if he would like to work as a bouncer Friday and Saturday nights at Shukran Hotel. He'd like that. Then I go down to my motorbike. Khalid comes running after me.

"Want to grab a Coke?" he asks.

"Why not?" I say.

"I've been to your disco at Shukran Hotel. You've got great music," Khalid says.

"Thanks," I say.

"You have to know – that Abdullah – he's a very dangerous man. He's been to prison. He only just got out after two years. Karanga Prison," Khalid says in confidential tones.

"What did he do time for?" I ask.

"Murder – everyone knows." Khalid nods seriously. That's not a bad rep for a bouncer to have. And I'm pretty sure the man didn't kill anyone if he only did two years.

"Get up on the back," I say. We go over to Shukran Hotel and have a Coke out the front.

"I could do a good job for you as well, when you have discos," Khalid says.

"Were you in prison as well?" I ask. He smiles, and we slap hands. He holds up his hand.

"No, but I've got a deadly weapon, courtesy of Big Man Ibrahim."

The next night I go there again. Two hours' worth of torture under Ibrahim's instructions. Afterwards I ask him about Abdullah.

"No, no – not murder," Ibrahim says. "The accusation was a lie. But Abdullah doesn't have the money to get out, so he sits for two years and waits for his trial. On the first day in front of the judge, the case is thrown out of court, because there is no evidence." Ibrahim laughs loudly.

"Two years for a lie," I say.

"Yes," Ibrahim says. "The Tanzanian methods – very hard."

It finally seems Marianne has given up on the idea of making me a better man. She is going to go off on her own:

"I'll go up and talk to them," she says. "Then we'll see what we can do."

"Alright," I say. She wants to go to Arusha and talk to a U.N. office there and then take a bus to Kampala and talk to another U.N. office – all of it something to do with refugees and internally displaced persons in camps. She wants to save those people. She's white – she's the reason they're suffering. I give her a lift down to the bus station in the morning. Am glad to see the bus drive off.

Marcus

GOD'S PUNISHMENT

One night a man and a woman from Claire's church knock on the door. The man speaks like Satan:

"It's God's punishment for your not being married. If you get married, you may just save the baby. If the child dies now, it cannot go to Heaven, and you won't go to Heaven either, because you're living in sin." Claire is weeping. The man opens his Bible and reads:

"'Thus saith the Lord: Behold, I will raise up evil against thee out of thine own house.' Two Samuel, Twelve Eleven."

"Come to our church," the woman says.

"I'm a Catholic," I say. "I can't leave my church, and Claire won't leave yours."

"You're endangering the soul of your child," the man says.

"But what if we were to get married at the magistrate's?" Claire asks.

"The magistrate can do nothing against the power of the devil," the man says. And Claire doesn't actually want to go to the magistrate – she wants us to go to church. And she doesn't trust my church, and I don't think her church is better than mine – I think they're all the same, the same dusty old bones.

"Marcus doesn't interfere with my faith. I won't interfere with his," Claire says to defend our position – we can't get married in two churches at the same time. Myself, I know those churches were started by men no different from me. They're all wrong.

"You must baptize your child – perhaps you can remove the evil from it and save it from eternal damnation," the church woman says.

"We've heard what you have to say," I say. "Now we want to go to bed. We have a child that is ill. We have work tomorrow."

"But perhaps . . ." Claire says when they've left.

"It's just lies," I say. "No child can be evil. We are not evil. God loves his children."

"The evil thoughts of the witch have entered the child. Only God can take them out," Claire says. I can tell her that witchcraft has no place in her religion, but I am too tired.

The next morning Claire goes on:

"We must baptize the child." I agree.

Two days later we are at her church, baptizing our daughter Rebekka, even though she's not so much a daughter now – just skin and bones. We give her sugar water with a spoon, but she vomits it out – from her mouth there's a smell of putrefaction, while her eyes are full of a sort of vacant despair.

I am at K.C.M.C. all the time; the doctors can't work out what's wrong. Until that last day. It's the day when Rebekka must have X-rays taken, ultrasound, all those things – to give us the final answers from the doctors. Claire takes her off. I go to hide in the bar. Screaming wakes me up:

"Marcus, Marcus – Rebekka isn't breathing." It's Claire's friend. I run to the house. Claire is bent over the sofa, screaming; she is pressing down onto the sofa – Rebekka's chest.

"It's Satan," Claire screams. "Rhema has sent Satan into my child." I hold Claire. She sobs. There is my daughter. Still.

"We were on our way up to the bus, but suddenly she wasn't breathing," her friend says.

We go to the hospital to get the death certificate and to church to arrange the funeral. So much to be done, and my limbs feels stiff. That night the church people return.

"You must join our church," they tell me. "The evil that has happened is due to you not being properly wed and in the right church."

I don't say anything. I want to get the funeral over with; afterwards they can have my answer.

"Marcus, you must be saved. Look at the things that have happened," the church man says.

"But it was evil spirits," Claire tells them. "It was a witch – she gave Rebekka satanic medicine and set the evil eye on her."

"You can only defeat the evil spirits by being saved," the church man says. "It's the evil spirits of the ancestors who are displeased – that's why they're punishing you."

I want them out of my house. How can God's man be talking about the spirits of the ancestors? – that's heresy. I tell them I will think about it. They leave, satisfied that I'm already living in their pocket.

"You must at least come to church on Sunday," Claire says.

"I'm going out for a while," I say and take my cigarettes with me. Claire starts crying:

"You're always using the bar as your church, but God doesn't live in a bottle."

"Yes, my God does live there, and when I empty the bottle, God enters my body." I leave. It's foolish to speak to Claire like that just because I am irked by these clerical fools – I ought to beat them with a rod.

WHITE SOLEMNITY

I whizz around town arranging it all: greasing the palm of the vicar to do his job, the coffin from the carpenters at Imara Furniture Factory, snacks for the guests after the ceremony. After my toils I take a break with beer and Konyagi. A big bloke comes over to me and sits down at my table, leaning over.

"You must tell your *mzungu* to stay away from Rachel," the guy says.

"Who are you?" I say.

"Tito," he says.

"You can tell him yourself," I say.

"If he doesn't stay away, I will harm him," Tito says.

"Harm?"

"Yes, harm," Tito says.

"He isn't my *mzungu*," I say. "I don't decide whether he runs after that girl or not.'"

"Now listen to me," Tito says. "If you don't . . ." I interrupt him:

"No. My daughter died yesterday and will be buried tomorrow. I don't care about you. I don't care about threats, about the *mzungu*, about the girl. Go away," I say.

534

"You've been warned," Tito says.

"*Tsk*," I say.

The entire family comes to the funeral; Solja, the dead daughter's namesake Rebekka, Katriina, *bwana* Knudsen. In life they are nothing to me anymore, but in death they stand by my side. Christian comes as well. At least he understands that much about the African system. If he fails me at the funeral, he will sow bad blood between us. His disgust at the screaming hysteria of the African women at the edge of the tomb is hidden behind his sunglasses; to the white man our grief is something primitive and barbaric.

Katriina comes over and puts her arm on my shoulder:

"Now baby Rebekka is at peace, Marcus," she says.

"Peace?" I say. "When white children die, they get wings and become angels in heaven. Black children become flies."

"Don't say that, Marcus."

"That's why we have fly swats," I say.

"No," Katriina says, shaking her head. I look at her:

"Invented by a white man."

GOD'S DISCO

"We can just about get enough money together to have the decks sent down," Christian says, "but it's impossible for us to pay sixty-five per cent import tax."

"Aren't there any *wazungu* who need Carlsberg sent down from Ostermann in the same shipment from Denmark?" I ask.

"No, there's lots of beer in Arusha, and there aren't any new *wazungu* coming down for a while. We're going to have to find a different way of doing it."

"I have an idea," I say and bring Christian out to see the bishop – Claire's bishop at the Pentecostal church in Majengo. Because churches don't pay duty, taxes, tolls. God is exempt from those things. There is an old Norwegian man who is part of the congregation – he has married a local woman and gets lots of things sent down from Norway. "He can set it up so we don't have to pay import taxes. And you can pay him for the local costs."

The Norwegian man has a small office in the bishop's building.

"Is it necessary that I go with you?" Christian asks outside the church. Sometimes the white boy thinks like an illiterate from the village.

535

"Yes – the church must see our beacon in the distance in order to help us. You must promise the bishop that you are ready to do something for him at any time. Perhaps they would like to rent the decks at religious get-togethers – then you will let them use them for free or always very cheaply. Just show them that you are here for them, and then we can get away with not paying taxes." And Christian says exactly what I've told him to. It works – they will help us.

UPRISING

Claire is lying in our bed, staring into the wall. Having so many worries has made her very thin. Perhaps she's decided to die like a stubborn native.

"*Fy fan!*" I say – damn, that's disgusting. But step by step we start to move again. We try hard to regain the energy to work.

At night when Claire is asleep, I get out my shoebox with my personal papers. It's inside the locked cabinet. Only I have a key. And I dig into the bottom, open the envelope and pull out the picture. My chocolate baby. "It's good," I tell the baby who is three years old now. "You are in Finland – you can grow up and be big and strong and pretty. Be healthy and go to school. You are my emissary, my agent in the white country." And I look at Tita and the baby, and I hold the picture out a little, so the drops that fall don't make it wet.

Claire's friends from church start coming to visit again.

"Ohhh – satanic," they say when they see my five framed pictures of Bob Marley on the wall along with one of Haile Selassie and one of Claire and baby Rebekka while she was still pretty and chubby. Jesus bleeds on the cross, but not in my home. "How can you live with those pictures?" they ask Claire carefully.

"We all have our own gods," she says. And she thinks Bob is alright to look at – you know where you are with him and he always sounds good too. Only when I make the bar my church and God does Claire complain.

Claire is strong. "We need something spectacular to sell in the kiosk and in Roots Rock to attract customers."

"Where will we get it?" I ask.

"In Kenya," Claire says.

"But we haven't got any Kenyan shillings and we've no way of getting them," I say.

"We will make batik," she says and buys fabric, wax, die and all the ingredients – she has acquainted herself with the technique through a woman her mother knows. The chemicals stink out the house, but the result is an explosion of colour.

NO-MAN'S-LAND

The Kenyan border is shut for political reasons, because the Tanzanian economy is so ruined by *mwalimu* Nyerere's dreams of socialism that everything would collapse if we got competition from solid Kenyan goods. But there is a market in no-man's-land on the Holili–Taveta border where we can sell our batik to the Kenyans. When we go back, we have to pay the import tax on all the Kenyan things we have bought. But we can smuggle things through instead.

Claire packs our large pile of batik, and we take the bus east through Himo and on to Holili. The road winds in long, gentle swipes through the billowing landscape, covered in shrubs and thorns. Cowherds with their cattle, sheep and goats – cornfields, beans. The bus drives up to a small hillock, and you can see far into the distance.

We enter no-man's-land. At the market the Kenyans come to buy sweetcorn, beans, batik fabric and second-hand clothes which come to Kenya from aid organizations in the west. Kenyans pay in Kenyan shillings. At the market the Kenyans have all the things we need, but not at wholesale prices – there is an extra mark-up. And then there's the import taxes on top.

We sell the batik at a good price, and in Taveta we buy soaps as such Imperial Leather and Lux, we buy Nivea lotion, Omo washing-up liquid, soap bars for washing clothes. In Kenya they have different brands of everything, you can buy proper cosmetics, salt is much cheaper and cooking oil too, there's Kiwi shoe polish, toothpaste, medicines like painkillers and cough syrup. Things that are ordinary in Kenya are luxury items in Tanzania.

In Holili we get on a bus to Moshi with our goods. We drive and wait for the border controls – police and customs officers. I have the banknotes ready, folded up in my hand. The bus stops, the customs officer walks down the aisle. I hand him the money discreetly – that's why he's here: the money is for his own pocket – not for the public purse which only feeds corrupt *mabwana makubwa*. The customs officer doesn't want to do a search, because the bus gets very hot when it's immobile on the road in the sun. The police and the customs officers would rather stand in the shade of the tree and wait for the next bus to come along, bringing gifts for their pockets.

My kiosk becomes the Garden of Eden. I have bought bus tickets, hired pedicabs, paid bribes – and still I make a good profit: fifty per cent. Right away we're back to our batik production. The kiosk is working, the chickens are growing. Claire's belly is growing as well, because we have been soft in the hard bed. Money is tight, but at least we're not just passengers hanging on the shirttails of a stupid white boy.

BLINDED

"You think that the *mzungu* is divine and can change your lives," I say, "but he's just a boy. The car he drives, that belongs to his father. The stereo in this shop – half of it's mine. He isn't a wonder." They look at Christian the way people at West Kilimanjaro used to look at Jonas – the forest king.

"He can get big decks for Liberty or Moshi Hotel from Europe," Khalid says. Firestone, our scrawny new hanger-on with the terrible stutter nods.

"You work for him yourself," Abdullah says. "You're just trying to keep us away from the good work he will offer us."

"I don't work for him," I say. "We are partners."

"Christian drives around in a Nissan Patrol with his *chiki-chiki* girl and has a good time, while you sit here, recording cassettes in Roots Rock all day long. You work for him," Abdullah says. I could explain it to them: the immigration people, the missing work permit, but I don't bother.

"We'd like to work for him," Khalid says. "When he gets the big disco decks, he will need more hands. Don't try to keep us out of the game." They leave. And I am trapped in the shop. When they meet Christian, I know they're talking about me. I have to do something. Christian comes to pick me up with the decks at night. I laugh:

"All the Swahili guys keep coming to the shop because they want to work for you. They think you will make them rich and famous and take them with you to Europe," I say.

"I am going to need more people when the decks arrive," Christian says.

"*We* are going to need," I say. "I've paid for it as much as you have."

"Well, technically I paid the better part of it," Christian says.

"Yes, but I'm the one who can get it into the country, and I'm the one who has to sit in the shop all day," I say.

"Yes, yes, of course," Christian says.

"You have to be careful about those Swahili guys," I say. "Right now they're nice enough, but if they smell blood, they will eat you."

"Give it a rest," Christian says. But I can't rest. Abdullah and Khalid have sown bad thoughts in the boy's head – I can hear them taking root.

Christian

Marcus has rented a taxi without a driver for the night. He takes me to Shukran Hotel, and we carry the decks inside.

"You must pick up Rachel at the shop at nine and then come down here," I say.

"Why?" Marcus asks.

"She wants to see it," I say.

"Is that a good idea, Christian?" he asks.

"What's wrong with it?" I ask.

"I'm just asking you to know that you're sure," Marcus says.

"If I'm sure I want you to pick her up?" I ask.

"Yes," Marcus says.

"Yes, I'm sure of it," I say and turn my back on him, going inside. Fucking hell, he is meddlesome – what the hell has he got against her? She's lovely. I could pick her up myself, but it's better I stay here, so people see me getting things ready for the disco, because the customers are more interested if it's run by a white man – never before seen.

The music has started, the lights are low, Abdullah is at the door, and the customers are filing in. Rogarth is here as well, even though I didn't actually ask him to come, but I still let him in for free.

Marcus arrives with Rachel. Her hair – she's had it done: tiny pitch-black kiss curls glisten on her skull. She is very attractive: pale beaded sandals, a long linen skirt which she has altered to slink around her thighs and arse. And a burgundy polyester shirt which accentuates her waist; the sleeves are short and show her plump arms. She comes up and presses against me, intensely but briefly. Then she lets go again. What does that mean?

"Would you like a Coke?" I ask. "I'll be done in just a minute."

"Alright," she says and sits down at a table. I fetch a Coke for her. I lean over and speak into her ear so she can hear me above the music.

"I think you taste nice," I say. "But I can't remember – where was it you said you were the tastiest?" She grins, and her breasts bob up and down, and I don't think she's wearing a bra – they defy gravity. The top two buttons of her shirt are open, so you can just make out the dark cleavage, and the fabric is stretched out between her breasts in horizontal folds. Even in the dark room I can make out the outlines of her nipples. She gestures towards her groin.

"This is where I am the tastiest," she says and laughs even more. The third button of her shirt springs open, so she puts up her hands to re-button it as I look down into the darkness between the globes. To guide the button into the buttonhole she has to pull the fabric tight around the pert weight of her breasts.

"So now you go to a disco at night," I say to Rachel. "What do you think your aunt will say to that?"

"My aunt thinks I'm taking an English class at the K.N.C.U. building," Rachel says.

"I can teach you to make trouble in English," I say, slapping her thigh because I want to feel it against my palm.

"Enough!" she says. "Tsk, you are bad." But at the same time she grabs my hand and keeps it in place on her thigh, which is warm with firm muscles under all the softness. I catch sight of Claire coming through the door, over to our table.

"Hi, Claire," I say. Marcus turns in his chair and sees her.

"Claire?" he says.

"Hi," she says. "I've come to see it."

"Sit down. I will get you something to drink," Marcus says.

"No, I want to see it," Claire says and turns her back on us, looking around the room.

"Tsk," Rachel says in a very low voice, probably because Claire wouldn't say hello to her. Marcus looks at me, very confused. Gets up, takes Claire to the bar.

"I am going to have to leave now," Rachel says.

"Oh, go on – stay a little longer," I say.

"But, then I will miss the last matatu to Majengo."

"We'll give you a lift home, I promise," I say.

"But not too late," she says.

"In a minute," I say. "I just have to talk to someone." I get up and go to the bar. Claire is standing there talking to Rogarth at the decks.

"What is she doing here?" I ask Marcus.

"She wants to see it," he says.

"No," I say. "She would rather be at home. She knows it's wrong for her to be seen in town so soon after her daughter's funeral. She can't even say hello to Rachel, who's sitting at our table. Tell me why she's here." Marcus sighs.

"She thinks that when I'm out with you, I do it so I can spend time with other girls," he says.

"Tsk," I say. "Does anyone think about anything but sex in this country?"

"No," Marcus says, shaking his head. And all the while Claire is trying to push her sister on me. Marcus shrugs. His grin is resigned.

"Why the hell can't she say hello to Rachel?" I ask.

"I don't know," Marcus says.

"Of course you bloody do," I say.

"She thinks Rachel is a bad girl," Marcus says.

"Bad how?"

"Claire says Rachel has been with many men," Marcus says.

"I've been with many women," I say angrily, even though I haven't been with nearly enough. "We can't all be as godly as Claire."

"No," Marcus says.

"She shouldn't be here, not with that attitude – I really can't stomach it," I say and go back to the table. Rachel isn't looking happy anymore.

"I'd like to go home now," she says.

"Don't worry about Claire," I say. "She's just very religious."

"Yes, but I have to go now. I have to go to work early tomorrow morning," Rachel says.

"Alright," I say and fetch Marcus who must drive the rented taxi. I've had a few beers, and the car has a steering-column gear lever which I haven't got a clue how to work. We go out in the darkness, into the cool air. Marcus goes over and unlocks the car. We drive Rachel home to Majengo.

Rachel. She is in my head when I wake up. Both my heads. My cock is rock hard. I must have dreamt of her. Christ, she is hot. Toast, coffee and cigarettes.

541

"Marianne called," Katriina says. "She'll be back tomorrow afternoon."

"O.K.," I say.

"Don't you even want to know how it went?" Katriina asks. How what went?

"Sure," I say. "How did it go?"

"Well it seems she can become an assistant to the person coordinating the U.N.'s refugee relief effort in the Great Lake area," Katriina says.

"Good," I say. "It's what she wants."

"What are you two going to do?" Katriina asks.

"Do?" I say.

"Yes. She is your girlfriend," Katriina says.

"She was my girlfriend," I say. "Now she's come down for a visit, and now she wants to leave. She does whatever she wants to do."

"I don't think that's quite how she sees it," Katriina says.

"No, I'm aware of that, but it's not like I asked her to come here," I say.

"I didn't invite you either," Katriina says.

"I can take off if having me in the servants' quarters is so abhorrent," I say.

"No, no, I'm just saying . . . I think you should have a talk with Marianne. You need to talk about what you'll be doing," Katriina says.

"Yes," I say.

"She probably wasn't expecting you to have several girlfriends," Katriina says. I raise my hands.

"Honestly!" I say and let my arms drop. I don't think it's any of her business, but for the sake of domestic harmony I turn around and go down to the servants' quarters.

I hear Katriina talking to the girls. Two hours later a taxi comes up the drive. Marianne, who is chattering about little, cutesy refugee babies, about procuring blankets and tents, about the unfairness of . . . well, pretty much everything the western world does. I nod without listening. Until she runs temporarily dry.

"I'm not going," I say.

"We'll just have to see each other whenever I have days off," Marianne says.

"If you're going to be saving the world, you'll never have time off," I say.

"Christian, you don't have to be a complete arse," Marianne says. And I ought to explain to her that her guilt about being white seems a bit misplaced. But I can't be bothered. I just want her to go. Just then Rachel comes walking up the drive.

"Hi," Rachel says.

"Hi," I say. "Would you like a Coke?"

"Yes, please," she says.

"Why does she come here? Send her away," Marianne says.

"You can't," I say. "That would be an insult. And wrong." I go into the kitchen to fetch a Coke – give it to Rachel on the veranda. Marianne has lit a cigarette and is wandering around in small circles on the lawn with her arms folded over her chest, staring at the ground. I light a cigarette.

"Just wait here," I tell Rachel, who gives me a vacant look. She's an African. Yes, she's going to wait. She's not leaving. The unpleasantness of life is something that must be dealt with stoically and with all the indifference you can muster. I go down to the lawn.

"What?" I ask Marianne, who turns around and yells at me:

"She comes here because she wants you. To take you away from me. And you give her a sodding Coke?!"

"Yes, I know that's what she wants. And you want to go to a refugee camp."

"Is that really what you want?" Marianne asks – on the verge of tears, I think.

"Right now it seems like a good idea, because all you do is nag." She sobs.

"But you're with me," she whines.

"Am I? You take yourself off to England to be a nanny, and I come down here, and suddenly you show up, and we have to go off and save the world hand in hand. That's not my plan. I didn't invite you." I stare at her. She stares at me, pointing towards Rachel on the veranda.

"I want her gone. I don't want her here while . . . Tell her. Tell her to go," Marianne says.

"You want her to walk all the way back, don't you?" I say. "You don't want me to offer her a lift, do you?"

"No, I don't want you to do that," Marianne says.

"'We have to be good, Christian. We have to make a difference,'" I ape. "But it's not like you're really that good to negroes. You're just out to emancipate yourself, or whatever the fuck the term is."

"You just want to fuck her," Marianne says. I turn around, call to Rachel in Swahili:

"Come, I'll give you a lift home." Go over to the motorbike. Rachel comes over and sits herself behind me.

I drive through the city centre, take the back road to Majengo and set her down.

"See you," I say and turn the bike, drive back to all the nonsense. And find . . . Katriina is sitting on the veranda. But no Marianne.

"What did you say to her?" she asks in an accusatory tone.

"Where is she?" I ask.

"She didn't want to stay. I've taken her to the Y.M.C.A.," Katriina says. "You have to go down and talk to her."

"O.K.," I say and throw myself back on the motorbike. At least she's out of my bed. At the Y.M.C.A. I talk to the girl in reception. Ask what room the white girl is in. She's not allowed to tell me. I pay her, get the room number, go up, knock on the door.

"What?" Marianne says.

"It's me," I say.

"Go away," she says. "I don't want to talk to you."

"For fuck's sake," I say. "What did you think would happen? We haven't seen each other for six months, and then you show up and tell me to go and work in a sodding refugee camp. No, of course I don't want to do that." I am leaning up against the door as I speak.

"You just want to fuck your little whore," Marianne says – it sounds like she's standing some way from the door.

"I haven't fucked her," I say. "And she's not a whore – she's a girl."

"Is she good in bed, that Little Black Sambo of yours?" Marianne asks. This is just too absurd for words.

"Yes," I say. "Much better than you. Not so self-centred."

"Does she tell you you've got a big white cock?"

"No," I say. "But I don't have to praise her humanitarian spirit for two weeks just to make her put it in her mouth." At least I hope that's true, because I haven't managed to make Marianne give me anything whatever – she just lies in bed like a dead flounder, and I have to work out the rest.

"It must be nice for you to have a little negro girl who depends on you for everything," Marianne says.

544

"She's got a job, damn it," I say and am about to say something else, but there's no point. I walk away from the door quietly – then I think I hear Marianne saying something. I go back.

"Marianne," I say, "you remind me of my mum, the way you ... you're so determined and ... bloody full of yourself, as you call me every name under the sun. You are so like her." I've told her about my parents, and I hope I hurt her.

"I'm through with you," she says from inside the room.

"That's it exactly," I say. "If it's not working, just put it behind you and find something better." I leave. Find myself a bar. Get drunk.

The next day I drive down to Roots Rock and then I stroll over to the shop to say hello to Rachel. The girl who is sitting at the fridge calls into the shop:

"Rachel, Rachel – your *mzungu* is here." She comes out – she is radiant. I take her hand and pull her a few metres away from the shop entrance.

"She has gone," I say. "The other girl."

"Did she leave?"

"Yes?" I say.

"I want you to come down and see my new room," she says. Her very presence arouses me.

"I'd like that," I say. "What time do you get off?"

"At nine."

Rogarth isn't at the coffee house when I arrive at eight-thirty.

"Are you hungry?" I ask. Rachel shrugs. "Have you already eaten?" I ask.

"A little," she says.

"Would you like something to eat?"

"Only if you're having some," Rachel says.

"I am," I say and drive up to the Y.M.C.A. roundabout and out along Uru Road to Gadaffi Bar. I order meat and grilled green bananas. A beer for myself. Rachel wants a Coke. We don't say anything while we wait for our drinks.

"Rachel, I'm not a wealthy man," I say.

"It doesn't matter if you're wealthy," she says. "I like you. It's not about the money."

"But . . ." I start. "You have to understand that I want to live here. In Moshi – Tanzania. I'm not going to go back to Europe or anything like that," I say. That's it: out in the open. And why am I saying all this shit? It's just crap Marcus has planted in my head. Rachel is looking uncomfortable. She's leaning forward, raising her shoulders and putting her lower arms together between her knees – the dark cleavage. She knows she's showing it off – I think. Her voice is quiet, and she's looking at the ground.

"Europe is good, because they have good hospitals and schools for everyone," she says. "That's good. But if you are here in Tanzania, then that's good as well. I am not interested in many cars and that sort of thing."

"What are you interested in?" I ask.

"I'd like to go to school and learn to speak English. Then I can get a better job in a shop or at a bar with a decent class of people and provide for myself," Rachel says and now she's looking right at me, her voice is steady, her big smile beaming. She's not sure of what I want – I think that's it. But she's absolutely certain of what she wants.

"I just don't want you to think that I'm rich just because I'm white," I say to finish the subject. Rachel chews and gives me a look I can't really make out. She swallows the food in her mouth, says:

"Money isn't important. So long as there's enough for a man to live like a man and not like a dog."

"That friend you share a room with – is she nice?" I ask.

"Salama," Rachel says. "Yes, she's alright."

I want to ask whether Salama is at home, but I don't say anything. We drive. I can feel her breasts distinctly against my back. She hugs me from behind. I can feel the weight and the softness of her upper arms. My arousal makes me go faster.

"Drive slowly," she says, laughing.

She shouts directions to me, and soon we're parked outside the door of what looks like servants' accommodation. Rachel greets with a smile a couple of women who are squatting and chatting outside one of the neighbouring houses. I weave a chain through the wheels and around the frame and close the padlock through its outer links.

She's standing at the door. "Come," she says. "Welcome." And steps aside. I go in. She pushes the door shut. Her friend isn't there – I wonder if it's by agreement. Across from the door is the window. No glass – just mosquito netting, bars and a finely meshed grille to stop anyone from reaching an arm in. The wooden shutters are padlocked. Under the window there are two rickety wooden chairs and a small dining table topped with a bouquet of wax flowers, nylon petals, a paraffin lamp in case of power cuts and a transistor with a broken antenna that has been replaced by a white wire winding its way up through the bars of the window. A laminated coffee table with crocheted doilies between the beds. A wardrobe up against the wall at the end of one bed and a series of wooden shelves on stacks of bricks on the other side of the door – kitchen utensils. A pot, a pan and a coal pan are pushed in under the foot of the bed across from the shelves. A light bulb is hanging on its flex from the ceiling, with an inverted paper bin as a lampshade – woven with big holes so the light creates geometric patterns on the walls. Luckily she's got a proper ceiling, so you can't hear every single sound that comes from next door. Pictures from western magazines are glued to the walls. I put my arm around Rachel's waist.

"Very nice," I say.

"Would you like a fizzy drink?" she asks and slips out of my grasp, getting a Coke from the bottom of the cupboard, opening it for me, pouring it into a glass which she puts on the coffee table along with the half-empty bottle and a battered ashtray.

"Thank you," I say and sit down on one bed. She must have fetched that Coke yesterday from the shop; perhaps she's borrowed the bottle – she may not have had a bottle to exchange for it.

"I need a shower," she says and gets a *kanga* from the cupboard. I sit and watch her. "You have to go outside," she says, pointing at the door – she wants to undress and wrap the *kanga* around her before she goes to the washroom at the end of the building.

"Alright – I'll wait outside," I say, smiling at her, as I go outside. I light a cigarette. The two women in the yard look at me once; then they ignore me.

Rachel opens the door slightly.

"It's alright – you can come in now," she says from inside, and I walk back in. She is standing right inside with her hand on the doorknob; a towel pressed against her chest with the other hand – ready for her shower. She's undressed and has wrapped the *kanga* around her. I too have my hand on the door, am standing in front of her so she must walk around me if she wants to go outside. You can't see her from outside.

She looks up at me. I put my free arm around her waist, on her lower back – the strong muscle of her buttocks against my palm through the thin fabric. Leaning forward as I pull her towards me. She leans back a little, away from me, without moving her feet. I kiss her mouth, suck the full lower lip in between my own lips, while I detach her hand from the door with an even pull – pushing it shut so that we are both of us invisible from outside. The meeting of our tongues – rough, warm, soft, moist. The hand with the towel is poised between our upper bodies. She pulls her mouth away. "Ah-ahhh," she says, shaking her head. "I need a shower." My hand on the curve of her powerful buttock.

"I want you."

"Yes, but you have to wait," she says. I grab the towel, lift it out of her hand and toss it onto the bed. Look down at her body. The swell of her breasts under the fabric. The knot where she has gathered the *kanga* between the dark globes.

"You are very beautiful." Kiss her again. My other hand is encircling one firm breast. Through the fabric I press the nipple – large between my fingers – pulling her towards me so she can feel my hardness through my trousers. Her hand reaches out and turns off the light.

"O.K.," she says, and now her hands are quick at the front of my trousers, pulling open the belt buckle, loosening the button, pulling down the zip. I pull at the *kanga* to make the knot open, the fabric slides about her body until I get it off her completely – it floats and falls away. The darkness isn't complete – light filters in from the veranda through the mosquito net and the bars above the door. I can smell the dry sweat under her arms; it excites me as I put my mouth to one nipple, sucking it, the taste of salt, sensing the black frizzy bush covering the curve between her legs. Her hands inside my trousers, down inside the boxers, grabbing my cock. Pulling my trousers to the ground with one hand she squats down and looks me in the eyes as she smiles and sucks my cock with long, steady pulls, pulling the foreskin all the way back and encircling the head with her mouth. All the while her eyes are locked on mine. Pink tongue with tiny, tiny bumps, circling the bright-red head; thick violet lips around the white shaft of the cock. She sucks me till I come, swallows my sperm, licks my cock clean squeezing my testicles, gets up lazily, smiling.

"Thank you," I say. That small tiredness; everything drops a few centimetres inside me. I step out of my trousers, which are bunched around my ankles; kick off my sneakers.

"Wait," I say. Press her towards the bed, letting my hand slide up between her powerful thighs; feeling the seeping softness, the itching pubes, squatting in front of her, the pungent and ripe smell of her sex.

I hold onto one thigh, letting my fingers sink into her flesh, lifting the other leg up onto the bed so I can get down there. Let my tongue travel up her inner thigh until I reach her cunt.

"Hhnnngg," she says. Eat it. Suck it, lick it, swallow it, her hands pulling my head towards her sex, small sounds. She pushes her pelvis quickly, rhythmically against my face. A wild taste. Frizzy hair itching my wet lips. Inside she is completely pink. I swallow. Hair against my tongue. Grab on to her buttocks to stabilize. Find her clitoris again, letting it slip in and out between my teeth, my tongue slopping against it. My cock is so hard again that it hurts. Guide my hand along her labia and smear moisture up towards her anus – suck at her cunt while I massage the sphincter, push in a finger. She is moaning now. The leg she is resting on starts to tremble. "Do it now. Come," she says and sits up abruptly on the bed – I only just have enough time to pull out my finger – and she crabs backwards, the muscles in her legs contracting, her breasts bob until she can lie down on her back, pulling me into her, drawing my body forward between her open legs. Her cunt glistens, dark and shiny, in the dim light. What does it mean that we're lying together – once I'm inside her? What is there on the other side? Does she expect that . . . my role – what is that? "You mustn't be noisy," she whispers. My cock aims low and thrusts along the crack between her buttocks and against the soft bedcover, but right away her hand is around me, guiding it into the soft wetness – so warm. The softness is . . . almost too much. I have just enough time to think that. Then she flexes. Locks me inside the walls of her cunt. Her hand is around the root of my cock now, now around my balls, the other around the back of my neck, suppressed moaning, guttural, her nails in my back, pressing my buttocks, drilling her fingers into them – hard. The jolts of her breasts on her upper body – supple. We find our rhythm. A film of sweat breaks out – our stomachs slide against each other as I thrust into her. We keep at it. It hurts. My legs are shaking with lactic acid. Thrusts. Until it comes. In waves. And I bang my way through the pain, contractions in my innards – explosion. I flex my back so I can suck her nipples, the smell of our fucking rises to the air, skin against skin – slick with sweat, she pulls my head up to hers, sucks my mouth, we are wet everywhere. Our teeth bump. Moan. I feel distinctly the last little bit move through me, push its way out, out of me, into her.

"Really good," I say. "Rachel, you are very lovely," I say. "I want you – every day," I say. She smiles broadly.

"My *mzungu*," she says. "He makes trouble." And there we are, wrapped around each other, the sweaty film on our bodies gradually drying. She nibbles my ear lobe. No-one can see us, but we're together now. I don't know what that means. A mosquito sucks blood from my leg; I leave it there – it ate from her earlier. Like me. I am looking forward to the next time. To having her sit on me so I can see her breasts dance. To running my hand up under her skirt, in between her legs, pushing her knickers to one side and finger-fucking her up against a car in a car park in the dark outside a nightclub.

I should have used a condom. She won't get pregnant – I hope. I let my hand glide down Rachel's buttocks – even when she's lying halfway across me the curve isn't sloppy like it would be on a white girl. Round, soft and firm at the same time.

Someone tries to open the door. Rachel gives a start.

"Rachel?" a girl's voice says.

"Hang on," Rachel says into the room, and to me: "That's Salama. It's her room." She gets up from the bed quickly, wrapping her *kanga* around her and grabbing her towel. Then she looks at me. "Get dressed," she says, opening the door a little. I have just enough time to see a pair of girl's eyes look in at me over Rachel's head as she slips through the door.

"Enough!" Salama says. "*Eh-eeehhhhh*." She laughs outside the closed door. Rachel laughs. I can hear them speaking quickly and in low voices, laughing again. I get up and look around the dimly lit room for my clothes. I would really like to join her in the shower but it's no good. The women outside will see me now when I leave. We were in here a long time before Rachel came out to shower. I start getting dressed. Feeling guilty. The white bloke who went with Rachel. But why feel guilty? Guilty of what? That's ... racism. She's a girl, I'm a boy. Lego – the colours don't matter.

I'm dressed. Tidy the sheets a bit. Smoke a cigarette. It tastes fabulous. Rachel returns. She seems a bit feverish.

"You have to leave," she says. "Salama needs her sleep."

"When will I see you again?" I ask.

"You come to the shop," she says, "and we'll see each other."

And I drive out through the cool air, shouting at the top of my lungs as I tear out of Majengo and up towards the Y.M.C.A. building, onwards. I drive home. Stop at the servants' quarters. All I want is to sit, nice and quiet, smoking cigarettes, thinking about the events of the night – going over them in my head.

"Christian?" Katriina calls from the veranda.

"Yes?"

"Come up here."

"Why?"

"Just come, will you?" she says. I get up. Cross the lawn. Marianne is sitting on the veranda. Katriina goes inside the house. I go up the stairs, stand in front of her and look at her without saying anything. What does she want now?

"We have to talk, Christian," Marianne says.

"Why?" I ask.

"We can't . . . say goodbye like that," Marianne says.

"Then we'll have to talk at the Y.M.C.A.," I say.

"Why?" Marianne asks in a weedy voice. I nod towards the house, the sitting room. "Alright," Marianne says and follows me to the motorbike without saying anything. I start it, drive us down to the Y.M.C.A., lock it, follow her to her room – she opens the door with her key, steps inside. I stay at the door.

"We want different things," I say. "There's no need to say any more. Take care." She looks at me.

"You too," she says.

I leave.

"How about tonight when you get off?" I ask Rachel outside the shop. "I can come pick you up?" She looks around nervously. Perhaps her boss gets angry if she stands about talking to me during work hours.

"Then we'll have to go up to yours," Rachel says.

"I don't think that will work. The lady of the house is angry with me," I say. Katriina. Not one word has she spoken to me since Marianne left.

"We can't be at my place," Rachel says. "Salama is there as well, and the neighbours have said bad things about me after you were there – the owner might decide to evict us."

"Alright," I say. "I'll work something out by tomorrow night."

"I can't tomorrow. I have to work," she says.

"But the shop closes at nine," I say.

"I've got a new job at a restaurant. It doesn't finish until eleven," she says.

"Then how about afterwards, when you've got back?" I ask.

"I have to go to work at seven the next day," Rachel says.

"I'm looking for a place of my own," I say.

"Yes," Rachel says, smiling. "I hope you will find it soon."

"Why do you need that new job?" I ask.

"Otherwise I can't pay for my English lessons," Rachel says. The shopkeeper has allowed her to take every day off from two till four, and she wants to sign up for an English course that runs at the K.N.C.U. building. But first she needs to find the money. If she is going to be working both days and evenings, I am never going to see her.

At night we drive down to Newcastle Hotel on Mawenzi Road and sit on the roof terrace. We buy chicken and chips and fizzy drinks. Sit and look out over the city. I can't seem to get on with it. Smoke cigarettes all the time.

"Rachel," I say. "I'd like to see you more . . . more often, alright. I'm trying to find a place to stay on my own – a small house – it's not easy. But I was thinking . . . if I pay for your English course, you wouldn't have to work nights."

"But you have to pay for six months before you can start," Rachel says.

"That's no problem," I say. "I've got it right here." I hand her an envelope with the money. She smiles.

"Thank you, Christian," she says and folds the envelope up without looking into it. Puts it in her pocket.

"Will you take me home now?" she asks. We don't have a place we can be together. There's no point in talking about it. I have to solve the problem. I take her home. She gets off on the street. I grab onto her waist – am about to kiss her. "Don't make trouble here, Christian. The neighbours speak very ill of me when they see it."

"O.K.," I say. "See you." I gas up, drive off. Shit. Shitting fucking shit.

On the pavement outside the shop she whispers to me:

"Christian, I have the day off tomorrow – all day. We could do something together tonight."

"Do you want to go to Liberty? Or to Moshi Hotel?" I ask.

"No, not go out," she says. "Just you and me. Together. We can make trouble."

"Yes," I say. "But where? Is Salama at home?"

"We can't be at my place," Rachel says,

"I know," I say. "We'll go to mine."

"Alright," Rachel says. "Come pick me up at nine."

I do. We pop round to Uhuru Hotel for a bite to eat before going back to the servants' quarters. There's a power cut. Rachel lights candles and a mosquito coil.

"Undress and lie down on the bed," Rachel says. I obey. She comes to the side of the bed. Strips naked in the flickering light. "You must lie still," she whispers and caresses me, kisses me everywhere. Fabulous. Trembling, tickling arousal, prolonged, painful – she holds me back the whole time, until it finally happens.

In the morning I go over to the main house to fetch a breakfast tray. Issa is standing there, ironing. He greets me but doesn't speak to me and doesn't offer to help. He is so deaf he can't have heard us, but I imagine the guard has been up all night. As I boil water and cut mangos into slices, Solja comes out into the kitchen. There are already two glasses of juice and two coffee cups on the tray.

"Got company, have you?" Solja asks.

"Mind your own business." I grin.

"Yes, yes," she says and leaves. I take the tray with me. We sit in the shade on the veranda outside the servants' quarters. Katriina comes round the corner. She is looking pale.

"I don't want her here," Katriina says in Swedish.

"That's not for you to say," I say.

"Yes, it is," she says. "This is my house."

"As far as I'm aware, my dad is paying the rent," I say.

"Do you think your dad thinks you should run around with those . . . You can't just use those girls," Katriina says. Her voice is shaking. I look at Rachel. Her expression is vacant.

"Use?" I say. "She's my girlfriend."

"Yes, right now she is. But what happens when you go back and leave her here?"

"I'm not going back," I say.

"That disco nonsense is making you next to no money. You will go back," Katriina says.

"What's your problem?" I say.

"You have to be careful, Christian. You can get your hands dirty when you mess around down here," Katriina says grimly.

"How about your hands, Katriina? Are they completely clean?" I ask. And that gets her. Her eyes shift. Her hands aren't clean.

"*Tsk*," she says and leaves.

I'm lying on my bed, smoking – waiting for the next development. It comes when Solja knocks on my door.

"You have to come up to the house," she says.

"Why?"

"You just do," she says. I go. Katriina is in the sitting room.

"You have to call your dad," she says.

"And what is he going to tell me?" I ask, because it's obvious that it's at her request.

"That you can't stay here anymore," Katriina says.

"Do you want me out by tonight?" I ask.

"Within the next few weeks," she says.

"I'll be off as soon as possible," I say.

"Good," Katriina says. Solja has gone to her room. I speak in a low voice, so she won't be able to hear me:

"I'm not Jonas, Katriina," I say. Her head jolts, she stares at me through squinting eyes.

"Get out," she says. "I won't have you in the house – not another minute." I leave. Sometime later Solja comes down to get a cigarette. She gives me an odd look as if there's something she wants to say. But she doesn't say anything. I wonder if she remembers the Land Cruiser on the back road in the dark – the one that was moving even though the engine wasn't running.

Rachel is sitting outside Roots Rock when I arrive that morning. Her face looks all wrong.

"What's the matter?" I ask.

"It's a big problem," she says, holding her hand up in front of her face, shaking her head, breathing in short gasps. I put my arm around her.

"What's happened?" I ask. She's crying. I pull her into the shop so people on the street can't stare at her. "Marcus, could you perhaps go for a walk or something?" I say. He gets up and leaves. Gradually I wheedle the story out of her. She owes someone money. When her big brother in Arusha died and she came to Moshi, they helped her – lent her some money, so she could survive until she found a job. Now they want it back. It's the equivalent of a few months' wages. She has already given them the money I gave her for the English course. I'm not sure about this. Am I being conned? But . . . I give her the money – I refuse to be distrustful.

"I'm going to have to go to work," she says.

"Will I see you tonight?" I ask.

"I have to work at the restaurant tonight," she says. She leaves. Marcus gets up from his chair outside the shop and comes in. Maybe he's heard us.

"That girl is totally scamming you," he says.

"Mind your own business," I say.

"Tsk," he says. I could punch him. I drive off. All the way to Karanga Bridge. Drive the motorbike in between the shrubs at the top of the slope and sit in the shade of a tree. Light a cigarette. I thought the idea was that Rachel would give up that job after I gave her the money for her course, and then we could be together in the evenings. But . . . I get it. This is Tanzania; if I get a house and let her move in, then I am the man and I get to call the shots, but right now all I am is a boy she's fooling around with. I haven't delivered yet, so I have no authority.

Late in the afternoon I drive down to Roots Rock to talk to Marcus. We have to do something to get the business up and running. But he's already shut up the shop for the day. I buy a fizzy drink at Stereo Bar, sit down outside. Then I see Rachel. She's standing outside the shop in a khaki skirt that clings to her round thighs, and a purple tank top in a synthetic fabric that fits tightly around her upper body, so her nipples are visible even from a distance. I go over to her.

"You can't be here now," she says, looking around nervously.

"Why not?"

"My boss, he is coming to pick me up. If he sees you, he will be angry," Rachel says.

"Why would he be angry?" I ask. Rachel sighs and looks at me.

"If he sees I am with a *mzungu*, he thinks I will leave the job soon, and then he won't want to invest in making me a good waitress at the restaurant," she says.

"But does he treat you alright?" I ask.

"He's a cousin of my family. He's just trying to help," Rachel says. "You have to leave now."

"I'll see you tomorrow," I say and go back to Stereo Bar's pavement restaurant. I sit there, waiting. At one point a newish Toyota Corolla drives up and stops outside the shop. Rachel gets in, and it drives off. If he is a cousin of her family and can afford a car, then Rachel ought to live with his family – isn't that the Tanzanian way when the young girl comes to the big city from the village? But the African ways are disintegrating – too many poor relatives come to the big cities; they have to make it on their own these days.

I drive up to speak to Marcus about business. We need more work. Claire comes out to greet me as custom requires. She's got very thin since the baby died.

"Marcus is out on an errand but he will be back soon," she says. But she doesn't ask if I would like coffee, or how things are with Katriina and the kids. Very rude. But alright, she's just lost a kid. The sun is hurting my eyes, so I go into the sitting room and sit on the sofa. She is at the dining table, writing in a copybook – tells me she is doing the accounts for the kiosk. My feeling is that a large share of the proceeds must be going towards Marcus' alcohol consumption.

"How's business?" I ask.

"Not very good – we can't live on the proceeds from the kiosk." I know she's referring to the fact that we're putting money aside to get the big decks sent down. But that's not something I'm going to discuss with her. Perhaps that's why she seems so hostile. "I feel bad for you, if she is your girlfriend," Claire says.

"If who is?" I ask.

"The one who says her name is Rachel."

"Why would you feel bad for me?"

"I feel bad for you. She is very bad."

"How is she bad?"

"She's a bad girl – I've heard people say that."

"Yes, I understand that – but how?"

"She uses different names."

"And?"

"When she's with a Christian, she uses the Christian name Christine. And when she's with a Muslim, then her name is suddenly Zaina."

"What are you trying to say?"

"She is very bad," Claire says.

"You think everybody is bad if they're not as godly as you," I say. She shakes her head and gets up.

"I feel bad for you – you could even die," she says and goes out to the kiosk. Stays out there. Finally Marcus returns and Claire comes back inside with him.

"What kind of cock and bull story is your wife trying to tell me?" I ask.

"Let's sit down on the veranda," he says and calls to the house girl to get her to put a couple of chairs outside. "I tried to tell you yesterday," he says in English, so Claire can't know what we're saying. "Claire speaks to people up here and down by the shop and around town. People say that the girl is called Rachel on some days and on others she's Zaina – if she's with a Muslim man; and if the man is Christian, then her name is Christine."

"Are you saying she's a whore?"

"She's a bad girl."

"You bleeding well think every girl but Claire is a whore."

"Claire has heard some very bad stories about her," Marcus says.

The story is that Rachel came to Moshi when her big brother in Arusha died. She lived with her aunt and worked as a waitress at a *mama's*, where she was found to be to the liking of the head of Tanesco in the Moshi District. He installed her in K.N.C.U. Hotel above Kibo Arcade in a room with a fridge and a stereo – his things. She had everything paid for: board, food, drinks, new clothes, lots of pocket money. The man's wife was ill, so he made promises to Rachel. But he never did pay the cash he had promised, so after two months she tried sneaking out with the stereo, but was stopped in reception because she wasn't the one paying for the room, so the things in it couldn't belong to her. Since then she's been meeting other men through her job as a waitress and at the shop. And Claire says she goes with them. For money.

"That makes no sense, Marcus. Why then would she have a job and live in a dump in Majengo? You think all girls are whores. You say that Claire's sister is a whore. And Claire thinks *you* fuck whores when we're working nights. And at the same time she wishes I would fall in love with her sister – who *you* say is a whore. I mean . . . what the hell are you thinking?"

"But at the same time that girl is trying to meet a good man who can take her away. That's why she has to be at the shop, so the good man can see her, because it puts the man off if she goes to the pumping bars in Majengo."

"I'm not having this, Marcus," I say. "You can't know this – who is she? What do you know?"

"She's dreaming of the good life with a man," Marcus says. "Preferably in Europe." I get up on the motorbike, flick down the kick-starter.

"All women dream of the good life with a man. You're the one who dreams of Europe," I say, starting the engine, driving off.

Marcus

THE COW AND THE CALF

Now I am a private detective. I launch an investigation into the little *malaya* who has bewitched my white boy. First I speak to Phantom, but he's given up keeping an eye on town life.

"Now I am Phantom the family man," he says because he has rented a small house in Soweto. The proceeds from his currency exchanges and smuggled goods must be good. A girl from his family's hometown in Ol Molog on the north side of Kilimanjaro has been brought here and impregnated. Phantom still has dreadlocks and sits in his small kiosk at the market all day long. "But soon I'll be gone," he says.

"Where will you go?" I ask.

"*Tsk*," Phantom. "The city has become very dirty. You can die here just because another man wants to own your shoes. I am going home to the mountain – the house I am building in Ol Molog will be finished next year," he says. Yes, we're none of us getting younger – I am twenty-two, and Phantom must be almost ten years older – we can't keep up with the city pace forever.

"Who can I talk to?" I ask.

"You know Big Man Ibrahim – he is very interested in all the ladies," Phantom says. Yes, Ibrahim, who lifted me into his pick-up when the water sprung as from a tap from my ankle. These days he is a karate instructor in the C.C.M. building and a very expensive bodyguard to *mabwana makubwa*. I find him.

"Marcus," he says. "The man with the two legs." Ibrahim grins. Now he has learned how to kill with his bare hands, life has become a great joy to him. Every second he wishes that someone will try to hit him, so he can use his tools. I ask him about Rachel.

"Yes, *chiki-chiki* – very nice *titi*," Ibrahim says.

"Did you talk to those *titi*?" I ask.

"No, no – I don't pay for the fruit I eat," Ibrahim says.

"Is she to be paid for?" I ask.

"I think Alwyn has some business with her," Ibrahim says.

"Does he sell her for pumping?" I ask.

"I don't know. But if you see her out at night, Alwyn's friend Tito is always close at hand so you don't try to snatch her up," Ibrahim says.

"Christian – the white boy – he is completely bewitched by her," I say.

"Really?" Ibrahim says. "Does he know that if you want to own the cow, you have to take the calf as well?"

"She has a child?" I ask.

"Yes, yes – a daughter came out after Faizal pumped her, but now the baby is gone," Ibrahim says. *Eeehhh* – I knew Faizal had pumped some little girl up and had kicked her so hard she ran away. But that it was Rachel . . . *tsk*. The child must be living with her family in the village while she tries to make a life for herself in the city. Ibrahim grins: "The white boy is great entertainment," he says.

Christian

I can't stand Marcus – all that nonsense. I sleep at the Y.M.C.A. for a night but am restless. Thoughts churning in my head. I miss Rachel, but she's also . . . weird. Or not weird, but . . . I just can't work out if she expects me to wait on her hand and foot because I'm white. And I think about the sexy way she walks – a bit lazy, but seductive. And all that nonsense Claire was talking – complete bullshit. And I can't get to spend time with Rachel because she's always working. Shit. Why would she work herself into the ground if she were a whore? Then she would have money. She's poor. She doesn't drink, she doesn't smoke, and most of the time she eats at work.

The next day I go up to Katriina to see if I've received any post, because I still use her P.O. Box. There's nothing.

Katriina says I should talk to Gösta's wife. Right now he's working on a big S.I.D.A. project in Uganda but he's built a large house in Shanty Town where his wife lives with their two young children. I call Uganda incessantly until I get a connection. Luckily Gösta is cooperative.

"I'll talk to my wife about it," he says and explains that his house has a small guesthouse in a corner of the grounds, away from the main house. "I may be able to rent it. But she's the one who decides these things. Go over and talk to her."

Katriina explains to me where it is. I go there the next day. The woman has spoken to Gösta and mentions a price that is on the steep side, but fair. Anders still sends me half of my dole money every month – a direct form of Danish aid. It's not a problem.

I can move in a few weeks later.

Shukran Hotel does well on Friday and Saturday nights, but it doesn't bring in much money. People in Swahilitown are poor, so we can't charge a nice entrance fee – if we do, no-one will come. We need to get hold of *mabwana makubwa*, but that requires a big place like Moshi Hotel or Liberty, and that in turn requires some heavy-duty decks. Rogarth and Khalid have become good helpers. They talk to a lot of people, get us jobs. We play at birthdays, weddings, school parties up on the mountain. We make ends meet, barely, while Marcus makes good money recording cassettes in Roots Rock. But I don't make enough to live the good life – I can only get by thanks to the kind offices of Anders.

I call Anders. He tells me that everything's gone according to plan. He's sent my decks by carrier to Oslo, where it will be included in the church's shipment for Moshi. He called them and was told that it had arrived safely.

"And I'm coming down to see you soon," he says.

"Yes, definitely. But hold off a few months until I've got things going. Right now I don't even have a proper place to live. But once the decks arrive, things will get up and running," I say.

"O.K.," Anders says. "But no later than Christmas."

"You've got yourself a deal," I say. Christmas is more than six months from now – that should be fine.

*

I drive out to the Pentecostal church and ask the Norwegian if he's heard anything about their shipment. No, nothing yet. He promises to let me know.

Then I drive up to Roots Rock, because Khalid's been talking about an empty warehouse a bit further out along Uru Road. Maybe we should think about renting it and having discos there.

"I will find the owner and speak to him tomorrow," Marcus says.

"Alright, tomorrow then," I say. "Then I'll come round tomorrow night and hear how it went."

"Good," Marcus says. "How are things with your lady friend?"

"I think things are fine," I say.

"Have you got to know each other?" he asks.

"What do you mean?" I say.

"Do you agree with me that it's important to be honest? If you are friends and spend time together, you have to tell the truth even if the truth is hard?"

"Yes, that sounds about right," I say.

"Did this girl tell you she has a little daughter at home in her village?" Marcus asks.

Blood drains from my face.

"A daughter?" I say.

"Yes, over a year ago she had a daughter by Faizal here in Moshi."

"The D.J. from Moshi Hotel?" I ask.

"Yes, and they were married and everything. But Faizal kicked her out, so now her daughter lives with her family in the village," Marcus says.

"Why did he kick her out?" I ask.

"I don't know anything about that, but suddenly I hear from a friend on the street that my white friend is running around with a girl who is married and has a daughter," Marcus says.

"But it's not like she's still with Faizal," I say.

"No. But she's running around with you and doesn't even tell you she has a daughter. That is not right. Maybe she has another boyfriend she's not telling you about," Marcus says.

"Are you saying she has?" I say.

"I don't know," Marcus says. "But you have to understand that the girl is telling you nothing."

I turn around and walk out of the shop – cold sweat pouring down my ribs. For crying out loud, what is she doing? I . . . I'm crazy about her, but she's not telling me what the hell's going on. Yes, it's not uncommon here that if a very young girl has a child she lets her parents look after it, but damn it – now Marcus is telling me that Rachel is married. To Faizal. And she's told me nothing. It's too much.

"Christian?" Rachel calls from the shop as soon as I step outside. I can't bear to look at her. My eyes tear up. I don't say anything. Get on the motorbike, kick-start it hurriedly, drive off.

Marcus

CRAZY BITCH

Eeeehhhh – time for shouting. The harlot is in my shop five seconds after the motorbike has driven off.

"What did you tell him?"

"*Tsk*," I say. "You try to seduce my partner with your miraculous pumping, but everything you tell him is a lie. You're married and have a child in your village. I hear stories about you pumping for money at K.N.C.U. Hotel. You're a dirty girl. A complete *malaya*."

"That's not true. That's just gossip," Rachel says.

"Isn't it true that you are married to Faizal and have a daughter?" I ask her, raising my eyebrows like a judge.

"*Tsk*," she says. "Faizal is a bad man, and my daughter is with my father while I work in Moshi. Why are you ruining my chances with Christian? He likes me," she says.

"He is bewitched by you," I say. "But I am his friend, so it's my job to tell him the truth when you lie. People tell me that you have a lot of dirty business with Alwyn and that crazy Tito. You have to stay away from Christian," I say. That Rachel is so angry she's shaking. She's standing at the door and staring at me and then she spits – a great ball of spit. It lands right on my shirt. And then she's gone. Crazy bitch.

Christian

I have to talk to Rogarth. I drive down to the industrial area near Majengo and honk my horn outside the ramshackle building where Rogarth shares a room with three other blokes.

"Christian," he says smiling as he comes out of the door – we slap hands.

"We have to talk," I say without turning off the engine. "Come on."

"O.K.," he says. Dives into the room to grab his jacket and gets up behind me.

"Where can we get a beer around here?" I ask.

"Majengo," he says, pointing ahead.

We sit in silence for a while. I look at Rogarth, look around, light a cigarette, take a deep breath.

"Marcus says that Rachel is living that life as well," I say as I look at the *malaya* sitting at the tables around us.

"Rachel? No, she's not like that," Rogarth says.

"How can you know?" I say.

"Why would she stand at a shop selling fizzy drinks all day when all she has to do is pump for a weekend and make a month's wages?" Rogarth says.

"Yes, that's what I thought," I say.

"That Marcus, tsk. He speaks ill of everyone and sits at the bar himself every night and says how he will be the boss of the biggest disco in Moshi soon."

"Shit. He could do fuck-all without me," I say.

"The important thing is to get the right place for a disco when you get the big decks. A place the customers will flock to," Rogarth says.

"Alwyn's decks at Liberty have almost broken down," I say.

"Yes, but the owner of Liberty is an idiot. He will never offer you a decent deal," Rogarth says.

"I know Rachel's got a little daughter. But she hasn't told me," I say.

"Yes, she's got a daughter," Rogarth says without showing any shock at the news or my knowing about it. "By Faizal," he adds. "But that daughter is at home in the village with her family so Rachel can live her own life. It's not unusual. It's not her fault that Faizal is so useless."

"How old is the daughter?" I ask.

"Halima," Rogarth says. "She's eighteen months, I think."

"Would you do that job for me?" I ask. "Find a good place for the big disco – somewhere we can get a proper deal?"

"I will find it," Rogarth says.

I am moving into Gösta's guesthouse. I borrow Katriina's Nissan and take my things up there in a few trips. That includes the transport crates my mattress rests on. I realize there's a revolver in one of them, but I need the box for my things and I don't want to give Katriina Jonas' gun. I buy a new padlock for the box and carry the key in a leather strap around my neck. Luckily the house is partially furnished. There's a sofa, an easy chair, a dining table with chairs, a bed and some kitchen utensils. After a few runs all my things are in place. Should I hire a house girl? I eat in town most of the time anyway. Perhaps I can get a girl to come twice a week and do the cleaning. I take a shower before I drive the car back to Katriina's, nick a few cans of beer and Coke from the fridge and a bottle of Tanqueray gin from the larder. I go over to *mama* Androli's and buy a big portion of lasagne, which I take home with me on my motorbike. I've got no music because my decks are at Marcus' or in Roots Rock. I eat, drink Africafé, smoke, listen to the cicadas and the ceiling fan twirling. This should be a good moment. My own home. But my head hurts and I've got no painkillers. Rachel – I don't want to think about her. What should I do? – I don't know. It's sad to be sitting here alone, and I'm pissed off with Marcus. He is lazy and a drunk and he badmouths anyone and everyone. The problem is the decks. He's the one who set up the contact with the Norwegian chap from the Pentecostal church. And I need those decks – otherwise I will have to activate my expensive ticket back to Denmark within the month. And what the hell would I do there? Do the second year of my H.F? I'm damned if I will. A car honks its horn outside the gate, the dogs bark. I open the door and look out. Rachel gets out of the taxi. I see a young guy coming out of the main house.

"It's for me," I call and walk towards the gate, the dogs at my heels. Rachel is standing outside the fence, the taxi is not moving, waiting for her. She probably doesn't know whether she's going back in it. Rachel looks scared. I open the gate. "Come in," I say. She turns to the taxi and speaks through the open window.

"Thank you, that's fine," she says, and the taxi drives off. She comes through the gate. Walks in front of me to my small house, into the lit sitting room. I walk past her and take my cigarettes from the drum table, sinking into the sofa. Rachel stays where she is.

"How did you find me?" I ask.

"I asked the daughter at the *mzungu mama's*," she says. Solja.

"When were you going to tell me you have a daughter?" I ask.

"I . . ." Rachel starts. She looks away, raises a hand to wipe a tear from the corner of her eye. "I was afraid you wouldn't like me," she says, snivelling.

"And you're married," I say, looking at her. She is standing there crying. It's terrible to have to watch. And she is so beautiful, but . . . and of course she had a life before she met me, but she bleeding well has to tell me these things. "To Faizal," I add. Rachel looks at me.

"He won't sign the papers and give me a divorce. He is a bad man." Rachel exhales, hides her face behind a hand, snivels. "I just wanted to . . . I wanted to tell you, but I was afraid to, because I like you," she says.

"Sit down," I say. She takes a few steps and sits down on the chair. I get up and fetch her a fizzy drink. Light a cigarette, even though I know it will make me dizzy. "What happened?" I ask.

"What?" Rachel says.

"With Faizal?"

"He drank, and he beat me," she says. "So I took my daughter Halima back to my father in the village."

"Halima," I say. "So she's going to grow up there?"

"I don't make enough money to keep her with me," Rachel says. I don't say anything. Get up and get out the gin bottle and a glass. Pour myself a big drink at the kitchen table. Down it and pour myself another one. Perhaps it'll take away my headache. Sit down on the sofa and light a cigarette, look at Rachel.

"I like you," I say. "But . . ." I say, gesticulating. I don't know what it is I want to say. Rachel gets up and takes my dirty plate and cutlery from the table – goes to the kitchen. Perhaps she's curious and wants to see the place. I can hear her rinsing the things.

"Christian?" she calls.

"Yes?"

"Can I take a shower?" she asks. Can she take a shower? I don't know. "There was no water in Majengo today," she adds.

"Do what you want," I say and drink from my glass. Hear the bath-room door closing, the shower being turned on. The thought of her in the shower makes me restless. Take another gulp of gin. Shit. I walk around the sitting room restlessly, smoking. My headache gets worse. I don't know what to do with myself. The bathroom door is opened, the calm patter of her feet coming down the corridor. Is she going to the bedroom? I suppose she's getting dressed. Outside it's completely dark. What should I do?

"Come here," she calls.

"What?" I say and go down the hall. The bathroom door is ajar, but there's a faint strip of light from the bedroom. I push open the door. She's lying on the bed, turned over onto her hip with her head resting on her hand, stark naked. The small bedside lamp is switched on, lights up her dark skin.

"Come here," she says.

"And do what?" I ask.

"Just come on," she says. I sit down on the edge of the bed, swing up my legs, lie down on my back next to her on the bedspread. She puts a hand on my stomach, starts moving it around, puts her face close to mine, touches my cock through my shorts, opens my belt as she nibbles my ear lobe, licks my ear. My cock goes hard. I reach out to the bedside cabinet for a condom. She doesn't say anything, but I think she is surprised; African men don't want to fuck with a condom. The woman getting pregnant – that's her problem. I suppose she's given it some thought. We haven't talked about it. She takes the condom from me and says, "See you later," before she pulls it onto my cock. Soon after she has taken me inside her and is riding me, nice and steady. My headache evaporates. My head feels light.

"Are you coming?" she asks.

"Keep going," I say. "Now," I say and she massages my cock inside her, milks me. I grab her hips with both hands and pull her pelvis up to my face while I crab down until I get her wet cunt on my face and can hold her steady with my hands and eat her out until she gets uneasy, rubs her cunt hard back and forth, so her pubes scratch my nose and cheek and tongue. When I look up I can see the undersides of her dark breasts bobbing around, her hard purple nipples, and right between them her chin, the open, panting mouth, the slanted eyes that look down as she grinds her cunt against my face. I can hardly breathe. She gets wet. Towards the end she fucks my face so hard I have to press the back of my head into the pillow, or her pubic bone would break my nose. She gets off, breathing heavily, lies across me, strokes my face, kisses me.

"Thank you," she says and takes the condom off my half-limp cock and ties a knot in it. "Wait here," she says and gets up from bed, walks naked through the house, now dark, while I lie there, wiping her juice from my face, relaxing. I hear the fridge door being opened and then shut. The sound of a cupboard door. Her footsteps approaching.

She kneels on the bed and pours beer into a glass for me, right in front of her dark breasts. Hands me the glass. I pull myself up on one elbow, drink.

"Thank you," I say and hand her the glass – she presses it against her nipples one at a time, smiling at me in the near-dark room. She puts down the glass, gets up, goes over and turns on the ceiling lights and the fan, walks lazily back towards the bed, lies down with her head close to my groin.

"I think there's more juice left," Rachel says and starts caressing my balls so my cock slowly stiffens. She reaches for the glass and takes a sip of cold beer, pulls my foreskin back so the head stands free in the cool air and I have just enough time to think about the colours – black, white, red, before she slides her lips over it. Shock. Cold beer surrounds my cock, carbonated bubbles tickle me. Then it becomes warm. She swallows the beer and massages me with her tongue while her eyes laugh up at me. She pulls my cock out of her mouth and sticks her tongue all the way out, tilts her head and licks long and steady up and down the shaft, pressing it hard against her tongue with her hand, pulling back her lips, letting her teeth glide lightly against it. She tilts her head to the side and looks me in the eyes. Then she starts sucking me, slowly, softly, moistly. She speeds up – thrusts her mouth over my cock. Works it with her tongue, sucks it, pulls her sharp teeth up it with just enough pressure. She lets go, looks at me:

"*Nitakukula*," she says – I'm going to eat you. My cock, my balls – my hair – covered in juice, and the air feels cool. Rachel presses my bent legs wide apart and pushes the backs of my thighs, so my arse lifts a little. She puts her face down, so I can only see her frizzy hair. The song of the cicadas is almost ear splitting. She licks where my cock is joined to my body. She lets her tongue play against my arsehole. The song of the cicadas is interrupted by a sharp sound from my groin. Spittle. Moisture. She spits in my arse and massages my arsehole with the tip of a finger while sucking my balls. She guides her finger slowly inside – attacking the root of the cock from within – and then she starts finger-fucking me slowly, while licking me in one long stretch from my arsehole, across the perineum, up along my cock, which she takes deep into her throat while her finger keeps up a steady, trembling pace. She makes the same journey with her tongue several times, then keeps my cock in her mouth, moving it in time with the rhythm of her finger in my arse – the two in synchrony. I start moaning. I can't help it. I hope I'm never going to come. She increases the speed. My arse contracts again and again around her finger, and the heat from gentle explosions pulsates into my abdomen. Her free hand finds my nipple and squeezes it, almost pulling at it – pain radiates and cuts into me. All my muscles are tense. I have never been here before. Roaring. I am roaring. My arse is completely clenched up. Her finger out, Rachel's breathing is shallow, quick. She's moaning while she grabs feverishly with one hand for my cock – the other grabs onto my buttocks, she is digging her nails into my flesh. Her black hand has a hard grip at the root of my white cock, as she guides her mouth over my glans in hard tugs, pulling her head away with her lips firmly pressed together, so it pops into the cool night air from her scalding hot mouth.

"*Ongeza*," I shout – do the job hard. "*Tena, tena*," – again, again. She keeps at it. My thighs are shaking, and the muscles in my stomach feel like a sack of burning bricks, while my arsehole keeps contracting to the rhythm of her cock sucking. I am dizzy – close to fainting. Her cat's eyes, almost closed, the delicate little nose – and the full lips around my cock. Up again. The cool air and then once more the warmth of her mouth and the pressure of her lips as my cock pops out again. It starts all the way up my spine and travels down through the vertebrae to my arsehole and my balls – they feel like they're on fire, ready to burst, blood rising inside them, my sperm starting to move as the pain becomes excruciating. My sperm swells, I moan as I stare at Rachel's red, moist mouth, which she keeps thrusting down over my cock. The pressure builds at the bottom of my balls, blood gathers, and the sperm rises, finds its way, explodes. Rachel's mouth moves upwards. I watch screaming as her lips let go, and there goes my sperm, landing on her cheek, my stomach, as her mouth descends once more. Rachel stops the rhythm. She's got my cock swallowed deep, moving her mouth up and down but without letting it out. She sucks, swallows, sucks again, sucks the cock, lets it out, circling her tongue around the glans. Then she stares at it. She wipes the sperm from her cheek with a finger and sucks it clean. She holds the cock at the base with her thumb on one side and her index and long fingers on the other, and pulls them upwards – pushing the last bit of sperm to the tip, where it glistens like a small white bead. She licks it off, puts her tongue back in her mouth and swallows. Then her eyes look at the sperm on my stomach.

"Some of it missed," she says, putting her face down, licking it from my abdomen.

"Ahhh," I say. She looks at me, smiling her tilted smile.

"*Nimeshiba*," she says – I am full. And then she laughs out loud and throws her voluptuous body over mine, so her breasts bob abruptly, and I pull her upwards so I can put my mouth to her breasts. I suck her hard nipples and she moans briefly. "No," she says. "It's sore." So I let go of it and I put my hand down to her cunt. "Careful," she says. "No more trouble." So I rest my hand against her, feeling the hair and the moist labia against my palm while my fingers rest in the cleft between her buttocks.

"Stay," I say.

"Yes," she says. And I fall asleep.

Rachel wakes me up very early. She is fully dressed.

"I'm off to work," she says.

"Do you want me to take you?" I ask.

"No, I'll just take a *matatu* on Lema Road," she says.

"Will you be back tonight?"

"If you like," she says.

"I do," I say.

That night I say I want her to move in. "I want you to take your things from Majengo and bring them here, and then I want you to live with me."

"What is the rent?" she asks.

"You won't be paying rent," I say. "If you move in, that means we're together. That means we're boyfriend and girlfriend. I'll pay the rent."

"But I want to work as well," Rachel says. "I want to keep my job at the shop and take English lessons in the afternoons," she says. Her salary would just cover the price of the English course – that's fine.

"Yes, of course. But no more working at the restaurant at night," I say.

"Yes," Rachel says, smiling. "We'll be together then."

"And then in a little while we'll have to see if we can get your daughter here – Halima," I say.

"Really?" Rachel says.

"Yes," I say. "She should be with you. With us." And Rachel leaps up and throws her arms around my neck, kissing me, holding me tight.

"I love you," she says. "You are a good man." I don't say anything to that. But I love her. We make love. It's . . . lovely. Rachel falls asleep quickly. She's had a long day. She looks like a child when she sleeps. Yes, she is poor. She has had almost no schooling. What does it matter? I am crazy about her. It's not just her body and the way she surrenders herself to me. Although that is a part of it. Of course her love for me is also a love for everything I represent, money included, all the possibilities. But in a way my love for her is the same; the fact that she is physical, uncomplicated, content with what I offer. Not like Marianne, who wanted me to save Africa. It's always a trade-off; there's a balance sheet. But Rachel is generous. She turns in her sleep. Can't our love be at least as good as any other? Can love ever claim to be free of anything associated with money – that can be bought with money? You are more popular in the world if you have a nice house, an expensive car, the right clothes. Is that any different in Denmark? Does white love have more depth? No, it's just as cold.

Marcus

FINAL WARNING
Tito comes to Roots Rock and buys a Coke from Patricia, who is manning the fridge. Tito enters the shop.

"I told you to keep your *mzungu* away from Rachel," Tito says.

"When the *mzungu* chases girls, I can't control him," I say.

"Rachel works for me and Alwyn," Tito says. "If the *mzungu* takes Rachel, he must pay us."

"You have to tell him that, not me," I say.

"I am giving you this final warning, because I hear they are sleeping together. If he doesn't stop it, I will ruin him," Tito says. Bang! Tito's hand has leapt out and smacked me. He is standing as calm as can be, smiling at me. "Be careful," he says. *Eeeeehhhh* – Christian is living in a jungle, thinking it is the Garden of Eden. He won't listen to me, so now he will learn the hard ways of Tanzania. All those stories about *mabwana makubwa* at K.N.C.U. Hotel – it is the truth. She is a complete *malaya*.

All day I am at the shop thinking about these complications. Christian has rented a small house up in Shanty Town, close to I.S.M. That is very good. But what happens to his *malaya*? If Rachel is good at bewitching him, she will soon be living in that house. I have to work hard at enlightening Christian, so he doesn't run himself into disaster.

Late in the afternoon he comes to take the decks to the night's disco at Shukran Hotel. I tell him about Tito's visit:

"The guys who guard Rachel, they have asked me what I'm doing with her, because she comes to Roots Rock every day. She is looking for you. They think I am trying to take her over, so I can make money selling her to other men. These men are dangerous – they can even kill." Christian looks at me with a very cross look on his face and shakes his head from side to side.

"Tsk," he says. "I won't hear another of your stories, Marcus. She's my girlfriend. She lives with me. No more nonsense. If you don't like her, that's your problem. If I have to hear more shit from you, we're done." He completely refuses to listen to me, so he must walk like a blind man through the minefield. Fine by me – go ahead.

Christian

Rogarth is on the decks. It's late in the evening, and everything is going as it should. We'll finish up in half an hour, and I draw Rachel with me outside on the dark street. We stand up against a car some way from the door, where Abdullah is lording it over the queue. Music is pouring out into the night. I kiss her, squeeze her breasts through her top, press my pelvis up against hers, put a hand on her thigh and pull up her skirt a little – I want to get my hand under it and finger-fuck her. I have an irrepressible urge to do it.

"No, not here," she says.

"What is it?" I ask.

"It's wrong to do in the street," she says. I hear a sound and have just enough time to turn my head before I am pushed, falling to the ground between two cars.

"You must stay away from that girl," some guy tells me.

"Let go!" Rachel shouts to another guy who has grabbed her by the arm, trying to pull her away with him while she beats at him with her free hand. I crab backwards and get to my feet as the first man closes in on me.

"ABDULLAH!" I shout. A blow lands in my face – hard. I stagger backwards against the car's bonnet.

"That girl belongs to me," the man says. "Everyone who pumps her must pay me – that includes *wazungu*." And I try to swing at him, covering my face with my left, but his fist slams a deep blow into my stomach and I double over, winded, as I hear Rachel scream:

"HELP! HELP ME!" The man laughs as I try to get up. He steps forwards and slaps me so I lean back against the bonnet. It races through my brain that he might kill me. No. There are too many people about, and it would be too bold a deed to kill a white man.

"*Toka!*" Abdullah says – he appears on the pavement, landing a kick to the man's stomach. Abdullah advances, hits out with something that resembles a karate chop. The man turns around – runs off. Abdullah runs after him. Rachel is screaming a little way off. I limp out onto the street. See Rachel standing alone on the other side as Abdullah gives chase. Abdullah comes strolling back. Rachel is sobbing. I go over towards her. Spit, breathe deeply. My stomach aches.

"Tell me who they are," I say. "What is this about?"

"I'm sorry," Rachel says. "It's a big problem." Abdullah is standing right next to us.

"Thank you, Abdullah," I say. "We'll be in in just a moment – you can wait at the door." He turns and walks away. I am standing in front of a whore. My whore. And she is crying, looking up at me with a pleading look on her face. I feel sick. She has . . . my head is throbbing from the blows, my temple is throbbing. And she has fucked . . . for money. All sorts of *mabwana makubwa* – for money. Marcus knew. Maybe Rogarth knew as well. He must have known. And Abdullah, Khalid, Ibrahim.

"Don't worry about those guys," Abdullah says. "I will talk to Big Man Ibrahim. We will tell them to stay away from you so we can run our business." I don't like the way he says our business, but now is not the time to address the issue. "I know many people who would do anything for a little cash," Abdullah says, grinning. Rogarth lugs my things out into a taxi.

"You go with us," I tell him.

"O.K.," he says.

"Shall we drop you off on the way?" I ask Abdullah.

"No, I'll walk. The night is afraid of me," he says, grinning. I give him a strained smile.

"Rachel," I say. "Get in the car." She leaps up and into the back seat next to Rogarth. I sit on the passenger seat. We drive all the way in silence. At the house, she gets out of the car but stays in the yard with her arms wrapped around her, while me and Rogarth carry the things inside. The taxi leaves. "Go inside," I tell Rachel. She goes inside. "Rogarth, wait out here," I say and go after her. I don't care that he can hear us. Then he'll know what's what when I speak to him in a minute. Rachel is standing in the sitting room right next to the door, by the wall, still with her arms about her.

"I am sorry, Christian," she whispers and sniffs.

"Sit down," I say, pointing to the sofa. She sits down at the edge of the seat with her legs together and her hands folded in her lap. It seems absurd – a bit late to be decorous. "Now I know everything about who you are," I say and sit in the chair across from her. "But I want you to tell me yourself so I know what it's like to hear the truth from you – for the very first time."

"No, Christian," she whispers.

"If you don't, I will kick you out on the street right now," I say.

"*Aaaiiiiiiihhh*," Rachel whines, gets up, goes over to the corner of the room, stands there by the wall, staring at the floor. Breathing heavily. She doesn't whisper – now she talks: "What was I to do? Starve to death? I have to live. I have a child. The child must live."

"How long have you been pumping *mabwana makubwa* for money?" I ask.

"My daughter Halima was ill in the village, so I had to send money for medicine – if not, she could die," Rachel says. I wanted her to answer the question to humiliate her, but I'm glad she didn't answer the question. I don't want to hear it. It makes me feel bad to use Tanzanian slang because I have . . . as recently as this morning I ate her out. I am a fool. I didn't want to know either, because . . . I want her.

"Perhaps you carry the disease in your *kuma* after being pumped without a sock," I say and I feel like Marcus is speaking out of my mouth.

"I don't have the disease. I have been careful."

"Perhaps Faizal gave it to you when he pumped you up."

"No, because Halima is well," Rachel says.

"Have you been pumping dirty men?" I ask.

"No," she says and slides down along the wall until she's sitting on the floor with her knees pulled up. I sit on the edge of the chair. She looks at me with eyes that are completely empty – tired. Rogarth is sitting on the veranda outside.

"So what now?" I ask. She doesn't ask me if she should go. If I tell her to go, she will do it at once without saying a word. That is how it is. She's an African. If I don't say anything, she will wait there on the floor until tomorrow if need be. I don't tell her to go. I get up.

Sunday Rachel has the day off. She serves breakfast to me as I sit at the small table. We don't say anything, but I grab her around the waist when she's poured me coffee. I lift up her top and kiss her stomach. Look into her eyes. She smiles and smoothes down my hair.

"My Christian," she says.

In the evening I drive down to speak to Marcus. Find him at the bar. I sit down.

"I ask you and you don't tell me to my face that you *know* . . . for a *fact* . . . that Rachel has been . . . what it is she has done. You hint at things, you give me rumours – what you think. Perhaps. Even though you *know*. What the hell kind of a friend are you?"

"I tell you everything, but you listen like a deaf man," Marcus says. That's just bullshit. I turn around to leave.

"You have to check your blood," he says behind me. I go back to him.

"Then let's find a doctor who can do it tomorrow," I say. He must bloody well know someone after all that time he spent at K.C.M.C.

"Alright," Marcus says.

Monday Morning. I drive – turn left on Lema Road. Not the road towards the town centre.

"What are you doing?" Rachel says. "I am going to work." I stop the motorbike on the roadside.

"Later," I say. "We're going to K.C.M.C."

"Why?" she asks.

"We need to test your blood. And mine," I say. I wait. She doesn't say anything. "We have to see if we have the disease – H.I.V./A.I.D.S. Do you understand that it spreads through sex the same way malaria spreads through mosquitos?" She still doesn't say anything. I take us there. We get off. Her cheeks are wet. I lock the motorbike. We walk towards the entrance. I take her hand, and she squeezes my fingers. I have an appointment and I paid the doctor in advance last night on the veranda at Moshi Hotel – otherwise we might be left waiting on the hard benches of the waiting room for hours. I tell a nurse we have arrived, and soon after she admits us. The doctor – he is black – asks us to be seated.

"Are the needles clean?" I ask. He raises his eyes and looks at me – completely silent for a moment.

"The needles are quite new," he says, holding out a handful of needles still in the plastic casings from the factory.

"I'm sorry," I say. He sighs.

"You are right to be cautious," he says and takes the tests. Gives us an appointment in three weeks – then he will have our results. Rachel starts crying again. I take her hand, lead her out, take her to work. Three weeks in hell.

Marcus

PIE IN THE SKY

Bwana Knudsen walks right into Roots Rock. "Marcus," he says, "I need to talk to you." We drive to Newcastle Hotel in his car. Go to the roof terrace. He orders food and beer.

"What is going on with Christian and this girl? Is it serious?" he asks.

"You have to ask Christian," I say.

"Yes, yes, but he's not thinking straight at the moment," *bwana* Knudsen says. "He reminds me more and more of Jonas." Shocking – hard and straight out, no falseness or the lies of silence. Should I ask the question? How did Jonas Larsson die? Was that a result of *bwana* Knudsen not thinking straight?

I don't say anything.

"Tell me – who is she? Is she a decent girl?" he asks.

"She is a poor girl from the village who can hardly spell her own name," I say, because it's not my job to tell him the rest

"Hmmm," *bwana* Knudsen says. "I thought as much." Yes, Rachel is almost like every other Tanzanian – suffering and ignorant. And most of them don't know they can fight to have better lives. But she knows it. She's almost unarmed. She has only one, perfect weapon, and she uses it. Isn't it her right to fight? Maybe she'll have more success than I've had. I explain it to him.

"She can be the girl who provides Christian with warmth and love," I say. "But she's not a good Chagga woman with a family with a good sense of business who can help provide a good living for the white man in a black country. Rachel is just a girl. How they live will be Christian's problem." *Bwana* Knudsen takes a long gulp from his glass.

"Yes, she won't be much help when he goes back to Denmark," he says, almost muttering.

"He doesn't want to go to Denmark," I say. *Bwana* Knudsen looks at me:

"The disco?" he says. "That's just pie in the sky – boys' dreams. If a man wants to make his way, he needs an education."

"I know," I say. "I've told him."

"I have to say I'm glad he's with you, so he doesn't get mixed up in anything. You at least know what's what." *Bwana* Knudsen looks right at me to make sure I understand: he wants me to watch out for his son. But where is my payment? I shrug:

"I help him, if he helps me," I say.

"Hmmm," *bwana* Knudsen says.

The fruitfulness on earth – me and Claire haven't given up on that work. Again and again I plant my seed, but it falls out – straight to the ground. We go to our doctor, but he can't find anything wrong.

"We should get married," Claire keeps saying. "Otherwise God won't bless us with fruitfulness." I am close to saying yes, just to shut her up.

BATIK MURDER

And who is that on the veranda outside my front door, sitting next to Claire? Doctor Strangler, Claire's former boss from when she was a house girl.

"Hi, Marcus," he says.

"*Mzee* Strangler," I say. "*Shikamoo*." Doctor Strangler gets up and shakes my hand.

"I am on an evaluation mission in Dar, but I just wanted to stop by Moshi and see the old places," he says.

"It's good to see you," I say and ask about his family.

"They're back in Australia. They're well. I was very sad to hear about your daughter – I wish I had been here," he says. Claire looks at me.

"Come with me and fetch fresh water for coffee," she says and goes inside. I tell the doctor I will be right out. Claire whispers very quickly in the kitchen:

"You have to ask him why we lost our child. Perhaps he can explain it.

"Yes," I say. Claire can't ask a man about these things, even if that man is a doctor. I sit outside with Dr Strangler.

"I saw your shop in town, and Claire tells me you're in the disco business with *bwana* Knudsen's boy, Christian."

"Yes," I say.

"Do you have enough to live on?" Dr Strangler asks. He is worried about Claire. "What happened to the sawmill project?"

"I was fired because the head of accounts wanted to have a shot at corruption and saw me as an obstacle," I say. Dr Strangler shakes his head.

"And what about that Christian? Is he going to be a D.J. in Moshi for the rest of his life? Is that a life, Marcus? It won't last – we all know that," Dr Strangler says. As straight as a sword he cuts through claims I have not even made.

"It's his father," I say. "*Bwana* Knudsen has allowed Christian to run free in Africa and let the boy's mother disappear. In Africa your eyes only see black things. What can he become? – a D.J. who flips records like a monkey. That's all he knows how to do."

"But you know more than that," the doctor says.

"Take your own children," I say. "You have pushed them to educate themselves and shown them how to work. My father was an alcoholic who knew nothing but how to hit people. So I ran away and ended up with *bwana* Larsson, Jonas. But Jonas has never counselled me, so I have become a confusion like he was himself, because he was all I had to show me how things are supposed to be done."

Dr Strangler laughs: "Just because Jonas was a fool, doesn't mean you have to be. You have to think about Claire as well."

"Yes," I say and get started on the unpleasantness. About how Rebekka died, and how my seed falls out. Dr Strangler begins an interrogation, almost like a police officer. What did you do? What is in your home? What do you eat? He wants to know everything. When I have answered his questions, he enters the house and studies every corner until he says:

"You mustn't make batik. The fumes from the chemicals are dangerous." The batik has two sides: it provides for us, but at the same time . . . Now we know. I have one more question, because I never made it to the white country.

"How are Dr Freeman and Vicky?" I ask.

"Vicky left Freeman for another man," Strangler says.

"What does that other man do?" I ask.

"He is the director of Freeman's hospital."

"Richer than him?" I ask.

"Yes, very much so."

"Of course," I say.

"Why would you say that?" Strangler asks.

"Freeman was rich here, and he gave Vicky the ticket to the white country. But once she arrived, she discovered that Freeman was only a small fish – there were bigger fish, so she went fishing."

"Ah, well, I doubt it's that simple," Strangler says.

"No, I'm just joking," I say and say nothing of the system – Dr Strangler can live and die in blissful ignorance.

Christian

Dad comes round and starts asking me questions about my relationship with Rachel, and I tell him to mind his own business. "I don't interfere with who you're seeing – how or why," I say. That shuts him up.

And now Rachel's in the shower. And now the big moment's come, even though she doesn't know it. I hear the bathroom door open, and her feet patter down the corridor to the bedroom. I go in. She's got a *kanga* wrapped around her, is fiddling with her hair. I turn on the ceiling lights. She turns around.

"What?" she asks.

"Take it off," I say, in a sombre voice, pointing at her *kanga*.

"Why?" she says and tries to smile, but it's not really convincing.

"I want to suck the bean," I say in Swahili.

"But . . ." Rachel says. My smile breaks through. I can't hold it back any longer.

"I spoke to the doctor today," I say. "The tests were negative." Rachel's mouth is wide open.

"Really?" she says.

"We're alright – our blood is perfect," I say. And then we're all over each other.

They have opened the Kenyan border again. There's no knowing how long it'll last, so I tell Rachel we're going on a holiday.

"We'll drive to your village so I can meet your family. Afterwards we'll drive to Mombasa, and on the way back I will drop you off at the village so you can take the bus back to Moshi with Halima," I say. Rachel smiles.

"You should know that they are very poor," Rachel says when we're underway. "The house is very bad. They live in the traditional way, with the cows indoors."

"It won't be a problem," I say. We could of course go and see them in the village during the day and then sleep in a guesthouse at night, but that would be an insult, and she knows it.

Rachel has two younger sisters from her stepmother's previous marriage. The motorbike is loaded with our bags, sleeping bags and presents for the family – clothes, mostly.

We sit at a table, eating.

"Do you think your father will serve *mbege*?" I ask, because I would like to be mentally prepared if I'm going to have to drink lukewarm millet-beer.

"No, he doesn't drink – it's against Allah," Rachel says.

"I thought you were *mkristo*," I say.

"At home I am *mwislamu* out of respect for my father who calls me Zaina. But in Moshi I am *mkristo* because my aunt is in the church," Rachel says. We laugh.

"One God and his prophet: Allah and Mohammad, God and Jesus," I say.

"It's almost the same thing," Rachel says.

"Yes," I say.

When we arrive, a lot of people gather round to see the white man who arrives with Rachel on his motorbike. But most of them leave when we go behind the fence that surrounds Rachel's father house. Her father shakes my hand. I greet him and converse in the politest Swahili I can muster. Ask about his fields, his livestock. Rachel has told me that he had to sell a cow to pay for Halima's medicine. Rachel gives them the presents she bought for them in Moshi, and then she goes into the kitchen hut to help her stepmother with the cooking. Halima is constantly staring at me with big wide eyes. Whenever I look at her, she laughs and totters over to Rachel and her stepmother on her fat little legs.

"She has never seen a real *mzungu* before," Rachel's father says. "Only in pictures."

"Yes, it's very strange – our skin is like dirty milk," I say, and he laughs. A good sign, I think.

Rachel explains to me that her sisters have been sent to stay with relatives so that there would be room for us in the house.

We eat a sumptuous dinner. And then like a flash it's time for bed. Rachel told me they get up early to milk the cows. It's obvious they've been around borrowing mattresses for us so we can be comfortable. Palm leaves have been scattered on the dirt floor in the main room of the house, covered by plastic sheets, and on top of that the borrowed mattresses. I have brought my own sleeping bag. It's not easy to fall asleep with the sounds from nature so close at hand, but in the end I drift off.

The next morning I wake to the sound of Rachel's stepmother grinding flour in a mortar. Rachel is milking the cows. The entire day here is spent grinding flour, fetching water from far away, gathering firewood, working with the livestock and the fields. I have mosquito bites behind my ears.

We have thin corn gruel for breakfast and papaya and oranges. I hate corn porridge but eat a little while under the stepmother's watchful eye. There's a small tin of Africafé on the table – brand new. There's also traditional African tea with milk and cane sugar – I'd really rather have that to wash the nasty flavour of the gruel out of my mouth. But I think the coffee was bought especially for me. It is confirmed when I open the lid – the tinfoil is unbroken. I break it, take coffee with sugar and milk. I doubt that it's something they usually have in the mornings. They may not eat breakfast at all.

Baby Halima isn't afraid of me anymore. She comes waddling over to me, wanting to be picked up. After breakfast I pull Rachel aside outside. I have Halima on my arm.

"Would it be good if I were to give them money?" I say in a low voice.

"No, don't do that. My father is a proud man," she says.

"Could you give him money as a contribution, because they've looked after Halima?" I ask.

"Yes, I can do that. But not while you're there," Rachel says. So I give her some banknotes and carry Halima around the yard while Rachel gives them the money. I explain to her father that I will be back with

Rachel in a few days, and then she will take Halima with her on the bus to Moshi, so she can stay with us.

"That is very good," her father says, smiling. And then we're off. Rachel is happy. I didn't do too badly, it seems.

Marcus

HARD SUMMER

It's summer and Christian has gone on holiday with Rachel in Kenya. We're still waiting for the big decks to arrive at the Pentecostal church. We have exchanged dollars on the black market, so Christian can buy new music in Kenya and the shop can go on being an attraction. I must run the shop alone for three weeks, while Abdullah runs the small disco. Every day I walk all the way into town with the L.P.s and Christian's tape recorder. How heavy is it? Like a man carrying a mountain. And then back right before nightfall.

Konrad is a Belgian bloke who is staying in *bwana* Knudsen and Katriina's house on Kilimanjaro Road while the adults and the girls are on summer holiday in Denmark and Sweden. Konrad borrows their car as well and Issa the cook. Sometimes I go up and talk to Konrad in the evenings – we drink beer and play Kalaha. He plays well for a white man, but he only wins when I make sure he does. Konrad starts early every morning and drives to a farm in Kahe, not far from T.P.C., where they employ him to grow beans that are flown back to Europe. One day he stops next to me as I am dragging things back to Uru Road.

"Get in," he says.

"Thanks." We drive off.

"Can't that music just stay in the shop?" Konrad asks.

"The Danish boy thinks it would be stolen," I say.

"That boy gives a lot of thought to his own comfort," Konrad says.

"Yes, the suffering of others is his pleasure."

"The way he treated his girlfriend – that was bad," Konrad says.

"His girlfriend? He's always buying her presents," I say.

"No, his white girlfriend," Konrad says.

"Well," I say, "he's bewitched by the black miracle."

"Does he pay you well?" Konrad asks.

"Mostly we've been saving up to bring his big disco decks from Denmark so we can make real money."

"Don't you get paid?"

"No, we're partners," I say, but now that sounds silly. Partners? I am the wheels, but who drives the car?

"Christian says you work for him."

"*Tsk*," I say.

"He's always got money, that boy. Money for beer, money for his black girl," Konrad says. This is white talk; once the problem has been faced, you grab your guns – ready for battle. In Tanzania it's hard to speak so openly about another man – especially when you are dependent on him.

"Yes," I say. "I understand that he's cheating me, but I have no options – no papers from school, no *mabwana makubwa* in my family. I have to show the white boy the hypocritical smile to get ahead."

"While he screws you over? Why don't you come out to the farm?"

"I'm no farmer. I can't grow things," I lie because I don't want to live a slave's life in the fields.

Some days I rebel. I only take half the L.P.s and carry them to the shop. But usually I take all the L.P.s, the tape recorder and Solja's Walkman – I can connect all of it to the record player and the amplifier so I can record two cassettes at a time. But business is worse than usual, because I.S.M. is closed and the better part of the whites have gone on holiday. Things are slow. Nonetheless, during the holidays I earn a reliable income, and I discipline myself. And at least money is going into *my* pocket.

BRAKES

The day of Christian's return to Moshi. He comes right over on his motorbike.

"How much did you make?" he asks.

I tell him the amount – honestly. Well, almost.

"Good. Then it starts to look like we might get the decks into the country. They're stranded with the customs officials in Dar. With that money we can go to Dar and grease the customs officers and get them to release them."

"The money isn't here. I've got it in the bank," I say.

"Then let's get it," Christian says.

"No, not right now. Let's do it like this: you're just back from your holiday, and I have been working nonstop. Give me two weeks holiday. And afterwards we'll sit down and talk things over."

"But it's important to get the things released quickly. And I've brought a load of new L.P.s from Kenya, and the kids are back at I.S.M. – surely this is a good time to make money."

"No. Enough is enough. I need a break."

"Alright then. Then let me take that money with me so I can work on getting the decks through customs while you're on holiday," Christian says.

"Stop. You're not listening. We will take a break and talk afterwards. And that money I made while you were away . . . we need to talk about that as well – we should add it all up. Plus the money we made playing discos. All that money should be added up."

"That's fine," he says. "I've got all the receipts and expenses written down, and you've got your accounts."

"Yes, but it really is about time. I've never had any pay. Salary. We need to work things out. What is the rent for the shop? What are the plans for the future? What salary do I get for my work, and what do you get for yours? That way we respect our business and the money in it," I say.

"That's fine, Marcus. But I need the money so I can get the decks released."

"No. Not until we have talked about everything. In two weeks," I say.

His face drops. Oh, oh, oh, ohhhh . . . Have I made a big mistake?

"Then I will take all this back to my house," he says. "I don't want it here." He starts disconnecting cables. I don't help him. He's about to take Solja's Walkman.

"No," I say. "That's Solja's. She lent it to me."

"She'd like it back," Christian says.

"I will give it to her myself," I say. He starts taking all the records. "No," I say. "You can leave my records here. And my decks as well." He doesn't say anything. In the end he can take nothing but his L.P.s and his tape recorder.

"I don't understand why you're suddenly acting like this," he says and calls for a taxi to take away his L.P.s and his tape recorder, while he drives behind it on his motorbike.

"Two weeks," I say.

FALSE
In the evening Claire's sister Patricia comes to see us. She also goes to the Pentecostal church in Majengo.

"Christian came and picked up the things from Europe. There were a lot of big boxes – they hardly fit in the car."

"They came?!" I ask.

"Yes," Patricia says.

"When did he pick them up?" I ask.

"The day before yesterday in the morning." *Eeehhhh*, the things are already at his house, but he tries to get hold of the money I have made over the summer, so he can pay some imaginary customs officials in Dar. Now I am angry. I take a stack of the money and put it in my pocket. My gamble must be a hard one. Straightaway I travel to Arusha. I seek out Mick the *mzungu*, who is almost an African because he's lived here his whole life. He used to buy cassettes from me when he was at I.S.M. Now he has a large garage in Arusha. Very capable.

"How are things with that Christian?" Mick asks.

I tell him about the situation. "That boy seems very confused," I say.

"Yes," Mick says. "He doesn't understand that so long as we're alive we have to keep moving." I don't understand what he means, but it is true; we have to keep moving.

"Yes. In the end he will move to Europe and leave his mess in Tanzania, with unemployed staff, and his local girl without either floor under her feet or roof over her head," I say.

"*Tsk*," Mick says and sells me a cheap run-down Yamaha motorbike, and I rush home to Moshi. I need that machine to save myself.

The next night Christian comes over with Big Man Ibrahim as a guard at his side. He has gone direct to Ibrahim like a little boy who has been smacked. Ibrahim who once saved my life will now help cause my destruction.

"It's important to get the decks out of Dar quickly," Christian says. "Think of all the money we can make." Christian tries to look friendly, as if I were a child that has to be told everything slowly.

"You won't get the money I made this summer to cover the expenses of your fake customs officers in Dar. You have already taken all the other money we made together. A small fortune. And the L.P.s aren't all yours. Some of them were mine, some we bought together – we will have to share them. And the decks we used to record the cassettes and play small discos – half of it was mine. I should get more money than you. And really – which of us was working? Me. *Eeehhhh*." Ibrahim takes a few steps forwards:

"If you don't hand over the money now, I will break you," he says. I don't look at Ibrahim – only at Christian:

"We will sit down and talk once my holiday is over," I say.

"I don't think we have any more to say to each other," Christian says.

"Christian's father would like to speak to you," Konrad says one morning. "He wants you to come to Uhuru Hotel at seven tomorrow." *Eeehhh*, the little boy has gone to his father for help in controlling the naughty negro. "What is going on with you and Christian?" Konrad asks.

"Why?"

"That Knudsen chap – he was very worried when he asked about you."

I meet *bwana* Knudsen at Uhuru Hotel. I come to the table. Knudsen is like . . . he is very busy, like he is on a television channel and all the viewers are keeping an eye on him. He is behaving in an odd way towards me:

"Sit down, Marcus. I just need to . . ." He goes to the bathroom, comes back, lights a cigarette, calls the waitress for more coffee. It isn't because there are people watching us. He sits back, heavily, takes a deep breath:

"What happened, Marcus, to your business? Between you and Christian? What are you fighting about?" I shake my head:

"I haven't been in a fight. I haven't fought at all. I have told Christian we will have to sit down and discuss how we are going to run this business. Together. Continue it. So we know how we are going to do it. Is that fighting?"

"Alright. Christian says you're asking for money," *bwana* Knudsen says. I am shocked.

"That's a lie," I say – straight out, like a *mzungu*. If we are going to have a talk in the white way, then he too must hear my harsh words. I tell him all about how Christian has been putting away all our earnings, and that I have barely been paid; that I made sure the new decks could be sent down through the bishop's office, but Christian now says that he must have money for his imaginary customs officers in Dar. "I've had it," I say. "Nearly every day I have problems with immigrations officials who want to be bribed not to kick your son out of the country. And I've told him how to remedy the problem, but he doesn't do it."

"Alright, I will see to that," *bwana* Knudsen says.

"But it doesn't help a partnership when one party is always working while the other gathers the proceeds for his own use," I say. "This isn't colonial times."

"But . . . you don't trust each other anymore. Then you have to end your mutual business in a civilized manner," *bwana* Knudsen says. How can this murderous man speak to me about civilization?

"Civilized?" I say. "I don't care about being civilized. He has used me to launch a disco business, and now he's pushing me out."

"That's not how Christian tells the story," *bwana* Knudsen says.

"Sometimes you tell a lie to help the people you love," I say. "If you find a dead man in a hot shed, you tell the police it was an accident, even though the man has been helped to his death."

"What are you saying?" *bwana* Knudsen – as white as a freshly laundered sheet.

"I too – Marcus Kamoti – helped tell the lie, because of my two white girls – I didn't want them to live a life where their father has been murdered. They must believe it was an accident," I say.

"White girls?" *bwana* Knudsen says.

"My girls. My daughters," I say.

"You don't have any daughters," *bwana* Knudsen says.

"Are they your daughters?" I ask. "Did you feed them? Dress them? Brush their teeth? They are my girls. I want to see them, but you have stolen them from me," I say. Because I don't understand why they've been taken away.

"You stay away from our girls," he says.

"You stole those girls yourself," I say. He is sweating. "You stole those two girls and their mother one night at a party. Do you think I'm blind?" I ask, getting up.

"I had nothing to do with that," *bwana* Knudsen. "I was asleep."

"If you walk in your sleep and murder a man, then you are still guilty," I say. He stares at me – looking very tired, doesn't say anything. It will shut doors to me; it is a mistake to do it, but I can't stop myself. I keep going:

"You don't want me near them, because I awaken the memory in you of Jonas and the madness that was. And about how he died, which you know all about." I walk through the door. Let him sweat.

Christian

Fan-fucking-tastic. The decks are in my sitting room. They arrived at the church; the Norwegian called. I picked them up. Safe landing.

"Now you can play at Moshi Hotel or Liberty," Rachel says.

"Yep," I say. Shukran Hotel is too small for the new decks. We have cancelled our contract and are going to find somewhere else. But Moshi Hotel already has Faizal, who has excellent decks that belong to an Arab. Alwyn has his crap decks at Liberty, and they've got next to no guests.

"But that place is full of psychos and the owner is a greedy cow," Rogarth says.

"Take the motorbike and drive around town and the area – see if you can find a place that would be good," I say. Rogarth sets out. He needs to find somewhere else for us, and he needs to be quick about it. Life has changed since little Halima joined us. Rachel has stopped working – you can't look after a baby and work fourteen-hour days. Otherwise, we would have to spend everything she earned on a nanny for Halima. Instead Rachel has found an English course she can attend in the mornings while I stay in with Halima. After her lessons Rachel does the shopping at the market and gets a *matatu* or a taxi home, and then I've got the afternoons to do my business. We have a young girl who comes twice a week and cleans the entire house as well as doing the washing and the ironing. The idea is that she can babysit Halima at night every now and then when Rachel wants to come with me to work.

Halima is a great kid, but our expenses have increased. Abdullah has been looking after the disco while we were on holiday in Kenya. It's worked out well enough, but now Marcus is acting up. I bring a stereo worth thousands of kroner to the table and have paid the better part of the freight with the money Anders sent me. But Marcus feels cheated; one minute he claims we are equal partners, but as soon as he has to contribute, I am an evil employer who steals from him. I'm done with that drunk.

Rogarth returns at sundown. He grins when I come out.

"What?" I say.

"I'll show you," he says, getting off the motorbike.

"Did you find something?" I ask.

"I might have – you'll have to see it and decide for yourself," Rogarth says.

"Where is it?" I ask.

"A bit to the east of town," Rogarth says.

"Majengo?" I ask.

"I will show you," Rogarth says. Rachel comes out with Halima on her arm.

"Don't stay away too long," she says. "You can't leave me with those decks at night."

"I won't," I say. "Two hours, tops." Because Rachel is right. There are two dogs on the property, and they can bark, but they're not really aggressive, and there's no night guard here. If anyone were to find out those decks are in the house, they might show up with *pangas* and a lorry at night.

"Rachel is right," Rogarth says. "If you're keeping the decks here at night, you need someone here to be awake."

"Yes, I know," I say, thinking. "Wait here." I go down to the C.C.M. building and Ibrahim's karate class, which I've given a miss since Halima arrived. Firestone is there, helping Ibrahim out.

"Can I borrow him?" I ask.

"For what?" Ibrahim asks.

"My house is full of decks – I just need someone to keep guard."

"Yes, of course," Ibrahim says.

"I-I-I-I-I . . ." Firestone says and skips about a little, making a karate chop at the air. "I will ki-ki-ki-ki-ki . . ."

"He will kill any *mwezi* that tries to steal from you," Ibrahim says.

"Yes, I will kill them," Firestone says, looking relieved.

"You drive," I tell Rogarth and get up on the back. He drives down to the Y.M.C.A. roundabout and takes the Dar road to the east. Past the exit to Majengo and a little further. He turns right at an Agip petrol station. Golden Shower Restaurant it says on a sign on the roadside. I have heard that you can have dinner here and that the food is not bad. But I've never been. We are on a dirt road that is perfectly alright, and right behind the petrol station Rogarth turns into a car park in front of the restaurant. We get off. There are only three cars parked here.

"The guy who runs it is half English; his mother is Chagga and his father English – it's the father who owns the place. People say he's mad," Rogarth says.

"Mad how?"

"Something's not right with him. Very aggressive. He can be sitting as nice as you please and suddenly he'll leap from his chair and hit you just because he feels like it."

"But it's the son who runs the place?" I ask.

"Yes," Rogarth says. We enter the handsome garden with flowers, shrubs, a well-tended lawn and pebble paths. The reason for the name – Golden Shower – is revealed: tiny orange trumpet flowers cascade from the eaves of the veranda. I pull down a few and suck out the sugary juice from the bottom of the trumpet. We ask for the manager at the bar. Order some food. Rogarth introduces me to him. David. Mulatto. I explain our intentions. He nods.

"I think we could probably give it a go, but you will have to discuss it with the owner – my father," he says.

Our food arrives – it's quite good.

"I imagine that we'd get a percentage of the entrance fee, and you get all the proceeds from the bar and restaurant," I say. David shakes his head.

"You'll have to discuss it with my father – he's here most nights. Try tomorrow."

"Alright, we'll be here tomorrow," I say, shaking his hand. The place is perfect. Enough room for a dance floor, tables in the garden where people can sit. The toilet's alright.

"The question is, will anyone come all the way out here?" I say.

"Yes," Rogarth says.

The father is there the following night. *Bwana* Benson. Very thin and sinewy, with unkempt greying hair. A bit emaciated. Bright purple open nylon shirt, dark gabardine trousers, polished brown leather shoes. Nicotine-stained fingers. We say hello.

"So, it's you boys who want to turn my restaurant into a brothel," he says, even though it's obvious he doesn't have enough guests – he needs us. He's nursing a beer – it looks like he's had a few already – but there is an inscrutably alert look in his eyes; perhaps that's just something I'm imagining because I've been told he is mad.

"We just want to play some nice music Friday and Saturday nights, so people can come out and dance."

"Dance?" he says, throwing back his head and laughing loudly, setting off a wet, throaty gargle of a cough.

"Yes. A nice bit of soul music, some reggae, a teeny bit of disco, some Zaire Rock," I say.

"Christian has good decks – a very good sound; much better than Moshi Hotel." Rogarth is standing next to me – we haven't been asked to sit down, and apparently he thinks he should be chipping in.

"Hmmm," the Englishman says. "And what do you imagine you should be paid for your trouble?" We discuss it for some time. "And how will I trust the numbers you give me?"

"You can count the guests or have a man sitting with ours at the entrance." The negotiations continue. We end up getting seventy per cent of the money from the door, but then we have to pay the bouncers and the guards for the car park. He's pushing it, but not too much – if we pull in the right sort of crowd, that is.

We drive back.

Marcus

LAST DANCE

Christian is at the shop, pulling a cable out from between the amplifier and the tape recorder, holding it up without looking at me. "Mine," he says and puts it in his bag. I am standing outside the door looking in at him. I take a firm grip of the sliding grille, pulling it shut in one swoop. "What?!" he shouts. I put the padlock through the eyelets and click it shut. He comes over. "What the hell are you doing, Marcus?"

"Do you feel it?" I ask.

"What?"

"Trapped," I say, getting out my cigarette pack. He rolls his eyes, sighs, says:

"Just open those fucking bars, will you?" I light my cigarette, blow smoke at him. He shakes the bars. "Give me a cigarette," he says. The bars are on the outside of the door, so there's no way for me to shut it as well. I throw the burning cigarette at his body, so he leaps back. "Damn it, Marcus," he says. "I will bloody well get Ibrahim to beat you to a pulp if you don't let me out right now."

"I'm going home for my coffee," I say.

"I will trash your things if you don't open up," he says, pointing towards my amplifier, the old loudspeakers, the tape recorder. I shrug, turn around and walk off.

"Marcus?" he says in a low voice. I can go back and let him out whenever I want. He is so white, he finds it embarrassing to call a black man to ask for help. He will close the wooden door from inside, hide himself from the customers at Stereo Bar, who are already getting up from the chairs on the pavement to see what has happened to this white man. At Coffee Bar I sit with this sad feeling. I have seen him grow from a boy to a man – I took him to his first proper disco. We started off going to kiddie discos at the Y.M.C.A., and later came the nights at Liberty in the good days. I taught him to dance; he stole beer and dollars and Marlboro for me from his father. And he tried to help me then, but he was only a boy. Yes, and now I see him as my naughty little brother. Greedy, naughty brother. My naughty, greedy little brother.

And I could have used force. Violence and force. When he was away on holiday, I could have taken all his L.P.s and everything and kept them in my house – locked away. Told the immigration authorities about him, and the taxman. Have him thrown out of the country directly. Yes, I could have said we did business together; he took all the money. I have my accounts: dates, amounts, totals – and some of them are in his handwriting. The accounts are at my house.

The steps I can take could even get him sent to Karanga Prison, but that would be like going against myself in some sense. And it would, ahh . . . it's like looking at a monkey; you can't shoot it – you feel sorry for it, you do. Because its eyes are like your eyes. So I stop; leave the coffee cup and go over – let him out of the shop.

"I hope you understand that what goes up must come down. You have to keep moving. You're facing hard times," I say.

He doesn't say anything.

Christian

I've agreed on a date with *bwana* Benson. I have bought a backup generator to run the decks if there's a power cut and have made sure it's up to the job. I am almost broke. With my very last money I get hundreds of small posters made, almost like fliers, A6 size. The reggae colours – red, yellow, green and black – the image from Bob Marley & the Wailers "Uprising", scaled down and with our name at the bottom: Rebel Rock Sound System. Plus a small map of how to find Golden Shower. I have bought an old sewing machine for Rachel. She sits at home, sewing yellow shirts for the entire crew – that's me, Rogarth, Khalid, Abdullah and Firestone. Rogarth and I will take turns D.J.'ing, Khalid will be at the door taking the money, Abdullah is the bouncer and Firestone will guard the car park; if good cars park somewhere without a guard, windscreen wipers and wheel caps will disappear. And someone who knows how to hotwire will stop by and drive off with the car. Not exactly something that would recommend us to the customers. At Golden Shower we will run cables for the loudspeakers over the rafters in the restaurant, so we can set up quickly. I won't run the risk of keeping my decks there all week – nor the loudspeakers – not even from early Saturday morning to Saturday night – who will take responsibility for their still being there? No-one. We drive around, walk or bike, to put up posters using sticky tape and tacks. We put up loads. People are *meant* to rip them down and take them home with them. The posh people in the city centre are not convinced:

"*Tsk*, no," they say. "You have to understand; there is no way you will get a big crowd out there – the big disco has to be in the city centre. Moshi Hotel has that market cornered."

We open on a Friday night. It gets dark. There is almost no light – no strobes. Only a disco ball to throw a few sparkles and a handful of fluorescent lamps. I am worried but at nine it happens . . . People start pouring in. They come from the slopes of Kilimanjaro – Old Moshi. They come from Majengo, even from Kiborloni. The Chaggas come to party – the proper sort of people. And I think about it: who is it that lives in the city centre in Moshi? – wealthy Chaggas and Asians in their flats. It's expensive – those people don't go to discos, except the men who go to watch ladies – and those men will drive to where women are: in a chauffeur-driven car or a taxi. Golden Shower is the right place. Or Swahilitown where the Muslims live, the half-Arabs, the people from the coast – but they are poor and not very fond of discos – and if they are, they want to go away from their local area: their families might catch them! We have the perfect location. Ibrahim comes in to see the opening act.

"It's a lovely disco," he says, smiling. Yes, the night is going really well. People are dancing and drinking and eating and dancing some more. No trouble at all. David is happy, even mad *bwana* Benson is smiling. We have a P.A. system with a twelve-band mixer. We can play insanely loud, and most of the time we play L.P.s so people get a clear sound. And Rogarth is a good D.J. No talking between the songs to show off – just music.

Once people have left, late in the night, David comes over and shakes our hands. We drag the decks out into a taxi.

"We need some breakfast," Ibrahim says, so we direct the taxi to Shukran Hotel and have breakfast in the café before the taxi takes me and Firestone home. Rachel gives me a good-morning kiss. Firestone crashes on the sofa, and I pass out on the bed.

Later I ask Rachel if she can get a babysitter so she can come down and see Golden Shower at night.

"No," she says. "I like discos on the mountain, but not in town – there's too much trouble." Perhaps she might meet the ghosts of her past there. I don't like to think about it. I smile at her.

"But aren't you worried the girls are trying to catch me?" I ask.

"No." Rachel is unconcerned. "Because now you have me and Halima, and you like us very much." She is right.

That night the music goes again. The rumour has spread. Golden Shower is packed, the money is pouring in, everybody's happy. I go over to Rogarth behind the two decks and look out across the teaming dance floor, putting my arm around him.

"Discos are much better in Tanzania than in Denmark," I say. He looks at me sceptically. "Because here everyone comes to the party: young, old, rich, poor, Africans, Indians – a perfect blend." I point towards a table. "Have a look at that old Indian there – you'd never see a man like that in a disco in Denmark. But here he comes to party."

"He's not here for the party," Rogarth says. "He's here to watch the animals – the black women. Is there one of them he'd like for his conquest? He has to come here, even though he can't dance and hates the music. All he wants is oldies from the 1950s. But how else will he get the young *malaya*? The young people go where their music is to be found, so that's where the old Indians go as well. They pretend to dance, but they almost fall over. I know all about their game from Moshi Hotel."

"But there are no dogsbodies here, are there?" I ask.

"No," he says. "Because we've just started. But next weekend, they'll be here."

Sunday night. Rachel lights a cigarette for me and sits up on the sofa, pulling her legs under her. She rubs my ear lobe as I smoke.

"When I met you at Liberty, Tito told you that you just came to pump the girls here. I told him no. That the *mzungu* isn't like that. But Tito said that the *mzungu* only wanted to pump me, and then he would go home; he wouldn't marry me and take me to Europe. One day he would disappear and leave me here. But I liked you. And you kept stopping by the shop even though you had your white girlfriend. But your white girlfriend went away, and you became my boyfriend. You couldn't stay away from me."

She's never spoken of Europe before, but now she feels secure enough. She knows I love her, even though I do my damnedest to shut up about it. So now she flags her dream: Europe. That cold miserable place. She is sitting absolutely still. I think I understand. I feel it myself: the human being – an adaptable animal. My brain adjusts to the situation, to the urges I have, the options that are to hand: I take them – I am part of it. Rachel is the same. I have come to terms with what she . . . was. I take one last deep drag of the cigarette, inhale and blow a pillar of smoke out into the air. She is the exact opposite of Marianne – we don't have to over-analyse every petty detail before we can discuss something. It's often hard to know what she's thinking. And I can see why Marcus said I would be better off with a Chagga girl from a solid family. But Rachel was the one I wanted.

"When I came to Moshi, all the girls in the offices on Rengua Road showed a keen interest in me. But you were never out to catch me," I say.

"How can I catch you when there are already four Chagga girls who work in offices and have good families and would help you with anything you wanted? And I'm just a poor girl from the coast who works for a *mama* and doesn't even have her family around?"

"But when you met me the first time, didn't you know I was interested in you?" Rachel doesn't say anything. "Didn't you?" I ask.

"Yes, but perhaps you were just interested in all black girls."

"Did you think I was one of them?"

"No. But I couldn't know. All I knew was that if you were really interested, you would come again." I don't say anything. "And when all the other girls have already opened the door for you before they even knew you, perhaps you might prefer to open that door which is still closed," Rachel says.

"Yes," I say, turning towards her.

"Do you think I can't stay away from you?" I ask.

"I do," she says, smiling.

"Hmmm," I say. And then we make love. The way she receives me, keeps me inside her. It doesn't have to be intense or last ages or be difficult getting started. It's just . . . her holding me, my holding her. Yes, we fuck like bunnies, but sometimes we just need to be close – like she wants to give me peace, like a gift. It is a gift. And she is happy giving it.

Marcus

SHITBAGS

When I had the recording shop, I was everyone's friend. Firestone, Abdullah, Khalid, Ibrahim, Rogarth. Now they walk the other way if I meet them on the street. They work for Christian at Golden Shower; and it works so well that Moshi Hotel loses half of its disco customers in no time at all.

"Why can't you do discos?" Claire asks.

"Because of my decks," I say. "They're not big enough."

"There are discos at some of the small bars with a single room and a tiny dance floor. You could play there easily enough," Claire says. She doesn't understand that the attraction isn't just good music – the white man himself is a draw. Even though we live in an independent nation, the negro is so colonized in his head that whatever is white is always going to be better.

Only Phantom remains my friend.

"Bob Marley's father was a white man," Phantom says. "But when the white man saw his dark, he was so frightened that he ran, and Jah chose the mixed child to be his voice on earth to help the oppressed rise. Never trust a white man."

And Claire is right. I have to do something. We only have the chickens and the kiosk. No-one in Moshi wants to buy things. The social trend goes one way only, and that is down – there is almost no money in circulation. At the same time the market in Kiborloni is flooded with second-hand clothes from Europe because the Europeans want to help the Africans with old clothes which destroy my economy and turn it to dust.

We turn Roots Rock recording shop into a clothes shop for snobs. The uppity families don't want to be seen walking through the dust between the small dirty stalls in Kiborloni, like dogs on a rubbish heap; their house girl might even be there to see the posh lady rooting through piles of clothes that have already been used by European people. That's why I send Claire's mother and sister as detectives to Kiborloni – they must find all the smart clothes which will appeal to the snobs in town. The clothes are adjusted, fixed up, washed and ironed, and then Claire sells them in the shop which we rename Princess. And we expand our stock to include make-up, bags and hair slides for the ladies. It works. But it's not enough to live on. Because suddenly I have an entire family in my keep. Me, Claire, her mother, her sister, a boy to man the kiosk, a house girl, tsk.

Claire finds young unmarried girls in Soweto, and she arranges a course for them where I teach them the art of batik-making. We pay a small wage, and then Claire will sell the batik in Kenya at a great profit.

I recorded all the good songs from Christian's L.P.s onto cassettes while he was on holiday. I have all the good music, even though I can only play it loud enough for a small room.

I find a bar in Majengo that is willing to pay me a little for a local disco. Phantom helps me at the door; we charge our humble fee. Raggamuffin Sound System – that's our name.

"Why should we pay?" the young chaps ask Phantom when they meet the demand for admittance fee. "That Marcus doesn't have the same good music the mzungu from Rebel Rock Sound System does at Golden Shower."

"Marcus has the same music the mzungu does," Phantom says.

"He doesn't have the good sound system," the chaps say.

"That's why it's cheaper here than at Golden Shower," Phantom tells them.

"But it has to be much cheaper. He is no mzungu D.J. He is just Marcus from the shop on Rengua Road. We know him already. You have to lower the price. It must be free."

"The price has already been lowered," Phantom says. "We have to make a living as well."

"You two are just idiots," the young chaps say. "We don't give a shit about your disco." The young chaps walk away. But there are grown-ups as well, who want to drink and listen to the good old-fashioned music without having to look at the malaya at Golden Shower. I play to them, and the night turns out well. The grown-ups are all on the floor, dancing.

Pszzziiiii . . . SPLOSH. Something hits a man on the floor and lands on the ground.

596

"*Kuma mamayo*," the man shouts, as he looks down himself. I can't see what it is. Something else comes flying through the open windows, hitting the wall, splashing onto the guests. They scream. It falls to the floor. I look: some plastic and something brown.

"It's shit," the man shouts, and everybody hides away from the window-openings, runs behind the bar and squats down. A new bag flies into the room; I duck down behind the table with my amplifier, record player, tape recorder. SPLOSH. The bag hits the wall behind me, and shit rains down on me. Phantom runs out into the darkness, but there are no street lamps – he can't see a thing. I turn off the music at once – the record player is still going round with a piece of shit on top of Bob Marley's "Natty Dread". A voice comes from outside:

"We don't give a shit about your disco." They've shat into the bags that people get in kiosks when they buy knick-knacks – the plastic is very thin and breaks easily. The shit-fire continues. All the guests run out of the bar, away, away, away from the shit – disappear into the night.

"Police, police, police," Phantom shouts – the police station in Majengo is just around the corner. We can hear people running away in the night.

"You have to pay for the cleaning up of that mess," the bar *mama* says. "Now my customers are gone as well."

"Shall I fetch the police?" Phantom asks.

"No," I say. "It's too late. The arseholes will have gone."

"I know who some of them are," Phantom says. "I know where they live. The police can find them."

"Yes, but now we have to pay to have the bar cleaned. The money we made is gone. We can't even afford to pay the police to do their job and arrest people."

Christian

The speakers boom with Isaac Hayes' voice, and the dance floor swims with eroticism.

"They can feel it at Moshi Hotel," Rogarth tells me. "I spoke to Faizal – he says their takings are plummeting."

"But that's obvious, isn't it? We're closer to Majengo, Old Moshi, Kiborloni – you need less money for transport."

David is pleased. His dad, *bwana* Benson, comes over to me. Benson hasn't said anything yet, but he comes to the bar for a few hours every night. Now he puts his arm around my shoulder and smiles broadly.

"It's going well," he says.

"Yes, our launch was perfect, wasn't it?"

"No," he says. "It wasn't going so well. But it is now."

"Why do you say that?" I ask. He gestures towards the bar where some expensive-looking girls are waiting, the way you would see it at Moshi Hotel.

"The ladies are here," he says. "This is why there's money to be made – it means we have caught on to the wealthy clientele as well. They dine, they drink, they buy rounds of beer to show off their wealth. We're doing well." He turns around and tells the bar *mama* in Swahili: "Bring a beer for our *mzungu*."

I begin to know all the bargirls and all the professional *malaya* in town. And I find out about things. People drink, the blokes get drunk, a tall man puts his arm around a girl at the bar, saying:

"Yes, she's mine now. She drank my beer. I paid for her."

"Remove that arm," she says, pushing him off. We're not at the fag end of Majengo – a papaya isn't opened by a single beer and a few coins. The girl is here to fish for a good man. But the tall man grabs on to her, pulling her close.

"Do you think you can drink my beer and then just leave?"

Bwana Benson goes over to the man, buys him a beer, gets in front of him and stares into his face – the tall man's eyes swim. Benson is a white man – reedy, but with a reputation, and I can see the doubt spreading across the tall man's face.

"Now you're drinking my beer," Benson says. "Does that mean you're mine? Can I do it with you doggy-style?"

"I didn't mean it like that," the tall man says and looks at the floor, embarrassed.

"You can't get a girl for a beer in my place," Benson says and walks away – comes right over to me.

"So now you've made my restaurant a boxing ring for drunks and whores – who will solve the problems if I'm not around?"

In the end we have to pay for another bouncer, in addition to Abdullah – our choice is Big Man Ibrahim. Everything quietens down.

The whores are a different thing altogether – the professional *malaya*. It's about money – they sell their papaya. And they have the gift of the gab – it's out of this world. Shameless. They talk about all sorts of in-crowd stuff. At first they try to make me a customer, but then they discover I've got Rachel, and they get used to me – start to trust me. They tell me things.

Chantelle, Tunu and Scola are their names. Chantelle – the most gorgeous woman in the world. Tunu – tall, thin, athletic – the chiselled face of a model. And Scola – a tiny pitch-black Satan with a constant naughty, condescending, cynical look in her eyes. She would sooner grab your balls than shake your hand. And I get to know them. I like Chantelle's blue eye-shadow, the large purple lips, the small delicate nose. Her skin is pale because she never goes into the sun. They try to tease me while we wait for the night to reach boiling point. They tell me about the different preferences they enounter, exchange experiences, boast of the presents they get, enlarge on various perversions, slander and gossip. About how fat, burping, snoring, farting, whinging, dirty, stinking and important their customers are. Tunu kicks off:

"My Sikh, he wants me to squat over his face shaking my arse as I touch his cock and balls, and he slaps my buttocks."

"Tsk. That's normal," Scola says. "My Arab wants me to stick my fingers up his arse while I eat his pump. Then he whimpers like a dog." Chantelle smiles sweetly:

"My man from Goa pumps my behind with his tongue, and then he wants me to wee in his mouth."

"Uhhh," Tunu says. "The behind is for things to come out of, not for things to be put into."

"What does our *mzungu* like?" Scola asks and lets a finger glide up between my buttocks outside my trousers. I smile at her.

"I like papaya; morning, noon and night." The ladies laugh and slap hands. It's different and yet the same.

"The fat man from Goa – the one with the sideburns," Chantelle says. "I must beat his behind – very hard – and tell him he's a bad boy. Once a week – every week."

"The very fat one – bald at the top of his head?" Tunu asks. Chantelle nods.

"Yes, that's the one," Scola says. "I used to smack him as well, but now he only wants Chantelle. He likes his women to look like a big *mama* when he gets his bottom spanked." Then it dawns on me:

"D'Souza!" I say. "Ahh no – that can't be right." They just look at me, raising their eyebrows.

Rachel nudges me in bed.

"You have to go pick up your friend," she says. I open my eyes, look out through the bars and the mosquito netting at the grey dawn.

"His name is Anders," I say.

"Anas," Rachel says as she goes to the kitchen. I sit down on the edge of the bed, rubbing my face. Anders. Yes. I smile to myself, get up and put on a lot of clothes – the early mornings are chilly. Rachel has already boiled milk and water on the cooker and made me tea. Now she's watching the toast on the griddle, which has been placed over the hot plates – she has just enough time to toast a few slices of bread on the waste heat once the kettle has boiled. I eat a mango, toast with peanut butter, drink tea with milk and cane sugar. Rachel sits across from me. Halima has gone back to her grandfather in the village for the next two weeks, because Anders will be here and we will be taking him out a lot.

"Do you have enough money to go into town?" I ask, because she's going shopping and to her English course at the K.N.C.U. building.

"Yes, I've got enough," she says. I get up and stand behind her.

"Thanks for breakfast," I say, bending down, kissing her neck. She reaches up and touches my hair, and I place the palms of my hands against the warm skin below her armpits, so my fingers feel the curve where her breasts leave the ribcage. "Shall we go back to bed?" I ask. She lets go of my head with one hand and tries slapping my thigh.

"Enough!" she says. "*Tsk*. Off you go."

When I come out of the bathroom, Rachel has gone back to bed. I can't see if her eyes are open. I wonder what Anders will think of her? The same thing I do? That she's irresistible? I look forward to talking to him. Miss talking to a white man who understands where I'm coming from . . . at least in part.

The sun comes up behind me as I drive towards the airport. I pass a Valmet tractor pulling two-wheeled transporters full of logs from West Kilimanjaro – where Marcus used to work. It's been a while since I last saw him.

There are very few people out. I end up behind an articulated lorry carrying flammable fluids as the road winds down towards the bridge across the river in the ravine just west of Moshi. The lorry spews out stinking black diesel fumes, and as soon as we have passed the bridge he waves me ahead – the all-clear. But I stay behind him. So many people die trying to overtake cars in this country. Annemette – she would have been seven years old now. There's only a narrow verge between me and the sharp rock face on either side of the road, which is all sharp curves, so the view is limited. The oncoming traffic goes rather fast towards the valley, and many of the vehicles have shoddy brakes. It takes powerful acceleration to overtake. It's risky.

I turn down towards Kilimanjaro International Airport. I've had so many experiences here: arrivals, departures. My little sister in the coffin. Mum. Myself – home . . . or home? I put it out of my mind. Pass the Merelani Township exit and stop by the bar at the entrance to the terminal area. Pay the parking charge and drive that final stretch to the airport terminal.

The plane hasn't landed yet. It starts getting warmer. I go over to the bar, drink a cup of coffee. The swallows fly swiftly and nimbly around in the building. There are posters on the walls: a red heart on a white background. In the heart it says TAKE CARE. Below it says BEWARE OF A.I.D.S. – but what is A.I.D.S. and how are you meant to be careful? It doesn't say anything about that, because it's taboo.

After my coffee I go to the roof terrace to see the Aeroflot plane land; Anders couldn't afford anything better. He comes out not long after. I call and wave.

"The White Negro," he shouts back. He looks beat up, but is smiling with relief. I go down. He sees me and comes to the window between the baggage reclaim and the arrivals hall.

"Jesus, what a trip," he says. "Great seeing you though."

"It'll probably be a while before the luggage arrives," I tell him. Anders goes over and changes the fifty dollars that is required on entering the country; at the official exchange rate – ridiculous. There's no power cut, but the baggage carousel has broken down all the same, so after waiting an age they simply throw the luggage through the hole in the wall; inside is another worker who shifts the suitcases onto the floor. Anders has followed my advice and taped his suitcases completely shut with brown sticky tape – that way the airport crew in Moscow thinks the bag belongs to a Russian and not worth breaking into.

"You must open it," the customs officer says.

"But my pocketknife is in the suitcase," Anders says. "I wasn't allowed to bring it on the plane." I can tell the customs officer is getting annoyed.

"Then you'll have to wait," he says. Anders comes over to me again while the officer deals with the other passengers.

"What the hell is this?" Anders says to me through the glass wall.

"Just take it easy," I say and remind him of what he should say; that he is here to climb Kilimanjaro and visit my dad in Shinyanga. Give the Y.M.C.A. in Moshi as his address. I greet the customs officer politely in Swahili. He answers me in English – a proper arsehole. I continue in Swahili: can Anders borrow a knife to open his suitcase? Now the officer runs out of English.

"Why did he do that to his suitcase?" he asks in Swahili. I explain about the Russians. "Oh, the Russians," the customs officer says, shaking his head. "Do you live here?"

I explain that I'm visiting my dad in Shinyanga where he is working for the *ushirika* – the co-op. But now me and my old friend from school want to climb Kilimanjaro.

"But you speak Swahili well," the officer says.

"Thank you," I say and tell him how long I have lived here. T.P.C. and so forth. Anders is squatting on the floor, sawing away at the tape with an ordinary table knife.

"Does he have a present for me in that suitcase?" the customs officer asks.

"I think it's just his clothes for the mountain climbing," I say.

"*Tsk*," the officer says and lights a cigarette. Then he suddenly smiles broadly, waves us off with his hand, turning his back.

"Thanks a lot," I say, and to Anders: "We're off the hook."

"What?" he says. "Didn't he want to see all my junk?"

"No. He just wanted to see if we were easy to scare. Let's get going." Anders comes out to me.

"Holy shit," he keeps saying as we move towards the car park. "I didn't sleep a wink, man. Eight hours at Moscow airport. The saddest place on earth. Concrete, concrete, concrete." He stops, looks around. "Wow, Christian," he says. Offers me a Prince. We smoke. It feels at once oddly inhibited and exuberant. I strap his suitcase onto the motorbike with rubber straps made from old car tyres. He is standing by, smoking. "I'm sorry about your dole."

"Oh well, don't worry about that – you did what you could," I say.

"Yes. I mean, I went to the desk at the Job Centre to get your stamp, and then the bitch took your card and told me to just wait a while. And there I was, sweating and keeping an eye on her while she went over and spoke to some other bitch, and they kept throwing me suspicious looks. Then the other bitch says: 'It seems we might have a small problem. Could you just come into the office, please?' Then I just ran – out, away."

"But of course. It was nice of you to even try. It really helped me. And you don't have to worry about money while you're here. I'll foot the bill – no problem."

"O.K., cool," Anders says and we get up, drive into Moshi. Now the traffic's busy, and there are women going to the market with baskets heaving with vegetables on their heads. "Negroes everywhere," he shouts.

We get home.

"Where's your girlfriend?" Anders asks. I tell him she's out shopping, at school. We smoke a spliff. He falls asleep on the sofa.

When Rachel comes home, he can't keep his eyes off her. She goes about the house, fixing things with her pert arse.

"Holy fucking shit," he says. She asks me in Swahili if he has a girl-friend.

"What's she saying?" Anders asks.

"Whether you have a girlfriend," I translate and give Rachel the answer: "No."

"Matilda might stop by later," Rachel says.

"I don't think Anders will take Matilda back to Denmark with him," I say in Swahili.

"He might," Rachel says.

"Matilda?" Anders says. "What are you talking about?"

"Nothing," I say. "It's just one of her friends from the English course that might stop by for dinner tonight."

"Oh. Is she attractive?" Anders asks.

"Yes," I say. Christ what a circus. Anders asks about everything. I try to explain it all to him: that Rachel has a child who has gone back to the village to visit her grandfather. That Halima normally lives with us. That Rachel is learning English. How my work is going – everything.

"You're practically a family man," Anders says.

"Yes," I say.

"Far out," he says.

"We'll go into town for a beer," I say once we've had supper.

"Alright," Rachel says. Matilda is on the sofa smiling broadly, waving a loose-limbed arm.

"Bye-bye, see you later," she says to Anders in her halting English. He points at her, says:

"Yes, we're going out sometime, you and me."

"Yes," Matilda says, giggling. She whispers something to Rachel, who laughs and slaps her thigh as I go out and open the gate, sit down on the motorbike. Kick-start it and turn towards the road, until I can feel the weight of Anders getting up behind me. Then I turn up the gas. The light from the headlights jumps over the bumpy road, the dusty plants, the endless darkness. I drive through town and out to Majengo. Stop in front of Jackson's bar, which is only a short distance from the police station and not too run-down.

"Let's sit out here," I say, pointing at the concrete veranda under a mouldering awning.

"Holy shit, she's hot – that Matilda," Anders says as the bar *mama* comes out. I order beers for us. "Do you think she's . . . ?" Anders starts.

"What?"

"You know . . . interested in me?"

"You bet she is. She's banking on you taking her with you to Europe." Anders gives me a serious look.

"Do you really mean that?" he asks.

"No, I don't mean that. But she does."

"For fuck's sake, I live on an estate in Aalborg – I'm a dustman."

"Yes, but you deal in amazing dust – European dust."

"But doesn't your girlfriend know I'm only here for a visit?"

"Rachel wants you to take Matilda home with you as well."

"Oh," Anders says. "I just want to . . . oh for fuck's sake. I just want to do it with a black girl."

The bar *mama* brings out our beer, pouring it into glasses. A barefoot kid in tattered, dirty shorts and shirt comes over to the bar; he's carrying an egg tray on his upturned palm. He comes over and stands next to us, looking at us but doesn't say anything.

"Would you like an egg?" I ask.

"An egg?" Anders says.

"I think it's something they picked up from the English – hard-boiled eggs with beer."

"Sure, why not – let me try one." I ask for two.

Two girls come strolling over with rocking hips in tight jeans. One of them is Salama, who Rachel used to share a room with. Salama stays in the background. She nods at me, but doesn't speak. Salama's friend comes over the fence. She looks at Anders. She looks at me. Smiling and in a low voice she tells me in Swahili exactly what she will do for Anders and how much it will cost – it's exorbitant. She can tell he's just arrived.

"You, sister!" I tell her. "I know the price."

"Yes," she says. "But it costs more for the *mzungu* because he's coloured."

"We were just talking," I tell her. "Not tonight."

"I'll see you later," she says in Swahili to me. And to Anders: "I love you," before she turns and walks away – swaying, rippling.

"Welcome to paradise," I say.

"I fucking love you too," Anders says to the darkness.

"She's a whore," I say.

"I realize that," Anders says. "And it seems I'm going to need a whore, since I'm not allowed to touch Matilda."

"No, I mean . . . you do whatever you do. What I mean is that she won't treat you right. She will do all the hands-on, actual stuff, but like a . . . machine – without feeling."

"Matilda?" Anders asks. He doesn't realize I'm talking about the whore – my Danish feels rusty.

"No," I say. "Matilda will give you everything, to reel you in. I'm talking about this whore here."

"Yes, she's a whore – you can't buy feelings, Christian."

"Are you sure?" I ask.

"But how about Matilda – why not?" Anders asks – and what is the logic behind it really? I'm with Rachel; why can't he be with Matilda?

"If you do it, you do it, but you have to understand that she will do it to get a ticket, and then I will have to hear her go on about you. For the next two years I will have questions thrown at me morning, noon and night about when you'll return."

"So you'll take Rachel home with you, when you return – that's what you're saying?"

"We'll get to know each other first; but yes, if I do go home."

"When you do," Anders says. I don't answer that. Am I to be a sort of pimp for Anders, so he can try going native? That will only make things worse. Black berries have the sweetest juice.

We toast, and I order more beer. And Konyagi. "The local schnapps," I tell Anders. Every time a girl walks by, he follows her with his eyes. I wonder if I should tell him about Rachel – what she used to be. Should I talk about A.I.D.S.? The risk? But I don't want to talk about those things, and I don't think Matilda was ever a dirty girl.

"I suppose it's the same game," I say. "It's just more obvious here."

"What game?" Anders says.

"When you're with a girl, then . . . one way or another you are going to end up paying to fuck her."

"How?" Anders says.

"In Denmark you pay for it as well," I say.

"I don't," Anders says.

"No, not in cash, but . . . with other things," I say.

"Yes, of course," Anders says.

"What I mean is that Matilda will give it to you for free in the hope that you will take her with you. And she will be cheated," I say.

"She will get something," Anders says. "I'm not the world's worst fuck."

I leave it at that. If he's going to fuck Matilda – well, then he is.

"How about your little sister?" I ask. "How is she – Linda?"

"They definitely pay – in cash – the men she's seeing."

"What do you mean?" I ask.

"The goodtime girl," Anders says.

"Is she . . . ?"

"Oh yes."

"Where?"

"Well, Linda isn't cheap – I don't think so, anyway. As far as I can make out she's a high-class whore. If you think banging a sixteen-year-old brat is high class."

I don't say anything.

We're playing at a secondary school in the Rombo district. We've rented Dickson's pick-up. I drive, Abdullah shows the way, and Rachel sits between us, while Anders, Firestone and Rogarth crouch in the back with the decks – wrapped up carefully in blankets and boxes so nothing is shaken to bits on the bumpy roads. Khalid isn't with us – he is at home in Swahilitown with malaria.

At six we arrive at the school in Rongai and start setting up in the main hall, while Rachel goes out to get us some Cokes. The power is down, but we've brought our diesel generator. It can only just run the stereo: no lights. Firestone is setting up the generator in the next room, so it doesn't interrupt the music. Rogarth is pulling cables for the speakers, while I place the decks on tables on the small stage, but we can hardly see a thing. I locate the caretaker, who gets us two paraffin lamps, and we hang them from the rafters – one at each end of the room. It's quite dark.

The room is hot as hell. Anders is standing with his back against the stage. He's in Africa for the first time. Christ, he's white. Alright, I'm white as well, we're the only white people for miles. But I forget about it, don't even think about it in that way, but he definitely is – all the time, because he isn't used to being the odd one out. He hasn't spotted me. I can tell he's high as a kite; wherever he turns his eyes, he sees blackness. A teeming dark crowd. It's surprising how scared he looks – like they're wild animals. I grab a couple of beers and go over to him.

"Let's go outside and get some air," I say. It takes us several minutes to push our sweaty way from the stage over to the door and outside. And outside it's absolutely freezing. We drink our beers, and Anders lights a spliff – Ibrahim has supplied him with weed. The altitude on the mountain. The thin air. They say that having sex on a plane increases the pleasure. It's certain that smoking *bhangi* at this altitude intensifies the effects. There's hardly any oxygen here. We sweat, and our sweat cools, the beer is cold.

"Are you alright?" I ask.

"Yes, yes," Anders says nasally, keeping the smoke in his air, bending backwards, exhaling.

"You be careful with that," I say. He hands me the spliff, staring right up at the sky.

"It's wild, man," he says. I hold the spliff even though I don't want to smoke before flipping records. I look up to see what Anders is looking at: the stars shining brightly in the black void, undisturbed by light pollution – not like in Europe. They are scattered across the vault all the

607

way to the horizon. We are surrounded by the cupola, and the stars seem so close we might pluck them out; the latitude means that you can stare right into the Milky Way, whose band of tiny little diamonds hangs like a fog in a wide belt behind the brighter stars.

We go back inside and move through the throng towards the stage. Anders pulls at my arm:

"Christian, you know, we *have to* get out of here." He is dripping with sweat, his eyes are wide open.

"What's wrong, man? Come on – we've only just got started here. We just got back in," I say.

"No. I have to be . . . I have to leave," Anders says. His voice is shaking. It's early – around ten. "I really have to get out of here, man," he repeats.

"Come on, it's only the spliff, Anders."

"Damn it, I mean, I swear – I just looked over at the entrance, and I saw . . ." He swallows. "I saw Gert come right through the door."

"Gert?" I say.

"My half-cousin's crazy half-brother. The one who beat me with a dead cat full of maggots. The one who raped and strangled a woman and stuck hunting cartridges and firelighters up her cunt and set her on fire to cover his tracks," Anders says feverishly.

"He's not here," I say.

"I saw him," Anders says.

"Alright, let's go outside and get some fresh air." We take the long way through the sea of people again. Anders' eyes are wide open; sweat's pouring from him like from a fountain. We get outside. In the light from the stars I can see some boys standing around the corner of the building – they become jittery when they see us, pull around out of sight.

"*Hamna shida*," I say – no problem. They probably have a bottle of *gongo*. Anders and I walk away from the building a little. I can hear that there are things going on in the dark, even though it's freezing. A girl giggles, and a boy's deep voice wheedles. I grab Anders by the shoulders, look into his eyes. He's shaking. "I want you to be absolutely honest with me, O.K.?" I say.

"Yes, man," he says.

"What's going on?" I ask.

"But . . ." he says, swallowing, squinting, opening his eyes again. "I am nothing now. I can disappear . . . without a trace. In Denmark I was . . . There was an . . . order to things." It's funny, but I don't laugh. "Can't we just bloody well leave?" he says.

"There's no lights on the motorbike, and we need the car to transport the decks tomorrow morning."

"Then turn off . . . Let's stop . . ." His voice is trembling.

"You think they can turn against you. That they'll pull their knives and eat you alive – is that it?"

"Yes. Yes."

"But they won't," I say, even though I'm pretty sure they would skin us alive if we stopped the disco now.

"No but . . ." He starts crying, catching my hands. "Promise me . . . no matter what you do, you can't leave me here. They will murder me." I can't help laughing. "You don't understand!" he shouts.

"Alright," I say. "We're going in to find Rachel."

"But how's she going to help?"

"She can help you," I say.

"Alright," he mutters and his shoulders slump into place. He's known Rachel eight days – hung out with her, eaten with her. And she's a beautiful girl – I've seen him throwing covert glances at her. Once we've worked our way back to the stage through the teeming mass of people, I manage to wave Rachel over to us. I pull them both behind the D.J.'s desk and get her to hold his hand, as I explain the problem to her.

"Tsk," she says. "That Arusha-*bhangi* makes people crazy." And then she hugs Anders from behind for four hours while he chain-smokes. The feeling of her meaty breasts against his back, her warm meaty arms around him, their hearts beating as one – the only consequence is that he will love her like mad for the rest of his life. But that can't be helped right now.

We get a bus to Arusha the next day – me, Anders, Rachel and Matilda. I've called Mick in advance and arranged that I can borrow his passport. If you haven't got a residence permit, you have to pay tourist rates in foreign currency, and I can't afford that. First we pick up the passport from the secretary at his garage – Mick isn't there.

We're going to stay at Arusha Hotel right by the Clock Tower round-about in the town centre. I leave Anders waiting in the hotel garden, while I go inside with Rachel and Matilda and take two rooms. The fact that it's Mick's passport makes no difference – all white people look the same. I rush back to the garage and return the passport to the secretary.

I find Anders in the garden. The girls are in their room, getting ready for a night out. Anders doesn't mention Matilda, but I can see what's on his mind. When they come down, we go out and find ourselves a restaurant, and afterwards we go up to Hotel Saba, which has the best disco in town. Getting away from Moshi is great.

Anders dances with Matilda. Afterwards they come back to the table.

"Fuck, I think the local girls are grinning at me," he says. "Is that because they want to come to Denmark with me?"

"I don't think so – they can see Matilda is with you," I say, laughing. He stares at me, shaking his head.

"I don't know . . . maybe that pot is fucking with my head."

"They think you dance funny," I say.

"Funny? How?" he says – disorientated.

"Like a sodding pillar of salt – a white man." He looks out at the floor – bodies writhing so they defy the physical laws of their skeletons.

"I can't do that," he says, shaking his head sadly. Matilda asks me what he's saying. I translate. Rachel and Matilda laugh. Anders shrugs.

"What the hell am I to do?" he says. "I'm from the north – our joints are frozen." In English he says: "I can't dance like an African." Matilda gets up and pulls him back out onto the floor, placing his hands on her hips, interlacing her fingers behind his neck, rotating her groin rhythmically against his crotch. Fingers are pointed and laughs erupt from both the boys and girls at the tables along the walls. Anders pays no heed – he's got his hands full. Eventually he gets his groove on. The night ends with the original plan turned on its head – my plan, the white plan; the girls' plan was more devious. I sleep with Rachel while Anders gets to know Matilda. She took charge on the dance floor – now he's beyond my control. That's her gamble.

"It's none of your business," Rachel says. No, it probably isn't.

"Well?" I ask the next morning.

"Amazing," Anders says.

Anders has left. I miss him. It was quite a bit simpler speaking to a Dane.

I bump into Marcus at Kibo Coffee House by accident. He comes over to my table. He sits down across from me, puts his hands together and gives a small speech that I think he's prepared beforehand.

"I've helped you get started on all the things you do here in Moshi, and then you kick me like a dog right before we were to taste the fruits from the tree we had planted together. Now you're eating all the fruit, and I starve. That's not right," he says. "It's only right that I should be involved in Rebel Rock Sound System. I can do a good job for you."

"Marcus," I say, "you're incapable of keeping a promise. It's always *kesho* with you whenever something has to be done." *Kesho* – tomorrow.

"Back then, it was because there were so many problems at home with baby Rebekka dying and Claire being very upset, so I couldn't work properly. But it's different now – I am very well," he says.

"You don't look very well," I say. "You look like a drunk. You don't eat anything, but every night you're at the bar drinking, so your family has no money."

"*Tsk*," he says. "You're not godly, Christian. You're an exploiter. Here you are in my country with no permits or paperwork. But I've got paperwork. I even have all the old accounts from the Roots Rock shop when you wanted to check how many cassettes Marcus recorded each day. When you wanted to steal every shilling I made to get your disco decks into Tanzania, and it was all one big lie, because the decks had already come through the church, the way I had made sure it would, and they were already in your house. Those accounts are written in your handwriting, and I've got them with me. Whenever I want I can go straight to the police and say: This white boy is here illegally without a work permit, without a residence permit, without rights. And he is running a large disco business in Moshi without paying so much as a shilling in tax." Marcus falls silent. He looks at me. This is blackmail. If I include him in my business, all is well. If not . . . he might report me.

"I'm not impressed," I say and leave.

When I return, I find Matilda has dropped by.

"Have you heard from Anas?" she asks. "Will he be back in Tanzania soon?"

"He only just left," I say.

"Perhaps he might send me a ticket – so I can fly to Europe," she says.

"I haven't heard from him," I say. Shit. Now I'm going to have to listen to that nonsense for months. I told Rachel – so that she might tell Matilda – that no plane ticket would come of shagging Anders to the brink of oblivion. But Matilda did it anyway – snatched her chance.

1988

Marcus

A SMALL PAIN

Claire has gone to Kenya to sell our stock of batik from the unmarried girls. I perform the duties of the peasant around the house. The chicken feed has been mixed with *pili-pili kichaa*. First I go to the chicken coop and remove the feeding troughs, which I fill with the *kichaa* mixture before I empty the water containers and pour *dawa ya kuku* into them. I hear a motorbike stopping in front of the house. The house girl says I'm in the garden with my chickens. Ibrahim steps out into the back garden – but no Christian.

"Marcus," Ibrahim says, "if you make trouble for Christian, you can die."

"Is he your *mzungu* now?" I ask.

"We are friends," Ibrahim says. "You had better stay away, otherwise I will work you over."

"He will cheat you as well," I say. "You will not get rich. He can't take you back to Europe."

"I can control that *mzungu* – I'm not soft like you."

"Really?" I say. Perhaps Ibrahim was envious of my life at the Larssons' when we were at school together. Now he has his own white toy: Christian. Ibrahim will learn that a white toy makes for disappointing entertainment.

"The accounts," Ibrahim says. "I need them."

"You won't get them," I say. Ibrahim comes over to me with his hand raised. "Now you're the white man's slave," I say. He slaps my face. BAM. And again – harder. PAH. Does he think I can feel a small pain like that slap? He will have to chop off my leg or cut open my stomach before I'll pay attention. "No," I say. "If I call the police, perhaps they might like to see the books as well? Perhaps they might like to extort the *mzungu*." Ibrahim puts a foot on top of mine and gives me a shove so that I fall backwards into the *kichaa* mixture and the aloe water. I am lying still on the ground. The house girl is watching us through the kitchen window.

"You damned chicken-farmer," Ibrahim says and walks off. He doesn't want me to call the house girl and make her run for the police at the Y.M.C.A. intersection. Ibrahim used to be my friend; when I almost lost my foot he carried me in his arms. He doesn't like beating me, but he is chasing his dream.

The day has the worst end. Claire returns with only a small batch of Kenyan luxury goods for the kiosk, because the Kenyans didn't want to pay good money for the batik the unmarried girls had made. Stylistically it was dull and the workmanship was poor: the dye didn't stick. *Tsk*.

Christian

Golden Shower seems to be going well, but we're not bringing in enough money, though I do think we have rather a lot of customers on the weekends. The money in the box divided by the entrance fee should fit with the number of people present, minus the Bensons' people and mine. It doesn't add up. Of course we have a few people who get in for free: people who have done us favours and a few friends. It still doesn't add up. I start counting. Who should I talk to? Abdullah is the bouncer, Firestone keeps an eye on the car park, and Khalid receives money at the door, because he knows maths. If there's something going on, they might all be in on it. I can't assume Khalid will have all the money missing from the kitty on him. He might have given it to one of the others. Who can I trust? I speak to Rogarth.

"I will look into it," he says.

"How? Who will you speak to?"

"No-one. I will spy on him at the door from the moment the night begins." And Rogarth does it; stands right inside the door, hidden behind a wall, keeping an eye on Khalid while counting how many people pay their entrance fee. Every half hour I go over and ask Rogarth. After an hour and half we have a result.

"He's a fool," Rogarth says. "The money is in his sock."

"Alright, you take over at the door when I bring Abdullah," I say and go get him. Acquaint him with the situation. Abdullah goes over and lifts Khalid from his chair, pulls him round the corner outside and holds him up against the wall while I search him. Khalid weeps while he delivers his whole I'm-so-sorry-but-my-mother-is-ill-and-I-needed-the-money-for-medicine-I'll-never-do-it-again speech.

"Get him out of here," I say. Abdullah drags Khalid down the road and gives him a kick up the arse, out into the darkness. Firestone is standing in the car park, grinning.

Khalid comes by the next morning. He begs to be allowed back. He is a good guy. It's business.

"No," I say.

"Come here and sit down," *bwana* Benson says when we arrive at Golden Shower on Friday afternoon to set up. I sit down at the table across from him. "From now on I will take forty per cent of the entrance fees," he says.

"The deal was thirty," I say.

"Yes. And now it's forty."

"Why?" I ask.

"Because I say so."

"But the place is packed every weekend. You make lots from the bar alone." He shrugs, smiles.

"Forty," he says, getting up and leaving. This is his place. Where else would we go? It pisses me off, but I swallow it. What can I do? And we still make a profit with the small discos on the mountain and when we play at Shukran Hotel with the small decks every now and again. I've got enough money to pay Ibrahim and Abdullah to be bouncers. And Rogarth has been taking the money ever since Khalid was dismissed. Firestone has worked as the parking attendant. I get my money. It covers food, fuel, rent, Rachel's English course, some pocket money, everyday expenses. But there's no money to spare to import parts for the decks when something wears out, so we don't have to rent things. I can't even get my hands on some strobes to fuck with the negro's brain a little.

On my motorbike to Swahilitown to pick Abdullah up. Feel dizzy and dehydrated – weary to the bone. Almost drive into the ditch, am afraid to overtake. Take Abdullah to the market and send him in to buy some *mirungi-khat*. Get a taxi to take the decks up to Golden Shower. Follow it, drag, drive, drag, set up, put away a hurried meal. By then it's too late for me to have a lie down. And where would I lie down anyway? Start chewing the leaves – have tried it a few times before as a cure against monster hangovers. They taste bitter, work slowly, a hum in my mouth. Find a kiosk around that carries Wrigley Juicy Fruit chewing gum; mill the sugary gum into the green lump of plant-matter. Like a rabbit. The boost starts kicking in. A slow amphetamine. Removes the taste of gin and tonic. The party has started at Golden Shower. I chew. Wake up. Drink like a fish in water. Stand behind the decks, slamming down the records, dance, laugh. I know it – have seen it before in others; my teeth are shining green in the fluorescent light of the disco. Feel just fine in the morning. We take my things back. In my head I have an intense desire to make love, but when I try to get things started . . . I can't.

"It can't do the job," Rachel says after she's touched me for a while. She doesn't approve of *mirungi*. Her breathing becomes even. I look at her back, at the ceiling. The fan is whirring. Feel worn to the bone. My heart is racing. When I wake up in the afternoon: excruciating hangover. How do I solve this?

"I can't work as a bouncer anymore," Big Man Ibrahim says.

"What?" I say. "Why not?"

"This disco business pays only pennies," he says. "I'm going to work in the mines in Zaire," he says.

"Damn, Ibrahim. Don't you know that's bloody dangerous," I say.

"I'm going to be an overseer – run a crew, send in the snakes. I won't be digging."

"How about Friday?" I ask. "Will you be there Friday?"

"Yes." Ibrahim smiles. "Friday is my last day. We'll have a party, and then I'll be gone – off to make my fortune."

"I'm going to miss you, man," I say. Ibrahim smiles at me, shakes my hand. Friday we party, and then Ibrahim goes away.

The trouble starts as early as the Saturday. Shouting. Hard-nosed little Scola gets into a fight with one of the young girls from Majengo – wild. Hair is pulled out, clothes are ripped – there is spitting, screaming, kicking aplenty. Abdullah comes over and grabs Scola from behind.

"You stay away from my fish," Scola shouts at the young girl.

"You're too old and worn," the girl shouts. "You can't suck the pump like a boiled sweet, because you think you're a posh lady. But you're nothing but an old *malaya*." And the girl slaps Scola, and Abdullah lets go his grip. I don't know why he does it, but we know Scola - she's been here from the beginning, and she's good company. Perhaps he doesn't like a dirty bitch like that hitting her. So he lets go of Scola, and she flies right at the other girl and splits her lip before I have time to get over there and shout to Abdullah over the music:

"Get that girl out of here now!" At the same time I grab Scola, and Rogarth, that idiot, turns off the music. I look up at him, but it isn't Rogarth - *bwana* Benson is standing by the decks and has lifted the needle off the L.P. - he looks at me with his yellow eyes.

"Dirty girls kill the mystery of the woman," he says in English with his working-class accent. "We need to believe in that - you and me. If we don't, there's nothing left."

Scola has calmed down - I let go of her and go over to Benson. "Where's Ibrahim?" he asks.

"He's left," I say.

"Come to the bar," Benson says. I follow, while Rogarth gets the music back on, but the atmosphere in the room has turned sour. We sit down on two barstools. Benson looks at me with his empty eyes, which nevertheless hold a certain ferocity - or perhaps it's just my imagination, because so many people have told me the man is mad. "The dirty girls come here and undercut my whores right in front of the customer - do you understand?" he asks.

"They are . . . whores," I say. "All of them."

"So are we," Benson says. "You are. I am. We too work for money. My whores, they give you something in return for your money. They are good at playing a role - professionals. But the bitches from Majengo: you pay them to make you ill, to feel dirty. I don't want my customers exposed to that. I won't have this kind of a problem again," he says and turns so that he's sitting with his elbows on the bar, lights a cigarette, drinks his beer - the audience is over.

Where does the woman end and the whore begin? The man who buys her - isn't he a whore as well? And the woman who is selling - she's trying to create a better life for herself with the one means at her disposal: her cunt. Is that alright? Is that her right? The money that changes hands - does it make a difference? The cunt is the means - a better life is the ends. All women use it. And the man who tries to make himself happier with the means he's got, he buys access to the cunt with his money. Is he made happy? What are the alternatives?

That night one of the bargirls is assaulted on her way home. She is beaten and raped by two men. A *malaya* makes money and can afford a taxi, but a bargirl brings life to the party. We let them in for free, because if the girls are lovely, men will come to the disco. Now they get angry. Two of them stop me on the street.

"Must we pay the bus ticket to be an attraction at your disco?" one of them asks – I've seen her often. "And when we try to get home, we're assaulted. Then we won't go to Golden Shower anymore, because it's outside the city centre. We will go back to Moshi Hotel, because at least there are street lamps."

She's right. We need them – otherwise the balance might tip back in favour of Moshi Hotel. So now I have to get involved in bringing the girls to the disco to keep it alive. And I need Khalid, I need Ibrahim, I need a new man.

When I get home, there's a Land Rover parked outside the house. Dad. He's on the veranda with a gin and tonic on the table. Halima is in his arms; he is lifting her into the air, blowing on her stomach to make farting sounds as she squeals with delight. Rachel comes through the door with a bowl of peanuts, sees me, smiles and waves. Where have I seen that picture before? Yes, it's usually a young black girl and an old white man. I drive up to the veranda, turn off the engine.

"Ristjan, Ristjan!" Halima shouts.

"Hi, Christian," Dad says.

"Hi," I say. "What are you doing here?" I go up and drop into a chair. Halima struggles out of my dad's arms and climbs up on my lap.

"Óbold," she says – she's trying to say football in Danish. Dad laughs.

"I wanted to meet your girlfriend and Halima – get to know them," he says.

"Why?" I ask.

"Well, I imagine she may the one who will be having my grandchild in time," he says. I make no answer. I ask about Shinyanga, his work. He asks me about the disco, but not the difficult questions – work permits and that sort of thing.

"Your mum asked me to say hi," he says.

"Oh," I say. "Well, you can say hi to her from me."

"She'd like to see you," he says. I gesture with my arms and grin.

"Well, I'm not going anywhere," I say.

"Christian. She is your mother," he says.

"I know that," I say.

"You could at least answer her letters," he says. I get letters from her, true. But they never really say anything.

"I suppose," I say, looking at my hands.

"You know, I was thinking we might all go down to the Chinese restaurant and have dinner together," Dad says.

"All of us?" I ask.

"Yes. Me and you two and Katriina and the girls."

"If we can get a nanny," I say.

"Rachel has already found one," Dad says. He can be a convivial bastard when dealing with people. If we pretend there are no problems, then there are no problems.

We're sitting there, all of us, having dinner at the Chinese restaurant. Solja is talking to Rachel. I am talking to Rebekka. Katriina and Dad are presiding over their assorted jumble of a family.

Bwana D'Souza steps into the restaurant with his chubby wife and their fat son.

"Mr Knudsen, Katriina!" he says with a big smile, coming over to shake Dad's hand while his chubby wife says hello to Katriina. Every time I meet D'Souza I see his fat brown face squeezed into Chantelle's buttocks while he shafts her with his tongue and she pisses into his mouth. It's bizarre, but I have no doubt that it's true. I don't say hello to him, he doesn't say hello to me. He doesn't like the fact that I move in circles many of the Indian *mabwana makubwa* frequent, all the while united in despising the negroes. I know too much.

I go on eating. Dad speaks Swahili to Rachel – asks about her village, explains what it is he does in Shinyanga – he's got quite good. Out of the corner of my eye I see D'Souza getting up and going to the bathroom. When he returns, he comes right over to our table.

"Mr Knudsen," he says, "I want you to know that there are many people who think that . . . it's not good that Christian is running around in Moshi pretending to be a local." Dad looks at D'Souza with surprise.

"Why is that not good?" he asks.

"He mixes things up – he's not supposed to be here running around with market dust at night. He should be in Europe, getting an education, a real job," D'Souza says.

"You can't say a thing like that," Solja says. D'Souza looks at her.

"It's the truth, isn't it?" he says.

"No, it's racism," Solja says, and Katriina looks at her – proudly, I think. Rachel stares ahead stiffly with empty eyes. Her English has got very good – she can follow the conversation.

"Do you think it's right that Christian is living here in Tanzania like a stupid local?" D'Souza asks rhetorically.

"What an odd thing for a man like you to say," I say.

"What's odd about it?" he asks, looking at me.

"You are known among all the fat *waafrika-malaya* in Moshi. You pay them to slap your bottom as if you had been a naughty baby." I let the words hang in the air – look up at D'Souza, whose face turns fiery red behind his sunburnt skin.

"This is madness," he says. "I have never heard anything so horrible." And he turns around and stalks back to his own family, throws some money on the table, shooing them out of the restaurant.

"Is that true?" Katriina asks in Swedish.

"Yes," I say in Danish.

"Yuck," Solja says.

"My dad wants to speak with you," David says the next time I go to Golden Shower.

"Is he in the bar?" I ask.

"No, in Majengo. At Jackson's bar," David says.

"But he'll be here later, won't he?" I say.

"No, you have to go down and speak to him now," David says. Oh shit – what else can he have to grumble about? Does he want a bigger cut?

"What is it he wants to speak to me about?" I ask.

"You'll have to ask him that," David says.

"Alright."

I drive to Majengo, park outside Jackson's, go inside. *Bwana* Benson is sitting at a table on the veranda. Though the open door I can see Chantelle sitting at the bar. She looks in my direction – looks somehow wrong. I wave at her. She doesn't wave back.

"*Bwana* Benson," I say. "What is it?" He signals with his hand that I should sit down. I do, starting to get my cigarettes out of my pocket. *PAH.* The slap of his hand hurts my cheek. I drop the pack onto the table. He is sitting there perfectly calmly. Start taking one of my cigarettes with his nicotine-stained fingers, staring at me with his piss-yellow eyes.

"What the hell are you doing?" I say. *PAH* – one more. He's fast. I push my chair back, stare at him, speechless.

"You're ruining her life when you mess up like that," Benson says. "She's losing her income because of you." Who the hell is he talking about? Rachel? Benson goes on: "He was her regular, and now he's beaten her up. She's lost the income that helped keep her daughter in school in Arusha."

"Chantelle?" I say.

"Yes, Chantelle," Benson says. "Fifty per cent."

"What?" I say.

"I'm taking fifty per cent of the entrance fee from now on," Benson says. I don't say anything. "That way I can clear up the mess you made and help Chantelle with her daughter," Benson says. I wonder if it's his . . .

"Alright," I say.

"Get lost," he says. I get up stiffly. Go to the door. I want to go inside to apologize. "Stay away from her," Benson says behind me. "She hits much harder than I do." I look through the door at Chantelle's back – the plump but narrow waist, her full arse on the barstool. She looks over her shoulder.

"*Tsk*," she says. "You can leave when you want. I have to live here." She turns her face away again.

"I'm sorry," I say.

"Get lost," Chantelle says.

Big day – Easter. It will be a big night as well. Rogarth arrives in a taxi to pick me up at ten because there are bound to be people coming to drink at Golden Shower from just after noon, and we have to be ready to play some background music. When we arrive, Abdullah is already there, ready to hang the loudspeakers from the hooks we have screwed into the rafters. We put up our lights, the decks are placed on our desk in the corner, the cables are connected. I flip the switch. The power amp is bust. Try the switch again. No lights. Check the cable, the outlet.

"What can be wrong?" Rogarth asks.

"I don't know," I say.

I get the metal casing unscrewed and lift it off, turn the thing on and listen to the internal power supply – it's humming.

"Alright – nothing wrong with the power," I say.

"But it's not playing," David says. No – no sound.

"Th-th-th-th-there's no lights," Firestone says pointing at the decibel display on the front. The machine is definitely on, but the diodes don't light up. That just . . . stinks.

"It's still early in the day," I say. "Let's go into town and find an electrician."

"We'll have at least four hundred people tonight."

"I know."

"Can't you just . . . rent something somewhere?"

"Where?" I ask. Of course I can't. There's only these decks, and the ones Faizal uses at Moshi Hotel. Liberty is finished – Alwyn's stereo is as dead as a dodo.

"Arusha . . . ?" David says.

"Easter comes to Arusha as well."

"I am going to have to speak to my father."

"David . . . We're going to try and fix this. Can't you just hold off *a little* on speaking to your dad?"

We drive down to N.V.T.C., the National Vocational Training Centre – a sort of polytechnic school for electricians and that. We find a guy who knows where we can locate the electronics expert. Rogarth takes off to pick him up. It's another hour and a half before Rogarth returns with the man. He smells of beer. He starts fiddling with the amplifier, sticking sensors from different kinds of meters into its innards. He smiles.

"What?" I say.

"I've found the fault," he says.

"Can you fix it? What is it?" I'm on my feet, standing next to him. He is holding a small glass cylinder in his hand.

"You've blown a fuse," he says.

"Alright," I say."Can you replace it? Do you have a new one?" He shakes his head, smiling.

"We don't have that sort of fuse here. Perhaps in Arusha."

"What do you mean – where in Arusha? Are they expensive?" I ask.

"I don't know," he says, shrugging. "Perhaps you might get . . . two or three for a dollar?"

624

A dollar, three fuses – that's . . . nothing.

"You should always have a spare," he says. I don't say anything. Hand him a few banknotes,

"Tits and arse, what are we going to do?" I shout into the air. Abdullah carries the amplifier outside – I walk behind him, a funeral procession, dead things. Rogarth has wandered off in the afternoon sun to get us a taxi. Four hundred people. Who have all come to Golden Shower, our disco, Rebel Rock. We're going to lose all that money. Benson will have a fit.

"There's nothing we can do," Abdullah says. A true African.

"Faizal?" I say.

"Faizal?" Abdullah says. "But he'll be back at Liberty tonight for the first time." I didn't even know that. Rogarth arrives in a taxi and gets out.

We drive over to Faizal, who is at home. Luckily he hasn't carted his stereo to Liberty yet. Phantom, the old *bhangi*-dealer is there. I launch right into it:

"Listen. Our decks are fucked. We'll have a huge crowd tonight and we've got no sound whatsoever. You have the decks. You'll have no people at Liberty on your first night. Perhaps you will when they learn that we've gone tits up." Then I start talking money. The price I offer Faizal is good. He shakes his head:

"I'd really like to do it, but you see, I've already arranged things with the lady at Liberty," he says.

"Have you taken your decks there already?" I ask.

"No, fuck that," he says. "I'd rather have that money." I give him half in advance, and we take his power amp with us in the taxi.

"You'll have the rest tomorrow," I say. "And the amplifier." Faizal nods, smiling as he stuffs the money into his pocket, and I think how it's a fraction of the child support he ought to have paid Rachel over the years.

At five we're back at Golden Shower. David isn't there. No-one knows where he is. Oh well. We set everything up – at six we finally get it to work. The stereo's playing, it sounds good, it starts to get dark.

"Let's go to the bar and get a Coke," I say, smiling. Saved by the bell. We grin at each other sheepishly. I go in first. There's David behind the bar with a strange look on his face. His dad is on a barstool with his back turned.

"It's working," I say. "We're all set for the party." *Bwana* Benson turns around. His eyes are gleaming. He must have been drowning his

625

worries ever since David found him before noon and told him we had no sound.

"Fuck off," Benson says. His eyes are yellow. I hold up my hands to calm him down.

"I am sorry there was a problem, but we're all set now. Everything's working."

"Get your crappy decks. Get your loudspeakers. And get out of my place," he says.

"But *mzee*, we're all perfectly set now," Abdullah says. I grab his arm with my hand:

"Abdullah, quiet," I say and shut myself up as well. Because the way he is now – drunk – I don't want to argue with him. And David is standing there behind the bar, leaning towards his dad, whispering desperately in his ear:

"No, Dad, come on. Everything's fine."

PAH, the man slaps his son; right in the face. I turn around and go over to the stereo with the others following me in a crocodile.

"Alright," I tell them. "Let's just grab our gear and get out."

And that's the end of Golden Shower.

"Can't we go down to Liberty?" Rogarth asks.

"No," I say. It's too late. Faizal has fucked over the lady from Liberty, and it's so late in the day she's bound to have found out by now. There's nothing to be done. The day is lost. We haven't got a place. I've wasted my money. "We'll go back to mine and have a small party," I say. First we go to *mama* Androli's. Sit there waiting while she rustles up some food for us. My head is spinning. I pay. We go back to the house. I pay the taxi. I haven't got much cash left. Rachel looks surprised to see us. I explain to her briefly what happened. She looks sad. "We'll have to talk about it tomorrow," I say. "Tonight we'll have a small Easter celebration away from life's troubles."

We eat, we drink beer. It's perfectly nice, but my head is aching. I roll a few spliffs, while Rogarth helps tidy the kitchen, make tea and coffee. I light up. Put the stereo together and put on an old Bob Marley record. My headache lifts. I find a bottle of Konyagi, pour out small glasses for myself and Abdullah and Firestone.

"*Insh'allah*," I tell Abdullah, raising my glass.

"*Shuri ya Mungu*," he says. Firestone doesn't believe in a God, as far as I've been able to make out, but Konyagi suits him well enough. He empties his glass and smacks his tongue. It's perfectly nice. We have tea and coffee, sitting outside on the small veranda, looking at the stars while Bob sings in the living room. Smoke another spliff. I go out in the dark garden. What just happened? I need to think things over – the details; the devil is in the details. I've had it too good for too long. But . . . there are many small things that go can awry, that are uncertain, wrong. How can I . . . ? A fuse throws me off kilter. A fuse that would cost a couple of kroner. It's mad.

I hand Faizal the second half of the money I promised him. Faizal has come in a taxi – I meet him outside, we sit down on the veranda, I fetch the amplifier and make some coffee for us. Halima follows me and hides behind my legs – she doesn't know who the black man is: her dad. Rachel stays in the bedroom with the door closed – she won't so much as see the man.

"My daughter, Halima," Faizal says and nods towards the girl.

"Yes?" I say.

"I want you to take her to Europe," he says.

"I'm not going to Europe," I say.

"No, not right now. But when you do go to Europe, I want you to take her," he says.

"Alright," I say.

"I'm serious," he says. "Living here in this shithole, it's very dangerous. I want you to take her."

"I intend to," I say.

"Good," Faizal says, smiling.

When he's gone, Rachel is pissed off with me. Asks me about what happened last night at Golden Shower, even though I've already told her.

"But what will you do now?" she asks for the third time in a row. "Isn't it better to go to Denmark?"

"I may have to go back to Denmark," I say.

"Perhaps your mother can help us," Rachel says.

"You're not Danish. If you come to Denmark and live there, they will kick you out. You can only come as a tourist for a few months – that's all."

"But . . . we're boyfriend and girlfriend," Rachel says.

"Yes, but we're not married," I say.

"No, but..."

"And why? Because you're already married. To Faizal. Why haven't you divorced him?"

"You know that he... I'm afraid that he might stand in court and say that I... I live with you. And then he can claim the child."

"But he doesn't want the child."

"Just as a form of revenge. His mother will come to look after it. And the authorities... then the authorities will look at you too; who are you? What are you doing here in Tanzania? Are you stealing the African man's woman and child? Have you got a residence permit? A work permit?"

"Rachel. Faizal would rather the baby lives with us and that we take her to Europe with us – he can't even afford to look after it. We make sure the child is well taken care of."

"Yes, but he might also ask for a payment for the divorce. If he makes a big noise about me in court, then that doesn't cost you anything. And I lose my child to his mother. But if Faizal is to be a lamb, he will want money first."

"Did he say that?"

"What?" Rachel says. "You're mad. Do you think I talk to that fraudster? Forget it."

Rachel comes into the sitting room, ready to go out. She stands in front of me.

"Will you take me to the court?" she asks.

"What are you doing?" I ask.

"Getting a divorce," Rachel says. I smile, shake my head, get up, put my arms around her.

"Rachel, it's Sunday. The courts are closed. We'll do it tomorrow." She pushes herself out of my arms – I can see that her eyes are wet.

"O.K.," she says and goes into the bedroom, shutting the door.

"The African has his village, his tribe and his family. The Indian has his religious community and his family. You've got your family," Mick tells me. We sit at a *mama's* not far from Mick's garage, eating pilaf, drinking beer. I have found the fuses and am about to go back to Moshi. "So you'll have to ask your family for help," Mick says.

"They won't help me."

"They'll be disappointed in you," Mick says.

"I have my friends," I say.

"Which friends?" Mick asks.

"People in Moshi."

"Friendship is a hobby for people who can afford it," he says.

"I'm friends with a lot of guys in Moshi," I say.

"No, you're not," he says.

"You take a very bleak view of mankind," I say.

"No. I'm telling it the way it is. Tanzania. You're not in Europe. When you fall, no-one will help you get up. Not being prepared only makes it worse. Do you have a girl?"

"Yes, Rachel."

"Is she your girlfriend?" Mick asks.

"Yes."

"A regular girlfriend?"

"Yes, damn it. We live together. Her little girl lives with us."

"But have you married her? Will you take her with you when you go to Denmark?" he asks.

I am about to tell him I won't go back to Denmark, but I know it's a lie – it will happen – he knows it. I hesitate. He continues:

"Many a sad fate comes from the white man's lust for black cunt."

I want to tell him that that's not how it is. But I keep my mouth shut.

I sit on the veranda in front of the house with my coffee and a cigarette. Halima is on the chair next to me mirroring my movements – she has a cup of milk and she raises an imaginary cigarette to her lips, sucking and blowing. I smile at her and put my Ray-Bans on her. She looks like an evil two-and-a-half-year-old voodoo priestess. I go out on the lawn and nudge a ball around. She comes out to me. We play football. She is good at running with the ball glued to the tips of her toes – it's impossible to take it without fouling her. Rachel comes out from the sitting room.

"I don't want you to play football with her," she says.

"Why not?"

"She's a girl."

"And?"

"Girls don't play football," Rachel says.

"You can see that they do – she plays like a dream."

"I don't want her to." Rachel goes over and picks up the child, who in her halting Danish says:

"Óbold, óbold, óbold." Halima starts screaming and crying when Rachel takes her inside. Sometime later Rachel comes out again:

"Don't you have things to do?" she asks.

"Relax, will you?" I say. She goes back in. "Can I have another cup of coffee, please?" I say. She comes out without a word, takes my empty cup and takes it inside. Fuck. She's nervous, because I haven't found somewhere to replace Golden Shower. And I'm on edge. Halima is sitting on the stone floor, banging Lego together noisily. Rachel is in the kitchen, staring vacantly out of the window. I hug her from behind. "It will be alright," I say. "We'll find somewhere else." She turns around and puts her arms around my neck.

"I'm just worried about how we'll manage if you don't find a place. And then where will we live?" she says against my neck, speaking quickly, and I stroke her back and blow into her ear.

"It will be alright," I say. "Don't worry."

It's a big fucking problem, but right now I can't fix it. I'm tired, need a change. Rogarth has gone up to the mountain to help his mum out repairing the crummy house they live in because his father is still in Karanga Prison. Ibrahim is in Merelani, whipping the snakes until they slink into the rock to find him his blue stones. I haven't seen Khalid since he got the boot. I'm worried about that. I drive into town and find Firestone. Ask him about Khalid.

"Kha-Kha-Kha-Kha-Khalid is w-w-w-working as a carrier on the m-m-m-m-mountain," Firestone says. "He takes c-c-c-c-classes so that sssssss-soon he can be a guide for *wazungu* who want to w-w-w-w-w-walk to the top." Good.

"Would you live in my house for a week?" I ask. Firestone nods. "I am going to Shinyanga on a small safari," I say. Firestone nods and gets up behind me on the motorbike. He won't bring anything. He doesn't have anything to bring. I take Rachel and Halima to the bus station on the motorbike. Halima is sitting in front of me on the fuel tank, secure between my thighs. She is holding on to the handlebars with her hands, and Rachel is sitting behind me with her arms wrapped around us both. I put them on a bus to Tanga. Tell Rachel to give Halima over to her family and come back at once – then we'll go up to my dad in Shinyanga together. But before she returns, my dad arrives in Moshi. Rachel comes home and says:

"You have to ask your dad for help." If my dad were an African dad and as well off as he is, he would help. Then he would invest in a place for me. I had thought of asking him, but I know he'll say no. He wants me to go to Denmark. To get an education. That sort of thing.

We're asked down to Katriina and the girls' – a big family dinner. Solja shows Rachel a picture book from Sweden, one Katriina keeps so she can show people what her country of origin looks like; it's all snow-covered mountains with rocks and romantic timber cabins, or green summery forests with flags flying, and maypoles and boats and old, pretty Stockholm, and villages with freshly painted houses, and blond children smiling happily – the Swedish Institute itself couldn't have been more complimentary. I sit next to Rachel on the sofa. She points to the picture of the houses:

"Do you have a house like that in your village in Denmark?" she asks.

"I don't have a house in Denmark," I say.

"No, but your family?" Rachel asks. I start to explain that the houses look different in Denmark, and that my family sold theirs before they left. My mum still lives in Geneva, and my dad will have to buy a new house when he returns. And then I notice my dad's expression – is it revulsion or terror? I don't say anything; how the hell can he expect Rachel to know? Shit. He goes to the kitchen.

We have dinner. Solja is railing against parents – her own and in general. She's ranting, she's got no respect for them. She wants to get out; as soon as she's finished I.S.M. she will leave the country, preferably to go to the U.S., she wants to study biology, but more than anything she just wants to get out – she can't stand the way we live here. She might be Samantha. But a wiser, more considered version.

After dinner I sit on the veranda with my dad – we have drinks and cigarettes in our hands. He has filled out quite a bit, but I don't mention it. Ask him if he can spare a little money.

"Christian, if you can't make it here, I think you should go home," he says.

"Where is that? Home?"

"Stop it, will you?" he says.

"No. You people dragged me here. I don't have a life in Denmark. It does fuck-all for me," I say.

"Just finish your *H.F.*, and you can decide what you want to do. Getting an education is important."

"And what about Rachel and Halima?" I ask.

"Well, erm . . ." he says and stops. He doesn't have an answer for that.

"I asked if I could borrow some money until I get back on my feet?"

"You can borrow some, but don't make a habit of it," he says.

The next day Dad borrows an enormous Land Rover, and we all drive to Tarangire National Park. Rachel sees the wild animals of her native country for the first time in her life – amazing, but true.

Rogarth comes round, walks up towards the veranda smiling – with Rachel, who went into town to shop before I got up. She comes over. I want to comfort her, take a shower with her, lie between the cool sheets with her, caressing her, because she's been so upset about our predicament. But she doesn't need consolation – she's not upset. Determined.

"I have set the wheels in motion," she says. What is she talking about? "The divorce. Now I'm going to fix you some food." She goes inside. Rogarth is still smiling.

"Yes?" I say.

"I have found the place," Rogarth says.

"Alright – where?" He shakes his head.

"You have to see it." So we eat. I let him drive the motorbike. We drive down to the Y.M.C.A. roundabout and out towards Golden Shower. He slows down right before the exit to Majengo and turns left – slowly – down through a ditch, across a dirt field to a building site – there are broken bricks, bits of timber, cracked tiles strewn on the ground. Royal Crown Hotel it says on the sign. A white wall with a curved entrance like a Mexican hacienda. Brand new. He turns off the engine, we get off, go inside. The hotel is completely empty, brand new, no activity. Odd that I haven't noticed it before – I take that road several times a week. It's a one-storey, quadrangle building, with a roof covering the tiled yard. There are tables and chairs – the dining area. Two of the wings have rooms. The wing across from the entrance has a bar, and one of the wings contains the kitchen and customer toilets. Not a soul to be seen.

"Have you spoken to the owner?" I ask in a low voice. Rogarth shakes his head.

"But I know who it is," he says. The place is perfect. Finally a young girl appears.

"What do you want?" she asks, almost hostile.

"Two Cokes," I say. "Outside." We go outside and sit down at a plastic table on the newly laid lawn between the building and the surrounding wall. She comes out. Rogarth asks where the owner is. She doesn't know. Leaves.

"It's been open for business for almost two months, but no-one comes," Rogarth says. Small wonder – the location is hopeless. If you're able to pay for that level of quality, you'd rather stay in the city centre, and if you're a pauper, you'd prefer to stay in Majengo. This place . . . perfect for safari companies if they need to spend a night somewhere before scaling the mountain, or once they've come down again. It would save them the long drive from Arusha. But he should have built a swimming pool. Without one they would rather drive all the way up to Kibo Hotel right by the gate to Kilimanjaro National Park, because that is high up, beautiful, old, authentic, from the days when the negro was colonized – that is what the tourist wants to experience.

"Who is the owner?"

"A retired police officer," Rogarth says. The amount of corruption he must have pulled off to be able to build this!

"A rich policeman?" I say sceptically.

"Not anymore – he hasn't made a penny from this," Rogarth says.

"Fuck. We ought to buy it," I say.

"Money," Rogarth says.

"Yes," I say. But if the old man would lend me the money – it would be a good investment. Rachel will get her divorce, I will marry her, get the residence and work permits sorted out, adopt Halima, we'll run the place. "Let's go," I say. Home. I keep calling Shinyanga nonstop until I get a connection.

"No," the old man says. "You've been here a year and a half. You say you've been working, and yet you haven't got a penny to your name. I won't throw my money out the window."

"Come on, Dad. I've just run into a bit of trouble. This will work if I own the place," I say.

"You're not allowed to buy anything in Tanzania," dad says. "Do you even have a work permit?" he asks. I haven't even got a residence permit – I get a new tourist visa every three months. I don't tell him that.

"I can buy it once I've married Rachel," I say.

"Are you going to marry her?" Dad asks.

"Yes," I say. "I am. Do you have a problem with that?"

"No, none at all. It's your life. As long as you know what you're doing," he says.

"And what's that supposed to mean?" I ask.

"If you can't make it in Tanzania, then how will you take care of her and little Halima? And you might decide to have a child together. That's a big responsibility, Christian. How will you manage? I think you're better off making your future in Denmark. And Rachel wants to come," he says.

A big responsibility, he says. Fuck – it's not as if it was a responsibility he shouldered particularly well.

"Rachel is getting a divorce," I say. "It will be a while before we can get married. I could easily have that place and run it, even if we do go to Denmark," I say. Even though . . . I probably couldn't.

"If you need money to pay your way here for a little while, I can lend it to you. But I won't buy you a hotel in Moshi. End of discussion. I won't," he says. "Apart from that, how are things with you? With Rachel and little Halima? Won't you come up for a visit?" Dad asks. He kicks me in the balls and now he wants a visit.

"Goodbye," I say. Hang up. Tosser.

Alright. Rogarth takes me up to meet the owner of Royal Crown Hotel in Old Moshi. We talk business. I squeeze him hard. He sells food and drinks; we get the money from the door.

"It's too much," he says.

"No," I say. "We can give you thirty or forty per cent if you like, but then we can't start until you've cleared away the rubble and built the access across the ditch from the main road." He's already spent an insane amount of money on building it and hasn't made a penny. "If we get all the money from the door, we will sort those things out for you. You won't be put to any inconvenience." He is amenable – we end up with a deal giving us eighty per cent of the money, and him getting twenty per cent.

I count my pennies, call the boys together. Off with the yellow shirts – it's time to get to work. First I have to sell the small decks to an Indian guy, otherwise I can't afford to get started; no more mobile disco for birthdays and parties on the mountain. But we should be fine – we get more than our fair share of customers. Rachel takes the bus to Tanga to visit her dad and bring Halima home. So it's Rogarth, Firestone and Abdullah.

Rebel Rock Sound System – everyone knows who we are. We spend our last money at Moshi Computer Centre; the owner designs our posters and prints them out. We spread them across town; on trees, on buildings, in shops. There is a big volleyball tournament in town with teams from all over: Zimbabwe, Zambia, Uganda, Kenya – boys and girls and lots of spectators. It ends on the day of our opening night. We offer free tickets to the gold medallists. The first night at Royal Crown Hotel. Everyone's there – all the volleyball teams and the spectators who know that the gold medallists are celebrating at our place. There are a hundred people outside, but the place is already packed – they party in the car park. Rebel Rock Sound System is up and running again. Friday and Saturday – which is the big night – until five a.m. And on Sunday when the older generation comes out – we play ABBA and the Beatles and Donna Summer to them. They leave at one or two, and we have a party of our own. We have worked all weekend. Take Monday off, breathe again.

Marcus

THE PRICE OF ELECTRICITY

Claire falls very ill with malaria, and the Princess shop in town doesn't go well, because her sister, Patricia, is no good at haggling. *Tsk*, living here in nonstop madness. Half my chickens die from an infection – we lose a fortune. I have to drive to the sons of *mabwana makubwa* and sell my very few good L.P.s. I invest every shilling in fabric, dye, wax, and chemicals to make batik. There are no small chickens under the stairs who can suffer a holocaust – the infection has already killed them. So the chemicals will only fume in Marcus' old lungs, and they will hang in tatters and rags.

I drive Claire to her mother's in Pasua. She will look after her until the malaria is gone. Send the house girl home – she lives in a village not far from Moshi, so it's better she is away from here at night when Claire isn't home, because otherwise the neighbourhood gossip will be ripe with stories of our ungodliness. I close the kiosk, so the kiosk boy can help me out in the toxic fumes. We're working with all the doors open so we won't get ill.

I smoke three sticks of *bhangi* straight away and spray the cloth with dyes and cover with wax and make sure the dye sticks by using chemicals and then boil the excess colour away – a long night, doped up on the chemical fumes. I wake up to an insane pattern. Soon we can sell this shipment in Kenya.

The electricity bill comes from Tanesco – it is sky-high. Our house girl is from a mud hut; she makes corn porridge for the kiosk boy and herself and leaves the cooker on; she sees it as a coal pan that will put itself out while she goes to the bathroom and does the washing. The electricity is wasted, to no avail. And whenever there's a power cut, she piles coal, like a mountain, into a coal pan.

I can't pay the electricity bill without selling the batik. I can't sell the batik until Claire is well, because only Claire can get the right price in Kenya – she is very good at that negotiation. Tanesco can even evict me from the house and take my underpants, if I explain my problem to them, because in their eyes I am only a little man. I have to force Claire from her bed and make her go to the head office with a false promise of greasing to get an extension on the payment.

We wait two days until Claire is almost free of her disease. Then we travel. Sneak across the border at Rongai; the same route as when the cattle is smuggled to the Kenyan abattoir in Oloitokitok. We take the bus all the way to Nairobi to get a better price. And we go to a disco. *Eeehhhhh*, they have the stuff; I haven't seen any of it in Tanzania. What we call disco is just a stereo and some records. Even our disco lights are bad for your eyes. In Nairobi there are completely good lights which make for lots of entertainment – they don't kill your eyes continuously, and they're beautiful. The disco in Nairobi is expensive for me and Claire, but sometimes a man needs to see something like that to learn how people try to improve on things. I need a reference like that, so that I can work instead of dream. It makes me happy – no longer so depressed about losing the disco business in Moshi. It wasn't European. I already knew – it was a shambles. And it was a fraud. Christian took the better part. I was the stooge. It was a combination of his means and mine, and he took advantage of me.

The kiosk will keep going, the chickens will grow big for the restaurant tables once more, I will plant my seed in Claire and make her belly swell. Money is tight, but at least we're not passengers hanging on the skirts of a stupid white boy.

Christian

From my motorbike I see Khalid walking down the pavement. When I fired him, he became a carrier on the mountain, but now it seems he has become a guide. He is wearing Scarpia mountain boots, which are significantly better than my footwear. They were probably bought in Kenya but would cost him several months' wages. And he's got Levi jeans and a T-shirt with the words NAGASAKI DREAMING on it; things he's been given as presents from the climbers. It means he isn't stealing, because you don't give a thief presents. And if he does steal and has been given presents anyway, he must be exceptionally charming. He doesn't see me and I don't stop to talk to him, even though I miss his work, his company. I'm glad he's doing well. But he stole from me.

Royal Crown Hotel is going well. Just as well as Golden Shower, and we get a larger cut which almost makes up for my having had to sell my small decks to finance the start-up costs. I am one man short, so I drive out and find Emmanuel at T.P.C. He promises to work for me on the weekends.

I have written to my mum like I promised Dad I would. Sent a picture of myself with Rachel and Halima outside our house. Now she writes she'd be happy to pay for the ticket if I come visit her this summer. "It's been years since we last saw each other," she writes. She still works for Médecins sans Frontières in Geneva but she can borrow her sister's house in Hasseris for the summer. "Then you'd be able to see your old friends from Hasseris Gymnasium." She doesn't acknowledge Rachel and Halima with so much as a single word. But I can use the plane ticket. I have to explain to Rachel that my mum can't afford three tickets because she is divorced from my dad, and he's got a new wife. Rachel doesn't understand why my dad won't help buy Royal Crown Hotel. We could run that hotel. How can I explain to her that he's hoping I will give this life up, go back to Denmark, finish my H.F., get an education and all that? Rachel is getting her divorce, but she says that there's a delay in court. I can't work out what she's thinking and how she sees the future, and I don't want to ask her right now. We're doing fine at the moment. Things are very stable. I play small discos on weeknights on some decks I borrow from a beatnik, an Irish teacher at I.S.M. – in return I must record cassettes for him and provide him with Arusha-*bhangi*. Sometimes we have discos on the mountain with the big decks, but then it has to be a weeknight and it has to be well paid, because otherwise it's not worth renting a pick-up and driving on the crummy roads. If the decks fuck up, I'm finished.

I need to get a better grasp on the situation. It is apparent to others as well that our gig at Royal Crown is working well. Rogarth is stopped on the street by some government officials who ask him what the *mzungu* is doing in Tanzania. "Does the disco business belong to him?" they ask. "No, it belongs to me," Rogarth says. I draw up a document saying that I have passed over the decks to Rogarth – that they belong to him. But I don't show him it. I don't trust him anymore. But I ask his advice:

"How can I get those papers?"

"They will ask for money under the table," he says. "And every time they are to be renewed, you will have to pay more, because you're not employed by a project or stationed here by a foreign government. All they see is that you're white, and then they want money," Rogarth says.

"So what do I do?"

"I don't know."

"I could marry Rachel," I say. Rogarth shrugs:

"Would you like to marry her?" he asks.

"What do you mean?"

"A girl from the village. Would she work in Denmark?"

"I don't know. I'm not living in Denmark," I say.

"But Rachel is still married," Rogarth says. I look at him. What the hell has got into him? Would he like to see me go under? Then he'd return to being one of four men sleeping in a room of twelve square metres? That's what he was when I found him.

"Why the hell doesn't she do something to speed the process up?" I ask.

"Faizal," Rogarth says. "Rachel is afraid to start the divorce, because she worries that Faizal could get the court's permission to take Halima and place her with his mother. Because that is very likely now that Rachel has broken the marriage and is living with a white man."

"But that's not true, Rogarth. Faizal wants me to take Halima to Europe, so she doesn't have to grow up in this . . . shithole," I say. Rogarth shrugs:

"Maybe Faizal will demand money in return for not causing trouble – because Faizal has got no money either."

"Do you think he's blackmailing Rachel?" I ask.

"I don't know," he says.

"Right," I say. "Well, thank you very much."

Christ, how African can you be?

Saturday night. Royal Crown is teeming. Rogarth is at the decks, and I am standing at the entrance keeping a watchful eye on Emmanuel, who is taking the money at the door. Abdullah is standing outside, flexing his muscles to let everyone know that any trouble they cause is an opportunity to get acquainted with his fists. A big new Range Rover drives into the car park. Ibrahim gets out with a bimbo on his arm.

"Christian, my friend," he says, hugging me. Big Man Ibrahim is wearing new clothes from head to toe, and his girl looks expensive.

"Your car?" I ask, pointing.

"Yes, yes, it's mine. I also have a big new Yamaha motorbike," he says. "We had a big harvest at my mine." I go inside with him and his girl. We sit down at a table. He orders beer for us. The bimbo goes to the toilet. Ibrahim winks at me. "Juicy, eh?" he says.

"Yes, very," I say. Ibrahim pushes his chair back a little and grabs his balls.

"Life is one big party," he says. "I have pumped the finest ladies in Arusha." I grin at him. He is proud of it. Boasting that you've banged whores by the cartload for money – I don't get it. But I like Ibrahim, because he was always so calm and self-assured, and he never tried to cheat me.

"Will you be going back to the mine now?" I ask.

"No, now I'm getting married. We are building a big house in my girl-friend's village," Ibrahim says.

"Are you marrying her?" I say and point to the toilet door, from which the bimbo has just emerged, heading back towards the table. Ibrahim laughs, leaning over towards me, putting a hand on my shoulder.

"No, no," he says. "She is just a little entertainment for the evening. My girlfriend is from a good family. I've already pumped her up, so the wedding is next week."

"What will you live on?" I ask.

"I will build a bar, and maybe I will buy a few *matatus*," Ibrahim says, smiling. Big Man Ibrahim. He dances with his bimbo, buys beer for me, Rogarth, Firestone, Abdullah, Emmanuel, shows off. I hope he'll do alright. I hope Ibrahim's future wife has a handle on money matters, because Ibrahim is best at fighting, chasing women and partying.

I am swimming at the Y.M.C.A. late in the afternoon. I see Khalid entering the covered terrace. He waves at me – I wave back. Once I have showered and changed, I go up to the terrace.

"Sit down here, Christian," Khalid says and asks the waitress to bring an extra cup, so I can have tea from the thermos.

"How are you?" I ask.

"Good," he says, without mentioning his smart clothes, the sunglasses that hang from his neckline, the money that allows him to hang out here.

"And the mountain?" He grins.

"I've become an assistant guide."

"Oh, but that's brilliant – you won't have to lug so much about then."

"I have to haul the white people," he says and shakes his head, smiling. "They're mad," he says.

"Mad, how?"

"Last week: I have an American girl – I have to help her to the top in the morning. We fall back. The sun is already rising. 'Where is that fucking peak?' she says. 'It's so damned cold, I'm freezing my fucking fingers off.' That's how she talks. Now myself, I am a Muslim – I haven't been brought up on fucking this and fucking that. But in the thin air everything is fucking. Your strength disappears, and a grown man can become like a baby. The American girl – she sneers and sits down on the ground. 'What are you doing?' I ask 'Get up – you'll die if you stay there.' Because we are paid to whip people all the way to the top, even when the customers say they want to go down, home, not take one step further. When we reach the bottom the next day, we get great tips if we have forced them to the top so they can get their diploma. They wonder how close they came to giving up. They think their guide was amazing. So the American girl, she says: 'I want to sit here in the sun and get warm, and then I want to get off this damned mountain.' I say, 'It's not far to the top. Walking will make your warmer.' Now she becomes ridiculous. She says, 'I can't feel my fucking fingers.' I look at her and say, 'Do like this . . .' And I show her; I take off my gloves and push my fingers down the front my trousers. She looks up from the ground: 'Do you want me to put my fingers down to your dick?' she says. 'No,' I say, 'I want you to put your fingers down the front of your own trousers.' I pull her up from the ground and pull off her gloves, and she starts to slowly push her frozen fingers down there, looking at me, very cross. 'All the way down,' I say, my face like a rock. 'Do you want me to stick my fingers in my pussy?' She asks, looking into my eyes, and I look into her eyes as well. 'Yes,' I say, 'Into your fucking pussy. It's fucking warm in there.' She does and starts crying, because the frozen hands start to thaw, and it hurts when the blood runs back. 'Your fucking pussy will make your damned fingers fucking warm,' I say. And she laughs and cries and says: 'You asshole, you fucking asshole.'" Khalid slaps his hands together. "The whites – they're mad."

I smile at him. Wait for it. Here it comes:

"But it's hard. A trip like that on the mountain – all your joints hurt afterwards." Khalid tells me of the cold, the pains in your chest, the poor salary, the dangers. "Christian," he says and stops for a while – looking down at the table and then back up at me, "if I pay you back, can I come back to Rebel Rock Sound System?"

"If you had paid me back first without asking me if I would take you back, then perhaps – but not when you want terms for paying me back my money."

"What do you mean?" Khalid says.

"If I have to promise that you can come back before you will give me back the money you stole, then you can't. But if you had just given me the money and apologized, then I think I probably would have taken you back."

"It's the same thing," Khalid says.

"No," I say.

"I invite you here, buy you tea and you insult me," he says.

"You're a thief," I say. He gets up, his hands bunched up in fists.

"You're the thief," he says. "In my country." His arm comes flying towards me. I push back and my chair scrapes against the concrete floor. Evade the fist, get up. He moves around the coffee table, his arms swinging like windmills, hitting my skull, my shoulders, my chest, but without any real force behind them. I duck, take one long step under the whirling blows and punch his stomach. And then again. He doubles up.

"You owe me money," I say, turn around and walk off. The following week he dies on the mountain. Poor weather conditions. Him and two

Europeans. And I feel seriously fucking guilty. Was I too hard on him? Should I have taken him back?

I meet Marcus on the street.

"I hear you dump your men on the mountain to die. It creates a foul atmosphere," Marcus says.

"He stole from me," I say.

"Yes, of course he did. He was living a sorry life in Swahilitown while you live in a house with a house girl and a motorbike and a girl to keep you warm at night. And you never pay enough."

Marcus

THE DISEASE

Dickson has fallen ill; he's shitting and puking nonstop – has a cold. Soon he will be only half as wide as before. His sister comes to the house to look after him. She is sitting on the veranda.

"Is he getting better?" I ask from my garden.

"Witchcraft," she says. "Bad people have cast the evil eye on Dickson, because he is successful and has been wicked with other men's girl-friends." But it's not an evil eye; that kind of talk is just hysteria, superstition, ignorance – a cover for the truth.

"What does the doctor say?" I ask.

"K.C.M.C. don't know what it is," she says. "We paid a fortune for their examination."

Claire has heard the conversation. When I come inside, she is very frightened.

"Do you think it is . . . the disease?" she asks. The disease – no-one understands it. There is very little information. The only thing everyone knows is that if you have pumped someone who has the disease, you get thin and you die. People with money send their sick relatives up to K.C.M.C., where they now have a giant death room. If there's no money, people keep their sick in the house and lie about their illness. It is very shameful if the truth is known.

"I don't know what's wrong with Dickson," I say.

"If K.C.M.C. can't find out what's wrong . . . it is like it was with baby Rebekka."

"Yes, when the doctors can't tell you what's wrong, you don't know what is the matter."

"Then perhaps it is the disease. Perhaps it was the disease that time with little Rebekka as well, because at the time hardly anyone had heard of it. Not even the doctors."

"If it is the disease, then they do know about it today. Even though they can't fix it, they can find it if Dickson has it and say, yes, that's it. But if they can't find it, then it's not the disease," I say. *Eeehhhh*, Claire makes me insanely afraid – I could be sick with fear. And yes, baby Rebekka was thin as well, skin and bones. And Claire is thin as well, because she goes by European fashion and eats but little. And I am thin because I have no stomach or intestines. We could die in a flash. I have read about the disease in a copy of *The Economist* which I bought second-hand in town. It comes in right through your pump when you put it in a sick papaya. Once you have it, you spread it to all your partners.

Claire can't sleep at night.

"Maybe that is why the baby will not stay in place in my belly," she says. "Perhaps we carry the disease in our blood."

"No," I say. "You heard Dr Strangler say that the baby problem was due to the chemicals from making batik."

"But he didn't examine us," Claire says. "So it was only a guess. You know it could be the disease." *Eeehhh* – she might as well say it outright: You, Marcus, have pumped other women while we've been together. Perhaps you have fetched the disease into your blood and have transported it into me.

We see Dickson sitting wrapped in a blanket on his veranda – he can't eat anymore – he's just a skeleton covered with skin. Every night Claire nags. There's crying and wailing, just like baby Rebekka when she was ill. Dickson dies soon after. I don't go to the funeral. He was a bad man – now he is underground.

I take Claire to K.C.M.C. and beg a doctor to test our blood and give us the honest truth. He agrees to the job. Then we have to wait three weeks for the answer. Claire lives in terror night and day. Finally we go back to the doctor's office.

"No, there is no problem. Your blood is good," he says with a big smile on his black face.

Christ Almighty, I get pumped that night – so hard I almost bleed.

1989

A SPIDER'S WEB OF LIES

A year later I see Rhema at the market selling *mirungi* to the Arabs and Somalis. She is very much afraid of me, because there have been evil thoughts from her towards Claire. Rhema thinks her grandmother's witchcraft sent my daughter Rebekka into the ground. I ask about my unknown son, Steven.

"It's very hard for me to keep him," Rhema says. I won't give her money – I want to know my son.

"Steven can come and live with us – that's the only way I can help you. I'll make sure he has everything he needs and I will send him to school when he is older."

Rhema agrees to it. Claire goes over to pick the boy up. We live with Steven in our house. It is strange, because we are strangers. But the boy likes us. That is good. On the weekends Rhema can come and fetch her son and spend time with him.

Finally I plant a seed that sticks, and Claire starts growing. That rouses satanic thoughts in Rhema; I see her fear when she picks Steven up on Saturdays. I talk to Phantom in the town.

"*Eeeeehhhh*," he says. "Rhema believes in the spider's web of lies; that she had a share in Rebekka's death, because she sent evil spirits towards you and Claire with her crazy grandmother. Soon Claire will have her own baby, and Rhema is thinking that Claire will kill Rhema's child to send the evil back."

"But I will send my son to school and everything," I say.

"Yes, but Rhema's family live on mystery and spirits. She is certain that Claire will kill her son in revenge. Rhema can't stop herself from thinking that way." Phantom says.

Christian

"When you're that noisy all weekend at the hotel, I have no customers in the rooms," says the retired police officer who owns Royal Crown. "You're costing me a lot of money." Before we came he had neither customers in the rooms nor at the bar. Now the bar is crowded every Friday, Saturday and Sunday night. He's raking it in. That will make a man greedy. Now he wants to increase his cut of the entrance fee from twenty to forty per cent. We settle on thirty per cent. And at the same time his own barman starts renting out the hotel rooms as bonking rooms. I can't quite work out whether the owner is aware of it. I tell the barman we will have to sit down with the owner and discuss it, because it brings more trouble – nice people don't want to go to a place like that, and the owner is an old man who is very concerned with his reputation, so we can't allow the place to develop in the wrong direction.

"No, no," the barman says. "I won't do it again." The owner knew nothing – the money has gone straight into the barman's pocket. But he puts a stop to it. And Royal Crown becomes the hippest place in town, and now it's such a hotspot, all manners of things start to happen: there are brawls, heavy drinking, drugs, *malaya* . . . it's all there. If you don't like drunken people, you shouldn't run a bar.

It's under control. The owner is on our side, because he's finally making money from his investment. My staff includes a man on the door, a bouncer, a D.J., a guard for the car park and myself. The owner only has two people in the bar. He reaps more than enough to supplement his police pension.

Whenever there's a fight, be it inside or outside the disco, the police come. And it's brilliant – the owner is a former police boss, they respect him. Things run smoothly.

But there's never a dull moment. I chew *mirungi* with Juicy Fruit gum to keep myself going on the weekends.

"It's only for a few weeks," I tell Rachel. "You'll come with me next time." I look at Halima and add: "You'll both come with me." She turns her back on me, doesn't say anything, crosses her arms, looks out of the window at the dusty garden. Of course she would like to go to Denmark, but Mum refuses to pay for more than just my ticket – that's it. "What is it?" I ask. She turns around with tears in her eyes – her face is set.

"Are you coming back?" she asks.

"Yes, of course," I say and get up – go over and hug her. Halima starts crying. I let go of Rachel and go over and lift up Halima. Go back to Rachel. "Yes, of course I will be back. Is that what worries you?" I ask.

"Yes," Rachel says. My grin is stiff as I nod around the room.

"Look – all my things are here. My decks, my motorbike, my Rachel and my Halima," I say. She sniffs and kisses me – she is scared. Marcus once told me that Claire's sister, Patricia, had gone out with an Australian man who went home to purchase equipment for a factory in Moshi and never returned.

"Don't leave me all alone in the world," she whispers. "Please don't, Christian."

I haven't seen my mum in several years. She borrows the house in Hasseris while Lene and her husband are in Provence on a car holiday. "You be nice towards your mother," Dad says on the phone the night before I fly out. I land in Copenhagen a week before I am to meet her in Aalborg.

In Copenhagen I can stay with my dad's older brother Jørgen in Østerbro. These days he is divorced, still head of a department in the Home Office, never at home. But he gives me a key, and I'm welcome to raid the fridge – the thing is, it's almost empty.

I have a few cut tanzanites, with papers, bought from an Indian in Arusha. And then I have the handful of uncut stones that I bought from Savio. And finally I have the big stone from my night in Zaire. I look in the phonebook, find a few jewellers. Go for a walk in Copenhagen and look at the shop fronts, feeling nervous. How do you go about it? I go home. Put on my pale suit and think about Rachel – I miss her, but at the same time I'm glad she isn't here. What would I do with her here? I use my uncle's aftershave. Go to the jeweller I have chosen.

"They could be stolen," the man says of the stones I have papers for. I point at the documents. "The documents could be forged," he says.

"Do you carry diamonds from De Beers?" I ask.

"Yes, of course," the man says, sitting up a little straighter.

"What about the Apartheid regime in South Africa? Governmental slavery is alright, but my stones that have been purchased legally in Tanzania you don't like," I say.

"Apartheid is finished," he says. "It won't be long now."

"Perhaps, but it's sure not thanks to you," I say and go out on the street. Can feel that I'm already losing momentum. Drink a Coke at a kiosk. It tastes like Moshi. Hurry on to the next jeweller:

"Would you be interested in purchasing tanzanites?" I ask.

"I . . . I might be," the man says cautiously. "If they are legal. Have you brought them?" he asks.

"Is there somewhere we can sit down?" I ask.

"Of course," he says. Shows me into the back room. I take the box with the cut stones out of my pocket and put the papers next to them. The man doesn't look at them. He screws an eye loupe into his skull, lights a lamp and grinds his teeth as he studies the stones one by one – his eye huge and submarine behind the loupe. "Yes," he says, taking out his loupe, looking at the papers. "They seem to be in order. Not the best quality of cut." He mentions his price. It's alright, but not quite good enough. I ask for more.

"You have to understand," he says. "We prefer to get them cut ourselves so they match our requirements."

"I understand," I say.

"Can you get more at that price?" he asks.

"Yes," I say. "As many as you like." He gives it some thought.

"What about uncut?" he asks.

"Let's agree about these ones first," I say, gesturing towards the stones.

"Alright," he says. "I'll take them."

"Good," I say and reach into my pocket. "And here we have the uncut ones." I put a small bag with stones on the table. He opens it right away.

"Oh, you can get these ones as well?" he says without looking at me.

"Without papers, yes," I say.

"Oh well," he mutters and examines them. "Where did you get them?"

"I bought them in the mining district," I say.

"So you haven't got papers for them?" he says without raising his face from the raw stones on a felt tray in front of him – but he does raise his eyes under his finely trimmed eyebrows, looks up at me, questioningly. "You have to understand," he says cautiously, "that in that case I can't pay as much for them."

"How much?" I ask. And he is game. We agree on a price. Then I pull the big stone from my pocket. He wants it. He would like to buy more.

"Come back at four – then I will have the money for you," he says. I shake my head.

"I'm sure we can go somewhere and have lunch at a restaurant close to your bank," I say. "Then you can nip over and pick up the money."

"I can't leave the shop," he says, even though there's a young woman out there.

"It has to be now," I say and start gathering the stones together. "I have a plane to catch." He gets up.

"Let's go," he says.

We have lunch. He goes to the bank, I get the money – he gets his stones. It's pennies in terms of making an offer for Royal Crown Hotel, but more than enough for the knick-knacks and new music I want to buy. I have to ask Mum if she wants to help. Show her pictures of Halima – see if she's still got blood pumping through her heart.

I track Anders down with the help of his dad, who still lives in Skelager-gaarden. He's got even more jigsaw puzzles on his walls now. Anders shares a small one-bedroom flat in the west end of town with an apprentice gardener. He himself is an unskilled labourer in a construction company, has just retaken his *H.F.* exams, plays the bass in a party band and talks of studying Building and Construction.

"Are you seeing anyone?" I ask.

"Sometimes," Anders says, smiling. "How is Matilda doing these days?"

"She's still asking: 'When is Anas coming back? When you see Anas in Denmark, please tell him I am missing him all the time' . . . and so on."

"She was bloody gorgeous," Anders says. "I haven't yet been with a white girl who was such an amazing fuck."

"Do you go to Gøglerbåden in honour of her memory?" I ask.

"No," Anders says. "I value my blood too highly for that."

"What do you mean?" I say.

"A.I.D.S.," he says. "I hope you know what it is."

"I only sleep with Rachel," I say.

"And she only sleeps with you? You're sure about that?"

"Yes. And she's been tested. I've been tested. We're both fine."

"Good," Anders says.

That night we eat at a kebab house then go back to Anders' place to adjust the mood before going to Jomfru Ane Gade. We talk about the old days at *H.F.*, about Anders' trip to Tanzania. We get drunk, listen to *L.P.*s. I can't really get round to asking Anders about his little sister, Linda, but suddenly there she is.

"I heard the negro was to join us," she says and comes over, throws herself at me, pressing her body against mine, kissing my cheek, laughs and lets go. Then she prances off to the fridge while throwing dirty looks at me. "Why haven't you brought your negro girls?" she asks from the kitchen, as she slams the fridge door. Anders sighs.

I look at Linda as she gibbers on. The way she is sitting, drinking from a bottle, making eyes at me, laughing. It reminds me far too much of Rachel – only, Linda does it like a vamp, full of ... irony. She mocks my desire to stick my cock into her – makes a joke of it. A proper little whore. But it's a twist on the methods Rachel is employing on me – or used to, because she doesn't use them quite as often anymore. Now she's just complaining about not going to Denmark. But what would she do in Denmark? Be a black Linda? At Gøglerbåden? What else could she do here? In Tanzania, yes – she has a function there, as my woman. She looks after the baby, and the home, and me. But here? She would be a passenger, a dead weight, a millstone around my neck, idle, useless, helpless.

We go out. Anders chats to a girl he knows. Linda gets close to me.

"So, have you missed me, Christian?" she asks. Her laugh is loud and high-pitched. I miss the days when Rachel used to flirt with me, but not in Linda's cynical way.

"Yes, I believe I have," I tell her.

"Boys like you are too easy by far," she says.

"Yes, I'm sure you can do better," I say. Her face closes.

"What has Anders told you?" she says.

"About what?"

"About me," she says. "What did that sanctimonious arsehole say about me?"

"He hasn't said anything about you," I say and think that a year and a half ago he said she was a high-class whore. Since then I haven't heard anything. But she doesn't seem high-class to me.

"Tits and arse," she says and turns away. Walks off, outside, disappears.

"What did you do?" my old dentist asks me, standing up.

"Do?"

"You have so many tiny cavities, and your teeth are brown ... all over."

"Coffee?" I say.

"It's not coffee," he says. *Mirungi* mixed with chewing gum.

"Can you fix it?" I ask.

"I'd like to know what it is," he says.

"It's what the Arabs know as *khat*. Green leaves with a mildly euphoric effect. Mixed with chewing gum," I say.

"Not great," he says, fixing the cavities and stripping me of the lion's share of the money I made from my tanzanites.

I go back to Anders' flat. Drink loads of black coffee to get my bowels moving. My intestinal flora is geared for Tanzanian conditions and my stomach has ground to a complete halt. My shit's turning to clay inside me. And I can't sleep at night, because it's so bloody light here. It's another few days before my mum arrives from Geneva.

"But, Christian," Mum says, putting her hand to her mouth, "you look almost like an Indian." I look down at myself. No. I look like a blond Arab. "Do you want to go out for dinner?" she asks.

"If you like," I say. And I'm just waiting. When will she say it? We eat, talk about nothing in particular. We get a taxi back to the house in Hasseris and make coffee. Get some cognac from the drinks cabinet. My mum doesn't disappoint.

"Have you thought about coming back and finishing your *H.F.*?" she says – her voice light and breezy.

"I live in Tanzania," I say.

"Yes, but you're not Tanzanian, Christian," Mum says.

"No, but not many people in Tanzania are," I say. She wasn't when she lived there. And the chap she fucked wasn't either.

"You can't live on the proceeds of a disco," Mum says.

"So far I'm doing alright," I say.

"Yes, so far. But not indefinitely, surely?" she says.

"No," I say. "Then I'll have to think of some other venture."

"But, Christian, that's . . . unrealistic," Mum says.

"Mum," I say, "I have four or five people working for me, I live in Moshi with my girlfriend Rachel and her little daughter Hamila. That's my life."

"But you must have an education. Then you can always go back to Tanzania and do it properly."

"What I do isn't proper?"

"I don't think so," Mum says, shaking her head. Originally I had meant to ask her if she would invest in Royal Crown Hotel. Naïve – that's clearly not where this is going.

"And Rachel and Halima – what about them? Do you want me to just dump them by the wayside?"

"No, but . . . I mean – have you ever thought that perhaps she might be with you because you've got money?"

"Yes, I have thought about that."

"And?"

"I don't see many U.N. employees marrying street sweepers," I say.

"What are you saying?" Mum says.

"I'm saying that trying to get ahead in life is normal. Rachel is normal."

"Yes, but she's just . . ." Mum stops.

"She's just what?"

"A village girl."

"Yes," I say. Mum takes a handkerchief from her bag and looks away, as she wipes her mouth. She lights a cigarette. I speak: "You might want to try meeting her. And she's got a daughter who's so much fun. Halima, that's her name."

"But it's not your daughter," Mum says.

"What's wrong with my family?" I ask.

"You come from two different cultures," Mum says. "She's practically illiterate."

"That's not the family I am talking about. You. And Dad. What the hell is wrong with you people?" I ask. Mum sighs:

"Don't you understand that she is only with you to get away from Tanzania – because you're white?" Mum asks. I laugh.

"And I'm only with her because she is black," I say. Mum shakes her head:

"Why do you have to be like that?" Mum asks.

"It must be a hereditary thing," I say.

"I was never that stupid," she says.

"In full daylight at Mama Friend's Guesthouse with Léon Wauters – that was proof of your good sense, was it?" I ask. She gives jolt, stares at me, looks away. "Was it?" I say again.

"You don't understand," she says, looking out on the street.

"Yes, I do. What I didn't understand was before that, when Léon asked for my advice." I leave it hanging in the air. She takes the bait:

"About what?" she asks.

"He told me a long hypothetical story about two people who were in love, but the woman was married to another man, so what was one to do?"

"That's not true," she says.

"Unfortunately – it is. When I asked him who he was talking about, he said it was him and Katriina." I laugh. Mum shakes her head – doesn't look at me – I continue in the same vein: "I thought it was a bit odd until I found León's used condoms in the bin, and you slapped me." Mum sniffs. Is that a trick? "So, yes, I have inherited my stupidity. You two have shown me how to be a fool."

"Just because your dad and I have had . . . You don't have to ruin your life because we have had some problems."

"There's nothing ruined about my life. I know what you're worried about. You feel bad about telling people that your son is a loser in Africa."

"That's not how it is," she says.

"Of course, Annemette would have been a far better person," I say.

"Don't," Mum whispers.

"That is, if you hadn't driven into that ditch." Mum gets up – screaming – grabs her glass and hurls it at me – misses. I just look at her. Leave the sitting room, go down into the basement, can hear her sobbing upstairs.

The next morning I get up early, go up and raid Mum's purse. Split. She'll be pleased. She will have bought absolution.

I feel disconnected from everything. I ought to be in Tanzania, but it's like Tanzania doesn't exist anymore. I am no-one here – invisible, anonymous. It feels great to hide among the masses, but it's also scary; I am completely insignificant here – no-one needs me. The pressure from having a business in Moshi rumbles inside me, because there are things to do and things to fix when I return. Right now I can hardly fathom that I am here in Aalborg and down there I have a completely different life.

Marcus

THE CHOCOLATE GIRL

I am sitting in the shade, drinking coffee outside Blue Café close to the market. I see a posh white lady on the other side of the street. It's . . . Tita! I push my chair further into the shade under the awning and lean back so the plants that grow around the coffee bar's terrace hide me completely. Tita is walking with a little girl – her colour is like milk chocolate. It's my child – five years old. Amazingly pretty and clean in a tiny floral dress and with little sandals. Tita looks like she always did. She is wearing sunglasses – very white. Maybe she is here to visit Katriina. Tita doesn't see me. I get up and walk behind them – at a distance. The chocolate child is dark-skinned, but her movements are those of a *mzungu* when she walks next to her mother; back straight and slightly stiff. I stop. Watch them walk away until they turn a corner. I turn back, order another cup of coffee, light a cigarette. I put on my sunglasses even though I am in the shade. Sunglasses aren't always about the sun – they are about hiding the truth of the eyes.

Later Katriina comes to Uru Road in *bwana* Knudsen's Nissan Patrol.

"Marcus, come – there's someone you should meet," she says.

"Just a second." I go inside and tell the house girl to polish my shoes very quickly, but to do it well. I put on my newest shirt, clean trousers. My shoes look much better. Off we go. Katriina drives us to their house. We turn down the drive. Tita is in one of the deckchairs next to the table just outside the door. The chocolate girl is playing with the dog. *Eeehhh*, I almost can't get out, my legs are that stiff. Tita has got up. She stands there, wringing her hands.

"Hi, Marcus," she says.

"Hi," I say, looking at the child, at Tita, back at the child. It is like me – Chagga face, good bones, muscles that sit perfectly, strong white teeth, full lips, and a nose that is just slightly flat. But golden-brown skin with freckles everywhere. Katriina has gone inside.

"Her name is Eeva," Tita says and calls the child in Finnish. Eeva comes over and holds on to her mother's leg; looks up at me shyly. Katriina comes out again and puts down a tray with bottles of Coke on the small table, but goes back inside at once. Eeva – the first woman in the world; because God made man and discovered that he was wrong, so He took a piece of his mistake and made his masterpiece.

"Eeva doesn't know anything," Tita says and looks down at the child. "She isn't old enough to understand." I look down at the child – smile the best I can, but my lips stick to my teeth. Tita says: "I don't know what to say to you, but I think . . ." She comes to a halt – keeps looking down. Then she looks up. "I thought you should see her." I sit down. I open a Coke and hold it out towards Eeva. She looks up at her mother questioningly before she takes it. I open one for myself and take a sip. Eeva holds her bottle towards me and looks. I touch my bottle against hers. She laughs – her eyes are dark stars. And it shifts something inside me so hard that I have to dry my own eyes and hide them behind my sunglasses, light a cigarette.

I look at Tita. She is pretty. So pretty. Slightly older, her *titi* sag slightly more, but very pretty. The child is pretty. Everything is good. Only . . .If only she had come sooner. Maybe we could have . . . but it's too late.

"I am happy," I say.

"Good," Tita says. I am an odd sort of *malaya* – I deliver my seed but receive no payment, and yet I am happy.

"You have to understand," I say. "I am happy that this pretty girl will grow up in Finland and not like me in Africa – the arsehole of the world. If she wants to meet me – that's good; I will meet her. If she doesn't, that is alright too." Eeva takes a sip of the cola, puts down her bottle and runs back to the dog.

"I am glad you feel that way, Marcus," Tita says. I think about how it is in Africa. If a black woman gets her hands on a white man, her entire family is happy, the rain starts falling. When they have children, the children will be the colour of chocolate. But if a black man gets hands on a white woman – *ehhh*, that is bad because the woman is the one with the money; the black man becomes her slave, and all Tanzanians look down on a man like that. You see the Tanzanian doctors at K.C.M.C. who studied in Moscow and brought home Russian nurses – no-one likes to see it; their children are the colour of dirt. And those Russian women don't even have money. It's the bad feeling of seeing the white woman dominating the black man who should be an emperor in his own home. But I can smile. Eeva has my blackness in her, and that makes her beautiful – my daughter.

"I'll just go get my camera," Tita says. I look at the child, who continues playing and sometimes looks up at me, but without saying anything. She doesn't know the English language. Tita returns. She hands me an envelope.

"It's photos of Eeva," Tita says. "May I take some pictures of you?" I nod. Position myself in front of the lush bushes. I take off my sunglasses.

"Eeva?" Tita calls and speaks to her in Finnish. Eeva comes over and stands right in front of me with her back turned. I put my hands on her shoulders. There are only the thin straps – and then the skin, which is warm against my palms; under that good muscles and pretty bones are arranged in a miraculous fashion. Tita takes the picture.

657

"O.K. then," Tita says, and Eeva runs over to takes a sip of her fizzy drink and then on into the garden. Tita sits down and looks from the camera to me: "It's just for . . . when she wants to know . . . Is that O.K.?"

"Yes," I say. "If you think."

"I do."

"What is it like being a mulatto in Finland?" I ask, sitting down again.

"It's fine," Tita says. But I can see – it's not fine.

"No problems?"

"Oh . . . well, some of the boys in her kindergarten call her a chocolate marshmallow. And say that she's got . . ." Tita smiles and holds a hand up to cover her mouth: "That's she's got pubes growing on her head."

"*Tsk.*" I shake my head.

"But she doesn't understand it. And it's not so bad," Tita says.

"And Asko?" I ask.

"He is in Nicaragua," Tita says. She asks about me – the accident. Am I doing alright?

"Yes. I'm doing fine," I say. Katriina comes out and asks if I have seen Christian recently? Whether things are fine between us?

"Yes – no problem," I say. Katriina must be loyal to her new husband's child. And the Knudsen man feels guilty because *mama* Knudsen disappeared in a way that made *bwana* Knudsen look ridiculous in the eyes of the world, and he kept his son in Africa – the confused boy. *Tsk*, a complete mess.

"Will you stay for lunch?" Katriina asks.

"Thanks, but no. I am already late for an appointment," I say. If I have to sit down to lunch with Katriina, Tita and the chocolate girl, it'll be too much for me.

Christian

It's seven-thirty when I get back. Firestone is sleeping in the chair on the veranda. I give him a nudge. He smiles and leaps up.

"Shhh," I say and sneak in to wake up Rachel. But the decks aren't in the sitting room. I go back out to Firestone. "Where are the decks?" I ask.

"Ah-Ah-Ah-Ah-Ah . . ." he begins.

"Abdullah has them at home in his room?" I ask. Firestone nods. "Is he still running the business as he should?" I ask. Firestone shrugs and nods. What is that supposed to mean? I go inside and wake up Rachel.

"My *mzungu*," she says and pulls me down into bed with her. She is warm and soft.

"What's with the decks?" I ask. "Why aren't they here?"

"They're at Abdullah's. He says he won't take them all the way up here every night. And Rogarth comes over every day and asks for you," Rachel says.

"Why?"

"I think there's maybe some problems with Abdullah."

"Problems, how?"

"I don't know exactly," she says. "But I think he might be taking more money than he should." I am absolutely knackered, but my adrenalin's pumping. I kiss Rachel, kiss Halima, give Rachel a large present full of clothes, perfume, nail polish and a Walkman. Then I pull my motorbike out from the sitting room and drive down to Abdullah – rouse him from his bed. He opens the door wearing only his boxers. It's probably only four hours since he came home from the night at Royal Crown.

"Ahh, Christian, my friend. It's good to see you again," he says. Hugs me. I ask how things have been. "Everything's fine. Abdullah has run the entire business – no problems." He stretches and yawns – the muscles roll under his skin. "Would you like some coffee?" he asks.

"No, no, I just wanted to be sure we hadn't had any major disasters." He finds my money – I can't imagine it's all there, but his theft seems so modest I am prepared to swallow his explanation whatever it is. He knows that – the man isn't stupid. I won't ask to see the accounts right now – that would be insulting, and he seems very confident. I can see that all the decks are stacked against the wall in his small room. I give him his present: a Walkman and a shirt. Proceed carefully.

"Do people still go to Royal Crown?" I ask.

"Lots of people," Abdullah says. "You just relax after your journey – I will take care of everything."

"You'd better get inside and sleep," I say.

"What will you do now?" he asks, slightly suspiciously, I think.

"I am going to go down to Shukran Hotel and drink some decent juice."

"Christian . . ." He says and gives me a serious look. Here it comes. He shakes his head. "Rogarth has given me a lot of trouble. A lot of trouble."

"How so?" I ask.

"He says that when you're away, he must be paid more money. Then I tell him that it's wrong to steal from you. But then he wants to take money from the kitty when Emmanuel is there, and Emmanuel doesn't know how to deal with Rogarth, so he lets him take the money. Then I tell Rogarth to get lost."

"What do you mean?"

"I run the business. He's a thief. I fired him."

"When did that happen?"

"Just after you left."

"Then who's the D.J.?" I ask, because Abdullah bloody well doesn't know how to flip records.

"My cousin Mohammed has been doing it," Abdullah says. I don't know any Mohammed.

"Alright," I say. I need information. "Let's meet tomorrow and talk – once we've both had some sleep."

"Yes," Abdullah says. "But if you talk to Rogarth or Emmanuel – you must know that they lie. They wanted more money, because you were away. But I didn't want to give them any more. They say I am a thief."

"Did you fire Emmanuel as well?"

"No," Abdullah says. "But he speaks ill of me – I can't work with him. But I wait until my partner is back from Europe – we will fix it together."

"We'll talk about it tomorrow," I say, patting his back – I'm damn well not his partner.

"You and me," he says. "We run that business together – no problem." I try to keep a poker face, while Abdullah's eyes study me close. It sure as hell isn't his business.

I rush up to Rogarth's mother's house in Old Moshi, but the neighbours say that she is dead, the children have been sent to live with some relatives in Dodoma. "How about Rogarth?" I ask.

"He is in Moshi," they say but don't know where. Fuck. That means he's got no place to live, no money, no nothing. I go all the way out to T.P.C. – so tired I feel dizzy. In the field workers' village I find Emmanuel outside his parents' small house. Even before I've turned off the engine, he's shaking his head sadly.

"Abdullah is the greatest thief of them all," he says. I get the full story. Emmanuel has been paid, but only half of what he was owed, and the sharing of the profits was dropped from the first day, when Rogarth was fired. I have made enquiries. Abdullah is using the money to buy building materials, because he wants to build a house in Swahilitown," Emmanuel says. Abdullah – that idiot. I drop Emmanuel off. Give him money for a *matatu* home and tell him to come see me the next day. Drive back home.

Rogarth is standing on the veranda when I come through the gate. He smiles a strained smile – the skin seems to be stretched over his skull, discoloured. An old backpack is resting up against the wall. I flick out the kickstand, get off.

"Rogarth," I say.

"Christian," he says. I hug him. Have just enough time to see how dirty his clothes are; he smells of smoke, dust, dried-up sweat.

Abdullah dumped African socialism and spent the proceeds on building a house in Swahilitown – that's the nub of the matter. I can live with that, cut him down, make him suffer for a while – because apart from that he's a good man. I tell Rogarth that. He shakes his head.

"I don't want to work with Abdullah again," Rogarth says.

"Why not?" I ask. Rogarth looks away.

"The first night after you flew out, Abdullah wanted to take the decks back to his own place and wouldn't pay us our salary – me and Emmanuel and Firestone. He says we are thieves, but he is the thief."

They have been waiting for me to come back and put things right. So I will have to choose: ditch Abdullah or keep him and build a new crew with the thief's friends. That would send a signal to Abdullah that it's fine to shaft me till I bleed.

"Firestone, can you go home – I'll see you later, yeah?"

He nods.

"Rogarth. Take a shower, give your dirty clothes to the house girl. Use our sofa. I'm going inside to sleep. Then we'll work out later how to get our decks back."

"Ibrahim is in town," Rogarth says.

"Do you think he would help us?" I ask.

"He would for money," Rogarth says.

"But he's got plenty of money from Merelani," I say.

"Yes, but his wife's family gives him problems – they have stolen from him," Rogarth says. Of course. Big Man Ibrahim is new money; a burly man with a flashy Range Rover, a fancy motorbike, a handsome wife – the expensive sort. He builds a gorgeous house in his wife's village. But

661

he's got no education and no understanding of money. He is having a big party while all his poor relations knock on his door for help. And he is African, so he has to help. His wife tires of him as soon as the money disappears. She is pregnant, but now she wants to divorce him. Then he loses the motorbike, his car, his house. And then he's back on the street where he started. The same old story.

"Alright, we'll find him later and get the decks," I say. Rogarth takes a shower. I go to bed and call Rachel. "Come here," I call from my pillow.

"Not when the house girl is here. And Rogarth," she says.

"Just close the door. Only three minutes. No trouble," I say. Rachel closes the door, lies down. I kiss her, lift her T-shirt and kiss her breasts, grab her arse, try to put my hand between her legs.

"No, that's enough," she whispers, and I fall back on the pillow. I don't fall asleep – I pass out from fatigue.

Four hours later I wake up with a rock-hard erection which immediately collapses when I become aware of the situation. Rogarth is sitting on the sofa with a cup of coffee, looking much better – wearing the same clothes, but they have already been washed, dried in the sun and ironed. I give him the sunglasses and the sneakers I bought for him in Denmark. We go down and find Big Man Ibrahim in town.

"If it came down to it, could you take Abdullah to the cleaners?" I ask him.

"How badly?" he asks.

"How much would it take?" I ask. Ibrahim names an outrageous sum. I'm white so I must have money. But I haven't got a lot of money. We discuss it at length – reach an agreement, but it's going to cost me. I rent a taxi, and we go back to Abdullah's – just me and Ibrahim. We smile as we get out.

"Have you talked to Rogarth?" Abdullah asks.

"Yes," I say and shake my head. "He told me a bunch of lies. I don't want to work with him anymore."

"That's good," Abdullah says. "We can easily run that business – you and me together. And my cousin Mohammed is a good D.J. – much better than Rogarth."

"We're having a party up at my place tonight," I say. "We've ordered food from *mama* Androli's, and we need to get the decks there so we can dance." Abdullah looks sceptical.

"We can just have the party here," he says.

"No, it's for my family as well. They're coming to see my home." Ibrahim has already started carrying the things into the taxi. Once my decks are safely inside I drop the bomb:

"Abdullah, you have stolen from me and from Rogarth and Emmanuel and Firestone. You can pay them back and apologize. Otherwise you're fired."

"You're making a mistake," Abdullah says. "You can't do that to me after all that I've done for you."

"You didn't stick to our agreement," I say.

"You'll regret this," Abdullah says.

"You be careful now," Ibrahim tells him, and we get into the taxi, drive off. A new enemy.

We have a lot of work. I really could do with having Abdullah here, but he refuses to apologize. One day I am hanging out at Coffee Bar, waiting for the others to show up. A guy with dark sunglasses comes over to me, stands at the end of the table.

"My name is Mohammed," he says. "Abdullah is my cousin." Abdullah. I've heard that his girlfriend dumped him when he couldn't afford to continue building his house in Swahilitown, which – it seems – was to have been on her family's land, so now Abdullah's investment in the building materials is lost. What an idiot.

"Sit down," I say. "Do you want some coffee?" He stays where he is.

"Abdullah wishes you two might still be friends," Mohammed says.

"I don't have a quarrel with Abdullah," I say. "But he has stolen from his colleagues. Do you know where he is?" I ask. I might try speaking to him. He's not a good enemy to have.

"I might do," Mohammed says.

"Abdullah still has a job with me, if he wants it."

"Abdullah says that after the way you've treated him, he will come back when you apologize to him."

I laugh:

"You want me to apologize to a man who spent my money on building a house in Swahilitown?"

"It was Abdullah's money. He worked for it," cousin Mohammed says.

"Listen," I say. "Abdullah is welcome to come and talk to me if he wants to. But the apology will have to come from him."

"Abdullah will be very sad to hear it. Do you know what Abdullah is like when he is sad?".

"Go away," I say.

"Just you wait," he says and leaves.

I am back behind the decks. I keep two one-shilling pieces on the head of the pick-up so the needle doesn't jump out of the groove when the dance floor is teeming at Royal Crown. The record player starts to shake, and the needle skips up and slides across the record with a screech as the coins fall to the floor. The entire stereo starts shaking. People scream. I get up from the chair I am sitting on. The floor is shaking as well – nothing is still. Then the power goes, and a load roar rises from the crowd. Earthquake. People start running. I stay where I am, holding on to the table. It calms down, while people run screaming for the exit – they are being crushed from behind, I think. And then everything is silent. Not even the cicadas make a sound outside. All creatures hold their breath. Kilimanjaro – there is life below it. The power returns. I check the record player, find Bob Marley, put on "Survival". Turn up the bass – heavy, so the floor vibrates. Everyone is relieved, people laugh, start dancing, the floor is trembling – but it's our doing. Everyone gets very drunk. But I can't get drunk. I have a knot in my stomach. Abdullah – he worries me. Now Ibrahim is my bouncer and my safeguard against Abdullah. But Ibrahim is a worry as well. He's got personal problems with his family who are still – it seems – screwing him over for the money from the tanzanite mines. And I need Ibrahim.

"Ibrahim is no good," Rogarth says. "He's selling brown sugar."

"Here?" I ask.

"Yes. His pockets are full of it, wrapped in banknotes. It makes people go wild," Rogarth says. And the wildness is increasing. People shag other people's wives, girls do it with other girls' boyfriends. Who is that with the fancy watch? Who is it complimenting your curvaceous body? The man who runs the hotel for the owner is given the boot, because the old man found out about the bonking rooms. He hears that his hotel is now spoken of as a very dirty place. I suspect that Benson has been badmouthing us. Royal Crown Hotel was to be the old man's goldmine during his retirement, and now it's becoming a headache.

"You're the ones who bring all those *malaya* to my place," he says.

"*Malaya*?" I say. "We don't bring any *malaya* here."

"I've been told you rent a taxi in the city centre every weekend to transport a lot of *malaya* from the city centre and Majengo to the disco here at my hotel. That is very bad," he says.

"Who says that?" I ask. "That is simply not true." Of course he is right that we pick up the bargirls in the city centre, because they are afraid to walk on the dark road to Royal Crown and they can't afford a taxi. The bargirls have to be here if the place is to be a success. They are lovely to look at, make some nice conversation, dance well. Alright, sometimes they fuck; they might even charge for it – that's their choice.

"People say that your bouncer sells illegal drugs," the owner says. He is angry because when you are an old man in Tanzania, it is important that you have a good reputation. He has had a respectable career in the police – now his name is being ruined.

"I promise you he doesn't sell drugs. And we will make sure there is no trouble. If you could get the police to come round when we have discos – that would be a big help," I say.

"No," he says. "It's not the police's problem. If you can't control it, I will have the police get rid of you." He turns his back on me and walks away.

I talk to Big Man Ibrahim, tell him to stop dealing, give him a raise.

The next night four young men show up and start a brawl at the bar. Ibrahim steps in and knocks two of them to the ground, the third one makes a run for it, and Ibrahim drags the fourth outside. I follow them. Ibrahim has the guy by the throat.

"Tell my friend why you come here, making trouble," Ibrahim says.

"We were paid to make trouble," the guy says – very frightened.

"Who paid you?" I ask.

"A mulatto – I don't know his name," the guy says.

"David – Benson's son," I say.

"Yes," Ibrahim says to me. "You take the food out of the mouth of Golden Shower – now he wants to make sure the old man kicks us out."

"*Tsk*," I say.

Marcus

DESTRUCTIONS

On the street I see Firestone – he notices me and quickly walks the other way. "Firestone," I shout.

"I-I-I-I am busy, Marcus," he says in a low voice and hurries away. I am a leper. All my old friends from Swahilitown are happy that me and Christian have gone our separate ways. They think that while I was there, I took all the gold. Now they can have it. But there is no gold. Only dreams.

At home I make sure the chicken coop is alright and check the kiosk and water the plants in the garden, and then I go to Dickson's bar to drink and relax – Dickson's lucky sister inherited it after he went to his grave.

Who do I find there? Christian.

"Hi, Marcus," he says.

"Hi, Christian," I say and sit down at another table. He is sitting at his table, I am sitting at mine. It's a local bar – guests don't come travelling from far away to drink here. If Christian has come, it's because he wants to speak to me. It's up to him to start the conversation.

"Would you like a beer?" Christian asks.

"Yes," I say. Christian gets up, takes his own beer, orders a beer for me from the waitress – a beer and a Konyagi – and sits himself down at my table. He asks me about Claire and the kiosk and the Princess shop in town. I ask about Rebekka and Solja, Katriina and his father, the house in Shanty Town where he lives with his personal *malaya*. Not with so much as a word do I mention the disco business. He is here because the Swahili blokes are giving him problems – any fool can see that. But he will have to be the one to say it. At eight-thirty I get up.

"Would you like to come round and have some dinner?" I ask.

"Yes," Christian says. He rolls his motorbike along with him the short distance over to my house and locks it with the chain in the front garden.

"Keep an eye on that machine," I tell the boy in the kiosk. Claire's face is completely blank when she sees Christian.

"Bring food for me and Christian," I say. Claire starts plating the food for us without a word. The food is strange – sticky rice and a bland sauce with hardly any meat.

"What sort of food is that?" I ask. "Are we pigs?"

"It's all we had," Claire says.

"Then it's better if we eat corn porridge like the negroes," I say. The food is bad because money is tight. And my son, Steven, won't eat it, even though Claire tries to speak to him in a hard voice – he just throws the food on the floor, and I start laughing.

666

"Why do you let him behave like that?" Christian asks.

"What do you mean?" I ask.

"You allow him to act up against Claire, and you just laugh," Christian says.

"I don't know why he behaves like that," I say.

"He behaves like that because he sees you laughing at your wife, calling her names and getting drunk, so he thinks that that's how a man should behave towards a woman."

"Do you think I should take him to the bedroom and let him speak to the rod?" I ask.

"You were never like this with Rebekka and Solja," Christian says.

"No, I was good towards them. Now I never see them, even though they live right around the corner."

"You can just go see them," Christian says. That boy knows nothing.

"What do you want here?" I ask.

"I came to . . ." Christian begins but stops.

"To what? To see me impoverished, eating pigswill with the stench of chicken shit in my house?"

"No, can't we just . . ." Christian says, sighing.

"Can't we just be friends, when you've stolen from me and cheated me and kicked me till I lie in the dust?" I say and keep at it: "It's you I should be taking to the bedroom to let you speak to the rod until you stop messing everything up." Christian gets up, walks out the door. I hear him unlocking the motorbike, starting, driving off. *Tsk*. Idiocy.

BABY-SNATCHING

Steven is in the house with us every day. After a few months of suspicion he has become very lively and chatty.

"He is very wild," Claire says.

"No," I say. "Not wild, but happy. We won't raise our children the African way with the rod, so that they are only afraid of us. We will be happy and alive with them, so the children are alive."

And at the same time Claire's belly grows with every passing day. Finally happiness is smiling on our family.

Every Saturday afternoon Rhema comes to pick Steven up, and every Sunday evening she brings him back. But this Saturday is different.

"If you want the child back, you will have to pay me," she says.

"What do you mean?" I ask.

"If you want me to return him tomorrow night, you have to pay me."

"Why?"

"That's just how it is," Rhema says. "The child is mine."

"I have looked after him for a few months now, haven't I?" I say. "I'd be happy to continue looking after him until he's a man. He will need to go to school for many years; you can let me see to that. But I'm not going to buy my own child."

"If you don't pay me money, you will never see the boy again," Rhema says. She takes the child. What can I do? The law says that until the child is eighteen, he belongs to the mother. And I have never admitted on paper that the boy is mine.

CATHARSIS

David the mulatto comes and picks me up at the kiosk. "My father wants to speak to you," he says. *Bwana* Benson has no customers at Golden Shower because the white boy is doing so well at his Royal Crown Hotel. Maybe he wants some advice on how to get his revenge? But Benson has another plan.

"I've got a permit, so you can go to Kenya. I want you to buy disco decks for me. David will go with you. When you return, I want you to be my number-one D.J." He even offers me an advance.

"I won't let you down," I say. We rush up to the border – the papers work. Straight to Nairobi. David carries dollars. We dash around town, find machines with a good sound. We find lights, we find music. Back to Moshi. Get started at once. We feel it right away. Christian's disco at Royal Crown no longer appeals to good people. His decks are worn. And good people want good sound – once more Golden Shower is the place for that. And I can still control the room as a D.J. – the atmosphere must be built with music until it's become a jolly party – happy, long, thirsty. None of Christian's people can do it. And Benson knows how to keep the dirty girls away; they can spread their diseases at Royal Crown – Golden Shower only has clever ladies who make you forget that money has changed hands.

Now Christian can miss me. I saw his problems with the immigration office and understood them long before he did. And his problems with the poor lice from Swahilitown as well. Through my friendship he could have evaded all those disasters. Christian wanted to be the boss of me, and I wasn't allowed any money – not even for a few beers. Whereas he is always chewing *mirungi*, smoking *bhangi*, drinking Konyagi, pumping his *malaya*. He has made his bed, now he can lie on the mattress, full as it is with stones and thorns.

Another darkness is lit up as well. Claire must rest her round belly for a few days, so I man the Princess shop with all the ladies' things. I sit outside with a Coke and a newspaper, my eyes hidden behind sunglasses.

"Hi, Marcus."

Solja? Solja!

"Solja!" I say and get up, knocking the bottle over, so the newspaper is flooded with sugary syrup.

"Hi," she says, giving me an odd look.

"Hi. I thought you had all left," I say.

"Left?"

"The house is empty."

"Oh that. Mum's moved to Shinyanga with Rebekka," Solja says.

"But then what about you?" I ask. "Would you like a Coke?" I open the fridge as she sits down.

"I am doing my last year at school," she says, lighting a cigarette. I put the Coke in front of her.

"But then where do you live?"

"I'm a boarder," Solja says, as if I'm very stupid – know nothing.

"Do they treat you alright?"

"Yes, it's fine," she says.

"But . . . how about Rebekka? In Shinyanga? It's just a huge desert with some sheds. Is there a school for her? Is there anyone for her to play with?"

"There are monks and nuns who teach the rich people's children," Solja says.

"Will she be brainwashed with God and the Virgin Mary?" I ask. Solja laughs:

"No, Marcus. I don't think it's too bad," she says. I ask about everything to do with Rebekka, like a nervous mother, even though I can tell that Solja finds it annoying. But I need to hear news of my little Swedish baby. We don't speak of Christian, who is still making his big mess in Moshi. I don't say anything about him. Solja doesn't ask. She stays for two cigarettes and a Coke, then she gets up and shakes my hand goodbye. My big white daughter like a stranger to her black father. *Tsk.*

STAB IN THE BACK

"Come on, have a beer with me," *bwana* Benson says. It is almost morning, the guests have left, the bar is quiet. It's only me, Benson, his son David and a man I don't know. I am drunk but still functioning.

"I will give you a lift home," David says.

"Alright, one more toast then," I say.

"It's good that we have customers again," *bwana* Benson says. "You have really brought them in with your music, Marcus." He raises his glass to toast me. "How about the white boy?" he says. "Will he stay in Moshi?"

"I don't know. He used me to launch his business, and never spoke to me again," I say.

"Yes, I understand. The white boy has got his work permit because his father's here and understands how the system works." *Bwana* Benson nods slowly.

"No, no," I say, drinking. "There are no permits. He is here like a ghost, full of tricks. Here on a tourist visa only, and with fake names on the disco licence. A fraud."

"Oh," *Bwana* Benson says. "Well, it doesn't matter about him anyway, because now Golden Shower is on the up and Royal Crown is going down."

It's only in the car I wake up, at the shock of the cool morning air. *Bwana* Benson is clever – he gives me beer, makes small talk, but in reality he is a snake in my mind, slithering after information. Who was the fourth man at the table? Was he immigration? Now he can blackmail Christian, if Christian wants stamps on his permits to stay. Then Christian will become poorer and his business will collapse. Or Benson might pay the immigration man to throw Christian straight onto a plane.

I could have blackmailed Christian myself, but no. That boy has been like a brother to me. A bad little brother. Sometimes he helps, at other times he will laugh if he sees his big brother stumble in the street. Perhaps I shouldn't have revealed anything to *bwana* Benson, but here in Tanzania Christian is nothing but trouble. He should be in a school in Europe. And while he ruins himself with African foolishness, he ruins other people as well. Me.

I wake up after only a few hours. The day is bad, because Marcus is a great fool who will never recognize the hypocrisy behind the smiling mask. I should have remained silent about Christian's affairs, *tsk*.

I am sitting outside the Princess shop, drinking a fizzy drink, reading the newspaper while Claire is once more behind the till with her big belly. The sound of his motorbike coming down Rengua Road is also familiar to me – I have taught myself never to turn my head at the sound of it. Now he parks in front of the shop and stops the engine, but he doesn't get off.

"Congratulation on your job at Golden Shower," Christian says. I don't look up from my new paper.

"I've been laid off," I say. Christian sighs – he thinks it's due to drunkenness. I look at him and explain:

"It's the same old story. First Benson steals my knowledge to build up his disco. Then the white man kicks my black arse to the kerb," I say. Christian looks away, kicks his motorbike into gear, drives off. No-one else can see it. His blood is already draining away like from a tap left running. Soon he'll be bled dry of juice, finished.

"Who was it?" Claire asks.

"Christian," I say.

"What did he want?" Claire asks.

"To be saved," I say.

"From what?"

"From himself."

Christian

I try not to think about the fact that the owner isn't happy with our disco. If only I could have bought that hotel. I have to put on the coal pan to boil water for coffee. Rachel returns with Halima. They are drenched. We help each other cook. It rains as evening falls, all night long, in the morning. Nonstop. The phone lines are down – the power's gone. No water in the taps, but plenty coming from above. Halima coughs. Rachel barely speaks to me.

Late in the afternoon Rogarth arrives on the motorbike – splattered with mud from head to toe. Behind him a taxi is slowly making its way through the flood of mud and water.

"The farmers will be pleased," I say, grinning at the sky.

"No, it's too much," Rogarth says. "The sweetcorn they have sown will be flushed right out of the soil." We know that no-one will come tonight, but the disco must run anyway. We load the decks and the music into the taxi. I get Rogarth some dry clothes to change into when we get to Royal Crown and put them into a bag. The taxi sneaks gingerly out on Lima Road and towards town. Rain falls on the mountain, gathers in streams, rivulets, rivers – makes its way down.

We're picking up Firestone on the way. We meet him and take Mawenzi Road towards the Clock Tower roundabout. When the road drops slightly before the post office, we see a river where the road used to be. The car park in front of Royal Crown is a lake.

"On the side of the road is fine," I say. I think the car would sink into the sawdust and mud on the car park. "Firestone, you'll have to go get some plastic inside the restaurant, so the things don't get wet." Firestone runs in, brings back an oilcloth, and we wrap the decks in it before carrying them inside out of the rain.

We set up. There's no power. I start the generator to see if it works and make sure there's enough diesel. No guests yet. We eat food from the hotel's kitchen; everything is chargrilled. A very few people start coming in, and the rain continues. We start the generator, light a few lamps, play soothing music – full of longing. Some of the ladies are here – they sit at the bar and have a nice time; no change in the weather, no hope of it letting up, no hope of making any money.

I am standing with Rogarth at the entrance, smoking – we look out into the pouring rain. The car park is a swamp, big puddles are forming even though we cleared the ditches of silt. I hear the engines before I see the three headlights through the darkness and the rain. They turn off the road. Off-road motorbikes. From the Merelani Hills. The guys turn off their engines outside the entrance but stay where they are without speaking. They are drenched, mud-splattered – their faces closed except for one whose eyes are staring wildly. I don't know why, but we go out in the rain and say hello.

One of the guys has an air of complete calm about him – you can detect no movement in him at all.

"My name is Christian," I tell him. He nods and shows his teeth briefly, but not like a smile – more like a twitch.

"Moses," he says. I nod. Moses? He stares vacantly ahead: "One hundred people died last night in Zaire – drowned in the mines when the floods came down from the mountains. One hundred at least," he says.

"Ah-ahh," Rogarth says. "*Pole.*"

Moses?

"Come on inside," I say.

"We don't have a lot of money," Moses says.

"We won't charge you," I say. They get down, lock their motorbikes calmly with chains in the rain. They can't get any wetter. The two others go inside with Rogarth. Moses stays under the shade of the porch. I offer him a cigarette which he accepts – light it for him. He pulls off his drenched jacket. His shirt sticks to his upper body as well. On his lower back, right above the waistband there's a bump in the wet fabric. A revolver. Moses. When the fat *mama* died. We were in the mine. I climbed up the ladder behind Savio. We came out of the mineshaft. The movement I saw . . . the darkness that moved. Moses. He got out of the pit as well – got away. He was below us on the ladder as we climbed out. But he didn't shoot. Perhaps he was afraid of being hit by my falling body. Maybe he was out of bullets. Rogarth comes back.

"What happened at the mines?" he asks.

"Last night," Moses says. "Everyone had gone down into the mines to sleep out of the rain. But all the water from the mountains comes running down the hills and gathers at the bottom of the valley. It's where everyone digs their tunnels – to start as close to the layer of good stones as they can. The water tumbles right down into the pits, the ladders are swept away. People drown in the darkness, hundreds of metres into the ground. People clamber over each other to get out. Only the strong survive – some of them. The rest, they're dead."

"But it was only water," Rogarth says. "It must have begun slowly?"

"No. Not just water," Moses says. "The water carries mud from the mountains and it gathers on the Simanjaro Plains south-west of the mines. When the plains are flooded, the water streams into our valley. It comes like a tidal wave. In the valley the wave hits all the piles of rubble – gravel, sand, dust – everything that has been dug up and is lying on the ground. And the wave carries mud and rubble straight down on top of us."

"And yourself?" I ask.

"Our shaft starts on higher ground – on the slopes of the valley. Very lucky for us." Up on the slopes – one of the worst plots because then they have to dig down further to get to tanzanite; but it saved their lives.

Rogarth passes round cigarettes, lights them for us.

"What will you do now?" I ask.

"We'll do very well now," Moses says.

"After the rains?"

"Now that the ground has been fertilized," he says.

"How does that help you? You're not farmers," I say.

"We will be finding many stones," Moses says looking far into the distance, into the rain, into the darkness. He turns around and goes inside. The ground has been fertilized. It dawns on me. With bodies. Rogarth follows him. I stay where I am. The sinewy bloke comes out – a big spliff in his hand. He looks calmer now.

"Great music," he says. "But it's not easy to dance today, even though the girls are lovely." He offers me the spliff – I take a draw; heavy Arusha-*bhangi*.

"Mmmm," I say. "How was the road down here?"

"We left this afternoon, slowly. The road is one big mire. We drove through the bush. Two and a half hours just to get to the airport and the main road."

Moses comes out – takes the spliff.

"Does being a middleman in Zaire pay enough to live on?" I ask.

"I'm not a middleman," Moses says. "I run a mine out there."

"Your own?"

"No – I own a share."

"How long have you been there?"

"Ten years," Moses says. He must have started out a snake. A decade spent chasing an elusive seam of indigo stone.

"Do you know Savio?" I ask.

"*Tsk*," Moses says. "Savio is a thief."

"Yes," I say. We go inside. The whores don't look like whores anymore, sitting as they do, chatting calmly at a table to the miners. We drink heavily.

Marcus

REDEMPTION

I go out the front door. Everything is glossy and green after the rains. The earth smells rich and fragrant. Who is standing there at the kiosk drinking a Coke, watching my door? Tariq from Swahilitown – Khalid's younger brother. I go over to him. "Give me a Coke and a Sportsman," I tell the boy in the kiosk. I offer Tariq a cigarette as well. "How are you? Have you joined the disco business?" I ask.

"No. That Christian is not paying them enough," Tariq says. "They think he's cheating them. And he killed my brother." I smoke my cigarette while Tariq pours out his heart on barren ground. "They were meant to get rich and travel with the disco. Arusha, Dar es Salaam, Kampala, Nairobi, Europe. Now Khalid is a dead icicle on the mountain."

"Dreams," I say.

"Rogarth wants to speak to you," Tariq says.

"Why?" I ask.

"He has a proposition. You must come down and meet him at Shukran Hotel tonight."

"The last time I saw him, he couldn't care less about me," I say. "I'm through with that business."

"But he has a plan that would help you as well," Tariq says.

"If he wants to talk to me, he knows where I live," I say.

"Rogarth is going to ask for your help getting rid of Christian, because the *mzungu* has cheated us all," Tariq says. But how can you get rid of Christian and benefit from it, when he is already poor? I'll help them with that, because I understand Christian very well. But I also understand that Rogarth had a profound interest in Rachel before Christian arrived.

"I don't care," I tell Tariq.

"But he cheated you as well that time with the recording shop, and he kicked you out of the business when his decks arrived," Tariq says.

"Yes, and I refuse to waste any more time on that *mzungu*," I say.

"But you could get back at him," Tariq says.

"I lost out back then. Now I spend my energy on surviving. Revenge will get me nowhere," I say. I have my kiosk and the shop, a child on the way with Claire and Eeva with Tita in Finland and Steven with a crazy woman in Soweto. My lungs are shredded by batik fumes, and every at night I breathe air that stinks of chicken shit. What else can I wish for?

"But we could take his things," Tariq says in a low voice, so that even the kiosk boy won't hear him. "We can take his tape recorder, his decks, all the records, his mixing desk, loudspeakers, strobe lights, disco ball – everything. Then we'll set up a new disco business – together. You can be part of it."

"Negro dreams," I say and go inside my house again. Christian. Now he is grown, and when he makes mistakes, they are grown in size as well. But he is still my little brother. It breaks my heart that he must suffer. Christian is in the swamp. These people can destroy him. And I too am in the swamp. Neither of us belongs there.

Phantom comes to my door. His Rasta hat isn't on his head; he's holding it in his hand and looking at the ground.

"What is it?" I ask.

"Have you heard?" he asks.

"What?" I say.

"Steven," he says.

"What about Steven?" I ask.

"He is dead," Phantom says.

"Dead . . . ?"

"In the floods."

"He drowned?" I ask.

"The house was washed away while they slept," Phantom says.

"But . . . what about Rhema and the crazy grandmother?"

"They saved themselves."

"*Tsk.*"

Two days before Christmas Claire gives birth to my new son. I am not blind. In the corners of the room I see it: snakedust – *eeehhhh* – carried straight from the witch doctor to my house by Claire's mother. Even the church-going ladies carry the bush inside them. With Rebekka all the faith and the hope rested in the lap of the church. But the love of God and Jesus and the Holy Ghost couldn't resist the witch's *juju* – the new baby must be shielded by the witch doctor, who calls on the protection of the ancestors via the snake's dust. The ancestors can ensure the integrity of the body, while the witch desires to open it to the invasion of evil spirits. But can we trust the ancestors? My father was not a good man – a prisoner of alcohol and madness. I sweep the floor.

"What will you call the child?" Claire's mother asks. A name cannot shield the child's soul. You can only hope.

"Redemption," I say.

Christian

We have a drought. The short rains never came – just one enormous cloudburst, which tore all the fields to shreds, so people had to plant and sow the seeds again. And the long rainy season will not come either. The earth starts to dry out. Not so much as one drop. People become irritable, the air is dry and hot – whenever there's the least wind, it is filled with dust. The sky is endless blue as far as the eye can see. All vegetation is left withered and grey. The sun bakes the soil until it becomes rock-hard and starts to crack. There is water from the mountain for livestock and people to drink, but soon even the streams from the mountain dry up, and out on the Maasai plains the cattle have started to die of thirst. Fewer people come to Royal Crown, and the ones who come are nervy. As soon as they put away a drink or two, the air is filled with aggression.

Brawls. Barstools flying through the air, screaming and shouting, punches are exchanged, kicks, broken bottles, beer everywhere, fists slamming into flesh as sirens approach from the Y.M.C.A. roundabout, where the traffic police always keep a car. A young man is lying on the floor – in the light from the strobes the back of his head flashes red with blood again and again. Eddy Grant is booming from the speakers. I feel someone grabbing my arm. The music stops, and the fluorescent lights come on – tables knocked over, broken glass, chaos. I look: a police officer.

"Come here," he says.

"Why?" I say. "I haven't done anything."

"You're running the disco – the fight is your responsibility," the policeman says.

"It's not my disco – I'm just a visitor," I say, pointing at Rogarth – we have agreed on that; he is the one who signs when you pay for the licence. "It's his disco. I'm just a visitor who helps him out a little."

"I know it's yours," the policeman says. "That dogsbody can't own big decks like that." I go with him to the car. The policeman points at me. "And you're wearing the shirt: Rebel Rock Sound System." I don't say anything to that. There are four police cars. Normally they only send the one car that is parked at the roundabout. Four cars – they have been bought and paid for: Benson. Rogarth is taken to another car by another policeman.

We go down to the police station and are taken to the office of a higher-ranking police officer – several distinctions on his uniform. Rogarth does the talking:

"I have done everything I can to keep the troublemakers away. What can my bouncers do when bad people come and push their way inside and grope the girls like animals? We try to stop them, but we are not police – we cannot control the entire world." And it's true – the police have no case. A brawl – that's very common.

677

"*Tsk*," the police officer says. "The *mzungu* works with the disco in Tanzania, and at the same time he says he is a tourist. But he's not Tanzanian. He's not allowed to work here. Where can we see his permit? Where are the papers that show it's alright? He's not allowed to run a business."

"It isn't my business," I say.

"No, it's my business," Rogarth says. "Christian is my friend from the old days. He is here on a visit and helps me out a little."

"You're lying," the policeman tells Rogarth. "We know that the *mzungu* has been here for a long time. He is living with an African woman in Shanty Town. He is living here almost like an African, but his papers aren't what they should be."

"Let me go home and pick up my passport so you can see the stamps are as they should be. I arrived a few months ago. I have a tourist visa. My dad lives in Shinyanga. I'm just here on a visit," I say.

"We can't let you go – you might run away," the policeman says. "If you are a tourist, you have to carry the passport in your pocket at all times. But you're anything but." And then he laughs out loud. He puts his hands on his considerable belly and laughs – loudly and engagingly. "*Eeehhh*," he says. "I know you now. You are the white boy from the killing-family. I remember the dead man – he would never pay for anything. But your father was quick to pay – so everyone would understand that the dead man fell and hit his head. Not a single other person was involved in the accident. Your kind creates such trouble in Africa – we don't like having you here at all. It's only when you pay up that we like you."

I don't say anything – my face feels wooden.

We're put inside a cell. Me and Rogarth with a few of the rowdies, probably paid for by Benson. They don't say anything. We don't say anything.

We are taken out of the cell before noon. Rachel is there.

"Let me give it to him," she tells the policewoman behind the desk. "It's his passport. He needs it." The policewoman holds out her hand: "I will give it to him. You are not allowed to speak to him." I have just enough time to nod at Rachel before we are escorted into the office. The policewoman comes in and places the passport in front of the policeman: a beetroot-coloured booklet will be my salvation. The policeman grunts.

"That's my passport," I say. "Please look in it – you will see that my tourist visa is everything you could ask for." Every time I've gone across the border to Kenya, the passport has been stamped with a new three-month tourist visa – sometimes by using a bit of greasing. But everyone does something illegal – it's the norm.

The policeman leafs through the passport a little without saying anything, without looking at me. He grabs the phone, makes a call.

"Come down to the police station, because we have a *mzungu* here – he can stay in the country, but he is not meant to do what he's been doing. He's not allowed to run a business."

I wait. They arrive half an hour later from the office on Boma Road. Very quick – they can smell money. They don't know that I'm broke. The immigration people enter the office. There are two officers, a woman and a man. And I know them. They used to go to Golden Shower a lot – she danced beautifully. His name is Lukas – I've had beer with him. They look at my passport.

"Uh-oh," Lukas says. "That is terrible. We can see exactly what it is you have done. You have . . . As soon as your tourist visa was about to expire, you have gone to Kenya and have come back with a visa for three more months. That is highly irregular." The lady gives me a stern look.

"We know you have even rented a house in Shanty Town. You have been living here for several years, but you have no residence permit. And now we hear that you run a disco, but you don't have a work permit either. If we call the T.R.A., I'm sure they will tell us you haven't paid taxes in Tanzania either, even though you live here."

Yes, you cow. You've bloody well danced at that disco. Bollocks. Who is my friend, and who is my foe? Lukas takes over:

"Our information tells us that before the disco you were involved in a recording shop on Rengua Road. A shop called Roots Rock. But you have paid no taxes, no duties to the authorities. That is very serious."

Marcus. This is his revenge. And that stinking immigration officer has had cassettes recorded in Roots Rock. I remember now. There's no way Marcus can benefit from this. Stupid. He is angry and drunk.

"What will we do with him?" the policeman asks.

"We will keep his passport and have him come in for a meeting," the immigration lady says. And they let me go. I have no money. Not a fucking penny. Rachel is standing outside.

"What shall we do?" she asks.

"Do you have any money?" I ask.

"You know I don't," she says. We take a *matatu* home. The motorbike is there. The things are there. Ibrahim has taken care of it. All hope is not lost. I open the Ostermann crate and take out my reflex camera. Get Rachel to put on a gorgeous dress – persuade her to show a little thigh, a teensy bit of breast. Shoot the rest of the film and put it in the fridge. Put in a new film, sleep a few hours and drive down to the Indian who runs the photo shop on Mawenzi Road, late in the afternoon. Sell the camera – for nothing really – but my options are limited. The small stereo was sold to finance the start-up at Royal Crown Hotel. That didn't pan out well. Soon I'll have nothing left to sell.

The next day I sit at a *mama's* not far from the immigration office. I wait. Lukas comes to have lunch. He's got my passport in his office.

"I can't speak to you without my colleague present," he says.

"Oh, go on," I say.

"You're welcome to come and see me at the office," he says, raising his eyebrows.

"Alright, we'll do it whenever you want," I say.

"What I want has nothing to do with it," he says. He's got my bleeding passport – what he wants is money. But it has to be done the Tanzanian way – not mentioned outright. I breathe deeply, try to be calm. Offer him a cigarette, light one myself.

"Would you both like to have a drink with me tonight?" I ask.

"We might," Lukas says. "Where will you be tonight?"

"At Stereo Bar?" I ask, because he's the one who will decide where I drink tonight.

"Perhaps," he says. "But first you must come to the office."

The office is a joke. Petty dictators, the lot of them. I sit on a bench up against the wall. There's a counter, and behind that there are a few desks where the immigration officers see to business so inexpressibly important that I have to wait for their attention.

"*Bwana* Lukas is busy," they tell me. I can see him sitting there and leafing through some papers in separate glass office – Lukas, it seems, is a big man. He will be more expensive than I can afford. I get up, go to the counter, address the staff. They don't look at me. Each of the desks is laden with stamps. One of the men comes to the counter and speaks to me while looking at the papers in his hand. He's not being submissive – they've got me by the scruff of the neck. He just wants to make the point that I am beneath his dignity. It's something they picked up from the good old colonial British civil service – that's the traditional attitude when exercising power: total condescension.

Finally I am admitted to Lukas' office. He leaves the door open. He doesn't offer me a chair. His female colleague enters. He speaks loudly enough for the others to hear it:

"We have approached the authorities – the T.R.A. and the government party office as well. You are here without a residence permit. But your father is collaborating with our country on a project in Shinyanga, so diplomacy requires that we speak to your father and the Danish embassy – to see if together we can clear up the mess you have made."

"Or you could just give me my passport – then I could get out of here," I say.

"You can't have the passport until we have cleared up the circumstances concerning the situation," he says. "We will summon you to a meeting when the investigation is complete." Lukas looks down at his papers. The audience is over. I think of my reserve capital – the last few dollars I have left from the sale of the tanzanites in Copenhagen. I can soon wave goodbye to those, one way or another. The drought is taking a big toll on everybody.

That night I sit nursing a beer at Stereo Bar from nine, even though I have no idea if they'll show up or not. I've always liked the small room with the high ceiling, the small booths between the mosaic-tiled concrete pillars facing the street. Now I'm just waiting. They arrive.

"We will sit out the back," Lukas says. I follow them out into the back yard where there are tables and chairs, and where meat is grilled. I order beer and *nyama choma* for us. Once that's arrived, they proceed straight to the matter at hand.

"If you help us a little, that will be alright. We can fix your papers so that you can stay," the woman says.

"How long can you give me?" I ask.

"If you can help us, it may be as much as a year," Lukas says.

"And how can I help you?" I ask. It will of course be a question of money, but I'm not sure how much. The woman looks straight at me, leans forwards and says:

"We need five hundred dollars."

I've got it. That's all I've got. But it's not unreasonable. A couple of months' salary for each of them. Normal. What they make a month isn't enough to feed anyone.

"Alright," I say. "Give me two days. Where would you like to receive your . . . present?"

"You can take us out to dinner the day after tomorrow," the woman says.

"Yes," I say. "Where would you like to eat?"

"Newcastle Hotel – on the roof terrace."

"Yes," I say and call the waitress. Pay the bill. Toast them, drink up. Drive back to Rachel.

"How did it go?" she asks.

"When hunger knocks on the door, the dogs will bite," I say.

1990

Christian

We had a good name. We had the decks. At Golden Shower and Royal Crown we pulled large crowds. But our options are shrinking.

"How about Jackson's in Majengo?" I ask Rogarth. He shakes his head.

"I've talked to him. He doesn't want people to have to pay an entrance fee. He says the space should be used by people to sit down and drink – if the space is used for a dance floor, then people will dance. Then they don't drink as much."

"But he'll bloody well get more people through the door if they can dance," I say.

"He says the place is already packed. They don't need to dance."

"Is there any place else with enough room for a dance floor?"

"Amand's up at K.C.M.C. – they have a small ballroom," Rogarth says.

We drive there on the motorbike. A bar with a small ballroom next door, a small garden where you can sit. Quite nice, really. The owner is a Tanzanian lady who used to be married to a Swedish man who died of the disease. His name was Åmand, but everyone refers to the place as Amand's, like an Arabic name. North of K.C.M.C. there are villages in the mountains. They might come down for the party. We agree and start things up. No-one comes. No-one. Perhaps word needs to get around first. The drought is contributing to the disaster. People have sorrows to drown – they don't want to spend their money on the door; every shilling must be spent on alcohol.

We are there for a few weeks, and slightly more people slow up, but they're mostly very young; it resembles a ruddy kiddie disco. Boarders from I.S.M. start showing up early on Friday and Saturday nights. Badly behaved youngsters – like I was myself; they drink beer and smoke *bhangi*. Deputy Head Thompson comes round to my house one Sunday morning.

"We can't have our students going off to your parties for a drink," he says. That man helped kick Samantha out of school – threw her to the lions.

685

"Get out of here, Thompson, or I'll set the dogs on you," I say. He gives a strained laugh, as if I'm joking. I can't be bothered to argue with him. I go inside and close the door, leave him frying in the sun. When I look out some time later, he is gone.

Amand's is too far off the beaten track; it's not just outside town – it's also too far from the main road. Golden Shower is flourishing again – everyone goes there. Benson is raking it in. I don't make enough – loads of bills, loads of people to pay, but no income. When things are going well, everyone shares in the business. They say: "We should share the profit, the same way we share the labour." When things aren't going well, the business is all my problem. "We can't work for you, when you can't pay our wages." Two and a half months. I am nearly broke. I have no use for Big Man Ibrahim. What do you need a bouncer for when you don't have any customers? But I can't send him away. He is too strong, and he is angry that his wife's family has stolen from him. The fact that he falls ill is in fact a blessing in disguise; he sweats, coughs, shits – the works. I sit by his bed in his stinking room and offer to get him a taxi so we can get him to K.C.M.C.

"Not K.C.M.C," Ibrahim says. "People die there." It doesn't look like malaria to me. It looks like it might be something else entirely. Something much worse.

"But you have to see a doctor," I say. "So you can find out what's wrong."

"It's just a bad case of malaria."

"Alright," I say. "Then what can I do for you?" Ibrahim wants to go home to the village – his parents' hut. They live on the coast, not very far from where Rachel comes from.

"I'll come back to Moshi when I am well again," Ibrahim says. I don't think he'll get well. I go to Chuni Motors and rent an old car. Drive Ibrahim all the way home. It's terrible. We have to stop several times because Ibrahim can't keep anything down. When we get there, he is lying shivering and sweating on the back seat and has shat himself. He shows me the way to his parents' house and I help his father drag him inside, while his mother stands wailing helplessly, slapping her face, crying. The disease is associated with such shame, but I can tell from the house that the family isn't absolutely impoverished, and his father seems like a good man, so perhaps they can help Ibrahim through his last days on earth.

"The lady at Liberty has had to sell up," Rogarth says. "The new owner is a man."

"Did you speak to him?"

"He asked me himself. I said: 'I don't know – you will have to speak to the boss.' So I think he'll be coming to see us."

Liberty has lain fallow for a long time. The bar with the veranda facing the street has done alright, but the disco in the back has been closed – there's no music. The Arab owner of Faizal's decks moved him to a hotel in Tanga, and the lady who owned Liberty wouldn't speak to us after the Easter disaster when we rented Faizal's decks and he stood her up.

But there's a new owner. A few days after he takes over he comes to my house in his beat-up car. Invites me to Liberty. We drive down and look at the room.

"I'll give you eighty per cent of the entrance fee," he says.

"One hundred," I say.

"At Amand's you don't get nothing," he says.

"That's right," I say. "I'm almost out of money. If I can't make any here, I will be on the next plane home."

"In that case I'd like to buy your decks," he says.

"I already have a buyer in Arusha," I say, even though it's a lie.

"Alright," he says. "You'll get a hundred per cent." At first it's just Rogarth and me moving the decks. But the others smell money the way jackals smell a carcass. They show up.

"I'll pull those cables for you," Emmanuel says.

"I haven't got any money to pay you."

"Money?" he says. "We're friends. Once we get the business up and running, we will all make money."

And Firestone is there, stammering and stuttering and helpful.

It's good to be back in business. Liberty – the first real disco I went to as a boy with Marcus. I remember seeing my dad in the company of Jonas Larsson, John from T.P.C. and a couple of fat old *malaya* at Kilimanjaro Hotel across the street. And then me and Marcus went over to Liberty and got drunk, listened to the music, danced. And now I'm going to be playing here myself. I'm looking forward to it – I have always loved this crummy, scarred room.

*

The first night. I'm standing in the glass cage right under the ceiling over the bar – gazing out on the dark, teeming dance floor, lit cigarette ends twirling like restless fireflies. The party is going full whack. Dig out a live recording of Linton Kwesi Johnson – drop it in.

"Ah-Ah-Ah-Ah-Ah-Ah-Ah . . ." Firestone shouts, as he comes running up the stairs to the D.J. cage. He stops in front of me, almost skipping: "Ah-Ah-Ah-Ah-Ah-Ah . . ." he stutters and stares at me with frustration. "Ah-Ah-Ah . . ." He comes to a stop once more, bunches his hands into fists, there are tears in his eyes. "Ah-Ah-Ah-Ah." I hug him, pressing him against me tightly. "Abdullah is here," Firestone says with surprise, opening his hands, looking down on them, looking into my face and smiling: "Abdullah has ch-ch-ch-chewed a lot of *mirungi*. He is wild. E-e-e-Emmanuel is out there – he is trrrrrrr-trying to stop him." The door is ripped open at the bottom of the stairs, and Abdullah appears, taking the narrow steps two at a time, the whites of his eyes showing, his bared teeth hurtling up towards me. Firestone stands aside, presses up against the wall. The air is moving, I take a step back, raise my hands – there's nowhere to go. I'm in for it now. Abdullah's fist hits me like a train, and the back of my head slams into the wall, and then he keels over. Firestone is ramming into him, and he bowls over almost in slow motion, across the decks, onto the record as it spins on the turntable. The music stops, I can hear the needle, the arm, the record – breaking; the table holding the decks buckles under Abdullah's weight, and then the glass of the small D.J. cage is shattered, broken by Abdullah's shoulder, and he falls silently in a rain of broken glass. At the bar people stare up at the D.J. cage without saying anything – they hear the glass breaking, the body falling. Move feverishly to the side. *DUFF* – Abdullah's body pushes them aside. *BAM* – Abdullah hits the floor, there's a clatter of broken glass around him, girls scream, people gather round the body, he groans, I look down at him. Notice that Emmanuel is standing next to me. His lip is bleeding.

"I couldn't stop him," Emmanuel says. I dash down the stairs, force my way through the crowd. Abdullah has sat up, is trying to get to his feet. I am standing in front of him, trembling on the inside.

"Watch it," I say. "Cool it."

"Stay where you are," Emmanuel tells Abdullah. "If not, I will kick you."

"I am calm," Abdullah says in a broken voice, holding his hands up in front of him.

"What do you want?" I ask. He's not looking too hot.

"Take me back," he says.

"You stole from me," I say.

"But I've lost everything," he says. "They took the materials for my house. My girlfriend's family. They have . . ." He comes to a halt. I could give him a job: he could keep an eye on the car park. I want to, but the others refuse to work with him. He cost them a lot of money, and he's unreliable. It's just business. "Otherwise I'll have to be a carrier on the mountain," he says.

"I won't have you back," I say. Abdullah leaps up, the heel of his hand rams into my face, I feel my skin breaking, cartilage cracks. I stagger back; a metallic taste flows over my tongue, warm and sticky, right as his foot flies up and hits me on my shoulder, and I am knocked to the floor. Emmanuel throws himself at Abdullah's back, grabs him and pushes, so they both fall over. Firestone throws himself on top of them. Blood is running down my chin as I force myself to stand up. Emmanuel is on his back with his arms around Abdullah's chest – trying to hold him as he thrashes about, sending Firestone flying. I'm at the bar, grabbing a beer bottle, breaking it against the edge of the bar, throwing myself to my knees by the struggling bodies, holding the broken bottle towards Abdullah's face.

"Stop," I say. He stiffens, stares at the jagged edges of the bottle, frightened. "You're leaving. Now, nice and easy," I hiss through the pain in my mouth. My thighs are shaking. Suddenly I can hear people again – they cheer and laugh around us.

Abdullah starts whinging.

"I will ruin you, you fucking *mzungu*. I will bring my friends. Just you wait," he says.

"That's what you told me the last time," I say. "I'm still waiting." Like a bad film. All of us – me, Emmanuel and Firestone – walk him through the room and down the hall, past Rogarth, who is still at his post working the door. We step out to the veranda bar, and Abdullah trudges down the steps to the dusty car park – out into the darkness, where he stops and speaks:

"I will come back with my guys, and I will break you – you will walk in the black country with your dirty skin of milk, and you will be poor, with nothing. You will know it, and I will see you bleed."

"Christian," Emmanuel says, "I'm going back to T.P.C. now."

"Now? Why?" I ask.

"I don't like this disco business – they're all hyenas," he says.

"Hold on a sec," I say, grabbing his arm. He stops, looks at me.

"At home in the village at T.P.C., Christian, I had a girl there – a lovely girl. Good. Hard-working. Clever. But I thought of Moshi, the discos, the good sound, the wild lights, the *chiki-chiki* girls everywhere and I wanted have a taste of them. But the girls here are dirty – *malaya*. And the guys are thieves. Hyenas," Emmanuel says, freeing his arm, going out into the darkness.

Slowly the party dies out. People saw a fight – it's been a satisfying night. For them. I have a broken turntable. And what about Abdullah?

"Do you think Abdullah will come back?" I ask Rogarth.

"Yes, of course," he says. "We have to stay here."

"But we have to get the decks home," I say.

"What about the speakers?" he asks.

"They stay here," I say. "It takes a full hour to get them down."

"Then he'll just break them," Rogarth says.

"How about Liberty's night guard?"

"No good," Rogarth says. We can't take them apart them – we haven't got the tools.

"I'm going to take a taxi back with the other things," I say. "If you stay here with Firestone, I'll come back, and we will stay here together until it's light."

"I will get a taxi." Rogarth leaves. I am standing in the empty room with Firestone. There's a guard who does the rounds at night, but he's an old man. Rogarth returns. We carry everything into the taxi; the working turntable, the tape recorder, the amplifier and all the music.

I take the things home, and everything is calm. Carry them inside the house while the taxi waits. I wish I had Ibrahim here, so he could stay at the house. The dogs aren't much use if there's an emergency. I open the old Ostermann crate where I keep my things. Dig down under cables and cassettes. Find the revolver, check that the safety's on, tuck it down the front of my waistband, pull the shirt over it. Rachel wakes up.

"What is it?" she mutters.

"I have to go back to Liberty," I say.

"Why?" she says sleepily into her pillow.

"There are some problems. I am going to have to stay there until tomorrow." Rachel sits up – wide awake.

"What problems?" she asks.

"Abdullah showed up and made a ruckus. We're going to have to stay so he doesn't return and steal the speakers. Or wreck them," I say. Rachel looks over at Halima, who is sleeping the sleep of the innocent.

"But what about me?" she says. "Abdullah knows where you live. If you're at Liberty, and he has seen you take the things home, he might come here and take them," she says.

"The night guard is here," I say. It used to be just the dog, but Moshi has got more dangerous with the drought – no-one has any money – so Gösta's wife has employed a night guard.

"The night guard will just run," Rachel says. It's true. If he gets scared, he will make a run for it.

"The dogs are here," I say.

"Those dogs are good for nothing," Rachel says. Shit. I have promised to return to Liberty.

"I will go back there, and then I'll come right back with the motor-bike," I say and go out into the kitchen, loading food and drinks into a woven basket – taking it with me. Back to Liberty in the taxi. I know the driver.

"There might be thieves at Liberty," I tell him. "I would like to investigate." He nods.

It's only because of their cigarettes that I notice them – three or four guys standing in the darkness right after the petrol station, not long before Liberty. There might be more of them if they're not all smoking. Sweat breaks out on my neck.

"Point your headlights at Liberty's entrance," I say and tuck my shirt into my trousers behind the revolver so you can see it sticking out of my waistband. He stops. "Honk four times," I say and reach my hand up towards the cabin light. "Can it be switched off?"

"What?" he says, hooting the horn.

"The light inside the car – I don't want it to go off when I open the door."

"It's not working," he says.

"I want you to stay here until they let me into Liberty," I say and pay him twice the going rate before I open the door. Get out of the car and stand facing the men with the cigarettes, who are now absolutely invisible to me in the dark. I stand there for a while to allow them to catch sight of the revolver in the glow from the headlights. I take the revolver in my hand and close the car door behind me, pull my basket of Sprite and cold samosas out through the open car window. Hold the revolver loosely in my right hand, keeping my hand by my thigh as I walk towards Liberty's door – I can't see the night guard anywhere. I hear movement somewhere not far off, but I can't see anything outside the beam of the headlights. The revolver is resting smoothly in my hand; I have my index finger on the trigger, rap the bottom of the handle against the door as I look over my shoulder.

"We will get you, *mzungu*," someone shouts a bit further up the street. It isn't Abdullah, but I've heard the voice before, though I can't put a face to it now.

"What?" someone says inside. It's Rogarth.

"It's me," I say. He unlocks the door. I push past him.

"Was there someone out there?" Rogarth asks.

"There are a few guys a bit further up the street."

"Wh-wh-wh-who . . ." Firestone shouts from the dancehall.

"It's Christian," Rogarth shouts back. There's a bat light on the floor a bit further down the hall. I catch sight of the night guard, who is sitting on a metal chair that has been tilted back against the wall.

"Why aren't you outside?" I ask. He gives me an empty stare.

"I haven't got a weapon," he says.

"*Tsk*," Rogarth says. The night guard doesn't care. He's got a *panga* and a stick, but he's spotted my revolver, and the seriousness of the situation has dawned on him. He is not paid well enough to get involved in anything this serious.

"I'm afraid they'll go up to Rachel," I say.

"Isn't the night guard there?" Rogarth asks. I gesture towards the night guard here. "That's not good," Rogarth says.

"There are dogs there as well," I say.

"That's not good enough," Rogarth says.

"I know. Perhaps we should send Firestone there – on the motorbike. He could take the back way through Majengo, because those guys are a bit further up the road here," I say.

"Firestone is no use," Rogarth says in a low voice. "He is very scared of Abdullah now – he can't stop shaking."

"Perhaps I should go back," I say. "Fuck. What a shit situation."

"Those guys outside – did they see the gun?" Rogarth asks.

692

"Yes," I say.

"I could go there on your motorbike – then they wouldn't know where the gun is; whether it's here with you or there with me," Rogarth says.

"And where will it be?" I ask. Rogarth doesn't say anything. I pull the revolver from my waistband. Hold it out towards him. He looks down at it in the darkness.

"No," he says. "I don't know about this kind of thing." I put the revolver back. I don't know either. I unlock the motorbike and pull it out from the hall where I park it when we play at Liberty. I tell the night guard to open the doors and go outside and see if there's anyone there.

"I'm not going out there," he says.

"It's your job – you're a night guard."

"I would rather not have a job then," he says. Rogarth goes over and opens the doors. I stand behind him with the revolver raised, my arm bent at the elbow so it's pointing right at the ceiling. Rogarth goes out – looks to both sides. There's still no power in the city centre. He turns to me, shrugs.

"I'll stand at the door and keep watch until you're clear," I whisper. I go back to Firestone. He is very quiet.

We smoke cigarettes and drink Sprite until it is light outside.

"Now would be a good time for you to go and see your dad," I tell Rachel. "Just until this business with Abdullah has been sorted out."

"But perhaps it would be better if we spoke to your father to see if he could get us a ticket to Denmark so we can run away from this mess," Rachel says. Denmark.

"No, damn it. We won't run away," I say, because I'm just not up to the task of trying to explain to her that my dad won't buy us tickets to go to Denmark, and that we wouldn't be alright there. I would, that's true – because I'm a Danish citizen – but she wouldn't.

"Alright, I will go and visit them for one week, then I'll come back," she says.

"Will you see Ibrahim while you're there?" I ask, because if it was a heavy-duty case of malaria and not . . . well, then he bloody well would have been back in Moshi by now.

"I'm sure I'll see him," Rachel says.

"Give him my best. And if he has got better, tell him to come back – I have a job for him."

Once Rachel is gone, I need try to concentrate on the job at hand. I have my residence permit sorted – bought and paid for, through the nose, on the roof terrace at Newcastle Hotel. The work permit – fuck that; Rogarth is listed as the manager. But Abdullah – how do I fix that? I drive down to the police station. Go right into the office of the officer who said I was from a family of killers. I throw it right at him:

"This Abdullah is causing me heaps of trouble. He is threatening me. Will you speak to him?"

"Abdullah? I don't know him, but he's a Tanzanian, so he has more rights than you," the policeman says with a smile. "You're just a tourist. It will cost you a thousand dollars for me to protect you just a little." Now he's laughing: "You will always have problems in life when you come from a family of killers. Your hands are red with the blood of the dead man."

I haven't got a thousand dollars.

I have put Rogarth up. I have taken the broken turntable to a repair guy in town. There is nothing we can do until it's the weekend again, and we have to be back at Liberty. I change into warmer clothes, and at the same time I move my passport from the shirt I had on into the pocket of my jacket. I have made it a habit to always keep the passport on me.

I drive to Arusha and up to Mountain Lodge to see if Mick is there – I need to speak to a white man. It's five when I get there, but he's still at work. I sit on the veranda and talk to Sofie. It feels great to speak Danish again. I ask after Mick.

"How is his garage going?"

"Quite well, I think. He's always working – it's not even certain he'll be back before late evening," she says.

"But will he go on living here at the lodge?" I ask. Because I'm surprised that he wants to live with his family.

"Yes, of course. Until he gets married, that is – I'm sure he'll buy a house in Arusha then," Sofie says.

"Is he getting married?" I ask.

"I don't know – perhaps at some point. He hasn't got a girlfriend as far as I know," Sofie says.

"Yes, if he doesn't like black girls, I suppose he might have a hard time of it," I say. Sofie laughs.

"It's not about colour. It's the laziness, the *laissez-faire* attitude, he's opposed to," she says. "You have to work hard here to make things work. When you have kids, they have to go to Arusha School, and that's expensive. You can't afford health insurance or anything of the sort. We have to stick together as a family."

I look around – the pretty, old house with bungalows at the back, the safari company Land Rovers, the well-trained staff. I envy their success, but they do work hard for it. I haven't worked hard enough – I realize that. My possessions are fragile – the objects; they break. My clothes are tattered, my shoes too, my sunglasses scratched, the tape heads in the tape recorder worn down, the records break. Is that normal for people? To be the things we possess? I am the turntable needle – if it doesn't work, I don't work. I have built my life on easily broken electronics. Perishable. And perishable relationships with other people, for whom I have become responsible. I look up. Stars start to appear on the black vault. Samantha – was this the life you didn't want – the one I have? But you could have lived like Sofie.

Sofie speaks again:

"But then, I'm a sort of negro as well," she says. "I'm half Greenlander, so I understand the Tanzanians perfectly; first the colonialists bossed them around, then they were left to fry in the sun – how can that not suck?"

I look up at the sky. It's starting to get dark.

"I'd better just drive the bike into the garage," I say and take my leave of Sofie.

I find Mick with his upper body buried under the bonnet of a safari truck. At his side is a gnarly old Tanzanian.

"Let's grab a beer," Mick says, and we sit down on a couple of old tyres in the garage yard. It's dark now, but the stars are out, and the moon is shining down on us.

"What is it really you're doing here, Christian?"

"I . . . I live here."

"Do you?" He looks round at his garage. "I live here. You're a refugee. You're trying to live some sort of teenage dream."

"For fuck's sakes, Mick, I work; people depend on me for their livelihoods."

"Yes, but from what I hear from Moshi, you're trying to cheat your way ahead. In the long run, man, that won't work." He looks at me. I wonder who he's been talking to in Moshi. It seems he can read my expression. He laughs: "Christian, Moshi is a small place. Your old partner – Marcus – I've known him for years. I always bought cassettes from him whenever I was in Moshi. Marcus has all the good music," Mick says.

"You come to Moshi?" I ask, because I've never seen him there.

"Occasionally," Mick says and lights a cigarette, smoking for a while in silence. I don't know what to say. I was going to ask him if I could borrow some money, but now I can't bring myself to ask. He looks right through me. Now he speaks again, calmly. But there's nothing calm about the things he says: "You're like Samantha – you try to dodge the hard things. You think it can be done, but things always catch up with you."

"I've got what it takes," I say. "I could have made it."

"When you haven't made it, that's when you know you haven't got what it takes," Mick says.

"It's just a few hiccups – it'll sort itself out," I say, even though I don't believe it myself.

"Yes, it will," Mick says. "The situation will resolve itself. Things will settle down. But there's no knowing that you'll come out on top – to me it looks like you'll end up bottom of the pile."

"I just need to get a bit of money."

"You have to think of them as wild dogs," Mick says.

"Who?" I ask.

"The people you work with and the ones who are trying to take over your business."

"I bloody well do," I say.

"No, you don't. Dogs. It's all about territory. When you walk past a dog at night, it will only attack you if you invade its territory. If you meet on common ground, it will only attack if you show fear, submission."

"What does that have to do with me?" I ask, even though . . .

"You're on their territory," Mick says. "They're a pack. You reek of fear. They have seen that you're vulnerable. You've been separated from your white pack, you're already bleeding. It's only a matter of time until you bleed out. Unless of course you make your way back to your pack. Europe," he says.

696

"But they're not my pack – in Denmark."

"No, I understand why you would think that. But the Danes don't know it," Mick says and laughs. "So they'll take care of you."

"You're white as well," I say.

"Yes, but I belong here. I have family, community – I'm a part of it."

"You're not a Tanzanian," I say. Mick points at a big pile of scrap metal in a corner under a lean-to.

"Do you know what that is?"

"Junk from old cars," I say.

"Yes. That's my store of spare parts."

"That pile right there?" I ask.

"Yes. It's a question of being self-sufficient. You need to inject things to survive here. You brought money which you invested – all well and good. Now you have squandered your investment. You haven't raised sufficient capital to rebuild your business in bad times. You're bleeding out. I grew up here. I understand the system. I would never have encountered your problems."

"I just need to get it sorted. I'll be fine then."

"I was taught by a guy who can fix a Land Rover with parts from a Peugeot," Mick says. "A guy who was self-taught. He's practically illiterate."

"Alright," I say.

"He is much better at it than I am." Mick points to the gnarly old man whose boiler suit is shiny black with motor oil. "That's him right there. He's my idol."

"I see what you mean," I say.

"No, you don't," Mick says. We don't say anything. Smoke. "Do you remember Panos?" Mick asks.

"Yes, of course," I say.

"Panos works at Heathrow Airport in London. He is throwing luggage around on double shifts. And he's with Parminder, who spends her time standing behind a British Airways counter," Mick says.

"Beautiful Parminder?" I ask.

"That's it exactly. She was married to a Sikh in Nairobi who beat her. So now Parminder has broken with her entire family and shacked up with Panos. And now they're working their arses off to put away money to build a safari farm in Ruaha," Mick says.

"But what about Stefano and his family?" I ask, because after what I heard Stefano's dad was ready to have Panos killed after he beat Stefano up for trying to rape Samantha.

"Stefano's family have all moved to China to run some big tobacco farms," Mick says. "The point is that Panos is preparing for this. He's working hard to save money for his investment. And he's found the right woman to help him. He's doing things the right way so he stands a chance of making things work for him. You're not."

"I see what you're saying," I say again.

"I can give you thousand dollars," Mick says.

"Really?" I say, because I haven't even asked. "I'm glad that . . ." Mick holds up a hand stop me. He digs into his pocket as he gets up. Hands me two hundred-dollar notes.

"Don't come see me again," he says and goes over and puts his body under the bonnet the way it was when I arrived.

A few days later Rachel and Halima return home.

"How about Ibrahim? Did you see him?" I ask.

"*Tsk*," she says and shakes her head disapprovingly. "Ibrahim is nearly dead."

"What happened to him?"

"He's got the disease. And in the village, they almost killed him," Rachel says.

"Stoned him?"

"Yes. The entire village – the men. Because Ibrahim has lain with another man's wife. So now they've stoned him hard – almost to death. And now he is dying in the hospital."

"But . . . the disease. Is he thin?"

"Yes, he isn't Big Man Ibrahim. He is like a skeleton."

"But how did he manage to sleep with another man's wife – if he was already ill?"

"For a brief while he was a little bit better, so he could get up from his bed. And he talks very smoothly to the girls, Ibrahim does. He owns a small shop, he's got two *matatu*, he's got a bar."

"If he's thin, then you know he's got the disease," I say.

"This is the village, Christian. They don't know anything about the disease – they just think it's a hard case of malaria."

"But I thought his wife had taken over all his businesses," I say.

"Yes, but they're still in Ibrahim's name, so people think he's a big man. Ibrahim's wife has the disease as well."

"What about their child?" I ask.

"The baby is alright. The wife's parents are looking after it."

The problem in the city centre just keeps getting worse – it's obvious to the authorities what we're doing at Liberty. Rogarth is stopped by the police on the street. Everybody wants a piece of us. The town is too small, and we are successful – at least that's how it looks. "Come on, we know you've got money. Give us some." Everything gets more expensive when you're white, and when you have money. We are met with inflated prices every time we want to buy something. When Rachel goes to the market, she gets white prices thrown at her. I start to live the same way as the white people I despised seven years ago when I moved to Moshi from T.P.C. with Dad. I thought they were paranoid, because they were afraid of the negro. I was disgusted with how they moved from their house to their cars, drove to their jobs, the school or the club. They brought the gardener with them to the market so he could carry their baskets, had meat brought to the door by the delivery guy. At the very most they knew a little of the cook having a family in a village, but they had never met them or seen his house or fields. They never spent time with the locals. They never tried to eat corn porridge and fish while squatting on the ground at a smoking bonfire. Or washed their arses with water. Smoked raw tobacco rolled up in newspaper. Never ate grilled cassava with mustard and chilli dressing on the cheap wooden seats in the cinema. Or drank *mbege* at the small shacks in the countryside. But now I get it. Moving around freely is impossible.

I let Rogarth take the motorbike and run errands in town; order posters, stick them up everywhere. Get light bulbs for Liberty so things won't vanish into a black hole for me.

Once again I walk on my feet. The hard-packed earth, the dust that rises in little clouds. It's not working. I'm on my way down Uru Road to speak to Marcus. But I don't want to. It's embarrassing. I'm ashamed – like everything is my fault. But that's not true. Should I forget about it? I turn around. Can see the lights outside the Y.M.C.A. – taxis parked outside. I go over and buy grilled corn on the cob from a guy who is standing outside a bar by the Y.M.C.A. buliding. He asks for an exorbitant price. I give him the right amount, speak to him in street-Swahili: "*Mimi sitake kuchuma mboga.*" I won't bend down to pick vegetables – I refuse to be shafted by him. Everyone sees me as a walking wallet they would like to get their fingers deep into. I go over towards the taxi drivers, and they all start calling to me in their halting English:

"Come here. Here. Taxi. Good car. With music." It's annoying that they don't get it; I came to Tanzania nine and a half years ago – I speak the language fluently.

I make a sign to the eldest of the drivers – a greying man with lined cheeks who is leaning against the bonnet of his taxi and hasn't said a thing. He stands up straight and goes round to open the door to me. The others grumble, but I can't be arsed to listen to all their crap and fight their attempts to rip me off.

Marcus

RELAXATION

Yes, a man needs relaxation after a long day's work. Just a drink or two, even though Claire is an enemy of that behaviour. She wants to keep me at home – eat, sleep, done. No joy in life. And the pumping; it used to be a juice – now she does that job like a log on the ground. I can't go to my local bar – my tab there is as long as the road to Dar. I go over and knock on the kiosk door and wake up the boy who mans it during the day and sleeps in it at night so nothing is stolen.

"Give me some money," I say.

"But *mama* Claire has already picked up the day's takings," he says sleepily.

"*Tsk,*" I say. The idea is that Claire runs Princess in town, and I run the kiosk. I don't want her meddling with my kiosk. And if I do need a little of the profits for some relaxation at night, then it's only so that I can build up the will to work the next day. I go straight back to the house and shake Claire awake. "Where is my money?"

"What money?" she mutters, her eyes full of terror from the rude awakening.

"My money from the kiosk," I say loudly, so the baby wakes up and starts his screaming.

"You're waking up Redemption," Claire says. "The money has been spent on corn flour and cooking oil and fizzy drinks so the kiosk can sell more." *Tsk*, Claire has run around with a taxi buying stock and has spent all the money in the kitty.

"Where is the rest of the money?" I say. By now Redemption is screaming like an ambulance.

"*Tsk*," Claire says. "You can look in my bag."

"Why are you so grumpy?" I say. "Can't a man be allowed to have a nice time now and then?"

"It's not every now and then," Claire says. "It's every night you go to the bar, as if it were your church."

"I just need a little relaxation – so I can sleep," I say.

"Other people can sleep without going to the bar," Claire says and comforts baby Redemption with her *titi*.

"Perhaps their wife is nice to them so they want to sleep with her, instead of finding a cold back," I say.

"I don't want to make trouble when I'm nursing – it's wrong. And I am tired from working all day," Claire says.

"You're always tired. But I'm not tired, so I have to go and talk to people and make some business."

"You'll be tired in the morning," Claire says.

"*Tsk*," I say and root through her bag. Out, away, down Uru Road to the Y.M.C.A., where there is now a large container bar with a kiosk; Gateway is its name. In my head I call it Get Away.

Christian

"Is Marcus in?" I ask the house girl at the door to his house.

"He is resting," she says. "I'm not allowed to wake him up."

I can see past her into the sitting room. There's a framed picture of Haile Selassie on the wall. Bob Marley as well. And then there are the family photos: Claire's baby Rebekka, who died; Marcus with baby Steven, who drowned; and another baby who I don't recognize. A faded picture of Katriina and the girls. Once he used to have a picture of me and him outside Roots Rock with our arms around each other's shoulders, cigarettes hanging from our lips, sunglasses – young, fresh, cool. Full of hope. That picture is gone now. He has no photos of Steven's mother, nor of Tita and their daughter. Or at least, if he does, they're not on display. There are no pictures of Marcus' parents and siblings. I know he's got some, taken by the Germans in Seronera when he lived there as a child. But they're not on the wall. He never speaks of them. His parents were bad. He broke with them, wanted to start his own family from scratch. He's done it and it's a messy one, because Marcus isn't much good either. Will any of his children keep a framed photo of him on their bookshelf when they grow up? Will Solja? Rebekka? I don't think so. All these photos will fade and burn, crumble and decay.

"Would you tell Marcus that Christian came to see him?" I ask the house girl, who is leaning against the doorpost and holding on to the door so I can't go inside.

"I will tell him," she says and closes the door. I drive home to pick up Rachel. We're going shopping at the market. I have invited Rogarth and Firestone for dinner. It's just the three of us now, since Emmanuel upped and left. Three hyenas. I have asked Rogarth to get a new bouncer, but he hasn't yet found one he trusts.

"The dog is ill," Rachel says when I get back. She shows me the dog – he's lying under a bush in the garden. Whimpers when we approach. The bitch is not far away, keeping watch over him.

"Did you tell them at the house?" I ask.

"Yes," she says. "They say it will pass."

"It's not our problem," I say, because I can't afford a vet. But having just one dog is a problem – you should always have two. A single dog can be killed easily, and then there's no alarm to wake up the night guard.

We drive into town. I want to avoid the Clock Tower roundabout, the city centre; don't feel like bumping into the owner of Liberty, the policeman, Benson or David, Claire, Marcus. We take the Arusha roundabout and turn down Arusha Road and then right down the one-way Kawawa Street – where Marcus was run over by Asko. And then down Chagga Street to the market, which is not far from Swahilitown. My eyes are hidden behind scratched sunglasses, scanning the surroundings for Abdullah, Tariq – enemies. I sweat. I drink a Coke in the shade, while Rachel argues with the merchants at the vegetable market – they know she's with a white man, and they would never believe that a white man can be skint.

At home I tidy up, play with Halima, help Rachel a bit in the kitchen. Rogarth and Firestone come over. I give them beer, put out salted cashew nuts and *chevdo* – Bombay mix. We listen to the soundtrack from "Shaft". There's a knock on the garden door. A small girl from the main house. Tears are running down her cheeks.

"What's the matter?" I ask.

"The dog is dead," she says.

"Has it been ill?" Rogarth says.

"Yes, since yesterday," I say. The little girl is still at the door. "Is there something else you must tell me?" I ask in a quiet voice so as not to frighten her.

"My mother says the *mzungu* must bury the dog," she says. I get up.

"Are there no men in the house?" I ask. The girl shakes her head. "Would you like a Coke?" I ask. She nods and comes over to me, taking my hand. We go out to the kitchen with Halima on our heels. I give the girl a Coke and explain the situation to Rachel, who is frying aubergines in oil.

I light a bat light and go outside with Rogarth and Firestone. Rogarth nudges the dog with his foot and looks worried.

"What is it?" I ask.

"It might have been poisoned," he says.

"How?" I ask.

"All you do is throw some poisoned meat over the fence," Rogarth says.

"Then the other one would be ill as well," I say.

"Not if the dog was greedy and ate it all," Rogarth says.

"I'll get a spade," I say and go towards the garage. Firestone goes inside our house. When I return with the spade, Firestone comes out with a knife in his hand. "What are you doing?" I ask.

"O-o-o-o-o . . . opening the dog," Firestone says.

"I thought you were a Muslim," I say. "Against dogs."

"Yes, but the dog is good now, because it's dead," Rogarth says. Firestone nods and smiles, squats right down and slices open the dog's belly, so its intestines fall bloodily to the ground. Rogarth holds the bat light while Firestone spreads the animal's intestines on the ground. Bile rises in my throat; I turn my face away and swallow. Light cigarettes – one for each of us.

"Here, Firestone," I say, holding my breath as I take a step over and hold the cigarette in front of his face. He takes the filter between his teeth and makes an incision in a large organ that connects to the gut. The stomach. The contents spill out on the ground, a stodgy mass which Firestone takes between his hands and works carefully.

"Anything there?" Rogarth asks.

"*Eeeeehhhh*," Firestone says. "Br-br-br-br-br-broken g-g-g-glass."

"*Tsk*," Rogarth says.

"What?" I say.

"You buy meat and mix it with tiny bits of broken glass. The dog doesn't notice, because it doesn't chew its meat, it just swallows it. The glass cuts the stomach and the intestines to pieces, so it bleeds internally and dies," Rogarth says.

"So someone did kill it," I say with a lump in my throat.

"Yes," Rogarth says. Samantha rises inside my brain. She is standing quite still – dead – looking at me. Her eyes are unreadable. Full of coagulated blood. I turn my back to the light so they won't see the tears that well up. I start digging the hole. The grave.

Marcus

ROMANTIC DISEASE

Rachel comes to my door one day – *eeehhhh*. Christian's *malaya*.

"I am *mwafrika* like you. I am your sister. And you understand these *wazungu* better than me. You can advise me," she says. But I don't understand the white people – perhaps I never did.

"Why would I help you?" I ask.

"You were the one who introduced that *mzungu* to me. And now he is causing me nothing but trouble. It's right that you help me," Rachel says.

"What sort of trouble?" I ask.

"He doesn't make enough money. I am worried he will suddenly disappear, and then I'll be alone with my little girl without a house or a job. What should I do?"

"Do you give him good love?" I ask. *Eeehhhh*, it makes her angry:

"*Tsk*, all the time miraculous, but he can't do the work of love when he is always chewing *mirungi* and drinking too much – my love has become just an another distraction from all his worries."

"You will have to think of something to get your hook deep into that fish," I say.

"You have to help me," Rachel says. I shake my head:

"Whether or not you're good to that *mzungu*, you are mistreated by him. And besides, I am through with helping people," I say. She turns around and walks away – over towards the container bar. I follow her with my eyes. Sometime later I see her walking down towards Uru Road with a young man – Rogarth. He is walking with his boss' *malaya* – while she is trying to find the way to manipulate the boss. This rich kid from T.P.C. has become adept at the ways of the poor since his father moved into Karanga Prison. But Rogarth still has a white man's belief in romantic love. Why is he interested in Rachel, who has already been pumped up by Faizal and who has been *malaya* for *mabwana makubwa* and for Christian? If Rogarth can prosper as a thief and fraudster, he could soon get a much better woman. It's a romantic disease that Rachel arouses in those boys.

Christian

I have persuaded the owner of Liberty to provide a bouncer until I find a new one. Firestone does odd jobs and keeps an eye on the car park as usual. I have gone all the way out to T.P.C. to pick up Emmanuel – have talked him into working the door. I don't know what to do. I am wearing a normal T-shirt now. No more yellow shirt. I let Rogarth take care of the decks, trying to make myself invisible. I desperately need money so I can give Rogarth and Firestone their salaries and pay the two months' rent I owe Gösta's family for their guesthouse, so they won't evict us.

Everything I got for the tanzanite stones has been spent. The money from Mick is gone.

I sit at a table, drinking Konyagi to calm myself down. A man in a suit sits down at the table.

"How are you, Christian Knudsen?" he asks.

"Errr," I say. "Alright. Who are you?"

"I'm from Immigration," he says. "You have a big problem."

"My papers are fine," I say. He shakes his head slowly.

"No. Your residence permit has been revoked. There has been a grave error in the handling of your case. You have to reapply."

"And what will that cost me?" I ask.

"Cost?" the man says. "A residence permit in Tanzania doesn't cost anything – if you are approved. And that alone is determined by the purpose of your stay here – does it benefit Tanzania or not?"

"What is it you say I have to do?" I ask.

"You must come to the immigration office on Monday morning," he says and gets up – leaves.

Monday morning I am sitting at the immigration office filling out papers. I'm admitted to the suit's office. He leafs through the papers, looks up at me:

"We will assess your case now," he says. "It will take us approximately a week, and you can come down and hear the result on Monday next."

"And what happens if you decide not to grant me a permit?" I ask.

"Then you will have twenty-four hours to leave the country." Soviet methods. What do they think this is? A spy movie?

"I am big-bellied," Rachel says when I come through the door. She is sitting on the sofa with Halima in her arms.

"What?" I say. "You're not big-bellied. You're gorgeous."

"Big-bellied," she says. "You have pumped me up."

"Are you pregnant?" I say, standing quite still in the middle of the room.

"I think so," Rachel says. "I haven't bled on time." She looks at me, her eyes unreadable.

"But we've been careful, haven't we?" I say, because since . . . since we had our blood checked out I haven't fucked her without a condom. Well, hardly . . .

"When you pump with a sock – that's not a hundred per cent safe," Rachel says: "And there have been a few times we've forgotten the sock."

"But you think you're pregnant. What does that mean? Are you or aren't you?"

"A woman knows these things," she says. Periods – eggs and blood, but I honestly don't really know how a cycle is supposed to go.

"Are you sure?" I ask.

"Almost," she says. "Are you leaving me?"

"No," I say. "No."

"But you're not happy," she says.

"Tsk," I say. "Right now there are so many problems. Everyone is trying to pluck me – like a chicken."

"I'm not," Rachel says.

"I know," I say. Do I?

"What are you going to do?" she asks, looking angry. The Tanzanian way – it's the man's job to provide.

"We'll have to see if we can get Liberty to work out alright," I say. "If that doesn't pan out, we will have to go up to stay with my dad for a while." I can sell the decks in Moshi – have a bit of ready cash. If we haven't got enough to pay for the plane tickets ourselves, he can help us with a top-up.

"What would we do at your father's?" she asks. "Will he send us to Denmark?"

"Let's just wait and see if Liberty is going to work out before we talk about Denmark," I say. Because, yes, my dad will send me to Denmark. I don't know what he'll do about Rachel and Halima. I haven't got a clue. And Rachel hasn't heard of the latest campaign by the immigration authorities. She doesn't know that I owe Gösta's family for the rent. She doesn't know we're at the edge of the abyss.

I am so fucking screwed.

Marcus

THE DEAL

Rogarth comes to my door with Firestone. The difficult years after his father's imprisonment have made him a tough guy. And the disco business turned out to be a mess. First Khalid died on the mountain, then Abdullah was kicked out. Big Man Ibrahim got thin and died. Now Rogarth is in charge of Christian's army of slaves, but the army is short of soldiers.

"Er, h-h-h-he c-ch-ch-ch-ch-cheats eeeeeveryone – he's nnnnot wo-wo-working, that *mzungu*," Firestone says. They have been giving me the cold shoulder for two years. Now they stand before me like beggars.

"He doesn't pay us wages anymore," Rogarth says. "We didn't know he was like that."

I told them, but to the African the white man cannot be wrong. The African has to feel the deception himself and see it with his own eyes first. But Rogarth knows both sides; he is a Tanzanian, he went to I.S.M. He ought to know better. Perhaps he is infected by romantic ideas about man's fellowship – or he has caught the white form of love, which makes him incapable of giving up his feelings for Christian's *malaya*, his path controlled from inside his trousers.

"So now you see that Christian is no good," I say. "*Pole.*"

"We would like to talk to you," Rogarth says.

"The house is for my family. We can't talk here," I say, staying at the door – very rude.

"Let's go over to the container bar," Rogarth says.

"I can't afford the bar," I say.

"Our treat," Rogarth says.

"Alright," I say and we go there – sit down at a table under the lean-to at the back, so we are alone. The waiter brings us beer.

"Y-y-y-your *mzungu* has ch-ch-ch-ch-cheated us c-c-c-c-compp-ppppletely," Firestone says.

"That's your problem," I say.

"Yes. But he's cheated you as well, and now he's cheating us," Rogarth says.

I don't say anything.

"Yes, and so . . . well, perhaps we might help each other," Rogarth says.

"Help each other do what?" I ask – not because I want to play at being stupid, but if Rogarth wants something, he's going to have to say it.

"We want payment, because he's cheated us," Rogarth says.

"I don't care – that's your problem."

"But he cheated you. Back then – with the decks and the money," Rogarth says – the very man who helped Christian do it.

"Yes. And when he was through with me, you went to him and bent over. Congratulations."

"Together we can take him down. We are offering you a means of getting even," Rogarth says.

"You can go ahead and get even all you want. I have a kiosk, a chicken farm and a family. I haven't got time for revenge," I say. "All I need is money."

"Chhhhrristian hasn't g-g-got any," Firestone says.

"But there might still be money to be made," Rogarth says. "But we don't know the whole story, so we're asking for your help. The money can be yours as well."

"He's got his decks – you will have to steal them and see if you can escape the police," I say.

"Yes, but perhaps he has contacts," Rogarth says. Here comes the truth. They're asking me because Rogarth is worried. What can Christian do? Does he have influence through his father in Shinyanga? Does his father know some *mabwana makubwa* in Moshi who can order the police to crush Rogarth like a beetle? Rogarth doesn't know – he needs me. Without these worries Rogarth would just destroy Christian – quick, quick, hard. And I think about my naughty little brother, Christian – he is out of his depth. But I would like . . . something. Without him getting hurt too badly. I would like to help them in a way that lets Christian get away in one piece.

"You could make money by taking his things," I say. "And I can help you avoid trouble with the police."

"How?" Rogarth asks.

"If I tell you, you won't need my help," I say and smile. Rogarth laughs out loud.

"Enough!" he says.

"But then we have to share the harvest," I say. "If not, I will sell you to the police for petty cash, or even for free."

"Yes. It's a deal," Rogarth says and shakes my hand. They know nothing. They don't know that *bwana* Benson has already set the immigration authorities onto Christian. They don't know that Christian is staying in Tanzania illegally. Christian has only discussed those things with me. Christian's fate is in my hands. If I squeeze, he will break.

Christian

Friday afternoon. Rogarth has just been here in a taxi to pick up the decks. After the vigil at Liberty we take the speakers home every night. On Monday I will get my verdict from the immigration office. Rachel is in the shower after walking home from town. She didn't ask me to pick her up. The bathroom door opens, and I hear her going into the bedroom. Halima is playing outside. I push open the door, go over and hug Rachel from behind, so my stiff cock rests between her buttocks. I need release.

"Stop that trouble," she says.

"No," I say. "I want you now." She sighs, pulls the *kanga* aside and lies down on the bed.

"Come on, then," she says. I drop my shorts to the floor, pull off my T-shirt and climb onto the bed, pressing her one leg to the side, so I can lie down between them.

"You don't need the sock," she says.

"Why not? Now's not the time for us to have any more children."

"I'm already pregnant," she says. "I haven't bled this month." My erection goes limp. I flop onto my back. She touches my cock. "Is it tired now?"

"It's a little surprised, but mostly it's happy," I say. "We'll see in a moment."

She puts her face on my stomach and caresses my cock and my balls. She sits astride my thighs and lets her soft breasts caress my cock. It rises again, and she takes me inside her.

Friday night goes alright at Liberty, but I am stressed out and tired when I wake up Saturday. Rachel goes to see a friend of hers with Halima. The kitchen stinks of old garbage. I look at the dustbin. The lid is broken, and Rachel hasn't emptied the bucket, and it's fuming in the heat. I carry it to the rubbish dump at the end of the garden and empty it. I stare at the rubbish. Between vegetable peel, leftover porridge and bits of bread I find bloody rags – Tanzanian sanitary pads. Then Rachel did have her period. I swallow my own spit. It's sad that she is lying to me – that she considers it necessary to hold on to me. Sad that she may be right. The saddest thing of all is that I haven't got her pregnant. My head aches.

I drive to the market in Kiborloni at noon, to avoid having to meet anyone. Buy some *khat* and go down to the river. The pain in my head compresses my brain. I smoke cigarettes and chew the bitter stalks. It dries out my mouth. Drive over to a kiosk and drink a Coke. Pop a few pieces of chewing gum into the lump and chew the cud. I don't know what to do.

Once more Rogarth comes round in the afternoon to pick up the decks.

"I need some money," he says.

"Of course," I say. He needs money for the taxi, to eat, a few shillings here and there to make the night run smoothly. Plus I owe him money. I give him as little as possible. I feel an urge to keep my last money with me in case . . . I might need it. Rachel and Halima are still with Rachel's friend. I take a long shower before I put on clean clothes – my Black Uhuru T-shirt with a safari jacket on top. Before I leave, I go to the bedroom and take the key from the leather cord around my neck, unlock the Ostermann crate, dig down through cassettes, photographs, papers and find the box. Open it and take out the revolver. Stick it down the back of my waistband. My jacket hides it. Make sure I have my passport in my pocket. Shiver as I am about to go through the door and turn around. Go to the fridge and take the undeveloped film from the door, putting it in my pocket. Root around at the very back of the freezer and grab the matchbox where I keep a few raw tanzanite stones. Out I go. Drive down towards Liberty in the gathering darkness. Everything is clear as day, all my movements are distinct when I've chewed *khat*. I will get through the night.

At the Clock Tower roundabout Firestone is standing waving at me. I pull over and stop.

"What is it?" I ask. He jumps up on the back and waves his arm quickly past my face as he stutters:

"G-g-g-g . . ."

I go. Stop outside Shukran Hotel. Firestone gets off and stands next to me. His breathing is fast and shallow, he is almost jumping on the spot. I realize that he felt the revolver as he sat behind me. No chance on earth of his being able to say anything coherent right now. I put a hand on his shoulder. Give him a cigarette, fire. Let him smoke, try to restrain myself.

"The p-p-p-p . . ." he says.

"The police," I say. He nods.

"They are abbbbbbuffhhh . . ." He swallows.

"They're at Liberty?" I say. He nods.

"They're looking for me," I say. He nods and smiles.

"I hhhhhhhh-have to g-g-g-g . . ." he says, pointing.

"You have to go back and help Rogarth," I say. He nods with relief. "Alright," I say. "Tell him to come down and see me at Jackson's in Majengo as soon as he can," I say. It's no further than he can walk, and it's under a different police jurisdiction, so they probably won't know what the fuss is about. But what's this all about anyway? The meeting with the immigration authorities isn't until Monday. I drive down to Jackson's. Order beer and Konyagi. Drink. Look around. It's a quiet night here. I haven't eaten today. Only a mango this morning. I have no appetite. It's because of the *khat*. A large lady comes and sits down at the bar. Chantelle. I go over to her, put a hand on her shoulder.

"Chantelle," I say, "I am sorry about what happened . . . back then." She looks up at me. Looks away again. Her skin feels warm against my hand. I sit myself down on the barstool next to hers. Our thighs meet. She is burning up. From nothing my cock goes rock hard. I want to be between those thighs – pump her, pull at her tits, suck at her mouth. "Chantelle," I say – my voice is thick, "let's go somewhere."

"What?" she says, looking at me. I point outside indiscriminately.

"Let's go somewhere, together," I say.

"Go home," she says.

"I want you," I say in a low voice, so no-one will hear me over the bar's scratchy radio.

"Go home to your own country," Chantelle says.

"I've got money," I say.

"*Tsk*," she says and turns her face away from me. I put a hand on her voluptuous thigh – stroke it. She pushes it away. "Stop that trouble," she says.

"But, I've got money," I say. A fat man gets up from a table and comes towards me. What does he want? He leans over against the bar, stares at me.

"When the lady doesn't want to talk to you, she doesn't want to talk to you," he says. I nod, get up unsteadily, go outside and start the motorbike. Drive off. Rogarth was supposed to come to Jackson's and tell me what's going on at Liberty. What difference does it make? I'll find out tomorrow. Drive round the corner to one of the dirty bars. Three young *malaya* are sitting at a table under the awning. They remind me of Rachel. Yes, Rachel must have sat there, fucked and sucked cocks at any bar that would pay her a few shillings. I sit down at a table. The bar *mama* comes over. I am going to have to eat something, otherwise I will collapse. I order fried meat and beer.

"Would you like some company?" the bar *mama* asks. "I've got some very sweet girls here tonight?" she says, turning slightly towards the *malaya* table. I give them a closer look. One of them is petite and shapely. It looks like a jagged violet snake is slithering across her face. A scar – perhaps a broken bottle.

"The small one," I say, drawing a line down across my cheek with my finger. "And a beer for her." The *mama* goes over to the girls' table, says something and goes to the bar for beer. The girl comes over to my table, shakes my hand.

"Deborah," she says. Our beers arrive. I tell her she's got a nice jumper on, that I like her hair – that sort of thing, because I don't want to know where she is from. We chat, drink beer – are we pretending to be an item? It's her scar that I like. But I have to pay for the beer. My fried meats are brought out. I have to pay for it too. As if we were an item. Is she dreaming of that? Does she know who I am? Or was the game just for the sake of the client? Me.

"Soap money," I say. "How much?" She mentions her price. "I'm not that white," I say.

"*Tsk*," she says. Lowers her price a little.

"Let's go." I start the motorbike, she gets up behind me, puts her hands on my hips.

"The first place over there is the best," she says. I stop in front of the fuck-hotel. I go over. There's a small office, a reedy man inside. At the back of the building there's an external gallery leading on to the rooms. Feel oddly light.

"A room until tomorrow," I tell the man.

"All night?" he says.

"Yes."

"Alright," he says, shrugging. I pay, even though he's overcharging me. He hands me the key.

"My motorbike – will you keep an eye on it?" I ask.

"I can't keep an eye on it," he says. "I'm not a night guard."

"Then I'll take it into the room with me," I say.

"What you take into that room with you – I really don't care."

I pull the motorbike up the two steps, down the corridor. Deborah unlocks the door, goes inside. I park the motorbike and close the door. There is a bedside lamp with a forty-watt light bulb. The walls of the room are whitewashed, but it's peeling. The concrete floor is crumbling. Wooden beds with foam mattresses – battered and stained. Deborah takes the sheet, which is folded up at the end of the mattress, and shakes it out, allowing it to fall over the mattress and the pillow. Then she undresses quickly and lies down on the bed.

"Come," she says. I undress, lie down next to her, touch her. She is very slender, almost skinny, her muscles small and hard right under her skin, which is firm, smooth, taut. My hands slide over her – her thighs, the outlines of her stomach muscles, the small hard breasts. She smells of chemical flowers – cheap perfume. Underneath it, a touch of dried yeast and old sweat. Her hand touches my balls – caresses them – my cock. But it won't stand. I get dizzy. Too much *mirungi*. With my tongue I follow the purple snake across her face.

"No," she says, grabbing my face between her hands. She moves it from her cheek, sticks her tongue into my mouth. It makes me gag – I pull away. She pulls at my cock. "You must do the work," she says.

"I can't," I say, removing her hand.

"I need my soap money anyway," she says. I run my finger over the scar on her nose and cheek – it's been stitched up unevenly.

"What happened?" I ask.

"Dogs," she answers.

"Dogs?"

"Men," she says. "Like you." I sit on the edge of the bed, so she can't see my face. Stare at nothing. Look back at her. Deborah. I like that scar – it suits her. She looks at me with empty eyes. I reach out for my trousers where I put them by the motorbike. Pull them towards me. KLONK – the revolver was under them; now it drops to the floor. I reach down for it, put it on the seat. I hear a gasp. I look at Deborah. Her eyes are wide open. I shake my head, pull out money. Hand it to her. She counts it, her body as tight as a spring, her eyes following my every move, as I get up, naked. Light a cigarette, take the revolver in my hand, sit down astride the motorbike. Move the revolver to my left hand. The metal of the fuel tank feels cool against my balls, my limp cock. Skin scrapes off my ankle as I kick-start the engine and turn up the gas. Deborah is out of the bed, pressing her top against her chest. I raise the revolver towards the ceiling and fire. Bits of plaster float from above, filling the poorly lit room with dust. Sweat is pouring from me. Sweat? It's tears. I lower the revolver. Turn off the engine. Look down.

"You can go now," I say. Out of the corner of my eye, I sense Deborah quickly picking up her clothes, grabbing her sandals in her hand and slipping through the door. Closes it behind her. The dust is settling on me. Why isn't Samantha here? I would like to talk to her now. I need to. Maybe she knows what will happen – she has experience of this kind of landscape. I miss her. Now I have almost become what she was – have I reached my final destination?

I sit on the motorbike. Smoke. The cigarette is made wet by the falling drops. Throw it away, light another. Try to breathe calmly. I have to do . . . something. Start pulling on my clothes. Can hear a car honking in the distance. It's approaching, constantly honking. Then it stops not far away. Still honking. People are shouting. What? I open the door slightly.

"Fire, fire. There's a fire at Liberty . . ." the voice calls, and more voices join in. Fuck. I quickly find the revolver on the floor, put it in place, take my cigarettes, pull the motorbike through the door, lift the kickstand and roll it down the gallery, around the corner, past reception, down the steps and away. Cars and people on bikes with passengers on the baggage carrier – all moving in the direction of the city centre. No-one wants to miss out on a fire. I blast off between the waves of dust and exhaust fumes from the cars, weave between people on bikes and people who are running, while I see the flickering lights in the distance. Across the train tracks, down the road and up towards the city centre. The smoke is tearing at my nostrils. Liberty is in flames. I have to stop in the middle of the road, where a large crowd blocks my way. The flames have leapt from the timber storehouse in the yard to the roof of the brick building facing the road, and the flames are gathering strength, lighting up the night – the sparks rising like fireflies. A fire truck has arrived, but only the one, and the jet of water from the hose is too feeble to even reach the roof. I pull the motorbike with me through the crowd; watch the hose winding over the wet ground – it's worn through, patched up; strips of inner tubing from car tyres have been wound around. Thin sprays of water spurt from it along its length – the water pooling on the rock-hard soil without seeping in.

I see the policeman. He sees me. I stay where I am with the motor-bike. He can come to me if he wants to. I haven't got anything left for anyone to take. But he doesn't come. Looks back at the flames. I flip down the kickstand, pull the key from the ignition, go over to him.

"*Shikamoo mzee*," I say. "What do you want with me?"

"You?" he says. "I don't want anything with you."

"I've been told you were looking for me," I say. He bursts out laughing: "*Eeeeehhhh* – you're so full of lies. Your own and those of others. And your friends are tired of you. That is very dangerous." He turns away from me and goes over and talks to some firemen who are standing about, looking at the bonfire. I get my cigarettes out of my pocket. Liberty's old night guard comes trudging over to me.

"*Bwana* Christian," he says, smiling. Is there anything to smile at? I hand him a cigarette. It's what he wants. What the hell? Light it for him. He sucks greedily.

"My decks and everything," I say to no-one in particular. "Gone up in smoke." The old night guard looks surprised:

"No, they left with the decks before the fire."

"How so?" I ask.

"It started in the dancehall, so they shouted that there was a fire. All the people ran out, and then they quickly carried your decks out the back door to a taxi on Kaunda Street," he says, smiling at me. "You are very lucky."

"Yes," I say. Go over and kick-start the motorbike. Drive back through the dark streets. All the windows are lit up. There's a taxi in the drive. What should I expect? I stop my engine a few metres from the veranda, where Rogarth and Firestone are sitting in chairs while Tariq leans against the wall.

"Christian, Christian," Halima shouts from inside the sitting room. I hear Rachel's muffled voice, and Halima starts crying, but the sound fades after a moment. Rachel has taken the girl into the bedroom. Closed the door.

"Listen," Rogarth says, comes towards me with his arms half raised in a gesture that is at once resigned and conciliatory.

"Listen to what?" I say. He stands right next to me, facing me. I am still astride the motorbike. He's the one. He has swindled me. Maybe Marcus helped him. "Do you have my decks?" I say. Rogarth doesn't say anything. He shakes two cigarettes out of his pack, lights the first and hands it to me. I take it and put it in my mouth. He drops the other cigarette to the ground and whips his hand up behind my jacket, pulling the revolver from my waistband, taking two steps back. Firestone gets up, smiling, and comes over to stand next to Rogarth.

"You're d-d-d-done for," he says, shuffling his feet in the dust.

"What are you doing, Rogarth?"

"Everything you have is mine," he says.

"You can't just steal my things. That's illegal," I say.

"Who are you going to tell? The police?" Rogarth says.

I don't say anything. Rachel – she faked a pregnancy. Rachel switched sides when she got nervous, thinking I wouldn't come through for her. First she tried saying she was pregnant. Then I would be sure to take her to Europe. Only, I didn't. She couldn't keep her cool, so she turned to Rogarth. Yes, she was – she is – right. I'm not working out. What can I offer her in Europe? – it's only the ticket she needs; up there she won't want to be with someone who's got nothing. Did Rogarth always have something to do with her being with me? It's not a pleasant thought.

"What about Rachel?" I ask in English. Neither Tariq nor Firestone speaks English well.

"She's with me now," Rogarth says.

"What's she going to do with you?" I ask.

"The same thing she did with me before you arrived. Pump," he says, grabbing his cock through the fabric of his trousers. The revolver makes him feel important. "Now, give that here," he says, pointing at my T-shirt with his free hand.

"What?" I say.

"Black Uhuru," he says. I look down at the T-shirt. The letters in the colours of the Ethiopian flag, encircled by white barbed wire. Rogarth smiles and points the revolver at me. And then he raises it higher – pointing at the black sky. PAW – the sound echoes towards me in the night.

"WOW!" Tariq shouts and laughs.

"What the hell are you doing?" I shout. Rogarth looks at me with empty eyes, holding the gun towards the others.

"Would you rather I gave it to Firestone?" he asks in Swahili.

"O-o-o-o-oh yes – give me the g-g-gun . . ." Firestone stutters.

"We want the motorbike," Tariq says.

"No," Rogarth says. "Christian needs that motorbike to go far away very quickly, so the rest of us won't go to prison for killing him, which we will if he stays, because any second now . . ."

Firestone roars with laughter.

"The white boy needs to die," Tariq says. Rogarth smiles at them before looking at me again. Rogarth raises his eyebrows. Speaks to me in English:

"Are you still here?"

I don't say anything.

"Time to go," Rogarth says. I kick-start, drive off.

Marcus

THE GREY BOY

Christian comes to my door, early in the morning. He smells nasty, he's dirty, his movements very nervous. I am standing on the raised terrace – Christian is standing down on the ground.

"I am sorry things have ended up like this between us, Marcus. I really need your help."

"What's the problem?" I ask.

"They've taken my things," he says.

"I have helped you many times, but you never help me," I say.

"Damn it, Marcus. If you'll go to the police for me, we can get my things back, and we can make it work again – you and me. I can write a piece of paper which proves that I have sold them to you."

"You call them your things and forget that I made the money to get them down here, so they're my things as well. You used me, and now you have lost them. And you can't even go to the police because you have no papers to prove they are yours. And you have problems with papers at the immigration office. No. We are not together. We are separated. And you are in the wrong country – my country."

"It's not your bloody country, you half-Swede you," he says, laughing.

"Yes, it is mine. I thought I was a Swede, but I'm not. It was only a dream," I say.

"Shit. For old times' sake, Marcus? I'm begging you."

"Are you admitting they were my things as well?"

"Hey, we can say they were yours, but it doesn't really help now that they've been stolen," Christian says.

"You will never admit that you took all the proceeds from the recording shop and brought decks down, and then you kicked me right out of the business."

"But . . . Alright, that wasn't right, the way that went on," Christian says.

"Not right?" I say. "I remember the fake customs officials I was meant to grease in Dar. While all the decks were already at your place in Moshi."

"Yes, I'm sorry," he says.

Claire comes out from the living room with Redemption on her arm.

"*Tsk*," she says when she sees Christian, but she doesn't say hello.

"Hey, who's that?" Christian asks.

"My Redemption," I say as Claire goes back inside.

"Good name," Christian says. I look at him. Smoke my cigarette.

"What's the problem?" I ask again. Christian sighs.

"The others have stolen my decks," he says.

"Who did?" I ask – only a wall separates him from his equipment, which is stashed under my bed.

"I don't know . . ." he says.

"No – you don't. You don't understand the reality that surrounds you. You're in between. You are nothing now; not black, not white, just a grey boy. The only way you can survive here is with money taken from your home in Denmark. You can't make it in your native country, because your brain is as stupid as the ignorant negro from the village. And when you are here, you cheat the wrong people, more blind than even the most ignorant negro." That's how I say it, like an axe of truth. He doesn't say anything. "You were looking for the easy way, but the shortcut to money drowns in a sea of lies."

"But did you hear anything, Marcus? I don't understand what happened."

"Your decks are gone," I say, "but you're still alive. You are lucky."

"Did you . . . ?"

"Yes, I made sure they didn't wreck your body. That was their plan. You are still in one piece – you can run for it," I say. *Eeehhh* – he is appalled. Now he knows what it was like when he cheated me; hauling vegetables in the sun, having chickens shitting in your house and breathing chemical fumes from the batik production, so your chances of a family is ruined.

"I ought to fuck you up, Marcus. I really should," he says. And I can see that he is serious – perhaps he will.

"Yes, you are from a family of killers; your blood is full of evil and hatred," I say.

"What the hell are you talking about?"

"How do you think Jonas died?" I ask. Christian just looks at me. "What was it that happened?" I ask.

"He dehydrated in the sauna – what does that have to do with me?"

"You think the oven will burn all night with the same wood that was put into it at ten?" I ask. "That at the same time the oven will spring open, hitting Jonas so he gets an enormous bump on the head?" Christian looks confused.

"I don't know, Marcus. I suppose he must have put more fuel in it, because he wanted to sweat, and then he tripped over the oven, because he was off his tits with drink," Christian says.

"Jonas argues with his wife, and your father tries to intervene – you remember that. And then Jonas walks off – very drunk and *bhangi*-mad – out to the sauna to sleep. Away from his wife, away from the noise of children. To sleep in peace without having to hear Marcus the negro slave make breakfast for his children in the morning."

"Yes, and so what?" Christian says.

"And then the oven burns in the sauna all night until morning with the door closed tight. Who put that wood on the fire? Who made the bump on his head? He was lying on the bench when I found him the next morning. So he falls and hits his head, and then he flies like an angel onto the bench – is that how it was?"

"I don't know," Christian says.

"What do you know?"

"About what, damn you? I was sleeping in your ghetto."

"Yes, but you know you were woken up," I say.

"Yes, and when I was, you were awake," Christian says.

"I was awake. In the larder, stealing Carlsberg."

"Then perhaps you were the one who put the wood in the oven and hit him over the head. You hated the man like the plague," Christian says.

"And how do I benefit from killing Jonas?" I ask.

"He doesn't exploit you any longer."

"I lose my job security, I lose my home, lose my motorbike, my food and my Carlsberg, lose touch with my Swedish foster daughters, lose my chance of a course in Sweden, lose my last chance of keeping in touch with my own chocolate-coloured daughter in Finland. I lose everything, go back to being a negro in the dust."

"I don't care about Jonas – he's dead."

"You don't see what's in front of you, Christian. Look closely: where does the rain come from, and who does it fall on? Who reaps the good crop?"

"I don't know."

"That's why you're too stupid to live here. You're not a negro. You're not white. You don't know what you are," I say.

"Neither do you," he says.

"Yes, now I do," I say. "I am the stranger." Christian looks at me for a while.

"Katriina?" he says.

"She loses her home, her money; can only go back to Sweden – a single mother with two daughters. No more living like a queen in Africa. No, I think Katriina is sleeping with her two girls in the big bed. Who then can have hit Jonas? Which of the party is left?" I ask.

"I was asleep. I don't know. Jonas died – not a great loss. It certainly wasn't me," Christian says.

"I saw your father go down to wake you up. What did he say?"

"I don't remember. That it was time to go," Christian says.

"You had to leave at six, even though you're asleep. Even though he is so drunk that his Land Rover fells trees in the garden as he reverses; even though there is a sofa in the living room he could sleep on. What else did he say?" I ask. Christian knows.

"I don't know," he says.

"You think I don't understand the Danish language? Rebekka made me speak like a Swede. I can understand my neighbouring country – I understand perfectly."

"Then what did he say?" Christian asks.

"We can't be here when the morning comes."

"Of course he bloody did. He was completely drawn into all those fights between Katriina and Jonas. Jonas was mad at him. He doesn't want to wake up on their sofa the next morning with a hangover and have Jonas call him every name under the sun and rant about how my mum binned him."

"Yes, your father was drawn in. Katriina drew him in – all the way," I say, making a nasty gesture with my arm and my pelvis.

Christian doesn't say anything.

"Even before Jonas died there was something between Katriina and your father."

Christian doesn't say anything at all.

"You sleepwalk through life. You're a stranger. You are wrong. Now I want you to get out of here," I say.

"And go where?"

"Away."

"Come on, man. I haven't even got money for petrol," Christian says. I get up, dig into my pocket, pull out a few banknotes, enough for petrol and food all the way to Shinyanga, put them on the seat of the chair, take my coffee cup, go inside the house and shut the door. The motorbike starts a moment later. I open the door. The seat is empty

Christian

Drive out of Moshi. Uru Road. Continue westwards towards Arusha. The airport is down there on the flatlands. I haven't got money for a ticket. Stop at a small kiosk on the roadside, drink a lukewarm Coke and stare at the mountain in the distance, smaller now. As I approach Arusha, I suddenly feel dizzy. My limbs feel wooden. I kill my speed. Can't go up to Mountain Lodge. Sofie would give me a bed – I think. But Mick – he doesn't want to see me, and I can't bear to see him. He was right. Find a guesthouse. Pull the motorbike inside. Lie on the bed. Stare up at the ceiling. Shake. Sleep uneasily. Wake up several times during the afternoon. When twilight falls, I go out. Find a street kitchen under a tree. Eat corn porridge and beans. I have to be careful how I spend my money. I've got enough for the trip, but petrol can be expensive in Serengeti. Drink tea with milk and cane sugar. Go back to the guesthouse.

I feel like drinking, but I shouldn't. Feel like smoking a stick, chewing some *khat*. All that shit was part of my undoing. I lie on the bed. The fire at Liberty . . . I swallow my slimy spit. They didn't let the night guard at Liberty in on their little number. Insurance fraud. Liberty's owner could have insured my stereo, even though it wasn't his. A bit of grease for the insurer – that would have been all it took. Perhaps the papers from my transport crate – they show the value in dollars of the things I got in through the church back then; the value of the record player and the lights I brought back from my visit to Denmark. The African methods for survival are manifold. In the crate was also the paper saying that I have made over the disco to Rogarth – drawn up so we could resist potential trouble from the authorities over my lack of a work permit. Why didn't I see Rogarth's intentions? That he would let me down? I have dug my own grave. And the fire: a new Liberty instead of the old warehouse. And who organized it? Rogarth isn't clever enough – if he was, he would have done it a long time ago. And Abdullah is all brawn. Tariq is just an overgrown child. No – can only be the original Garvey Dread: Marcus Kamoti.

Darkness. Wake from my slumber. My body itches. I can smell myself and the mattress, the insects I have crushed in my sleep. Get up in the darkness. Find the light switch. There's no power. I draw back the curtains. The faintest grey light pours in. Monday morning – they're expecting me at the Immigration office in Moshi. I quickly put on my clothes, go out, leave the key to my room at the front desk next to the receptionist's woolly head, resting on his arms while he snores faintly. Go back and pull the motorbike with me out onto the road. Open the tank and shake it. I will have it filled it up at the last petrol station before Serengeti. They'll know if there's petrol to be had in the park. If not, I will have to buy a jerry can and strap it to the back. I kick-start the bike. Drive off in the grey light. Freeze like a dog. The sun comes up as I reach the outskirts of Arusha. Stop at a café on the roadside. Eat chapatti, a hardboiled egg, drink tea with milk and cane sugar until I'm stuffed. Think about me and Marcus on a motorbike going to West Kilimanjaro. The same cold, the same diet. I will miss the mountain. Leave the township and drive through Maasai country towards Serengeti. They have had rain here. The tarmac road winds between gentle green grassy slopes. Fill the fuel tank in Karatu and eat a few stale sandwiches. Am registered and pay at Lodware Gate. Drive right past Ngorongoro without stopping to reach Seronera before it's late. Get there. Dry and dusty. A German Ph.D. student lets me spend the night on the floor of his hostel room. I get something to eat. A shower. Rinse my clothes of dust and wash my T-shirt with hand-soap – it stinks. Fill the fuel tank in the morning at the lodge. A safari company driver tells me the road through the western corridor is still passable, because so little rain has fallen. Drive through the scalded flatlands, nice and easy. Out of Ndabaka Gate, lunch in Lamadai. In Ngudu I have a sleepless night in a guesthouse with bedbugs. Start early the next morning. Am dehydrated. Grey. I stop in the town centre. Ask a man for directions to the *ushirika* headquarters; the cotton union my dad works for. I find the place. Ask for *bwana* Knudsen. Am shown towards an office. Knock on the door.

"Yes – come in," he calls in English. I open the door.

"Hi, Dad," I say.

Twenty-four hours' worth of sleep, and the world feels like gravity has been revoked. Katriina doesn't say anything. I read out loud to Rebekka, who goes to a missionary school just outside town – taught by monks and nuns. I sit listening to Miles Davis through headphones for the better part of a night. The next afternoon Dad picks me up at the house. We drive out of town. Perhaps he wants to speak with me. But he doesn't say anything.

"How is work?" I ask. Dad sighs. The cotton union is the most important workplace in the region. He has to program their new accountancy system and teach them to use computers. But there's not much support to be had:

"The boss has told me that if I create a system without cheating, the employees will cause it to break down. So that's just great," he says. We drive through endless cotton fields. Dad points out three large wooden warehouses between the fields. Two of them are almost burnt to the ground. "The accounts say that those two warehouses were full of cotton, but it had all been sold under the table to private buyers. Everyone knows it, but to make the accounts add up it seems the bosses felt they had to burn down the buildings."

"To account for what had happened to the cotton?" I ask.

"Yes – all gone up in flames. Next year it will be harder; an empty open-air storage area isn't quite the same as a stocked storage facility."

I don't say anything.

"It'll go tits-up anyway," Dad says. "The smallholders will lose their investment, while the bosses build new houses."

"Insane," I say.

"It really is," Dad says. "I've been here for ten years, and everything I touch turns to dust." I share that experience. Dad is paid well for turning things to dust. The western world buys absolution – but for what? No-one wants to pay for the dust I have made.

"Then why do you stay?" I ask.

"I don't know," he says and gives a brief laugh. "It's a lovely place. And there is the odd person who learns from me and quickly sets up their own private enterprise so that they can make money."

Dad has filled out a bit. He seems relaxed. The troublesome woman is far away – my mum. Now the rain is falling on Katriina; the simple woman who is grateful and has real children – better than his own, one of whom is dead and the other is even more hopeless.

We eat. The conversation steers well clear of all conceivable mine-fields. Everyone has something they could hold against each other – silence is the safest strategy. I help Rebekka with her homework. Katriina bakes bread in the kitchen. Dad is programming a leaky accountancy system.

Dad goes to bed early – he has a meeting in Mwanza in the morning and will inquire about transport for me. Transport to Denmark by some route or other. I am in the sitting room, reading. Katriina comes out of the kitchen. Hands me a large gin and tonic. Sits down.

"What are you going to do now?" she asks. "In Denmark, I mean?" I laugh.

"Live and die," I say.

"Where?" she asks.

"In my own skin. Where else?"

"Yes, yes," she says. "But what will you do for a living? Will you go back to school?"

"I don't know," I say and look at her. Ask the question: "I would like to know how Jonas died."

Katriina says that she tried to wake him up, get him on his feet to get him to bed but that he had fallen against the sauna oven and had hit his head.

"Why did you want to get him into the house?"

"I didn't want Solja and Rebekka to find him out there when they woke up," Katriina says.

"You expect me to believe that?"

"It's the truth," Katriina says.

"I think you hit him over the head," I say.

"No," Katriina says.

"Then what?"

"I got him on his feet, and then he tried to . . . to grope me. So I pushed him off, and he stumbled onto the oven and got a gash on the back of his head."

"Why not call for a doctor?"

"Why would I?"

"He was your husband," I say.

"No. Not for a long time," Katriina says.

"You put extra wood into the oven. Marcus told me."

"To dehydrate him and make him really ill," Katriina says.

"And then he sodding well went and died," I say.

"Yes. He dehydrated," Katriina says.

"No," I say. "That wasn't all."

"Perhaps he fell again," she says.

"I would like to know what happened," I say.

"It doesn't matter," Katriina says.

"It does to me," I say.

"It wasn't your father," she says. "Perhaps it was Marcus." I just look at her. She looks out of the window at the dark night – her eyes have a faraway look: "I went out to look in on him – Jonas. He had drunk himself to sleep and was lying on one of the benches outside the sauna. So I put extra wood in the oven and pulled him into the sauna."

"Did my dad help you?" I ask.

"No, he doesn't know anything. I was going to wake him up to get him to help me. But I didn't," Katriina says.

"Help you carry Jonas inside?" I ask.

"Yes," Katriina says.

"Into the house?" I ask.

"No. The sauna."

"Wasn't that where he was lying?" I ask.

"I told you. He was on one of the benches outside," she says.

"Then how did you get him inside?"

"I got someone to help me."

"Marcus?"

"Yes," she says.

"Did he know you could kill Jonas by letting him dehydrate?" I ask.

"Perhaps – I think so. But I just told him I didn't want to have Jonas in the house."

"And he didn't wake up?"

"No."

"And then you bashed his head into the oven?" I ask.

"No," she says. "We put him down on the bench, and I told Marcus to go and wake you up. And once Marcus had left, I beat Jonas over the back of the head with a rock."

"With a rock?"

"Yes," Katriina says.

"Why?"

"Because he was useless. And I didn't think the coroners down here would be much good," she says.

"And then you woke my dad?"

"Yes. And told him it would be best if you left."

"Does my dad know what you did?" I ask. Katriina smiles.

"No," she says.

"Do you think he would like to hear that you murdered your husband?"

"Your father is my husband now," Katriina says.

"All the same," I say.

"I think he's happy."

"Happy? Really?" I say.

"I'm pregnant," she says, smiling.

Shinyanga is a large city with one-level housing and nothing to do. No cinema, no club, two restaurants, no discos. There are hardly any white people here – fewer than ten within the city limits – so everyone stares if I move around. In the mornings I take Rebekka to the missionary school outside the city on my motorbike. I go for long rides through the cotton fields. I love that machine. Bultaco 250cc. Dad says I should leave it for Solja. It's alright – she'll really like it.

The area is so very poor. Old people are accused of witchcraft and driven away from their villages, so their families won't have to feed them – there isn't enough food to go around. They sleep under trees in the wilderness; starve to death.

Saturday night. Katriina has asked a French couple for dinner – they're both doctors and work at the hospital in Shinyanga.

"We're drowning in A.I.D.S. patients," the man – Laurent – says.

"And orphans living with their grandparents, and they're all of them malnourished," Odile says. I have seen the children in the villages – distended abdomens, grey skin and reddish hair.

"How did it go so wrong?" Katriina says. Laurent shakes his head:

"If you look at the geography, it's really very simple. The disease starts somewhere in Congo and is then spread along the highways by lorry drivers who pay for sex. And by schoolteachers who travel to conferences in other towns. Afterwards they go home and fuck their wives and fuck their students in return for good grades. And the next time the teachers go to a conference, their wives fuck other men, and the students fuck each other. There's no television in Tanzania," he says with a resigned laugh.

"But they could use protection," Katriina says.

"African men don't want to use a condom," Odile says.

"Plus there's the rapes," Laurent says.

"What rapes?" Dad asks.

"If an African man is told that he is H.I.V. positive, the witch doctor tells him to go out and have sex with a virgin because she will cleanse him of the disease," Laurent says. "I've seen cases where H.I.V. positive men went home and raped their ten- or twelve-year-old daughters in order to get well."

"Now the Tanzanian doctors have issued a ban against telling people they are H.I.V. positive. Because one of the most common reactions is for the infected men to go out and have sex with as many women as possible to take them with them to the grave," Odile says.

"But surely you have to tell them that they're . . . contagious, dangerous," Katriina says.

"But the African doctors are right, you know," Odile says.

"Right about what?" Katriina asks.

"You tell an African man he is H.I.V. positive and will get A.I.D.S. and die, and until then he must use a condom or he will infect people. And the first thing he does is go out and fuck anything and everything that moves in order to take them down with him. It's a psychological mechanism we don't understand. But we can see it happening all the time," Odile says, shaking her head.

"But are people really that promiscuous?" Dad asks.

"Yes," Odile says. "In this area you work when you sow and again when it's time to harvest. The rest of the time there's nothing to do." Dad tells her about the night guards. "My point exactly," Odile says. I think about Marcus and Claire.

"Suppose you had an infant who died of A.I.D.S., and both the mother and the father were H.I.V. positive – would you keep the cause of death secret from the parents because you assume the man would go out and spread the disease?" I ask.

"I never tell an African man he is H.I.V. positive. It's not a risk I'm prepared to take," Odile says.

"So you never tell them if you test a man and he's positive?" I ask.

"No," Odile says. "And what if you did tell him? You can't get a condom for love or money."

"Abstain from sex," Dad says.

"In Africa?" she says. "What other fun is there for them to have?" Not them. Us. Dad looks at Katriina. She has been fucked by Jonas who, in turn, fucked anything with a pulse. And Dad's fucked her without a condom – if not she wouldn't be pregnant. I look at Katriina, who looks at Dad. There's a lot of looking down and shifting in one's seat. I think about Ibrahim's malaria, Marcus and Claire's emaciated little Rebekka,

Tita, who was fucked by Marcus, my mum who cut and sucked blood from the gardener when he was bitten by a snake at T.P.C. But most of all I look at my hands, where a few blood vessels stand out. We were tested, me and Rachel – the doctor said we were fine. Breathing around the table suddenly sounds shallow. It only lasts a moment, then everything is back under control again – on the surface. The blood is running through our veins, out of sight – no-one knows what secrets it may carry.

Dad does all he can to get me a plane ticket. He very much wants to send me back to Denmark. It will be hard to make a life there – but here it's just impossible.

He's got travellers' cheques and enough dollars to buy me a ticket with K.L.M. from Nairobi to Rome, where the plane has a stopover. But he hasn't got enough to get me all the way to Amsterdam. He himself will take me the five hundred kilometres north to the border crossing at Nyabikaye, east of Lake Victoria. From there I can catch a bus to Nairobi.

"I can't get through to the bank in Denmark and get them to transfer money to the travel agency in Nairobi, and this ticket is the best the travel agent in Mwanza can do," he says after a long day on the phone.

"It's cool, Dad," I say. "It's fine."

"Good," Dad says. "I've got enough Kenyan shillings for you to be able to get a ticket to Nairobi and have a little money to spare. And I can give you about a hundred dollars. Then you'll have to hitchhike or get a train from Rome. Do you think you can do that?"

"Yes," I say.

"Take this," he says and hands me a piece of paper. I look at it. It's Mum's address in Geneva. I put it in my pocket. "She'd like to see you if you behave," Dad says. I look out of the window. I can tell he is still looking at me. "Things happen," he says. Wisdom pouring from him.

Dad drops me off at the border two days before my flight. That gives me time for any African complications on the way to Nairobi. We hug each other.

"Take care of yourself, Christian," he says.

"You too," I say. "Good luck."

"Write to me," he says.

"I will." I let go of him and walk towards the border control – pull my passport from my pocket. All the stamps are in order – bought and paid for in Moshi. There's a nightbus to Nairobi. I will be in Jomo Kenyatta Airport tomorrow before noon with about thirty-two hours to kill before my flight. I have a few stones in my shoe – under the sock, between my toes; raw tanzanites. That way I won't lose them if my bag is stolen.

I get a window seat and sit squashed against the body of the bus, held in place by an elderly *mama*'s fat thighs. The bus is alright, and I've done it before, so I know you need to go thirsty – there's no breaks for peeing. Nod off a little, but sleep evades me. Smoke cigarettes while the *mama* snores gently beside me. The bag is at my feet. I have an undeveloped film of Rachel smiling and showing a bit of leg. And baby Halima playing football, sitting on the motorbike with corn porridge all over her little face. I look out at the dawn, as the tyres sing against the tarmac. The landscape is hazy – there are tears in my eyes.

"*Pole*," the *mama* says next to me.

"*Asante*," I say.

Marcus

I drink my morning coffee on the veranda and look out over the dusty residential area, my kiosk – which is looking oddly crooked.

It lands in my head; one day I will be asked by my own children: "Why are you drunk?" I thought that they would be afraid of me, so I could hide completely from the bad feeling. Not be disturbed. But there will be a time when they will ask me. And it is a hard thing to know – that the reign of terror continues. I am almost done, dry of juice and running on empty as I continue my path through life – downwards, because what can I do? Claire, I can't let her down. She can't survive on her own with Redemption. He must be mine as well. He is mine. But will there be a resurrection? Will he turn out like me? – the plant that withers while it grows. When he grows up and leaves this home, it will be time for me to die – then I will have completed my disastrous assignment on earth and can go back to dust.

"Come and take Redemption," Claire calls from inside the house. She needs to do her hair and lather on the make-up before she goes to work at Princess. The house girl will man the kiosk while I drink my coffee. "Come on and take him," Claire calls.

"*Maku, maku*," he whines. Perhaps I should listen to the crisp music from the fine machine in my house. I am looking for a man to buy it from me – I am done dreaming about discos. But Redemption should dance. I go inside and find the L.P., put it on. Redemption smiles up at me as I take him outside. Put him on the veranda, take my coffee and sit down on the chair. Redemption bounces on his chubby legs as Bob sings: "*Emancipate yourself from mental slavery. None but ourselves can free our minds.*"

Claire comes outside:

"Don't you make that child mad about music," she says. "It only leads to disaster." I raise my hand and stroke Claire's back. She smiles at Redemption as he dances. This is his song. Redemption will make his own disasters. I hope they will be good for him.

Christian

I eat some chapatti at the bus station in Nairobi – drink some tea. Buy bananas and toasted peanuts and bottled water. Eat a hardboiled egg. Take a *matatu* to the airport.

I go to the toilet. Open my bag and take out a small cardboard box with seashells and corals, collected on the beach outside Tanga with Halima. We gave my dad the box, and I've taken it from his bookcase in Shinyanga. Little Halima. Rachel. I have to swallow. I quickly put the raw tanzanites into the box, put the lid on, pop it into my bag, zip it up.

Walk around and smoke cigarettes. Am hungry, but I'm almost out of Kenyan shillings and I don't want to waste my dollars. Pick up a Kenyan newspaper from a table. TRIBAL WAR IN EUROPE one of the headlines on the foreign-affairs page reads. Yugoslavia is in flames – rape, genocide, streams of refugees – the Kenyan journalists probably had a great time writing that headline. Finally they've got our number – we're the same: barbarians.

I'd like to go into the departure hall, but it's more than twenty-four hours until check-in for my plane starts. But K.L.M. opens a check-in desk for an earlier departure which goes to Amsterdam via Athens.

"Couldn't you let me in, please?" I ask, holding up my mouldering Diadora bag; all I own in the world. "I've only got this one – only hand luggage." The pale Dutch lady looks at me. I am dirty, smelly, my stomach is rumbling – a pathetic sight. I am aware of the situation – she finds it upsetting to see a member of her race in that state; it's that part of her feelings I am trying to appeal to.

"Alright," she says, stamping my ticket. I go into the departure hall. I haven't got enough money. There will be food on the plane. In a day.

The Kenyans know a thing or two. There is soap and paper in the bathrooms. I take off my Black Uhuru T-shirt, wash my hair in the sink, my neck, my armpits. Dry myself with toilet paper. Wet the T-shirt in the sink and put a little soap on one end. I itch downstairs. Go into one of the cubicles, lock the door and drop my trousers. Use the soapy end to wash myself, the other end to wipe off the soap. I am dizzy with hunger. Can't get all of the soap off. Pull up my trousers. Go out to the sink with no top on and rinse out my stinking T-shirt. Go back into the cubicle, drop my trousers and try to get off the rest of the soap. Black Uhuru is covered in arse-sweat – I decide not to ponder how that symbolism could be construed. Clean, freshly ironed old-man's underpants with flies, taken from Dad's wardrobe in Shinyanga. There's no rubbish bin, so I dump the T-shirt behind the toilet. Go out to the sinks and take off my sneakers; wash my feet in the sinks. An African man in an impeccable suit comes through the door – he doesn't dignify me with so much as a glance; he goes right into the cubicle where I left my T-shirt. My socks are on the floor under the sink. They stink. I kick them over to the corner, leave them there. Clean socks, a clean T-shirt – all my clothes belonged to my dad, and they're all I have because I didn't take anything with me from Moshi. Brush my teeth for a long time. That's as good as it's going to get. Go out, down the lino-covered halls; the spicy smell of Ethiopian, Somali and Kenyan women. Consider borrowing a deodorant from the Duty-Free shop, but if I'm caught, they will make me pay for it. Buy myself a pack of Marlboro. Feel lightheaded with hunger. The cigarettes taste unbelievably nice. Perhaps I could get a job washing dishes at a restaurant? Then I could get something to eat as well – a hot meal. The fact that I'm thinking like that, does that mean I'm on the cusp of a nervous breakdown, or is it a good sign? I think about it – what are my options? People leave heaps of leftovers on their plates at the bistro, but I can't bring myself to go over and eat them. I've got just enough Kenyan shillings for a cup of tea. The place is busy. I buy the tea, carry it to a table where there are two plastic trays with plates, chips left on both of them. Without checking if any of the other customers are watching me, I gather the chips on one plate, add extra ketchup and salt, shovel loads of sugar into my tea. Consume my meal, chewing it slowly. The nutrition has to last.

I am about to faint as I walk down the runway to the plane.

"I'm sorry," I tell a stewardess with chestnut hair and full breasts. "I feel like I might pass out. Could I get a fizzy drink or something . . . ?"

"Yes, of course," she says and goes to the galley. "Are you afraid of flying?" she asks.

"Yes," I say.

"Would you like some nuts with that?"

"Yes, please," I say. She hands me a bag of salted almonds and a 7 Up. I go to my seat. The almonds are amazing. I force myself to chew each one for a long time and only take small sips. The nutrients are pouring into my veins.

Finally we take off. Goodbye, Africa. Warm and sneaky. If I don't think about it, it will be alright. Fall asleep. Dream . . .

"Stop!" What? Myself? The stewardess is leaning over me, grabbing both my shoulders.

"You're dreaming," she says.

"What?" I say. Am close to tears. Inside the dream it was white, black, red and grey.

"I don't know," she says. "You were screaming."

"I'm sorry," I say. Her lovely scent, the starched uniform, her gorgeous body pulling away from mine.

"That's alright," she says. "It's probably your fear of flying. Would you like something to drink?"

"Yes, please," I say.

"7 Up?" I nod. Wish she were still holding on to my shoulders. What do dreams tell us? Black has a particular significance for me.

We approach Italy. I dig into my pockets. I've got ninety-seven dollars. There's a note in there as well. I unfold it: Mum's address. Put it back into my pocket. My tanzanite stones in my pocket. Of course there's a Danish embassy in Rome, but what's the point? If they check up on me, I may get asked to pop home to face a charge for benefit fraud. And I've heard they're not as nice about sending people home these days. Can a sentence for benefit fraud be served in an open prison with billiards, television and good food, I wonder?

We are served food. It's cramped on monkey class. I carefully unwrap the small portions. Eat every scrap. I call for the stewardess. It's the same lady.

"Could I have another portion?" I ask. "I'm very hungry." She takes my tray.

"I'll see if we have any more, sir." My neighbour pretends the exchange never happened. Particularly when I get the new tray and put the sandwich into my bag. Ninety-seven dollars. Rome–Aalborg. We land. The passengers for Rome get off. A blonde stewardess walks slowly down the aisle counting the passengers. Not long after a voice is heard on the speaker:

"Any more passengers for Rome should leave the aircraft." We all give each other scrutinizing looks, shrug, shake our heads. My neighbour looks at me.

"Rome?" he says.

"No, I'm not for Rome," I say. The blonde stewardess is counting us again – another is checking the bathroom while the cleaners whizz through the cabin, collecting rubbish bags, hoovering. My stewardess is speaking to the steward, nodding towards me.

"Blind passenger," my neighbour says, putting his hand into the inner pocket of his jacket. "I've tried it before. Now they'll ask us to get out our boarding passes." My stewardess is on her way down the aisle again – she isn't counting.

"No," I say. "Let me out."

"Are you for Rome?" he asks. I don't say anything. He gets up so I can squeeze out. The stewardess stops a few feet away, waits for me to get my denim jacket out of the overhead locker. Never trust a white person. I walk towards her.

"What happened to your fear of flying?" she asks in a low voice with a small smile.

"I am trying to get over it, but it takes practice," I say.

"It's not easy to get a lift these days," she says. I nod. She smiles at me, very briefly – coquettish. Then it's gone and the stiff mask is back in place as she turns around and walks down the aisle ahead of me towards the plane's open door.

"Wait," she says when we reach the pantry. She goes to the cupboards and pours the contents of two lunch-trays into a duty-free bag, puts two 7 Ups in there as well and three packs of cigarettes. She hands me the bag. A black person would have gone out of there empty-handed. She smiles. I love her. I will love her for the rest of my life.

"Thank you," I say.

"Good luck," she says.

"Thank you." I nod, turn around, walk through the door, down the stairs. Across the black tarmac.

JAKOB EJERSBO made his literary breakthough with *Nordkraft*, a best-selling novel about young people and heroin addiction set in his native Aalborg. From 1974–7 and 1983–4 he lived in Moshi in Tanzania. He died in 2008 after a ten-month battle with cancer. The Africa Trilogy, published after his death and based on his experiences in Africa, was to prove a phenomenal critical and commercial hit in Denmark

METTE PETERSEN'S previous translations include *My Friend Jesus Christ* by Lars Husum, and *Exile* and *Revolution*, Books One and Two of The Africa Trilogy.